The Book of Jezebel

𐤎𐤐𐤓 𐤀𐤉𐤆𐤁𐤋

RM Watters

Philosopher's Stone Books

Bringing history & magic to life.

Philosopher's Stone Books is an imprint of Frequency 3 Media, LLC.

Designed by Rebecca Watters
Images used in the cover art licensed from Shutterstock, Inc.
Image of Jezebel's Seal, 1484-1 YZBL Jezabel, © Zev Radovan
Main title and heading typeset: LHF Ascribe Regular
Title page typeset: LHF Essendine 2
Body typeset: Century Schoolbook
Section dividers: LHF Saratoga Ornaments 2
Author's note, dedication, and quote typeset: Perpetua

A catalogue copy of this book is available from the Library of Congress:
Library of Congress Control Number: 2023950738

ISBN 979-8-9895577-6-9

For my children:
the lights of my life.

Author's Note

Historical accuracy is difficult to achieve with a narrative set in the 9th century BCE, so I have taken many liberties in crafting Jezebel's story. While I have done painstaking research and striven to be as historically accurate as possible, not much is known about Jezebel, Ahab, and their children outside the Biblical narratives with which many of us are familiar. Archaeology has shown they were real historical figures who ruled in ancient Israel. The historical Jezebel was highly literate, although none of her writings are known to survive. (Her opal scarab seal has survived, however, and it can be seen in the Israel Department of Antiquities.) The letters she writes to her daughters in the novel are entirely fictional, and the letter she wrote to the nobles of Jezreel about Naboth is only known from the Biblical story—no copies of the letter have been found, so I have taken some creative license here.

The wedding song in Chapter 1 is based on Psalm 45, which some scholars believe was written for the marriage of Ahab to Jezebel, due to it referencing the 'daughter of Tyre' and the 'ivory palace'. For narrative purposes, I have taken creative license by adding direct references to Jezebel in the fictionalized original of the psalm. While it is not mentioned in the Biblical narratives, there is archaeological evidence that Ahab made a temporary truce with Hadadesar of Aram when he fought alongside him and the other kings in the battle to recover Irhulani's kingdom from Assyrian domination.

While the Biblical narrative vilified Ahab based on religious views, archaeological evidence suggests Ahab's reign was prosperous. He did a lot to improve infrastructure, not only in his palaces but also in the cities and the roads, and these improvements benefited the majority of his people. It was an overall peaceful reign known for its pageantry and festivals and increased learning, much of which was heavily influenced by the Sidonian culture Jezebel brought with her when she married Ahab. (It is unknown how old Jezebel was when she married Ahab, but in the ancient Levant it was normal for girls to be married between the ages of 12-15.) While the historical Ahab had many wives and concubines, Jezebel is the only one whose name and origin is known. His children with Jezebel were Athaliah, Ahaziah, and Joram, but it is entirely possible that they had other children together whose names were not recorded because they did not become kings or queens.

Religious beliefs and practices of the Canaanites are also not well-known, beyond what the Biblical narrative tells us. It is known, however, that blood and sex rites were a common practice in Canaan—particularly with the cults of Ba'al and Astarte in Phoenicia. Temple prostitution was a real practice looked down upon by Yahwists but, given the archaeological record, there is strong evidence that it was a sacred act that was practiced only by priests and priestesses. And while the Biblical narrative makes claims to the contrary, there is no evidence whatsoever of child sacrifice performed in Ba'alist temples. Archaeologists have found cremated remains of children (and some adults) in the ruins of Ba'alist temples, but it is more likely this was part of their funerary rites and not a result of child sacrifice.

As for Jezebel's family, apart from her father and brother who both ruled the Kingdom of Sidon (Phoenicia), virtually nothing is known. Her father was a priest of Astarte before he became king of Tyre, and because the practice of making royal women priestesses was common in those days, there is reason to believe Jezebel was a priestess and likely high priestess. Her mother's origins are unknown—her name and relationship to the kings of Assyria were invented for the purpose of this story, but it is not unthinkable that she may have been of Assyrian origin. There is also no historical evidence for Jezebel being related to Hadadesar of Aram, so I have taken many liberties with their relationship. It is not unthinkable that they might have been related, however, because royal families have always intermarried for the purposes of strengthening alliances, gaining access to trade, and increasing the wealth of their kingdoms. The belief in royal blood being superior to that of commoners was also strong in that period—so much so that Egypt's royal family often married their own siblings—and that belief remained strong throughout human history.

Finally, a note on language. Akkadian was the lingua-franca of the ancient Levant. It would have been spoken predominantly at all royal courts in the region. Therefore, most words and names used in the novel are based on their Akkadian equivalent. In some cases, the Phoenician or ancient Hebrew equivalent is used instead. Ancient Hebrew (sometimes known as Proto-Hebrew) is an older form than Biblical or Modern Hebrew. Ancient Hebrew used the Phoenician alphabet. Like most Canaanite languages of the time, it did not include labio-dental fricatives **f** and **v**, which only came into use in Hebrew after the Assyrian conquest. To aid the reader, I have included a **glossary** in the appendix.

"Time's glory is to command contending kings,
To unmask falsehood, and bring truth to light."
William Shakespeare

Table of Contents

Part 1 – On Prophecy

Part 11 – On Covenants

Part 111 – On Sacrifice

By the time you receive this message, I will most likely be dead. The enemy has infiltrated our ranks. Your brother the king has been slain. The traitor is on his way to slay me even as I write this to you now. My daughter: the safety of our people, the future of these realms, and the preservation of our divine bloodline rests in your hands. You must do whatever it takes to preserve the last of us. Draw on your strength.

May the gods continue to bless and preserve you, my daughter.

Part I

On Prophecy

1

The Road to Shomron

The storm coming in over the sea was sublime. Rolling peals of thunder compelled me past potted palms that danced and swayed, toward the wide arched windows in the windswept corridor outside the Queen's chamber after she dismissed me for the night. Only the second highest in the fortress at Zour, my mother's private apartments always had the best view from the gallery overlooking the sea and part of the city on the rocks below. I had spent so much of my childhood there, racing wildly down the broad corridor, only to fall prey to the supreme beauty of the endless sea, pausing from my play so that I might take heed of her call.

While I stood gazing out the window now, strands of dark hair came loose from braids and tight coils, whipping and stinging my cheeks and nose. Squinting against the wind and errant locks, I ignored the call of my nursemaid to come away from the window. I was drawn to the magnificent power on display before me: a broad, billowing tower of dark blues and greys rising over the raging sea, cut through with white-hot bolts of fierce lightning from within. It grumbled as the storm toiled its way toward a landfall that would, the further inland it went, absorb its strength, and ultimately tear it to pieces.

I felt in some way that I was connected to this storm, as if it conveyed the torrent of conflicting emotions coming from within my being: excitement at the prospect of my upcoming marriage and the satisfaction of fulfilling my duty and my destiny, along with the trepidation of leaving my home and my family, of going to a foreign land to be the wife of a king, a man whom I had never met, and all that came with it. It was a great honor that I was to be the first of his wives; an even greater honor that I was also to be his *Melkah*, his queen and chief of his wives. My husband's kingdom would become my kingdom, his home my home, his people my people. I understood this from a very young age, having been reared toward this destiny

1

from birth. It had been my mother's life, and her mother's life before her. My aunts had the same experience and, if I had any daughters from my marriage, it would become their life, too.

Royal marriages were about securing alliances and strengthening dynasties; there was no concept of anything else, no reason to believe it could or should be any other way. I was happy to do what was expected of me and to build, if not love, then at least contentment in my marriage. If no joy was to be found with my husband, as was sometimes the case, then I could hope to find support and friendship from among the other wives and concubines my husband would acquire. The others, when they eventually came, would be under my care and guidance as well as my command, for he had no living mother to take on that responsibility. I was second only to my husband; they were beneath me. I smiled at the thought.

Suddenly, a crack of lightning struck the shore, causing massive shards of the rocky cliffside to fall into the sea and drawing my attention to the white-capped waves that threatened to tear off even more in its fury. Perhaps one day the whole city would fall into the sea, I mused darkly. Of course, if that ever came to pass, I would not likely be here to be a part of the experience. I realized then that this could be one of the last times I ever gazed at the sea, which had been a constant fixture in my life from the moment of birth.

The seat of my husband's kingdom was deep inland and high in the mountains. I had never known a life without the sea, on which my father's people depended for trade and sustenance. I had always loved it, and yet I had also taken it for granted. The sea would always be there, but I would not. What if, like my mother, I never returned to the land of my birth? Sadness filled me then, to take its place among all the other emotions I was trying so hard not to feel. But I was the daughter of a king. More than that, I was a descendant of the gods themselves, and an incarnation of Ashtarti. Sentiments, especially those which led to self-pity, had no place in my life.

Aware of my duty, I lifted my chin and tightened my jaw, breathed in the salt air, and closed my eyes against any tears. I was the goddess, made flesh. I would not cry now and smear the kohl that lined my eyes, letting the guards and slaves and even my nursemaid see that I was also human.

I slid my gaze sideways without moving my head, daring a glance at my nursemaid who stood across the corridor and continued

2

to urge me away from the window. Her expression was one of growing concern, but I was not afraid of the storm. If anything, I felt energized by its raw power and magnificence, and it sparked a playfulness in me that I had not felt in days. It took my fourteen years of practiced willpower to hold back the smile that threatened to betray my amusement, pretending not to hear her over the rising winds and growling thunder. Nevertheless, it was not the smile but the tears I sought to hide from her when I turned my gaze back toward the angry sea and continued to ignore her warnings.

She of all people knew me, better than even my parents, and she would scold me if I showed any weakness of character – lest my father hear of it. Ever conscious that he was seen by some as a usurper, Ethba'al of Zour, King of Tzidon would abide no weakness from any of his offspring. This was especially true for me. As the only daughter of his chief wife and consort, Azra of Assyria, I was to bring glory to his family and people by my marriage to the new king of Yisrael, cementing an alliance that would bring peace and prosperity to both great kingdoms. I could not now, on the evening before my departure, bring shame upon him.

With that in mind, I finally decided to heed my nursemaid's warnings and turned away from the window. She squinted and pursed her lips as I returned to her side. "How many times must I tell you not to tarry by the window when it storms?"

At last, I allowed a faint smile to break upon my lips and I met hers with a mischievous gaze. "What do you think it means?"

"What do I think *what* means, Yezeba'al?" she asked, her affectation of displeasure betrayed by the hint of a smile on her lips. She always hated that I had the power to amuse and disarm her whenever I was disobedient. I was grateful she would continue to serve me in my new home. A priestess of Ashtarti and spiritual guide as well as my childhood nurse, Daneyah would continue to be of great comfort to me in the years to come.

Looking to her for wisdom, I said, "A storm on the eve before my departure? Surely, it must mean something." My whole life had been an amalgam of signs and premonitions.

Tucking an errant lock behind my ear and fixing my sleeve that had slipped from my shoulder, she said, "Perhaps it is a parting gift from the Ba'alim, to wish you well on your journey and in your coming marriage."

3

I permitted a half-smile. "Perhaps," I conceded as I paused to meet her gaze before passing through the doorway. I did not want to admit that a part of me feared it was not a gift but a portent of things to come.

The morning of my departure for Yisrael was clear and perfect, showing little sign of the storm that had passed through the night before. Instead of taking the long road that was used by traders, we travelled south by sea from Zour to the port at Yapo, in the Sharon Plain. This was on the western side of the mountain range of Kerem-el: the vineyard of El, the father and patriarch of the many gods that were venerated in that region long before I was born. Olive groves and vineyards covered the rocky slopes; at the northernmost tip of the range, which we passed while out at sea, the highest peak was a sacred place that overlooked a bay where fishermen and sailors could take shelter during storms.

Unfortunately, I did not get to see the vineyard of my divine ancestor, because I was sick for the better part of the voyage. I had spent my whole life gazing at the sea from my father's palaces, had grown up surrounded by tales of my courageous seafaring people, but I had never been out to sea until that day. My initial excitement at finally being able to sail on one of my father's ships ended the moment my stomach began to churn with the persistent rise and fall of the waves. It was Daneyah who noticed me looking ill, just before I leaned my head forward and began to throw up over the side of the ship – much to the shock and horror of my mother, who was standing nearby. Suddenly, I was being whisked away by my attendants and had to spend the rest of the journey miserable in bed, eager to return to steady land and ashamed of my weakness.

It was a relief when we reached Yapo, where Akhab's Lord Steward – *abarakkum* – and an armed escort came to meet and welcome us on our ships that were moored in the harbor for the night. The Lord Steward was a brown-haired man called Obadyah; while he was outwardly polite, I sensed the steward's distrust and saw, when he thought he was not being observed, the way he looked with disdain upon the four hundred priests and priestesses of my entourage when we assembled to continue our journey the next day. They were to remain in Yisrael, where they would continue to serve me as High Priestess and keep the light of the Ba'alim from dimming in the hearts of my husband's people. That was the greater part of my mission, and one I thoroughly believed in, but Obadyah and some of his men looked at us as if we were an invading army. I realized then that the road toward peace would be long and precarious.

On the journey from Yapo to Shomron, my father rode on the back of a horse with Obadyah and some of the other men. Most of our entourage walked, but my mother and I sat on curtained litters carried by slaves; their great muscles bulged and shined with sweat in the scorching sun. Through kohl-lined eyes, I discreetly admired the strength of their bronzed forms while I opened the sheer curtains to dissipate the heat. When the dust and the smell of their sweat became intolerable, I drew the curtains once again, thankful that the heat brought out the scent of myrrh on my skin. As I cooled myself with an alabaster-handled fan set with ostrich plumes and peacock feathers, I wondered if the slaves were troubled by the heat and their work or if they were somehow made for these conditions the way a horse was made to pull a chariot.

I began playing with the scarab pendant, carved from a large opal, which hung from a beaded necklace around my neck. The opposite side of the scarab was my seal, carved with Egyptian symbols of divinity and *l'yzbl*: "belonging to Yezeba'al." I never took it off, except to bathe, sleep, or stamp my correspondence. No one else was allowed to touch it on pain of death. Whenever I did take it off, I handled it myself or kept it locked away in a small cedar box.

Dropping the scarab with a thump over my chest, I leaned over and looked back at Daneyah. She was riding a short distance behind on the back of a donkey with the other priestesses, most of whom were on foot. She looked exhausted, her face red, her brown curls plastered to her cheek and the side of her forehead covered with sweat. Her plain white mantle, draped around her haphazardly, looked as if it might come loose from her hair at any moment, to be lost beneath the shuffling sandals of weary handmaidens and the hooves of beasts of burden. Travel was tiresome and exhausting.

"Music," I called to a group of priests who walked alongside my litter, carrying flutes and drums and stringed instruments.

"Yes, my Ba'alah," their leader answered pleasantly, even though he looked wretched and miserable covered in dust and sweat.

5

Then he raised his lyre and began to play. Soon, the others joined with their instruments, each of them playing their parts. I closed my eyes and breathed deeply to relax and enjoy the pleasant melodies, letting the musicians choose what songs to play.

Traveling for most of the day, we followed a road that went northeast through the plains and forests of Sharon and continued into the mountain range. Having spent all my fourteen years sheltered inside the walls of my father's palaces in Tzidon, I was curious to observe the open plains and rugged mountainous terrain from my litter as we trudged slowly along the way.

Although it was dry that time of the year, it was not the desert I had been led to believe. The soil was rocky, but the mountains were covered in shrubs and cut through by jagged valleys that acted as natural corridors. There was no sign of any people, but one could sense eyes watching as we passed. Bandits or murderers could easily hide within the rocky crags and caves that dotted the slopes and no one would know they were there. With our rich clothes and endless train of opulent wealth, we would make an appealing target. I was grateful for the armed guard that surrounded us. Their diligence allowed me to relax, take in the scenery, and watch the wildlife.

Beautiful golden jackals ran between the bushes, pausing now and then to watch warily as we passed. Herds of wild elephants occasionally roamed in the distance. Whenever we paused to give water to the horses and livestock, I could hear the grunting of wild boar. I even smiled at a pair that chased each other in play as I relaxed within the shade of my curtained litter, stroking the smooth feathers of a peacock, who had been taken out of his traveling cage to rest upon my lap. He cooed and purred as I scratched under his beak. The peacock and his mate had been brought to me when they were only chicks, a precious gift from a faraway kingdom where their kind prospered in nature. They had hatched several young since then in my father's garden at the palace in Tzidon. I insisted on bringing the original pair in the hope that their offspring would prosper in my new home, as well. It was said the great and wise King Shelomoh kept peafowl at his palaces in the days when the two kingdoms of Yisrael and Yehudah were one, so I knew they would be welcome in my new home.

Having spent two days at sea and two more traveling by land, we reached the city of Shomron on the third day. It was a glorious city set high upon the hills; from its center rose the crown jewel of Shomron, the sumptuous royal palace that was built by Akhab's father, Omri, during his prosperous reign. After depositing us at the governor's mansion outside the palace complex, which would be our lodging for the night, Obadyahu left us. We were given the remainder of the day, as well as the night, to rest before my presentation to the king.

As we settled in, I was taken to the bath that had been prepared for me with fragrant oils. My handmaidens, most of whom were priestesses, scrubbed thoroughly to remove the dust that had built up in our two days of travel through the mountains and plains. Then began the first of the preparations for my wedding. Upon my feet and hands and cheekbones and chin, delicate patterns were drawn with the dark brown paste made from powdered henna leaves. The same was applied to my belly and breasts, for only my husband to see. It would last throughout the various festivities of the following days and only begin to fade once I had been a wife for yet a few days more.

When the color had set and the paste was wiped off the surface of my skin, I smiled at my reflection in the gold disk of my ivory-handled mirror; the handle was carved in the shape of a crowned cobra from which a lotus bloomed. When I admired the henna patterns, I imagined the touch of a lover's fingers tracing them and hoped that my husband would find them to his liking.

That night, from my open window at our temporary lodging, I looked up at the palace that would soon be my home and tried to imagine what my life would be inside those walls. Daneyah's daughter Kora came to stand beside me at the window. Nursed together at her mother's breast, we were as sisters; she was more sister to me than any of my father's other daughters. His Melkah's only daughter, I was his favorite. Having been identified as the long-awaited reincarnation of Ashtarti at the time of my birth, I had been kept apart from my half-sisters and felt no kinship with them. Most of them hated me because I was exalted over them, even over those who were my elders. As such, I had always been closer to Kora, the only one of my handmaids who was not a priestess of Ashtarti.

Admiring the palace from afar, she pondered aloud, "The 'Ivory Palace'. I wonder if it's truly made of ivory?" When I did not

7

reply, she turned her gaze upon me, placed a hand on my shoulder, and offered a comforting smile.

I covered her hand in thanks and looked up at the palace again, taking a deep breath and letting it out slowly. "What will he be like, the king who is to be my husband?"

Kora stroked my hair which had been left loose to dry before it was combed out for the night. She had always loved touching my hair, which fell in soft waves and was easier to care for than her own tightly curled locks, which she often kept hidden beneath a kerchief. After gently tugging at my hair in a playful manner, she tilted her head thoughtfully, and said, "I've heard he is young. If you accept him tomorrow, you are to be his first wife." She paused and giggled mischievously. "I hope he knows what to do on your wedding night..."

I chuckled as warmth spread over my nose and cheeks, and then I cast my gaze downward. Looking out the window to avoid meeting her gaze, I said, "He is a man and a king. I am sure he knows what to do."

"No doubt they've prepared him for it – if he did not already figure it out for himself."

"He has sixteen concubines, so I've heard."

"Well then, he's certainly not ignorant of the female body." She passed her gaze over mine, which was more developed than hers even though she was older than me by a few months. She took after her mother: tall, thin, and fair, compared to my voluptuous curves and olive-complexion. Smiling, she said, "No doubt he will be pleased with his latest acquisition." When my cheeks grew warmer, she laughed. "Yezeba'al, am I making you shy?"

I looked at her sideways. "What do you think?"

"Are you scared?"

"N-no. Just..."

"Nervous?"

I nodded. Then I bit my bottom lip, while she looked out the window again. After a pause, she turned back to me. "It will be all right. You can still turn him down if he is not to your liking."

"I know. And I am prepared to do so, if I do not feel that we could work together to bring peace to this tumultuous kingdom."

"Or if you don't find him attractive enough to bed." Despite my amusement, I hissed through my teeth, but she only continued to

8

laugh. "You'll probably enjoy it. At least, I've heard it can be enjoyable if the husband is not a brute. Your mother told you...?"

"What to expect, yes." The warmth spread across my face again, as I thought of the demonstration I had been made to watch, in preparation for my marriage. After spending most of my last day in Zour at the Temple of Ba'al, where I was declared High Priestess, I was taken back to the palace and escorted to my mother's private quarters. There, a priest and priestess of Ashtarti demonstrated everything that a man and woman can do together in the marital bed. I had not told Kora because I always wanted to protect her innocence. Being neither a priestess nor a wife, she did not need to know these things. Even now, all I said was, "She talked with me our last night at Zour before I went to my chamber for bed."

"And...?"

I looked at her and almost rolled my eyes. "And I know as much as one can know, without actually...doing the act myself."

"So, tell me about it. Please, Yezeba'al, I want to know. My mother will not tell me anything, and you are the closest thing I will ever have to a sister."

"I'll tell you when I know more about it for myself."

She heaved a sigh and leaned back on the windowsill, twisting her neck to look out into the city. It was dark except for the lights coming from the windows of people's homes, and the fires from watchtowers that lined the walls. I wondered how the rest of our entourage was faring in their camp outside the city, grateful that I did not have to spend another night in a tent.

I looked at her again when I felt her eyes on me, and she observed, "You're so serious tonight. You're usually more vivacious."

A barely concealed smile betrayed my amusement. "I'm going to be made a queen in two days' time. Tomorrow I will be presented to the king with my dowry and my entourage. Forgive me if I'm a little more pensive than usual."

"Are you a bride going to her husband or a prisoner on the way to meet his executioner?"

Now, I rolled my eyes and smirked. "I'll know by this time tomorrow, I suppose. And then I promise I will tell you more about it."

Kora giggled and threw her arms around me, letting her chin rest on the back of my shoulder. I embraced her in return and rested

9

my head against hers with my eyes closed, allowing myself to enjoy this moment of peace on my last night before everything changed forever.

Early the next morning, I was awakened before sunrise. My thick, dark hair was smoothed and combed through with hot oils before being braided and intricately woven, coiled, and pinned to the back of my head. Most of my hair would be hidden beneath a headdress, so the hairpieces made from my own hair that I often used were not needed this time. Then I was arrayed in richly woven cloth, dyed purple in the manner for which my father's people were known and lined with gold. Finally, my eyes were lined with kohl and my lips painted crimson – the color of fresh blood in a sacrifice.

Once I was dressed, I knelt before an altar that Daneyah had set up and consecrated in my chamber that morning. While she and my mother supervised, I anointed myself with holy oil, burned incense, and bowed three times with my forehead to the floor. Then I sacrificed a pair of doves to the Ba'alim.

The first dove was calm and unsuspecting as I took him from his cage, gently stroked his feathers, and lifted the gold ceremonial dagger. Having witnessed her mate being sacrificed, the second dove began to grow restless as I clutched her in my hand and, in one swift movement, carefully slashed her breast with the freshly sharpened blade. Like the first, it was a clean kill, the blade having pierced its heart – a proper sacrifice.

The doves' pure white feathers were smeared with fresh blood when I prepared them as burnt offerings upon the altar before two small jewel-eyed ivory figures: what the Yahwist zealots referred to as idols, claiming that we worshipped the figures themselves instead of real and living gods. They did not understand our ways. The figures were not our gods – they were representations of the goddess Ashtarti and her divine consort, Hadad, whom we referred to most often by his title, Ba'al, and occasionally by the epithet that had been given to him by the people of Zour: Melkorat, 'King of the City'. The figures provided a focal point, a tangible means for us to reach out to the Ba'alim, who were with us in spirit. Their jeweled eyes, ruby for

Ashtarti and emerald for Ba'al, provided a conduit through which the gods could watch us perform our acts of communion and worship.

While my offering was being made at the governor's mansion, my father and brother were at the Temple of Ba'al which Akhab had constructed near the palace at Shomron as a wedding gift, so I could continue to practice my religion and perform my sacred duties as High Priestess in my new home. There at the temple, my father made the customary sacrifice of bulls, sheep, goats, and quail upon the altar that had been consecrated to our Ba'al. Later I learned that Akhab attended the sacrifice but did not take part in the ritual; for, although he was not a zealot, he was faithful in his devotion to Yahowah and did not wish to anger his jealous god.

My own offering of the two doves, I would later present to my husband for us to eat during our nuptial feast. For now, I left them on my private altar while I pressed my hands together and bowed three times, in the slow and reverent manner which I had been taught. With each bow, I whispered prayers of thanksgiving and asked them to bless my union. Then I rose and returned to my handmaidens, to finish being prepared for my presentation to the King of Yisrael.

A cloth-of-gold mantle that was so long and heavy it would need to be carried by my handmaidens during the full length of the procession, was pinned to my hair beneath a headdress made from the same gold of Opir as my jeweled collar, rings, and bracelets. A gold medallion set with a polished sapphire – a symbol of the sea, on which my father's people had long depended – hung from the headdress on the center of a thick gold chain lined with tiny gold droplets that dangled over my forehead and shimmered when they caught the light.

Finally, moving slowly and with the help of Kora, I slipped into golden sandals that were fitted exactly to my feet. The narrow gold thong would not obscure the intricate swirls and designs of my henna tattoos and the small gold rings on my toes. Now, I looked every bit the daughter of a king who was soon to be another king's wife.

Once all was in order and the time came, we assembled in the courtyard, which was filled not only with the people who were part of my entourage but the many lavish gifts that were part of my dowry. One of the gifts was a bedframe of cedar wood inlaid with ivory. It

11

was to be my bridal bed and the bed I would use for the rest of my life; the mattress rolled, and the frame disassembled to be carried upon a cart every time we travelled. As I passed by the cart that morning, I could not help but to look at the elaborately carved bedframe and think about what my first night upon it would be like.

My father, dressed in all the splendor of a priest-king and standing in a golden chariot, noticed my gaze fixed upon the bedframe, and teased, "Do not be afraid of a bed, Yezeba'al! Upon it, you shall perform the most sacred duties of a priestess of Ashtarti for your husband alone."

While he laughed, I turned my gaze toward the ground and smiled modestly, while my mother put her arms around me, and said to him, "Stop – you will embarrass her, Melekh! She is still a maiden – praise Ba'al that she has been preserved from her own folly!"

If my mother was concerned about my father embarrassing me, she had chosen instead to slay me with her last comment as she led me to the litter that awaited me near what would be the end of the procession. I looked at her in horror, grateful that no one else had overheard the remark – or if they did, they chose not to show it. When she saw my resentful expression as I settled into my chair, she said quietly, "Do not pretend it is not true, Yezeba'al. I thank the gods every day you did not spoil yourself. You will thank them, too, when your husband is pleased by your ignorance of the act."

She left me then to ride in her litter directly behind my father, who would lead the procession in his chariot. The King and Queen of Tzidon were surrounded by armored eunuchs. Highly trained warriors, they eschewed married life in favor of a life of service to the king's household. Being eunuchs, they could be trusted in the presence of the king's wives and daughters, the only members of the male sex who were allowed to be alone with us, apart from kin. I was taught from birth to trust them with my life, for they were expected to give theirs to preserve mine, if ever the need arose.

After the king and queen came my younger brother and heir to the throne, Ba'alesar, driving a miniature version of the chariot my father drove. He was only ten years old but had been learning how to drive a chariot for three years already, so he was well-prepared to be a part of this procession and make my father proud. When all this was over in a few days' time, he would return with my parents to Tzidon – without me. Feeling a sting in my eyes, I tried

12

not to think about it. I had to stay the course, wherever it would take me.

Following my brother on foot were my twenty score priests and priestesses, led by Daneyah on her richly dressed donkey; then the officials, ministers, and any other high-ranking members of the royal court who had come to Shomron for this auspicious event. Anyone invited would not have dared to refuse such a great honor. They were there to represent my father's kingdom and show their support in his alliance with the new King of Yisrael. Also, there for support of a different kind and following in their wake, were the entertainers: dancers, acrobats, singers, musicians, and big men pounding a steady beat on drums hung over their shoulders on thick leather straps.

Finally, came all the servants carrying the endless trail of gifts: livestock, doves and quails in cages to be sacrificed at the temple in the coming days, furniture, ivory carved in the Egyptian style that was popular in Tzidon, rich cloths and silk rugs, large chests of cedar and ebony inlaid with ivory and filled to the brim with cups, plates, bowls of gold and silver and other precious metals, jars and sacks and small boxes full of incense and oils and spices, an ornately carved cage bearing my peacock and peahen, sapphires and rubies and emeralds and pearls and other precious stones, weapons enough to fill a king's armory, and many more gifts to further enrich the kingdom. Many of these gifts were obtained in trade with faraway exotic kingdoms that could only be reached by ships capable of traversing vast distances across many seas, increasing their value, and showcasing the wealth of my father's kingdom. At the end of all this came the last and greatest of treasures: the bride in all her regalia, to be delivered to her king.

Carried on my litter and surrounded by my armored eunuchs, I sat on a cedar chair inlaid with ivory, my back straight, head held high. In my lap, I clutched an intricately carved ivory coffer containing frankincense and myrrh. This last gift would be presented to my husband as a gift for the Temple of Yahowah on Mount Gerizim, as an offering of peace between our deities.

My fingers ached as I clutched the coffer close to my waist. It was like an anchor against the effect of nerves and the weight of my own sumptuous regalia. I could hardly move or turn my head, for the golden mantle and headdress were extremely heavy; it required a

13

great deal of concentration to keep from being pulled down by the mass of it. By the time we reached the palace, my head, neck, and shoulders ached, yet I could show no sign of discomfort. My expression remained fixed and calm, despite the roiling chaos underneath.

The grand procession moved slowly through the city streets, lined with people tossing flower petals and leaves, waving fan palms, shouting joyous welcomes to the Canaanite princess who was said to be a living goddess. I managed to pass my gaze from side-to-side, to glimpse the people of Shomron – soon to be my people. Most of the faces I saw were warm and filled with joy as they offered blessings for a happy, fruitful marriage. Those who were already followers of my gods prostrated themselves before me as I passed. Many others seemed curious and eager to catch a glimpse of the girl who was to be their new queen. However, there were some faces I noticed from among the crowds who did not look kindly upon me.

As the procession moved through the gates that were open to the palace complex, we passed a group of men holding staves and dressed in rags or animal skins. Their faces were set with eyes hard as stone, with grimaces and hissing and curses upon their lips. They were strangers to me, and yet I knew them. Having been prepared for this mission, I was aware of this new cult of Yahowah that had taken root in the southern kingdom of Yehudah and was rapidly growing north into Yisrael. Yahowah was one of many gods worshipped in the region, but he was a fierce and jealous storm god who demanded of his followers to be the only one they prayed to and worshipped. His followers were tolerant of those who worshipped other gods, for the most part, until this new sect of Yahwist zealots began not only to demand exclusive worship but to claim the other gods were false and condemn all who worshipped them. I was a foreign princess who worshipped foreign deities. Worse than that, I was a priestess said to be the incarnation of the goddess herself; to the zealots, I was most unwelcome. Swallowing hard, I averted my gaze and tried to ignore them. This was an auspicious day, and I would not allow a few angry old men to get in the way of it.

As I reached the crowded courtyard at the back end of the procession, followed by still more armored guards, the largest building in the palace complex came into view. Situated on a foundation hewn with wide stairs leading to the pillared entryway

14

and flanked by a guardhouse on one side and a secondary pillared entryway on the other, it rose high above all the other buildings in the city, seeming to reach into the clouds. I knew that was where my future husband awaited me. Would he be pleased with his bride?

My stomach twisted and I took a trembling breath, preparing myself for this final stage of the journey. Still following the gift-bearers, I was carried up the stairs through the great entryway and into an antechamber lined with some members of the king's court. From there, we followed through another pillared entryway into the great hall, a vast chamber with a high ceiling. Clerestory windows ran along the tops of the east and west walls, allowing the grand chamber to be lit by the noble sun throughout the day. This was the public audience chamber, from which the king would conduct most of the affairs of his kingdom. Today it was filled not only with his family, ministers, courtiers, and foreign dignitaries, but with my family and the members of our entourage who had all filed in before my arrival.

At the far end of the hall, upon a raised dais, the King of Yisrael was seated on his great throne looking bored. No doubt he would rather be in the field practicing the art of war, riding his horses, or driving his chariot than sitting indoors to watch this seemingly endless show of wealth and prestige being paraded before him. I observed him, partially obscured behind the diaphanous curtains of my litter, and wondered what he was thinking. Perhaps he thought our procession was overdone, that it was cultivated to mask the unsightliness of his bride. He had probably been told that I was comely, but dignitaries often exaggerated the beauty of princesses being offered in marriage treaties. I was confident in my own beauty, but worried his tastes may not align with my appearance. If he had sixteen concubines, even if it was said I was the most beautiful woman in the world, how could I compare to them in beauty and form? I did not want my husband to be disappointed, especially now that I had seen him for myself.

While he was, indeed, young as I had heard, he had a full beard that was trimmed close to his strong jaw but left longer at his chin, in the fashion of the day. His hair fell in dark brown curls, cut short around his face but growing longer as it fell past his ears and down to his shoulders. His skin was perfectly bronzed from the many hours he must have spent outdoors. His nose was straight and distinctive but not overly prominent; his dark, heavy-lidded eyes

15

were almond-shaped and were neither too close nor too far apart; his brow was thick yet shapely and upon his forehead rested a golden diadem, the symbol of his lordship. Beneath his sumptuous robes, I could imagine he had a fine form to match the face, and I was eager to look upon him. He had the appearance of a god, and I was pleased.

My servants arrayed all the gifts before him, leaving an opening at the front of the dais for the presentation of his bride. When the litter was brought down on the floor, my father came to stand before me, obscuring my husband's view as I rose from my chair, still bearing the ivory coffer. Kora and the other handmaidens helped me step down without losing my balance. I glanced to the side where my proud mother stood with all the dignity of a queen who had likely been presented to my father in this same manner. Her right hand rested on her son's shoulder, as he stood by her with his jaw tense, likely to conceal a yawn that desperately wanted to escape. He was so young to be a part of this, but I was grateful that he had come.

When my father stepped forward and began to walk the aisle toward the dais, he climbed the steps to meet Akhab, who had risen from his throne and come forward. The two kings grasped each other by their forearms in a gesture of unity and friendship. Then my father stepped aside and held out his hand to present me to my husband. Keeping my head high but my gaze lowered, mindful not to make a single misstep, I was led forward to complete my short walk to the dais, as our herald announced:

"Yezeba'al, High Priestess and Virgin Consort of Ba'al, comes before Your Lordship, Akhab, King of Yisrael, bearing gifts and expressing great joy at this union. It is her will that there be peace between our peoples and our gods for all time to come. She therefore asks, Melekh, that you accept, as a token of the peace she brings, these precious offerings of frankincense and myrrh to be delivered to the Temple of Yahowah on her behalf."

As it had been practiced so many times beforehand, I knelt before the king and set the ivory coffer on the floor. Bowing with my arms stretched out in front of me, I gently pushed the coffer across the floor toward him as I dropped lower, until the sapphire medallion that hung over my forehead touched the floor. I had been instructed to pause and wait for several seconds in this pose, while one of his servants came to retrieve the ivory box and bring it to him for inspection. My neck was aching from the headdress and mantle that

16

were bearing down on me as I waited patiently, distracting myself from the pain by staring at the floor. I watched a tiny ant crawling along one of the cracks and wondered if ants felt pain as we do.

When it came time for me to rise, still ignoring the pain, I slid back to a kneeling position and lifted my head to behold my husband and my king. I nearly faltered when our eyes met. His previously bored expression was now replaced by one of intense curiosity. For a moment, I could neither think nor take a breath. I felt as though I knew him; as if I'd known him long before this moment and, rather than meeting for the first time, we were merely being reunited after a lengthy separation. Every part of my being was filled with joy, and I longed to run to him as my soul cried out: *It is you, my beloved!*

Finally exhaling, and aware of the hundreds of eyes that were now fixed upon me, I remembered my duty and carefully rose to my feet. Meanwhile, the king proclaimed in a speech that he had surely practiced many times: "O beautiful, virtuous, benevolent Daughter of Tzidon: I, Akhab, Melekh Yisrael, accept your offering and humbly ask that you accept me as your husband and lord this day."

Although I had not known exactly what he would say, this speech had also been practiced many times before I left my father's kingdom. It was, in part, a script we followed as expected of us – nevertheless, as a high priestess and a princess of Tzidon, I still had the right to reject his offer and return to my father's kingdom. It seldom happened, as duty often overcame preference, but it was my right, and in coming I was prepared to exercise it if I did not find the King of Yisrael to my liking.

Tearfully meeting his gaze, I smiled spontaneously. Breaking with the script I had been prescribed, I answered, "Ba'al, I am yours."

As the peoples of our kingdoms who were present there erupted into cheers and praises, my father came to me and, with tears shining in his smiling eyes, he took my hand and led me up the dais. He brought my left hand to the right hand of my husband, and I became his wife, the wife of the King of Yisrael. My heart overflowed with joy as we stood side-by-side and the hall erupted into another wave of cheers the moment our clasped hands were raised before the two royal courts, to show all who were present that we were united as man and wife.

While standing before the nobles and our families in the Great Hall, we were blessed with incense and anointed with sacred oils.

17

Although the practice of taking multiple wives was permitted among kings in Yisrael and elsewhere, only the king's first marriage was given the official blessing and anointing by priests. The later wives would be wives in name only, bound to the king by law but not by the spirit. Unless Akhab denounced me or raised another in my place, or if I failed to give him an heir, I would always remain his one true wife.

Yisrael's High Priest had come to Shomron from Mount Gerizim to perform the marriage ritual. An aging man with a long dark beard streaked with gray, and dressed in robes made of the finest materials, he performed the ritual with all dignity and respect. This gave me hope, for if I was accepted by the High Priest of Yahowah in Yisrael, I thought that my acceptance by the people was assured and that I might win the favor of Yahowah alongside that of my own gods.

That was until an old man leaning on a walking stick came forward and pointed to me with a fierce gaze. "You, O daughter of Tzidon, are the wife of our king: the king of our people, the people of Yahowah, the Lord God of Yisrael. Hearken to the Lord; give fully to him in your heart and in your mind, in your body and in your soul, and he will bless you. But if you withhold your heart from the Lord: if you offend him with idols and false worship..." he paused and spat on the floor. Shocked by this, I startled and grimaced, as the old man continued, "...he will curse you and your husband's kingdom. So let it be."

This old man, as I would later find out, was one of a group of Yahwist prophets who had been invited and encouraged to come bear witness to our marriage. Although not members of the priestly caste, like our own Ba'alim prophets, these men held a great deal of respect among the followers of Yahowah and were often welcome in the courts of princes and kings who sought to please the god of Yisrael and Yehudah. However, they often ran the risk of displeasing the rulers whose favor they sought, as was the case with this man.

Akhab was outraged. He immediately stepped forward to demand the prophet's removal from the palace and commanded him be taken to the dungeon for his offence. I watched my father's jaw tense and his eyes become narrow slits as he stared at the prophet with fire in his gaze. He almost smiled as the old man was escorted out of the palace, flanked by two guards with their weapons drawn.

18

Once the prophet was removed, Akhab raised his hands, "My wife, my honored guests, I beg pardon for this intrusion. I was unaware that this prophet, whom I have long respected, has been taken in by zealotry. Rest assured; he will be duly punished."

My father bowed his head. "This is why we are here, Melekh. And I assure you that my daughter is not afraid of these zealots. She is pleased to stand beside you in your mission to rid your kingdom of false teaching. I have the utmost faith in your union."

"As do I," said Akhab, turning to me with that curious gaze once again. When he smiled, I could not help but do the same, even as I lowered my eyes out of modesty. He took my hand, brought it to his lips, and said, "Yezeba'al, it is time for our people to meet their new Melkah."

He offered his arm. I took it and then he led me down the aisle as the entire assembled court prostrated themselves to us. He took me to a staircase that led to an upper corridor where there was a great window overlooking the city. A shofar was blown to announce us to the people. Being so close when the shofar was blown, I flinched. Already, I hated the sound of shofars even more than I hated the sound of horns. The noise grated on me; I would never get used to it.

The king saw my expression and offered an apologetic gaze, covering my hand with his in a comforting gesture. Then he was pulling me forward – there was no time to waste now that the shofar had sounded. When the people saw us, it was clear that many of them had been waiting for this moment. More cheers and praises arose from the city beneath us when they saw the king raise my hand, clasped in his. We smiled and waved and threw coins to the people, who scrambled to catch them and lift them off the streets. This done, we paused and met each other's gaze. In that moment, I believed that everything I had come here to do would be accomplished.

At last came the feast, which began with my offering of the roasted doves to my husband for us to share. While we ate the doves, the priests and priestesses of the Ba'alim offered their blessings and prayers for our marriage. My father joined them in his role as priest-king to speak of the union of Ashtarti and Hadad, the divine couple whose marriage was seen by their followers as the ultimate expression of marital bliss. Likening us to them, he finished with a

19

joke: "May this great king not disappear into the underworld, of course. I'm sure my daughter would not be pleased to lose her husband every time the rains cease."

Those who understood the reference, and who bore a sense of humor, laughed at his joke. Even my husband chuckled, and answered graciously: "I assure you, Melekh, I have no intention of leaving my lovely wife without a mate each summer. I should like to spend each day with her for many years to come."

Seated on a cushion at the head table, my un-sandaled feet pulled under me, I smiled and looked down at my hands in my lap, as warmth spread across my nose and cheeks. Glancing at Akhab, I saw him gazing at me, and my heart quickened. Wishing to hide my awkwardness, I reached for my cup of spiced wine sweetened with honey and sipped generously. The tingling that began in my head and spread throughout my body was a welcome sensation. Under the watchful eye of Daneyah, reinforcing the rules of my strict mother, I had never had so much wine in such a short amount of time, but I enjoyed my newfound freedom to imbibe.

That was until my husband reached out his hand and took my cup to prevent one of the servants from refilling it. "Not too much or you will be sick in the morning – there is no water in this wine. And we still have three days of feasting to get through."

Offended that, as my husband, he would think himself my master and treat me as a child, I could not hide the irritation from my gaze. He saw the look but only smiled. "Trust me; I've done it myself more than a few times – regretted it every time. But like an idiot, I had to try it again and again to be sure. Ah, there – you have a lovely smile."

My smile was brief, however, as I looked at my empty cup with a sigh. I did not want that sensation to fade.

Akhab seemed to read my mind. "It feels good now, yes?"

I looked at him from the side and gave an affirming nod.

"Ah, but then you wake up feeling like you wish you had died. And if you had far too much you will not even remember what you did the night before, and you have to live with the uncertainty when those who do remember tease you and make jokes at your expense. Not worth the morning death wish. I do not want that to be your experience. But...I will not stop you. I only tell you now so you will know my experience and may use it to make your own decision, if you wish."

At last, I conceded. I raised my palm to the next servant who came around to fill my cup. With a dutiful bow, he took his pitcher and moved on to the next. I saw Akhab watching me from the side with a smile. "You made a good decision, Yezeba'al."

I hoped he would not see my maidenly blush in the dim light of oil lamps that surrounded us. Unable to bring myself to look at him directly, I admitted, "You are gifted in the art of persuasion, Melekh."

"I thank you for the sincerity of your compliment. However, an orator is only as persuasive as the openness of his listeners. The greatest orator in the world cannot convince a man whose mind is closed to his message. At least, that is what my father taught me – and in my short experience as king, it has proven true."

"Omri was a wise man."

Akhab smiled but his gaze took on a faraway look. Then he began cutting his meat, and said, "He was a good man. Taught me many things, some of which I've found useful."

I smiled while he ate a bite of herb-roasted lamb. Then I became aware of my parents watching us and my smile faded. My father had touched my mother's arm to draw her away from the conversation she was having with one of her ladies, and then she followed his hand pointed toward us as he whispered something to her. They both smiled and nodded approvingly. I lowered my gaze, pretending not to see them.

Thankfully, everyone's attention was soon diverted when my husband's Chief Scribe appeared, having been charged with the task of composing a wedding song to recite at the feast. At the king's summons, he came anxiously to bow before us, bearing a sheath of papyrus in his ink-stained hands.

"Aharon, what have you composed for us this night?"

"Melekh Akhab, Melkah Yezeba'al," said the scribe with another bow, before speaking not only to the king and me but also to the assemblage of courtiers and guests, "I must confess that when I was charged to write a new song for this glorious occasion, I found my tongue went dry, my fingers ceased to work! It was as though I had never known words; I became mute. But then, Melekh, Melkah, as I bore witness to the splendor of this wondrous occasion, and to the beauty and grace of Melkah Yezeba'al being presented to you,

21

Melekh, the words that had for so long evaded me suddenly began to spill forth. My mind began to overflow as a spring that had been, at last, unblocked from its natural flow! And I am eager to share with you, all of you, what I have written this night – and assure you, it is an improvement from what I had originally prepared for this occasion!"

Akhab wiped his fingers on a cloth and, smiling, raised up his hands. "Then we are eager to hear it!"

Aharon the scribe gave a nod, and then turned to the music director. The director also gave a nod, the musicians prepared their instruments, and Aharon turned back to us. "The tune you will recognize, Melekh, for it is set to 'The Lilies', but the words are my own. May it please the king."

With that, the music played, Aharon cleared his throat, and the song began:

> *My heart overflows with a glorious descant*
> *As I recite this song for my king and his bride:*
> *My tongue is a pen, and I a skillful poet.*
>
> *Akhab, most excellent of the sons of men!*
> *Forever you are blessed by the greatest of the gods:*
> *Your lips have been anointed with Yahowah's grace.*
> *Mighty king, with sword strapped to your thigh:*
> *Ride on, victorious; in all your majesty*
> *You bring truth, meekness, and righteousness.*
> *Display remarkable deeds with your right hand.*
> *Sharp are your arrows in the hearts of your foes:*
> *Kingdoms fall beneath them and tremble,*
> *While Yisrael's throne shall go on forever.*
>
> *Yours is a rod of fairness:*
> *With it you bring justice to your kingdom,*
> *For you have cherished righteousness,*
> *You have loathed iniquity.*
> *Therefore Yahowah, the God of Abraham, your God*
> *Has anointed you with the sacred oil*
> *And raised you with gladness above all other men.*
> *Aloes, myrrh, and cassia perfume your garments.*

22

In the Ivory Palace, you have been made glad
With stringed instruments played to your glory.
The daughters of kings are among your concubines,
And your Melkah, in gold of Opir, stands at your side.

Listen, daughter, with an open heart
And with gladness follow these, my words:
Forget your people and your father's house,
That Melekh will be inflamed by your beauty,
And you will honor him as your husband.
O daughter of Zour, who comes bearing gifts,
The richest among people shall beseech your favor!
The princess of glory, enshrouded with gold:
In richly colored clothes adorned you are led,
Among virgins, you are brought before the king.

With exultation and great joy, the maiden is led
To the bridal chamber, where the king shall enter
As he enters his palace the victor of a great war.
Your sons shall take the place of their father:
You shall bear him princes of all the earth.
Yezeba'al, you shall live forever, immortalized by my song:
In all generations your name shall be remembered.
The peoples, with gladness, will praise you with thanks.

The song ended; Aharon bowed low to us while my husband showed his approval by rapping on the surface of the table with his hands. Others were soon to follow the king's approval in a like manner. I smiled graciously and nodded to Aharon the scribe, but kept my hands folded in my lap.

When the rapture died down, my husband cleared his throat. "You have done well, Aharon. Of course, this is why you were chosen. I imagine you will soon be asked to modify this song to be used at the weddings of other kings and great men, as well – I hope you will ask to be paid for your endeavor!"

The scribe, overjoyed, offered a second bow. "You do me great honor, Melekh."

23

The king smiled, gave a nod, and raised his hand. Aharon took the cue, bowing repeatedly as he backed away until he was far enough to turn around. I glanced at my husband with a smile, for the first time feeling an eagerness for him rising from within my body when I thought of him entering me as a victor of war... I shuddered and looked away; grateful no one could read my mind.

With the conclusion of the scribe's lyrical poem, the dining portion of the feast ended, and the celebration continued with music and dancing and song. It was a celebration that would last for days, breaking only for us and the guests to sleep, among other things. As dusk fell on that first night, however, I could see my husband's interest in the entertainments waning. I hoped his interest in me had not also waned, but an occasional glance in his direction provided reassurance when I found him watching me. He offered a smile which I modestly returned before looking away in shyness, thinking of what I knew was soon to come. *Please, let him be satisfied.*

When it was time for me to be escorted to the bridal chamber, an announcement was made that the king and his bride would be departing, but that the festivities would continue well into the night for all who wished to stay. At that point, the king's sister Atalaya came to retrieve me. Normally, in these situations, the king's mother would take that role but, as she was deceased that role fell to Atalaya, known to the family as Aya. She took me aside and brought me to my family so they could extend a final blessing for my wedding night.

My husband stayed at the table a moment longer, sipping at his wine and watching me discreetly. Then he got up and, followed by his men, went off to prepare for our first night together. I watched him disappear, hoping he was not dreading the consummation of our arranged marriage. Or worse, that he would spend this night with one of his concubines.

While my parents and Daneyah gathered around me to offer a final blessing, Aya stepped aside to give us privacy. I noticed some of the prophets of Yahowah, who stood at the far end of the hall, watching the festivities with scorn. Loosened by wine, I laughed at their disapproving gazes. "They are such miserable creatures."

My mother looked up and my father turned to see who I was looking at, while Daneyah merely lifted her gaze and smirked. Then my father said, "Yahowah has them chained like animals to their fear of incurring his wrath."

"Apparently, they are not allowed to have any fun," said my mother with a careless shrug. "Our gods are not so dull."

"Their god is like a petulant child," I said, "throwing himself on the floor before his nurses and demanding their attention. I do not know how they can stand to worship him."

My father smiled at this and placed a hand on my shoulder. "I have no fear of my Yezeba'al being swayed into worship of this jealous god. She will not forget the gods she has served all her life or turn against them in scorn."

My mother tipped her head to him. "You have taught her well, Melekh." Then, as my father stepped away, she gazed at me with glistening eyes and placed her hands upon my arm and on my cheek. "Remember what I told you, daughter, and all will be well. I pray he is good to you, and that you may find enjoyment in the act."

One of the conditions of my marriage contract was that I would not be housed with the king's other women. Whether they were wives or concubines, kings' women were typically housed in shared quarters with each other, the kings' children, and all those who were appointed to tend to their needs. As the High Priestess, however, I required my own suite (or house, if one was available) and absolute freedom of movement within the palace complex. It was necessary for me to perform my regular duties at the Temple of Ba'al and to afford me a reasonable expectation of privacy for one of my station.

At my father's palaces in Tzidon, I had my own residences near the temples where I studied, worked, and prayed every day with the other priestesses until the day I left for Yisrael. While he was unable to grant me a house of my own, Akhab had agreed to grant me my own quarters within each of his palaces; I was pleased to find my suite at the Ivory Palace of Shomron spacious and sumptuously decorated in anticipation of my arrival. My bridal bed was also there; I almost did not recognize it with the frame assembled and the mattress covered with luxurious cushions and richly colored bedlinens, ready to receive its bridal couple in their divine union.

After my mother's final words to me at the feast, the king's sister led me and Daneyah to my bridal suite. Apart from the priestesses who would be attendant on me that night, we were escorted by our ever-present eunuchs. Being not men, they would remain present in my bridal chamber even as I was stripped from my ceremonial robes to be prepared for my husband. I was so used to them that I was only vaguely aware of their presence, and because they were not true men, I had no fear of them. They were trained to avert their gaze and remain as still and silent as possible unless they were needed; there and yet not there, they seemed more a part of the room and its furnishings than they were human. They would leave once my husband had arrived, but they would stand directly outside the chamber to keep watch throughout the night.

While I watched the dancing smoke of incense and inhaled its aroma, Kora and my handmaidens removed my veil and the gold ornamentations I had been wearing since that morning. It was a relief to finally have them taken off and the soreness in my muscles massaged out. Standing naked in the middle of the chamber, I glanced over and thought I had seen one of the eunuchs watching me, but if he had been he looked away before I could catch him. I stared at him for a moment to see if he would turn his gaze toward me again, but he kept his gaze fixed at the wall across the chamber. I thought I must only have imagined he was looking at me – he was not a man, after all. What interest could he possibly take in a woman's body?

After being undressed, I was taken to sit at a dressing table while the braids and coils that had taken hours to weave were undone in minutes. My hair was gently combed until it shone like the silk curtains that adorned the latticed windows. The rich silks were illuminated by the flames of countless oil lamps that hung from metal stands and fixtures on the high walls. Sitting patient and still, I watched the flames flickering while my maids continued to prepare my body to receive my husband, wiping the sweat and dust from my skin, and polishing all the way to my fingertips. Once complete, Daneyah came to anoint me with oil of myrrh, the scent of which always surrounded me. Trying not to think, I was unable to silence the hopes and fears that were as numerous as the lamps.

Before I left my father's kingdom, apart from the demonstration that I had witnessed, my mother had admonished me to give freely to my husband and not be afraid of his advances. I knew my duty as a wife and was curious about the act of love; I wanted to know a man. Nevertheless, I was afraid of what I did not yet know. I hoped the king's outward show of graciousness would transfer to our marital bed, but I knew that was not always the case.

Perched on the lush cushions of my bed, wearing only a diaphanous veil of gold silk wrapped around my naked form, my noble bearing faltered when my husband appeared, and the maids and eunuchs left us alone in my bridal chamber. I could neither hide my trembling nor the maidenly blush that warmed my cheeks, while he approached me with the confidence of a man who had known many women before me. He slipped off his richly adorned robe and let it fall to his feet, revealing a well-toned and evenly bronzed physique. Then he removed his loincloth. I turned my gaze to the floor and tried in vain to steady the quickening of my heartbeat and the sharpness of my breath. It was not that I had never seen a naked man before – it was the knowledge of what his nakedness meant as he stood before me that caused me to look away.

He sat beside me, his weight on the cushions pulling me closer to him. Not yet touching, our bodies were close enough for me to feel the tingle of his heat. I inhaled the spices from the oils that anointed his skin – myrrh, aloe, and cassia. I was pleased by his scent. I felt his gaze on me and watched, from the corner of my eye, his hand rise toward me. I braced for his touch just before he gently moved my hair and the veil from my shoulder, gliding his fingers down the length of my arm and continuing to peel the veil away. My face grew hot as he revealed my form to his gaze, and his fingertips grazed the side of my breast on its journey. I exhaled, not knowing for how long I had been holding my breath.

I heard an express of air from his nostrils, and then his voice rose calmly to break the silence. "I will be gentle with you, Yezeba'al. You are my wife. I want you to enjoy this as much as I will."

For the first time since he appeared, I lifted my gaze and was comforted by the warmth I found in his, although I quickly cast my gaze away. Still vaguely trembling but somewhat more at ease, I smiled faintly at his reassurance and gave a nod.

Then he looked down at my tattooed hands, which were clutching the veil in my lap to hide the last of my nakedness. "But I will only take you when you are ready."

Relief that I would not be forced upon was mixed with disappointment that he might leave without knowing me. When he got up and bent to retrieve his robes from the floor, I pushed past my fear and forced myself to speak. "Wait!"

He stood erect and turned back to look at me, a question in his gaze.

"Please. Stay."

Without a word, he nodded and dropped his robe, and then he returned to sit beside me once again. I held my breath as he carefully reached to lift my chin, passing his thumb over the tattoos, and admiring them just as I had imagined the previous night. Then he looked up. He caught me watching him, only this time I did not look away. For the first time, I really looked into his eyes, and I was amazed by the intelligence in his gaze. He seemed momentarily stunned, perhaps by the forwardness I displayed in meeting his gaze so intently, and yet I detected no displeasure on his part. If anything, I sensed he was as taken in by my gaze as I was by his: as though our souls were meeting with a kiss.

He smiled faintly and tilted down my chin so he could brush his lips against my forehead. I closed my eyes and sighed, and then he tilted back my head to kiss the tattoos on my cheekbones. My body responded to his touch. I shivered, goose pimples dotting my flesh.

"Are you ready for me, Yezeba'al?" It came in a whisper and sent further chills through my body that excited me. I gave a nod of acquiescence.

He smiled and continued to hold my gaze while he brought his hand up to my breast, stroking with his thumb and squeezing gently. My lips parted, and I gasped, as the ache between my thighs grew stronger. My eyes stung and I nearly pulled away, but I held fast to both my duty and my growing desire, and at last stopped clutching at the veil upon my lap.

When I looked down then, I saw his part swollen with yearning. Quickly averting my gaze, I glanced discreetly from the side but could not withhold a smile when I saw that he was well-endowed. He chuckled and took me by the arms, and I allowed him to lay me back on the cushions. I squeezed shut my eyes, bracing for whatever came next.

He took his time and kept his promise. Lying next to me, our bodies touching, his fingers traced the swirling henna designs upon my breasts and belly that would lead him ever downward to my most sacred parts. For now, he avoided that secret place, instead coming back up to press his lips to the open spaces between the lines of

28

henna. I twitched when his lips brushed against my waist. His breath was warm upon my flesh.

I inhaled sharply when he brought his mouth to my breast and, with his tongue, traced the most tender part. Every bit of me was calling to him; not only my body but my soul cried out to him, and he seemed to hear it.

"Do not be afraid," he whispered, holding my gaze when he took my hand and directed it to his part. Accepting what he offered, I looked into his eyes with intense longing and tightened my grip. With a sigh of his own, he moved himself to me, and I knew that he was pleased. Growing in confidence, I continued touching him, and his passion increased. He brought his hand to my thigh, gripping firmly yet gently, and began kissing me hungrily as, more and more, I became an eager participant.

He seemed to know when I was ready. He held my gaze when, at last, he touched between my thighs. I gasped, raised my hips, and opened my legs to him, trembling violently and desperate to be taken. He smiled and then moved upon me to enter. The pain was sharp and sudden, yet brief. Crying out, I clung to him as tears filled my eyes. Then I inhaled deeply and whimpered as he continued.

He moved slowly at first, still meeting my gaze, and gently wiping the tears from my cheeks. Then he let his forehead touch mine, and gently rubbed his nose and lips against my cheek. We shared one breath as our bodies found a pleasing rhythm. Our union truly seemed divine, as though our souls mated with and through our bodies, which were perfectly formed for one another. By the time we finished our first coupling, we had both been equally satisfied.

2

The Mind of a Man

The next day, I became the anointed Queen of Yisrael. Before the ritual began, however, there was some dissent among the men at court who were opposed to the idea of a female ruler. While I had the support of my husband and some of the prominent members of his court, and even the High Priest of Yahowah who had agreed to perform the rite, the act of anointing me as co-ruler with my husband was not well-received by the majority. Most outrageous to these men was that I was a foreigner and, according to the laws of their land, the sacred oils used to anoint kings and priests were forbidden to be used on outsiders. Standing beside me and the High Priest on the dais as we prepared for the ritual, my husband met their outrage with reason, first by arguing that I was already an anointed priestess.

"The same sacred oil used to anoint kings and priests in Yisrael," he explained to his court, "is daily used by the Ba'alist priests and priestesses at Tzidon and elsewhere. Their priests taught our priests the sacred recipe; it has been in use by them long before it came to be used by the Yahwist priests here. Just this morning, I witnessed my wife anointing herself with this same sacred oil before she went into communion with her goddess. She has done this all her life – am I to tell her now that this is forbidden? What right do I have to tell an anointed priestess that she may not continue to anoint herself, as she must to perform the rituals that are a vital part of her sacred duty?"

This was met with silence, and the men who had only a moment ago been so vocal looked down at their feet. The anger on their faces had not dissipated, but it was clear they had no suitable response. It was only later that I would learn who these men were: uncles to my husband and noblemen of Shomron, some who served as ministers at court. Despite his youth, my husband seemed to know how to deal with the stubbornness of these older men and was not

30

afraid of going up against them because he firmly believed in what he was doing.

"Now," Akhab continued, "as the holy oil is used daily by my wife in her role as High Priestess, I see no harm in letting it be used to anoint her as Queen of Yisrael."

"It is one thing to anoint her as your wife, Melekh," said one of the men, "but to anoint her as your equal, to place her over us as though she were a man and a king…what right has a woman to rule over men? She has not the mind for it!"

"What do you know of my wife's mind, my lord? I was unaware that you had access to the minds and hearts of other men, let alone the hearts and minds of their women!"

This evoked a few chuckles from some members of the court, and so the man fell silent. Even my father, who did not laugh easily, smiled at my husband's jest. I watched him whisper something to my mother, who stood among the other priestesses, the only women allowed to be visibly present when the court gathered in the Great Hall to witness my anointing that day.

Now that he had disarmed our opponents, Akhab became serious again. I admired his youthful yet commanding presence, while he addressed the whole of his court: "It has never been unknown to any of you that this was my intention, as part of the marriage treaty, for Yezeba'al to be my co-equal in the governance of my kingdom. You did not object when the arrangements were discussed. Now is not the time for you to raise your objections, after it has already been agreed upon. That you would wait until this moment to object tells me that you were not listening then, or you listened but you did not understand, or perhaps you are intentionally being disruptive by waiting until now to voice your opinions and insult my wife and her family who are my guests."

The anger that rose in his voice at that last part silenced most of the men, but when my husband began to turn away, one of them shouted, "But this has never been done before in the kingdom of Yisrael!"

At this, my husband grinned. "Good, then this will be the first! Clearly, it is long overdue."

With that the clamor died down and the ritual was able to proceed. My husband returned to his throne, while I was made to kneel upon the dais before his court for the same ritual that was used

31

to anoint and crown kings. For this, my robe was opened to reveal my breast while the High Priest anointed my heart after first anointing my forehead and my hands. Then the High Priest placed the crown of the kings of Yisrael upon my head while my husband watched proudly from his throne. That done, I stood before the court and vowed to serve them and the people of Yisrael to the end of my days. Then all the men of the court were made to prostrate themselves before me in the way they paid homage to their king.

I watched the same men who had just voiced their objections begrudgingly kneel and prostrate themselves, making note of their faces. I did not yet have the experience of court intrigues to understand how best to deal with these men, but I already understood the importance of knowing one's enemies and learning their ways.

Following the anointing ritual, the court dispersed so their preparations for the second day of feasting could begin. While my husband took my father, brother, and some of the other men out for sport, my mother and I met with Obadyahu and Asa, one of Akhab's brothers. Asa was the youngest member of the council who served as Akhab's Minister of Ceremonies. He and the steward were helping us with the logistics of a performance I had planned for the banquet that afternoon.

"What will the performance be, Melkah?" asked Obadyahu, ever the picture of civility.

My mother answered for me. "It is a sort of play with dancing and song, that tells the story of the union between Ba'al and Ashtarti. Yezeba'al will be performing it with some of the other priestesses."

Obadyahu looked at me with a blank expression, but I could sense the distaste for our plans. A hint of his true feelings came out when he said, "It is most unusual for a queen to perform plays, but I have no doubt Melekh Akhab will be most pleased. He is rather fond of the arts."

"I thought he was fond of sport?" asked my mother.

"He is," answered Asa, with a cheerful countenance. Although he was clearly younger, he resembled Akhab most of all their brothers, of which there were many. Looking at me, he continued, "You will find my brother is fond of a great many things and excels at all of it. He is as much a musician and poet as he is a warrior and athlete. No doubt he will even write poems and songs for you, Melkah – although, I doubt he will ever perform them publicly."

My mother sniffed. "The king hardly strikes me as being shy."

"When it comes to his artistry, he is incredibly private. He never thinks any of it is good enough, but I tell him all the time he is as gifted as Dawid – if not more so, in fact."

For the first time, I spoke up. "I hope he will be pleased with my performance."

Returning his gaze to me, Asa said, "Oh, no doubt he will, Melkah. No doubt everybody will."

Obadyahu cleared his throat, and I saw him give Asa a warning look. I pretended not to notice. Thankfully, my mother knew how to smooth out the awkward moment. "Well, thank you both for your assistance. We had better return to the Melkah's quarters to dress and prepare for her performance. Shalom."

They responded in kind, and then she whisked me away. I was grateful for her wisdom in handling the situation, although she could not help but to tease me. "I believe *Akhimelekh* Asa is enamored of you, Yezeba'al."

"If he is," I replied, "it is most improper. I doubt my husband would take kindly to his brother becoming infatuated with me."

My mother only chuckled, and then we proceeded to my quarters where Daneyah and Kora would be waiting with the other priestesses attending to me that day.

While the previous day's festivities reflected the more subdued nature of Yisrael with its Yahwist sentiments, the second day's festivities were to reflect the ways of Tzidon; in particular, my devotion to Ba'al as the incarnation of his divine consort. My mother had downplayed the significance of my performance when answering the steward's question. More than simply telling a story, it was actually a sacred ritual dance – one that could only be performed by the priestesses of Ashtarti. It was said to be the dance the goddess herself performed at the court of El when she chose his son Ba'al to be her husband.

Dressed in a rich costume, I was to lead the other priestesses in the dance. When we were still at Tzidon, I chose the twelve who would accompany me. My mother directed while Daneyah instructed us in the choreography and taught us the meaning behind every move and gesture, which were meant both to entice and inform. Nothing was without purpose. The dance was sensual in nature because the sexuality of the goddess symbolized the fertility and abundance of life on earth. Together with her chosen consort, Ba'al, Ashtarti was the creative force within the universe; all life depended on their sacred union.

When the banquet opened, I gathered with my mother, Daneyah, and the other priestesses just outside the hall. While the other priestesses overflowed with excitement, I peered through a screened window that looked into the hall from the corridor. Akhab was seated on a cushion at the head table, talking with Asa and my father. The court musicians were playing their own music, waiting for the cue that it was time for our dance to begin, at which point my own musicians would take over to accompany us.

When the moment came, the music suddenly ceased, and a hush fell over the hall. Then the priests of Ashtarti filed in with their instruments and began to play. The other priestesses went in ahead of me and began to dance, whetting the observers' appetites as they leapt, twirled, and moved their bodies like water flowing from a spring to nourish the land. The men watched with great interest, some of them even daring to reach out to touch a priestess who came near, only for her to leap away and continue her dance unsullied.

Then came the cue for my entrance. Stomach churning, I pushed through the discomfort and went into the banquet hall when the doors were opened to me. All eyes were on me as I began to dance, surrounded by my priestesses, slowly making my way toward the head table where my husband sat transfixed. My father leaned over to explain what every stage of the dance signified, but Akhab was likely not listening. He never took his eyes off me after I appeared – and, according to Daneyah who told me afterward, neither did any of the other men. She said they were captivated, but I only saw my husband, for it was he who was the subject of my desire.

At the end of my routine, the music stopped, and I met my husband's gaze while reciting one of the sacred poems of Ashtarti to her Ba'al: the purpose of which not only acknowledged Akhab as my husband but also declared before all the assembly that he was Ba'al

34

incarnate. This last declaration was not required; in fact, my mother had cautioned me not to say it unless I was certain of his worthiness.

Earlier that morning, after my husband left me and I had finished my communion with Ashtarti, I went to the temple and consulted with the priests of Ba'al. They agreed with my assessment of Akhab and were pleased. I recognized him the moment our eyes met, and I knew by the perfection of our union the previous night that I was not mistaken: if I was truly Ashtarti then Akhab was Ba'al.

Now, standing before him with tears quickly forming in my eyes, I recited the words of the poem that I had read so many times in the hope that they would draw my beloved to me. Much of the poem recounts the goddess crying out in the wilderness for a lover to come to her, to fill the emptiness within her – a euphemism for sexual union. At the end of the poem, her lover at last appears, and the final line speaks of her joy in finding him: "Ba'al, you have come! / I give my soul to you, my god. / I give you my body. / Ba'al, I am yours!" After speaking these words from my heart, I dropped to my knees and prostrated myself before Akhab, not as my king but as my god in the flesh.

The sudden silence in the hall was noticeable. Still prostrated, I discreetly lifted my head to survey the reaction. Everyone was staring at me and Akhab in various states of surprise. Some seemed impressed and some appalled, while others seemed to approve when they began to nod and mutter in agreement. It was not uncommon for kings to declare themselves gods, but in Yisrael it had never been done before. Akhab himself seemed surprised and looked around as if fearing an impending attack. I half-expected the Yahwist prophet from the previous day to appear and denounce me, but no one said anything until at last my husband said, "Rise, Melkah."

I obeyed and looked directly at him, fearing he might be displeased with me. Instead of being angry, though, he continued to look at me curiously while stroking his beard. He did not seem wholly opposed to the idea of being a god incarnate, although I sensed it would take time for him to accept and believe it. By proclaiming him Ba'al incarnate, I was opening the door to him becoming my High Priest, which would allow us to perform the most sacred of Ba'alist rites – if I could convince him to agree to it. That would soon become my most important challenge.

The third day began with another ritual. This time, in my role as High Priestess at the Temple of Ba'al in Shomron, I consecrated the kingdom of Yisrael and its people to the goddess Ashtarti. Then I blessed some of the priests and priestesses of Ashtarti before I sent them out to minister to the people. One of their missions was to construct shrines in gardens, groves, and grottos throughout the kingdom, where men could come to seek communion with the goddess through her representatives on earth.

Most of my husband's court were followers of Yahowah in those days and, while they did not understand our ways, they were not yet opposed to them. This was because zealotry had not yet made it into the upper echelons of society. They understood that we were not there to replace the god of Yisrael with our gods, but rather to preserve the old ways. They were increasingly being threatened by the new cult of Yahowah that had begun to take hold within the kingdom. Followers of the Ba'alim faced rising threats and violence from Yahwist zealots, especially those who were outside our fortress walls in the villages and towns of the southern provinces. The priests and priestesses whom I sent out in pairs knew the dangers posed by these zealots, but they were committed to spreading the goddess's message of love and healing to all who yearned for it.

The consecration was followed by another day of feasting and revelry. This time, I presented my husband with a wedding gift that had been made by one of the finest craftsmen in Tzidon. It was a gold cup in the shape of a winged bull. The bull was seated, with his wings artfully wrapped behind him to create the cup from which its bearer would drink. Akhab was delighted by the uniqueness of this cup, and marveled at the artistry that went into making it. He was not merely being polite. From that day on, wherever he traveled, the cup went with him and he treasured it, using it at every meal.

Although they were welcome to stay for as long as desired, once the three-day feast had come to an end, my family and their entourage bid us farewell to begin their journey back to Tzidon. I embraced my father, mother, and younger brother with stinted tears, and although it was hard for them to leave me, they knew that I was happy with the king. Everyone could see that we were a harmonious couple.

In those places where our gods were venerated, the recitation of the story of the union of Ba'al and Ashtarti, and the likening to the divine couple and their devotion to one another, was customary at all nuptial feasts. But for Akhab and me, it turned out to be true. We talked in the privacy of my quarters where he began spending most of his leisure time. We made love whenever we desired, worked and studied together, learned about one another, and came to understand that from the start, ours was a union of souls. It was fortuitous that we were so well-matched, as though the gods themselves had created us each for the other. I would soon come to find that we were alike in mind as well as body. Our intellectual capacities were equal, our tastes often aligned; where we differed, still we were complimentary rather than contradictory.

Akhab realized this early into our marriage, as well. He soon developed a respect for me that was rare even in the more egalitarian cultures with which we were familiar. However, it would take much effort to prove my capabilities to his court, for they were not accustomed to women taking any part in governing a kingdom. Each day the court was in session, typically four days per week, I sat in my ivory-inlaid chair to the right of Akhab's throne, dressed in my richest robes and jewels, lips painted red, eyes lined with kohl: a beautiful decoration as queens were expected to be but nothing more. If his mother had still been alive, she would have sat in that honored place and I to his left. The *Gebirah*, Queen Mother, would have had more say in the government of his kingdom than I would have been granted but would still have acted with little authority and always in the shadow of the king. Although Akhab had tried to change that with my anointing, my part as his queen was still to be present but silent.

At first, this was a blessing. In those earliest days, I was content to remain seen and not heard. Unless it was part of a performance, I was never comfortable being put on show. The elaborate costume I wore was not only for looks; it provided a shield between me and my husband's court, like armor on the battlefield. So many men, so many eyes upon me and not all of them welcoming. So many energies swirling about, some of them pleasant but many of them piercing and abrasive. Solitary by nature, I wanted to run and hide, but I knew my duty and had been trained for this. To some extent, I even knew how to use my own essence to shield myself from unwanted energies, although I was still learning.

When I entered the Great Hall on my husband's arm each day, he was my rock and my fortress. Whenever I felt weak or uncertain, I looked to him for comfort and reassurance. He placed a hand over mine and offered a tender smile to put me at ease. I inhaled deeply and exhaled slowly as we walked together up the steps of the dais to be seated upon our thrones. It was always a relief when the cymbals were struck and the appointments began, for then I became virtually invisible to those who had come to see the king.

While the men talked and debated the affairs of the kingdom, I observed it all, but my mind often wandered. I took in my surroundings, admiring the tapestries and ivories adorning the whitewashed walls, the iron braziers that stood at the corners of the dais; flanking the doorways, the potted palms added a touch of green and swayed in the breeze that came through the open windows and doors. My eyes traced the gently waving fronds, falling on one of the slaves who knelt at the base of the palm. He was a young boy, no older than ten or eleven years of age. He reminded me of my brother, except he was fair in complexion with shorn flaxen curls sprouting from the top of his head. Around his neck, resting loose upon his collarbone, was the typical iron collar that marked slaves from servants and other freemen. His garment was a plain tunic of undyed course fabric, probably flax, although I could not tell from that distance.

The boy kept his face lowered, his expression empty, and then for a moment something caught his gaze – a gleam or reflection of light – and he looked up. Our eyes met briefly from across the chamber and a look of alarm passed over his face before he looked down once again. I saw him trembling and noticed a tear sliding down his cheek. Aware of the power my rank held, I felt sorry for having frightened him in our moment of shared curiosity. I was grateful no one else noticed him, for he would have been dragged into the courtyard and beaten with a rod for having dared to look at me. I tried to project a message to him with my mind, promising that his secret was safe with me. I do not know if he received it, but he soon

38

stopped trembling and his tears dried when no one had come to beat him. I shuddered, thinking for a moment what it would be like to be in his place.

Whenever I longed to escape the confinement of the Great Hall with its smothering energies and uncomfortable audiences – typically elders or noblemen who had come to the king to settle their feuds or resolve their bitter complaints – I looked high above them all. I admired the intricately carved ceiling, hung with lamps and braziers that could be lit during feasts that took place in the night. Now they were cold and empty, but they were so high I wondered how anyone could ever reach them to be lit. Then I swept my gaze to the side to watch falcons and other birds that perched in the clerestory windows, preening their feathers and observing us as I observed them. I thought it must be a beautiful thing to be one of them, soaring above danger and the petty problems of human life.

Once when we were staying at another palace, I witnessed a bird take flight from one side of the Hall to the other, letting its droppings fall on the prominent nose of one of the courtiers waiting for his chance to see the king. He was a nobleman and elder at Yezreel, called Nabot, who owned a vineyard and often came to court when we were staying at the fortress there, or the palace at nearby Megiddu. Akhab was constantly having to mediate between Nabot and those who had dealings with him, for he was a troublesome neighbor and dishonest businessman. When the bird released its droppings on his face, I had to stifle a laugh; thankfully only Akhab and the Lord Steward noticed, being near enough to hear me while the audience continued without interruption.

In between audiences, I leaned over to tell Akhab what had happened, and he laughed heartily. The Lord Steward, meanwhile, stood before us, waiting patiently to inform the king of his next audience.

While Obadyahu stood on the steps of the dais during audiences, he often moved about, stepping down to retrieve documents, scrolls, and clay tablets, or small gifts and tokens that were presented to the king or myself by those who came to see us. He was our mediator, maintaining a necessary distance between us and those who were granted audiences with the King. Unless they were summoned, the Lord Steward was the only member of the court allowed to ascend the steps of the dais and approach us directly, to

39

deliver messages and gifts into our hands or receive directives which he would impart to the servants or ministers or other members of the court waiting below.

To the side of the dais but close enough to hear all that was being said were the Chief Scribe and his aides, who varied in number each day. The Chief Scribe was the same man called Aharon who sang to us so beautifully at our first nuptial feast. At court, he sat cross-legged on the floor making note of all the proceedings in case they were needed for later review. Aharon was young like Akhab, and his father had served King Omri for most of his reign. When Aharon's father passed away, he began to serve Omri but had known Akhab all his life. Aharon was an odd man: keenly intelligent and gentle by nature, but with peculiar mannerisms and no sense of humor.

I once made a joke when we were working with him in Akhab's study, but he stared at me as if confused. I thought he must have hated me, for I knew he was devoted to Yahowah. When he left us alone together to continue his duties elsewhere, Akhab explained that it was nothing against me, for Aharon did not seem to have a capacity for humor, and sarcasm went over his head. Yet, he was loyal and dutiful and knew the law and workings of the court better than anyone – except, perhaps, Obadyah whose own expressionless face often unnerved me.

When I asked Akhab if the *abarakkum* was also incapable of humor, like Aharon, he laughed. "No, Obadyah truly is a humorless man. In truth, I have never much liked him, but he is capable and knowledgeable about a great many things and served my father before me. Without him, I could not have transitioned so smoothly into my role as king. We do not always agree on things, but we both have the kingdom's best interest at heart and that makes him tolerable. I can always count on him."

Now, as Obadyah watched me and Akhab laughing together about the bird and Nabot, I wondered if my husband's trust in him was misplaced for he seemed not only humorless but hostile beneath his indifferent veneer. It unnerved me, and I glanced around to ensure that our bodyguards were nearby.

At the front of the dais were four armed eunuchs; standing against the wall behind us and flanking a doorway hidden by curtains were two others. The eunuchs who served us at court were statues of flesh, alert and focused. Armed with swords that would only be drawn

40

if needed, they bore in one hand heavy spears that rested upon the ground at their feet, the points of which rose high above their heads. There were other guards, and my eunuchs, positioned around the dais and throughout the hall, particularly by the doors. At the first sign of trouble, they could be moved into immediate action, surrounding us, closing and barring the great wooden doors, and striking down anyone who posed a threat to the king or myself.

Beyond the guards who stood at the foot of our dais was a stone banister parted only in the center aisle, behind which stood the ministers of court. These were the highest ranking men below the king, many of them his brothers, uncles, and cousins who had been appointed in their distinguished roles to help divide the many duties of managing the kingdom. There were twelve ministers, but each of the twelve had their own attendants, who were not permitted to speak unless called upon.

Behind the ministers, separated by another banister, were the courtiers: governors, other princes who were Akhab's kin, or elders of noble families granted favor and permitted to attend court to bear witness and take part in its proceedings from time to time. There were no women on the main floor; those who came with their husbands, fathers, and uncles, or were high-ranking widows who came of their own accord, remained cloistered behind screens in an antechamber or up in the gallery. They were allowed to watch but never to speak unless brought before the king on one of the rare occasions women were granted an audience.

The most important of Akhab's ministers, although he worked mostly in shadow, was the Lord Treasurer, at the time one of Akhab's uncles, of the same name. He was an aging man with grey beard and kohl-lined eyes who dressed in simple robes compared to those worn by many of the other ministers and courtiers. With the exception of a gold amulet that marked his role and a simple diadem to indicate his station, he was otherwise unremarkable in his manner of dress. This was deliberate. It was in his best interest to avoid looking as rich and powerful as he was, for his proximity to the royal coffers could not be overt.

The elder Akhab took his role seriously, handling the exchange of resources within the palace and advising us on matters related to expenditure. Along with his brother, the Minister of Trade, he had been one of the most vocal supporters of Akhab's union with me. When I first came to Yisrael, however, he treated me as if I was only a foolish woman with no understanding of the way our economy worked; it impressed him to find that was not true. It was during a heated debate in the king's study, to which I was witness, that I had first proven myself to him. I had intervened, siding against my husband, for I believed his uncle was right in that matter.

The elder Akhab seemed shocked when I calmly explained to my husband what he had meant, breaking down the issue and the proposed solution. Akhab at once understood after I explained it in my own way, and the solution was immediately put into place with great success. When the two Akhabs expressed their surprise, I reminded them that, as a daughter of Tzidon, I was well-versed in arithmetic, trade, and economics. Over time, the Lord Treasurer came to respect me and to work with me as an equal, and I, in turn, respected him for his knowledge and experience.

The next most important of the ministers was one of Akhab's half-brothers, Abram, who was his general and the Minister of War. He was an irreverent man, young and full of himself, but skilled as a warrior and leader. Akhab trusted him above all others to oversee his military and advise him in matters of war. He was also a womanizer and a drunkard who often boasted of his prowess in bed and on the battlefield. During many feasts, Akhab had to warn Abram against speaking of these matters in front of me, but I found him amusing as much as he was distasteful. When he saw me trying to hide my amusement it only encouraged him. He often winked at me when making his jokes and boasts, but he was loyal and devoted to his brother and never once tried to overstep. He simply enjoyed making people laugh and, even though I did not care much for him in the beginning, I came to appreciate his acceptance of my gods and raucous sense of humor.

At the time, he and young Asa were the only two of Akhab's brothers who served as ministers. The rest of them – these ministers of law, agriculture, commerce, foreign affairs, building, religion, and so on – were mostly his uncles, all of them older men and many of whom had little respect for me or my foreign ways. I often found myself at odds with them as I began to take on more of an open role in governing the kingdom alongside my husband. It was only in later years, as many of them were forced to retire or died off and were replaced by younger men, that I began to face less opposition. But it would never truly fade even from those whose respect I had earned. Long-held views and tradition were not easy to overcome. Akhab was always the exception, and as I continued to impress him, he encouraged me to take more of an active role in managing the kingdom beside him.

My first opportunity to reveal some of my capabilities came before the whole of Akhab's court when a foreign dignitary arrived in Shomron to present the king with the second of his wives. They had travelled from the ends of the earth to reach the administrative center of our kingdom, where we hosted all official state visits from foreign monarchs and their dignitaries. The King of Zhou was struggling to maintain a firm hold on his kingdom and hoped that he could secure as many foreign trade opportunities and alliances as possible to bolster his power, against the wishes of most of his nobles. Zhou already had dealings with Tzidon; now, the king had sent one of his brothers to represent him on this mission, which was made possible by my marriage to Akhab.

Their procession was smaller than my own, but still quite impressive, and the princess who sat upon her litter was exquisite in her finery. Her gold headdress was in the shape of a nesting swan, its wing tips raised at the back and its head tucked down against its breast. From the sides of her headdress were three strings of beads carved from gemstones and precious metals, which hung beneath her chin like a dazzling curtain. She sat upon silk cushions, held a bowl of riches in her lap, and kept her gaze lowered and expression serene. I could see the faint tremor, though, and knew her fear. Having come before her, I would soon take her under my wing and help her feel at home in this land that must have been so different from her own.

The Zhou dignitary was middle-aged and portly beneath his sumptuous silks, and although he smiled broadly, I could sense his distaste for this mission. His disdain was made worse perhaps by the fact that my husband and his court had no knowledge of the Zhou language. In order to communicate with us, he had a translator in his entourage: an apparently well-travelled man who looked at us with genuine kindness and showed some familiarity with our customs. What was unknown to everyone assembled that day was that there was one person in Akhab's court who could speak and understand

43

their language, only she was invisible to all the self-important men who had gathered in the Great Hall for this momentous occasion.

After processing into the Great Hall at the head of his entourage, the dignitary bowed with his arms outstretched when he reached the foot of the dais. His heavy-lidded eyes scanned us both, settled briefly on me with a look that suggested he had heard tales of my beauty but was not impressed, and finally rested upon my husband the king. He met the king's gaze with a smile, but I could feel the contempt hidden beneath.

"King Akhab," his voice resonated as he spoke in his native tongue, "I am Ji Xiao, Prince of Wu. My brother, Ji Yi, King of Zhou has charged me to represent him on this revolting mission."

Without intending to, I gasped aloud. My husband looked at me oddly for only a moment before turning his attention back to the dignitary, while I looked at everyone assembled and saw that no one from my husband's court reacted to what was said. If it were not for the discreet snickers from some of the prince's entourage, and the princess's momentary expression of embarrassment, I might have thought I misheard.

The prince paused, allowing the translator to repeat what he had said in Akkadian. It was translated exactly, except for the one word 'revolting', which the translator changed to 'auspicious'. Again, I doubted I had understood correctly – after all, my understanding of Zhou was far from perfect, and I had no occasion to practice since coming to Yisrael.

My husband smiled at the translator's message, and said, "Welcome to Shomron, my Lord Ji." I sighed, wishing someone had explained to my husband the naming practices of Zhou, as he continued without any awareness of his blunder. "We are pleased to have this unique opportunity, which my wife," he indicated me, "Melkah Yezeba'al was able to facilitate through her connections at the courts of Zour and Tzidon from which she hails."

He paused to give the translator time to repeat his message to the prince, who listened carefully and glanced briefly at me with disinterest, before turning back to my husband with his well-practiced smile. At the end of the translation, he bowed graciously but as the meeting slowly proceeded, his contempt for us and for his mission became more apparent. His patience with the need to translate everything also began to wear thin.

44

"In honor of this travesty," the prince continued in his own language, "the foolish king sends Princess Hu, his most beautiful daughter, to be the wife of this filthy desert king, Akhab ben Omri – truly a waste of a flower worthy only of a true prince of Zhou."

My lips parted and my brows raised, but no one was paying any attention to me – except the princess, still seated on her litter, who seemed to realize in that moment that I understood what was being said. Our eyes met and for the first time since she had been brought in, she smiled faintly – perhaps relieved there was someone at Akhab's court with whom she could speak in her native tongue.

Seeing her watching me, I nodded a discreet reassurance, as the translator spoke in trembling voice. "In honor of this glorious occasion, His Majesty the King of Zhou has sent his most beautiful daughter, Princess Hu, the flower of Zhou, to be the wife of the noble Akhab, King of Yisrael."

When the translator nodded to him, the prince continued, "This is a waste of time. None of the other nobles support this mission. I cannot understand why our king is eager to open trade with a kingdom of rocks and dirt – what is here to benefit our people?"

Clearing his throat and looking more uncomfortable with each of the prince's proclamations, the translator said, "Our king is eager for the union of our peoples, that we may benefit greatly through trade for many generations, and he has the support of all his nobles. Is it not a glorious opportunity for our people?"

"We should crush this kingdom of dust; instead, we make allies. Truly, I believe my brother sent me on this senseless mission to punish me for making love to one of his wives in our youth, before she became his." He smiled proudly, and continued, "He has always resented me for having seduced her with my prowess, for I am more handsome and courageous than my brother the king and have had more women than he."

Chuckles arose from his entourage, and the translator's eyes grew wide. A bead of sweat rolled down his forehead as he considered an alternative translation. "I am proud of our heritage and honored to share it, and to represent our handsome and courageous king on this glorious mission to bring prosperity to our kingdoms."

I could not believe what I was hearing and released a short burst of air in an attempt to stifle a contemptuous laugh. Again, Akhab looked at me, this time with a questioning gaze – perhaps realizing for the first time that I understood what was being said. Even the princess lost her composure now, but she hid her expression behind her hand and pretended to cough as she lowered her head.

The prince, none-the-wiser, continued, "Nothing good will come of this alliance..."

At last, I could not remain silent. My ire betrayed itself in my tone, as I raised my voice to address the prince in his own tongue: "How long will you continue to insult my husband and his kingdom, Lord Xiao?"

Gasps and murmurs immediately rose from every corner of the Hall, and all eyes were turned on me. The prince's smug grin faded, and his expression became that of a mouse cornered by a cat. I was pleased to have stunned him, for the first time feeling what it was to have a man's power. When he did not speak, I said, "Have you forgotten your own tongue? Honestly, I wonder what the king's wife ever saw in you – if indeed what you say is true. You call my husband filthy, but I can attest to his cleanliness. He smells of aloes and of myrrh, cassia and qaneh-bosem, while you stink of fish-rot and conceit. I can smell you from here."

Some of his own men chuckled, only to catch themselves when he whirled around to glare at them. The princess was struggling to hide her own laughter, hiding her mouth behind her hand, and I thought it was beautiful the way she laughed with such graceful modesty the likes of which I had never seen. Her uncle glared at her before turning back to me with anger on his lips. "You dare to insult me, woman?"

"If I am not mistaken, Lord Xiao, you insulted my husband first."

Now, he laughed and turned to his entourage. "Mighty King Akhab has his wife defending him because he cannot defend himself."

"The only reason he is not gutting you himself at this moment is because he cannot comprehend what is being said – but I do understand, and I will be sure to tell him every word unless you prostrate yourself and beg for his mercy."

At this, the prince looked uncertain, perhaps even doubtful.

"One word from me," I continued, "and the doors will be closed to this chamber, and you and all your men will be cut down where you stand. Your blood shall paint the floors of this hall red, and we

46

shall dance in it while the beasts and the insects dine upon your flesh."

"Why should they listen to you: a woman?"

"They will do this, for I am beloved of the king, and he trusts me in all things. I will tell them you have threatened to murder the king and to ravage his kingdom. Your name will be cursed throughout the kingdom of Zhou, for you will have failed in your mission as your brother's honored representative. You will give him an enemy where he sought a friend. He will not mourn you, for his daughter the princess will tell him it was your fault the mission failed. She will receive all credit for having saved it and prevented a war between our peoples. All this will happen, and more, if you do not show repentance. Now, beg."

Trembling, the prince dropped to his knees and fell before the dais, rambling apologies and begging for mercy. My husband looked to me in shock, while the translator struggled to keep up with the prince's lamentations, most of which even I could not understand. Finally, my husband rose, and the people of our court prostrated themselves before their king, as was custom. Akhab's voice boomed, firm yet tender, when he said, "We kings of Yisrael are known for our mercy. You and your men will be spared." He glanced at me, still unsure of what had just happened, and continued, "Arise, noble prince; you need not fear me this day, for you are forgiven."

I smiled with keen satisfaction as the prince pulled himself to stand and straightened his robes, trying to regain something of the dignity he had lost. He pressed his palms together and bowed to my husband in gratitude, while Akhab returned to his throne to resume the meeting. The prince maintained a respectful discourse for the remainder of his visit.

Later, having retired with my husband to the privacy of my quarters when court was dismissed, we skipped supper to make love instead. Afterward, we lay beneath the covers in my bed, and he looked at me with admiration as he stroked my arm. "You have never been more beautiful than you were today, parlaying with that man and making him beg for mercy." We shared a snicker, then he continued, "but I am still trying to make sense of what happened."

47

I sat up and reached for my cup on the table beside the bed. After quenching my thirst, I said, "Lord Xiao was insulting you, because he knew you could not speak his language."

"But you can."

I nodded. "In Tzidon, we trade with a great many peoples and my father insisted we must also be familiar with their tongues to avoid being cheated. When I was a girl, I had a tutor from Zhou who taught me a great many things about the world. He was a kind man, but he was unusual amongst his own kind, which is why he remained with us at my father's court instead of returning to his own land."

"Why is that?"

"The people of Zhou think they are better than everyone else." I gave him a pointed look, thinking of his own people who had a similar mindset.

"Hmm, sounds familiar," he admitted, rubbing the back of his neck.

"So, I put him in his place."

"You did well," he said, sitting up and taking my face in his hand. He kissed me sweetly and I hoped he would seduce me, but instead he took a drink, and asked, "How many tongues do you recognize?"

I gave it some thought then counted on my fingers, as I listed them off: "I speak, read, and write Tzidonian, Akkadian of course, Egyptian, Hebrew, Greek, Aramaic, and Sanskrit."

"Sanskrit? What is Sanskrit?"

"The language of the people of Opir."

"Ah. Where your peacocks are from, yes?"

I smiled. "Akhab, I am not finished yet."

"There is more?"

I nodded. "Although I am not literate in Zhou, Kushite, Italic, or Celtic, I am proficient in speaking them. I wanted to learn more, but I did not have time before I came here to be wed."

"I have never heard of some of these languages."

I recounted on my fingers, whispering the languages to myself. "Altogether, that's..."

"Twelve," he finished, without me needing to list them again. "I thought I knew many tongues, but you know twice as many!"

"My father knows all the languages of the world, I think. I only know these few."

"That is more than I know," he said, gently stroking my hair and the side of my cheek. "You are a wonder, Yezeba'al."

I met his gaze with a faint smile, but then I was suddenly overcome with shyness and turned my face away as warmth spread through my cheeks. He lifted my chin, encouraging me to look at him again. Feeling awkward, I said, "Education was important to my father. He had us all in the classroom almost as soon as we were weaned from our nurses."

Akhab chuckled at this, and asked, "You know more about the world than any woman I have ever known, and more than most men even. I thought my education was enough, but now I am starting to wonder what else I have missed. What did your father have you study?"

For a moment, I was amazed by his interest. Then I began rambling excitedly, while he listened with a smile and a gleam in his eye. "We were tutored in languages, arithmetic, trade, and geography mostly. But we also learned history, literature, and philosophy. We had tutors that came from all over the world. But we learned from those close to us, as well. From my mother and Daneyah, I learned all the fundamentals of our religion: the hymns, prayers, and rituals, what they mean and how to perform them as High Priestess. Of course, there are certain rituals I was not allowed to perform, being still a virgin, but I was taught about them nonetheless." I paused and met his gaze, uncertain. "I can...teach you all these things, if you would like to learn them."

"I would love to learn all these things. The world I know seems so small in comparison."

"Anything you do not know I can show you. I brought many scrolls and writings with me from Tzidon – they are still locked away in a chest, most of them. I have not looked at them since I arrived, I am ashamed to admit."

"Every time I think I have learned all there is to know about you, I learn something new and astonishing. You have the body and soul of a woman but the mind of a man."

"Women are as capable of learning as men, if they are given the chance, Akhab. I am not so unique."

He brought my hand to his lips and then laced his fingers through mine, and said, "Then you will show the world what a woman can do, if given the chance." He released my hand and turned over on

49

the bed to reach for his cup. After taking a drink, he turned back to me, and said, "You truly impressed the men today – as good as any skilled diplomat. You must not be afraid to speak your mind at court. You have much to say, and we have much to learn from you."

"I do not think I was very diplomatic today," I confessed. "I insulted him and chastised him for having insulted you."

"What did you say?"

"I...told him he stank of rotting fish."

He wrinkled his face. "I see. That is not good for diplomacy."

"It was a reference to his land. Wu is on the coast, facing the sea, if I remember it correctly. But he deserved it, for calling you a filthy desert king."

"What? This is not even the desert! We are in the mountains, not the desert."

I laughed. "That is what upsets you, husband? Not the 'filthy' part?"

He shrugged. "I am a man – I do not mind getting dirty every once in a while. I especially enjoy getting dirty with you..." He climbed over me and tickled my sides. I laughed and attempted to squirm away. Then he began kissing and touching me, and at first, I was an eager participant. Then I remembered the new princess and how beautiful she was, and I turned my face from him to hide my pain.

He stopped. "My love, what is it? What has happened?"

At first, I was afraid to tell him the truth, but he had never been angry with me, and so I decided to trust him. "I am not your only wife now."

He sighed and fell back onto his side next to me. "You know that I must take other wives, Yezeba'al. But you will always be my true wife and my queen."

"She is very beautiful."

"She is," he agreed, putting his hands on me. "But not as beautiful as you, Melkah."

"There will be others."

"And none of them will ever compare to you, my beloved."

"You do not know that for certain."

"Perhaps not, but I can be confident in my assessment, for I have known many great beauties and none of them are half the

50

woman you are turning out to be – each day, you astound and enlighten me."

"My beauty will fade."

"Impossible," he said. "Yours is a beauty that shines forth from within. I see it not only in your face and your body, but also in your mind and when I look into your eyes. I see the beauty of your soul. That will never fade, and it is beyond compare."

Growing more confident and playful, I said, "I am a goddess, you know."

"So, I have been told," he said, looking at me with a shrewd grin. "And I am starting to believe it."

This raised my hopes, and I asked, "Will you agree to become my High Priest, then? Ashtarti needs her Ba'al."

He sighed and looked at me, fond yet somewhat sad. "I cannot. I am the king of Yisrael – of the people of the covenant. I must serve Yahowah. But together, we have united our two religions, to bring peace between our gods."

"Your god does not want peace, Akhab." I met his gaze when I said this, but then I sighed and turned away from him.

He slid closer and put his arms around me, his body warm and strong against mine. After kissing my shoulder, he said, "My love, you must understand. I do not reject your religion, but to practice it would be to reject my own."

I turned back to him, laying with my hands upon the cushion beneath my head. I met his gaze earnestly. "Will you forget me when you go to her, Akhab? When you consummate your marriage with her tomorrow night?"

His voice was gentle when he said, "Oh, Yezeba'al, I could never forget you." Then he placed a hand upon my breast and fondled my nipple between his fingers, as he whispered, "You are my queen and my goddess..." He brought his mouth to my breast with a single kiss, and continued, "...the woman I love above all others." He paused to kiss again. "Nothing could ever change how I love and desire you with every part of my being – to be one with you in the soul and in the flesh."

He pulled himself over me and began gently biting and sucking at my breast. I released a trembling sigh as he moved his lips across my flesh, up to my throat, while his hands drifted to other

51

regions. Eager to be one with him, I surrendered to my husband and lord.

The following morning, I went to the women's quarters to see how the princess was faring in her new home. In all our residences at Shomron, Megiddu, Yezreel, and elsewhere, the women's quarters were laid out in much the same way, with only a few minor differences. In each palace complex, they occupied an entire building, accessible only by a single entrance guarded by eunuchs. No man was allowed entry into the women's quarters unless accompanied by the king, and that rarely happened. The king rarely went to the women's quarters, for he spent most of his leisure time with me. While my quarters were separate from those of the other women, they were near enough that I could go to them whenever they needed oversight by their queen.

My quarters consisted of many chambers, including a dining room, a sitting room, a large private bath, a prayer chamber with a small altar consecrated to my gods, a private terrace, and a personal study; all of which I had to myself. I enjoyed the peace and quiet there. Although the women's quarters were more extensive than my own, they were shared by all the other women and their children, and it always felt cramped in comparison. On the first floor were the women's bedrooms and the nursery, which included a dining hall for the children and their nurses and guardians. The guardians were also eunuchs, but they specialized in overseeing the care and early military training of the king's sons when they were too old to be in the care of nurses. The king's daughters, of course, stayed with their nurses until they were wed and, unless they shared them with some of their sisters, often chose to keep their nurses with them in their new homes.

On the ground floor, the residents of the women's quarters had a communal bath, a large sitting room, and a dining hall. These chambers were wrapped around the women's gardens on three sides. The gardens were accessible from the centrally located sitting room, through double doors that led to the veranda. From there, short steps went down from all three sides of the veranda and into the gardens, which gave the women plenty of room to spread out.

The gardens had channels and fonts drawing water from nearby sources. These provided more opportunities for the women to bathe and the children to play. On the hottest afternoons, they cooled themselves in the water. The garden was peaceful and bustling, depending on which part of it one occupied. The sounds from the gardens were often of laughing and splashing, the trickling of water, voices in conversation, and loud calls of the peafowl I kept in the gardens at our three main residences.

Of the king's women, I was the only one with access to the other gardens. I alternated between them depending on whether I wanted to socialize or to be alone, always in the presence of my eunuchs either way. I spent a great deal of time in the gardens, enjoying the fragrant flowers, the sounds of nature, and the cool breeze that danced with the swaying boughs of terebinth, palm, cedar, oak, cypress, fig, almond, olive, and pomegranate trees. The fruit-bearing trees provided treats for the people and wildlife throughout the year, and many provided shade from the hot sun as well as high places for the peafowl to rest alongside the less colorful native birds.

As the king acquired more wives and all his women continued to bear children, the women's quarters became the most densely populated part of the palaces. For now, though, there were mostly concubines occupying that wing of the palace, along with those of their children old enough to leave the nursery at Megiddu, where the majority were kept. A few of King Omri's widows – those without children to take them into their homes – remained as guardians and midwives to Akhab's women, but there was no *gebirah* among their ranks. As such, I had taken the advice of Akhab's sister, Aya, to appoint one of Omri's childless widows as the mistress of the women's quarters. Although she was the youngest of Omri's widows, being in her mid-twenties at the time that I came to Yisrael, Maryam was above all the others, answerable only to me. She was gracious and fair as Aya had promised, and although she served Yahowah, we never had an issue with each other.

When I entered the women's quarters that day, Maryam came to me in a hurry. Whatever she was going to say, however, was forgotten momentarily when she took in the style of my dress, the neck of which was low and revealed the crease of my bosom. It was one of the fashions worn by the women of Athens, normally adorned with a cloak. It was a hot day and, unless I was going to be out in the sun, I did not wish to be encumbered, so my shoulders were left bare.

I always found it amusing when my husband's people were shocked by the different fashions I wore, especially those which exposed one or both of my breasts. That was still less shocking to them, however, than the time I showed up to court wearing Egyptian regalia, complete with a snake-headed diadem. The priest of Yahowah who served with the ministers at my husband's court nearly fainted, although to be fair it may have been the heat. Maryam never seemed troubled by my outfits, but until she became accustomed to my penchant for dressing in fashions from around the world, she was often stunned by the sight of me.

Once her moment of surprise passed, she curtsied and whispered, "Melkah, I am relieved you are here. The princess has been weeping all night. She does not speak our language and none of us can speak hers. She has only her maidens to speak to and tend to her, but they do not know our customs. I do not know what to do."

I placed a hand over hers and nodded my thanks, then immediately went to find the princess. She was still lying on her bed, awake but staring miserably at the flame of a lamp on her bedside table as her maidens swirled around her in confusion and concern. They immediately fell to the floor in prostration when I entered, for they had been with her in the Great Hall the previous day when she was presented. No doubt they recognized me, although they, too, were momentarily stunned by my clothing. Their robes, in contrast, kept them completely covered.

"Beautiful princess," I called in her tongue. "Do not be sad. Forgive me if I have neglected my duty toward you."

When she heard me, she leapt from the bed and came to her knees before me, where she clung to my hand and pressed it to her lips as she wept. "Oh, my Queen, I do not mean to be ungrateful. Only, I am lonely and afraid. I do not know the language or customs of this land. The other wives all stare and laugh at me because I am so different."

I placed a hand over her head and stroked her hair, as she rested against my waist the way that a child would rest against its mother, although we were likely the same age. Then I took her by the arms and bade her to rise, lifting her chin so as to look into her eyes. "We are not so different. You are also the daughter of a king. And

54

those women are not the king's wives; they are his concubines, and they are beneath you. If they have laughed at you, I shall deliver a swift retribution upon them."

"They are not his wives?"

"You will be his second wife. I am his first."

She paused, and then asked, "Your father is the King of Tzidon?"

"Yes. There were many people from all over the world in my father's court."

She giggled and covered her mouth in that particular way that I would come to find was customary for women of Zhou, as showing one's teeth was considered immodest. "My uncle, the Prince of Wu, does not like anyone who is not from Zhou. He thinks you are all ignorant barbarians – but you put him in his place."

"I hope I did not frighten or offend you, princess."

"Me? No, I was delighted. I have never liked that man. I do not know why my father tolerates him – even if they are brothers."

"Your father is merciful, as are the kings of Yisrael."

She shook her head. "My father is not merciful. He boiled a man alive for less than what my uncle has done to offend him."

I raised my brow and my lips parted. "Boiled...alive?"

She nodded. "In a cauldron. He was a rival prince to one of my father's closest friends." She shrugged. "That was before I was born, of course."

"Of course... Then is it true, what your uncle said...about one of your father's wives?"

"Oh yes," she answered. "Everyone in the court of Zhou knows about it. She was executed when their affair was discovered, and her children were banished, for the king could not be sure they were his own. That is why I am surprised my uncle is even still alive, but men are more easily forgiven for their sins than women, is it not true?"

I nodded regretfully.

She continued gravely, "It is a story that is told to remind us all what can happen if we are ever unfaithful to our husbands."

"Which you will never be," I said, taking her hand and leading her to sit at the table nearby. I paused to tell one of the servants to bring us some wine and fruit, and then I turned back to her and continued in her own tongue. "The king is a fine husband and is known for fairness and mercy in his kingdom."

55

"What is he like, King Akhab?"

Thinking of him fondly, I answered, "He is gentle and noble and kind, strong and true... There is no man as worthy as he."

"You love him," she observed.

I gave a single nod, lowering my gaze as if sharing a secret I should not confess.

"And he loves you?"

Again, I nodded.

"You must hate me, then."

"I could never hate you. We will be as sisters – like Ashtarti and Anat, who were both the wives of Ba'al, my god. And we will promise to always help one another. Will you agree to that?"

"I agree," she answered with a lovely smile. I admired her intelligent eyes. Her hair seemed darker than mine against her pale skin, although I am certain it was no darker. When it was combed out, I would find it shined like polished ebony and was as straight as the spears carried by the king's guard, while mine fell in waves and sometimes curled at the ends.

"You are lovely," I observed, remembering what she had said about being different. "Never let anyone tell you otherwise."

"Thank you," she answered with a faint blush.

"What are you called?"

"Hu," she answered with a wrinkled face.

"You do not like your name?"

She shook her head. "My mother called me Fang-Hua."

"Fragrant flower," I said in Akkadian. She looked at me, mystified. Then I returned to her language, to explain, "It is the meaning of your name, in our tongue. Fang-Hua – would you like me to call you that?"

She smiled and gave a nod. "Yes, please, my Queen."

"Then henceforth, you shall be known to us as Fang-Hua." I turned to the other women and told them, "She is the Lady Fang-Hua. Her father is the King of Zhou. She is to be treated with the utmost respect, for she is second only to me in this court. Do you understand?"

The concubines and even Omri's widows all nodded, and those who had laughed at her betrayed themselves by their looks of shame. "For now, I will forgive those of you who mistreated the Lady Fang-Hua, for you were not aware, but if I hear any more talk of mistreatment by any of you the consequences will be most unpleasant."

Again, they nodded hurriedly, their faces growing red with shame. When I turned back to Fang-Hua, she was watching me with great interest. I told her what I had said, and then added, "I shall teach you to speak and understand the language. It is not so difficult to learn."

"Thank you, my Queen." Then she looked at me quizzically. "If I may...?"

I gave a nod, for her to continue.

"How do you know the language of Zhou?"

"I learned it at my father's court, in Tzidon. Many languages are spoken there, and I had a tutor who came from Zhou. But I am not literate in your language – I can only speak it."

"I can teach you, if you would like?"

"I would like that very much." I smiled, and then an idea came to me. "You teach me to read and write Zhou, and I shall teach you to read and write and to speak any language you desire, starting with Akkadian, which is the language everyone speaks in all the royal courts of these lands. I shall also teach you to speak and understand Hebrew, which is the language of the common people of this land. Many of our servants and slaves speak it exclusively, so you will need to use it when you are speaking to them."

From this was born the idea to teach all Akhab's wives and concubines to read and write. Many of them, I would come to find, did not want to learn. Some of them even thought it was sinful, but those who were interested took to it eagerly. Naturally, when word got out that I was teaching literacy to the women, it was not well-received at my husband's court. Nevertheless, I would not be deterred and Akhab approved of their learning.

Whenever other women joined us as wives and concubines to the king, I quickly assessed which of them would be open to literacy and began their tutelage as soon as they were ready to take on the challenge. I enjoyed teaching them, and it gave me something to do when I was not with my husband or practicing the rituals of my religion. It was especially important when Akhab's other wives began to bear legitimate heirs for his kingdom while I had only miscarriages, each one more devastating than the last. Teaching and study kept me from being consumed by my sorrows. Besides, it was

57

something I could share with my husband that none of his other wives could. While they brought him children, I brought him learning.

Sitting on cushions in my private quarters, we often had scrolls of papyri with the writings from both our religions scattered across the table. They were held open by figurines carved from wood, stone, and ivory. He was enchanted that I could read and write, so unlike the women in his society, and delighted that we could engage in spirited debate without it turning to animosity. We tried to understand each other's way of thinking, but I admit it was harder for me to understand his religion than it was for him to understand mine.

"If Yahowah is king of the gods, why do the other gods not fall in line under his power and authority?"

"No, no, no," he replied, shaking his head, and holding up his hand. "It is not that he is the highest or most powerful of the gods — he is the *only* God, meaning there are no other gods, Yezeba'al. They do not exist."

I laughed. "How can that be? No other gods."

"You are laughing at this?"

"Yes, of course I am laughing. It is ridiculous. You are telling me that *one* god created everything that exists, without the help of any other gods? Everything in all creation: on the earth, in the sky, in the sea, and the heavens? One god, and no one else?"

"That is what they believe, yes. That is why the zealots are so adamant."

I tilted my head, intrigued by his answer. "And you? Do you believe this?"

He sighed and ran his fingers through his hair. "I do not know. Sometimes, I believe. It is what I was taught by my tutor, Eliyahu; what is said in the stories and the sacred scriptures written by the prophet Moshe." He pointed with his fingers to one of the Hebrew scrolls. "While it is only a story, it speaks of Yahowah creating all the heavens and the earth."

I took the scroll and looked at the passage he was referring to, and then I laid it on the table. "Look, here it does not speak of Yahowah creating anything. It speaks only of Elohim."

"Elohim is another name for Yahowah. It is referring to his powers of creation. That is why it is in the plural."

58

I looked at him skeptically. "El is one of the gods, but he is not the only god. Yahowah is one of his sons and a storm god – how can you not know this?"

He sighed and stroked his beard thoughtfully.

"And Elohim refers to many, not one. He and all his sons and their families; even their servants and lesser kin might be included in the House of El."

"A royal house? Like the House of Omri?"

I pointed to another passage. "Look, here it even quotes the gods, the Elohim, saying, 'Let *us* make man in *our* image.' If Elohim is only one god, the same as Yahowah, and there are no others, then who is he speaking to, that he says this?"

Akhab took up the scroll and scratched at his chin through his beard as he examined it. After a moment, he sighed and set down the scroll then finally sat up and crossed his arms over his chest. "I do not know. But you are a very good debater."

"Akhab, do not try to change the subject with flattery."

"I am not," he insisted, although his mischievous smile suggested otherwise. "I am only saying what is true. You have backed me into a corner, Yezeba'al. I do not know where to go from there."

Suddenly, I was no longer interested in debate and suspected he was not, either. Drawing on the tabletop with my fingertip, I suggested, "You could...take me to the bed. You know where to go from there."

He rose from the cushion and came to stand over me. Looking up at him with a naughty smile, I took his offered hand and let him pull me to my feet. He slid his arms around my waist, drew my body to him, and brushed his lips against the side of my neck. My lips parted with a trembling sigh. I closed my eyes and offered my neck to him with a delicate tilt of my head. Then he lifted me in his arms and carried me to the bed.

After making love, we laid together in quiet harmony. I had never known such peace as that which I felt in those moments, wrapped in the strength of his arms and listening to his heart beat a steady rhythm. The peace was broken, however, when his deep voice rose from the silence to ask, "Do you truly believe I am a god incarnate?"

For a moment, I was speechless. It was the first time he had spoken of it since the day I made the pronouncement at our wedding feast. After the last time I had tried to broach the subject, I was afraid to bring it up again. Now that he had spoken of it, I was emboldened. I sat up in the bed and looked at him directly. "Do you think I would have made such a claim if I did not believe it to be true?"

I let him sit with the question for a moment.

"I opened myself up to scrutiny and criticism when I made that claim. I did not make it lightly. I absolutely believe it. You are not merely *a* god incarnate – you are *my* god incarnate. My Ba'al. My divine consort. The other half of my being." Now, I took his hand and brought it to rest over my heart. "We are as one, Akhab. Don't you believe it?"

"I want to believe. A part of me believes." He began to stroke my naked flesh, as he continued, "I believe that you are the other half of my being but...to be a god incarnate. It seems impossible."

I lowered my face and fought the urge to weep.

He turned onto his stomach and rose onto his elbows to place his hands upon my thighs. He seemed to realize I was hurt, and perhaps it was an attempt to lift my spirit when he said, "I do not know if I am a god, Yezeba'al, but I know that you are a goddess, and I shall worship you for the rest of my days."

He then began to kiss my thighs, and soon I was relieved of my disappointment. Eager to be seduced, I allowed him to lay me on my back so that he could delight me in his worship.

3

Ten Thousand Kingdoms

Akhab had a lot of stamina and a strong sexual appetite that only I could match. Although he had many concubines and, as a king, it was necessary for him to take other wives – three, apart from me, within the first year of our marriage alone – I was the one that pleased him best and with whom he spent most of his nights. Our closeness was often remarked upon by others, many in admiration, although some were concerned by his obvious preference for me. As the years passed, his affections never wavered, no matter how many other beautiful and capable women were presented to him. When he took to wife a daughter of his cousin, a girl named Leah with whom he did not even bother to consummate the marriage, gossip began to spread that I had bewitched the king with sorcery. We heard these rumors and laughed them off, until the day when Eliyahu, called the Tishbite, came before the king to denounce me before the whole court at Megiddu during the third year of our marriage.

In those early years, when I was young and still adjusting to my role as Melkah, many prophets came to Akhab's court to chide me for my vanity and devotion to the gods of my father. I had been warned about these zealous prophets and their staunch followers who often walked about in rags and stirred up dissension among the people; how they spoke to even their kings as if they were above them, for they claimed they received the word of Yahowah directly to their ears. How any king could permit such people to roam about their land, let alone welcome them into their courts, I could not understand.

Nevertheless, I tried not to take offence as I ignored their arrogance and bore their abuses in relative silence. I did not need to speak to these men. Each time they came, my husband jumped to my defense in anger and sent the prophets away with threats of imprisonment and exile. He never made true of those threats, however, for fear of incurring the wrath of their god. His inaction had only emboldened them. As I witnessed more prophets come to rebuke my husband before his whole court, my outward show of patience finally began to wane. Resting my chin on the thumb of my left hand with my elbow on the arm of my chair, I often drummed my fingers on the right as they assaulted us with a barrage of lectures, insults, and bold accusations. By this time, I knew that eventually my husband would tire of it and send them away, but that nothing would change as long as he believed in Yahowah's supremacy over the other gods in Yisrael.

When Eliyahu came before us on this particular day, my husband sat upon his throne and greeted him warmly. Seated in my chair at the king's right hand, I observed the warmth between them and hoped perhaps this one would be different from all the others. Akhab had told me that Eliyah was his tutor when he was a boy, for he was a learned man who once served at court as a scribe and scholar. Now, after aligning himself with the zealots and rising to become their leader, Eliyah had the appearance of a wild man: long unkempt grey hair and beard, poorly hewn animal skins wrapped around his body and held in place by ropes, he walked about in bare feet. Observing him as he approached, it was hard to imagine he had ever been fit to serve at court, but Akhab assured me he was once a very different man.

Eliyahu came to us that day to speak for some of the ministers of the court. Those ministers had been too cowardly to address the king themselves, for they knew his devotion to me grew stronger with each passing year. They also knew Akhab still bore some affection for his erstwhile mentor, whom he had once looked up to and wanted to emulate, so they went to Eliyah and implored him to speak to the king on their behalf. Unlike those conspiring ministers, the leader of the zealots was a man of conviction, unafraid to speak his mind.

"Melekh Akhab," said Eliyahu as he rose from his knees, "I give you thanks for receiving me."

"We may not always agree on a great many things, Eliyahu, but my old tutor will always be welcome at my court."

"Ah yes. I recall, Melekh, in my days as a court scholar during the reign of your father, you were the wisest and most capable of my pupils. You showed great promise as a youth by your intellect and strength of character – until your interest in women became greater than your interest in learning."

There were some chuckles from the courtiers. I glanced at my husband from the side. He was stroking his beard and smirked. Then he said, "I assure you, Eliyah, I still have a keen interest in learning. But I know you did not come all this way just to reminisce about old times. What brings you to Megiddu on this fine morning?"

"Very well, Melekh," he replied with a bow of his head. Then he straightened and began pacing before the dais with his fingers pressed together. "I come before you today on a mission of great importance, although it pains me to stand before you now for this purpose. You see, it relates to your love for women, which has indeed overshadowed your love for a great many other things, as is often the case when young men discover the delights of the female body. I was, myself, once a young man. As you were always my favorite student, I hoped that inclination would pass as you grew into a man, but I have heard otherwise."

Akhab snorted and looked at me. "Can you blame me when you behold my Queen? She is not only the most beautiful woman in the world, as any man with eyes can see – she is also wise and possessed of a keen intellect. How many men can boast they have a wife who is not only a lioness in bed, but can also hold their interest in the study and the field?"

More snickering from the courtiers arose, and even I could not hide my amusement.

For the first time since he approached, the prophet looked at me, but it was with scrutiny rather than admiration. "Indeed. It is she that is the reason I have come. You see, Melekh, it is said that you do not give equally of yourself among your wives: that your Melkah receives more attention than all the rest combined. That you have even left the management of the kingdom in the hands of your *abarakkum*, ministers, and scribes, that you might go and lie with her in the middle of the day!"

I had to look away and pretend to cough to hide a grin. Meanwhile, my husband leaned over, and whispered, "I would take you now, if I could."

"Do you think it would make him go away?"

He laughed and reached for my hand to bring it to his lips, while the Tishbite continued listing off our apparently long list of

63

sexual sins. "That, upon the Queen's summons, you obediently go to fulfill her carnal whims!"

"Oh, that you could summon me now," Akhab breathed.

"...that you have lain with her in strange and unnatural places, outside the privacy and decency of the marital bed!"

I beckoned to my husband with my finger, and when he leaned in again, I whispered, "If he is trying to shame us, he is only making me burn with desire for you."

"I am grateful for the thickness of my robes to hide my own." He pulled at them. "Women are lucky in that way, I suppose."

I sat back then cleared my throat trying to appear serious. It finally took discreetly biting the inside of my bottom lip with the points of my teeth to keep from smirking, as the prophet went on.

"...and that you have even known her when she was unclean, in the manner of heathens." He spit on the ground in disgust. Moving swiftly and silently, the young slave kneeling on the floor nearby moved to wipe it up.

Looking at the floor where he spat, I grimaced. When I first came to my husband's kingdom as a young bride, I wondered, *What is it with these zealots and spitting?* By now I had come to realize it was the custom of some of the staunchest followers of Yahowah to spit upon the ground at the mere mention of other gods. As the debate between true and false worship was one of the premier topics of the day, they kept the slaves busy wiping up their spittle from the floor. I sighed heavily and looked away to hide my disgust.

The prophet's list complete, Akhab cleared his throat, and I could see him struggling not to laugh. "Well, it seems you have compiled quite a record of our apparent sins, Tishbite. I wonder, who has been lurking and hiding behind every wall and window and column and rock and tree to witness all these...carnal acts I have committed with my wife?"

Snickers resounded from among the ministers and courtiers, particularly from Akhab's brothers. I lowered my face to hide my amusement once again and, by sheer force of will, managed not to laugh aloud. It seemed it was only the old men who found our behavior offensive. The young men seemed impressed and likely wanted to emulate us with their own wives and concubines.

"This is no laughing matter, Melekh. You have been inflamed by the sin of lust, bewitched by the Queen's painted face and immodest dress!"

Aware that all eyes were now turned on me, I straightened my posture, while my husband rose from his throne and fixed the prophet with a fierce and steady gaze. No one was laughing now. "Are you accusing the Queen of sorcery, Tishbite?"

"Does she not claim to be a priestess of her false gods, Melekh?"

Tired of being talked about, I raised my voice to speak for myself. "I am High Priestess of the Ba'alim in Yisrael, the living embodiment of Ashtarti and her representative on earth."

The prophet spat. "Blasphemy!" There were rumblings of talk from within the court, but they quickly died down when the prophet, leering at me as if he knew he was setting a trap, raised his voice to ask, "Do you anoint yourself with sacred oils and cut your own flesh to draw blood for rituals to your gods, Melkah?"

Unafraid of his snares, I declared, "I do."

He spat. "Sorcery."

"No more than the rituals of your priests and holy men."

Before the debate could go on, my husband cut in. "A priestess is a holy woman, not a sorceress. We are not putting the Queen or her religious activities on trial, Tishbite. She needs neither prove nor disprove the verity of her rituals, for they are her own, and I will not interfere in her belief."

"There is only one true God, Melekh. All others are false, as are their rituals and prophets." He spat on the floor again. "Your Melkah worships wood and stone and entices the people of Yisrael to do the same, but I speak for the one true God."

"If my gods are not real," I said calmly, "what has your god to be jealous of? If my gods are but wood and stone, they are no threat to your god; therefore, he is either jealous of nothing or of his own creation, for he claims to have made all things. If he made these things, let him destroy them in his jealousy. Else, let him be silent, for his carrying on to me is proof that my gods do exist, for a true god has no need to be jealous of nothing."

Eliyahu looked at me hatefully as those of our court who worshipped the Ba'alim, or whose minds and hearts were leaning in that direction, began to mutter in agreement. My husband gazed upon me with a proud smile, and for a moment I thought I caught a glint of belief in his eye. It gave me hope that he could yet be converted.

For now, however, he was still eager to appease the god of Yisrael. When the prophet opened his lips and began to speak, Akhab raised his voice to cut him off. "We are not here to debate the merits of one religion over another. There are those who believe differently, yet they do not point in our faces and denounce our god as you zealots do theirs. They accept him as one god alongside their own, and we would do well to learn from them in this, for acceptance promotes peace and the wellbeing of kingdoms."

The prophet was again about to speak, but then my husband raised his voice, deep and strong. "You have accused the Queen of sorcery before the whole court who are gathered here to bear witness to your allegation. On what grounds do you base this accusation?"

"It is known that a woman who paints her face to appear more beautiful than she is by nature, does so with the intent to pervert and seduce."

"If a painted face is a form of sorcery, then it is a wonder we are not all worshipping the Ba'alim by now."

This drew some laughter from those gathered. The Tishbite looked down at his bare feet and, shaking his head, mumbled to himself. I watched him closely, trying to discern if he was touched by madness. Then I spoke: "You condemn me and accuse me of sorcery for painting my face, but queens and noblewomen have always adorned and painted themselves in such a way. Even the wives and concubines of Shelomoh and Dawid – will you condemn and accuse them of sorcery, as well?"

"They were swayed to follow foreign customs, unaware of the wickedness of their ways. They may be forgiven for their ignorance, but you are not so ignorant. You adorn yourself to seduce the king and lead him to sin."

"The Queen is my wife, and I am drawn to her quite naturally. She has no need to seduce me."

"You are Melekh Yisrael, king of the people of the Covenant. Your wife is a Canaanite idolatress and makes no secret that she is a priestess of her Ba'alim..." He paused to spit. "...and that she promotes their worship in the kingdom."

66

"I have permitted the Queen to worship freely, as I have for all people in my kingdom."

"She is seducing you and the people away from the one true God! She has distorted your vision so that all you can see is the falsity with which she presents herself before the court – as false as the idols she worships!" Spit. "See, even now, how you turn away to gaze upon her unnatural beauty!"

"Is it forbidden for a man to gaze upon his wife? I do not recall that being among the laws of Moshe and Abraham."

"She has made of herself an idol by the unnatural beauty of her painted face, that you might be led astray! She even admits that she considers herself the embodiment of her false god! And you make jokes of this, Melekh, but soon others *will* follow your example and turn from the Lord God to worship this idol in a woman's form." Spit.

Akhab scoffed. "The Queen *is* beautiful with her painted face, yes. But I tell you that what you see here is nothing compared to the beauty of her natural face – and *I* am the only man who ever gets to see it. She has seduced no one." He returned to his seat but paused before sitting and turned back to say, "You are treading on dangerous ground, Tishbite. Do not try my patience."

With that, he sat on his throne and took my hand and brought it to his lips. That should have brought the issue to an end, but Eliyah the Tishbite was a stubborn man who did not give up easily; like all prophets, he thought himself to be right in all things. This Tishbite was the worst I had seen of them, however, and I wondered at his boldness. He seemed a man possessed by an angry spirit.

"It is no secret that our Lord Yahowah, the God of Yisrael, *the one and only God*, detests a man for the overuse of his wife for pleasure. It is why he allows for a king to take many wives so that he may know them, and they will bear him many sons. For no other reason should a man know his wife."

My husband reached for my hand, wove our fingers together, and said, "My other wives have been fruitful – they have no need of me, for their needs have been met. The Queen has yet to produce a more fitting heir, so we must keep trying." Still holding my hand, he squeezed it gently.

Looking at my husband in gratitude, I smiled pensively. He knew I felt inadequate because, after three years of marriage, I had not yet been able to carry a single pregnancy to term. Repeated

67

miscarriages had begun to take their toll, and I wept bitterly at every loss I endured, while his other wives and concubines continued to bear healthy, living children.

Outwardly, I rejoiced with them; after all, I bore them no ill will and was happy that my husband had many heirs to secure the kingdom, even if I could produce none. But I was sensitive to the talk that I knew was circulating at court. My husband was always eager to shield me from criticism and rebuked any who had spoken ill of me, but I knew more than he realized and often grew melancholy when I thought no one was looking. In the privacy of my chamber, whenever I lamented my failure to give him a child, he reassured me that it did not lessen his love for me. He even joked that it gave us more reason to know each other as often as possible.

Even when I was at my worst, Akhab could always make me smile. Our natural playfulness together often turned to love making. For us, it was not merely a carnal act, as our detractors believed – it was a spiritual act of healing that restored us from the many issues weighing on us every day. In the land of my birth, this would have been understood and accepted as part of the natural order, a harmonization of the masculine and feminine energies that were a necessary part of creation, but here it was a foreign idea, as unacceptable as my gods were to the zealots.

The Tishbite scoffed and suddenly his voice rang through the hall, startling me and some of the courtiers. "That is still no reason to show favoritism to the Queen! Your abundant affection for her is well-known, Melekh, and affection for a wife is pleasing to the Lord, but too much affection risks adoration. Be careful, lest you incur the wrath of the Lord by replacing true worship with *false idols!*"

His gaze burned through me when he said these words, and spittle flew from his mouth again. I held his gaze and raised my chin in defiance. Meanwhile, my husband yawned. "I tire of these censures, Tishbite. I will not apologize for loving my wife; neither will I apologize for exalting my Queen."

"If you will not fear the Lord God of Yisrael, Melekh, then perhaps you will at least fear the resentment of your other wives?" Standing now in a curtain of sunlight that entered through the clerestory windows on the western wall of the great hall, he grinned like a madman.

Akhab sighed loudly. "Are you a prophet or are you a fool? I resent your mockery."

"You may not appreciate my sense of humor, Melekh, but I speak true as much as I speak in jest. While it is God's wrath you should most fear, showing preference for the Queen will only spark jealousy and competition from your other wives."

At this, I laughed aloud, and the prophet's gaze turned to me in surprise before reverting to his usual disdain. "There is no competition to be had." And I smiled gleefully.

"Is that confidence, Melkah *Yezebel?* Or is it pride that I hear?"

The Tishbite was the first to bastardize my name in deference to the god El, whom the zealots insisted was the same as Yahowah. It was also a vulgar joke, a clever play on the Hebrew word for dung: *zebel.* While I only spoke Hebrew to address the common people of Yisrael, most of whom did not understand the Akkadian we used at court, I understood very well the double meaning. Soon, it was customary for all zealous followers of Yahowah to do the same. It irritated me but I was wont to ignore it. I would not be provoked by petty insults from my inferiors.

"I am a queen: it does not matter what you hear. Know your place."

He looked at me with a smile, as if in challenge. "A queen, yes, but still not a man. Know *your* place, Daughter of Tzidon."

Akhab bristled, but I saw him watching me with a gleam in his eye and a faint smile, which he hid from the others with his forefinger. I had often impressed him with my speech; by now, he knew when to step in and when to let me fight my own battles.

With a smirk, I raised my brow, tipping my head as if conceding a loss. Then I sat up straight and fixed the prophet with an icy gaze and a wicked smile. "Yes, I am a daughter of Tzidon. I am a woman, and that makes you think less of me. But listen well, old man: where I am from, *no* man is above me."

The prophet laughed and raised his hand and turned to the others to be sure they were listening. "The Queen thinks herself equal to a man!"

"I *am* equal to a man – the King – and greater than most."

I sat back with a bitter smile and shook my head as the court suddenly erupted into fits of hissing and booing and men shouting curses upon me. These were the same men who had opposed the king raising me to co-equal status three years earlier; now that I had declared myself his equal before all, their anger was reignited. Watching them now, I sighed heavily. I had been sent here to bring peace, but as time passed, I kept thinking how impossible a task had been placed into my hands. These prophets of Yahowah did not wish for peace with any but themselves, and they were constantly at odds with the king because of it. Sometimes, I wondered if my presence there only made matters for him worse.

The king rose from his throne now and demanded silence from his court. But as the din began to fade, the prophet seemed to want to incite further chaos by proclaiming, "See how the Canaanite woman speaks to a prophet of the Lord!"

He glared at me, as more shouts erupted from among the ministers and courtiers. I saw my husband scanning to take note of them when the prophet pointed directly at him. "Melekh Akhab! Have you no faith in the God of Yisrael, that you would allow your woman to speak in such a way while in the presence of men?"

"My *Queen* has every right to address the court, as she sees fit! You are the one who has overstepped his place!"

"Your *woman* is a Canaanite and an idolatress, and she will bring the wrath of the Lord upon us all!"

Finally unable to hold back from the build-up of three years of enduring this harassment, I rose from my chair and raised my hand to stop my husband from speaking in my defense. He bowed his head and stepped back, while I stepped forward to stare the prophet down from upon the dais. "I am Melkah Yisrael and High Priestess of the Ba'alim! And you will speak to me as such, or you will leave this court at once! I will not be talked to like a child being scolded by her nurse, especially when you are the one who is like a child screaming and demanding to be heard!"

Once he had provoked me to anger, his passion waned. Now, he could gloat, and he spoke with composure. "Your pride and arrogance will be your undoing, *Yezebel*."

I gritted my teeth, and said, "My name is Yezeba'al, Melkah Yisrael!"

The last of my composure frayed, I turned and stormed off through the archway on the wall behind the dais. It opened to a staircase and corridor that led to our private apartments. Followed close behind by Zarek, the captain of my eunuchs, I trembled violently as I walked down the corridors and up the sets of stairs, eyes burning, until I was far enough away that I did not need to fear I would be overheard in the Great Hall. Then, unable to go any further, I wailed and dropped to my knees. I began pulling at the jeweled collar at my neck, and my headdress, desperate to take them off so I could breathe. I wished for my head to stop pounding.

Kora must have heard me, for she suddenly appeared and came to help. Soon afterward, Daneyah came to my aid, as well. Upon my coronation, I had elevated her from nursemaid – a position of which I no longer had use – to court advisor to the Queen, a position that had not existed previously. The appointment had not been well-received by the same ministers with whom I was frequently at odds. They objected to it, on the grounds that she was a woman and a foreign idolatress. I reminded them that I was all these things, and it was my will that she be given this position. My husband supported her appointment and put an end to their grumbling. As my advisor, Daneyah had been in the throne room to witness many of the prophets' abuses against me over the years, and she had been there today, as well.

In the past, she had often complained about these prophets and their treatment of me: no man or prophet, no matter how high he was raised, would ever dare to speak to the King and Queen of Tzidon in such a way. In my father's kingdom, a man who had displayed such open arrogance before his superiors would be killed for such offenses, or at least imprisoned, but my husband had a strange reverence for and even fear of them that I could not understand. Daneyah resented his patience with these outspoken prophets and suggested that the time would come when he would need to choose between me and his religion. I hoped it would not come to that.

Kneeling on the floor beside me and wrapping me in her embrace as I wept on her shoulder, Daneyah stroked my disheveled hair and whispered reassurances, as she did when I was a young girl. "You did well today, Yezeba'al, standing up for yourself against that awful man. I am proud of you. Today, you have at last become a true Queen." Then she lifted my chin and smiled warmly before she rose and helped me to my feet. We walked slowly to my chamber, followed by Kora carrying my crown and jewels, and the ever-present eunuchs who were silent witnesses to it all.

Washing my face, brushing out my hair, and stripping me of my outer garments, Daneyah and Kora put me to bed and tended to me with unguents and fragrant oils, massaging them into my aching limbs until my husband appeared. Then they took the vials and containers away, covered my body with the bedlinens, and moved aside for him to come to me. Having dismissed his court for the day, and finally able to shed the weight of his kingship, he knelt beside the bed and wept over me, apologizing, and begging my forgiveness for not sending the Tishbite away sooner.

Weeping fresh tears, I said, "Why do you spare these prophets when they abuse me so? For three years I have borne their insults and their cruelty with grace and modesty, as you have asked of me."

"I know, I know, my love, and I was wrong. *I was wrong.* I see now, and that is why I have sent them away."

"My father would have killed them for less."

Akhab sighed heavily and looked away. Then he shook his head. "I am not your father, Yezeba'al. And this is not your father's kingdom."

"No, it is *your* kingdom – and you should not tolerate the abuses of lesser men!"

"These men are prophets of the Lord, my God. I cannot have their blood on my hands. Do you understand this, my love?"

"No, I do not understand. They are not priests – most of them are filthy peasants who claim to speak to Yahowah and to be his messengers."

"A prophet can come from anywhere, highborn or low."

"They are madmen, and troublemakers. They will turn your people against you if you let them continue in this way."

"Yezeba'al, I have sent them all away. And I will not permit them – any of them – to return unless they come to me in true repentance."

I stopped and sighed. "Do you promise they will not return to harass us?"

"I promise, love, they will not return. I have banished all Yahowah's prophets from my court, even those who claim not to be zealots. If they want to come back, they must show true penitence for their ill-treatment of you, my Queen."

Still laying with my cheek resting on a cushion, I turned away and breathed deeply. Akhab continued to gaze at me in contrition, gently stroking my cheek with his thumb. I looked to Daneyah, who was quietly helping Kora with her work, while the slaves and servants came in and out to assemble our supper on a table. It was set up near the archway that opened to my private terrace, overlooking the garden. I had forgotten that we had asked to dine in my bedchamber that night, but now I was no longer in the mood for eating. Craving privacy with my husband, I slipped on a robe and sent them all away. They nodded dutifully and went out, Daneyah pulling the door closed as she left, and then I sat on the bed with my legs crossed.

Akhab smiled sweetly and, when I held my arms out to him, rose to meet my embrace. I wrapped my arms around his waist and closed my eyes, resting my head against his torso and listening to the sounds of his body. He moved to sit on the bed beside me then brought his fingers to my chin, raising his thumb to caress my bottom lip.

"You are more beautiful than all the gold of Opir, my sweet Yezeba'al: my Rose of Shomron."

It was a hinting reference to the Rose of Sharon from the Song of Shelomoh, which was read each year at the time of Pesakh. Apart from my familiarity with it from attending the temple of Yahowah with the rest of the household, I knew it best of all the sacred readings because Akhab often recited the most beautiful and sensuous parts of the song to me as a precursor to love-making.

I smiled faintly and lowered my gaze. "You were kind to say that I am more beautiful as I am now than when my face is painted, although I am not sure anyone who is against the practice was convinced."

"I said it because it was true. You are more beautiful like this, in the way that only I know you."

I met his gaze and attempted to smile again but was not able to hold it.

"Oh, my dear, sweet Yezeba'al. What makes you so sad?"

"I am beautiful now, but what will you think of me in a few years when I am old and my beauty begins to fade?"

73

He raised his hand to brush hair away from my cheek, gazing at me still. "You will grow old, that is true, as we all must succumb to age in time. But your beauty will never fade, not to me, for I see the beauty of your soul that is beyond compare."

I smiled and, as he moved to kiss me, closed my eyes to enjoy the moment our lips came together. Then, as he pulled away, I opened my eyes again and breathed deeply.

He moved to lie on his stomach, resting on his elbow with his jaw in his hand, looking up at me with a smile as he toyed with my fingers. "Do you know what attracted me to you the first time I saw you those three years ago, when you were presented to me?"

I shook my head.

He chuckled and his eyes took on a faraway look as he remembered. "It was how seriously you took everything, the way you were carefully thinking through every step, your face fixed in intense concentration. The grace and care you put into every move, and the sincerity and determination of your character are what most impressed me. Of course, your outward beauty was without question, and perhaps that is all the others saw when they first beheld you, but it was the woman I saw beneath all the paint and regalia that I fell in love with that day – and I have loved her ever since, in fact growing more to love her with each passing day."

"Do you speak of me or of someone else entirely?" I teased.

He raised up on his knees and, with a growl, grabbed me and pulled me to lie over him. We kissed and tussled, and I shrieked when he began to tickle the sides of my waist. Then we stopped and were lost momentarily in each other's eyes before he sat up and drew me into another tender kiss.

Intoxicated by my love for him, I lingered with a smile even after he pulled away to lie back against the cushions. When I heard him sigh, opening my eyes I found him looking toward the table heaped with bread and fruits and cheese and steaming meats. Pitchers of wine from the royal vineyards sat ready to be enjoyed, with an extra wineskin placed nearby in case we wanted more when the pitchers were empty. Everything smelled delicious and I became aware of our bowels grumbling in earnest.

We got up and went to the table to eat together before our supper grew cold. Keeping our dinner conversation light, we laughed together over gossip and silly things, sipped wine, and made eyes at each other until we had eaten enough to be satisfied. Then we chewed on a mixture of herbs and honey to sweeten our breaths and went out onto the terrace to look at the stars.

We talked quietly and he pointed to some of the brightest stars, naming them and their constellations. I told him what they were called in Tzidon, and we mused at the differences. After a while, I shivered from the night air. Seeing this, Akhab removed his outer robe and slipped it around me. Then he pulled me into his arms. I leaned back against him, closed my eyes, and breathed deeply, grateful for the warmth of his body against mine.

In the silence, troubled thoughts began to take hold of my mind once again. Unable to quiet these thoughts, I pulled away and went back inside. Akhab followed. "My love? What troubles you?"

Pulling off the robe he had wrapped around me, I draped it on the foot of the bed and went to sit at the head. There, I slipped off my sandals and pulled up my feet to sit with my legs crossed again. I wanted to curl up beneath the blankets and hide, but Akhab came to sit before me and reached for my hands, gazing at me earnestly. "Please, Yezeba'al, tell me what you are thinking about."

I inhaled, still trying to form my thoughts into words. "Is it true, what they say about me?"

He pulled his hands away and let them rest in his lap in a helpless gesture. "What have you heard?"

"They say that I am barren."

"You are not barren – you have been with child many times…"

"They say that Yahowah has cursed me for not abandoning the gods of my father. That I will not bear a child for as long as I live unless I turn away from them and send the Ba'alim priests and priestesses – my friends – away."

He sighed and ran his fingers through the curls that hung over his forehead and framed his face. It was clear that he had heard the same, but that he had chosen not to tell me what was being said when I was not around to overhear it. I waited, aware that he was only thinking of what to say.

Again, he sighed. "The other day, when I was overseeing the care of my horses, Obadyah came to me. He said that some of the ministers – I'm not going to say who, but you can likely guess which ones – came to him and asked him to speak to me on their behalf." He paused to take a deep breath and looked at me as if trying to decide if I should hear the full truth about what had been said. Seeming to decide against it, he lowered his gaze and shook his head. "They are fools, and I said as much."

"What did they want him to say to you?"

When he did not answer, I reached for his hands, taking both in mine. "Akhab, tell me what was said."

"Th-they wanted him to try to convince me to...set you aside and raise another wife as queen."

I inhaled sharply and tightened my hands into fists, trying not to cry.

"– but he told me this, not to convince me, but so that I could know what they were scheming and respond appropriately. Of course, I was outraged. I slammed my fist against the wall in the stables – that's how I really bruised my hand. I'm...sorry I lied to you about it. I did not want you to know before I'd had time to consider how I would deal with them."

"You *will* deal with them, this time?"

"Yes, of course I will. Now that I have a witness who can speak against them."

"Am I not a witness? And my ladies who have also heard the things that have been said? You forget that a woman is as capable of bearing witness as a man."

"Yes, of course. But it is not as easy here as it is where you come from to convict men on the words of women, right or wrong."

"You are the king! Your word is law!"

"My word is bound by the laws of this kingdom, and it cannot be so easily changed or undone. I am but one man, serving under the laws and traditions of those who came before me."

I sighed heavily and looked away.

"My love, I am sorry. I should have told you sooner. I did not want you to be hurt by what they said, or fear that I would even consider replacing you – because I want you to know, I would never consider it."

I kept my gaze low and willed myself not to cry. "Maybe you should consider it." My voice wavered and, despite my effort, a single tear escaped its lonely imprisonment.

"Yezeba'al," my husband cooed, reaching to take my face in his hand. I swatted his hand away.

76

"No, Akhab, maybe they are right. Maybe I *am* unable to bear children. Maybe you should dispose of me and raise another in my place. You have many worthy and capable wives to choose from."

"None are as worthy and capable as you."

"They have given you children — sons to strengthen the dynasty and carry on the family line. They have done their duty as your wives, but I..." My voice broke and I bent forward to hide that I had begun to weep. He moved to console me, but I would not allow it. I managed to compose myself again, and I met his gaze, even with tears in my eyes. "I came here to bring peace, but all I have brought is discord because they hate me so. If I cannot bring peace to this kingdom, and cannot give you heirs, then I have failed as your queen."

"You have not failed. There is still time."

"When it is time for you to name a successor, his mother will rise above me anyway. You may as well do it now and get it over with. I can...learn to be satisfied being just another wife."

"As long as I live, you will be the one by my side. You are not just another wife, Yezeba'al. You are the most astounding woman I have ever known. Your courage and wisdom have been remarked upon by those who see it — and they do see it. Do not be troubled by the talk of weak men."

"It is not only the ministers and gossipers that trouble me, Akhab. There is more. I know the prophets of Yahowah say that I am a danger to the kingdom — that it will fall because of me."

"Those damnable prophets! All they ever do is stir up chaos and dissent. If anyone is a danger to the kingdom, it is them! You are a harbinger of peace, while they are the ones causing trouble and playing on the weaknesses of envious men. You are right to distrust them, and I have been a fool to ignore their provocation for so long. You have more wisdom and better judgment than the prophets. You have more intelligence than all the ministers at court combined. You — a mere woman of seventeen years — you have more wit than them, you are more capable than them, and they know it. And that is why they hate you — they feel threatened because they know I see it, too."

He touched my cheek and gazed at me tearfully. "You have brought knowledge and wealth to this troubled kingdom, brought light into the wilderness where we have gone astray. More than that, you have brought joy and comfort to my lonely heart, touched my soul

77

in a way that no one else can. And my body..." He chuckled when I smiled and turned my gaze away. Then, growing serious again, he took my hand, and said, "You are good for me; and what is good for me is good for my kingdom."

"But if what they say is true – that I will be the cause of the kingdom's fall..."

"I would let *ten thousand* kingdoms fall before I would ever turn my back on you! Do you not understand how much you mean to me? Have you not listened to all that I have said?"

I started at his sudden burst of anger. When he saw how he had frightened me, he ran his fingers through his hair and exhaled. Then he lifted my chin. "Look at me. Do not avoid my gaze." I did as he commanded and saw that he, too, had tears in his eyes yet spoke firmly and with conviction.

"You are my Melkah, Yezeba'al: my beloved, the most exalted among women. Let them talk. Let them be consumed by their envy of you. And let the others be the bearers of my children, if that is the will of the gods – you will be the bearer of my heart for all my days. The others are as cattle to me. You are the one I love."

Overwhelmed, I fell into his embrace. He kissed me passionately and soon all our troubles were forgotten, as we made love well into the night.

The next day, Akhab publicly rebuked his ministers and exalted me before his court. Those who had been involved in the secret dealings, as revealed by the steward, were called out for their duplicity. Most of them were his uncles, but now they were traitors, and they knew they had been exposed. They trembled openly when the palace guard suddenly appeared and blocked the exits, so that the ministers who had spoken against me could not escape. Those men were seized, stripped of their ranks and honors, and sentenced to a life of imprisonment.

Abram and Asa laughed openly as Akhab rebuked those elder ministers, eager to see their fall. The Lord Treasurer turned his face from them, while the Minister of Trade watched his half-brothers being led away and shook his head at their shame. Of the twelve, they were the only four ministers who had not been part of the schemes, for I had earned their support.

Coolly observing all this from my place at my husband's side, I was pleased. In the past, I had complained to my husband about these men, but with little effect, for they had persuaded him with their silver tongues and their flattery. Now that he had seen what their manipulations had done to me and had the word of the Lord Steward and the Minister of War, to whom they had appealed, he acted swiftly and with a vengeance.

Before they were taken away, they were brought to the foot of the dais and forced to kneel, the blades of their captors sharp against their throats. I rose and came forward to look upon them all and to address them as their Queen: "For three years, I have forgiven your slights, ignored your snickers whenever I passed, and put up with your backhanded compliments. As Melkah, I have showered you with gifts and shown you endless kindness, even while enduring your petty jealousies, yet still you would conspire against me. Know this: while my husband intended to have you executed for the crime of treason, I entreated him to grant you clemency in the form of a lighter sentence. While you rot in our dungeons, your families will retain their property and continue to live in the prosperity to which they are accustomed, but the kingdom will go on without you and you will be forgotten."

I looked to my husband. He gave me a nod, and then I waved, and commanded, "Take them away."

With their positions now vacant, the king gave me the right to fill them with whomever I deemed worthy. Naturally, I filled them with my friends and supporters – some of Akhab's brothers and the Ba'alim priests and priestesses who had consoled me throughout the many ordeals I had faced since coming to Yisrael. Any members of the court who did not approve of their appointment surely did not dare to raise an objection after what they had seen performed that day. Now there was a fair balance in the court between the different gods whose interests were constantly at play within the kingdom. Akhab was pleased with my choices, as I chose them not only based on friendship but on their individual qualifications, and with that meddling prophet also out of the way, I felt that we were entering a golden age of peace and prosperity within the kingdom.

It was a familiar scene: another gilded bride being led to the king in a procession bearing many gifts. Not nearly as many as the gifts I came with when I was in the new bride's place, to be sure; yet every gift was chosen from her family's treasury to showcase their prestige and given as part of her dowry for the betterment of Yisrael. The main difference, however, was not in the gifts but in my position on the dais beside the king: as his queen, I was present for each marriage that followed mine. My presence was necessary, not only to support the king, but also as a reminder to the new wives that I was above them. Yet even with my rank and Akhab's promises, I knew that each wife who bore him a son while I had none made my favored position increasingly tenuous.

The presentations of royal wives were always grand, but those who came after me were also performed alongside the other duties of the kingdom. This was in stark contrast to my own, which had been given a precedence that warranted a four-day cessation of the court's regular activities. There would still be a feast now, but the celebration was subdued, marked by mores and protocol. Because of my rank, I retained my place by the king's side at the head table while the new bride sat among her family and attendants until the time came for her to be escorted to the bridal chamber.

It was rare in those early years for Akhab not to consummate his marriages on the first night, unless he did not desire his new bride or thought she was not ready. Since I was the highest-ranking woman in the king's household, it was my responsibility to welcome and prepare each new wife to receive him as her husband. It was a duty I bore with as much grace and humility as I could muster, for it was an honor to be the highest among them. I had always known that I would have to share my husband. It would have been selfish to think I should have him to myself, but at least I could content myself in knowing that I had his heart.

This newest bride, Zubira, had come from D'mat in the resource-rich kingdom of Kush. She had a dowry nearly as large as mine and had been presented to the king in gold and richly embroidered robes to rival those of Tzidon. Of all Akhab's wives, she was the one who had the most potential to oust me from my lofty position as his chief wife. I would not hold that against her, but I could not help being aware of it as we received her into our ranks.

Like me, she worshipped her own set of gods and goddesses. While I directed the other wives and handmaids in preparing her, she clung to one of her idols carved from ivory. She was said to be the same age I had been when I came to be the first of Akhab's wives, and her height seemed to support it; only after she had been stripped of her regalia in the privacy of the bridal chamber did I notice that she looked younger and trembled fearfully. But I could see the intelligence in her eyes that looked around at everything and everyone with a mix of curiosity and uncertainty, and I was eager to make her feel at home. I needed her to trust and look up to me, not only for her own sake, but to prevent us from becoming rivals.

Gently, I stroked the top of her head, where her shorn curls had been smoothed against her scalp with resin to be kept hidden beneath the elaborate braided wig she had worn for her presentation to the king. Now the wig rested on a stand and, with the paint removed from her face, she looked even younger and smaller than she had appeared when dressed in all that regalia.

"Sweet daughter," I whispered, "do not fear the king. He is a kind and gentle man to his women and children."

As I looked at her body, I was certain that she was younger than we had been led to believe. I met Fang-Hua's gaze while we worked together to prepare her and noticed that she looked just as troubled. Then I took her aside, and whispered, "I wonder if the representative from D'mat was truthful about her age when he arranged this marriage."

"It seems impossible now," she agreed. "The girl is still a child."

Zubira's brother, the new king of Kush, seemed eager to be rid of his sisters, hastily marrying them off, as I had heard, so as not to be burdened with their care while trying to grow a family of his own. Zubira was the youngest, and purportedly the prettiest, of his sisters. It was always said in these arranged marriages that the girl in question was the prettiest, but in her case, I could believe it because she was one of the most beautiful young girls I had ever seen. If only she did not look so young.

"Can you send a message to the king?" asked Fang-Hua.

"I can't." Tears bristled in my eyes. "It is against protocol."

81

"You are his Melkah – he will listen to you."

"The king will not take her when he sees that she is too young to be a wife, but I cannot interfere with what has already been planned. If I do, it will be seen as jealousy. The decision *must* be his. But I know him. He will not go through with it."

She nodded and then we returned to Zubira, who was trying her best to maintain a dutiful expression. But as I returned to her, I saw the way her eyes glistened. When a tear broke loose, I discreetly wiped it from her cheek. She looked at me with fear, but I smiled and stroked her cheek, leaning in to press my lips to where the tear had been. She offered a grateful smile as I pulled away.

Looking to be sure no one else was near, I leaned close to her, and whispered, "Zubira, listen to me: the king is an honorable man. He will only take you if you are ready." I paused and looked at her dubiously, "Are you ready?"

She shook her head, and another tear slipped down her cheek.

"Tell him that," I whispered, gently wiping the tear away. "Do not be afraid. If he does not see it for himself, you must tell him you are not ready. He will listen." I paused as Leah came near, and then I spoke in a full voice. "The king will be good to you, as will I. We are your family now and this is your home. If there is ever anything you need, come to me. Yes?"

She nodded and sniffled, and then I backed away to let the preparations continue. When a messenger came to inform me that the king was on his way, I gathered the four other wives who had been chosen to help prepare her, and we left her alone in the king's chamber with her attendants and a pair of eunuchs to guard her while the others followed us. While we walked in the corridor, Fang-Hua followed close behind me, but the other wives whispered and giggled behind our backs. I stopped abruptly and turned to narrow my gaze at them. "You will maintain decorum and show Zubira the same amount of respect as you were given when you arrived."

"Forgive us, Melkah," said Leah, the instigator of most of the problems I had with the other wives, for she was petty and quarrelsome. She was fourteen but stood a whole head taller than me. She had already been married to Akhab for a full year but had yet to conceive a child by him because he never summoned her to his chamber. I had heard it said that she was still a virgin, but I did not

82

ask Akhab if this was true because I did not want him to perceive it as jealousy.

Her father was a priest of Yahowah and a cousin to Akhab, and that gave her precedence over some of the other wives, but she would always remain my inferior and she hated me for it. Even though she spoke to me now with a dutiful bow of her head and a bend in her knees, I knew that she would not show such deference toward me if not obliged. I held back a great deal of my frustration with her; one thing I would not tolerate, however, was disrespect toward the king's other wives, especially ones of higher rank than her own.

"Do you take issue with Zubira, Leah?"

"No, Melkah. It is only that..." She giggled. "Well, her skin is so dark."

"Ba'athu has dark skin, and you did not criticize her when she arrived."

Leah looked down at the floor but then lifted her pale green eyes to meet my gaze. "Ba'athu is not a royal wife."

"What is your point, Leah?"

"It is only that Zubira will stand out among us. I do not think any of the king's wives should stand out from each other. Except of course you, Melkah."

I drew my lips into a tight line and squinted at her. "Stand out, where exactly? I am the only wife who is ever seen by the public after marrying the king. Once you are here, you do not exist except to bear more children for him."

"His *only* children – I mean, since you haven't borne him any."

My hand rang against the side of her cheek and then I took hold of her arm, twisting it behind her and grabbing her by the hair at the back of her head. "What gives you the right to make such comparisons, hmm?"

"I'm sorry! I'm sorry! I did not mean it!" She whined like a dog.

I grabbed at her tiny stomach, digging my fingers into her flesh. "I do not see you getting with child anytime soon. The king does not even want to touch you." With that, I shoved her away from me.

Three of the other wives watched with barely concealed amusement but one of them, Hawwa, moved to comfort her the moment my back was turned. Without turning toward them, I raised my voice suddenly: "*Don't* give her comfort when she has brought this on herself!"

Hawwa obeyed immediately. "Yes, Melkah."

Now I turned back to Leah, having composed myself. "You will show Zubira deference, as befitting the daughter of a king – which *you* are not. Do you understand, Leah?"

Her fair hair was disheveled, loose strands sticking to her ruddy cheeks that were wet with tears. She turned her gaze to the floor. Her voice was shrill and hoarse and trembling. "Yes, Melkah. I beseech your forgiveness."

"Granted," I answered, although I stared her down to be sure she was indeed subdued. Then I turned and continued down the corridor. They followed close behind, in silence.

We passed the king in the courtyard on his way to the chamber where his new bride awaited him. We should not have been there to see him but had been delayed by Leah's nonsense. Akhab looked dutiful as he approached, flanked by his bodyguards. When he saw me as we passed, our eyes met with yearning. It took all my strength not to reach for him, and my heart cried, as it had with every new wife, but I knew my duty and would not allow jealousy to take hold in my heart. Especially now, as I prayed for Zubira's sake, he would not consummate the marriage.

He would never do such a thing, I told myself. *When he sees her close enough to judge her age, he will not stay.* But I had heard horrific tales of men taking wives so young and not waiting until they were mature to consummate the marriage. It was rare and it was frowned upon, but it did happen. What if I had been wrong about my husband's character?

After leaving the other wives in the women's quarters, instead of returning to my own quarters I went out to walk in the king's garden where the calls of peafowl alerted from within the trees at my arrival. The mated pair who had been part of my dowry had, indeed, been fruitful. Now there were several peafowl dwelling in the gardens of our palaces: living treasures in a kingdom where they did not exist by nature. I felt a kinship to them; like me, they were foreigners who had made their home in a strange land. Apart from that, I loved their vibrant colors and smiled sadly that I could not see them in the dark of night. Now all was quiet as they settled back into their sleep within the branches of fruit trees.

84

Apart from the anguish I felt at my husband taking yet another wife, something I bore in solitude and shame, my heart was heavy with anxiety. This fear grew each day I carried yet another child I was sure to lose. I brought my hand to my lower abdomen, touched the firm bump that had only just begun to form, and wondered how long I had before this one ended prematurely. Leah knew of my pregnancy troubles, and she knew I was with child now. I felt some shame that I had allowed her to get a rise out of me, but her one talent seemed to be in finding a person's weakest point and pressing on it.

Seized by the urge to weep, I sat on the edge of a pool and hung my head, allowing the tears to fall into the water so they would not smear the kohl around my eyes. I did not want anyone to see that I had been crying when I returned to the palace.

I lifted my face and gazed at the half-moon. Admiring the stars, I recalled what the prophets of Yahowah had said and wondered if it was true.

Overcome, and careless of the eunuchs who were hidden in the shadows to watch over me, I went down on my knees and leaned against the font, my arms outstretched, and my palms turned upward. "Yahowah, god of my husband's people...I ask for your favor this night. If it is true that I worship falsely, if that is why I have been cursed to lose the children I conceive of my blessed husband, please spare this one. Prove to me you are greater than my gods, and I will serve you. Let me keep this child, and I will offer him up to you. I will raise him to know you and give praise to you alone for all my days." I leaned forward and clutched my abdomen. "Please, Lord, let me keep this child."

The rustling of leaves pulled me away from my whispered prayer, and soon a cat appeared. It purred as it approached, and I reached out to stroke its soft fur, comforted by its presence. Then I remembered that cats were revered in Egypt. While she rubbed her face against my fingers, I asked, "Are you a sign from Bastet? Has she blessed me with her favor?"

The idol Zubira had been holding had the head of a lion. Perhaps she was a follower of Egypt's fertility goddess. If so, had I pleased the goddess by my care toward one of her followers? I would have to ask Zubira if her idol was Bastet, or if there was a different lion-headed goddess who was worshipped in Kush.

When the cat jumped up onto the side of the pool for a drink, I looked up at the palace. The oil lamps in my apartments were lit, the flames waving in the breeze like fingers beckoning to me. Inhaling deeply, I pulled myself up and returned to the palace to prepare for bed. When I arrived, though, my husband was there waiting for me. I gasped in surprise and ran to his embrace.

"What are you doing here? You should be with Zubira."

"I could not stay away." After kissing my lips, he held my chin to scrutinize my face. "Where were you? Have you been weeping?"

"I went for a walk in the garden. I was praying…to Yahowah."

I turned my gaze away in shame and wiped my cheeks – my fingertips were blackened. I cursed under my breath and wiped them on my outer robe. Then I used the edge of my mantle to wipe the rest from my cheeks.

Meanwhile, Akhab looked at me with brows raised and the hint of a smile. "Yahowah? I thought you hated my god."

"It is not your god I hate – only his prophets."

"I know, love," he chuckled. "I was only teasing."

He kissed me once more before I pulled away. I went to my dressing table and began pulling the pins from my hair, dropping them with a clang onto the surface of a gold tray. "I asked him to spare this child. If it is true that I am cursed by him, then only he can help me. And I have promised to serve him if I am able to bear this child."

"What would your father think of this?"

"I do not care what he would think. If it is right and good, then I will do it. I cannot bear to lose another child. If I am at fault, then I must correct my error and beg forgiveness."

He smiled faintly and looked down, while I began stripping off my dress. I draped it over the screen I did not bother to use, as there was no need to hide my body from my husband. Then I paused to examine my reflection in a tall mirror that had been among his gifts to me upon our marriage. My breasts were fuller, and the tiny bump of my abdomen was larger than it had been the last time, which gave me hope that this pregnancy might be successful. In the mirror, I saw my husband admiring my form.

"So, Zubira?" I asked, with a glance over my shoulder, hoping he would see neither the jealousy behind the question, nor the concern I felt for her.

86

He sighed heavily. "What about Zubira?"

"Does she not please you?"

"She is only a child."

Although I agreed, I wanted to be sure I knew where he stood on the matter. "She is the same age that I was when I was presented to you."

"She does not look it." He turned his face from me and sighed once again. "I could not go through with it. I took one look at her before I turned and walked away. I suppose now I should have said something, but I was angry."

I did not bother to hide my relief. "I believe you did the right thing. I do not believe the representative spoke truthfully about her age when he arranged this marriage."

"Would you...explain all this to her, Yezeba'al? Tell her I do not feel she is ready to perform the duties of a wife, but that I want her to be comfortable here, and happy. I do not want her to feel rejected because I left without a word."

"I will tell her this. Oh, my love, I knew you would not go through with it!" Then, fearing he would perceive jealousy, I said, "But she is beautiful. Perhaps when she is older."

"Yes, she is beautiful," he agreed, "but she is not a woman. And when I saw this for myself, I came to find you."

"But why did you come to me? You have other wives who could please you." I turned away as I said this, attempting to hide the smile which betrayed my pride at knowing I was the one he craved.

"They do well enough," he said coming toward me. "But they are not you: my Rose of Shomron." When I turned to face him, he drew me into his arms and gazed at me with a knowing smile. "Perhaps Eliyah is right – perhaps you have bewitched me." He dropped to his knees and put his hands on my thighs. "But if that is true, then I am a willing captive."

He pressed his lips to my belly, wherein our child grew, while I slid my fingers through his hair. Then he lifted me, laughing, as he climbed to his feet and carried me to the bed. He laid me gently on the cushions and began removing his robes.

I wanted him desperately, but I was also afraid. "No, Akhab – we cannot. The baby..."

"We have abstained every time before, yet it made no difference. And I have spoken to other men who have made love to their wives throughout their pregnancies with no trouble. It is not a cause for miscarriage, love. I promise you it is safe. It will not harm the baby. But if you are not in the mood..."

He began to pull away, but I held his arm and looked at him with a conflicted gaze. Then he climbed over me and began kissing his way down my waist. I shivered and looked at him with a naughty smile. "Is it not a sin to Yahowah, for a man to know his wife when she is already with child?"

"It is, according to some of his prophets. But even they do not know everything, and they are not always right."

I was about to speak again, but he placed his fingers over my mouth. "Hush, woman; and let me please you as you have so often pleased me." He continued making his way further downward, whispering playfully, "Bless me, Ba'alah: let me drink of your sacred, life-giving water." Then he began gently biting the outside of my thigh.

Giggling, I opened my lap and granted him the favor for which he asked. When he began, I inhaled sharply, closed my eyes, and tangled my fingers in his hair.

4

Strangers in a Foreign Land

My faith in the Ba'alim had truly been shaken by fear, and so I sent my priests and priestesses of the Ba'alim away the following day. Even Daneyah was among them, and it was the most difficult parting because she had raised me as her own. She admitted she did not agree with my decision but understood my need to protect my unborn child – that perhaps Yahowah would come through where our gods had failed me. "But should the time come that your mind is changed, Yezeba'al, we will be waiting for you to call us back to you." Then she kissed my forehead and wished me well and followed the others out of the palace. She would stay at one of their residences in the city, which they were permitted to keep even though they had been expelled from the royal court.

All their positions at court were filled by more of the men of House Omri, as there were many pressing matters which required the aid of the king's council. The most important was a new alliance with the southern kingdom of Yehudah, which would bring much-needed peace between the two kingdoms that had once been united under the reign of King Shelomoh. There were two conditions to the alliance: the first was to be fulfilled immediately by Akhab, who would have his sister Aya wed to the new king, Yehoshapat. While he already had many wives and concubines, Yehoshapat promised to make Akhab's sister his queen. Although the King of Yehuda was in his thirty-fifth year, Aya was fond of him and agreed to the arrangement. The second condition to that treaty was to be fulfilled in the future: that once Yehoshapat named a successor from among his sons, that son would be wed to the finest of Akhab's daughters, presumably mine if I had any, since I was his queen.

In order to fulfill the first term of the treaty, it was necessary for Akhab to escort his sister to Yerushalayim for the wedding. Although we differed in our religious beliefs, Aya had been tolerant of my devotion to the Ba'alim. And while we were the same age, she had been a mentor to me when I first arrived in this foreign land. She had become a friend to me, in fact, in the years following my marriage to her brother. It was not easy seeing her leave so soon after I had sent Daneyah and many of my other friends away.

"I will write to you often," she promised. "I will not forget the kindness you showed in teaching me."

"I still cannot believe that, as the daughter of a king, you were never taught to read and write. In Tzidon, that would never happen."

She smiled and looked down, reaching to touch my abdomen as if in blessing. "If you bear any daughters, I know you will teach them the same. I pray Yahowah blesses you in this way, with many sons and daughters."

"And may he bless your marriage." I looked down and touched my abdomen, and said, "If I have any daughters, I shall name one of them for you."

Her smile turned to a grin. "I would be honored to be her namesake. And I would want you to send her to me when she is old enough to wed. There is the second condition to this treaty that must be fulfilled, after all."

"If it should come to pass, we will honor our part in the treaty – and I can think of no better guardian for any daughter I might have, than you, my dear sister."

We embraced tearfully, and then I went to my husband. He held me by the waist and kissed me. Then I gazed at him, realizing this would be the first time we would be separated for an extended period. "Come back to me, Akhab."

He smiled and touched the tip of my nose. "It is a short journey to Yerushalayim, and we will be surrounded by my armed guard the whole way. You have no need to worry, Yezeba'al. I will return to you." He touched my abdomen. "And to our child."

"If your god blesses me, I will change my name to honor him."

"Imagine what Eliyah the Tishbite would say to that! He will practically have named you himself!"

Although I smiled, I admonished him: "You are not to speak a word to him unless I say it."

He chuckled. "I promise, I will not say a word to anyone unless you permit it, Queen of my Heart."

He brought his hand to my cheek and kissed me once more, as if for the last time. Then he forced himself to pull away and went to his horse after checking that his sister was safely in her litter. I stood back and, with Captain Zarek and what was left of our senior officials at court, saw them off to the sound of shofars. Looking back at me from his horse, Akhab saw my face wrinkle at the sound. He laughed and kissed his hand to me, and then turned forward.

As soon as they were out of view, we went in to prepare for our own journey that would be made the following day. While my husband traveled south to Yerushalayim, the court moved to our fortified palace at Yezreel, a few hours to the north. Although it was considered our military center, the fortress of Yezreel had many of the same amenities as our palaces at Megiddo and Shomron, including a walled garden. The garden at Yezreel was smaller than those of our other palaces, but I kept several of my peafowl there as at the others.

When I arrived at Yezreel, one of the first things I did was go to the garden to see them. Entering the garden, I saw one of the peacocks perched on the wall between our garden and a neighboring vineyard that belonged to the courtier, Nabot. The peacock cried out the moment he saw me and opened his wings to glide to the ground, then ran to greet me as he always did whenever I arrived. I laughed in delight and pulled some grapes from the bowl one of my ladies carried for that purpose. He ate the grapes from my hand and purred as I stroked his feathers and told him how beautiful he was and how much I had missed him. When the grapes were gone, he gently nibbled at my fingers and called for more, which I gladly provided as my ladies threw grapes to the other peafowl who had gathered for one of their favorite treats.

Once all the grapes were dispensed, I made my way into the fortress to rest after my journey. This was the one evening I had to myself, before it was time to open court early the next morning. In my husband's absence, it was my duty to hold court and tend to matters-of-state or administer local justice as needed. It was his decision to leave me in charge, as I was present at most court proceedings in the past and was aware of how to run the kingdom in his absence. It was not easy, though, to contend with those who were not accustomed to working with a queen instead of a king.

When he had announced his decision at court the day before leaving for Yerushalayim, it had been received with much grumbling and even outrage from the ministers who would not be accompanying him on his journey. The Minister of War was the first to speak up.

"*Akhu*," said Abram, diplomatically, "surely any one of us would make a more suitable regent? Normally, it is the Lord Steward..."

"It is my decision," said Akhab, calm but firm. "I choose the queen. She is more suitable than all of you combined."

I had to hide my amusement, pretending to cough and turning my face away. No doubt they knew what I was doing, but modesty was more suitable in that moment. They, apparently, did not care for his quip.

"This is not the way that things are done!" the Lord Treasurer shouted suddenly, in one of his rare outbursts. I was honestly hurt by his reaction, for I thought he had more respect for me.

After this, the king's council erupted into chaos, grown men shouting over each other and none of them listening to the other. I covered my ears and wished I could vanish, wondering if it had been a mistake to send my own council away. I missed them terribly at that moment, but then I reached down to touch my abdomen, reminding myself of why I had done it.

When Akhab finally managed to return order and convince the ministers to work with me in his absence, it had taken much effort. I stayed out of it, letting Akhab do all the work, for the other men already saw me as meddlesome and I needed their support if I was to have any success in my regency.

Although I dreaded my first day of holding court at Yezreel without the king, it went smoothly at first, and I thought perhaps it would not be so bad to run the kingdom for the short time he was away. That was until Nabot appeared before me. Nabot supplied much of the wine to the region and was one of the wealthiest men in Yezreel, although it was said that he cheated his business partners. There were many larger and more productive vineyards further away from the city, including our own. That he could have amassed such wealth, as was apparent by his sumptuous manner of dress, from a vineyard that was not as good as many others in the region, suggested that the rumors about him were true.

When Nabot appeared early on that first morning, having arrived early enough to be among my first audiences of the day, I was seated in the king's throne to signify my position as regent. It was clear by his haste that he was eager to see the sovereign, but when he saw me occupying the king's throne instead, his already disgruntled expression changed to one of hostility. As he approached, he turned his gaze to Obadyah and did not even bother to bow before me when he stopped at the foot of the dais. Seeing this, I raised my eyes to the ceiling, took a deep breath, and exhaled slowly.

Nevertheless, I remembered my duty and greeted him with a benevolent smile. "Shalom, Nabot. What brings you to the king's court this day?"

He shifted from one foot to the other, cleared his throat, continued to avert his gaze, and said nothing.

I glanced at Obadyah, who looked at me nervously. After what happened to the ministers who had conspired against me, it became clear that Obadyah was beginning to fear me. I might have relished this new development; instead, it made me trust him even less. It is fear, after all, which drives the milkmaid to crush the spider in the barn.

Clearing my throat and forcing a smile, I tried again. "Shalom, Nabot. How can the court serve you this day?"

Again, he said nothing. The attendant ministers and courtiers began to twitter and Obadyah shifted uncomfortably, as Nabot looked to him as if waiting for him to speak.

I tensed my jaw, closed my eyes, and breathed deeply. Then I turned to the Lord Steward. "*Abarakkum*, extend the court's greetings to Nabot, and inquire as to his needs."

Obadyah looked uncertain. Giving him a nod, I made a gesture with my hands for him to proceed. Clearing his throat, he turned to Nabot. "My Lord Nabot, the Queen extends her greetings and asks that you express your needs to the court, so that we might serve you this day."

As expected, that did the trick. Nabot immediately stepped forward and, addressing Obadyah, began his complaint. "*Abarakkum*, you may tell the Queen that her damned birds have once again breached the walls of the king's garden and ransacked my vineyard! They have eaten an enormous amount of grapes from my vines and have cost me a great deal of profit because of it!"

Now, I wished my husband could deal with Nabot, but since it had fallen to me and had to be dealt with, I could not let it fester. Clearing my throat, I attempted to keep my tone firm yet gentle.

"Lord Nabot, I apologize for my peafowl coming onto your land and eating from your vineyard. I am afraid they are quite fond of grapes, you see."

At last, he turned a furious gaze on me. "This is the third time I have had those damned birds ruin my harvest! Do you know how much they have eaten of my grapes? How this will cost me?"

Ignoring his outburst, I asked, "Do you have enough left for the harvest, that you will be able to maintain the vineyard and cover your costs?"

His lips parted and he turned his head before straightening and clearing his throat. "Yes, I do have enough for the basic needs... But that is not the point! It's those damned birds of yours not staying where they belong!"

Now, I took a deep breath, attempting to control my temper. Once composed, I lifted my gaze toward him and again forced a smile. "My Lord Nabot, do you forget you are speaking to your Queen?"

"I know who I am speaking to — you are a woman and a Canaanite, and worse than that, an idolatress!" He spat on the ground at his feet.

I smiled bitterly. "Yes, well, despite all that I am also your Queen. And, as the king is currently away attending to his affairs in the kingdom of Yehudah, at his command it has fallen on me to manage the affairs of our kingdom here. As such, you will address your concerns to me, showing the proper courtesy and respect, as you would if you were in the presence of the king."

"Well, if you are in charge of the kingdom now, what are you going to do about those damned birds that are always coming onto my property and eating the fruit of my vineyard? How can you help me? Do you even understand anything in the way of business and agriculture? Are you even capable of understanding?"

"I understand a great deal about these things, and the bottom line is that my peafowl have cut into your profits. As before, the Royal Treasury will reimburse you for the loss, provided you admit our Minister of Agriculture onto your property, that he may assess the damage. With the help of the Royal Treasurer, they will determine a fair compensation — with your input, of course."

Nabot squinted at me, his lips set, yet finally placated. Somehow, I had managed to control my temper throughout the ordeal, and I was relieved that it was over.

"*Abarakkum*, direct Lord Nabot to the Minister of Agriculture and the Treasurer. My Lords, you are to accompany Lord Nabot to his vineyard at once and, when the damage has been assessed and a consensus reached, compensate him in full."

The ministers nodded dutifully, as Obadyah stepped down to direct Nabot toward them. Before he went away, however, Nabot turned back to me with renewed animosity. "Those birds are a nuisance! Apart from their destructive tendencies, they are loud and vicious! One of my gardeners was hissed at and bitten by one of the damned beasts when he attempted to shoo it away!"

Fixing him with a pointed stare, I said, "Perhaps if they were treated with respect, they might not be so vicious?"

For a moment, he seemed flustered by my response. Then he grumbled, "Vain, ostentatious creatures. They are too colorful and think too highly of themselves!"

I smirked, scanning his own colorful plumage with my gaze. "They are God's creatures, like any other."

"You speak of the Lord Yahowah as if you are not an idolatress!" He spat on the floor. "What do you know of God's creation?"

"I know that you believe in one god, Yahowah: and if he truly made all of creation, as it says in the writings of the prophet Moshe, then he made peafowl just as he made the chicken or the cow. Therefore, they should be appreciated for their beautiful representation of his masterful artistry."

"They do not belong here! They should be sent back to wherever they came from!"

At that, I rose from my throne and fixed him with a fierce stare. I trembled with rage now. "You mean, like I should?"

For the first time his face showed true fear. Raising his hands, he offered a bow, and said, "I meant no such thing, Melkah."

"The peafowl stay and if there is any further issue with them in your vineyard, we will continue to make compensation, as needed. Shalom, Nabot."

I started toward the throne but stopped and turned back. "Oh, and Nabot?"

He turned to listen, perhaps hopeful that I might change my mind.

95

Taking my seat on the throne, I said, "You may want to consider a command of your god from the Book of Debarim: that when you gather the grapes of your vineyard, the excess should be left for the stranger, for you were also once strangers in a foreign land."

I looked down to straighten my skirt and indicated with a delicate wave that I had finished. Then Obadyah shuffled him and the two other ministers away, so I could attend to my next audience.

Although I had the large bath for basic cleansing in my quarters, at each of our palaces I also had a small rectangular bathing font installed in one of the anterooms to my bedchamber. This was a ritual font, where I could take warm salt-baths in water that was heated in a nearby cauldron before being poured into the font. The salt was added with herbs and sacred oils. This type of ritual bathing was customary in Tzidon; to my husband's people, it was just another strange and foreign custom. But after he tried it for the first time, Akhab was convinced of its merits. Not only did it ease tension and soothe aching muscles, it also cleansed and regenerated the soul. After the day I had, such regenerative powers were needed.

Reclined in my bath that evening after supper, I watched the steam rising from the surface of the water and inhaled the scent of lilies, roses, and myrrh. Kora was attending to me, and I told her about all the things that had happened at court, in particular my confrontation with Nabot which had occupied my mind for much of the day.

"Did he truly call the peafowl vain and ostentatious? Because the peacocks have colorful feathers?"

I nodded and looked down at the petals and fragrant herbs floating on the water amidst droplets of oil. "Although, I think he was referring to me as much as he was referring to the peafowl. But you have likely seen how he dresses, Kora. If I am vain and ostentatious then so is he. I should have reminded him that even the great King Shelomoh kept peafowl in his gardens at Yerushalayim. I wonder, would he think my penchant for bathing frequently also vain and ostentatious?"

She giggled. "He would say it is…in excess, hmm?"

I chuckled and closed my eyes, resting my head on the edge of the bathing font. Then Kora said, "He is such an awful little man."

I opened one eye. "You mean Nabot?"

She nodded. "I have seen him about many times, always scowling – I do not believe I have ever seen him smile."

"Neither have I. Nobody likes him at court – he is always at odds with someone. I truly believe he goes around looking for things to complain about. And it is said that he is a cheat. None of the other nobles care to do business with him, but often they do not have a choice because his vineyard is close and the wine cheap." I sat up with a sigh and stretched my arms out of the water, the petals and herbs sticking to my flesh. I cupped my hand to pour water over myself. Then I paused to raise my hand to my forehead, water dripping onto my face. "Ugh, I have such a headache."

Kora moved to sit on the floor near my head and began massaging my shoulders. "You are tense, Yezeba'al."

"Is it any wonder, after dealing with men like Nabot all day?" I gently swatted her hand away. "It is no use. Do not bother." Then I leaned forward and held my abdomen, groaning a little at a particularly sharp stab that took me by surprise.

"Are you ill?"

"I have felt like this all day. No doubt it is all the pressure having gotten to me."

She looked at me warily and I knew what she was thinking.

I held up my hand. "It is nothing. I am certain of it. It is only the strain of running this kingdom. I do not like running the kingdom without my husband."

"You are very good at it," she offered. "Even when you were sitting beside your husband, my mother has told me about how well you conduct yourself, how you wrangle with the obstinate, how you soothe the troubles of those who will allow you to be as a mother to them, and how you think through all these difficult matters to offer the most reasonable solutions possible – as good as any man."

I looked at her, incredulous. "Truly? She tells you all these things?"

She nodded solemnly. "I can only imagine what she would say, if she was here to see you now, running the kingdom yourself."

I sighed. I felt remorseful for having sent her away, missing her affection along with her counsel. "She must hate me now."

"She does not hate you. Even now, when she writes to me, she asks after you. She misses you but continues to speak very highly of

97

you, not just to me but to all who will listen." She paused and tilted her head, looking at me with an earnest gaze. "Does this surprise you, Yezeba'al? That the priestess who raised you as her own would be proud of you?"

Trying not to think of it, fearing I might waver in my resolve, I sprinkled more water on my arm and looked at the flames of the oil lamps dancing from their fixtures on the walls. "I suppose not." I turned my gaze back toward her with a mischievous smile. "Only, I did not realize you spent so much time speaking of me when I am not around!"

With that, I skimmed my hand across the top of my bath just enough to flick water at her. She held up her arms and giggled, and then I splashed her again, until she cried out, "No! Yezeba'al! Stop! You're getting me all wet!"

Laughing, I said, "That's the point!" Then I sighed and sat back, twisting my hands together and staring at the latticework on the window. "How things have changed for us, Kora."

"Do you miss it? Our life before...?"

I shrugged. "Sometimes. I miss some things, I suppose. Being respected, for one. But most things, no. I am happy here with Akhab. I cannot imagine my life without him. I love him so."

"If only you did not have a kingdom to run?"

I raised my brow, smiled, and tilted my head in acquiescence. Then I sighed once more and pulled myself to stand. Kora rose to fetch me a cloth to dry myself, but when she returned, I was staring down at the stream of blood running down my leg and pooling in the water below.

She gasped. "Oh, Yezeba'al!"

Trembling and fighting the urge to cry, I reached for her hand for support as I forced myself to step out of the bathing font. She wrapped the long, thick cloth around me and helped me to my bed. Neither of us said a word. We had been through this so many times before. There was nothing to be said that had not already been said, and I could not bear to hear it again.

She stood by watching as I settled in, pulling the cloth underneath and around me, so it could absorb the blood. There would be so much by the end, of course, but there was no knowing how long it would go on – it could take a few hours or even a few days for the whole ordeal to be over.

"Shall I fetch the midwife?" she asked gently. Most of the midwives were stationed at Megiddu, but we always had one travel with us wherever we went. Normally, I kept a priestess-midwife, but this time it was one of Omri's widows who came with us instead.

Pulling my blankets around me – was it the cold or the blood loss that caused me to shiver? – I nodded solemnly. It was only when she left that I gave into my sorrow and wept bitterly.

When it was confirmed that I would lose the child, a messenger was sent to Yerushalayim to inform Akhab that I had taken ill and was being moved to the palace at Megiddu. The nature of my illness was kept from the official message, but I knew he would return right away. There was only one reason I would be moved to Megiddu after being taken ill; I had little doubt he would understand what was happening. It would take two or three days for the message to reach him and at least the same for him to return with his entourage, so I knew not to expect him for several days. Meanwhile, the court was closed and everything in the kingdom came to a halt until the king's return.

My priests and priestesses were harkened back to court the moment I knew the god of my husband's people had abandoned me. Ever faithful, they returned without malice or spite, requiring no act of contrition for having sent them away. Bearing sacred incense and chanting solemn devotions, the priestesses raised their arms to pray for intercessions that I knew would never come. Still, it was a comfort for me to hear their sweet voices raised in prayer, and the sacredness of their ritual made it easier for me to cope throughout the ordeal.

Daneyah, Kora, and some of the wives with whom I was close attended to me with dampened cloths and fragrant oils, while the priestess-midwives did their part until it was finished. As with the others, the remains of my unborn child were wrapped in swaddling and given to a priest with payment for the offering and taken to the Temple of Ba'al. There, the remains would be burnt upon the altar with prayers and incantations asking Ba'al to preserve the soul of my child from the ravenous hunger of Motu: the Void, he who eats the souls of the dead. Then the soul of my child, thus preserved, might return to me in a new form. This was the way for all children who died before they reached the age of maturity. Unfortunately, the

99

priests and prophets of Yahowah were horrified by the practice, calling it an abomination since they did not understand our ways. The zealots even claimed that we sacrificed our children to a bloodthirsty god, which seemed strange to me, for I had never seen a god command more blood to be spilled in his name than Yahowah.

In the cycle of life and death, Ashtarti was life, and many of her priestesses served as midwives to help bring new life into the world. As Ba'al was her counterpart, it was his priests who ushered the dead back to the underworld to await their next life. It was necessary to keep the balance of masculine and feminine energies from being tainted and disrupting the life-death cycle; thus, men were not permitted inside the birthing chamber, and unsanctified women were not allowed into the temples of Ba'al, not even to attend the funerals of their children. A mother's grief could prevent her child's soul from making the necessary journey to the underworld, so even I could not attend. From my terrace of our palace at Megiddu, I watched the smoke rising from the Temple of Ba'al as the body of my child was consumed upon the altar. I closed my eyes and a single tear slid down my cheek. I then said a silent prayer to my gods.

Daneyah sat with me. She must have seen the tear, for she reached for my hand. "You must not lose hope."

"I am being punished."

"No, Yezeba'al."

"The Ba'alim are displeased with me," I said heavily, "for appealing to Yahowah and sending you and the others away."

"You are Ashtarti incarnate. You cannot displease the Ba'alim the way that a simple mortal such as myself can."

"I abandoned Ba'al and now he has abandoned me."

"I do not believe that. If I do not hold it against you, when I am nothing compared to the infinite perfection of his being, how could he? Continue to make your offerings to Ba'al, and the priests at the Temple will continue praying for Ba'al to bless you—"

"As long as my husband refuses to be the one to offer up these prayers," I said bitterly, "it will never come to pass. I am Ashtarti: 'she who conceives but does not bear living offspring'. Why is that?"

"Why is what?"

"Why is Ashtarti unable to bring forth living offspring? Why is it that the rains do not come in summer?"

"Because Ba'al is in the underworld – Ertsetu."

I gave a firm nod. "It has been revealed to me. The answer is in my name: *Iye-ze Ba'al?* Ashtarti's cry in the wilderness. Unless Akhab accepts that *he is Ba'al* – until Ba'al is awakened in him – she will continue to send our children to him in Ertsetu, to remind him that she needs him to return and restore the balance of life."

She gasped, seeming at last to understand.

"Ba'al must be *here*, fully awakened, or it will only ever half work: I will continue to conceive but not bear living offspring. Ashtarti needs her counterpart to complete the cycle. Without balance, there can be no life."

"Yezeba'al, this revelation is a gift from the Ba'alim. Do you see now? It is proof that they are not displeased with you. And they will help you if you do not lose faith."

I fell silent then, unable to argue with this simple truth.

After a few days, I was well enough to return to Yezreel. There, I put on my simplest outer garments, so I could sit in the women's garden. While I took in the sun and fresh air, some of the other wives kept me company and tended to my needs, while some of the king's concubines tended to theirs. Many were engaged in conversation or working on some activity, but I mostly kept to myself and watched my peafowl roam about, catching beetles and worms from within the trees and floral shrubs. I saw my favorite peacock strutting himself on the wall between the garden and Nabot's vineyard before spreading his wings, rising up, and gliding to the other side for an illicit treat.

After the peacock disappeared over the wall, I looked at Fang-Hua, with whom I was closest. She was beautiful and intelligent and had earned the king's favor as her grasp of Akkadian improved enough for her to converse with him on more philosophical subjects. She was second only to me, but she never sought to compete and respected me above all the others. Of course, there was another reason she did not compete with me for the king's favor: Ba'athu.

Ba'athu was one of the king's concubines. She was also the favorite of Fang-Hua. Now, they sat on cushions talking and laughing, and as I watched them together, I witnessed a tender moment shared between the two. I knew of the special relationship between them, as there were between many of the wives and concubines, who had found more than companionship from among our ranks. The king knew of this, as well, but he permitted it because it did not threaten the legitimacy of his heirs. Of these affairs, Ba'athu and Fang-Hua were the most devoted to each other, much like Akhab and me. I often thought that if Ba'athu had been born a man, she would have made a fine husband for Fang-Hua. Realizing this was mere fantasy, I looked away with a heavy sigh.

Zubira sat on the ground nearby and played with her doll that was as richly dressed as she. Its hands and face were carved from the wood of the ebony tree, its features painted, and from the top of its head sprouted tiny braids adorned with miniature beads to resemble her own magnificent wigs. Although she was as regal as the rest of us, while I watched her play, it struck me that she was still a child and should never have been considered ready to be a wife. I had always suspected she was younger than we were told. Finally unable to quell my suspicions, I called to her by name.

She looked up from her play and, when I beckoned, got up and came running to me with a smile. Still holding her doll in one hand, she bowed, and then waited for me to speak. It occurred to me she was better behaved and more respectful than most of the other wives, apart from Fang-Hua. She had been raised well, even if her brother had lied about her age to get her married off sooner.

"Zubira, my dear child, I wanted to thank you for always being so good and so sweet to me."

"Thank you, Melkah. I am honored by your favor." Despite her formal speech, her eyes sparkled when I met her gaze. I smiled for the first time in days.

"Come," I said, holding out my arms. When she moved to embrace me, I brushed some of the braids that had fallen over her face and pressed my lips to her forehead, as she leaned into me. After tickling her sides to get her to laugh, I squeezed her once more and then released her. Then I confessed, "Although we are as sisters, I feel as though you are a daughter to me, Zubira. I hope this does not displease you?"

"I am very pleased, Melkah."

"You have my permission to call me Yezeba'al, at least when we are not in more formal situations."

"Thank you," she answered. Then she lifted her doll to move the braids from its face as I had done for her. "You remind me of my mother. She was very loving and kind, like you."

"How she must miss you."

She shook her head. "My mother died when I was very young."

"I am sorry, Zubira."

"You do not need to be sorry, for she is with me every day now, and can never be parted from me." She touched her necklace, a beaded collar in the Egyptian style. I suspected it had belonged to her mother.

"Was your mother Egyptian?"

She nodded.

"I thought so. That is why you have such a devotion to Bastet."

I thought about the night of Zubira's arrival, about the cat that had come to me in the king's garden. *I should have sought Bastet's favor, instead of Yahowah's. She would not have commanded me to abandon my gods to prove my devotion to her.*

Pushing away such bitter thoughts, I asked, "How old were you when she died?"

"It was a few years ago. I think I was seven."

"How old are you now?"

She fell quiet and looked at the ground, shifting on her feet.

I took her chin, gently, and studied her closely. "Zubira? How many years have you? Speak truthfully. You are safe with me."

When she looked at me, a tear slipped down her cheek. "I am sorry, Melkah – I mean, Yezeba'al."

"Why are you apologizing?"

"Because I have lied to you and to the king. I am only eleven years of age, not fourteen."

I released her chin and sat back in my chair. "You did not lie to us. The man who represented you lied. But it is no matter because I am glad you are here. I like you very much. And I hope you are also happy here?"

She nodded. "You and Melekh Akhab are very good to me, as are most of the other wives..." I knew she was hinting at Leah, whom I had already reprimanded several times for mistreating Zubira since that first night. "The king says that when I am older, he will...make me his wife, but for now he wants me to be as a daughter to you and

103

to him, and I like being your daughter. I do not know if I want to be a wife, but perhaps someday I will want to be."

"You do not want to be a wife? Were you not given the choice to come here to marry the King of Yisrael?"

She shook her head. "But it is all right, because I did not wish to stay with my brother and his wives. When my father died, my brother let his wives abuse me. He always hated me, even when he was only a prince and my father was king."

"Why did he hate you? How could anybody hate a girl as sweet as you?"

"Because I was my father's favorite child. He loved me most of all, above even my brothers, and said that he wished I could become king because I am smarter than them, and stronger too. That is why my brother hated me most of all and could not wait to be rid of me when he became king." She met my gaze with a mischievous smile now. "And I could not wait to be rid of him."

I admired her spirit, so like my own. "Your father was a wise man to encourage his daughters to be honest and true, and to see the value in a woman of wit and charm. Never lose that spark, Zubira: it is a mark of intellect and strength of character, too often frowned upon in this strange land."

"I shall not lose it, I promise, Yezeba'al – for I shall look to you always as an example of what a woman should be."

I laughed and leaned back, saying to the other wives in jest, "Did you hear that? This girl knows who she is speaking to."

From behind me, Leah murmured, "She knows how to flatter the vanity of a queen. So what?"

Hearing this, I pulled myself up and whirled around to face her. She was standing, weaving at a loom. "What did you say, Leah?"

At first, she appeared fearful of my wrath but soon took on an air of defiance and continued weaving. "I said what I said. I am not the only one to think it, even if I am the only one with courage enough to say it."

I scoffed. "You are only jealous that I am Akhab's Melkah, and you are not – everybody knows it, even if I am the only one to say it."

She gasped and stopped weaving when I stepped closer to her.

"You think you are the only one with ears, Leah? You have made no secret of your envy of me. People do talk, and I have heard about all the things you have said concerning me: how you believe you would be the better queen, and how you complain about my closeness with the king."

Her pale cheeks burned red. "He is only closer with you because you have bewitched him with your vanity and your false gods!"

"Call it vanity if it makes you feel like the better woman. I care not what you think of me. I see right through your pretentious act of piety, Leah. And so does the king. It is why he never summons you to his bed."

Her lips parted, she faltered, and then she ran from the garden in tears. Watching her flee, I stood satisfied that I had finally said what I had for so long held back. Then I noticed the other wives watching from the cushions where they sat. The only one not staring was Hawwa who had been appointed my cupbearer. She stood beside me, holding the tray with my cup of wine, eyes to the ground beneath her sandaled feet. I looked squarely at all the women now. "If you take issue with me, you are welcome to leave my presence now. I will not be surrounded by flatterers and false companions."

Without word, they went back to what they had been doing, and I finally returned to my chair. Then Fang-Hua remarked in her straightforward way, "You have only said what all of us have been thinking about Leah for so long, Melkah."

"It is true," agreed Tamar, a daughter to the King of Ekron. She was the fifth wife to join me in marriage to Akhab. "And I can assure you, Melkah, that the only others who agree with Leah are not among us here. They are some of the lowest concubines – not to offend you, Ba'athu."

Ba'athu raised her hand and shook her head, no offence taken.

Tamar continued, "and they only agree with her because she is their source of gossip from among the wives."

"She should be one of them," said Amat, my cousin who, with her sister Tabuya, had married Akhab as part of a treaty with Elam a few months after I became his queen. Together, they were his third and fourth wives. Tabuya was ill and heavy with child, so she was not with us in the garden that day. Both she and Amat hated Leah almost as much as I did. "She is a tiresome girl with no sense of decorum."

"She looks poorly on all of us who are not from here," added Fang-Hua, "especially if we do not worship her god."

105

"It is true," Ba'athu agreed, and then she bent to kiss Fang-Hua on the lips and the two were lost in each other's gaze. I smiled faintly and turned away, not wishing to intrude.

"And she barely eats," said Tamar, who was full-figured even when she was not heavy with child. "Have you seen how scrawny she is? Like a reed!"

There were many laughs at this, and although I also found it amusing, I said, "All right, that's enough. We do not need to make ourselves into hypocrites and gossipmongers. It is unbecoming of royal women."

I took a sip of the wine that Hawwa kept for me on the tray. She was the only one who never said anything against Leah, and although she was loyal to me, I knew she felt sorry for the girl. I appreciated her unwillingness to participate in gossip and offered her a grateful smile. Of all the wives, Hawwa gave me the least amount of trouble. Were she not so timid, she would have made a good leader among the wives, for she had the nature of a true peacemaker.

Meanwhile, Amat said, "You are right, Yezeba'al. And that is why you are the best woman to manage us. You are reasonable and fair, and you guide us well, only rebuking us when it is warranted."

"Thank you, Amat."

"What Amat says is true," Tamar nodded. "You know, my cousin Batsheba is married to the prince Yehoshapat – well, I suppose now he is Melekh Yehoshapat – and anyway, she has told me that his mother, who I guess is now Gebirah, is horrible to them. She is a tyrant over all his wives and beats them for even the smallest of infractions. I admit, I am worried for Aya, being sent to his court to marry him. She is a sweet girl, and the Gebirah is a wicked woman."

Although this troubled me, I did not wish to think of Aya suffering unfairly. "As she is sweet, we can only hope that Aya does not incur the Gebirah's wrath."

"That's the thing," said Tamar, "they do not even have to do anything wrong. She will find something to be wrong or make something up when she is in a particular mood. They say she has only gotten worse since she has begun the end of her time...you know, when the bleeding stops for good."

I said nothing, only took another drink while the other women gasped and giggled. Then Tamar continued, "What I am saying is

106

that you are at least fair – you are hard on us only when we truly deserve it. And you look after us in so many ways, like a mother. For one thing, you have taught us all to read and write. I cannot imagine the Gebirah of Yehudah doing that."

"She likely does not know how to do it herself," I observed, feeling somewhat sorry for the woman, although I had never met her. "Perhaps if she could read and write, she would not be so angry all the time."

"You mean, like Leah?" suggested Fang-Hua. "Since she is too good to learn how to read and write, perhaps that is why she is always so unpleasant? She has nowhere to direct her pent-up energies."

Smiling, I tipped my head in agreement. Leah was the only one of Akhab's wives who did not want to learn from me, but that was no surprise because her father, Akhab's cousin, was also a priest at the temple on Mount Gerizim. Sometimes, I wondered if her father had wanted her to marry the king in the hope that she could lure him away from me and my foreign influence.

Not wanting to go down that path in my conversation with the others, I said, "You know, Fang-Hua, I like your perspective on this. I often find study to be a good way to direct my energies into something useful that I enjoy." Most of the women wrinkled their noses in disagreement, but I laughed. "All right, perhaps not as good as sex, of course...but almost." I raised my cup with a naughty grin, while the other women laughed and agreed. Then I brought the cup to my lips, as their conversation took off in another direction.

When I set the cup back on the tray, there was a sudden commotion and I turned to see the king striding toward us. I gasped while the other wives rose to their knees and prostrated themselves. Hawwa, still holding the tray, bowed her head. The king offered them all a brief wave but came straight to me, bending to kiss my cheek.

"My love, I came as fast as I could – rode straight through each night." He knelt and took my hands and gazed up at me tearfully. "The messenger said you were ill, and I knew right away what had happened."

Forcing back tears, I leaned into his embrace and rested my forehead against him. He kissed the top of my head and stroked my hair and whispered gently to me. I nodded at his reassurances of love and devotion – that nothing had changed between us – and then I lifted my head to offer a weak smile. But then I became aware of the other women watching us, and my smile faded.

Although it was well known that Akhab favored me and being so drawn to each other we were so often touching, kissing, and caressing openly, he had never shown an overabundance of affection for me in front of his other women. Unlike many kings and princes who delighted in their women competing for their favor, Akhab sought to avoid arousing envy and jealousy, by avoiding flirtation. Whenever one of his women attempted to coax him into flirtation in front of the others, he rebuked her openly and she lost his favor for a time. His care for us all kept a sense of peace and harmony in the women's quarters; any conflicts and problems with jealousy between his women were caused internally through no fault of his own.

He seemed to realize himself then, and suggested, "Come, let us go in and lie down. I am exhausted from travel." I nodded. Then he helped me to stand, saying to the other wives, "Return to your duties."

They meekly obeyed. Then he walked me to my chamber within the fortress, where he laid me in bed and then began stripping from his tunic. Watching him, I suddenly asked, "How did you arrive without us knowing? I did not hear the shofars announcing your return."

"I wore a plain cloak for a disguise," he said with a grin.

"Naturally," I replied with a fond smile. "You and your disguises."

"It is the only way to avoid being recognized as king! You should try it with me sometime. We can go into the market and buy fruit, as if we were a common laborer and his wife."

I threw my head back and laughed, and then I shook my head and placed my hands on his waist when he came to me. Stripped down to his undertunic, which was plain and fit closely to his body, his warmth was comforting to me. I pressed my lips to his waist. He slid his fingers through my hair and gazed down at me, bent to kiss my lips, and then he climbed into the bed, and we settled in to rest.

Closing my eyes, I nestled into my husband's arms with my head upon his shoulder, listening to his heartbeat. It was the most comforting thing to me, especially when I felt so weak and fragile as I did then. Only with him did I feel safe enough to be vulnerable.

I must have fallen asleep, because when I opened my eyes again, it was dark, and the chamber was dimly lit by only a few lamps. Akhab was gone and, were it not for the tunic he had taken off earlier, still draped across a wooden chest, I would have thought I had dreamt his return.

There was a gentle rapping on the door then, and I realized it was that which must have roused me. I sat up with a stretch, and then called, "Enter."

It was Kora. "Ba'alah, the Chief Scribe is here with a message for you."

While he was in our employment as Chief Scribe, Aharon was technically in service to the Lord Steward, and often did his bidding. Obadyah himself had once been a scribe before being exalted to the role of steward and then promoted to the loftier role of Lord Steward. It was likely that Aharon would one day rise to take his place if he served faithfully and learned his role well enough to be trusted with such an important position.

I reached for my robe to cover myself appropriately. "Admit him. And Kora? Stay with me, please."

She nodded and then went out to bring in Aharon, who would likely be waiting in the antechamber. It took only a moment and, before long, my door was opening once again.

"Melkah," said Aharon, pausing in the doorway to bow before proceeding further into the chamber.

"Aharon," I said, holding out my hand so he could press the back of it to his lips in deference. "My lady tells me you have come with a message?"

"Yes, Melkah. It was a message for the king, but he...has commanded that he is not to be disturbed. *Abarakkum* Obadyah asked me to deliver this message to you instead."

There were few things which warranted such a command, and I did not like to hear this. I could not help but to wonder if that is why Obadyah was so quick to send this message to me, knowing I would be hurt by it. Nevertheless, I maintained my dignity, ignoring my own thoughts. "What is the message?"

"The rest of the king's entourage has arrived from Yerushalayim, along with his effects. Everything is in order – nothing missing or damaged."

"Thank you, Aharon."

109

He offered a bow and turned to leave, but then I called to him, and he turned back to me. "Yes, Melkah?"

"Where is the king?" I tried to sound only vaguely interested, getting up and walking to my dressing table. While he hesitated, I sat on the stool there and began casually combing my hair as I waited for his answer.

"The king is...in his chamber, Melkah."

Closing my eyes, I breathed in and exhaled slowly. Fighting the tremor in my voice, I continued running the comb through my hair, growing somewhat more hurried. "With whom?"

"Uh...the Lady Leah, Melkah."

The comb stopped abruptly, and my fist tightened around the lock of hair I had been combing, such that my fingernails were digging into my palm from the other side. Realizing myself, I took a deep breath, turned my back toward him, and continued dragging the comb through my hair. "Thank you, Aharon. You are dismissed."

He gave a nod and Kora escorted him out, and then she swiftly returned to me without needing to be called. She knew of my feelings for Leah, and of all the trouble I had had with her – some of it, she had even witnessed for herself. Perched on the side of the bed, she sat up straight and put her arms around me, resting her cool fingers on my hot forehead and letting me weep with my head against her shoulder. Fearful of my growing desperation, she would not leave me alone for the rest of the night.

5

Your God is My God

The next day, I refused to see the king. He had been informed that I would not be joining him to hold court that morning. So, he attempted to come to me during the break in the afternoon, when the heat was most intense, during which time we often lay together. Only now, I stayed locked in my chamber and refused him entry. As he knocked and implored, and then pounded on the door from the other side, finally threatening to break it down if we did not open it, Daneyah and Kora looked at me in fearful astonishment. It was Daneyah who had to tell him through the door that I did not wish to see him, and I could tell by her expression she did not enjoy her task.

Finally, his anger faded, and he began to weep, begging to understand how he had offended me. Hearing this, my pride was shattered. At last, I relented and told Daneyah to admit him. When she opened the door, the king was on his knees and leaning against the doorframe with his forehead on the back of his forearm. He seemed to have given up hope, but now looked up and smiled faintly through his tears. As he came to me, I rose from the bed and nodded to Daneyah and Kora, who immediately left us alone. Then, allowing my own tears to be seen, I opened my arms to him.

"What have I done to offend you, my Queen? I do not understand why you would be angry with me?"

Annoyed that he did not know and not wanting to have to tell him myself, I huffed and pulled away from his embrace. I went to sit on the side of the bed and turned my face from him. He came to sit beside me and took my hands, but I pulled mine away and turned my face the other way.

"Yezeba'al, my Queen, my Rose of Shomron... Please, tell me what I have done? If I am a fool because I do not know, then I am a fool, but I need you to tell me so that I can make penance to you, my beloved."

111

Part of me wanted to tell him what was in my heart but putting it to words was not easy. I was torn by duty and sentiment; words made it seem childish, and yet I could not help feeling as I did. I wanted to be truthful but wished he could just know so I would not have to say it and put words to my selfishness.

Finally, I said, "When I woke up last night, I was alone, and the bed was cold beside me. And then Aharon came to me with a message, and when I asked him where you were and who you were with..." I paused and closed my eyes. Then I opened them and turned to him. "How could you leave me, knowing what I had been through? How I had need of you to comfort me, only to find that you had left me to be with another woman – and not just any woman, but the one whom you know I hate?"

"Leah," he said with a sigh, turning his face to the floor.

"How could you go to her when I am grieving the loss of our child? You do not even like her! Or have you only been telling me that because you wanted to please me? Have I been the fool to believe everything you say?"

"Yezeba'al, you know it is true. I do not care for Leah at all; I have never lied to you about that or about anything."

"Then how could you choose her over me, at this of all times?"

He sighed heavily. "I went to her because I was reminded that she has not yet conceived and that I have been neglecting her, which is true, but that her timing was right for me to try with her. It is my duty as a husband."

"As it is your duty to try with me?"

"You know that it is not the same!"

"Do I? How can I be certain?"

He rose from the bed and threw his arms out in frustration. "Because with you I desire it! I crave you even when we are apart. I do not crave them unless I see their bodies naked before me, but I crave you even when I cannot see you. I see you in my mind and feel you in my heart. When I am with them, unless I am drunk, it is you I am thinking of! I stay away from them until I am reminded of my duty! I take them only then when they are most fertile! You know that, Yezeba'al – otherwise, I am with you. By choice, I am only ever with you!"

My anger turned then to weeping, and he came to me and pulled me into his embrace. Holding me and petting me and kissing

112

me, he continued his reassurances. "Look, I am touching you even now, when by the laws of Yahowah, you are unclean. With the others, I am content to follow those laws and stay away from them, but with you I do not care about any of it, because to me you can never be unclean. Everything about you is perfect and beautiful to me. I love you more than life itself. I would do anything for you."

"Then why will you not do what must be done for our children?"

Sitting back and rubbing his face as if exhausted, he lamented, "What children, Yezeba'al? You have been with child so many times, but we have no children together."

"Five. We have five children together, Akhab – lost before they were even born, yes, but I remember each one and grieve for them all. They are as real to me as any child born. Even if nobody else sees them, I see them. And I mark all the days of their loss on my heart as your other wives mark the days of their children's lives on theirs."

He buried his face in his hands and sighed heavily. "I'm sorry, love. You are right. I did not think of them in this way, but of course you would think of them, as their mother. But I...what can I do? How can I help you or them?"

"I have told you what you can do, Akhab. You say you would do anything for me, but you will not go to the temple of my Ba'al. You will not make an offering to my god; you will not ask for his favor."

"I pray to Yahowah every day, asking him to bless us, to bless you with his favor."

"And what good does that do for us? How has Yahowah blessed us? He is not a fertility god! He cannot help us! He will not help us, Akhab. Only Ashtarti and Melkorat can give us the children we are asking for, but I have been the only one asking for their favor – you have not done your part!"

"You are asking me to abandon my God."

"No, Akhab. That is not the way of my gods to demand such exclusive devotion. They are not like Yahowah; they are not jealous gods."

"It does not work that way here, Yezeba'al. If I turn to your gods, then I am abandoning Yahowah. That is the way of it, because that is what he demands of his followers."

Overcome, I fell to my knees before him in tears. "Please, my love. I did all you asked: I have gone with you to the temple on high

113

holy days. I have worshipped your god alongside my own. And in a moment of desperation, I gave myself completely to Yahowah. I turned away from the loyalty and support of my friends and the gods they worship, the gods I worshipped my whole life. I did all this, hoping that it was true, and that Yahowah would help me, but he did not. He could not. But I am not asking you to turn away from your god, only to turn to my gods in our time of need. Only they can help us. Please, Akhab, do this for me. For us, for our children, that they can come to us as they have been trying to do."

He got up and moved away from me, going to the window to look out and wiping tears from his cheeks. I stayed on the floor, feeling defeated. And in that moment, I hated Yahowah for his pettiness, that he would not allow his followers to seek the favor of other gods who could help them with their troubles where he could not. "Will you not go to my Ba'al, Akhab? Not even once?"

Still gazing out the window, he said, "I do not know. I will…consider it. But I need more time to think it through and decide. I cannot give you an answer while my conscience is troubled. I beg of you only patience. But now, I must go. I must hold court. The ministers will be waiting, and there is much work to be done. Always so much work to be done." He turned to me, imploring with his gaze. "Will you join me?"

I turned away. "No. I am in mourning for my child – and for my husband, who will not mourn with me."

He sighed heavily and then I heard his footsteps as he walked away. Still kneeling on the floor, I doubled over and wept.

For the next few days, I continued avoiding my husband, by keeping busy with my work at the Ba'alim temples and absorbing myself in study. Then one day, I went to the garden where I knew the other wives would be taking the evening air, as it was the time of day when the air cooled, and the peafowl were most active. Many of the women and their children enjoyed feeding, petting, and admiring them. Everyone was always amazed when the peacocks lifted their tail-feathers on display and danced in their attempt to woo the peahens. Even after seeing it for many years, I was still amazed by it, too. Watching the peafowl always made me feel better.

I was looking forward to a peaceful evening when I stepped through the archway and came upon Leah on the terrace. Her back was to me, but I could see she was holding Zubira's doll and keeping it out of her reach, as the girl cried and begged her to give it back. Two of Akhab's concubines stood by, watching and laughing. Nobody moved to help the girl. From down in the garden, Tamar noticed and rebuked Leah, but Leah ignored her and continued taunting Zubira.

"You do not need this doll, little girl. What kind of wife still plays with her dolls? Anyway, it is an ugly doll – as ugly as you."

Having heard rumors that the king was losing faith in me, and that he summoned Leah to his bed each afternoon when he would normally come to me, I was still fuming. Seeing this now only further enraged me. Some of the other wives saw me and they watched, mouths agape, as I moved toward Leah without a word. The concubines saw me from the corners of their eyes and immediately cast their gazes to the ground and backed away, remorseful because they knew they had been caught. Seeing me coming, Zubira stopped reaching for the doll and began wiping the tears from her eyes.

That was the only warning Leah had before I dug my fingers through the hair that was pinned upon the back of her head and pulled her down so that I could snatch the doll from her hands. She howled in pain as I tossed her aside. Then I returned the doll to Zubira and whispered instructions to her. She nodded in understanding, smiling gratefully, before running to Fang-Hua near the center of the garden. Fang-Hua pulled her into her arms in a protective manner, while I whirled around to unleash more of my wrath upon Leah.

The wretch was pulling herself off the ground and leaned against the wall, weeping. She held the back of her head, while I tore into her. "You call Zubira ugly, Leah? *You* are ugly: as ugly in spirit as you are in body. Pale as a corpse! Thin as a reed!" I took hold of the tassel at the end of the sash around her waist and dropped it dismissively, sneering at her. "Look, you have no shape, no curves for bearing strong and healthy sons for the king. Akhab has no desire for you – when he is obliged to bed you, he must think of me in order to perform his duty. He only took you as a favor to your father, who feared he would never be able to find you a husband because you are so ugly and formless. That is why the king never called you to his bed."

115

She gasped, stricken by my assessment. Then her usual defiance suddenly took hold. Standing to her full height, she spat, "You are an evil woman, *Yezebel!* Everybody knows that you will bring the wrath of Yahowah upon us!"

Laughing at her echoed insults, I demanded, "What gives you the right to speak to me that way? I am the daughter of a king."

"My father is a priest of the Lord God, who is above all kings!"

"My father is a priest and a king. I am a priestess and a queen. No matter what you do, you are still beneath me."

"You are a priestess to no one, because your gods do not exist!"

Again, I laughed. "Your god is a storm god who thinks himself their king and wants to be the only one, but he is as pathetic and sniveling as you."

She sneered. "You are only jealous because the king spent the first night of his return with me in his bed and has called me to him every day since!"

"By obligation, not desire."

"It certainly seems like desire, as he lays over me and comes into me, calling my name and saying how beautiful I am, more beautiful than that witch *Yezebel!*"

"It is not the king's custom to make proclamations while he makes love – are you sure it is the king, and not some proxy he appointed to lay with you in his stead, because he is so disgusted by you?"

She screamed and finally lunged at me, pulling my hair, and attempting to scratch at my face. I fought back with equal ferocity, screaming curses and obscenities at her in my father's language. There is no knowing for how long this went on before suddenly we heard the king's voice, deep and firm, shouting a single command: "Enough!"

We stopped immediately, both of us turning to face his burning gaze and bowing our heads in shame for having lost control of our honor. Although I had only been defending myself, I was aware that I had behaved appallingly, embarrassed that he had seen it. I wondered what had brought him there when he was supposed to be holding court. Then I glanced up and saw Hawwa standing beside him. She must have gone to fetch him when the fight broke out between us. Obadyah was also there, and the king turned to him to

116

issue some command. With a nod, the steward hurried away to carry out his orders.

I jumped when I heard the king's voice once again, sudden and hard: "Yezeba'al! With me, now! Leah, you are to wait here until you are summoned. I will speak with you next."

Raising my head proudly while keeping my eyes lowered in shame, I walked behind the king, who led me to his study. It was where he spent hours poring over maps and official documents, answering letters, and similar administrative duties which were his least favorite of all. I spent many hours sitting there beside him, absorbed in study and keeping him company while he worked, but I had never been summoned there at the receiving end of his wrath like some of his other women.

When the door was closed and we were alone in the chamber, he stepped close to me. While I kept my gaze to the floor, I could feel the coldness of his gaze upon me. Even without shame, I could not bear to have seen the look in his gaze at that moment. Then suddenly, he struck me across the cheek with the back of his hand. Akhab had never struck me, and I was in shock.

"Is this what happens when there is no Gebirah to keep order among the king's wives? Have I raised you too high, Yezeba'al? I curse the day I made you chief among my wives!"

Although the barb struck deeply, I kept my head high and refused to give into the urge to cry. "You are unfair to me, Melekh. I am not the one who is to blame."

"Are you not? You avoid me. You refuse to speak to me, jealous of my being with her as a wife. Am I to believe it is only a coincidence that I now find the two of you in the garden shrieking and tearing into one another like a pair of jackals? What brought this about, if not for your jealousy?"

"Leah is a wicked girl."

"She is a devout follower of Yahowah. Her father is a priest."

"She does not know her place!"

"Neither do you!"

Closing my eyes, I tried to stop a tear from breaking free, but it slid down my cheek. I breathed slowly to calm myself so that I could explain to him what I had been dealing with. He was unaware of it because I would not trouble him with the internal disciplinary issues

117

of the women's quarters. That was my responsibility. But now that he had been dragged into it, he needed to know.

"For the past year, she has given me no end of trouble by her haughtiness and petty jealousy – as petty and jealous as the god she serves!"

"Her God is my God."

"That is not the issue!"

"Is it not? You brought it up."

"Her piety is false! She is always stirring up trouble from among the women, breeding dissention between them, and turning them against one another."

"Against each other, or against you?"

"This is not about me, Akhab! She has been harassing Zubira since the day she arrived! Ask the other wives! Ask them what she has been doing to the poor girl! Ask them, and they will tell you all that I am telling you and more!"

He paused to examine me, stroking his beard as he always did when he was considering. "Why don't you tell me then since you are here. Tell me what happened today: why it took such a bad turn that Hawwa had to break protocol and send one of the eunuchs to fetch me while I was holding court. Start from the beginning."

Finally, I told Akhab about what had happened. He listened patiently, pulling at his beard, and nodding occasionally. When, at last, I had finished recounting the whole tale, he inhaled deeply and pulled me into his embrace. Kissing the top of my head, he wept and began apologizing for laying his hand on me in anger. My cheek still stung from the force of the blow, and I hoped that his hand did not leave a mark there, to further my shame.

Nevertheless, I forgave him and kissed him, and having been so long without knowing each other, we were soon carried away by our passions. He lifted me onto the desk, knocking things to the floor in his haste. I will not call it love-making, but after so long without knowing each other, it filled our need all the same and was equally satisfying.

Afterward, leaving the slaves to straighten up the chamber, we went out together and he spoke to Leah in front of me and the other women. She said nothing about Zubira and the doll, until he asked her about it. Confronted with the truth, she broke down in tears and confessed her guilt. As punishment, she was banished from

118

participating in any of the remaining festivities that year and commanded to serve Zubira each day from sunrise to sundown until I deemed it sufficient.

Then, with all the other women there to hear it, he told me that if any of them ever gave me so much trouble again, I was to bring it to his attention and let him mete out the punishment. His open support further cemented my authority in the women's quarters, leaving no question for those who refused to obey a "Canaanite idolatress." I was the highest among them whether they liked it or not.

Affairs in the women's quarters remained calmer after that day, and soon we were busy with more pregnancies, miscarriages, and births, starting with Tamar giving birth to a son. He was the third she had given to Akhab, the first two being twins: Natan and Mikhael. I congratulated her and admired the newborn son, as his brothers were brought in by their nurse to see him. While the nurse held Mikhael, I took Natan and held him over his mother and newborn brother. Then I answered Natan's babbling as he reached out to touch the hair on the infant's head.

Hawwa was found to be with child soon afterward. This would be her second child, the first having been a daughter. Ba'athu had given the king one daughter and one son, and she would give him two more sons over time. Amat and Tabuya, my cousins who had married Akhab together, had also given birth to sons by him a year later, born within days of each other. Tabuya had a stillborn daughter at this time and was now in mourning, while Amat was still trying to conceive again. Fang-Hua, meanwhile, had given birth to her second son only a few months earlier, the first having been born a year before. There were also many children who had been born to him by his concubines, several before our marriage and many more since. The nurseries in the women's quarters were always full and busy with the children and their nurses. I went there often to look into the wellbeing of the king's children and their mothers, and I knew each of them by name.

Although his duties as king kept him so busy that he could not give special attention to each child individually, Akhab loved all his

119

children and presented their mothers with many gifts upon each successful birth. When they lost a child, by disease or accident or chance, he went to the mothers to comfort them himself, and grieved each in his own way. In the privacy of my chamber, I often comforted him upon these losses, as there was no one else to think of him when they were so deep within the grief themselves. It seemed a small thing for a king with so many children to lose a few here and there, and certainly some affected him more than others but, like any father, he felt each loss and rejoiced at each new birth. Of all his women, it was only Leah and me who had not borne the king at least one child. But this would soon change.

Maryam, as the head midwife, had the important duty of keeping track of the women's cycles and informing the king when the time was most optimum for him to conceive with each of his wives. It was a role that was normally occupied by the highest-ranking woman, typically the king's mother. Without a Gebirah, that rank fell to me but, as one of his wives, it would not be appropriate for me to take on that particular role. She was also the one who informed me of each new pregnancy, miscarriage, and illness among the king's women. When one of them was in labor, I was summoned in the last stages to oversee the births of his heirs.

I was seated at my writing desk one afternoon, in the small antechamber attached to my private quarters. I had converted it into my own personal administrative office – something that queens of Yisrael did not normally have. Nevertheless, I insisted upon it because I needed a place to keep up with my correspondence, conduct business related to the needs of the temple and women's household, continue my studies, and write my own poems, stories, prayers, and hymns to share with the other Ba'alim priests and priestesses, and with those of the king's women who enjoyed such things.

I was in the middle of writing a letter to congratulate Akhab's sister, Aya, on the news of her first pregnancy when Maryam came to me, escorted by Kora. She waited for me to pause, and when I looked up, I could see that she was troubled. Setting down my stylus, I sat back in my chair. "You have news from the women's quarters, Maryam?"

Wringing her hands, she nodded slowly and continued to stare at me as if dreading what she had to say.

120

Sighing heavily, I asked, "Is it a pregnancy or labor?" When she did not answer, I added, "Or is it a miscarriage? Have the women been fighting amongst each other? Is one of them sick? Come on, out with it."

"Melkah," she finally began, "the Lady Leah is with child."

Upon hearing this, I sat for a moment staring into the fire of the oil lamp on my desk, feeling the anger build from within. Then suddenly it broke, and I yelled out in rage, squeezing my hands into fists and pressing them into my lap. After letting it out, I took a deep breath and managed to compose myself, smoothing my dress, breathing steadily, and checking that my hair was not out of place.

Then I turned back to my desk and lifted my stylus, dipped it in the inkwell, and bent over the letter to continue writing. "I shall inform the king of this blessed news. Thank you, Maryam."

She bowed and left me alone, and then I dropped my stylus and sat back in my chair once again. Laying my head back, I stared up at the ceiling for a while. Then I got up the strength to go to the women's quarters before going to find the king and deliver the news.

He was tending to his horses at the stables – one of his favorite places to be when he was at leisure. He had a great love for horses and chariots, many of which he inherited from his father, but many more which he had acquired on his own since becoming king. He had built an impressive force of charioteers, who practiced vigorously and often. He and his men enjoyed the sport of it, going out frequently to hunt, but they would be quite the force to reckon with should they ever be called to war. So far in our marriage, while there had been some minor rebellions, one very recently in the south, he had never been called to war. I was grateful for it.

Some of the men were out driving their chariots now, and I watched them as I approached the king. He was seated by one of his prized chariot horses, examining its hooves. When he heard me coming, flanked by four of my most-trusted eunuchs, he looked up and smiled warmly. "Have you come to ride with me, wife?"

I watched him examining another hoof, and answered stiffly, "No, Melekh. I come bearing news."

Satisfied, he lowered the hoof and patted the horse's thigh. The horse whinnied in response and began moving about. It seemed agitated and I watched it warily, while my husband got up and began washing his hands in a basin held up by a young stable boy. "Is the news so grim?"

Grateful the horse was being led away by one of the stable hands, I said, "Lady Leah is with child, Melekh. It was confirmed today by Maryam. It is predicted that the child will be delivered at the end of the spring before Pesakh."

Drying his hands, he dropped his gaze and nodded slowly. "Well, this is blessed news. Thank you for delivering it to me."

I remained frozen in place, looking at the ground and not knowing what else to say. I should have congratulated him, but I could not bring myself to say those words. Akhab stepped closer to me and slid his arms around my waist, drawing me to him. Despite my frustration and my desire to be angry with him, my body responded to him as it always did. Nevertheless, I refused to give him any sign of assent.

"Yezeba'al, this is a good thing. If all goes well, it means I may never have to lie with your archenemy again."

When I lifted my gaze suddenly, he was smiling mischievously. My anger softened the moment our eyes met, and when he kissed me, it abated completely. Then he rested his forehead to mine, and we shared one breath for a moment, before he stepped aside and took my hand. "Come with me."

"Where are you taking me?" I asked, turning to hold my hand up so my eunuchs would not follow.

"Somewhere we can be alone together, my Queen."

Although I chuckled, I insisted, "I am not in the mood for a dalliance, Akhab."

"Still bristling with envy?"

I stopped suddenly and looked at him with furrowed brow. "I want to be a mother, Akhab – not only because it is my duty as the wife of a king to bear sons. I want to be a mother – to have children of my own to love and cherish."

"Well, if you want children, my love, we must keep trying." Lifting me up and over his shoulder, he laughed at my half-hearted protests. My mantle fell to the dirt as he carried me into the chariot house.

"Akhab!" I cried, lightly pounding on his back with my fists. "Akhab, where are you taking me? Put me down!"

"All right, Ba'alah," he said, bringing me down inside one of the chariots. There was little light inside the building since he had closed the doors on the way inside. The only light came in from a few small clerestory windows, but they were insignificant compared to the ones that brought the sunlight into the great halls of our palaces. I stood at the front where the driver would stand and, after my eyes adjusted, looked around at the endless rows of chariots. Meanwhile he stood at the back and laughed heartily.

"This is a strange place to take your wife to make love, Akhab."

"Is it? I thought it might be interesting for us to try something new."

"And if someone enters?" It was a false protest – we had made love in many places where we might have been discovered and had never much cared either way.

He grabbed me around the waist and growled. "You'll be making so much noise, they wouldn't dare." Then he took me by the face and kissed me hungrily. Afterward, he stepped back and patted the body of the chariot in which we were standing. "This is my newest chariot. It arrived only just this morning."

"It is impressive," I replied with little interest. I was disappointed that he had not continued his advances.

"It is not just another chariot, Yezeba'al – it is my chariot, the one I will drive if I must ever go to war. Since you are here, I thought you could help me bless it. As the only woman to ever stand in my chariot, you will bring me good fortune every time I drive it."

Smiling playfully, I asked, "Well, do you just want me to stand in it, or did you have something else in mind?"

"I was thinking…would you like to be the first one to drive it?"

"Me, drive a chariot?"

"Yes, my love. I came here to take it out for a test drive, to see if it is as good as its maker claims. Perhaps you would like to try it with me?"

Although a part of me still wanted to be angry with him, I at last gave into his charm and agreed to his madness. He hopped out of the chariot and helped me down, and then we walked together to find the master of his chariots to prepare it for our drive. I had never driven a chariot before, but I had ridden in them with my father when

I was a little girl. I had enjoyed the thrill of racing around the field in one, and I wondered if I would enjoy the thrill now that I was older.

Going out with Akhab, I insisted that as it was his chariot, he should be the one to drive it first. He was a masterful charioteer, and he enjoyed pushing everything to the limits, doing stunts and sharp turns and seeing how fast he could make it go. At first, I was terrified, and I clung to him as the chariot moved faster than I thought it could safely go, but by the end of our first run I was laughing and exhilarated and had forgotten about all my woes.

When we were stopped, he offered me the reins. "All right, now it is your turn. Go on, take them. I will show you how to do it."

I hesitated. "No, Akhab, I do not wish to drive a chariot. I will not have the strength to maneuver it."

He raised a brow and clicked his teeth. "Your Ba'alah is the patron deity of horses and chariots, and yet you will not drive a chariot?"

"She is also the patron of sailors, and yet I was seasick the entire voyage between Zour and Yapo, much to my mother's horror and my father's disappointment."

"So, you are not a sea faring Asherah. Perhaps you are meant to be Ba'alah of the Plains – you married me, after all. But if you do not wish to know the freedom of driving a chariot, I cannot force you to do it."

I wanted to argue, but when I opened my lips there was nothing I could say to dispute his logic. Laughing at his ingenious method, I met his smiling eyes and satisfied grin. "All right, I will do it. But you have to stay with me – I will not drive it unless you are with me."

He placed his hands on my shoulders and kissed my cheek. "I shall be with you the whole time, wife. I shall never leave you."

Akhab was a patient teacher. Standing directly behind me, he showed me how to hold the reins and directed me on how to use them to steer the horses, practicing with me while the horses were held in place by a pair of stable hands. Being so close together in this manner was incredibly sensual and I was soon covered in goose pimples while I turned my head to gaze at him. Seeing the look I gave him, he kissed me, and said, "Not yet, love. First, you must drive the chariot."

"How do you know what I was thinking?"

"Because we are the same, you and me." Smiling, he braced himself on the body of the chariot and pointed ahead. "Now, drive the chariot so we can make love."

He gestured to the stable hands, who moved away from the horses, while I closed my eyes. I was about to start when he took my face in his hands. "You cannot drive a chariot with your eyes closed, Yezeba'al. At least, not until you are skilled with it, and provided you are familiar with your surroundings. You expect the horses to do all the work?"

I stuck out my tongue at him and he snickered. Then we resumed our position, and this time I kept my eyes open. With a flick of the reins the chariot lurched forward, and we were soon gliding across the field together. Still braced on the body of the chariot, he kept us both from falling over, and I felt safe being able to lean back against him as the chariot moved. When I felt as if I might lose control and kill us both, I brought the horses to a stop in the middle of the field. I was shaking when I handed him the reins. The charioteers who had been practicing earlier now watched from the side of the field in amusement, and they cheered.

"That was good," said Akhab. "Look, they are impressed."

"They are impressed because they have never seen a woman drive a chariot before, not because it was good."

"It was good. You could be an imposing force in a chariot, my love."

"I *will* be an imposing force if you take me somewhere we can be alone."

He grunted and then took the reins, driving us to a secluded place within a lush, wooded area near a stream that ran from the spring that supplied the city with fresh water. No one was allowed in this area unless appointed by the king, for it was part of the royal grazing ground for his horses. Unless they were looking for a missing horse, even few of those men came this far. As such, it was the perfect place for us to find privacy and solitude.

When we stopped, he unhitched the horses so they could graze and drink while we sat together in the chariot, in the shade of trees and looking out at the stream. Akhab sat with his back against the wall of the chariot and pulled me to rest on him. With his arms around me, we stayed like this together for some time, enjoying the peace and the silence. The only sounds were the flowing of the stream, the occasional breeze blowing through the trees, the movement of animals, and the rhythm of each other's bodies as we kissed and shared tender caresses that would eventually grow more heated. Far away from the palace, in a little world of our own, it felt like we were in our early marriage again, before all the other wives and the pressures and the miscarriages had begun to fray at us.

After that day by the stream, I was feeling more myself again and at peace with my duties as the chief wife of the king. I was also feeling more charitable. When it came time for us to move with the court to Megiddu, instead of riding in my litter, I rode on the back of Akhab's horse with him, instead offering my litter to Leah. This surprised everyone, but I insisted because she was with child and the cushions in my litter were more comfortable than the ones in hers. She accepted begrudgingly, and I could not help enjoying that she had the best view of me and Akhab riding together. It was a small price for her to pay for all the trouble she had given me. When she finally tired of seeing us share the occasional kiss or caress, she drew the curtains closed. To my satisfaction, they remained that way for the rest of the journey.

Over the months, Leah's pregnancy progressed well, and the midwives predicted a favorable delivery. Of course, the only midwives Leah permitted to examine her were those strictly devoted to Yahowah, but I always brought Daneyah with me when I went to check on her and the other wives who were at varying stages of pregnancy. Having some experience as a priestess-midwife from her early service at my father's palaces in Tzidon, Daneyah was the only one who suggested Leah might have difficulty, because she had such narrow hips. Not trusting the opinion of a foreign idolatress, Leah's favorite midwife only scoffed at this and said the girl was blessed by Yahowah's favor and would not have any trouble.

Being with child, Leah was released from her duties toward Zubira, and now she had her favorite concubines appointed as her ladies, serving her every whim. The other wives began to grow tired of Leah and they often complained of her to me, but her behavior was nothing for me to chastise. So, I shrugged it off and gave them some ideas on what they could say to her. They appreciated my advice and were always happy to report when it had worked.

Beneath all her blustering, I had come to realize that Leah was unbelievably fragile and, rather than hating her, I began to pity her. The other wives, however, still had to live in close quarters with her. As she got heavier with the growth of her child, she began to spend less time in the garden, so it became something of a refuge for them. It was in the garden that I heard most of their complaints, while relaxing on the large cushions and rugs that had been laid out in the grass, often while the king's older children played around us.

"She is more imperious than ever," said Tamar, who was holding her youngest son in her lap. He was able to sit up now, and she was dangling a toy for him as she continued. "As if she has been touched by God or something because she is having a child. We have all had children, so what? She is nothing special."

Sitting beside her, Amat whispered to her, and then she gasped in realization. I knew what was being said and raised my hand in reassurance. "It is all right, Tamar. I understand, and I agree with you. But I say, let her have this moment. It is all she has, really, when you think about it."

Leah had spent so much time alienating herself by her poor behavior that she had no one, except perhaps Hawwa, while we had the support of each other. She had her sycophantic followers from among the concubines, but even they were beginning to feel the weight of her tyranny and had grown more distant whenever they were not serving her. Leah did not have any real friendships. And she certainly did not have a lover, I thought as I looked over at Ba'athu and Fang-Hua. They were lying on a rug, lost in their own little playful world together, as lovers often are. I smiled faintly, thinking of myself and Akhab.

"Well, when you put it that way, Yezeba'al," said Tamar, looking in the same direction, "I suppose you are right." Then she looked toward the terrace and scowled. "Ba'al Zebul, preserve us — here she comes."

We all looked and saw Leah, heavy with child and moving with difficulty, being helped by her ladies down the steps and grumbling the whole way. I turned back and raised my eyes to the heavens with a heavy sigh. Upon seeing her, Zubira got up and came to nestle safely beside me on my cushion. I put my arm around her and moved braids from her cheek to kiss her there, and then I got her laughing as I tickled her sides.

Meanwhile, Leah finally reached us. Because she was too big to get down on a cushion with the rest of us, a stool had to be carried out for her to sit on. The slave who carried it followed her command on where to place it, and it was no surprise that she positioned herself directly in my view. She was likely hoping to upset me by displaying her pregnant form, but I was no longer bothered by Leah's childish behavior, as I was secure in my position as Melkah and the king's favorite. We all continued talking and laughing, playing with the king's children as they came and went. We paid no attention to Leah as she huffed and sighed and fussed and squirmed about.

"Ugh, I cannot wait for this child to be born," she finally announced loudly. "It is so much work, and everything hurts me." She paused to be sure that she had been heard, and then added, "But I should not complain because Yahowah has blessed me with a child."

At the same moment, I was accepting a flower from Fang-Hua's eldest son, little Ishaq, who had run up to give it to me with a kiss on the cheek before running off to rejoin the others in play. I smiled at the gift, twirling it in my fingers and admiring its petals, while saying simply, "Yahowah is a storm god, not a fertility god. He cannot bless you with a child. He can bless you with rain. And a war, perhaps. The king has blessed you with a child." Then, "He is the one who had to work for it, after all."

Leah scoffed. "Well, how have your fertility gods been working for you? How many times have you miscarried? You may be the king's favorite now, *Yezebel*, but you will never bear him a child because you will not repent of your wicked ways, and eventually even he will tire of you."

Ignoring her barb, I handed Zubira the flower. When she got up to carry both the flower and her doll away, I looked directly at Leah, and said, "The king will not tire of me because it is not for making children that he lies with me...in my bed, in his garden, on his desk, in his chariot..."

The women gasped and some of them giggled, while I continued, "Whenever and wherever he has need, I am there to give him pleasure and healing through the act of love, as *only* I can do."

When I paused, Fang-Hua asked, "You have made love to the king in his chariot?"

128

I smiled proudly. "Yes, I helped him bless it when it was new. He made me drive it first, but then he drove us out to the stream, where I climbed on his lap and showed him what an imposing force a woman can be in a chariot."

There was more laughter and giggling from most of the women. Then Ba'athu observed, "That explains why he was taking you out in the chariot so often when we were still at Yezreel."

Amat wondered what it would be like to make love in a chariot, while Tamar observed that she had never even stood in a chariot let alone driven one. Soon they were asking me about what it was like to drive one, and had I done it only once? I told them I had driven the chariot many times since then, as the king had been teaching me nearly every day. By the time we left Yezreel, I had become proficient, but I did not believe I could ever drive the chariot without Akhab riding with me because it took a great deal of strength to manage.

Most of the women agreed that they would never want to try, but Ba'athu and Tamar were intrigued by the idea of women driving chariots. Meanwhile Leah sat brooding over her failed attempt to upset me. She continued to fuss and grumble at her ladies until she finally had enough of not being the center of attention. That was when she got up to hobble away, her ladies rushing to follow.

A few hours later, while I was dining late with Akhab in my chamber, Maryam came to inform me that Leah was in the final stages of labor. When I moved to get up from my cushion, Akhab reached across the table and placed his hand on top of mine. "Must you go now? You know she will not even want to see you there, and you probably want to be with her even less."

He was right, but I sighed and pulled my hand away. "I must go, Akhab. It is my duty to observe the births of your heirs."

"Leah's child will never be my heir. I have plenty. And if you have any, they will take precedence over all the others. You have my word."

"My love, she is your *wife*, not a concubine. Even if her child is lowest among them, he is one of your heirs, and I must be there to witness his birth." I got up from the table, while Kora hastily brought my mantle and pinned it to my hair. When she finished, I told her to summon Daneyah and send her to assist.

129

Meanwhile, the king picked at his supper. "If only my mother were here to take this burden off your shoulders. You should not have to do this for each and every one."

Pulling my mantle around me, I said, "If your mother were here, she would likely hate me, because she was so devoted to your Yahowah."

"She would have had to put up with you, because I love you more than I could ever love another – more than I loved her, even."

I bent to kiss him, and then I searched his gaze. "Wait here for me?"

He took my hand and nodded. "I will be here when you return, my love. And I shall long for it every moment."

I smiled as he pressed my hand to his lips, and then I pulled away and followed Maryam to the women's quarters. The eunuchs who guarded the entryway to that isolated section of the palace opened the wide double doors to let us pass. As soon as they were opened and we started down the corridor, I could hear the screams coming from the birthing chamber.

I looked at Maryam and saw her troubled expression. She admitted, "It was not going well when I left, Melkah. I had hoped it would have changed by the time I returned with you."

My face set, I swallowed hard and gave a nod, as we continued to the chamber. When we arrived, Leah was standing in the middle of the chamber with her legs spread apart, holding the handle at the end of a rope that dangled from the ceiling. Unable to stand on her own, she was supported by her two faithful concubines, while the midwife she had appointed knelt on the floor at her feet, careless of the blood and fluid pooling around her. I had attended many births, but I had never seen so much blood. I nearly vomited from the strong odor of blood and fluids but managed to suppress the urge.

Ba'athu and Tamar were standing by Leah to offer comfort and reassurance, while Hawwa dabbed at her brow with a cloth and Fang-Hua stood by with a cup of water for Leah to sate her thirst. The other midwives Leah had approved to assist were gathered around, offering advice, and urging her not to waste her energy on screaming. She refused the stick that was offered for her to bite down on, to help with the screams, and when they tried to put it in her mouth, she let it drop again and again. Letting out another shriek, she whined in agony. She almost fell, but her ladies continued to hold

130

her up and Tamar brought her arms back to the rope, gently urging her not to let go of it.

"I...need...to lie down!" Leah whined. Her face was red and covered with tears. "Please, let me lie down! It hurts! Oh, it hurts! Please! I don't want to do this. Don't make me do this!" She saw me then, and she let go of the rope to reach for me, while her ladies struggled to hold her up. "Oh, Melkah! Please, make the pain stop! Make it stop!"

Confused and trying to hide the fear and horror that I felt in seeing her this way, I went to take her hand and caressed her forehead, gently shushing her. "It is all right, Leah. It will be all right. You can do this."

"No," she wept, shaking her head and falling into the arms of her ladies. She was pale and trembling and covered in sweat with no color in her cheeks. "I cannot do this. I cannot."

Suddenly, her eyes shot open and a yell began to rise from her throat as another contraction gripped her. Again, she screamed, and finally the midwife directed the ladies to take her to the bench to rest while she checked on the progress. It was about this time that Daneyah entered, and she came straight to me. Neither of us spoke a word.

Meanwhile, breathing heavily and exhausted, Leah leaned against her ladies who sat beside her and continued supporting her. Then she looked at me. "Don't you have herbs? Medicines that can take away the pain of labor? Please, Melkah. I have heard that your people have these things. I need them. I cannot take the pain any longer. I cannot do it; I would rather die than suffer another moment of this."

I shook my head apologetically. "I am sorry, Leah. I do not have anything that I can give you."

"No, but you must have something! Please, I am desperate— ah!" She held her swollen abdomen, overtaken by another contraction. Soon, she was wailing again while her ladies and the other wives attempted to calm her.

When the contraction ended, she rested for a moment, and I thought she had fallen asleep in the arms of one of the concubines until she looked at me through slit eyes, exhaustion in her gaze. "Please, Melkah... Have mercy on me, please."

Fearing that if she died, I would be blamed after giving her one of my herbal remedies, I shook my head firmly. "I will not give you anything, Leah. I cannot." Then, taking her hand, I said, "You must do this, Leah. You can do this. Your body is made for this."

She began to wail once again and leaned into the arms of her ladies while they rocked with her, and Maryam stepped aside to consult with the other midwives. At first, they spoke together quietly, as if they did not want anyone else to overhear, but then they became animated and argued bitterly. Daneyah caught my gaze and shook her head. I feared it was as she had said.

Finally, Maryam came to me and gave a brief bow. "Melkah, I fear Lady Leah cannot push the child out – it is too big and her hips too narrow – but if it does not come soon, it could be smothered in the birth canal. As you are the queen, I must ask, what would you have me do?"

My lips parted and I turned my gaze toward Leah. She was so pale, not a drop of color in her cheeks, despite all the effort that went into the labor. If I had once told her she was pale as a corpse, it was nothing compared to how she looked now. I knew she had lost too much blood and was dying. I had hated her – oh, how I had hated her – but now, faced with this, I regretted all of it. I did not want this. And I did not want the burden of making this decision, but I had to do it because the midwives could not act unless I gave them the order to do what needed to be done.

This was not the first time I had to make this decision, when the lives of mother and child were in danger. I had made this decision so many times before without hesitation, but now it felt as though I was guilty of murder. There was a chance she could survive the procedure – it was not always a death-sentence – but the survival rate in these cases was low. Nevertheless, if they did not perform the procedure, the deaths of both Leah and her child were almost a certainty.

"It is...the king's child," I said weakly. "You must save the child."

She held my gaze and nodded gravely. Then she returned to the other midwives, gave the order, and they went to work. By the time they went to lift and carry her to the narrow bed, Leah was barely conscious. It took both concubines and three of the midwives to get her laid out so they could begin the procedure. I watched as they began feeling for the position of the baby, but when they pressed the blade to her abdomen I turned away, covering my ears against the last of her screams. Daneyah put her arms around me, and whispered, "It is not your fault. You cannot blame yourself, Yezeba'al. It is not your fault. You did not do this to her."

I nodded and buried my face in her shoulder to hide my tears, but as she rubbed my back and continued her reassurances, I could not help but wonder if I had done this to her. Had I not wished ill on her so many times when I was angry with her? What if, in my jealousy, I had manifested this curse upon her? Was it possible to curse someone without meaning to do it?

The child was pulled from its mother's womb while she lay dying, but by the time they had gotten to it, too much time had passed. The child's flesh had turned blue and their attempts to revive it failed. It would have been a son. As I watched their attempts to revive him, I felt as cold as his mother's corpse, which lay covered by a blood-soaked linen. It was so hard to believe that only a few hours earlier, she had been complaining in the garden, and now she was gone, as was the child she had been so proud to bear.

"Akhab," I said, standing over him. The night was almost over by the time I returned, and he had fallen asleep in my bed waiting for me. I was exhausted and would have loved nothing more than to lie down beside him, but I had to tell him. Anyway, I could not sleep after what had transpired that night. I glanced at Daneyah, who was closing the door after entering, and then turned back to my husband and shook him gently. "Akhab."

He yawned and rolled onto his back. His eyes blinked open, and he smiled. "Hmm. Yezeba'al, you were gone for so long."

I stood back as he pulled himself up to sit on the edge of the bed, rubbing the sleep from his face. "So, tell me: do I have a son or a daughter?"

My gaze to the floor, I forced myself to say the words I had been dreading. "There was…a complication, Melekh. The child was too large. He had grown too much in his mother's womb and she… The midwives did everything they could to save them both but…when it became clear that Leah was… She had lost too much blood, you see, and…"

133

Daneyah came to me just in time to catch me, as I began to collapse. I nearly fainted, but with the help of the king she brought me to sit on the bed. Akhab held me up and nodded to Daneyah, holding up his hand to let her know he would take care of me from there. She bowed in deference to him, but asked, "Ba'alah, do you wish me to stay?"

"I will be all right, Daneyah. Thank you."

She nodded, and then she bowed once more and departed. When we were alone, Akhab turned to me and took my hands in his. "Was the child able to be saved?"

I solemnly shook my head.

He sat for a moment in stunned silence, and then he got up and went to the window to look out. The sun was not yet rising but there was a sliver of color along the horizon to the east. Soon it would peak over the hills and it would be day, but for now the sky remained at its darkest. The stars were brilliant on a bed of endless black. I looked past my husband to see all this, too numb even to wonder what he was thinking or feeling in that moment.

When he turned, I looked up to meet his gaze, fearing he would be angry with me. Would he blame me for what happened, as I blamed myself? Instead of blame or resentment, though, I found only a man lost to the seeming unreality of what had happened. "She was...faithful to Yahowah...and he abandoned her."

Wishing to comfort him, I said, "He did not abandon her, Akhab. He could not help her. No one could help her."

"No, you are right. He could not save her life..."

Feeling steady now, I got up and turned my back to him. "The women are preparing the...bodies...for burial. I have sent word to *Abarakkum* Obadyah to make the preparations for a funeral in the manner that has been commanded by your god and..."

"Yezeba'al," he said, taking a step toward me now.

I turned toward him but avoided meeting his gaze. "If you would like to go to them, to see them..."

"Yezeba'al," he said again, coming to take me by the arms. Then, holding my hand, he led me to sit on the bed. "I will not go to see them. I do not wish to gaze upon the dead."

"They are your wife and child."

"You are my wife."

"It was a son."

"I have many sons."

"She was...so young and I..."

"There was nothing you could do."

Finally, I met his gaze. My eyes were filled with stinging tears. "I am sorry, Akhab."

"It was not your fault. It was the will of the gods."

Angry at his callousness, I pulled my hands from his. "Don't you feel anything for her? Anything at all?"

"I pity her," he admitted, "but I did not love her. I could not love her. I cannot love any of them, Yezeba'al – not the way I love you. There is no one but you." He took my hands in his and lifted my chin to meet my gaze. "You are my Queen, the most exalted among women. High Priestess of Yisrael. Asherah incarnate. And you need your counterpart."

He got down to kneel before me now. I looked at him with curious uncertainty and waited for him to continue. "I do not know if I am Ba'al incarnate, as you say, but you have chosen me and, in my stubbornness and fear, I have dishonored and rejected you. But I am ready now, Ba'alah. I will go to the Temple of Ba'al. I will prostrate myself before your god and make an offering upon his altar. I will do my part. I will seek his favor. Your god is my god, your goddess, my goddess. Let us see if they can bless us where Yahowah has failed."

"Oh, Akhab."

Finally, the tears broke free, and I got down on my knees before him. He put his arms around my waist, and I took his face in my hands and kissed him tenderly. We laughed and wept with our foreheads together, forgetting everything else. At last, the cycle would be completed, the energies balanced. And as I lifted my gaze, I saw out the window the streaks of morning light were breaking through the darkness.

6

Where is my Prince?

While preparations for the Feast of Yom Kippur were at their height throughout the kingdoms of Yisrael and Yehudah, at the Ivory Palace in Shomron we were making preparations for a feast of a different sort. It was the Feast of Ba'al, celebrating his annual reunion with his consort upon his return from the underworld – one of the two most sacred feasts in our religion. Temple profits were always at their highest around high holy days. A greater number of Ba'alists came not only to make the usual sacrifices but also to receive the special services of the priests and priestesses of Ashtarti who were there to provide healing and enlightenment through the sex act. Only men needed to receive this service, because it was believed that women did not need to seek a union with the divine to achieve enlightenment; unlike men, women came by it naturally and could open themselves to enlightenment without the aid of man.

So, while unsanctified women were not allowed into the temple, any man seeking enlightenment could go to the Temple of Ashtarti for this service at any time, day or night. It was also for this reason that, while a woman could become a priestess by making a vow to the Ba'alim before the people, as I had done in my twelfth year, for a man to become a priest it required him to undergo a symbolic death and resurrection. This was accomplished through the act of ritual sacrifice and divine union performed by a priest or priestess upon a consecrated altar.

Once fully consecrated to their holy lives, priests and priestesses of Ashtarti served men of the community. They did this by taking them into either the special chambers at the temple or the secluded gardens, groves, and grottos set up for worship outside the temple, to bring them the temporary relief of a union with the divine. The followers of Yahowah were especially appalled by this service, likening it to prostitution, because they could not understand the difference between sex as a carnal act and the sacred sex performed by our priests and priestesses.

It was in performing this role many years ago at the Temple of Ashtarti in Tzidon, that Daneyah came to be with child. Wanting to have her child, she left her position at the temple and took refuge at the palace, offering herself into my mother's service. Still nursing Kora when I was born, she was appointed to nurse me as well, since my mother was occupied with the duties of being queen. My mother and Daneyah had known and loved each other before that time, so it was not an unusual choice. And in the kingdom of Tzidon, having a priestess-nurse was preferred, particularly in royal households, as it was thought that much of a person's nature and belief was brought to them through the milk they received in infancy. I became as a daughter to Daneyah, as well, and she had always told me when I was growing up that the Ba'alim had given me as a gift to two mothers.

Seeing the preparations for these celebrations once again gave Daneyah cause to reminisce, and on the eve of the feast, I listened with interest as Kora took down my hair and combed it out. Tamar and Fang-Hua had come to sit with us and were curious about all the rituals, symbols, and their meanings. My role as High Priestess especially fascinated Tamar because it was not a role that had previously existed in Yisrael.

"But how does a high priestess differ from a high priest – other than what is between their thighs, I mean?" This was met with some chuckles, by me and the others. "No, but I am serious. Are they not coequal, as you have said? And why are the other priests and priestesses of the Ba'alim not also married to one another? Or are they? I am confused."

Tamar's interest in my religion was pleasing to me, so I was not offended by her questions. They were asked with the desire to understand rather than to challenge or refute. With patience, I explained, "Provided they have undergone the necessary period of discernment, any woman can make a vow as a priestess, and any man can be made a priest through his union with a priestess, but the priests and priestesses are not required to be committed to one another because they are only agents of the Ba'alim, not the Ba'alim themselves."

"And what does that mean: to be agents of the Ba'alim?"

137

"They represent the Ba'alim in their service to the people, the way that a regent represents the king in his absence." This was met with expressions of understanding from the others, as I continued, "But, as a regent does not become the king simply by representing him, neither does a priest become a high priest. The same rule applies for a priestess. They may be used as vessels for the Ba'alim to act upon the earth, such as when they provide healing and enlightenment through sexual union, but they are not and can never become the true living embodiments of the divine."

"And that is what high priests and priestesses are?"

I gave a nod of assent. "That is why, for a man to become a high priest – even if that man is a king – it can only be done through a union with the High Priestess, who is his consort."

"So then," asked Fang-Hua, "can the High Priest create other high priestesses?"

"No, because divine power cannot be transferred from a man to a woman the way it is transferred from a woman to a man. The High Priest only receives his power through the High Priestess. And he must be worthy." I smiled fondly. "Akhab is worthy."

"And who does she receive it from?" asked Tamar. "You – who did you receive it from, I suppose is what I am trying to understand."

"From Ashtarti Herself, as I am of Her bloodline."

Both Fang-Hua and Tamar gasped, while Daneyah and Kora nodded support. Then Daneyah said proudly, "Her mother can trace the family line all the way back to the Ba'alim, through her mother, who was daughter to Abdashtart, the true King of Zour, and his blessed queen Azba'alah: both of whom were descendants of Ashtarti and Ba'al Hadad."

"Why do you call him the true King of Zour?" asked Fang-Hua.

"In a time long before any of you were alive," Daneyah continued, "Abdashtart was murdered by the four brothers who ruled as usurpers until the last of them was killed by Yezeba'al's father, Ethba'al. Ethba'al then earned the right to kingship and was rewarded for avenging Abdashtart by marrying his granddaughter: Yezeba'al's mother, Azra. Of course, that was in the time before Azra's father, the King of Assyria who was a son-in-law to Abdashtart, made enemies of his own daughters' husbands by demanding they pay him tribute. Ah, but here I am rambling... What were we originally talking about?"

138

Kora said somewhat impatiently, "Yezeba'al's descent from Ashtarti, Ama."

"Ah yes. Her descent can be proven through records that have been preserved since long before that time and are kept in all the royal houses who can claim such descent. Through the daughter of Abdashtart – Yezeba'al's maternal grandmother, who was Queen of Assyria and mother to many daughters who have themselves become queens – many royal houses can now claim descent from the Ba'alim."

I gave a nod to Daneyah, thanking her for the rather detailed explanation. Then I said, "And any of the daughters of those royal houses may become high priestesses, if they have been properly trained and have committed themselves to the priestesshood. Of course, not all Her descendants have the aptitude for it. That is why Amat and Tabuya are not priestesses, for example, though they are qualified by their blood."

"So," asked Fang-Hua, "that means that not anyone can become a high priestess?"

Again, I nodded. "Only women who are descended from Ashtarti through the maternal line can become high priestesses. It is Her divine blood that allows a high priestess, through consistent practice and meditation, to access Her powers and use them to act out Her will upon the earth. But they must first commit themselves to Her service. And even with commitment and practice, a high priestess can only attain the fullness of Her powers through the union with Her divine spouse: Ba'al Hadad, Melkorat. That is why her husband, if he is worthy, must become a high priest – and it can only be done through these rituals, performed by the High Priestess on the first night of the Feast of Ba'al. Unlike the traditional awakening ritual, which can be done as often as needed, such as in times of drought, the making of a high priest cannot be done at any other time of year."

Tamar thought carefully about it, and then asked, "When you say that these rituals will make the king into a high priest, what does this mean? Why is he not automatically a high priest because he is married to a high priestess?"

"Ba'al must be awakened in him, through the spilling of his blood upon the altar, to shed his former self and be transformed. This is why he must accept the invitation of the High Priestess by his own free will. It cannot be forced upon him by anyone, not even Ashtarti

139

herself. The king, being already of the spirit of Ba'al and now having accepted this role, will no longer be a mere mortal when the ritual is complete."

"But...you are not simply Her representative," said Tamar. "I have heard it said that you *are* the goddess herself, incarnate in the flesh." The chamber fell silent, and Fang-Hua stared at me in awe. Then Tamar asked, "Is it true? Are you Asherah – or Ashtarti as you call her in your father's tongue? Are you the Queen of Heaven herself?"

I met Daneyah's gaze. Thankfully, she stepped in to answer. "Yezeba'al is indeed the goddess incarnate. There had long been a prophecy that one would come from her line who would be the goddess returned to us in human form, and that she would be a great queen and give birth to many children whose descendants would spread throughout the world and bring peace and prosperity to many nations."

"If I can give birth to any children," I said suddenly, lowering my face in shame.

"You will give birth to many children, Yezeba'al," Daneyah said firmly. "It has been prophesied – and I have seen it for myself."

"What if I am not the one the prophesy spoke of, after all?"

She smiled slightly. "You are the one. All the signs have pointed to it. You must not lose faith." Then she turned to the others and said, "There were many signs spoken of in the prophecy that appeared at the time of her birth and throughout her infancy, which led us to believe she was the one."

"What were the signs?" asked Fang-Hua.

"There have been too many to count and to name them all," Daneyah replied. "I shall tell you about them all, in time. For now, I will speak only of the first and most important sign, the one that heralded a great blessing from the Ba'alim. On the day she was born, a great star appeared in the sky and remained visible for a full year, even in daylight. It had a long tail, much like that of the peacocks she so loves, when they are draped behind them as they walk."

Fang-Hua gasped. "My father's people have seen these stars. They do not see them as a sign of blessing, but as a warning or curse from the gods when they are displeased with us."

Daneyah shook her head. "Not to us. To us, they are signs of the favor of the gods. When they do come as warnings, it is the *love*

140

of the Ba'alim which provokes them to warn us that we may be prepared. But not all of them are warnings. This one was very specific and had long been predicted to indicate the return of Ashtarti. We knew by the shape of it, what it meant, and immediately suspected it was Yezeba'al. That is why she was given that name, for it is the cry of the goddess herself: 'Where is the Prince?' Once it was confirmed, after many more signs, she was kept apart from the king's other daughters, to shield her from envy and protect her from corrupting influences. She was given her own residences, close to the temples at Tzidon and Zour, so that she could be prepared for her destiny."

"Did you know this all along?" asked Fang-Hua, looking at me.

Again, Daneyah answered. "When Yezeba'al was a girl, until she came to Yisrael she was dressed and carried through the streets for the Feast of Ashtarti every year, so that the people who had awaited Her return could venerate Her in human form. I remember how well she always conducted herself: a tiny girl in all her gold raiment and jewels. Even as a small girl, it was clear that she was not like other children. Her mind and heart and soul are different from the rest of ours. She often exists in a state between worlds, both here and there." She lifted her hand to indicate the heavens.

"We have noticed," said Tamar. When I smiled, everyone knew it was acceptable to laugh at Tamar's joke.

Then Fang-Hua asked, "So, she was a high priestess from birth?"

Daneyah shook her head. "She was raised to understand her true divine nature from birth, but she still had to willingly offer herself in devotion to the goddess before she could be made High Priestess. We did not want to force her down that path, but rather to open it and let her decide whether to take it. When she made her vow as a priestess of Ashtarti, that is when she became qualified to be made High Priestess, and her purpose became clear."

It had been a long and lonely path toward understanding and accepting my divinity, as I remembered it. Other than Kora, I was indeed separated from all the other girls, unless they were priestesses of Ashtarti. My many half-sisters, on those rare occasions when I did encounter them, looked at me as if I was a pariah. Sometimes I resented my parents and Daneyah for taking me away from them, for keeping me apart, but I knew now they had done the right thing. This was my burden to bear, and I had learned to live

141

with it. *No blessing exists without adversity; that is the nature of duality.*

"So, if She is in you," asked Tamar, "if you are the incarnation of Ashtarti – why must you still worship Her?"

"I worship Ba'al. I do not worship Ashtarti."

"But do you not pray and make offerings to Her?"

"I venerate Her and give Her thanks for Her wisdom and guidance. You see, the whole of Her essence is too great to fit into a single human form. Only a small part of Her is in me – a single spark from a bonfire, if you will. That part must be strengthened and renewed through communion with the divine whole from which it comes, or it will be extinguished. Prayer and meditation help me to do that, and just as we must honor our earthly parents, so too must we honor the divine from whom we are created."

"Extinguished? Does that mean you will...die?"

"The soul that is within me – that spark of the goddess – will become depleted the longer I go without communion with Her. When that happens, the body may not die, but the mind and the heart and the soul begin to wither. Sorrow begins to grow in its place and, like the roots of a weed in a garden, chokes the life out of it. Then what is left of that spark becomes desperate to escape the confines of the body."

Fang-Hua gasped and her eyes grew wide. "You mean...?"

"Self-annihilation. Yes. That is what I mean. And that is why it is so important for me to commune with Ashtarti, so that I am not driven to such desperate acts."

With that, the questions ceased. Our time together was over, for their attentions were turned to my ceremonial raiments, which were now being laid out by Daneyah and the other priestesses. It was around this time that the king also arrived at my chamber, however, and all the other women departed.

After greeting me, Akhab pulled me into his embrace and kissed me tenderly on the mouth. I knew he was desirous. "No, Akhab. You know we cannot tonight – it is a holy day that must be observed. You can spend the evening however you like, but I must be pure for my communion with Ashtarti and save my strength for our reunion tomorrow night. You know what you have to look forward to."

Looking into my eyes with a naughty smile, he growled, "Can I not have you now as my wife, and still have you tomorrow as my goddess?"

Although I ached for him, too, I diverted his advances and remained firm. "No, Akhab – you know you cannot. I have already explained all this to you. If you are in need, you may go to one of your other women tonight, for I must spend my night in prayer, meditation, and fasting. Surely, one of your wives is in a fertile state tonight."

He brought my hand to his lips and scanned my form, covered only by a thin and slightly transparent underrobe that accentuated the curve of my hips and shape of my breasts for an appreciative male gaze, such as his. "All right: to the lilies I go. But I will think only of you, my Rose of Shomron."

"Try to think of them, little bee," I suggested, gently pulling my hand away. "It will make it more enjoyable for both of you."

"Is there one you suggest for me tonight?"

I gave it some thought. "Hawwa."

He groaned.

"You have not been with her in a while."

"Hawwa is sweet, and I am fond of her, but she is without passion. I do not think she finds any enjoyment in the act."

I looked at him in disbelief. "Truly?"

"Yes," he insisted. "She lies there while I do all the work, as if she is waiting for me to get it over with. I cannot enjoy my time with her. At least the others try... But they will never be as good as you."

Sitting at my dressing table to anoint myself with the sacred oils used in meditation, I smiled at his reflection in the mirror. "I do not know how any woman cannot enjoy the act of love – especially with you as a lover."

Akhab stood behind and put his arms around me to take hold of my breasts. "That is why I want only you, Yezeba'al. You enjoy it as much as I do. Your body and mine... We were made for each other."

It took all my strength not to give in to him, as he rubbed his nose against the side of my neck, inhaling the scent of the anointing oils. When he brought his lips there and began kissing down to my shoulder, I let out a faint moan as the urge to be with him intensified. I allowed myself to enjoy it for only a moment and then got up and

143

walked away to slip another robe over my body – as much for myself as it was for him.

Watching me with his charming smile and a look in the eye that he knew could get me to do just about anything, he said, "Cover your body with a robe, wife. It does not matter. I know what you look like underneath. And even if I did not, I could still imagine it."

Trying to hide my amusement, I hissed through my teeth. Nevertheless, he started toward me. Smiling, I held out my hand to stop him in his tracks, my palm to his heart. He pressed his hand over mine and gazed at me with longing, but at last relented. "All right, I shall wait for you, my goddess. I only beg of you one last kiss and then I shall depart."

Letting my hand fall to my side, I tilted my head back invitingly and he came to take me in his arms one last time. As he kissed me hungrily on the mouth, he let his hands stray to places they should not go. I laughed and tried to pull away, but he kissed firmly and would not release me until he had gotten his fingers where he had wanted them to go. Then he pulled away and held up his naughty hand. "To leave you as desirous of me as I am of you, my Queen."

"You did not have to do that, you know," I chided. "I think of you constantly when we are not together, remembering all my times with you and longing for the next."

"Tomorrow night," he said with a satisfied grin. Then he bowed with his arms out. "I am sorry that you must wait for me, my Queen."

Giggling, I threw one of the cushions at him and he blocked it with his hands. As the cushion fell to the floor, he pranced away, laughing. I shook my head, then returned to preparing myself for the long night of darkness and loneliness that awaited.

In Tzidon, I witnessed many of the rituals and celebrations associated with the Ba'alim feasts. In Yisrael, I had also hosted small-scale celebrations with Ba'alist nobles and my priests and priestesses, but the king had always stayed away. While he eschewed my feast days in favor of his own, I still joined him on his pilgrimages to the temple on Mount Gerizim each year for Yom Kippur and

Pesakh, although these feasts were dull in comparison to the feasts I remembered from my youth.

"It is no wonder you dislike festivals," I once told him, after first witnessing the most exciting feast his Yahowah would permit. "I must show you a true celebration one day. I can assure you that once you have witnessed the delights of a Ba'alim feast, you will never wish to return to this."

At the time, he had merely laughed and shook his head, saying that was why he could never join my celebrations, for it would be too tempting. Then he kissed me and told me to enjoy them for both of us. Now at last, he had not only agreed to join me, but accepted the invitation I extended to him years before, to take an active role at my side. Once Ba'al was awakened in him, I knew he would come to fully accept his divinity.

Observation of the eve of the Feast of Ba'al was well underway in the city of Shomron by the time the sun rose the following morning. Beginning with the appearance of the evening star at dusk the night before, woeful cries of *"Iye-ze Ba'al?"* meaning "Where is the Prince?" could be heard echoing throughout the streets as the people, led by the priests and priestesses, began the first stages of preparation for the feast to follow. For my part, I spent most of the night in meditation and communion with Ashtarti, listening to the cries of the people that echoed my own name. After the meditations, I laid down for a few hours of rest, during which I had many strange dreams. Then I was awakened when Daneyah and the other priestesses came to dress and prepare me for my role as High Priestess.

As on the day of my wedding, I was washed and anointed with sacred oils. My hair was combed and pinned up on the back of my head, but it was not nearly as elaborately dressed as it had been on the day of my wedding. Instead of a long and heavy mantle, I wore only a thin gold veil that hung down my back to the waist, pinned beneath a simple gold headdress in the shape of a crescent moon. The points of the crescent were turned upward so that it appeared as if I had two horns growing from the top of my head. The first time I had been prepared for my role as High Priestess at this feast, my first year in Yisrael, I was enchanted as I beheld my reflection in the mirror. After applying the kohl around my eyes, I was startled by how much I looked like my mother in that moment, as I remembered her, the first time I watched her dress for this feast.

My headdress, earrings, arm bands, bracelets, rings, anklets, and toe rings were of the finest gold of Opir. There could be no other metals used for this ceremony, as it was believed that any other metal would interfere with the ritual or even cause harm to my body. All of it was gold, except for some of the jewelry set with stones associated with the healing properties of the Ba'alim, such as ruby, amethyst, lapis lazuli, garnet, obsidian, and clear quartz. Beneath my collar, resting over my heart as always, was my opal scarab seal. The opal was a stone of intuition, healing, and passion, while the scarab was a symbol of regeneration.

Below my jeweled collar, my shoulders and breasts were tattooed with henna designs – seals to ward off any harmful or unclean spirits that might try to attach themselves to my essence. Only the Ba'alah herself could pass through these seals, and they were to provide the only covering for my breasts and shoulders, which were otherwise left bare. Finally, resting below my exposed waist was a gold belt, which held up a thin white skirt that fell to my feet but was open at the sides all the way up to my hips. Just visible from one of the slits was the ceremonial dagger strapped to my right thigh, used for the ritual sacrifice.

This was all I would be wearing for the nights of the feast, when I fully became the true living embodiment of the goddess, come to awaken her beloved from his time in the underworld. The ritual was a reenactment of the life, death, and resurrection of the first Ba'al, Hadad, who was murdered by Motu. When Anat, Ba'al's sister and one of his wives, went to avenge him, Ashtarti – his favorite wife and consort – awakened him. Restored to life by the power of the sex act, he returned to Ertsetu to kill Motu and preserve the souls of the dead from Motu's insatiable hunger. From that story, the ritual was born and carried through the ages by their descendants and followers. His awakening each year ushered in the autumn rains that would replenish the land after the four months of drought that came with his absence each summer. Many ordinary priests and priestesses performed the smaller rituals, but only the High Priestess herself could awaken Ba'al through the final, most mystical of all Ba'alim rituals: the physical union between Ashtarti and her Ba'al.

My mother, as High Priestess of Tzidon, had performed this ritual each year with my father at the Temple of Ba'al in Zour, but I had never been allowed to witness it because of my youth and

146

virginity. However, I had been taught about the ritual and its meaning and was instructed on how to perform it. Since coming to Yisrael, I had performed this ritual in effigy every year now at the Temple of Ba'al in Shomron. But this year was different: I would not have to perform the sacred rites upon an effigy of Ba'al, for I now had a true, living mate to be my divine counterpart.

As I had explained to the women in my chamber the night before, Akhab had agreed to be consecrated as High Priest. The role that had long been empty in Yisrael would be filled at last, by the only man who was qualified to fill it. By nightfall, through my rituals, my husband would become fully aware of his true nature as the living embodiment of Ba'al. And while I prepared for my part, he was being prepared at the temple by his priests.

While all devoted followers of the Ba'alim could participate in the festivities in the city, the most sacred ritual of all was performed in secret. The temple was closed to the public that day so that the altar of Ba'al could be cleansed and reconsecrated for use in the ritual. Having been made to drink a concoction that would temporarily place him into a death-like state, Akhab – wearing only a loin cloth, gold wristbands, and leather sandals – would be laid upon the altar. There, I would meet him at the end of his ceremonial journey to the underworld.

At the appointed time, I was taken to the temple in a covered litter. This ensured that the people would not see me before it was time for the Ba'alim to be revealed to them. Being carried through the streets, although I could not see anything outside my litter, I could hear the continued cries of the people: "*Iye-ze Ba'al?* Where is the Prince?" As twilight approached, the cries became more desperate with the rising anticipation for his awakening.

In an antechamber at the temple, I was made to drink a sacred herbal concoction that would put me in an altered state and allow the whole essence of Ashtarti to fully inhabit my body for the duration of the ritual. Then I waited astride the horse that I would ride into the ceremonial chamber when it was time for me to awaken my prince. Surrounded by my priestesses, who gently stroked the horse to keep it calm, I felt charged by the spirit of the goddess coursing through me as the herbs took effect. It was an amazing feeling: not possession, for it was not a foreign entity inhabiting my body, but completion, as I felt more connected to my true self than I had ever felt before.

147

When all was in place at last, a hush fell over the frenzied crowds. We entered the ceremonial chamber to the steady beat of drums played by priests. The heavy doors were pulled open, and my priestesses filed out into the chamber to join the assembly of more priests waiting there. When the drums stopped, that was my cue to enter. As I urged my horse forward, the priests and priestesses crossed their arms over their chests and knelt to me – the goddess incarnate – with their heads bowed.

"*Iye-ze Ba'al?*" I demanded, casting my gaze around at all who were assembled.

"*Iyu-shm, Ba'alah,*" they replied, meaning, "He is there, Ba'alah," and they raised their arms toward the altar, behind which stood a large emerald-eyed statue of Ba'al Hadad in the form of Melkorat. Lamps and incense burned throughout to light the way as I rode toward the altar, where my husband lay beneath the gaze of Ba'al as if dead. It was a relief to see him there, in place of the cold and lifeless effigy.

When I reached the steps at the base of the altar, I dismounted with the help of Daneyah. She then took the horse to the stable masters, who returned it to the antechamber to prevent its interfering with the ritual sacrifice. Striding carefully, I climbed the steps to the altar and paused to regard the statue that represented my consort-god. Then I turned my gaze to my true consort.

Not yet fully awakened, Akhab had begun to stir. Over his chest, he clutched an ankh and a ceremonial axe – symbols of life and death. After removing those from his hands and setting them aside, I touched his cheek and smiled down upon him. His eyelids fluttered as he tried to speak, but I placed my fingers over his lips. I said again, "*Iye-ze Ba'al?*" to remind him where we were and what we were doing, as it was not yet time for him to fully awaken. He fell still, as the drums began to pound a quiet, steady beat. That's when I climbed upon the altar and straddled him, in preparation for the sacrifice.

Reciting the prayers and incantations, I pulled the ceremonial dagger from its place at my thigh and raised it high above my husband. The freshly sharpened blade had been coated in sacred oil of myrrh, which would dull the pain and aid in healing. Then in one swift movement, which we had practiced several times with a blunted weapon in preparation for this day, I placed my left hand over his throat to protect him lest the dagger slip as I brought it down to slash his breast over his heart, cutting just deep enough to draw blood. The slash brought him fully to awareness. He jolted and cried out, while I placed my left hand over the bleeding wound and pressed the blood upon the altar. I then raised my bloodied hand into the air to make the sign of blessing: a bull's head, formed by the two outer fingers extended upward, with thumb and inner fingers folded together in between and facing forward. Then I announced, "Ba'al is in him!"

At this, the clergy, assembled in their ceremonial vestments, stood up with their arms raised to proclaim: "Ba'al is risen! Ba'al is risen! Ba'al is risen!"

As the cries were repeated within the chamber, I returned the dagger to its sheath. My husband looked up at me as if returning from a daze. Perched over him, I smiled at his return and could see in his eyes that he, too, had been changed. It was him, only it was more of him than I had ever seen, and I knew I had been right in my decision to make him High Priest. The ritual had worked – but it was still only partially complete. Without his full consecration, the spirit of Ba'al that had been summoned by the awakening would leave him in search of another form. The union of Ba'al and Ashtarti needed to be consummated immediately for the ritual to be complete.

This was the part we had been waiting for – the most sacred, secret part of the ceremony. Only the most senior priests and priestesses could attend to witness the union of Ba'al and Ashtarti in human form. Now, led by Daneyah and her male counterpart, a priest of Ba'al named Anniba'al, the rest of the assembly surrounded the altar and began the ritual chanting that would usher in the reunion of god and goddess.

The herbs I had imbibed earlier would help me to overcome any natural modesty that could prevent my completing the final and most vital part of the ritual. My sensations were also enhanced by them, so I would be more likely to reach ecstasy during our union. Without us both reaching ecstasy, the Ba'alim energies within us would be unbalanced. I was confident, though, because my husband seldom failed to bring me to ecstasy even without the concoction to aid me. Now, infused with the complete essence of Ashtarti, I was possessed by a desperate need for my consort that compelled me to move his loincloth aside and take hold of his risen part as the chanting intensified around us.

Trembling with desire, I came over him and we were united in the flesh, before all the priests and priestesses who had come to witness the divine union. Charged by the spirit of Ba'al, Akhab clung to me, kissed my breasts, and cried out as I ravished him. In my heightened state it was only a matter of time before I had reached ecstasy, at almost the same moment as him, and our voices carried throughout the chamber together as a hush fell over the assembly. Exhausted by the end of it, I fell over him and then we lay together, still trembling and clinging to each other, breathing heavily.

It was only when one of the priests threw open the doors and proclaimed to those waiting outside the chamber, "Ba'al is risen!" that we came back to ourselves and remembered what we were supposed to do next. As the priests and priestesses repeated the chant, I climbed off my husband and stepped onto the cold stone floor. Then I helped him to rise, and we were taken to an open litter to be carried together in a torch-lit parade through the streets of Shomron. The parade route was lined by armed guards, and the procession was led by our priests and priestesses who made the sign of blessing to the crowds as they proclaimed: "Ba'al is risen!" Hearing this, the people raised their hands in blessing and shouted the same in return, and this went on all the way from the temple to the palace.

When we reached the palace, those members of our court invited to our celebrations prostrated themselves until we had passed. Then, the litter was set down inside the Great Hall where Asa, our Minister of Ceremonies, awaited us. When my husband acknowledged him, Asa announced, "All is prepared for the feast, *akhu*. The entertainers are in place and ready to begin, at your word."

"Thank you, Asa," my husband answered, placing a hand on his brother's shoulder. "We will begin soon – but first, our people must see us."

Asa nodded and, as we passed, I saw his eyes scan my form. He had long harbored an infatuation with me, but he was as devoted to his brother as I was to my husband. He would never have dared to do more than look, and I would never discourage a man from merely looking. His admiration was reciprocated by a single nod and a smile, the only gifts I would give in acknowledgement of our mutual understanding. Akhab saw the way his brother looked at me and placed a hand on my hip, continuing to draw me toward the stairway that led up to the terrace overlooking the city.

150

Daneyah preceded us and, as she stepped out on the terrace, raised her left hand in blessing to the people of the city. "Good people of Shomron!" she announced. "Behold: Ba'al is risen!" Then Akhab and I stepped forward together, as we had on the day of our wedding. In the light of torches and oil lamps, we raised up our left hands to share the sign of Ba'al's blessing. Raising their left hands, the people returned our blessing and proclaimed in rapture: "Ba'al is risen! Ba'al is risen! Ba'al is risen!"

As we accepted the adoration of our people, my husband and I looked at each other and smiled. Then the people of Shomron – all who had come out to witness the celebrations – dropped to their knees and prostrated themselves before us. And when we had stayed long enough for them to be satisfied, we stepped back and returned to the great hall to begin the celebration, where our guests awaited us.

The Feast of Ba'al went on for the following three nights, with breaks in between for all the revelers to sleep and recover from each night of the festivities. Unlike all the usual court functions and somber Yahwist festivals, I brought Kora out of her role as my handmaiden so that we could enjoy the feast together as we had in our youth. The king had also decided that those of his women who wanted to join in the revelry were permitted to take part, so long as they were accompanied and observed at all times by widows of Omri. Along with the eunuchs, these childless widows now served as guardians to protect the chastity of Akhab's wives and concubines. One elder guardian was assigned to each young woman present. Only the soberest of Omri's widows were chosen for this vital position, and they took their role seriously, as it was important to maintain the integrity of the dynasty and its heirs.

Not all the women wanted to take part in the festivities, but those who did were permitted to join us. Many of them were excited to be included for once: Amat and Tabuya, who had worshipped the same Ba'alim their whole lives; Fang-Hua and Ba'athu, who had recently converted; little Zubira, who was still learning about my Ba'alim and found them to be like some of her own gods; and Tamar, who worshipped the Ba'al of Ekron but was also interested in mine.

151

Hawwa, while she would not condemn us for our worship, did not wish to be converted and wanted nothing to do with any of the Ba'alim feasts. She was content to stay in the confines of the women's quarters with those of the king's concubines who were of a similar mindset. We had no interest in forcing them to conform, as long as they left us alone. The feast would be more enjoyable without the presence of those who did not share our belief, after all.

For that reason, while anyone in the city could participate in the public festivities, the celebration at court was exclusive. Any members of the court who were not followers of the Ba'alim and had no interest in converting were not invited to participate in the festivities. Most of them would have left the city during this time, anyway, traveling to the Temple of Yahowah on Mount Gerizim for their own sacred feast. Defenses were raised to prevent thieves and miscreants from taking advantage during a time of celebration, but all the usual court functions ceased. Only our Minister of Ceremonies, the Lord Steward, and a handful of scribes continued to carry out their administrative duties at the palace during the three-day feast.

While my husband and I had taken leading roles on the first night of the festivities, on the last two nights Akhab took a much less active role, while I opened the festivities with a ritual dance, accompanied by some of my priestesses. Not simply a beautiful and sensuous dance; like the dance I had performed during our wedding festivities, nothing was without meaning. Each movement of the sacred dances served a purpose and had been carefully preserved from the time when Ashtarti herself came down from the heavens to teach them to her daughters here on earth. While I danced, Akhab observed our entry from his throne, tended to by Asa and the Lord Steward. Obadyah kept his gaze averted, but my husband and his brother eagerly watched my every movement. When my dance was finished, I went up to meet my husband on the dais, where we stood together and welcomed our guests. Then we stepped back to enjoy the festivities from our thrones, while Asa slipped away to ensure the revelry continued without interruption.

Food and drink were plentiful, laid out on banquet tables or carried on trays by servants. Meanwhile, slaves waited on their knees with their backs to the walls, ready at a moment's notice to clean up any messes that were made from spills or the results of excess,

152

inevitable at such raucous affairs. Most people had the wherewithal to step out into the courtyard when they had imbibed too much, but those who were less experienced tended to have more accidents than those who had learned to read their bodies and get out in time. From my place on the dais, I noticed Kora slip out once or twice, and was surprised because she had always been so modest. Nevertheless, I was so preoccupied between my husband and the entertainments that I never noticed her return.

Musicians played lively melodies on drums, flutes, and stringed instruments while our guests – already drunk on spiced wine, aroused by the atmosphere of revelry, and intoxicated by the delights of qaneh-bosem and other sacred herbs – danced and sang and made love to each other openly. Priests and priestesses even took part in orgies in the antechambers that were set up for such purposes. Throughout all this, in the center of the hall, lavishly costumed entertainers performed dances, pageants, magic tricks, and acrobatics meant to tell the stories of the Ba'alim, and to inspire the revelers with awe.

Watching all this from his throne, Akhab looked up at me and smiled. "You were right, my beloved."

Perched over him, I looked down, and asked, "Oh? What about, my love?"

He took my hand and pressed it to his lips. "Once I have seen the delights of a Ba'alim feast, I can never be satisfied with anything less."

With a chuckle, I looked out at the fire eaters who were currently performing their most daring tricks to the gasps and cries of wonder from our guests. "I told you one day I would show you a real feast. I never break my promises."

He smiled and then lifted his hand. "And look at my brother – I have never seen him more alive than he is on this night."

"You have finally given him purpose."

"He had purpose before," Akhab insisted.

I wrinkled my brow, with a skeptical tilt of my head.

"What? There has always been music and entertainment at my court."

"But not like this."

"All right, that is true. And Asa has been waiting for an opportunity like this for his whole life, I believe." He fell silent for a moment, and then said, "You know, my brother is infatuated with you, Yezeba'al."

"I know," I answered, glancing down at him with a smile. "He has written a great many poems and songs that I am certain are about me."

"I have noticed," said Akhab, observing his brother from afar. "So has half the court, I believe. He has made no secret of his...admiration for you."

Now, I cleared my throat. "Has there been gossip?"

"No," he said with a shake of his head. "Everyone knows that I trust you, Yezeba'al. Your loyalty is without question. It has merely been remarked upon, how infatuated he is with you, and that he seems to have little interest in other women at court. Of course, part of it is attributed to his devotion to Ashtarti – he is one of your earliest converts, after all."

"I believe he was the first, actually. Certainly, the first of your brothers."

"He is in his twenty-first year. I believe it is time for him to take a wife, and perhaps to make her his muse instead."

"Do you have a lady in mind?"

"I was hoping you might have some suggestions. You know the wives and daughters of our courtiers better than I do."

I smiled in amusement. "I will think on it, my love. Perhaps when this feast is ended, we will talk about this more?"

He nodded and we continued watching the various entertainments.

By the third night of festivities, we were beginning to tire of it, however, so we became less observant of the feast and more intoxicated with each other. My fingers tangled through my husband's curls while I tickled him playfully behind the ear, toyed with his earring, and stroked the side of his neck. We exchanged hungry glances from time to time and I leaned down to whisper in his ear, my breath warm and moist as I told him what I wanted to do to him and what I wanted him to do to me. I felt the vibration of a hum from deep within his chest and he smiled, wrapped his arm around my hips, and slipped his hand beneath my skirt to rest upon my thigh. His fingers inched closer to that sacred place, until the ache for him finally became too much for me to withstand. Uninhibited by the combined effects of wine and qaneh-bosem, I climbed onto his lap

154

and straddled him. Bending forward to kiss him, I was pleased by the sensation of my bare breasts against his own naked flesh. When he grabbed at my thighs and began lifting his hips to me, I moved his loin cloth aside, eased him in, and braced myself on the back of his throne. We were lost to the throes of passion until Akhab suddenly opened his eyes. The Lord Steward was coming. He grimaced as he dodged through the crowd of dancers and drunken revelers on his way toward us.

Akhab groaned and, when I turned to observe what he had seen, grabbed me more tightly and urged me to continue. Averting his gaze, Obadyah waited at the foot of the dais for us to finish. Then, breathless and satisfied, I climbed off my husband's lap and returned to the arm of his throne while he readjusted his loincloth and gestured for the steward to come forward. Stepping onto the first tier of the dais, the steward bowed low. "Melekh, Melkah, I apologize for this interruption, but a youth has arrived with a message from one of the prophets. He requests an audience."

"Now?" my husband declared, raising his hands at the festivities surrounding us.

"I am afraid so, Melekh."

"Send him away. If it is so important for him to interrupt one of our most important feasts, then he will come back when it is over."

Obadyah swallowed hard. "He said it cannot wait, Melekh."

"Who is this prophet, his master? Is he a prophet of the Ba'alim?"

I interjected, "If he was one of ours, my love, he would know better than to interrupt our feast – or he would already be here taking part."

The steward admitted, "He is a prophet of Yahowah, Melekh."

"Ugh, why should I permit him? I banished them all from my court more than a year ago, after that zealot, the Tishbite, insulted my Queen and accused her of sorcery."

Tilting my head, I wryly suggested, "Perhaps he has come with an apology for the way they treated us?" Then I turned to the steward. "What of this messenger? You say he is a youth?"

"Yes, Melkah. He calls himself Elisha."

Akhab wrinkled his brow and scratched at his beard. "I thought he called himself Eliyah?"

I giggled. "No, my love, Eliyah is the prophet's name. Elisha is the messenger." I turned to the steward. "Is he not their leader?"

"I believe so, Melkah," said the steward.

"Then who in the name of Ba'al is Elisha?"

"His messenger, Melekh," the Lord Steward replied.

We burst into laughter while Obadyah stood by helplessly. "He insists that his message is urgent, Melekh – that it cannot wait."

I sensed Akhab was about to tell him to send the boy away – his look of scorn said as much, as he shifted in his throne, but I placed a gentle hand over his fist. "Let the boy come. Let him deliver his message. The sooner he gets to say whatever he has come to say, the sooner he will leave, and we may continue the night's revelry. I am sure he is harmless."

Akhab's anger softened when he met my gaze. He took my hand, squeezed it, and brought my fingers to his lips. "Very well, my love. As always, you know best."

I leaned with my arm around his shoulders again, as he looked at the steward. "If he wants to come here, let him come and see all that the Ba'alim have to offer to the faithful."

While we continued giggling, the steward gave a nod and retreated. Then Akhab gently pulled me down to whisper in my ear, "I imagine he'll come barefoot and dressed in filthy animal skins, like his master."

I chuckled. Then I straightened and folded my hands into my lap to wait for this messenger to appear before us, wondering how closely he would resemble my husband's prediction. We watched the dancers that were now performing, but soon lost interest and began fondling each other until we noticed Obadyah returning with the messenger. Then we sighed and put on an air of seriousness as the boy called Elisha approached.

He was, indeed, a youth but he was not dressed in the ropes and animal skins that were typical of the prophets of Yahowah. His tunic and cloak were of a fine quality, like those worn by landowners and their families. I lowered my gaze to his feet – not barefooted at all, he wore sandals made of fine leather. My brows raised in surprise and my gaze shot up to examine his features. His face was clean, his hair neatly trimmed, and he had the hint of a mustache just starting to come in on his upper lip. He was tall and slim, but not emaciated. He might even grow into an attractive man one day.

156

As the youth approached, I raised my chin and waited for him to show some form of deference, but he did no such thing. Instead, the ferocity in his dark eyes was tempered only by his curiosity. When I met this with a warm smile and a delicate tilt of my head, his ferocity instantly melted. It seemed to me that he also had some color in his cheeks, and I wondered if he had ever seen a half-naked woman before.

Noticing the youth's eyes tracing my form and focusing especially on my tattooed breasts, my husband chuckled. Then he addressed him in Hebrew: "You like what you see, boy? That is my wife you gaze upon. But go ahead; look freely. I am proud when others admire what is mine alone."

The youth instead cast his gaze to the floor.

Akhab laughed, while I smiled, amused. Thinking the youth would not understand, I spoke Akkadian. "Careful, husband; you will incite him to break the tenth commandment of his god."

"By his face, I would say that he already has, from the moment he laid eyes upon you." Then my husband switched back to Hebrew. "Well, boy, what have you to say to us?"

Looking up again, Elisha asked in perfect Akkadian, "You are the king and queen?"

While I was surprised, Akhab smirked. "Do we look like paupers to you?"

"Akhab, be nice to the boy," I said playfully. "He is on an important mission."

My husband sniffed and leaned his elbow on the left arm of his throne, while I continued to occupy the right. "Well? Deliver your message. As you can see, we are rather occupied and would like to get on with our evening."

"My message...?" The boy lowered his gaze and now I was certain the bridge of his nose began to turn red as more people took notice of his presence. "It is not my message, but a message of one Eliyah, prophet of the Lord. He wants me to tell you that he is coming."

"Yahowah is coming here – to my court? Well then, I hope he arrives in time for the festivities."

While we snickered, the youth faltered. His mouth hung open and it seemed to take a moment for him to understand my husband's mockery. Once he understood, the redness spread from his nose and

157

to his cheeks, and then he narrowed his gaze. "Not Yahowah. Eliyah is coming."

Meanwhile, my husband had begun to play with my scarab pendant. The tips of his fingers brushed against the tops of my breasts. He barely turned his gaze from me, when he asked, "And who is this Eliyah, that I should take note of him?"

"He is a prophet of the Lord God of Yisrael. He has been chosen by the Lord to lead our people and proclaim his message to all who would hear."

"Oh, you mean the Tishbite? Yes, I remember him. I believe I banished him when he called my wife a sorceress. I suppose that is why he has sent you, to plead his case?"

"He has sent me to prepare the way for him."

"To prepare the way," Akhab repeated with a smirk, dragging his hand down my breast and across my waist until it rested in my lap. He gently squeezed my thigh, shifting in his seat. Feeling the heat of arousal once again, I wrapped my arm around his shoulder and fondled his earlobe. I wished the boy would leave, yet I was vaguely interested in what his master had to say. As infuriating as he could be, the Tishbite *was* entertaining – until he went too far. Perhaps, after being away from us for so long, he would be more polite.

Elisha, meanwhile, sighed and kept his gaze fixed on my husband. "He awaits my return. Will you permit him to come?"

Akhab sighed heavily and turned back to the youth. "Where is he now?"

"He is outside the palace walls, Melekh. So, will you see him?"

Akhab waved carelessly. "Bring him to me. Let us hear what he has to say that we have not heard before." Then, as an aside to me, he said, "This better be interesting."

While Elisha turned and hurried away, Akhab took my hand and pressed it to his lips. It would take time for the youth to get all the way out to where his master waited, so we returned our attentions to the performers and revelers. By now, our passions had cooled, so we sat quietly and watched the dancers finish their routine. Then Asa directed them away while some acrobats came forward to perform and the musicians played another lively tune. I laughed and clapped along with the music, and soon others began to clap along with me. As we watched the acrobats perform increasingly elaborate and dangerous tricks, the musicians began to beat their drums and play their instruments to heighten the suspense, and I realized I was holding my breath.

Just before its dramatic climax, the performance was interrupted by a burst of wind that came through when the heavy doors were pushed open suddenly, and a wild man walked briskly into the hall. He was followed by Elisha and flanked by two more of his followers. Here was our barefooted prophet cloaked in animal skins. The Tishbite had always been slim beneath his tattered cloak, but now he was so gaunt that he appeared to be malnourished.

I leaned down and lifted my hand to shield my lips, whispering to Akhab, "I thought Yahowah provided for his prophets?"

He sniffed at my joke, and said, "Perhaps he will do us all a favor and starve to death before causing more trouble in our kingdom." Then he settled back into his throne, while the herald announced the approach of Eliyahu the Tishbite, while leaving off the names of his followers, who seemed to have come only to bear witness.

Without any sign of deference, or waiting for the king to address him, Eliyah called out, "Melekh Akhab, thank you for admitting me in the midst of your celebrations! Although, I am surprised to see you still here at Shomron, that you are not on your way to Mount Gerizim for the Feast of Yom Kippur, to make penance to the Lord."

"Shalom, Tishbite," said my husband, holding out his hands. "The Feast of Ba'al is upon us. It is that which you interrupt, but I believe you already knew that. Have you come to see the wonders of the Ba'alim?"

"I have been charged by the spirit of the Lord, and I have come to wonder at how far you have strayed from the righteous path under the influence of your foreign queen." Casting his gaze around the chamber, he added, "Indeed, you have fallen. It is as the messenger said."

"Fallen? My dear Tishbite, no — I have been raised higher than any king in Yisrael before me. Have you not heard the people shouting and proclaiming in the streets: 'Ba'al is risen!' For, I have truly been awakened. The Queen has opened my eyes, so that I may see and understand my true nature."

"Your eyes may be open, Melekh, yet you remain blind to the error of your ways."

159

Akhab scoffed. "On the contrary, I have never seen more clearly than I see now."

"Is that so, Melekh? And what do you see?"

Regarding him coldly, Akhab said, "I see a madman standing before me, claiming to speak to *Serapim* and do their bidding in the name of his jealous god. A troublemaker, who has been going about my kingdom and attempting to turn the people against me. I have even heard it said that the words of Eliyahu the Tishbite were the driving force behind the rebellion that arose last spring in the southern parts of my kingdom, which I was forced to put down while my queen was still mourning the loss of our child."

The Tishbite's thick grey brows rose, and he looked to me in surprise, while I looked away. "I am sorry to hear of this, Melekh. Truly."

Raising his voice, my husband continued, "As it was only your words and not your person that led the rebellion, you are not to be held accountable this time. But let me be clear: if it happens again, you will be."

Eliyah smiled bitterly and held out his arms as he bowed his head. "Very well, Melekh. Would you permit me now to tell you what I see?"

Akhab assented with a careless wave and rested with his hand upon my thigh once again. I smiled to him and then turned my attention back to the prophet, eager to hear what he would have to say now that he was charged by the spirit of his god, as he claimed.

Ever mindful of his gathered audience as more of our guests became aware of his presence and ceased their merrymaking, Eliyah handed his staff to Elisha and paced the floor in front of us. He started calmly but grew more irate as he went on. "What I see here before me is a debauched assembly and a king, led by a wicked queen, who has raised himself higher than any son of man should ever be risen!"

Now he stopped pacing and turned to point an accusing finger at us. "You have made of yourselves idols of false worship! I have even heard it said that you are now claiming to be the divine made flesh!" At this, he tore the front of his cloak, to reveal a chest that was covered thickly with hair – was it his own hair, or yet another layer of animal skins?

Any remaining revelry stopped entirely now, and the chamber fell eerily quiet as the prophet dropped to his knees. He began twisting, thrashing, pounding on the floor, and raving like a lunatic. "You surround yourselves with drunkenness, depravity, and fornication, and call it a high holy feast? There is nothing holy or sacred about what I see here before me on this cursed night! You have turned your father's palace into a den of iniquity! You say you have been raised high, Melekh, but I say that never was there a king lower than you, who ignores the warnings of the prophets and permits his wife to lead his people astray!"

Pausing to wipe spittle from his lips, he reached for Elisha, who immediately came forward to bring his staff and help him to stand. Then he leaned on his staff, momentarily catching his breath and waving the boy away, before turning a fiery gaze on me. I was still seated on the arm of my husband's throne, when he said, "I see here a woman that calls herself a queen yet clothes herself and behaves as a harlot! A woman whose husband calls her his equal yet allows her to sit higher than himself, and to fill his court with idolators and temple prostitutes! I say before you all, *Yezebel* will bring the wrath of Yahowah upon this kingdom, upon this very house! She is not a queen, but the demon Lilitu incarnate!"

I leaned closer to Akhab, and whispered, "Who is the demon Lilitu?" I had read every religious and spiritual text I could get my hands on, so it surprised me that there was a character with whom I was not familiar. If she was a demon, however, I knew she must have been a powerful goddess, for the Yahwists were in the habit of calling all the other gods demons when they did not deny their existence entirely.

Slouched on his throne and stroking his beard, Akhab shook his head and waved off my question for later, as the prophet pointed an accusing finger at him. "And *you* are a weak king indeed to allow her to dominate you and provide her with the tools she needs to bring down your father's kingdom! You call on your missing god and ask him to return the autumn rains? As the Lord God of Yisrael lives, before whom I stand, there shall neither be dew nor rain these years, except by *my* word!"

I watched my husband's jaw tense, and he dug his fingers into my thigh while his left hand tightened on the vacant throne arm. Then I removed his hand, rose, and looked around at the members of

161

our court and the entertainers, all of whom were frozen in wonderment at what they had seen and heard. Attempting to lighten the mood once again, I lifted my arms out and raised my voice so that it would carry across the whole of the chamber for all to hear. "Yahowah has his prophets throwing tantrums in his name."

I brought my hands together, and suddenly the whole assemblage burst into laughter. Then I turned to see my husband smiling up at me. He reached for my hand and drew me to him, saying in Akkadian, "This is why I love you, Yezeba'al, my Queen. You always know the right thing to say at the right time."

Our shared laughter was brought to an end when Eliyah's voice rose, fierce and strong: "You – a woman and a foreign idolatress! You would dare to utter the name of the Lord?"

"Careful, prophet," Akhab warned. "You are already on unsteady ground by your earlier incursions, and now this interruption of our festivities. The only reason we have permitted you to speak at all is for our amusement – but this I do not find amusing."

Eliyah cast his gaze around at the assemblage, and then he spat upon the ground. I was surprised it had taken him so long when the last time he was here he had practically given our floor a new shine. "That is what I think of your festivities, Melekh Akhab!"

While one of the slaves came to wipe up his spittle, Eliyah stepped over the boy and pointed directly at me. "And you, *Yezebel*, know this: the Lord God of Yisrael has cursed your womb! It has withered like a barren field and will produce no living heirs of your body. The kingdom, if it survives long enough, will fall to the offspring of your husband's other wives and you will die broken and childless!"

It was this second curse that left me speechless and my husband enraged. Rising from his throne now, Akhab ordered the guards to seize the Tishbite, but the prophet pulled something from the leather satchel at his waist and threw it to the ground. It burst into a cloud of smoke as the whole court erupted into chaos. My eunuchs and the king's bodyguards immediately surrounded us on the dais, weapons drawn and ready to attack should anyone approach us, while Akhab pulled me to his body protectively. Meanwhile, with the aid of the smoke and the chaos, the prophet and his followers slipped away into the shelter of night, managing to evade capture. It was clear by the haste and ease with which they had escaped, that

162

they had planned for it ahead of time – and that they had help from the inside.

When the smoke cleared, the captain of the guard came to us, holding out his hand. "I found this, Melekh, where the prophet had been standing. He must have used it to make the smoke and create the diversion for his escape."

"What is it?" asked Akhab, releasing me. Both of us moved forward to see what the guard had found. They were tiny ceramic shards. Akhab picked at them, lifting one to examine what appeared to be part of the rim of what had once been a ceramic vial, the remnants of a wax seal still visible along the outer edge.

"Alchemy," I said upon seeing this.

Akhab looked to me. "You know what this is?"

"Egyptian magic. I know of it."

"The prophet uses sorcery, after he accused you of doing the same?"

"Not sorcery," I said. "It is merely a trick, one of those once known only by the Pharaoh's priests. Now it is a common entertainment at the courts in Egypt, Tzidon, and elsewhere."

Tightening his lips and breathing through his nostrils, Akhab snapped his fingers to call the other guards to him. "Find the madman. Detain him and bring him to me."

The men nodded and went off in search of the Tishbite. When they went away, my husband stepped aside to speak with Asa, Obadyah, and Aharon, who had been enjoying the festivities until the prophet's interruption. Meanwhile, Kora, Daneyah and some of the other priestesses came to me. I assured them I was all right but let Daneyah embrace me, and I rested my head upon her breast, as we had done since I was a small girl. Then my husband returned to me, asking, "My love, are you all right?"

I nodded and pulled away from Daneyah to take my husband's hand. "I am not afraid, my love. I put my faith in the Ba'alim, to overcome any curse Yahowah has placed upon my body, if what the charlatan says is even true. Either way, it does not matter. Now that the ritual is complete and you stand beside me awakened to your true form, nothing can stand in our way – not even some petty storm god and his mad prophets."

163

Daneyah chuckled. "They certainly do not make a good case for their Yahowah, ranting and raving at everyone in such a manner. Who wants to worship a petulant child?"

I and the others laughed but Akhab, who returned to his throne, was still brooding. Wanting to bring him comfort, I went to sit on the arm of his throne again, raised my arm to rest above his head and brought his hand to my breast. He fondled me for only a moment, but then sighed and dropped his hand. "I have had enough of these zealot prophets. They have gone too long unchecked to have one grow so bold, as he. I was wrong not to do something about them sooner."

I got up and stepped away, and then I turned and looked at him playfully. "What will you have done to them, Melekh?"

At last, I managed to get his attention, and he looked at me with desire in his gaze. "What would you have me do, my love?"

I thought for a moment. "Seek out and destroy all the lesser prophets who have incited rebellion and committed treason against us."

"The lesser prophets," he said thoughtfully. "And this Eliyahu the Tishbite? He is the worst of them – should he not also be destroyed?"

"For the Tishbite, do not make a martyr of him for his followers to venerate. Send him to the dungeon, where he can preach to the spiders and vermin. He will certainly eat better there, too."

The others laughed, while Akhab rubbed his beard again, as he always did when he was contemplative or brooding. Then he sighed. "No, I'll have him dragged before me and kicked, like the dog he is – the better to teach his followers a lesson."

At some point throughout all this, Kora had gone off to the side and was in conversation with Aharon until Obadyah went to scold him. I could not hear what was being said but was surprised when I looked up to see Obadyah so animated, having lost his temper with the young scribe. I watched curiously, wondering if it was because he found Aharon enjoying a Ba'alist feast when he was, technically, a Yahwist like his master.

Then Akhab snapped his fingers and called to Obadyah. The Lord Steward came at once, dragging Aharon by the collar of his tunic, while the king waved away the gathering that had assembled around us. While they dispersed and returned to the festivities, I

164

attempted to meet my husband's gaze, but he was stewing once again. I pouted my lip and sat on his lap, leaned across his shoulder, and took his face in my hand. "Where is my Prince?"

Pulled at once from his reverie, he looked up at me with a sad smile. "I am sorry, beloved. I do not mean to ignore you."

"Oh, my love, has the dog's barking left you cross? Do not let him ruin our festivities. I am not worried, and neither should you be. Let the soldiers deal with the Tishbite." I leaned into him and walked my fingers up his thigh. "We have better things to do."

He met my gaze and smiled mischievously, and we giggled together. Meanwhile, Obadyah had been standing nearby, waiting for the king's order all this time. He cleared his throat nervously and interrupted our playful banter. "Melekh, what would you have me do?"

"Ah, yes," my husband answered with a sigh. Then he glanced around to be sure only Obadyah, Aharon, and I were present to hear what he had to say. "I am going to make a new law. Aharon, when I am through, I want you to go at once to the other scribes – rouse them from their beds if you must – that they may begin drafting my decree."

The Chief Scribe bowed his head and waited for the king to find his words.

"The decree is going to say something like this: 'Let it be known that preaching or prophesying in the name of Yahowah is hereby outlawed in this kingdom and punishable by death'."

Obadyah nearly choked. "Melekh?"

"Yes, and I want the decree to focus specifically on punishment of those who incite rebellion. I do not care so much about the worship of the common people – it is those troublesome zealots that must be dealt with. Have it written tonight, that I may go over it in the morning and make any necessary changes. Oh, and do not speak to anyone of this matter, apart from the scribes you trust most. I do not want the people to know until the decree has been issued, so that the prophets will not have time to go into hiding."

We knew that Obadyah was a Yahwist, so it was not surprising that he seemed troubled by the king's pronouncement. Nevertheless, he was mindful of his duty. After a brief delay, as he grappled with the weight of his charge, he bowed obediently. "It will be done, Melekh." Then he gave a stern look to Aharon before turning on his heel and walking away.

As the Chief Scribe followed his master to do the king's bidding, I watched as he passed by Kora, and noticed him glance in her direction. Then the two of them exchanged a look that I knew all too well. Suddenly, the memories of so many brief and subtle moments between the two, hardly notable at the time, came together in my mind.

Getting up from my husband's lap, I went to Kora and, as her back was to me, tapped her on the shoulder. When she turned to face me, I stepped in the other direction with a grin, and then she turned the other way to see me and laughed. "Yezeba'al, I am glad to see you are still able to be yourself tonight. I was afraid that after the wild man's curses, you would be inconsolable."

I sniffed and twisted my mouth in bitter amusement. "The Ba'alim will bless us with a child – I feel it now. I am confident that it will come to pass, no matter what that filthy madman and his petulant god have to say."

She smiled faintly and I noticed the distracted look that overcame her as she lowered her gaze. Sidling up to her, I asked, "So, what is this between you and Aharon?"

With a sharp intake of breath, Kora's eyes grew wide, and her face took on the color of having been too long in the afternoon sun. Then she averted her gaze. "There is nothing between us."

Tilting my head playfully, I said, "Come now, Kora. I saw that look he gave you, which you returned. You have not said anything to me of this – how long has this been going on?"

"We…well, I mean, you have been so busy and…there is much to be done, so much for you to worry about, that… It did not seem like something you would need to be troubled with when you have a kingdom to manage."

"You are as a sister to me. If you are in love, I should be the first one to know about it – other than the one you love, of course. Does your mother know?"

"I have not said anything to her about it. She does not need to know, because she treats me like a child, even though I am older than you."

166

"I know, and I am sorry she does this to you. I think it is because you are her only child. She wants to protect you and keep you innocent."

"Perhaps I do not want to be innocent."

I regarded her with a knowing smile. "So, have you made love to him yet?"

Her face, having previously returned to its natural color, was immediately inflamed once again and she lowered her gaze to hide a smile. "We have...a number of times. But only very recently. He is a good man, Yezeba'al. I know that a lot of the other servants and people at court mock him because of how serious he is, and he sometimes is a bit strange, I admit. But he is a talented singer and musician and writes the most beautiful poetry! Oh, I am so very fond of him, and I believe he does love me."

"Then why is he sneaking around with you in the dark? He should take you as his wife and be done with it."

"He would never have dared to ask!"

"Well, never mind that – you let me take care of it. He has been a loyal servant to the King's court for many years, and he should be rewarded for his service."

She covered her mouth and gasped, and then she threw her arms around my neck. "Oh, Yezeba'al!" Then, regarding me with tears in her eyes, "Truly, you would do that for me?"

I gazed at her fondly. "Of course, I would, Kora. You are my sister before you are my handmaiden, as it has always been between us." Pausing to reconsider, I poked her with my elbow. "Well, no longer a hand*maiden*, I suppose." She covered her mouth to hide her laughter, as I said, "Anyway, that has never changed, even if I am now a queen and...distracted by my own charming husband."

"And running a kingdom beside him," she added. "That is no small thing." I tilted my head in concession. Then she took me by the hands, and said, "Now, I know that before all this happened, you and the king were...occupied. And I know that right now Aharon is going to carry out the king's orders, but we have made plans to see each other tonight, so if you do not mind, Yezeba'al, I would like to ask permission to return to my chamber to prepare."

"Yes, of course. I shall let you go, then. Have a glorious night, Kora." I winked and she stuck out her tongue at me, as I slipped away and returned to my husband.

He had been watching us curiously, and as I sat again upon his lap, he asked, "What was all that about?"

"Nothing for now. I shall tell you all about it in the morning, but for now, my Ba'al, why do we not bring this feast to an end so we can return to our chamber for the night?"

He growled in agreement and kissed me, and I was glad to see his mood had not been completely ruined by our encounter with the raving prophet. While the last of the revelers stayed in the Great Hall to finish out the festivities, my husband returned with me to my bed, where together we ended the feast in much the same manner with which it had begun.

7

Increase of Faith

By order of Ba'al Akhab, Melekh Yisrael and Ba'alah Yezeba'al, Melkah Yisrael: Preaching and prophesying in the name of the god Yahowah is hereby outlawed in the kingdom of Yisrael. Any person, man or woman, who speaks against the king or queen and incites rebellion within the kingdom of Yisrael through preaching or prophesying in the name of Yahowah is to be arrested and brought before the king and queen with witnesses to testify. Those found guilty of sedition are to be executed according to the laws of this kingdom; they are otherwise to be imprisoned. Furthermore, any person, man or woman, who is caught willfully harboring preachers and prophets of Yahowah known or believed to be guilty of seditious preaching is to be stoned and then hanged by the neck until dead; thereafter, his property and all his effects are to be confiscated, forfeit to the royal House of Omri. Let it be known.

The carrying out of the king's orders came swiftly, after facing only a brief delay while we worked out the minor details. The first morning after the feast had ended, before holding court, I sat with Akhab at the desk in his study, while Obadyah, Aharon, Daneyah, Anniba'al, and our most trusted ministers gathered to discuss the terms of the new law. Aharon took note of our discussions and determinations and then, while we held court, organized them into a draft of the decree. The following morning, the king and I looked over the draft together and scribbled down our suggested changes, which Aharon then applied, again while we held court.

This drafting and redrafting went on for a few days before it was finalized on a clay tablet and then distributed to the scribes so they could make copies of the decree to be sent out to every city, town, and village within our kingdom. The decree would be read aloud to the people before being posted in town centers: a reminder to any with the capacity to read. The decree was overall well-received – there was only one minor rebellion in a remote town that was put down without the king's intervention – but it was not as effective as had been intended. The prophets typically congregated in and around the major cities, where their messages could be heard by the masses and nobility alike, but by the time our decree was issued, word had gotten out about the new law and many of them had disappeared before they could be arrested.

We wondered which of our ministers might have betrayed us, but the majority of them were now Ba'alist. Even the few remaining Yahwist ministers showed distinctive loyalty and held the disruptive zealots in contempt, so it was suspected that one of the scribes might have sent a warning out before the decree was issued. At any rate, it was a minor inconvenience and produced only a slight delay. We knew it was only a matter of time before the whereabouts of many of these preachers and prophets would begin to surface. The numbers of these men, and a few women, were not as high as we had anticipated, but they were enough to keep the court rather busy over the next few months. The results were impressive, though. With fewer agitators stirring up trouble, stability began to return to our kingdom, allowing us to focus on improving the lives of our people as well as tending to more important personal matters that had arisen.

First there was the issue of finding a wife for the king's brother, Asa. There was no shortage of eligible maidens ready to be made wives, and because Asa was an attractive man with a striking resemblance to the king, he was much admired. The issue, however, was in finding for him a young lady who could cure his infatuation with me and put the king's mind at ease. I began at once to speak with the ladies at court with daughters of marriageable age, and in very little time found several suitable candidates. They were brought to court to be interviewed by me in the private audience chamber, while their hopeful mothers stood by urging them to answer my questions without fear. After discussing the most suitable candidates with Akhab, we finally selected a girl who bore a slight resemblance to me in looks. Then Asa was summoned to the king's private audience chamber, where Akhab informed his brother that he had arranged a marriage for him.

Asa did not take the news well. When the brothers fell into a terrible argument, Obadyah sent Aharon to find me. I was instructing some of the women in a writing lesson when a eunuch came with the message. Placing Tamar in charge of the lesson, I went out to see Aharon, who was waiting in the heavily guarded antechamber to the women's quarters. He seemed relieved when I appeared. When he told me about the fight, I went immediately to smooth things over between them.

I entered the king's study without warning and found the two royal brothers shouting at each other, such that neither of them could possibly have heard what the other was saying. They stopped immediately when they saw me, and I demanded, "What is this? Is it my husband and his favorite brother prepared to kill one another? What has brought this about?"

"Asa is not pleased that I have found a wife for him."

I looked to my brother-in-law, and asked, "Asa, are you not pleased to take a wife?"

Unable to meet my gaze, Asa's cheeks reddened. "It is not that I do not wish to take a wife, Ba'alah. It is the reason behind his decision that angers me." He paused and glanced up to meet my gaze then looked away once again. "It seems my brother fears I am too smitten with you. I have made no secret of my admiration, I know, but I have assured him, I would never dare…"

"I know, Asa," I gently interrupted. "You are an honest man; Akhab knows this, as do I. But you are at an age now when it is appropriate for you to take a wife, and as you have not shown any interest in…suitable ladies…the king has taken it upon himself to choose one for you. It is customary for the king to arrange the marriages of his unmarried brothers and sisters, after all. Do you object to the lady he has chosen for you?"

"I…do not know the lady he has chosen. I have never met her before."

I sat on the desk and took my husband's hand. He rested it on my thigh, while I smiled sweetly and spoke to his brother. "You have not met her, but I know the girl and her family well. I believe Rachel would be the perfect wife to a man with your skills and talents. She is comely. And she loves music. She sings beautifully. She would be the ideal muse, I believe, and would appreciate your talent as much as I do – more, in fact, because she would be your wife, and your adoration of her would be more acceptable."

Akhab squeezed my thigh, and said, "She looks a lot like you, actually."

Asa scoffed and glared at his brother. Then he turned to look out through the cedar-screened window. Eventually, he turned back to us. "Fine. I will accept this marriage, but do not think for a moment I do not see what you are up to with this, *akhu*. I am not a fool."

"No one ever said you were a fool, Asa."

"Just tell me when we are to be wed, and I will be there. Now, if you will excuse me, I have much work to be done."

The king waved his hand and Asa was gone. I climbed off the desk and went to sit at my husband's feet. "You did well, my love."

"No, Yezeba'al, *you* did well. I should have had you present from the start. You have always known how to speak with my youngest brother. It helps that you are close in age, I suppose."

"It helps that I am the object of his infatuation." I rose on my knees and rested my elbows in his lap, holding his face in my hands and drawing him into a kiss. Then I said, "Do not worry about Asa, my love. When he sees his new bride, he will be content."

This proved true. When the day of the wedding arrived, not long after, Asa and his bride took to each other quickly. While the two were pledged to each other in a small ceremony attended only by the two families, Akhab and I looked on proudly. She did not cure his infatuation with me completely, but she at least gave him a new focus for his passions. His songs and poems began to be dedicated to his new wife in my stead and, while her slight resemblance to me did not go unnoticed, the court's whispers about Asa's infatuation with his brother's wife were soon put to rest. While this marriage was only just beginning, however, one of the king's marriages was about to come to an end.

Troubled by her conscience after hearing of the curses of the prophet Eliyah and the king's new decree, and following the success

172

of the Feast of Ba'al, Hawwa requested the king's permission to be released from her duties as a wife and return to her father's house. Although Akhab had no passion for Hawwa, he was fond of the girl. We both found her gentle nature and peacekeeping attributes to be quite useful in the women's household. While he was disappointed in her decision, Akhab granted permission for their marriage to be dissolved. Before she was allowed to return to her family, though, she had to be examined to ensure she was not with child. Also, her two daughters would have to remain at Megiddu with the rest of his heirs.

Originally, he had considered letting her take the two girls, the first being two years of age and the second only just learning to crawl. Had she only been a concubine, it would have been permitted. However, the advice of his counsel reminded Akhab of the necessity for his legitimate heirs to remain within his household until marriage. The decision made, she agreed to abide by it. I was present when Hawwa went to the royal nursery to say farewell to her daughters and bless them. They were both too young to understand what was happening. Remaining in the care of their nurses, their lives would hardly be changed, but I knew that their mother's heart was breaking. Her life would never be the same.

When she came to me after turning away from them, she kept her gaze to the floor and bowed her head, asking me to look after them in her absence. "They are your daughters now, Melkah. Please do not let them forget that I love them."

"Hawwa, are you sure you want to do this? You can stay here and be a wife of the king without having relations with him. He will respect you if you ask for it."

"Thank you, Melkah, and I know that he would but I..." Still looking at the floor, she shook her head and sighed heavily. "I will not condemn you and the king for what you believe, but as it conflicts with my belief, I cannot stay."

"Hawwa, the new law does not affect the ability of you or anyone in the kingdom to worship as you see fit – it is only those who actively seek the destruction of our kingdom and condemn us for our belief that are under penalty. Many followers of Yahowah are still employed with us. They will not be prevented from worshiping as they choose, as long as they remain loyal to us."

"I know, and I am grateful for that, Melkah. I would never speak a word against you or the king. You have only ever been good to me, but I must do what my conscience dictates. I want to live a quiet life in prayer and seclusion at my father's house. That is all I have ever wanted, and I believe it is the will of Yahowah that I devote my life to him in this way. I am grateful that the king and you, Melkah, have agreed to allow it."

She glanced at her children who were playing together with their nurses and half-siblings who were of a similar age. Her voice cracked, as she continued, "And I know that my daughters will be well cared for here at the palace. I ask that you love and raise them as if they were your own."

"You know that I will, for all the king's children are as my children. I will speak highly of you to your daughters and tell them how you loved them enough to leave them where they could be raised as king's daughters, as is their right. And I will ensure they are taught about your god as well as my own, that they may know who you serve."

She looked up at me, and her eyes flooded with tears. I could feel that she wanted to embrace me, and so I opened my arms to her, and she fell into them. "You have been a good wife and loyal companion, Hawwa. I will pray for you every day."

"As I will also pray for you, Melkah."

I touched her face and gazed at her fondly, as though she was one of my sisters. Then she turned and hurried away to meet with her father's servants who had come to take her back to his house. So, while the king finalized his divorce from Hawwa, the court prepared for yet another wedding. This time it was not the king or one of his brothers being married: it was the Chief Scribe.

Rewarding Aharon for his loyal service to the kingdom, he was raised to the position of second steward – a rank just below that of Lord Steward – and given permission to take a wife of his choosing from among my handmaidens. Without hesitation he chose Kora; of course, she assented. They were married and given houses with their own staff: one each within the walls of our residences at Shomron, Megiddu, and Yezreel, where they could live and raise a family together while still being near enough to continue their service to us. They were intensely happy, and I was amazed at the change marriage brought to the awkward former scribe, who seemed a new man. He was still odd in some of his mannerisms, and perhaps a bit more anxious than he had previously been, but his love for Kora was obvious and his loyalty to us increased. He also enjoyed his work of helping Obadyah and the other stewards in managing the king's household, which was about to increase.

Within weeks of the Feast of Ba'al, I began to feel the all-too-familiar signs of pregnancy. It was soon confirmed that I was with child and would be delivered around midsummer if all went well. Rather than being besieged by fear, however, this time I was filled with hope. Over the next few weeks, it almost seemed as if everyone at court and within the king's household held their breath, but I was confident because I knew the union with my husband was complete. As the weeks passed without incident and my condition began to show through layers of robes, everyone relaxed. Soon the whole court was abuzz with preparations for the birth of a new heir.

While the king had many sons, the birth of a son to his Melkah would displace them in the line of succession unless the king himself deemed otherwise. There was no knowing for certain if my child would be a son or daughter until it was delivered, but the Ba'alim priests and priestesses who were gifted at prophesy all said the same thing: the signs favored the birth of a son to the queen. I was pleased and Akhab hopeful that he would have a new son to declare his successor. So, even though our autumn rains had not come as they normally would that year, our minds remained fixed on the glory of our kingdom's future.

With the approach of summer came the preparations, not only for the birth of our child, but also for the other most important of our Ba'alim feasts: the Feast of Ashtarti. As was customary, we had returned to Shomron for the feast at the end of spring, even though I was now heavy with child. I fretted over the timing for fear that the child's birth might interfere with my ability to carry out the rituals of this sacred feast, but Daneyah assured me that, as my child was not due until a few weeks after the feast, it should not prevent me from carrying out my duties as High Priestess.

Before the feast, however, and upon our return to Shomron, our first order of business was meeting with a representative from Ashkelon. The diplomat had come for the finalization of a treaty that would provide protection from the Kingdom of Yehudah for them, and access to another seaport for us. The terms of the treaty also included the arrangement of yet another marriage for Akhab, to a niece of the King of Ashkelon. Wasting no time in settling the treaty, the king's niece Abbigail arrived with her retinue and the marriage hastily concluded with the signing of the treaty.

At this point, there was no need for a great celebration. Once Abbigail had become yet another of Akhab's wives, the day's business continued as usual. I remained at my husband's side, while the girl was taken to the women's quarters to settle in and await a time for our husband to consummate the marriage. That would not be for several weeks, until after our return to Megiddu, for Akhab now refused to consummate any of his marriages until after I had inspected the new brides to ensure they were old enough to be wives. Besides, there were more important matters that warranted his immediate attention now; in particular, the upcoming feast over which we would preside.

Since he was new to his role as High Priest, Akhab was still learning the intricacies of our religious duties, the differences between the rites we carried out, and the meanings behind all of it. Also, because I was so heavy with child, I needed to consider how the sacred rite of our sexual union could be carried out without losing its legitimacy and efficacy. We were resting in bed together after our supper that night when I raised the issue and expressed my concern, but Akhab did not understand.

"We make love all the time," he remarked. "The only difference is that we will be on the altar in the temple."

"No, Akhab, that is not the only difference. For *this* rite, I am supposed to be the one on my back. I forgot to explain this to you."

He smiled and I knew he was imagining it.

Meanwhile, I continued, "The only issue is that, with the child so heavy in me, I cannot lie on my back for very long, and certainly not upon a stone altar. We will have to do it with me sitting up, but you must still be in the dominant position, and I must lie on my back at the moment of ecstasy. Daneyah has assured me that it will still work."

"But does the position truly affect it?"

"Everything affects it. That is why it is so important that the ritual be done correctly." He still looked confused, so I said,

"Remember what I told you about the powerful nature of sexual energy? How it must be channeled equally?"

"Yes, of course."

"As I have explained, everything exists within the framework of the duality between Ba'al and Ba'alah, male and female. Even our rituals must reflect that duality: when I awaken Ba'al in you, I am on top because it is part of your being raised – Ba'al comes up from the underworld through the altar and enters through the base of your spine."

"Yes, I remember." He shivered and smiled at the thought.

"So, when Ba'al is to leave for his return to the underworld, to keep the balance of energies in this cycle that the feasts and their rituals represent, I must be underneath while Ba'al passes from you and through me on his way back to the underworld. That is why we do it this way – to complete the cycle. Any other way will disrupt the balance; the cycle will be broken, Ba'al will be trapped between worlds, and the energy will overflow. It could be disastrous."

"But you have performed these rites without me these past years...and I know that for the awakening of Ba'al, you have used an effigy in my place. If for this rite I am supposed to mount you...how did you do it before you had me to perform with you?"

"I used a...sacred ritual object, made for this purpose."

He still looked confused, so I climbed off the bed and knelt beside it to reach underneath. He sat up among the cushions and watched curiously as I pulled out a long, narrow wooden box and placed it on the bed. Still not meeting his gaze, I opened it to reveal a solid gold object in the rudimentary shape and form of a man's part. "This is what I use."

When I glanced up at him, his expression showed a combination of intrigue and shock. Then as I put it away, he said, "Do you...use it at times other than the ritual?"

Rising after hiding it again beneath the bed, my smile betrayed nothing. "I do not need it when I have you." Then I climbed back into bed and laid in his embrace with my head on his shoulder and my arm resting on my belly. He kissed my forehead, and I moved my hand over his heart. "I prefer the feeling of you inside me, of your hands on my body, and the warmth of your flesh. I prefer the power of your soul and mine, as they come together through us and in us. There is nothing that compares to that, Akhab."

177

He tightened his arm around me and because he fell silent, I thought perhaps he might be thinking of something equally poetic to say. He may not have been a true poet like his brother Asa or a musician like his ancestor King Dawid but he was gifted in music and poetry and wrote many songs for me, although he seldom shared them with anyone else.

Instead of responding poetically, however, he asked, "So, when you do the ritual...do you use it on yourself?"

"Ugh!" I pulled away and struck him on the shoulder with the back of my hand.

Raising his arms to shield himself from another potential attack, he asked, "What? I am only asking about how it works!"

"Yes, I use it on myself. Now, can we please not talk about it any longer? It is embarrassing."

"But you use it in front of the other clergy."

I hissed and lifted one of the cushions to hit him with it. Then, putting the cushions back in order, I said, "During the ritual, I am in an altered state. I am hardly aware of them."

He fell silent, and I thought the subject was finished until he asked, "Can I...watch you use it some time?"

"Akhab! It is a ritual object! The clergy do not watch me use it for their own arousal – they are aware of the sacredness of what is happening when I use it in that way."

"I understand this, but if you only use it for ritual purposes, why do you keep it hidden in your chamber under your bed, hmm?"

I made a sour face, which made him laugh. Then I answered, "It takes practice in order to use it the right way."

"So, you do use it outside your rituals... I would like to see this."

"You are a deviant!" I said, and I punched him once again on the arm.

Laughing, he grabbed my hand and pulled me into a kiss. After only a moment of resistance, I gave in. But then, wanting to put him in his place, I grabbed him by the wrists and climbed over him. When I released him, he caressed my belly, feeling the movements of our child in my womb, and kissed me there. Then he lay back again and gazed up at me. "You do not need to be ashamed of this, my love. I find it interesting. I did not know these things existed. Women are...more industrious than I realized. But if you wish to keep it private, I understand."

"Perhaps some time I will let you see when I use it, but I do not use it often. I use it only when I cannot have you instead, so that will make using it in front of you more difficult."

"Then I will have to make you desperate for me but not allow you to have me, so that you will have no other choice but to use that instead."

"But would you not rather have me yourself?"

"Of course, but I want to see it. And when I see it cannot satisfy you the way I can, then I will take you."

Grinning playfully, I suggested, "We do need to practice how the ritual will be performed..."

"Tonight?"

I shrugged. "Well, if you are not in the mood..."

"Wait, I did not say that," he replied, grabbing to stop me from pulling away. I giggled as he climbed off the bed and let him pull me to the edge. He lifted the hem of my gown and began kissing and gently biting my thighs.

We practiced for much of the night.

The next morning, after my husband left to meet with Asa to finalize the plans for the feast, Kora came to help me prepare. She was also radiantly with child by now, although a couple months behind. We were delighted to be pregnant at the same time and excited to feel and show each other the movements of our children within our wombs. We giggled when, upon our embrace that morning, my child kicked just as we came together, and her own child responded with the same.

"Your child is going to be strong, Yezeba'al," she said. "That was quite the kick that even my own child felt!"

I chuckled and placed a hand over my enormous belly. "This child is very active. Sometimes, he moves so much that it seems as though there was a war taking place within my womb. I wonder at the trouble he will give his nurse. I pray he will be milder once freed from this vessel that confines him. He will be a warrior, like his father."

179

A worried look came over her, and she placed a hand over mine, still resting on my stomach. "You do not think he will give you trouble upon his birth?"

Shaking my head, I smiled. "No, it will not go as it went for poor Leah." I paused and whispered a prayer for her soul. Then I continued, "The midwives have assured me that my hips are wide enough. The birth should go swiftly and easily, although they are concerned that his position is constantly changing. It seems he has not settled in to await his birth just yet. When they feel for him, he is first here and then there. He is constantly thrashing about. But the prophecies speak favorably of his birth, so I am not worried."

I breathed deeply and gazed out the window at the beautiful morning with a smile. "I am at peace, Kora, for the first time in years. And," glancing down at my swollen belly, "I am looking forward to this blessing I am about to receive."

"But first," said Kora, "we have a feast to attend – and you are presiding over it with your husband the High Priest. I do not envy you, you know, mating with your husband in front of the other clergy twice a year."

"It is a sacred rite, and I am honored to do it."

"I could never do it. I am glad I am able to keep my relations with Aharon private. I do not think he could do it, either."

Laughing, I said, "Well, that is why you and he are not High Priestess and Priest."

"And thank the Ba'alim for that! We would not want to be!"

We laughed together, and then she helped prepare me for my bath so I could cleanse my body in preparation for the day of prayer and meditation that lay ahead. In contrast to the Feast of Ba'al, the Feast of Ashtarti began at dawn instead of dusk, but it was just as sacred and required the same amount of bodily and spiritual preparation. However, it was not as joyous, because it was commemorating the time when the curse of Motu forced Ba'al to return to the underworld. Like a husband going off to war, his last act before leaving was to have one final union with his consort before their four-month separation to follow.

The sexuality of Ashtarti was a focus of her festival, not only because a woman's body was the conduit through which all life was created, but also because it was through the sex act that Ba'al was able to move between the two realms he inhabited. As such, it was

180

necessary for us to carry out another ritual coupling at the Temple of Ba'al that morning, while the highest members of the clergy again surrounded the altar with their drums and chanting.

Despite my initial concerns, we managed to carry it out perfectly. I felt the energy of Ba'al pass through me and out, as it was intended. After our coupling, a robe was placed over me, and then I gave a blessing to my husband, who I could see was more exhausted than usual. This I was told to expect, as he had gotten used to the abundance of energy he had received from Ba'al these past months; now that there was less of his essence in the body, it would take more time for him to recover.

I could feel his sorrow, so I took his hand to offer comfort and encouragement. We went out then to see the people who had come to Shomron for the feast. Just as it was done for the Feast of Ba'al, we were carried on a litter through the streets of Shomron to the cheers and blessings from the people, who we blessed in return. This time, however, the parade ended when we reached the Temple of Ashtarti that was on the other side of the city, near the main gate.

Akhab helped me from the litter and then we went inside Asharti's temple to initiate the new acolytes who had completed their discernment and were ready to begin training for this most blessed vocation. Then they were ushered to the back of the chamber while their predecessors came forward to be accepted fully into the ministry as priests and priestesses of Ashtarti. Akhab and I stood by the altar as the previous year's acolytes were brought forward to kneel before their god and goddess in human form. They made their vows to me, and I gave them their blessing.

Afterward, the new priestesses were taken aside to kneel in front of the acolytes, while the new priests were made official by the conferment of power from their elders. This, of course, was done through the sex act. Akhab and I sat enthroned on the dais as, one at a time, a more practiced priest or priestess took the new priests to the inner sanctum where the altar of Ashtarti was hidden behind curtains. The new priests were allowed to choose which of their elders would bless them in this way; one young man dared to ask for me, even as my husband sat enthroned beside me. Thankfully, Akhab was more amused than offended. He said, "Young man, you may have the High Priestess when she selects you to replace me as High Priest. Until then, you must be satisfied with one of her priestesses instead."

181

Laughter erupted from those around us, and then the cheeky young man dutifully selected one of the available priestesses. She led him to the inner sanctum where their coupling took place. While they were engaged, I led the rest of the clergy and the new initiates in prayers and hymns, renewing the consecration of Yisrael to the goddess and asking for her favor. There was another reason for this: it helped to mask the sounds of lovemaking that often arose from behind the curtains at our backs.

There were a lot of new priests this season, so this process went on all afternoon. It was actually a relief when it was finished. Then we went outside the temple to sit upon thrones that had been set up beneath a gold-fringed canopy on a dais in the square outside the Temple of Ashtarti. Daneyah and Anniba'al, as our spiritual advisors and most trusted assistants, stood on the dais near our thrones while we observed the next stage of the celebrations.

The new priestesses, all of them still maidens, performed a sacred dance around the pole that had been constructed in the center of the square, while the new priests encircled them and chanted. The pole was made from wood and carved with symbols of the Ba'alim and representations of their faces, one on either side. Representing the sacred union of the Ba'alim, it was a reminder of the healing and enlightenment that were available to men through the gift of sacred sexuality, as taught to us by the first Ba'alah to walk the earth many generations before us.

Having been instructed by the elder priestesses in preparation for this day, once the dance was completed, the maiden priestesses were taken into the temple, where they would perform their first acts of sacred sex with men who came to them for this blessed gift. Through this act, enlightenment and healing were achieved when the men's souls passed through the underworld and back at the very moment when they reached ecstasy. This served as a symbolic death and resurrection like that of Ba'al in his annual cycle. Although this service was always available with the priests and priestesses who were inducted in previous years, it was only during the Feast of Ashtarti that newly vested priests and priestesses began their sacred work. This year, there were more than ever, and temple profits were soaring as wealthy men paid more to be the first to receive the blessing of Ashtarti through them.

The new priests and priestesses would also replace older ones, who had already served the required four years and were now moving on to take on other roles in their devotion to Ashtarti. Priests usually served as musicians, scribes, and tutors to royal and noble houses, while priestesses often served as midwives, nursemaids, and mentors for the same.

Those who wanted to continue serving the men of the community as they had for the past four years were permitted to stay at the temple, if there was room; if not, which was the case this year, they were given a place at another temple, or went out to serve in the gardens, groves, and grottos consecrated to Ashtarti for that reason. It was a great honor to serve the goddess in this manner; her priests and priestesses were highly respected by those who understood their divine purpose.

Aware of the sublime gift they had been given, new priestesses were always eager to shed their virginity and begin their work. As the maiden priestesses disappeared into the temple, Daneyah leaned over to say, "I remember my first time like it was yesterday."

I often wondered what it was like to be a regular priestess and perform these acts for the multitudes. While a part of me was curious about it, I was grateful that, as a royal daughter and high priestess, I needed only to serve Ba'al himself, though my husband. Looking up at Daneyah, I asked, "Do you miss it?"

"Sometimes," she answered with a faint nod. "Not all the men who came to me were pleasing – in fact, many of them were not to my liking at all – but it was an honor to share with them the gift of enlightenment and healing through the act of love."

Akhab reached for my hand and brought it to his lips. "As my beloved Ba'alah does for me nearly every day."

"Nearly?" asked Daneyah with a raised brow.

Smirking, I answered, "I cannot always perform my sacred duty as the wife of a king, but I make up for it. Some days, we make love several times a day."

"Most days," he answered, with a roguish grin.

I smiled proudly and said, "You must take a break sometimes, my Ba'al. I would not want to wear you out. Besides, if you only ever have me, your other wives will become lonely for you."

"Some of them, perhaps. But then, quite a few have each other and I am certain they do not become lonely for me that often."

Daneyah chuckled. "The Queen of Tzidon often felt that way. I must admit, she was fonder of me than she ever was of her husband the king, or any man."

While my husband laughed heartily, I smiled, thinking fondly of my mother. She had accompanied my father and brother to visit us two months previously and were overjoyed to see me swollen with child. They were even more pleased that my husband had converted to our religion and become a high priest. It was the first time they had come to see me since I was married, but after our joyful reunion, my mother had spent most of her time locked away in privacy with Daneyah. Meanwhile, my father and brother spent much of their time out with Akhab and the other men in the field, racing and performing mock battles in their chariots. I had gone to watch, but then felt some regret that I could not be on the back of a horse or driving a chariot with them. I enjoyed being with child, but the loss of activity was starting to make me grow restless. At least there were the three nights of feasting to look forward to – if I did not tire out too quickly to enjoy them. This seemed to be happening more, the further my pregnancy progressed.

Sighing heavily, I turned to watch the long line of men filing into the temple. Outside, elder priests and priestesses waited to collect the men's offerings before they allowed them to pass through the threshold. They also had to keep count of how many there were so the others would not be overrun inside. There were only so many priests and priestesses available for the service, and only so many chambers where the service could be performed. When the temple reached capacity, the remaining men were turned away and told to come back tomorrow. The exchange of energy was so powerful, especially with Ashtarti coming through them, that the priests and priestesses were only allowed to perform the ritual sex act once per day. I was grateful that, because Ashtarti was *always* in me and my service was only to one man, I did not have such limitations imposed.

Watching all the men being turned away as dusk fell, I rose from the throne and prepared to return to the palace. I was impressed by the number of them who had come that day – it was a great deal more than the previous year. Despite the curse of the Tishbite and the lack of rain, devotion to the Ba'alim was higher than ever in the kingdom of Yisrael. And that devotion would only continue to climb

184

with the blessing we were about to receive in the birth of a child that the prophet had sworn would never come.

After the customary three days of feasting had run their course, we returned to our palace at Megiddu. Newly built, it had become the favorite of our palaces. We were beginning to stay there more frequently when not required at Shomron or Yezreel. Megiddu had the best gardens in Yisrael as well, due to Akhab's implementation of the most advanced modern water system, and views of the surrounding countryside were magnificent with its thick forests and lush plains. The surrounding palaces and estates belonged only to our most loyal family, friends, and administrators; many were our fellow priests and priestesses who served at the Ba'alim temples there.

Megiddu was also the perfect location for tournaments. I was out in the field watching the king and his men competing with their chariots, when the pains of labor began. I knew it was beginning, but I also knew that there was plenty of time before it would become urgent, and so I watched the men finish their routine and waited for the winner to be declared. Of course, it was Akhab who was declared the winner, not because he was king but because he was truly the most skilled with a chariot. Even his brother Abram could not best him, although, it was Abram who almost always won the archery competition.

The men congratulated Akhab on his victory, and then he came to me while the field was being prepared for the next round. He was dripping with sweat when he pulled off his helmet and bent to kiss me on the cheek. I squealed and pushed him away. "Akhab, no! You stink of horses and sweat! At least wipe yourself off before you kiss me!"

With a hearty laugh, he stuck his hands into the basin of water that was brought to him, and then he wiped the water from his face and beard. Shaking his head and still snickering, he said, "Forgive me, wife. I thought the sweat did not bother you – that is certainly not the way you feel about it when we are in the throes of passion."

"Then it is different!"

185

"How is it different?" he asked, handing the cloth back to the servant boy. "Sweat is sweat, my love."

"It is different," I insisted. Then I paused and inhaled sharply as the pains intensified. Daneyah and Kora came to me immediately, but I waved them away.

Akhab also took notice. "Yezeba'al? Are you all right? Is it time? Do we need to return to the palace?"

Breathing through it, I clenched my teeth and nodded to reassure him. When the pain had subsided enough for me to speak, I said, "It is fine, Akhab. There is plenty of time before it is critical, but I think it *is* time for me to return to the palace and summon the midwives to the birthing chamber."

Daneyah gently chided me, "You should not have come here in the first place, Yezeba'al. I told you that you should be resting."

"And I told *you*, I have no desire to be confined to my quarters like an invalid. Besides, I wanted to be here to support my husband."

"You will support him by taking care of his heir and the vessel that bears him."

I braced myself as another pain took hold but still managed to hiss at her to show my displeasure at being reprimanded. When it had passed, she and Kora helped me to stand, and I was taken back to my litter. Akhab informed his men what was happening, and the rest of the competition was put on hold, while he accompanied my retinue back to the palace for the blessed event. Akhab rode alongside my litter the whole way, holding my hand and fussing over me. I looked over at Kora, who was riding a donkey on the opposite side of my litter, and said, "Why are men such babies about this whole thing? They are not the ones who have to do all the work."

We chuckled together, but then Daneyah rode up next to Kora, and said, "The king is worried about the wellbeing of his queen — there is no harm in that."

"I know, and I was only teasing." I looked over at Akhab, who had heard all of it, and was smiling in amusement.

"She is right, though," he said. "You should listen to her — it is why you appointed her to be your advisor."

"She never listens to me," Daneyah quipped.

I stuck out my tongue at my husband, but then I was seized by another pain. They were coming closer together, and I began to wonder if I had indeed waited too long to say something. Thankfully, we were getting close to the palace now.

As soon as we arrived, the slaves carefully set the litter on the ground in the courtyard. I was immediately surrounded by those who had come to whisk me away to the birthing chamber, having been informed by a messenger sent ahead. It became more difficult to walk now as the pains intensified, but I insisted on not being fussed over, permitting only Daneyah and my husband to help me whenever I needed to pause to let the pains pass. However, the moment we reached the women's quarters, my husband was made to wait outside, for no man was ever allowed inside the birthing chamber, not even a king.

Kissing him once more before going in, I said, "It will be all right, my love. I will see you again soon, with our son to behold."

Then I let them usher me in and close the door as he paced in the corridor outside. He was surrounded by brothers to support him but unable to do anything until he heard the good news. I cannot imagine how tense he was waiting out there and listening to the sounds from inside without understanding what any of it meant. Whenever one of the women had to go through the door to fetch more water and clean linens, Akhab was there, trying to look in through the open door. He had never shown such interest or concern for any of his other wives, and I heard the priestess-midwives twittering at how unusual it was for a king to be so concerned about these matters. But knowing he was there gave me peace and I was determined to make him proud.

Standing in the center of the chamber, I held onto the rope that dangled in front of me, while Kora and the other women tended to me. Trying to focus on the task at hand, I was comforted by the prayers and incantations being chanted by Daneyah and some of the other priestesses in attendance. I cried out only when I could not bear the pain any longer. Instead of screaming as I had seen many of the other women do, I focused on directing my energies into pushing whenever my body gave me the urge, while the midwives continued to reassure me that it was right and good. When, at last, the child's head passed through, the rest came swiftly and soon the chamber was filled with the sound of my newborn's first cries.

At once, I was taken to rest while the midwives tended to the child, cleaning and swaddling it before they brought it for me to inspect. I reached for my child when I saw them coming, and as she handed him to me, Daneyah said, "You have been delivered of a healthy and strong daughter, Ba'alah."

There was a moment of surprise, and even of slight disappointment I admit. But when I looked at my daughter's tiny, red face, wrinkled and whimpering, all that was erased, and I was filled with the purest love I had ever known. I took her in my arms, laughing and crying as I gazed at her, and said, "She is beautiful. Ashtarti has blessed me with one of her daughters to raise in her image."

Daneyah caressed my hair, while one of the widows of Omri went to admit the king, aware that he was still waiting anxiously outside and desperate to see that I was all right. Having changed from his battle armor and cleaned up in the time we were apart, he came straight to me, kissed me, and I lifted our child for him to see.

Before he could speak, I declared, "You have a daughter, Melekh."

The same stages of surprise, disappointment, acceptance, and love shaped his expressions. Then he sat beside me and held us both in his arms, kissing me on the cheek, and smiling down at his daughter. "She is beautiful, like her mother."

I was going to respond but, suddenly, I was seized by more pains and a pressure so intense that it took my breath away. I groaned, and immediately one of the women came to take our daughter from me, while the king looked at me in concern. Hurrying over to us, Maryam explained, "Nothing to worry about, Melekh. It is only the afterbirth."

"Ah, yes," he replied, although it was clear by his expression that he did not know what that was, and that it was disturbing to think about.

While Maryam knelt, I spread my legs and raised my hips for her to inspect, and I looked at my husband with an awkward grin. "See, this is why it is not customary for a man to be present in the birthing chamber until it is all finished."

Before the king could say anything in reply, Maryam cried out in surprise. "Aiee Yah! There is another child coming!"

After a moment of surprise passed through the chamber, there was a flurry of activity as the women shuffled the king out and prepared for me once again to give birth. There was not even time enough for me to be taken to the rope in the center, but there was no need for it either. The second child came more quickly and easily than the first, and before I knew it, I heard one of the midwives cry out, "It is a son, Ba'alah! And he is strong and healthy, too!"

While my son's cries arose and echoed through the chamber, I closed my eyes and breathed in with a smile. Now, I felt vindicated. The Tishbite's prophecy had been wrong: while he said I would never be delivered of a living heir for the king, I had delivered two in less than a year from the time his curse had been spoken. We had still not had much rain, but none of that mattered because I had a son for the king.

After the birthing was finished, my children were cleaned and I was brought to rest on a bed of cushions upon a raised bedframe – not as fine as the one in my chamber, but still better than the bench I had been seated on before. Then the king was brought in once again. He was beaming with joy, having been informed that the second child was a son even before he was allowed to see us. But in the moment when the door had been opened while Maryam delivered the news, I witnessed my husband and the men who were waiting there with him break into cheers. He embraced one of his brothers, and then the door was closed while the midwives continued tending to me and my newborn twins.

The birth of our twins was announced to the people and, from the chamber where I rested and visited with my husband later that day, we could hear the people celebrating and rejoicing in the streets of our city. It was quiet inside the chamber, though, and a peaceful atmosphere surrounded us as we admired our children and laughed together about that surprising moment when our son appeared in the birth canal.

Akhab was holding our daughter while I held our son, and he gazed at her with tears in his eyes. "A son and a daughter; both at once. The Ba'alim have been good to us, making up for so much loss, all in one blessed moment."

"They were trying to come to us," I replied, smiling down at my son, and stroking his cheek. "When at last they could make it, they wanted to come together because they had been forced to wait for so long."

189

He met my gaze with a loving smile. "You have done well, my Yezeba'al. I am sorry it took me so long to do what was needed. Thank you for your patience with me."

I leaned my head back and he knew it was an invitation for him to step forward to kiss me. As he bent over me and our lips came together, our daughter who was still in his arms began to fuss. I held my arm out to take her. Then he took our son from me, as Daneyah approached. "She is probably hungry for her first meal. Shall I fetch the nurse, or do you want to be the one to feed her?"

When I met her gaze, she smiled knowingly. Then, as my husband looked on with our son in his arms, Daneyah instructed me on how to coax my daughter to latch on, so that she could take her first meal. When she was satisfied and had fallen asleep, Daneyah took her from me and suggested I try it with my son. He had not made a fuss from his father's arms the whole time, but Akhab handed him to me. Then he took our daughter again, and Daneyah instructed me to put my son to the other breast. "You may feed them both from either side, but you must always make sure both sides get the same amount of feeding time, or your breasts will grow to be different sizes and remain that way when the milk dries up."

Akhab raised his brows and met my gaze in horror, while I laughed. "Do not worry, my love. I shall not turn into a deformed cow! I will be sure to keep them balanced for you to enjoy – besides, I want them to remain beautiful, too."

He laughed, and then he came to sit on the cushions beside me. Together we watched our son take his first meal. Soon, both our children were sleeping, and we switched again, so that I was holding our daughter while Akhab held our son. "He will be the milder of the two. I get the feeling that his sister will be the more difficult one."

With a chuckle, I leaned my head against his shoulder, as my gaze fell on our daughter. "She is the one who had to be first. It is no wonder it always felt as if there was a battle going on inside my womb – likely it was she, fighting for dominance."

"Then she will be just like her mother," Akhab said with a laugh. "Ah, but we shall love them both equally, and no doubt they shall love each other...even if they do try to kill one another from time to time."

"As is the way of royal siblings."

"All siblings when you think about it. Look at the story of Qayin and Hebel. And they were not even twins."

I chuckled, and then said, "You know, my mother was a twin. It was her sister that married the King of Elam and is the mother to Amat and Tabuya. Although, my mother and her sister were identical."

"Amat and Tubuya – they are also twins?"

"No," I laughed. "Amat is a year older than Tabuya. How can you not know this? You are married to both of them."

"I...do not pay attention to these things. It is of little consequence to me. As long as they are women – and look it – that is all that matters. I married them at the same time, so I thought perhaps they were twins."

Shaking my head and smiling, I fell silent, and began stroking my daughter's cheek with my forefinger. She was clutching my thumb as she slept, and I was amazed at the strength of her tiny fist. I thought then of the treaty with the King of Yehudah, and how we had promised to uphold the second half of the treaty by marrying our first daughter to his successor when she reached marriageable age. Akhab's sister, the Queen of Yehudah, had given birth to a son named Yehoram nearly two years before, and I knew that if both of them reached adolescence, my daughter would marry him as soon as she was old enough to wed.

It seemed so far from now, but I knew it would come all too quickly, and I pulled my daughter closer to me then. Was it wrong of me to feel some hesitation, when it was the duty of princesses to marry in this way, and the duty of their mothers to let it be done as it was done to them. Had my own mother felt this way when I was promised to Akhab? Perhaps one day I would ask her, but for now I did not wish to think of it.

Breaking the silence, I said, "Speaking of your other wives being old enough... Zubira has begun to bleed."

He shifted our son's weight in his arms and sighed heavily. Daneyah came to retrieve the baby, while Akhab asked, "And do you believe she is ready?"

Inhaling sharply, I asked, "Do you?"

He looked away and shook his head. "No, I do not."

"Good, because neither do I. So, when Maryam comes to say something to you – which she will soon, because she believes the

191

marriage should be consummated, even though I have told her I do not think it is right…"

"I will tell her it is your decision to decide when Zubira is ready."

I nodded once. "Thank you, my beloved. And I will let Zubira decide, because it should be her decision to make."

Akhab put his arm around me and looked down at our daughter. "It is hard to believe that in twelve years she will be a woman. The time goes so fast, now that I am getting older."

I rolled my eyes and snorted in amusement. "Akhab, you have only twenty-six years. You are not old."

"No, but I am getting older and in only a few years more I will be considered old."

I scoffed. "Did not your Metushelak live to be over nine hundred years old?" He saw the way I was smirking, though, and was aware that I did not believe what the scriptures said concerning the longevity of early mankind. He poked me in the side, and I laughed, but then our daughter began fussing. "Look what you did, waking her like that – you naughty king."

Daneyah came to take her from me. Then Akhab slipped both his arms around me, laid me on my back, and climbed over me, saying, "I will show you what a naughty king I am!"

I laughed while he kissed my breasts, but Daneyah chided the king, "Not until the bleeding has stopped!"

Looking up at Daneyah like a child being scolded by his nurse, he said, "What? I am not going to take her when she has only just given birth. I only want to play with her a little, as much as she will permit."

She saw the way I was smirking, and then narrowed her eyes at him, betraying little of the amusement that I knew she was hiding. "Nothing down *there*."

"I promise, Daneyah. I will not."

"Good," she said, finally letting the trace of a smile break free. "Carry on then, Ba'al."

Then she turned away, while we giggled and had as much enjoyment of one another as possible without compromising my wellbeing. The women tending to me, and to our newborn children, averted their gaze and went about their business. And when I had finished giving my husband satisfaction I laid down to rest, asking him to stay with me. Although it was morning, he had tasked Obadyah and Aharon with managing the needs of the court for the day, so he agreed to stay without hesitation; it was the first time he had ever set his duties to the kingdom aside for the birth of an heir. Exhausted, because we had not slept since before the pains had begun the previous day, we fell asleep quickly and slept for the better part of the day. Then after a brief awakening to eat and adore our children, we slept again through the night.

8

The Trouble with Storm Gods

With the birth of our twins following the king's conversion, the number of converts to our religion tripled, for it proved to many the power of the Ba'alim. Men whose wives were struggling with fertility issues came to Ba'al, now making sacrifices and leaving offerings upon his altars all throughout the kingdom. They also sought out the temple priestesses who taught them how to please their wives, for it was part of our teaching that if a woman is pleased by her husband, she is more likely to conceive. Many of them received their blessings as quickly as we received our own, in whom we delighted.

Keeping my promise to my husband's sister, we named our daughter Atalaya, while our son was given the name Akhazyah, after one of Akhab's brothers. Our children were blessed together in my chamber at Megiddu, while Akhab and I looked on proudly, with two of Akhab's brothers and their wives attending as witnesses. During the sacred naming ceremony, incense was burnt in censers that were carried by priests around the chamber to ward off evil spirits. Meanwhile, the priestesses sprinkled water over our children's foreheads, one at a time, as their names were pronounced over them for the first time.

As she had been born first, Atalaya was the first to be given her name. She was held by a priestess over a small basin of cleansing water as another priestess sacrificed a sacred dove to Ashtarti, whose ruby-eyed figure looked on as it was burnt upon the altar that I had set up for my own private religious needs. I had similar altars in my quarters at each of our residences. After Atalaya was blessed, it was Akhazyah's turn to receive his name in the same manner, only this time it was a quail that was sacrificed to Ba'al and burnt in the same way. While the sacrifices burned, the priests and priestesses raised their hands over the altar and chanted quietly, asking our gods to accept the sacrifices for the protection of our children as we promised to have them serve the Ba'alim all their lives.

With the naming ceremony complete, it was time for the court to return to Shomron for administrative duties that could not be performed at Megiddu. We would only be at Shomron for a few weeks, but our newborn children had to be left behind at the palace at Megiddu, where they would stay with all their siblings in the nursery. Until they were old enough to endure the difficulties of even a few hours travel between palaces, the king's children always remained at Megiddu. Apart from it being our favorite home, it was furthest away from enemy territory, making it the safest place for the king's heirs to be raised. While Shomron was our administrative center, and Yezreel our military center, Megiddu was the center of our family life.

It was difficult for me to leave my children, who were still only a few weeks old. This was my first time without them. I knew they would be well cared for by their nurses, but I still worried and lamented that, by the time we returned, my own milk would have dried up so I would not even be able to feed them again myself. My husband teased a little, suggesting he could help ensure my milk did not dry up. Then he became serious again, reassuring me that we would have more children soon enough to nurse at my breast, and that our son and daughter would be waiting for us when we returned in a few weeks.

"They will not have forgotten their mother."

"They may not forget me, but neither will they remember me."

I looked past the curtains on my litter to watch the last-minute preparations taking place before our departure. Then I sighed and sat back. "They are not old enough to remember me, which I suppose is a good thing. They will not miss me nearly as much as I shall miss them."

He bent to kiss me, and then said, "They could never forget the woman whose heartbeat they heard every day for all the months they were growing inside you. They will remember you. It is only a few weeks."

I smiled and then, as he went to mount his horse, settled into my cushions where I would ride out the journey to Shomron. It was a thirteen-hour journey, split between two days of travel, but less difficult than it had been at the start of our marriage. The roads were

195

more advanced now, thanks to Akhab's interest in improving infrastructure throughout our kingdom. He had a keen mind for engineering and architecture, and I often teased that he would have made a good engineer if he had not been born to be king. He was always interested in the latest technologies, and even helped design some of the improvements himself when he met with the architects and engineers who oversaw these projects. Unfortunately, no amount of advanced technology could reduce the heat of summer, and my fan did little to assuage me.

Even worse than the heat was the ache in my breasts as the milk swelled with no babies to feed. By the second day of our journey, I was in so much pain that I was nearly in tears. When we stopped at a wayside to give the men and animals a break, Daneyah suggested I express some of the milk to relieve the pressure, which I did while Kora and the other handmaids surrounded my litter for privacy. Afterward, I went into the miqwah to cleanse myself, grateful to wash the sweat and dust from my flesh.

When we resumed our journey, I drifted off only to be awakened by the sound of shofars blaring the command to stop and hold. My litter halted on the road and the slaves carrying it stood at attention, awaiting further orders. I looked around, asking sleepily, "What is it? Why are we stopping?"

Just then, my litter was brought to the ground as my eunuchs closed in, surrounding it with their backs to me and weapons drawn defensively. I tried to see past them, and called out, "What is happening?"

Captain Zarek and Eliezar, his second-in-command, came together through the line of eunuchs and stopped before me with a bow. "Ba'alah, there was a large group of men spotted on the road ahead. They are bearing weapons and demanding to speak with the king."

"Akhab! Where is he now? Tell me he did not go to see them!"

"He is speaking with his officers, Ba'alah. They are deciding what to do."

I started to get up. "I must speak with him. Let me go to him."

"Forgive me, Ba'alah. The king has commanded us to stay in place. We cannot allow you to leave the safety of your litter."

"Nonsense. If we are ambushed, my litter is the least safe place for me to be, because they will know to look here first."

"Forgive me, Ba'alah. It is the king's command."

"*I* command you! You are beholden to *me*. Let me go – I must see the king."

The captain and his second looked to each other, and then Captain Zarek whispered to Eliezar, who gave a nod and went away. He slipped through the circle of eunuchs, who parted only long enough for him to get through. Then Zarek said, "He will ask the king what to do, Ba'alah."

I settled back into my litter with arms crossed and sighed. Soon the king appeared, followed by Eliezar. Immediately, I climbed out of the litter to meet my husband.

"My love," he began, but I cut him off.

"Akhab, you will not go to these men! They must not make demands of their king. Who are they? What do they want with you? It could be an ambush."

"I know, my love. And I will not go to them alone."

"You cannot go to them at all! Are you out of your mind?"

He took me by the arms, and said calmly, "Yezeba'al, I must speak with them so we can pass safely. They pose more of a danger to us if I do not meet with them and hear what they have come to say. But it is being arranged now. I can meet with their leader at a safe distance, with my bodyguards and a contingent of soldiers nearby. But you must stay here with the other women, where it is safe."

"Safe? Trapped in my litter and surrounded by eunuchs? You might as well point me out to our enemies, and say, 'There she is – the Queen!' for they will know just where to find me if they wish to do harm or take me as a hostage."

"I am leaving enough men here to protect all of you. I have given orders on what to do if we are attacked."

"You make it sound as if you are going to war."

"They are armed men," he replied, but he took my face in his hand and met my gaze. "I must speak with them and try to placate them, so it does not come to that."

My eyes stung, but I pushed back the urge to cry. "Let me go with you."

"Out of the question!"

"If you are going to face them, then I am going to face them with you."

"No, Yezeba'al. You will stay here where it is safe."

"I will not let you face these men alone! If I am there, perhaps they will be less likely to harm you. A woman's presence can be enough to settle the hearts of angry men."

He sighed heavily and ran his fingers through his hair. "They are followers of Yahowah, and there are zealots among them. They will not look kindly on you, my Ba'alah."

"I do not care. Let me come anyway. Let them see me, and we will see if their hatred remains strong in my presence."

There was a moment of hesitation, when I thought that he was going to relent, but then he shook his head firmly and put on his helmet. "No. You will remain here with the women, where it is safe."

He walked away and I tried to follow, calling after him, but the eunuchs stepped in my way. Furious, I beat on their shoulders with my fists and demanded they let me pass. Although the eunuchs were not as massive as true men, they were solid muscle beneath their armor, and my tiny fists had no effect on them. They were under the king's orders and, while he had raised me to be his equal, in that moment it was clear that his orders were to be obeyed over mine.

Finally, I sighed and returned to my litter to wait. Daneyah and Kora were permitted to come to me, at least, so I was not alone in my fortress of eunuchs. When I saw them coming, I asked, "Daneyah, Kora, do you know what is happening?"

"Aharon is with the king," Kora reported. She, too, had been riding in a litter but looked exhausted and was still heavy with child. Observing her, I wondered if she should not have remained at Megiddu, but she had insisted on coming. She had another month or two before her child was due and was insistent not to be confined to her bed. I was not about to be a hypocrite by demanding she stay behind.

"And the Lord Steward?"

"*Abarakkum* Obadyah is also with them," she confirmed.

"They have gone to see those men," said Daneyah.

"Could you see them? How close are they? How many are there?"

She shook her head. "There was only the messenger, brought to the king by his scouts after speaking with the Lord Steward. I could not see anything more."

"He should have let me go with him."

"That would not have been wise, Yezeba'al," countered Daneyah.

I sighed heavily. "You sound like my husband."

"He is wise to protect you."

"I do not need protection."

"Oh, then I suppose we can send these eunuchs away? Shall I give the command?"

I pursed my lips and crossed my arms over my chest. "I do not appreciate your tone, Daneyah. I am not a child – I am your Queen."

"Forgive me, Ba'alah, but when you are acting like a petulant child, I will speak to you as such." I gasped, as she continued, "You have no armor, no weapons, no training in battle – if these men intend to start a war against the king while he is on the road, the last place you need to be is at his side."

I huffed, but this time said nothing. She was right, but I was not about to admit it.

"Do not worry, Yezeba'al. The king will return to you."

It seemed like an hour passed before the shofars sounded again. There were different ways the shofars and horns were blown, which communicated different messages to those who were aware of their meaning. This time, they announced the king's return.

Kora placed a hand on my shoulder and smiled, while I gave a sigh of relief. I got up from my litter as my eunuchs began to relax their guard now that the danger was past, and then I saw my husband. He came straight to me, removing his helmet, and I ran to throw my arms around his neck. I did not even care that he was covered in sweat. He was about to speak, but I was so overjoyed at seeing him that I pressed my lips to his mouth, taking him by surprise. He placed his hands on my waist and relaxed into the kiss.

When I pulled away, I said, "Akhab, I was worried sick."

"I am all right, my love," he answered, touching my cheek.

"What happened? It is safe – the men are gone?"

"Yes, it is safe and yes, they are gone."

"Who were they? What did they want? And how did you make them leave?"

He took my hand and I walked with him to the shade of a tree, where some of the other men had gathered to escape the heat of the glaring sun. "They were landowners and farmers, mostly."

"Landowners? You said they were armed."

He gave a nod. "They were armed, yes. And they had hired mercenaries among them."

"What did they want?" I was too confused to be outraged.

"They knew we were on the road to Shomron, so they came to speak with me. They were angry about the drought and blamed me for not following Yahowah." I scoffed, while he continued, "but they were easily assuaged when I offered to pay them for their losses. They went away, satisfied."

"That is not the way that things are done!" Now, I was outraged. "They should have come to court to request an audience, not confront you on the road with armed men!"

He nodded again and gently took my arms, glancing around at the others who were watching and listening. "I agree. But there they were and there were enough of them that it would have been unwise not to listen."

"You should have rebuked them," I said bitterly, crossing my arms over my chest. "They had no right to confront you like that."

"What else was I to do? Go to war with them?"

"If I had been there..." I stopped when I saw the way he was smiling at me now. "What? You find this amusing, Akhab?"

"No, my love. Only I am certain that leaving you behind was the best course of action, or you might have provoked them to war by your stance."

"Sometimes men need a firm stance, or they will walk all over you. Do you truly believe paying them to go away will solve the issue of their disobedience? Now that you have given them something, they will come back to demand more when they are no longer satisfied."

"And if that comes to pass, I will deal with them then, but for now my priority was in protecting you." He took me by the chin and drew me into a kiss. I wanted to be angry, but I could not argue with that, and I softened to the gentle sweetness of his lips.

When the kiss ended, my eyes filled with tears, and I searched his gaze. "Was this not a rebellion?"

He chuckled. "No, my love. It was a show. If it had been a true rebellion, they would not have bothered to talk – they would simply have attacked us. But they did not, which is why I knew if I gave them recompense, they would go away and we could continue our journey without incident." He touched the tip of my nose, but I turned my face away. Then he smiled and pulled me into an embrace.

200

"Keeping you safe is worth all the riches in the world. I would sell my soul to protect you."

"Do not say things like that."

"I love you, Yezeba'al, my Queen."

I looked away, annoyed that he had me where he wanted me. "I love you, Akhab." Then I turned to him and tapped him on the chest. "But I am still angry with you."

Now, he laughed aloud. Then he said, "We must regroup and continue our journey. That set us back quite a lot and we must make it to Shomron before dusk."

I returned to my litter as the rest of our entourage reassembled, but I was still troubled by what had happened. It seemed a small enough matter, as far as Akhab was concerned – not a true rebellion, and easily dismissed. But I knew that they would not be satisfied for long, and I sensed it was only the beginning of a far greater problem. As we carried on and I looked to the cloudless sky, I prayed that I was wrong.

Despite our successes with the Ba'alim feasts and the rise in converts to our religion, that incident on the road made it clear that the kingdom was beginning to feel the effects of the drought. Throughout all the rainy season of that first year since the Tishbite's curse, it had only rained once, and many crops had failed. The following year was even more dismal, however, for there was no rain at all. My son and daughter learned to take their first steps upon dry, cracked earth in a garden that had once been green and lush. After two years of drought, my peafowl began to suffer immensely. For the first time since I had brought them to that land, more of them died off than were born. They were not desert creatures, so they were especially weak to these conditions.

I supposed Nabot was pleased to have fewer of my peafowl eating of his grapes, but then there were fewer grapes for them to eat. That only made him more irate when the few who remained came into his vineyard. But soon, they began disappearing, and when one of the nobles of the city made a complaint about Nabot, the report included an incident where Nabot had tried to cheat the man on an order of wine for his party by replacing some of the vessels with the freshly slaughtered carcass of a very large bird that he said was more valuable and would more than make up for it.

When Akhab showed me the report, I was shocked. An investigation uncovered other similar incidents, many of which had gone unreported because the people in question accepted the trade without complaint. Others had purchased the meat from Nabot's servants, after being told of its rare value, but had been unaware that they were serving the Queen's peafowl at their tables. They insisted they would never have bought the carcasses had they known, but it seemed unlikely as the people of Yisrael were incredibly conscious of everything they ate and drank, and where it came from. We did not hold it against the people who purchased the meat: they were not to be blamed for Nabot's guilt.

Once these reports came through, we sent men to search Nabot's property and interview his servants. This infuriated him, but there was nothing he could do. Traps were found in his vineyard, positioned near the wall that bordered our garden, and one of the men even found a bloodied fragment of a peacock's feather in the place where animals were slaughtered for their meat by his servants. I was devastated and wept bitterly, demanding Nabot be brought before us to answer for the slaughter and unlawful sale of our animals. Having proof of his crime, he was summoned to our court the next day, and he came to us with his usual sanctimonious airs.

When he appeared, the king and I were seated in our thrones, and the Lord Steward pronounced the charge: "Lord Nabot, you have been accused of stealing and slaughtering the Queen's peafowl and selling them for profit."

"They were on my land, Melekh. They spend more time in my vineyard, *stealing from me*, than they do in the Queen's garden."

Suddenly, the king's voice rose from beside me, deep and strong; it echoed through the vast chamber, causing many of the people to startle, including myself. "Animals are not capable of committing theft! But as the animals were the property of the Queen, you have committed theft against her! How do you answer to that charge?"

"By law, women may not own property, Melekh."

My husband tensed his jaw, as he reconsidered. "Very well, then you have stolen from me, for what is the Queen's is also mine. How do you answer to that?"

202

"They are not oxen or sheep, Melekh. The law does not speak for them, because they are not of this land. They are not worthy animals."

"It does not matter what you think of the peafowl – you had no right to take them and end their lives! And even less right to sell them for profit!"

"While the people of your kingdom go hungry for lack of grain, you are concerned for the lives of some birds you keep for the Queen's pleasure? They serve no purpose in your garden! They do nothing but steal my grapes, and now there are so few for them even to steal! While the Queen weeps over some pretty birds, I am struggling to pay my workers fair wages, so that they can feed their families! So, yes, I sold them, but it was not for profit: it was to pay my workers. I kept not one shekel for myself."

I observed the finely embroidered clothes he always wore. They were nearly as rich as the king's and were today even decorated by some of the feathers of my own peacocks, no doubt with the intent to further provoke me. Unwilling to give him the satisfaction, I kept my voice calm when I said, "Perhaps if you sacrificed some of your own luxuries, you would be able to pay them better."

"My luxuries? Some of my best plants have begun to shrivel, their grapes withered on the vine and their vines turned to dust! I have had to rely on the grapes from my lesser vines to make any profit, but they are less sweet and do not bring in the same profit. They are not enough to make up for what I have lost these past two seasons. I have sacrificed a great deal already! So yes, I killed some useless birds – and I used them to pay some of the workers for their families to eat. I am not ashamed of it. Charge me for them, I do not care. I would do it again."

"We have all made sacrifices," said Akhab. "We are aware of the suffering of our people, and we have given much from our own coffers and granaries to alleviate their suffering. Regardless, Nabot, instead of seeking recompense for your losses, you have broken the laws of this realm concerning the theft of property. As such, you will be charged according to the law once the value of the property has been determined."

Although the theft of peafowl was not covered under the laws of Moshe, their worth was determined by their value as an exotic luxury animal. Our Minister of Trade could attest to their value because he was responsible for procuring more peafowl from Opir every year or two, so that the flocks would not become weakened by inbreeding. Their value alive turned out to be more than Nabot had charged for their meat, so that was the value we attached to them for his fine. The greedy landowner was fuming when he left the court, bearing the weight of his penalty, but I felt little satisfaction in the matter. Already, there had been so many problems because of the drought. If it continued much longer, I feared we would have more than just my peafowl to worry about.

Eventually, even some of Akhab's own uncles and brothers, who owned estates throughout the kingdom, came to our court to express fears about the coming planting season. They were led by Akhazyah, after whom our son was named, although he was known to the family as Akhaz. He had been one of the earliest to convert, but now he was starting to doubt his conversion, asking, "What if the curse of Yahowah is true? What if he is punishing us for putting our faith in other gods, against his command?"

While the king had his own misgivings, which he communicated to me when we were alone in our chamber, he publicly maintained an air of confidence. "Two seasons of drought may be followed by several seasons of abundance. Drought comes and goes – it is nothing new here, for there have been draughts in every generation. We must not let fear take hold in our hearts, Akhaz."

"It is not about fear, Akhab! It is what has already happened – ever since you turned to the Ba'alim and urged the rest of us to follow you, the rains have not come! It was bad enough the year before, and now, after your latest building project, it has only gotten worse!"

He was referring to an obelisk the king had commissioned, which was erected at Yezreel, in the square overlooking the market. In the Egyptian manner, it was carved on all sides with writing and glyphs that told the story of the love between Ashtarti and Melkorat, and of their reincarnation and reunion through me and Akhab. It was a beautiful gift to me, to commemorate the birth of our twins. Those who worshipped like us welcomed its addition and often went to the obelisk to touch it in the hope it might heal or bless them. The people of Yezreel left offerings to the Ba'alim all around the obelisk when they could not travel to Megiddu or Shomron to make their offerings at the temples there.

204

Akhaz himself had once appreciated the obelisk, but now his faith had also been shaken by fear. "If it is not true that Yahowah is the only god, why have the rains stopped?"

"Yahowah is a storm god," said Akhab. "His command over the weather does not make him the *only* god."

Akhab's uncle Amar, who had never converted to our religion, spoke up now in scorn: "Your Ba'al is also a storm god, so why can he not simply make the rains come?"

Akhab sighed heavily and pinched the bridge of his nose between his eyes. Keeping his tone steady, he explained as he had so many times before, "The storm gods are at war over our kingdom. Until the war is over, the rains will not come."

"Yes, and who started that war?" said Amar. "And for what?"

Akhab's voice resonated through the chamber. "Yahowah started this war when he refused to let us seek the aid of other gods for things he cannot help us with! Is it a coincidence that the moment I turned to the god of fertility that the heir I longed for was provided? And not just a son, but a daughter also, both at the same time – proof of the superiority of the Ba'alim to Yahowah in these things. He may be able to command the rains, but he could not give us the children we desired."

Jumping in, Akhaz argued, "Your conversion resulted in the births of the Queen's son and daughter, yes, but at what cost to the kingdom, Akhab? Should the rest of the kingdom suffer this drought, just so one woman could have children that your other wives were capable of bearing?"

"You dare," my husband began to raise his voice in anger, but I calmly cut him off from my seat beside his throne.

"Yahowah has a hold over our kingdom only because his followers have allowed him to reign here for so long and keep the Ba'alim out. Once the Ba'alim have been firmly reestablished here, by the continued increase of faith, the rains will come again. It is only a matter of time."

Amar, who disliked me intensely, scoffed. "Are you also now a prophetess, Melkah?"

"She is High Priestess of the Ba'alim and Ashtarti incarnate," my husband snapped, "not a mere prophetess. You should refer to her as Ba'alah."

"I do not worship your Ba'alim," said Amar. Then he spit on the floor. I sighed and laid my head back, while he continued, "And I will certainly not worship your wife."

Akhaz said, "Enough, *Abakhu* Amar. We all know you are faithful to Yahowah. You need not continue reminding us."

"Then tell your brother the king not to command me to worship his wife and give her the title of her foreign gods!"

"Forgive him, *akhu*," Akhaz said to the king, who offered an impatient wave. Then Akhaz turned to me, and asked, "You see rain for us, then, Ba'alah?"

"When Yahowah has been purged from this kingdom and no longer has power here, the war between storm gods will end and the rains will return. It is a certainty. But until the zealots have been eliminated, we will continue to suffer this drought. Therefore, if you know of the whereabouts of any zealous prophets of Yahowah in this kingdom, be sure to make it known to us and you will be handsomely rewarded for your service, *Akhimelekh*."

While Amar continued to glare at me, Akhaz smiled graciously and thanked me. At last appeased, they were escorted out so the next audience could be ushered in. While this exchange took place, my husband looked to me and reached for my hand. Taking his, I smiled, and he brought mine to his lips. "You are the greatest queen Yisrael has ever known, my beloved Ba'alah."

"Only because you have permitted me to stand beside you, my Ba'al."

"Only because you have the mind for it."

"Even so, how many kings would be courageous enough to give away a portion of their power to their queens?"

"Perhaps if more queens were like you, more kings would allow them to do the same."

I scoffed. "I do not think that is true, because few kings have the ability to humble themselves before their equals, particularly those of us that are women – in this kingdom especially. You are the exception."

He looked to the entryway, where Aharon was speaking with those waiting to be our next audience. Sighing, he then pressed my hand to his lips once more before releasing it, and asked, "Do you believe the rains will return with the next Feast of Ba'al?"

"I hope they will, my love," I replied. "But I fear that as long as Yahowah still holds our kingdom in his clutches, it will not be possible. If we want the rains to return, he must either be appeased, removed from power, or taught to play well with the other gods."

Akhab sniffed, and a bitter smile formed upon his lips. "You know that for him, there is no compromise: he will not be appeased unless all followers of the Ba'alim are eliminated and the kingdom closed to all outside influences."

"He may be a god, but he understands nothing about what it takes to maintain a kingdom, and even less about the way of diplomacy."

"No, I think he understands it, my love; he simply refuses to follow it, as other gods have done before him. If he cannot have this kingdom for himself alone, he will stop at nothing to destroy it."

I tipped my head. "Then he must be eliminated."

My husband sighed, the weight of kingship heavy upon him. "Then we must continue to pray that more of his zealous prophets be revealed and brought to justice by the time of our next feast, so the people do not all lose faith."

I gave a single nod and turned forward, worrying that he had also begun to lose faith in the Ba'alim. If the rains did not return soon, though, it would not matter how many children I could bear for the king, because there would be nothing left of the kingdom for them to inherit.

By the end of summer, plans for the Feast of Ba'al were well underway, and the people were eager for his awakening in the hope that it would bring the rains. Despite my certainty that it would only come to pass when Yahowah was expunged from our kingdom, I carried out my rituals and made offerings to the Ba'alim, believing they were our only hope. They had brought us our children, which they could do without interference from Yahowah, but because Ba'al Melkorat was also a storm god, his presence in Yisrael was a threat to Yahowah's dominance in a way none of the other gods had been before. It had become clear by now that we were, indeed, caught in the midst of a great war between two powerful storm gods, vying for control over our kingdom.

207

Even with fewer of Yahowah's prophets wandering the kingdom, by the third year of drought there were several small uprisings, and the king was constantly sending men to put them down. Once or twice, they grew so bad that he had to take his own contingent of charioteers to put them down himself, which he hated to do because he did not wish to go to war against his own people. The landowners who had stopped us on the road two years previously were among them. This time, because they rebelled, their lands were forfeited to the king, so the payment he had initially given them was returned in greater sum. Their vineyards and estates would continue to prosper for us if the drought did not last long enough to permanently destroy the worth of the confiscated lands.

After putting down a rebellion nearby, by the time he returned to Yezreel Akhab was beside himself with worry. Within days of his return, he lost several of his horses, and many more were starting to show signs of starvation, as the water from the spring that nourished their grazing lands had dried up. "This drought is draining the life out of us," he lamented. "We cannot go on like this forever."

"The channels in the gardens have ceased flowing entirely," I reported. "It is terrible, not having the water to cool ourselves in the evening. The children have missed playing in it."

"It is even worse in the city. The people need to travel further and further to get water just to cook and clean, as the spring that feeds the channels and cisterns is unable to produce enough for their needs. It is not simply an inconvenience for them – it is a matter of life and death. But there is more. I want you to see just how bad it has become."

He took me out in a chariot, drawn by one of the horses that was still strong enough to pull it, and showed me the stream where we often went to make love. Due to the excessive heat, my preoccupation with the twins, another miscarriage, and now my latest pregnancy, we had not gone out to the stream in well over a year. I was shocked to see how the once broad stream was now barely a trickle. The grasses and wildflowers that once surrounded it were gone, and the trees had all withered.

"Everything in the land is dying. We must do something. If I lose all my horses, I lose more than half my army. We cannot drive chariots without horses."

I placed a hand on his shoulder. "Do not lose faith, Akhab. The Ba'alim are with us."

"They helped us with our children, but they cannot help us in this!" The suddenness of his outburst caused me to jump, and I clutched the bump in my abdomen protectively. He quickly realized himself and took a deep breath to calm his anger before he continued. "We need help, my love, but we will not find it with the rivals of Yahowah." He put both his hands on my abdomen. "The Ba'alim have been good to us, and I will not abandon them, but Yahowah is too powerful here. We must do whatever it takes to preserve our kingdom."

"What can we do?"

"We must find water somewhere," he answered, scanning the horizon. "It cannot be like this everywhere."

He took up the reins again, and I braced myself against the body of the chariot. Seeing that I was secure, he flicked the reins, and we started back toward the stables at the palace. Leaving the horse and chariot in the hands of the stable master, we went into the palace where the king summoned Obadyah and Aharon to his study. While they devised a plan to find water and grass for the horses and mules to graze, I stood looking out through the cedar screen and watching a vulture circle over the city. Down in the streets, a pack of dogs was in the process of tearing apart a dead cat. The vultures and the dogs had plenty to eat, with more animals dying of thirst and hunger.

I shuddered and turned away from the window, as my husband was saying, "I know you have another child, Aharon, and your wife will not be pleased to have you leave her so soon after his birth, but we are in grave need of whatever help we can get."

I came to stand by my husband and leaned against the side of his desk, where he sat. He slipped his arm around me and rested his hand over my abdomen. I placed my hand over his and smiled faintly when the child kicked. Akhab pressed his fingers more firmly into my belly to acknowledge the movement, as he continued, "Our animals are suffering now, but soon it will be our children who will suffer."

Aharon bowed in understanding. "Yes, Melekh. Of course, my wife will understand the need for us to go."

"I will explain to her, if she gives you any trouble," I offered.

He bowed his head. "Thank you, Melkah. Kora respects you greatly and will listen to anything you say. Even her mother has commented that she will sooner take her advice when it comes through you than when it comes directly from her."

I chuckled and gave him a nod, "That sounds like Kora, indeed."

Aharon bowed, and the king said, "Go. Take the rest of the day to tend to your families. Meet me at the stables in the morning. We shall depart at dawn."

Aharon and Obadyah backed out of the chamber with the customary bows, and then I turned to my husband and playfully tussled his curls. "Will you come to me at Megiddu when you are done searching for water?"

"Are you moving there while I am gone, wife?"

I gave a nod and rubbed my belly. "It is time for me to make my way there in preparation for the birth."

"You still have two months, do you not?"

"Yes, but this is the time when most women are made to lie in waiting, in their beds. I will not be an invalid, but I must be at Megiddu soon, for with each passing week it becomes more difficult to travel in this condition."

"Then I shall come to you at Megiddu, wife," he said with affection in his gaze, while he brought my hand to his lips. "You will have Kora with you?"

I nodded. "She is eager for my return. She hates being laid up, unable to work. Be sure to bring her husband when you come."

"He would come even if I did not give the command. I know he is eager to return to his wife and children. He talks of them constantly! Although, in that, I am certain we have much in common, for you are ever on my mind."

"I am grateful to Aharon for his love of my dearest friend and companion. That she can enjoy the same happiness that I have with you brings me much satisfaction."

Akhab hummed in agreement. "It is a shame we cannot convince Aharon to follow the Ba'alim, even with his mother-in-law being a priestess of Ashtarti."

"He is a loyal man, Akhab," I replied, slipping my arm around his shoulder. "His loyalty to Yahowah cannot be held against him as long as it does not compromise his loyalty to you."

"He is a good man. I have much respect for him. He will make a good replacement for Obadyah one day." Then he turned to me and

210

pressed his lips to my belly. "And you are a good woman, to bear no ill will for those not following your gods."

"Our gods, remember?"

"Ah, yes. Forgive me. I only mean…"

"I know what you mean, Akhab." I took his face in my hands and slid my fingers into his hair, disrupting the crown that rested over his temples. He lifted the crown off and set it on his desk, and then he tugged at the ends of my sash to pull me to him. I climbed onto his lap, straddling him, and pressed my forehead to his. We kissed, and then I met his gaze sadly. "I will miss you when you go. You only just returned."

"I know, my love. But you understand why we must leave."

"Yes, I understand, but that does not mean I will not yearn for you every moment you are away."

Growling, he clung to me, and asked, "Is it wrong for me to want to make love to you when the court is waiting for us to open it?"

"They can wait for a short interlude while I make love to you," I said with a grin, pulling at his tunic.

The next morning, Akhab and his two most-trusted stewards set out in search of water and a new grazing ground, all three of them going separate ways. Akhab and Aharon both took a small contingent of soldiers and bodyguards to protect them on their way, but Obadyah insisted he would travel alone, claiming he did not wish to draw attention to himself as an agent of the king. I withheld my suspicions.

When the men were gone, I returned to our palace at Megiddu where I was pleased to be reunited with my children, who were now two years of age. Once I was settled in, I took Atalaya and Akhazyah to visit Kora and her children. Her daughter Ruta was only a couple months younger than my two, and she had a one-month-old son called Shmuel. While Kora sat on the floor with the three older children, I sat in a chair holding Shmuel and cooing at him.

Suddenly aware that my attentions were diverted from her, Atalaya got up and came to show me the toy horse she had just taken from her brother's hand. "Look, *Ama*."

"Yes, I see," I answered. "What is that called, Tala?"

"A horse."

211

"Very good," I replied. "Now, you should give that horse back to your brother, because it was wrong of you to take it from him."

Furrowing her brow, she clutched it to her chest, and said, "No! Mine!"

Akhazyah got up then and toddled over, apparently deciding to take matters into his own hands. He offered her a toy ox in exchange, but she shook her head defiantly. Finally losing his patience, Akhazyah dropped the ox and tried to take the horse from his sister, latching onto it with both hands, but she clung to it fiercely and bit him.

"Atalaya!" I handed Shmuel to his mother, and then took my daughter's arm and slapped her hand. She began crying and fussing and trying to pull away, as I scolded, "You do not bite people! Especially when you are in the wrong! Now, give me the horse."

"No!" she growled in rage and hurled the toy horse across the chamber. Then as Akhazyah ran to retrieve it, she ran to Kora and hid behind her, sticking her tongue out at me. I stood with my hands on my hips, shaking my head and trying not to smile at her antics. "You better hope *Rebitya* Sabanba'al does not see you behaving in this way," I said of my daughter's nursemaid. "She would not tolerate it."

"Perhaps neither should you," Kora suggested with a smirk.

Now, my smile broke free and I sat on the chair again. That's when Atalaya came to throw her arms around my waist in apology, and I gently moved some hair from her forehead. "I cannot be too hard on her – she is my daughter, after all."

"She takes after you, that is for certain."

"Too much, I fear," I said with a laugh. I pulled my daughter into an embrace and kissed her cheek, which she accepted reluctantly. Then I released her, and she ran off to play. "Zyah is tough, though. He will only let her push him around so much before he stands up for himself. You should see the quarrels they get into in the nursery!"

"I have heard. My mother has told me. The last time she was there with you, she said they were on the floor, grappling like animals!"

"It is true. It took three of the nursery staff to pry them apart! I could not believe it. Although, that time it was Zyah who started it. He picks on her, too. I am not certain which of them is worse, but

212

their quarrels never last long, at any rate. They may fight like jackals from time to time, but they adore each other."

I indicated with my hand to where they were on the floor, playing again as if nothing had happened. Now, Akhazyah offered the horse to his sister willingly, but she decided she no longer wanted it, so it was left on the floor while they played with some of the other animals from the wooden ark that was a favorite in the nursery.

Thinking about the story of the great flood, I said, "We could use a portion of the water from that flood. Too much rain then, and now not enough. Yahowah is a temperamental god."

"As storm gods typically are," Kora laughed. Shmuel began to fuss, so she brought him to her breast to placate him and sighed. "Do not worry, Yezeba'al. The men will find water and grass for the animals, and soon the rains will come again. This drought cannot last forever."

I nodded in agreement. "I am sorry we had to take your husband from you."

"It is all right. It cannot be helped."

"How are things between you?"

"We are well, thank you," she answered. Then she said to Ruta, who had come to offer her a toy, "No, thank you. Go and play with the prince and princess."

"You should have accepted it," I said as I watched Ruta toddle away in disappointment. "It was a gift."

"I never thought of it that way. Hmm. Next time."

"Speaking of gifts...Akhab and I were thinking of something we could do to honor you and your husband's loyalty toward us."

"You have already given us so much more than we could ever ask for, Yezeba'al."

"Nonsense," I said, shaking my head. "I thought it should be something different. Would you and your husband ever accept an invitation to dine with me and the king?"

Her brow raised. "You mean, privately? Not at court with all the others?"

I answered with a nod.

"I...do not know. I mean, I would love to but...Ahru is terrified of you."

"Truly?" I admit, I was slightly amused.

213

She gave a nod. "The only thing he fears more than you and the king is his god – and maybe Obadyah."

I rolled my eyes and shook my head. "Yahwists. I do not understand how anyone can worship a god they must always be afraid of. I much prefer our gods – they are so much kinder and more forgiving."

"I think he is afraid *not* to worship Yahowah."

"He could worship this table for all I care, as long as he is loyal to us. He serves Akhab well, and we both agree he will make a suitable replacement for Obadyah one day." She smiled, perhaps thinking of the added benefits she would receive as wife of the Lord Steward, while I continued, "Sometimes, I wonder how we ever got by without him – even if he does lack a sense of humor."

She chuckled. "He may not find humor in things the way we do, Yezeba'al, but he knows how to have a good time." When I looked at her incredulously, she giggled, and said, "Just not in a way that you would understand."

I snorted. "I shall have to take you at your word, Kora, for I cannot imagine it. He is all work, all the time – even when Akhab has offered him a day off that was not the Shabbat, he has refused to take it. The man would work himself to death if not for the Shabbat – I am glad my husband has decided to keep observing that tradition."

"I suppose that is why Yahowah commands it of his followers – to keep them from doing that." She sighed. "Ahru does like to be useful."

"He must see me as an immoral woman."

"Not immoral," she insisted. "Simply...misguided."

I raised my brow. "He has said this?"

She hummed thoughtfully, "More like...implied it. He does not like some of the rituals we perform in our worship, for example, but he sees it as a product of our birthplace and our upbringing rather than a flaw in our being. He does not condemn us, though – not like those hateful zealots. I do not think he would have married me if he did."

"I am surprised he has not tried to convert you to his way of seeing things."

"Oh, he does," she laughed. "But I think... Sometimes, I think he pities us. That is why I say he sees us as misguided."

"It is still hard to believe you are married to him," I mused. I would have said more but was caught off-guard by my unborn child suddenly shifting around and wreaking havoc on my insides. I inhaled deeply and placed a hand over my abdomen.

"Are you all right, Yezeba'al?" asked Kora. "Can I get you a drink?"

"No, I am fine, Kora. Thank you." When the child finally settled in, I sighed in relief. Then I asked, "Will you come to dine with us at court tonight? Your mother will be there, and she would love to see you."

"No, I do not think I will. If she wants to see me, she can come to my house any time. It is not far for her to walk." Her tongue dripped with acid, which surprised me.

"Is everything all right between you?"

"She has not come to see her grandchildren in two weeks. Always, she says she is too busy to come, but I know you do not have her working so hard and her duties at the temple are minimal."

"Hmm. She has been...otherwise occupied. I think it is the new woman she is seeing."

"A new woman? What about your mother – I thought they were devoted to one another."

"Another priestess from the temple," I explained. "She never sees my mother – they have agreed it is only right for them to release each other from their bond, so they may spend time with other women."

"It seems fickle."

I shrugged. "They maintained their devotion for years, but it is difficult under the circumstances, and I can understand their decision. Daneyah was hesitant, at first, but this new woman has potential and I believe they are truly in love. Can you blame her for falling in love with a woman she is able to see every day? To seek comfort in her presence?"

"No, I suppose not. It is only that...she has not told me about any of this. Of course, she never tells me anything. I think she is angry that I married Ahru – she has not been the same toward me since."

"I know she does not like that he is a follower of Yahowah, but I do not believe she holds it against either of you in any way. She is quite fond of him, from what I have seen."

"Well, she is kind to his face, yes," she agreed, "but I think she secretly hates him and wishes that I had not married him."

"She has never said such a thing to me, Kora. She is simply preoccupied. You know your mother as well as I do."

"You know her better, apparently."

"Come, Kora."

"No, Yezeba'al – it is true. She favors you. She always has. I do not hold it against you, of course. It is not your fault she is this way – the fault is entirely her own."

"You are too hard on her," I said.

"She has always been hard on me, so I suppose now we are even."

I sighed and looked down at the floor. Akhazyah came to me, seeming to sense I was upset and wishing to comfort me. "Ama sad?"

"No, Zyah, Ama is not sad. Ama is happy that you are here. You are always so good to your Ama." I lifted him onto my lap and brushed his soft curls away from his cheek, to kiss him there. Then I looked at Kora. "You will not come?"

"What is the occasion?"

"No occasion – only a feast for my friends, of which you are one."

"Most of your friends are priests and priestesses, and I am not a priestess."

"No, but you are my friend, and the one I love most. That is why you are my most trusted handmaid. Who else could put up with me, anyway?"

She looked at me from the side and I could see she was hiding a smile. "Well, you know how I feel about parties. I have never been one to shine. I prefer smaller, more intimate feasts."

"All right, but if you change your mind, you are always welcome. And I still want you and your husband to consider dining with me and Akhab sometime."

"Thank you, Yezeba'al. I appreciate the offer. Of course, we will dine with you; just not tonight."

I nodded in understanding and rose, holding Akhazyah at my side, one of his legs resting over my bulging abdomen. He clung to me, his little fingers twisting around my mantle and rubbing the soft fabric as he brought it to his mouth. I ran my fingers through his

216

thick, dark curls, and said to Kora, "Well, I shall leave you to rest. I must return the children to the nursery and prepare for the feast."

"Are you sure you do not need me to come and help you prepare?"

"Yes, I am sure. You are still on leave, until you are fully recovered."

"Which will be when? I am fine, Yezeba'al."

"Which will be when the bleeding stops, and you are not exhausted from small tasks."

"You and my mother both treat me as if I am fragile."

I touched her forehead, tucking a loose curl beneath her mantle. "You nearly died this last time, Kora. You are not fragile, but we are concerned for you. Until you get your strength back, you will not return to the palace for work."

"Do you miss me, at least?"

"Of course," I said with a laugh, taking Atalaya by the hand and leading her toward the doorway. "The other handmaidens are nothing compared to you. I am starting to rethink allowing the daughters of noblemen serve me – they cannot do anything right. They do not understand my ways, like you and my priestesses do."

She smiled. "All right, then I am satisfied. I look forward to returning to you."

"As do I. Take care of yourself, Kora. I will return tomorrow for another visit. Shalom."

"Shalom, shalom," she replied, waving to the children as we departed.

The feast at the palace was well underway when the doors opened and the king strode in, followed closely by Obadyah, Aharon, and some of his men. Daneyah was seated on cushions with her lover, who was singing a bawdy tune and playing on the lute, while Anniba'al and another priest were in a corner, making love to one of the priestesses of Ashtarti. Ignoring them, I perched on the edge of the table, joking with a few of the other priests and priestesses, who were passing around a smoking bowl of qaneh-bosem. Being with child, I was not taking the bowl and smoking directly, but I enjoyed breathing in the fumes that swirled around me, nonetheless.

When the king entered, the others stopped what they were doing and prostrated themselves. Even Anniba'al and his lovers paused from their lovemaking to pay homage, although I am certain they were not pleased to be so interrupted.

The moment I saw my husband I got up and ran to greet him with an embrace. We kissed, but when I pulled away, I saw the grave look upon his face. "Akhab? What is it?"

Speaking quietly so no one would overhear, he said, "Eliyah the troublemaker has reappeared."

"Truly? And have you arrested him? Is it finally over?"

He shook his head. "No, my love." He paused and turned to the assemblage. "You may rise and resume the feast." Everyone seemed relieved to continue where they left off while I followed my husband.

Upon reaching his study, Akhab gestured for Obadyah, Aharon, and his men to stay outside. Then he closed the door and drew me toward his desk, speaking in a hushed tone, "The Tishbite came upon Obadyah on the road and bade him to speak to me. He did not come to me to start trouble."

"When has he not started trouble? The man is a nuisance. How did he know where to find you?"

"Obadyah led me to him – in great fear for his life, mind you."

"Was he threatened by the madman?"

He shook his head. "Not afraid of Eliyah – afraid of me."

"Why would he fear you?"

"He was afraid I would think that he knew of Eliyah's whereabouts all this time, but of course he would never betray me in such a way."

"Would he not?"

He was about to speak but stopped suddenly and ran his fingers through his hair. Then he closed his eyes and inhaled deeply. It was clear that he had already considered it. "Yezeba'al, I know you have never liked or trusted him, but Obadyah is an honest man. He and his father both served my father before me."

"I am only saying that perhaps you should consider it." He sighed heavily, while I continued, "We know someone from inside our household has helped the Tishbite before. *Someone* helped him and his followers escape the night when he came to our feast. *Someone* alerted the zealots before the law against them was passed, that they

218

might flee or go into hiding. Somehow, the Tishbite and his followers always seem to be one step ahead of us. The only person in our court who is connected to each of these incidents – the only one for certain who has the knowledge and position to get away with it – is your Obadyah."

"Yes, I know all this, and I have considered it. But if that is the case, I will deal with him later. At present, the most important issue is the lack of water in our kingdom, and the Tishbite offers a solution."

"Yes, I am certain I know his solution: he will lift the curse when you cast me aside and abandon our gods in favor of Yahowah alone."

"That is not his solution."

"Of course, it is. If there is one thing every zealot has in common, it is that they are intolerant of the worship of other gods. They will fight anyone to the death for it. I cannot believe you did not arrest him."

"You know I was not pleased to speak with the Tishbite after the last time we saw him, Yezeba'al, but he swore that he came in peace and goodwill. I cannot arrest him for asking to speak with me."

"Is there a limit on sedition? He always asks to speak with you, Akhab, and you always permit him. You should have cut him down right there, for all the trouble he has caused us. You are too soft on him. You have always been."

"He was very dear to me once, a long time ago..."

"I know, you have told me how he was a teacher and mentor to you when you were a boy. But, my love, he is not the same man he was then. Even you have said how he has changed since he joined the zealots: gone mad. Why do you humor him like this?"

"You said we should not make a martyr of him, Yezeba'al. I only wanted him arrested and imprisoned, not executed."

"Then why have you not arrested him? Where is he now? Free to roam about our kingdom, causing trouble and turning our people against us? Is it he who has been the harbinger of all the rebellions you have had to put down in recent months? Surely, there is no other zealous prophet of Yahowah left in our kingdom after the rest have been uncovered."

He shook his head. "No, for he left our kingdom until he was commanded to return to speak with me."

219

"Commanded by whom?"

After hesitating, he answered, "Yahowah."

I rolled my eyes and scoffed.

"He was, believe it or not, hiding in Tzidon, your father's kingdom."

"Why would he go there? He hates my father's people as much as he loves his Yahowah."

"He does not hate them. He hates your gods, perhaps, because he does not believe in them. But more than anything, he hates those of my people who turn to the Ba'alim when he believes we should remain faithful to our covenant with Yahowah."

"*Your* covenant?"

"My people's covenant," he answered, turning away from me. "You know I do not agree with it, Yezeba'al, but I am of the people of the covenant. They are my people, and I am one of them, even if I do not believe as they do."

"I am not so certain of that." I turned to gaze out the window, observing the lanterns of a caravan moving toward the city. It was strange that they should travel in the dark of night, but they must have thought it prudent, as they were close, although they would not be permitted within the walls until the gates were opened again at dawn. They would have to camp outside, with all the other latecomers.

Akhab came to stand behind me, and he slipped his hands around my waist, holding my belly as I leaned back against him. "You know I am faithful to our gods – and to you. Forgive me, Ba'alah, for giving you cause to doubt me." He bent forward to kiss the side of my neck and I nestled my head into his shoulder. I thought he might try to seduce me, but instead he said, "There is more. I never told you his solution: why the Tishbite wanted to meet with me."

I pulled away and turned to face him. "To tell you that you have broken the commandments of Yahowah? That you have gravely sinned by your worship of the Ba'alim? What is new that he has to say? The man is more predictable than the sun."

"He had a proposition for me."

"Why do you let these men dictate to you? You are their king. Dictate to them what they should do, or else cut them down for their disobedience!"

"We need the favor of Yahowah for the rains to return, or else we need to prove to the people once and for all that the Ba'alim are greater. There is no other way."

"Prove they are greater? And how are we to do that? Was the birth of our twins not enough? And the one I now carry, due in less than two months from now? What more proof is there to show that the Ba'alim are greater than Yahowah? He commands the rains, but he could not give us our children. Only the Ba'alim could do that."

"He wants me to gather all the priests and priestesses of the Ba'alim in our kingdom and lead them to a meeting ground on the mountain of Kerem-el, in two weeks' time, on the eve of the full moon."

"What for? What does he want with them?"

"He wants to compete with them before all the people."

"Compete? He is one man alone. How can he possibly compete with all the priests and priestesses of the Ba'alim?"

"They will make offerings and ask for the rains to return. He will do the same for Yahowah. He swears that when it is over, the rains will come again. This is our chance, Yezeba'al – our chance to put an end to this war, once and for all."

"You realize this one man is the reason the war is not over? If you cut him down, the last of the zealots to stand in our kingdom, that will prove that Yahowah is not greater than our gods. The fact that he is the only one left standing is proof enough of the might of the Ba'alim, yet still the people waver. It is their lack of faith – and yours – that keeps this war between the gods in effect."

At this, he slammed his hand upon the surface of his desk, startling me. "Damn it, Yezeba'al, I do not waver in my faith!"

"Do you not? Is it not your lack of faith which permits this madman to remain alive within our kingdom? You had the chance to cut him down and put an end to all his troublemaking, yet you have chosen instead to give him everything he asks for! And for what? What good will this petty competition do? I do not trust this Eliyah, and neither should you."

"It is not for me that I give him what he asks, but for the people, who *do* waver in their faith. If I cut him down, a man for whom they have long had respect, they will not be convinced of anything except our ruthlessness. If they need a show to convince them, then let them have this show. Let this one man have his competition and let him fail before all the people, and then they will see that he is a fraud and they have been misled. And when he cannot have his way, he will either give up and go away, or he will make his last mistake."

I thought about the mountains of Kerem-el, which I had passed through many years ago on my way to be a bride in my husband's kingdom. "Those mountains are dangerous, Akhab. There are many caves and hidden passages for men to hide. What if he has gathered more followers to hide there, to make an ambush against you and start a rebellion? You could be killed! You should go with an army, not with our priests and priestesses."

Akhab shook his head and took me by the arms. "No, my love. He will not harm me. I am the king, anointed by his god. Whatever he feels for me now, he will respect that. It is not in his nature to break the laws of this realm."

"He has broken the laws of this realm by speaking against us."

"He has stopped speaking against us, my love. Remember, he did not lead any of the rebellions."

"He did not need to lead them – his words were enough to strike fear into the hearts of the people. He may be a madman, but he is cunning, and he knows the power his words have over them. Do not tell me he did not know that he was feeding the flames of their rebellions whenever he preached against us and our gods."

"That was in the past, Yezeba'al. Now, he has come only for this competition, so let him have it. Let him be proved wrong."

I sighed, unable to quell the uneasiness I felt over this plan. "All of them? He wants you to bring all the priests and priestesses in this land? It must be in the hundreds. And Daneyah – must she go, too? Must she be among them?"

He gave a nod. "Yes, he is adamant that it must be *all* of them, so he can show all the more that he and his god are greater. It is all nonsense, of course, but it is what he has asked. And Daneyah must certainly be there, for she is well known by him and by many, because you have raised her as your advisor at court. He will know if she is not there."

"This is what makes me uneasy, Akhab. He would not want all of them to come if he did not believe he could win this competition. If, indeed, there is even a true competition to be had. Surely, he must have some plan laid out. He has made the terms; he has chosen the

222

meeting ground. He knows the mountains better than we do – he and his followers know those valleys and caves the way your armies know the field, but this is not the field, Akhab." I shook my head. "Everything about this feels wrong. You have seen what he is capable of, with his trickery and his knowledge of Egyptian magic."

"I will be there with a battalion of soldiers, and many of our people will be there, as well. He would not wish to harm the people, for he will not be able to prove his point if he harms any of them. Neither will he prove anything by harming an anointed king, so you need not worry for my safety. He will have his followers there to witness, no doubt, but he will not make battle against us. How could he, even if he wanted to? He is old, and even with a mass of followers, they would be outnumbered." He paused and lifted my chin to look in my eyes. "Do not be afraid, Yezeba'al. I will return to you, and we will at last be victorious. This war will end, and the rains will come – I am sure of it."

I gave a nod and let him draw me into a kiss, but I was not sure of anything in that moment. All I knew was that this whole arrangement filled me with unease, and that I did not trust Eliyah the Tishbite to act honestly at this game he was playing.

9

Proof of Guilt

By the time Akhab left with Daneyah and his men, Kora had recovered enough to return to her work at the palace. She was indeed eager to return, content to leave her children in the care of their nurse who was better suited for the daily care of infants than she. Kora had not inherited her mother's love of the same. She much preferred her work of commanding the handmaidens, overseeing the care of my robes and jewels, and tending to my needs. It was that which suited her, that for which she was made, as she often said, and so she was there at my side on the day when the rains returned.

It was late afternoon when the heat of the day had finally broken, and the women were outside in the dusty remains of the garden with the king's children. I had a headache and stayed inside where I could rest upon a cushioned long chair, while my children nestled into my arms and kissed me, perhaps thinking that their love alone would cure my ails. I smiled and returned their kisses, assuring them that they were indeed enough, although as the evening approached my headache only continued to grow worse. When Atalaya and Akhazyah began fighting over their place in my arms, their nurses finally came to retrieve them, scolding, "You must let your poor mother rest! How can she feel better with quarreling like this?"

"It is all right," I murmured, although I was relieved to be left to rest on my own.

Kora came to me with a cup of water – a coveted luxury in those days of drought – and bade me to drink. "It will help ease your pain."

"It is not for thirst that my head aches, Kora."

"Still, you need to drink, Yezeba'al."

I was too weak to protest, and besides I knew she was right, so I sat up enough for her to administer the water to me. When I was ready to pull away, she tipped the cup forward and giggled when

224

some of the water spilled over my chin and onto my breast. Had Daneyah been there, she would surely have scolded Kora for wasting water in such a way. I could almost hear her saying it, as if she was there, but I knew she must still be at the mountains with all the other priests and priestesses, if they were not on their way home by now.

Kora set the cup on the table beside my chair and brought a damp cloth to my forehead, placing it over my eyes to shield them from the light. I clutched her hand in thanks as I laid my head back to resume my rest. I listened to the sounds of the king's children at play, the murmur of the women's voices, and the occasional calls of the few remaining peafowl drifting in through the windows from outside the chamber. I could also hear the breeze and was aware when suddenly the wind picked up, coming in through the screens and pulling at the curtains. This was followed by a distant rumbling.

I lifted the cloth from my eyes and raised my head. Kora and the other women also turned to listen. I asked, "Was that thunder?"

We all looked at each other then, almost afraid to speak, lest our awareness of it cause it to dissipate. The voices coming in from outside became more animated, and the peafowl cawed excitedly. Kora came to take the cloth from my hand when I sat up and slid my feet into sandals, rising to go to the doorway and look out. Just as I approached the threshold, the first drops of rain began to fall. My lips parted, as I watched the children spring up and begin shrieking and dancing in the rain, while the women pulled themselves up and joined them. Only a few ran for cover.

When I felt little arms wrap around my legs, I looked down to see Akhazyah clutching me, while Atalaya stood in the doorway peering out. My children had never seen the rain, so they did not know what to think of it. Atalaya looked to me, questions in her gaze. I smiled and gave her a nod to reassure her that it was safe, as her nurse came to scoop her up. "Shall I take her out to see it, Ba'alah?"

I nodded and brought my hand down to my son's cheek, his big brown eyes gazing up at me for reassurance. "It is all right, my love. It is rain. We have needed this rain for so long."

He looked out and tipped his head back, following the trajectory of the rain coming down from the sky, as if he could still not believe what he saw. Even with all the times I had seen rain, after so long without I could barely believe it myself. Finally, I took his hand and, laughing, led him out into the garden. Kora and his nurse

225

followed us, and we all stood together in the rain, letting it drench us. I laughed. We all laughed, in joy and disbelief.

Akhazyah pulled away to go jump in one of the puddles that was forming, and his nurse followed him. I put my arms out and closed my eyes, my head tilted back as the life-giving water poured down on me. And I thought, *Cleanse me, oh gift from the heavens. Cleanse me and let me be worthy.* Then I opened my eyes and looked at Kora who was watching me, and I said, "It is finished. The war is over at last."

She came to place her hand in mine, and we stood together holding hands and laughing in the rain, as we had done many times when we were children. Then the sounds of horns came over the noise of the storm, announcing the king's return. I looked at Kora with a grin and gasped, then I raced into the palace, while she chased after me. "Yezeba'al! Be careful! You might slip and fall and hurt yourself!"

I nearly did but managed to catch myself on a doorframe. Then I met her gaze with eyes wide and laughed, before I kicked my sandals off and carried on, and she continued to follow me. "Yezeba'al! The baby! If you fall you will hurt the baby!"

Sure of my step, I ignored her as I would have ignored Daneyah when I was a girl. I ran through the palace until I came upon my husband just as he was entering. Drenched in rain as much as I was, he saw me coming and opened his arms, and as I crashed into him, he managed to keep us both from falling. I was giddy and did not notice the dejected look on his face, as it was momentarily replaced with an affectionate sparkle in his eye.

"The rain! Akhab, we did it!" I took his face in my hands and kissed him firmly on the mouth, while he placed his hands about my waist and waited for me to calm down. Then I pulled away, still smiling, and noticed his expression. "Akhab? What is it? Do you not see, it is raining." I looked around. "Where is Daneyah? And all the others?"

He broke down then and dropped to his knees. Clutching my legs and weeping before me, he repeated, "I am sorry. I am sorry. Oh, my love, I am sorry."

I noticed Obadyah now, standing by the doorway with his head hung and an anxious look upon his face. Then I looked at Aharon, who had gone to his wife and was holding her by the arms and speaking quietly to her. Suddenly, Kora shrieked and began to

226

fall, but Aharon clutched her to him and would not let her fall. I began to tremble, and my eyes filled with tears. I did not know what had happened yet, but I knew I would never see Daneyah again.

What follows is Akhab's account, as spoken to me, of what happened when he arrived with the Ba'alim priests and priestesses at the meeting place on Mount Kerem-el:

It was early morning when we arrived. Eliyahu was there, preaching to a great mass of our people, some whom I recognized as his followers and others who had come to see what, if anything, would come to pass. I had dismounted from my chariot at the base of the mountain, leaving it in the hands of Abram and his men who were told to stay and wait for a sign that they should come. Flanked by my bodyguards, I continued on foot with Obadyah, Aharon, Anniba'al, and Daneyah close behind. We were followed by all the other priests and priestesses who had come to be with us that day.

When he saw me approaching at the head, Eliyah raised up his hand, and called: "Melekh Akhab! Good of you to join us at this moment! I was just speaking to the people of their faithlessness to the Lord our God!"

"We are here, Eliyah: all the priests and priestesses of the Ba'alim – all of us, save for one, the High Priestess, my Queen, who is heavy with child and unable to travel at this time."

"No need, Melekh! I do not require her presence – neither do I require yours, except that you should bear witness to what happens here today. I need only the prophets of your gods to perform their rites."

"They are not prophets, Eliyah – they are priests and priestesses, anointed and ordained. They are the only ones who may perform these rites."

The prophet merely looked at me and smiled, an open-mouthed grin. He might have laughed, but he was too far away for me to hear if he did. Then he raised his voice again, as if he read my mind: "Come closer, Melekh. You and your men. You should stay close to me where you may hear and observe without getting in the way."

227

Shifting my stance and casting my gaze around at all the crags and high places that surrounded us, I answered warily, "I would prefer to stay here, where I may be of assistance to my clergy, should they require it."

Eliyahu shook his head, and this time I heard him snicker. "There will be no need. All that I require, they may perform without the help of their king or their...ah...high priest, as you call yourself."

I might have answered his barb, if not for Daneyah – good, faithful, virtuous Daneyah – who looked to me, and said, "It is all right, my Ba'al. Let him have his way for now. We will manage." Then with a smile – you know that smile, Yezeba'al – she said, "You do not know the rituals anyway, so your presence among us would only be a burden."

I chuckled, despite my nerves. Then I gave a nod, before I climbed the rest of the way up to the rock where Eliyah stood above the people. I bade Obadyah, Aharon, and my bodyguards to follow me, while the priests and priestesses filed into the meeting ground with Daneyah and Anniba'al at the head.

Once all were settled, Eliyahu said, "I hope you will indulge me, Melekh Akhab, while I finish my sermon to the people?"

Although I was eager to get on with whatever he had planned, I raised my hand to permit him in the hope that all would be done sooner if he had his way. Aharon stood beside me, ready to take note of what he heard, and the prophet continued where he had apparently left off:

"How long will you waver between two opinions? If Yahowah is God, follow him; but if Ba'al, then follow him." When none of the people spoke, he continued, "Only I remain as a prophet of Yahowah; but the Ba'al's prophets are four hundred and fifty, as you see here. So, let them give us two bulls. And let them choose one bull for themselves, and prepare it, and lay it on the wood, and put no fire under it." He indicated a large pile of wood that had been placed in the center, by the remains of an altar, around which the people had gathered to listen.

While I observed our surroundings, Eliyahu continued. "Then I will prepare the other bull and lay it on the wood, and put no fire under it. And this being done, call upon the name of your god, and I will call upon Yahowah's name: and the god that answers by fire, let him be God."

228

As I listened, the people nodded their agreement, and one of them called out to the prophet, "What you say is good." But I watched warily, for the first time feeling that something was wrong.

He turned to the priests and priestesses, eyed them carefully, and then he urged: "Go on; choose one bull and prepare it first, for you are many in number and I am only one."

Something about the way he said this, and the way he smiled to himself, unnerved me. A part of me wanted to call out for them to stop, but then I feared the people would see it as a weakness on my part. And, I admit, I was curious to see what would happen if it went on, hoping against all reason that we would have victory this day.

Meanwhile, Eliyahu continued, "And when it is prepared and lain upon the wood, call upon the name of your god, but put no fire under it. And let us watch and see if your god answers with fire. You have until sundown, and then it is my turn."

So, they did as he instructed, and chose the largest of the bulls for their sacrifice. Daneyah and the priestesses arranged the wood and prepared the altar, while the priests took the bull and led it toward the wood. There they held it in place, while Anniba'al took the dagger from his belt and slit its throat. The blood spilled upon the altar and the bull fell. Then they prepared the bull and carried it to lay on the wood upon the altar.

While the Ba'alim priests and priestesses worked, Eliyahu began to prepare an altar out of twelve stones he had gathered – one each to represent the twelve tribes that were formed by the sons of Yakob, he explained, and he dedicated this altar to Yahowah. After this, he did something very strange: he dug a large trench around the altar. I wondered, what was the purpose of this trench, as he then began to arrange the wood and bade some of the people who were his followers to bring the other bull forward. Then he pulled a knife from his belt and slit the bull's throat so that its blood spilled upon the altar, and it fell, as had the other one. He prepared it in much the same way as the priests had done before, placing the bull upon the wood arranged on the altar he had made.

When both bulls had been prepared and placed upon the wood of their altars, the Ba'alim priests and priestesses surrounded their altar and their offering, and, raising their arms to the heavens, performed their ritual dances. They chanted and sang and called out: "Ba'al, hear us!" and many other such lamentations and prayers, but

229

of course no one answered them because that is not the way that it is done.

This went on for hours and, as the sun rose to its peak, its heat bearing down on us, I drank much water. When I could not stand it any longer, I went off into the brush to relieve myself and was feeling hopeless. While I was in the brush, Eliyah rose from where he had been seated upon the rocks. He laughed and called out to mock the clergy: "Cry aloud, for he is a god. Either he is deep in thought, or he has gone somewhere to relieve himself, or he is on a journey, or perhaps he sleeps and must be awakened."

I tensed my jaw and sighed heavily, as I knew he intended to mock me in this also, but I would not be moved by his taunting. Instead, when I had finished, I returned to where I had previously sat, holding a mantle over my head to keep the midday sun from burning my face. Sweat poured down my forehead, and I had to wipe it from my eyes several times with the mantle. But I tried to limit my drinking now so I would not need to keep going into the brush.

It was after the Tishbite's taunting that Daneyah and Anniba'al determined to enact the ritual of the awakening, as it is permitted without the High Priest and Priestess to perform the full right: spilling their own blood upon the altar in the hope that it would suffice. Then the others came in pairs, one man and one woman each together, to do the same. They did this, but nothing happened, and I leaned over to say to Obadyah and Aharon, "Of course it will not work like this. They need me and the Queen to enact the full rite. Doing it this way is incomplete. Besides, it is not the way of Ba'al to light a fire out of nothing. This is lunacy."

"Of course, Melekh," answered Aharon, his tone cheerful despite the grim expression on his face. He looked at Obadyah, but the Lord Steward said nothing.

Obadyah continued to watch in growing discomfort. As you know he has never cared for these rites of the Ba'alim and is squeamish to all the blood of sacrifices. At last, he walked away and went behind the brush to retch, returning only once the spilling of blood had ended. By then, the priests and priestesses had settled in to meditate and pray, chanting wearily as the day wore on. Still nothing happened. Many of the people had also stopped watching, having grown bored. They turned to each other to converse and play games, now, but Eliyahu remained on his perch upon the rocks, watching it all with contempt. He was not troubled, for he knew as well as I knew that all their prayers and rituals would not bring fire. Surely, so did they, yet they continued until evening when it was time for Eliyahu to make the evening offering, as he had planned.

Only then did he rise. Leaning upon his staff, he called to the priests and priestesses, "All right, all right, that is enough! Your god has failed to heed your call, and now it is my turn to call on Yahowah. Perhaps you may try again tomorrow when the sun rises?"

He laughed while the priests and priestesses, exhausted by the exertions of the day, seemed relieved to stop. While they went off to rest nearby, Eliyah called to the people, "Come near to me!" And when the people came near, he commanded those nearest to him, who were his followers: "Fill four jars with water. Then pour the water upon the offering and upon the wood." They went and did as he commanded, and then he commanded them to do it twice more, until the water had soaked the altar and the wood and filled the trench all around.

That being done, he bade them to stand back with the others while he raised his arms toward the heavens, and cried out, "Yahowah, God of Abraham, of Yizhak, and of Yisrael, let it be known today that you are God in Yisrael, and that I am your servant, and that I have done all these things at your word." He glanced about, his eyes scanning the mountain peaks and the horizon beyond. Then he continued, "Hear me, Yahowah! Hear me, that this people may know that you alone are God, and that you have turned their hearts back again!"

Suddenly, fire began to soar through the air from above. It seemed to come from everywhere and all around us in a sudden fury, and it fell upon the offerings and consumed everything in a great inferno: the wood and the stones of the altar, and even the trench that had been full of water was now full of flame, so that all around could feel the heat upon them even without being near. Being night, it was now bright as day while the fire burned.

I rose to my feet and stepped back, as did Obadyah and Aharon, while the prophet laughed at the wonder he had performed. At first, the people stood amazed, and some backed away in fear. But once the initial fear was past, they dropped to their knees and prostrated themselves, and cried out that Yahowah is God and begged his forgiveness for having been led astray.

231

"You wish for Yahowah's forgiveness!" Eliyahu called out to them. "You will have it if you follow my next command: Seize the prophets of Ba'al! Do not let any one of them escape!"

The whole gathering fell into a frenzy. My men surrounded me with their weapons drawn. Aharon and Obadyah stayed close to me for fear, while the people who were gathered seized the priests and priestesses of the Ba'alim. No soldiers among them, yet they were many and they were seized by fear of having displeased the God of Yisrael. And at Eliyahu's command, led by his followers who had swords and bows with arrows, they chased the priests and priestesses down to the valley of Kishon and cut them down and left them there to rot upon the earth. By the time the night was over, not one of them was left standing, as I discovered once the frenzy died down and the people had dispersed.

Throughout all of this, I was safe, and no one moved against me, but I wondered where all my soldiers were. Why did they not come? Then I saw the man who, with his horn, should have sounded the alarm, but he had joined the people in the attack and no longer served me. While all this went on, I was brought to my knees, and I fell to the ground, exhausted and trembling. I wept at my failure to protect them, knowing Daneyah, whom you loved most, was among them. I must have fallen asleep in my distress, for suddenly I was awakened to the sound of Eliyahu's voice, calling my name. I opened my eyes and saw that it was dawn, as the prophet said, "Get up, eat and drink; for I hear the sound of a storm approaching."

His tone was sanctimonious. He knew he had defeated me. Even without an army, he had won. And then he took his staff and walked up into the mountains, followed by Elisha and the others of his followers. I admit, I was hungry, and my thirst had grown, and so I ate and drank and tried to understand what I had seen. My faith was shaken, but my reason continued to argue against the truth of it.

After a time, I sat staring where the fire had burned. The stones and the dirt around them, and in the trench, were blackened, and there was no sign of the wood and the offerings left behind – all had been consumed in the blaze that had burned throughout the night. I was numb to what had happened. I listened for the sounds of a storm as the prophet had claimed to have heard, but I heard nothing. Then the sound of footsteps came to me, and I turned to see

232

a boy I recognized as a servant of Eliyah, but not Elisha. The boy regarded me with pity, and he said, "My master says to tell you to go down and prepare your chariot, that you must leave before the rains come so you are not caught up in the storm."

There was then the sound of thunder coming from the direction of the sea. And so, I went down to where my men had been left waiting. They had all fallen asleep, unaware of that which had come to pass. I roused them in anger that they had not been watching and listening for a sign, for if they had not fallen asleep, they would surely have seen the fire in the mountains and come to investigate. They could have stopped the people from slaying the priests and priestesses of the Ba'alim. Yet, somehow, they had slept through it all and had not even been awakened to the sounds of their screams and lamentations as they were being cut down and torn to pieces by the mob.

Still rubbing the sleep from his face, Abram explained that they had been offered drink by some of the people, who had come to them bearing wineskins and friendly faces. He was ashamed he had not been suspicious. But for thirst, he might have sent them away. Now, he was certain that the wine had been tainted for that purpose.

There was no time for me to chastise him further, for as the men prepared my chariot, the winds were picking up and the sky was darkening. The storm moved fast and soon the rains began to fall – light at first, as I mounted my chariot, but then growing heavier the faster we rode back toward Megiddu. Eliyah must have left before he sent the boy to speak to me, for he was suddenly there at the entrance to the city when I approached in my chariot. Else, I do not know how he could have arrived before me.

"Yezeba'al, my beloved, my Queen," said Akhab, dropping to his knees before me and taking my hand in his. I was seated in a chair, cold and still and shaken by his report. We were in my chamber together, with Kora who had come to hear the report. She sat weeping quietly at the other end of the chamber, Aharon standing silently behind her with a hand upon her shoulder.

The majority of the Ba'alim priests and priestesses who were killed by the zealots on Mount Kerem-el that day were the same ones

233

I brought with me from Tzidon. I had known many of them since infancy, Anniba'al and Daneyah in particular, and they were very dear to me. Not only were they among my closest friends and most ardent supporters, they were my connection to my homeland and my heritage. Losing Daneyah was bad enough, but losing all of them at once was like being severed from everything that was the foundation of all I had ever known and loved until the day I became Akhab's wife.

Apart from being devastated, I was also angry. Yet, I was still in shock and unable to speak, so Akhab again tried to reach me. "I am sorry, Yezeba'al. You warned me. You knew he could not be trusted, and I should have believed in you, but instead I cast my lot with him and lost. My love, can you forgive me?"

He laid his head upon my lap, and I placed my hand upon it, letting my fingers tangle in his hair and caress his scalp, even as I sat staring at nothing. I was still coming to terms with everything that had happened. It seemed so unreal. Daneyah was gone. Dead. Slain by the hand of the prophet, or by the people who followed him – it mattered not, for he was to blame as much as I was to blame for the deaths of the prophets of Yahowah. For only a moment, I thought perhaps I was also to blame for all that had happened, for I knew I had angered the god of Yisrael.

"If you are to blame, then I am to blame also," I finally managed.

Kora looked up from her weeping. "You cannot blame yourself, Yezeba'al. Nor you, Melekh. My mother died for what she believed – she would not have gone any other way."

Akhab rose and sat in a chair, while I said, "Thank you, Kora."

Still shaken, my husband stared into the flames of an oil lamp on the table nearby. "I saw the fires with my own eyes, Yezeba'al. They rained down from the heavens…"

"It did not rain down from the heavens, Akhab," I said, rising from the chair and turning to him. "It came down from the mountains, likely by the hands of his followers. Shot from bows, on flaming arrowheads, no doubt. Somehow, they managed it, but surely it was not the work of Yahowah."

"Yes, of course," he agreed, hesitantly. "I know that, but…it looked convincing to those who do not know any better. The people saw and believed – that is what matters, for they have turned the tide against us."

A wave of sorrow nearly overtook me as I thought of Daneyah, but then a wave of anger pushed it away. "Vile trickery! He and his followers – they planned this travesty. He chose the day and place and method by which they would be tested."

"It is clear that he set the whole thing up," Akhab muttered, returning to his sense now. "He knew in advance how it would all turn out."

My anger continued to rise. "He came out the victor by his own charlatanry!"

Akhab sighed. "I still do not understand it though, how he lit the pyres when they were drenched with water. It was as though the water itself caught fire!"

"Are you certain it was water or was it something else?" asked Kora, making me remember something from our youth.

"It looked like water," Akhab shrugged.

"No, it was not water," I insisted. "It was more of his Egyptian magic; I am certain of it. You remember, Kora? The magic tricks the magicians put on at the courts in Tzidon?"

She nodded, momentarily distracted from her grief. "Yes, they had earthenware jars full of what looked like water but was not. They showed us first an empty jar, and then they poured the waterlike substance into the jar and set it aflame. The heat was so powerful that the jar burst and even the flaming shards were consumed by the time the flames went out. When I saw this as a girl, I thought they were gods, but I know better now. It was not water, but some other substance."

"We already know the Tishbite is an alchemist. The smoke he made to escape from our party, and now this..."

Akhab nodded, understanding now.

Then Kora looked to Aharon, who had also been listening intently. Even he had been tricked by the prophet's show. "Now, do you believe? Are you still convinced that your Yahowah is the one true god, when his prophets use alchemy and magic tricks to perform their feats? And murder hundreds of his rivals – innocent men and women, Ahru!" She fell to weeping again.

"Those prophets we have killed were guilty of sedition," I put in, when I saw the moment of doubt on Aharon's face, "but not one of those killed by Eliyah's men was guilty of any crime other than to believe differently than he."

235

"They were not even armed," said Akhab. "They had their ceremonial daggers, but nothing more by which to protect themselves. And my useless soldiers, sleeping through it!"

It was then that I was seized by a sudden dizziness and a pain in my womb. I stopped abruptly and clutched my abdomen, grasping the back of my chair to steady myself. Akhab immediately leapt from his chair and came to me, and Kora came also, while her husband watched with concern but dared not approach.

"Yezeba'al?" said Kora, gently taking the king's hands from me.

He let her take over, aware that she was better qualified to help with women's matters, but asked, "What is happening to her?"

Kora touched my abdomen. It was hard from the contraction. I was in so much pain that I could not speak, but Kora explained, "She is having pains of childbirth."

I clutched her and managed to speak. "It is too soon."

"I know," she replied calmly. "Let me take you to lie down. You have been under too much distress for your condition. Perhaps if you rest, it will all pass."

"What can I do to help?" asked the king, his face beset with worry.

"Summon the midwives, although there are few of them left," Kora answered solemnly. "Most of them were priestesses of Ashtarti."

As I took to the bed, I saw the way she hardened herself from the pain of loss, and I realized for the first time the measure of her strength. Then I looked to the king, and said, "The midwives, those who are left – summon them, please."

"Yes," he answered, shaking off his concern so that he could be of some help to me. Then he bade Aharon to go to the women's quarters and ask for the midwives to be sent to my chamber. Then he sent the other men away as my other handmaidens appeared, summoned to me by Kora who had gone to fetch them from the next room. They all surrounded me and began to do what they knew they must. I tried to remain calm so as not to make the condition worse but could not rest because my anger continued to boil. Akhab did what he could to comfort me, but his presence was more disruptive than useful. Nevertheless, he refused to leave me. Eventually, I commanded a wineskin be brought for the king and told him to sit down so that he would not get in the women's way as they worked. He listened and seemed grateful not to be expected to do anything.

The storm was still raging outside by the time the midwives at last appeared. Leading them, Maryam came to me, and said, "Try not to worry, Melkah. For now, you must rest." Then, explaining more for the king's benefit than for my own, she said, "It is common for storms and distress to cause false signs of labor, Melekh. Most likely, she will not be delivered too soon, and the pains shall pass."

The pains did not pass, however. They only grew worse throughout the night. By the time the grey skies were lit from behind by the rising sun, it was clear that my labor had begun, and I was taken to the birthing chamber to be delivered. Everyone tending to me, including Kora and the other wives, performed their duties solemnly and without comment, for we all knew that I was giving birth to a dead child: born too soon, it was unlikely the child would survive long enough to draw its first breath.

Near midday, a son was delivered and died shortly thereafter, despite the best efforts of the midwives to sustain his life. Without the priests of Ba'al to perform the funerary rites at the temple, since those who remained were mere acolytes, I had to implore my husband to do it in his role as High Priest. He had witnessed these rites and knew, generally, how they were performed. One of the acolytes who had nearly finished training to become a priest helped to guide him through it, and so the rites were observed in accordance with our sacred traditions. My poor son's soul could be guided to the safe keeping of Ba'al in the underworld, until the time came for him to return to us in a new form.

After the funeral, I was still in mourning over the deaths of Daneyah and the others, and now that I had lost my child also, I was fuming. When the king returned from conducting the funeral of our son, he found me staring out the window at the smoke still rising from the Temple of Ba'al, bitter tears flowing down my cheeks. I did not turn to him when he entered, but I knew he was there.

"Yezeba'al. It is done. Motu will not devour the soul of our son. He will return to us."

I nodded. Then I wiped my tears and at last turned to him. He came to embrace and kiss me, but I pulled away, unwilling to be comforted. "Summon Aharon."

"Aharon?"

"Yes. I have a message I need delivered. Tell him to come here."

The king nodded and gave the command to one of the eunuchs who went to find Aharon. When he arrived, I stopped pacing before the window and turned my fury toward him. "You know where to find this Eliyah the Tishbite, Aharon?"

Trembling, he answered, "No, Melkah. I have no idea where he is!" He hesitated, though, and then confessed, "But I know one who does."

Kora looked at him, stricken. "You know who has been helping the zealots? Have you also been helping them?"

"No, my love! I swear it! But he is my master. He commanded my silence, and I am sworn to obey him in all things."

"*Abarakkum* Obadyah," I said, my suspicions confirmed. I saw my husband bury his face in his hands, the weight of guilt upon him. I would tend to him later.

Keeping his face lowered in shame, Aharon nodded. "If I am to be executed, Melkah, please in your love for her, spare my wife and children."

"Nonsense, Aharon. There will be consequences, to be sure, but you are not to blame for this. It is your master the Lord Steward who is guilty."

"Do you have proof of his guilt?" asked Akhab, his voice heavy with grief.

Aharon shook his head. "Only my word, Melekh."

"We shall soon have our proof," I retorted. "Aharon, go at once to Obadyah, and when you find him, tell him that I am going to kill the prophet Eliyahu. Tell him that you heard me say: 'As he has slaughtered my friends, so let it be done to me and worse by the will of the gods, if I cannot make him as one of them by this time tomorrow!' If it is true that Obadyah has betrayed us, he will make sure that his prophet has fair warning. Now, go! Take this message and do not return until it has been delivered!"

Aharon nodded stiffly. After briefly looking to his wife, who gave him barely an acknowledgement, he hurried away. Then Akhab said, "Why do you send a warning? Is it so important to entrap Obadyah, that you will allow our greater enemy to flee once again, as he has always done?"

"This is about more than proving Obadyah's faithlessness, Akhab. If the prophet flees, then he proves himself a coward and a liar. For if he truly believes in his god, then let him face us. Let him stand before us with no plan in mind and see how far his god's favor extends before my wrath! When the people see that he is a fraud – that he flees from us, instead of putting his faith in Yahowah to preserve him – they will know better than to follow him."

"I fear you give the people more credit than they deserve, my love."

"Then let them all burn! Let them all be cut down by their own foolishness! Let them become martyrs by their own god's hate! I will not rest until that man and *all* who have aided him lie dead!"

My anger brimming forth, I shoved the small incense burner and oil lamp from the table. Thankfully, neither had been lit, or the silk rug upon which they fell might have gone up in flames. The women of my chamber came immediately to clean it up, as Akhab took hold of me and pressed me to him. I clung to him and wept bitterly.

As expected, Obadyah was observed leaving his residence not long after Aharon departed from delivering my message. The Lord Steward was arrested at the city gate upon his return a few hours later, after sundown. The next morning, disheveled and dirty after a night spent in the dungeon, he was brought before the court to face judgment. The king and I were seated on our thrones, dressed in full court regalia, and Aharon now stood in the Lord Steward's place upon the dais. Once the staidest man I had ever met, Obadyah now looked at us all in fear and confusion. I enjoyed watching him squirm.

"*Abarakkum* Obadyah," the king said from his throne, "you were seen leaving the city yesterday afternoon, though you were not given leave from your duties. I was told you rode as fast as your horse could carry you, and that several hours passed before you returned." He paused and fixed the former Lord Steward with an icy gaze. "Where did you go in such haste?"

"T-to visit an ailing relative, Melekh. My cousin, who lives in the village."

239

Akhab hummed. "That is interesting. I was not aware that Eliyah the Tishbite was a relative of yours, let alone a cousin!"

At last, Obadyah seemed to understand that he had been lured into a trap. His eyes shot over to Aharon, recognition and even betrayal burning in his gaze. Then he admitted, "He is not, Melekh. I... It was..." He hung his head, perhaps realizing any attempt to cover up his guilt was futile. Instead, he dropped to his knees, and implored, "Please, Melekh! Have mercy!"

"For what?"

A heavy silence hung over the court as Obadyah looked at the king in confusion. Then he turned to Aharon. Then to me. I glared at him with the hint of a smirk – a cat, pleased to have caught a mouse. He quickly looked away. The Hall was deadly still as everyone waited for him to answer. I could hear him sigh before he at last confessed. "*Abarakkum* Aharon came to warn me of Melkah Yezeba'al's wrath against the prophet Eliyahu for what...happened in the mountains of Kerem-el, and for...the loss of her child. I swear to you, Melkah, I did not intend for any of this to happen!"

I turned my face from him, as much to hide my pain as to reject his plea. Akhab reached for my hand. He held it firmly, as the traitor continued, "Please! I only wanted to warn him so that he would be safe. He is not only my friend but a prophet of the Lord my God. It was never my intention to harm anyone – I only wanted to do what my conscience demanded was right and just!"

"Following the law is right and just," said the king, still holding my hand. "Do you not agree, Obadyah?"

The former Lord Steward tightened his lips without reply.

"You are aware," my husband continued, "of the law against aiding and abetting zealots and seditious prophets, are you not?"

"Yes, Melekh."

Akhab gestured to the scribes. The one who was chief among them came forward with a scroll and gave it to Aharon, who brought it to the king. Akhab unrolled the papyrus and glanced at it, to be sure it was the correct one. He then returned it to Aharon with a nod. Aharon handed it to the scribe, who now brought it to Obadyah.

The king asked, "Tell me, Obadyah, do you recognize this scroll?"

Obadyah nodded. "Yes, Melekh. It is mine."

"Then tell the court what it is."

"It is... a ledger. An account."

"Of what?"

"Of...money I have borrowed."

"That is an awful lot of money for one man to borrow, Obadyah. Have you taken to gambling in your spare time?"

There was some laughter from amongst the ministers and courtiers, all who knew Obadyah was the last person in Yisrael who would take up such a habit. It would be easier to believe a horse took to gambling than the straightlaced former steward.

"N-no, Melekh."

"Speak up," the king commanded, his voice booming. "No one can hear you."

"No, Melekh."

Akhab nodded. Then he said, "I know your wife has been fruitful, Obadyah. How many children do you have together that are still living?"

The former steward looked at him warily, suddenly fearing for his family. Nevertheless, he answered, "Eleven, Melekh. Sons and daughters both."

"And they are all still living at home, unmarried and in your wife's care?"

Obadyah nodded. Of course, we knew his family well. His eldest daughter served as a handmaiden to me, in fact: a great honor for the daughters of noble houses who hoped their daughters would secure suitable marriages by my recommendations of them to eligible men. But when her father was arrested the night before, her service to me was terminated and she was sent back to the care of her mother.

"Surely, you can afford to care for your family and cover the needs of your household on the wages and gifts you have received in your tenure as Lord Steward?"

"You have been most generous, Melekh."

"Then tell me, Obadyah, how you have managed to incur such exorbitant debts in only three years? The same number of years, in fact, that the law against seditious prophets has been in effect. That is interesting." He paused. When he received no answer, he asked, "It is three years since you began keeping that ledger, yes? Or, rather, I should say it was *Abarakkum* Aharon whom you made to keep track

241

of your debts for the past three years, as part of his service to you. Is that not true, Obadyah?"

Again, the traitor glanced at Aharon with heat in his gaze. Nevertheless, he admitted, "It...is true, Melekh."

"So, in three years you have gone from being a man with no debt – in fact, you had been quite prosperous as I recall – to owing more money than a man could pay back in several lifetimes even with the wages of a Lord Steward. That is a considerable sum, Obadyah."

"It is, Melekh."

"Where has all that money gone, I wonder?"

He waited. No reply. The accused merely lowered his gaze.

"Shall I rephrase the question? What have you been doing with all the money you have been borrowing these past three years, Obadyah?"

"Giving it to those who are in need, Melekh."

"Your ailing cousin, I suppose? Must be quite the unusual treatments he is receiving in his physician's care, to be so costly – and, apparently, ineffective."

There was no answer, apart from the twittering of courtiers who enjoyed Akhab's dry sense of humor. Unfortunately, Akhab was not enjoying it as much as they were.

He sighed heavily, pressing his thumb and forefinger to the bridge of his nose. I reached out to him. He gave me a grateful smile and squeezed my hand, bringing it to his lips. Then he released my hand and turned back to Obadyah. "We know what you have been doing with that money, Obadyah. Why prolong the inevitable and waste the court's time with more lies? You already confessed to helping the Tishbite, by warning him of the Queen's wrath. Are we to believe you were not also giving money to him and the other zealots? Money they used to buy smuggled weapons and alchemical ingredients: those same weapons and ingredients which were used to slaughter the priests and priestesses of the Ba'alim on Mount Kerem-el?"

"I...did not know the money I gave them would be used for such things! I thought it was being used to feed and clothe the prophets of Yahowah who were hiding in the caves there. And to buy medicine when they were ill."

"That is a lot of food and medicine. They must have been living as kings in those caverns. And being very ill – like your cousin in the village."

Obadyah shook his head and held out his hands. "There were at least a hundred of them. I did not know they were amassing these weapons and planning these deeds. Please, Melekh, I swear to you – I did not know!"

"Yet, you knew that you were breaking the law."

"Please, Melekh! Have mercy on me! I only wanted to preserve their lives! I did not know what they were planning! I did not mean for anyone to be killed! I...believed in their innocence!"

"Innocence," I said, speaking for the first time since the traitor appeared. "If they had been innocent, there would have been no need for you to hide them. There are many prophets of Yahowah still living openly in Yisrael, for they have not broken the laws of this realm. If they had been innocent, Daneyah and Anniba'al and all the other four-hundred or so priests and priestesses of the Ba'alim whom they slaughtered without mercy would still be here. So, tell me, Obadyah, what should be done to you and all those responsible for the slaughter of *innocents*? Shall we extend to you the same mercy your zealot friends denied them in the mountains of Kerem-el, when they cut them down for worshipping a different god? You beg for mercy now – but would you offer the same, if you were in our position and it was your god's priests who were slaughtered in their stead?"

The silence that followed was such that we could hear the voices of children playing in the palace gardens. It was a strange contrast to the heaviness of what we were dealing with at court that day. Momentarily distracted, I thought of the child I had just lost, the child whose laughter I would never hear. I faltered, nearly swept away by a wave of fresh grief. Akhab noticed and reached to take my hand again. I assured him I was all right.

After composing myself, I said, "No. You will not find mercy here. You know the laws of this realm better than all the men and women who have already died for the same crime. You think your life is of more value than theirs? That you should be granted clemency when they were not? You knew the penalty for aligning yourself with zealots, and yet you did it anyway – at great cost, not only to your family who will now be responsible for paying back your debts, but to every ordained man and woman of the Ba'alim who were not spared

243

when your beloved prophet called for the people to slaughter them in Yahowah's name. You made your choice, Obadyah. Now you will face the consequences, like every man and woman whose death warrants you delivered to their executioners when caught committing the same crime for which you are now charged."

I turned my face from him, and then the king gave the final command. "Obadyah, for the crime of aiding and abetting seditious prophets, as the law is written you will be beheaded in the square at sundown. May Ba'al save you from the jaws of Motu."

The king waved his hand to dismiss his case. Immediately, Obadyah fell to the floor and wept, crying out for his god to save him, claiming he had been a loyal servant. But Yahowah did not hearken to his calls. As the traitorous steward was executed in the square at Megiddu, Akhab and I watched from our thrones that had been placed at the top of the stairs leading into the Temple of Ba'al. Afterward, his body was taken to be burned upon the altar as an offering to my god. By offering his soul in service to Ba'al, perhaps he would be spared from permanent death. It was a small act of mercy, for we believed that all souls deserved to be spared from Motu's voracious appetite.

The matter was not ended with the death of Obadyah, however. Akhab sent his brother Abram with four hundred and fifty armed men – the same number of Ba'alim priests and priestesses who were slaughtered – to search the caverns in the mountains of Kerem-el and cut down every zealot they could find. But by the time they reached the place where Obadyah had helped Eliyah hide the zealous prophets, they were all gone. All that remained was their refuse and a great many earthenware jars that bore traces of an odorless liquid that looked like water but was capable of devouring earth when set to flame.

Part II

On Covenants

10
Envy of Kings

Following the slaughter of our Ba'alim priests and priestesses on Mount Kerem-el, we had to send to Tzidon and request more be sent to replace them, for the temples and shrines could not be managed by acolytes and the High Priest and Priestess alone. Understandably, it was difficult to find those who were willing to come to Yisrael after what had happened; those who did came with a religious zeal to match that of our opponents. Perhaps that is what was needed because, after stories of what Yahowah's zealous prophet was capable of doing had spread, zealotry was on the rise in the kingdom of Yisrael. Hoping to stifle it, we doubled down our efforts to locate Eliyah the Tishbite and his band.

Nevertheless, Eliyah remained at large, and I regretted having given him fair warning of my vendetta. At the time, Obadyah was an easy target for retribution, and it was necessary to remove the traitor in our midst, but we could have caught Obadyah some other way. Sorrow combined with a sense of arrogance (I admit) and righteous indignation had clouded my judgment. The loss of another child, this time after an agonizing delivery, did not help matters.

Soon enough, however, I was with child once again. Our anger at the zealots faded as pride for our ever-growing family increased.

First came Hannah, so named for she was a gift of life after so much death. She was followed within the year by a son, named Yoram, who quickly became a favorite of his father, although Akhab adored all our children and doted on them sometimes too much. This was especially true of Atalaya on whom he doted constantly whenever she was around him. I once teased, "She could get you to do anything, without question. You spoil her."

He responded by getting up from the floor and pulling me into his arms with a playful growl, "Not as much as I spoil her beautiful mother." I laughed and he became distracted, kissing and stroking me, until Atalaya became jealous and pulled at his robe.

She was now four years old, precocious, and increasingly demanding. "Abbu, come play with me! Ama is supposed to be resting."

It was true, for I had only given birth to Yoram a few days previously. It was a difficult labor, for he chose to come out backwards and upside down. It would take some time for me to recover, but at last I was feeling well enough for my other children to come see me and their new brother. He was now feeding at the breast of his nurse nearby, and Akhazyah was there standing on his toes to get a closer look.

When Atalaya led her father away, I returned to my bed, where milk-drunk Hannah was sprawled across the pillows, fighting sleep. The moment I lay down, she came to lay across my lap. While I stroked her hair, I called to my eldest son, "Zyah, come here."

"I want to see the baby, Ama."

"Akhazyah, listen to your mother," Akhab said firmly. He was now stretched across the floor, leaning on one elbow with an ivory horse in his other hand.

Zyah meekly obeyed, coming to lay on the bed with me. He nestled in when I pulled him into my arms. He adored his father, but he was sometimes afraid of him. Akhab was harder on him than he was on the others, because he was most likely to be his successor, so my eldest son often came to me for comfort. Even now, Akhab eyed us together and shook his head. "If I spoil Tala, you spoil Zyah."

"You are too hard on him," I answered, brushing curls from my son's forehead and kissing him there.

"He was disobeying you."

Zyah burrowed his face in my breast and started pulling at the front of my robe, but I brushed his hands away. He and Atalaya were weaned when Hannah was born, but it had been difficult with him, especially when he witnessed me nursing his younger siblings. When I would not let him nurse, he growled and pulled at the strings until I slapped his hands away. Then he whined but finally gave up, instead sucking on the sleeve of his robe.

As Akhab witnessed the small battle over my breast, he clicked his tongue. "You see, this is why I say you have spoiled him more."

"I do not let him have his way," I answered with a hint of resentment.

248

"You do sometimes. Otherwise, he would not still try it."

Meanwhile, Atalaya stood over him with her hands on her hips, and chastised, "Abbu, you are not paying attention. You are supposed to be the horse!"

"Oh, yes," he answered, turning his attention back to the ivory figure in his hand. He pretended to gallop it up the front of her robes and made imitations of horse sounds, and she laughed.

"You're silly, Abbu!"

He cast his gaze to mine, and we shared a moment of pride and admiration. Then Zyah shifted in my arms and accidentally kicked Hannah in the head. She had at last succumbed to a nap but now awoke crying. Her nurse, who was mending some of the children's robes nearby, got up and came to retrieve her but I held up my hand and reached for her myself. I pulled Hannah into my arms, and said, "Oh, did your brother kick you? It was an accident, my Hannah."

I kissed her forehead and then she settled in with her head on my breast, while Zyah gently stroked her curls and tilted his head to look closely at her face. "I'm sorry, Hannah. I did not mean to."

She closed her eyes and turned her face toward my breast, sucking on her thumb to comfort herself. Not wanting her to ruin her teeth, I pulled her hand away from her mouth and offered my breast instead. She accepted, but that only upset Zyah, who started to whine, "Ama, please! I am thirsty too!"

"Then you can have juice, Zyah."

His nurse came to collect him then, and he fussed dreadfully as she pulled him away, while I ignored his pleas. When she handed him a ceramic cup, he tossed it on the ground, and it smashed. The nurse began to chastise him, while one of the servants came to clean up the juice and ceramic shards. Meanwhile, Akhab gave me a look, but I duly ignored it, and then I had to remind Hannah not to bite while she nursed. Her wide brown eyes looked up at me apologetically and she kept nursing, careful not to use her teeth, while I gently stroked her forehead and smiled down at her.

Hannah was a delight, but her blessed life was cut short when, in her third year, a fever swept through the region. Not just our kingdom, but many were affected. I, too, had fallen ill, and so was not told of the death of Hannah until after I recovered enough. The fear was great that I might succumb to the fever in my grief. Her funeral was conducted by Akhab himself, while I lay in fevered delirium, staring out the window at the smoke rising from the temple and wondering if the gods had abandoned us. It seemed the smoke from the temple was endless. The wailing of women could be heard within the palace and throughout the city for days, so it had not occurred to me that it was one of my own children being returned to the underworld that day.

The twins also fell ill, but thankfully recovered quickly, and Yoram was blessed not to be touched by the fever at all. Fang-Hua was taken from us, along with the youngest of her two sons, and we all mourned their loss – especially Ba'athu who was devastated by the loss of the woman she loved and promised to look after Ishaq, her eldest son. Zubira, who had only just given birth to her first child by the king, managed to survive the fever but her newborn was taken, as were many of the king's other children and several of his concubines. No one was spared: the faithful of Yahowah and the Ba'alim alike succumbed to it, so for once it was not yet another excuse for the prophets of our two religions to lay blame on each other and claim it as a punishment from the gods. Everyone in the region was grieving.

A year after the fever took Hannah from us, I gave birth to a son who was given the name Ethba'al, after my father, but he died within days of his circumcision and became yet another one of our children sent back to Ba'al in the underworld. Still, we had three who grew in strength and health each year, and, despite several miscarriages, another was to join them soon enough. I was in my twenty-ninth year in the fifteenth year of Akhab's reign when another son was born to us, while my brother was visiting from Tzidon.

Esar, as I called my brother, delighted in his niece and nephews, and spoiled them terribly with gifts every time he came to visit us. He was now a father to many children of his own with several wives, and this time he brought his eldest son on what was an unofficial visit to our kingdom. Mattan, as my nephew was called, was ten years old, the same age as the twins, and he played well with his cousins. When he met them for the first time on this visit, he did not at first know that Atalaya and Akhazyah were twins. I was still heavy with child, seated on a chair in the garden and visiting with my husband and brother when we overheard an exchange between Mattan and Atalaya.

Mattan had been talking to Zyah, when suddenly he turned to Atalaya and asked, "Tala, is it true that you are Zyah's twin?"

"No," she replied with a smirk. "He is *my* twin, for *I* was born first."

Akhab, Esar, and I burst into laughter, which made Tala smile proudly. She was already developing a wicked wit and quite pleased with herself that she could make even the adults laugh aloud. Of course, Zyah wished to outdo her in this as in everything else so, with a smile, he insisted, "No, you are my twin because I am a son and sons are more important than daughters."

Akhab raised his brows and Esar's lips parted into a smile, but I was not amused. "Zyah! That does not make a difference! She was born first and, therefore, you are her twin. You get to be your father's successor – let her have what she can, so at least it is fair."

Zyah looked thoroughly chastened until Tala made a face at him. He responded by snatching the veil from her head and running off as she jumped up to chase after him. Their cousin watched with great interest as they taunted each other, laughing and racing through the garden. Then Zyah climbed into a tree and left her veil stuck upon one of the branches before leaping down. She grabbed at him, but he managed to dodge out of the way, giggling. Mattan offered to fetch the veil for her, but she only laughed before climbing the tree to fetch it herself. Then she jumped down and walked by Zyah, who was still laughing. She waved the veil at him, saying, "Next time, I shall make you wear it and paint your face to look like a girl."

"Then I shall draw a beard around your mouth with kohl so that you look like a boy."

"Fine. Then if I'm a boy, that makes me the eldest son – and that means I shall be Abbu's successor in your place."

Zyah bowed with a laugh, and said, "As you wish, Melekh Atalaya!"

She swatted at him, but then they embraced. It was clear they adored one another, even if they were in perpetual competition.

After his siblings' battle concluded, six-year-old Yoram looked up from the fortress of sticks he was building and asked, "Ama, if Zyah gets to be king then what do I get?"

"You get to be the one who is most cherished," I answered with a wink.

Akhab spoke up, "Yoram, if you learn well to be a great warrior, when your brother is king you will be his most trust general and his Minister of War."

"What is a Minister of War?"

"It means you will command the king's armies and know everything there is to know about wars and battles. You can help him make important decisions when the time comes for him to defend and strengthen his kingdom."

"Like *Abakhu* Abram?"

"Yes, like *Abakhu* Abram."

Yoram smiled. "I want to be like him."

"One day, my son, you will be. But first, you must learn to shoot, wield a sword, and drive a chariot. Do you want to practice shooting now?"

"Yes, Abbu!"

"Then go and fetch your bow and a quiver of arrows, and you can show your *Akhamu* Esar how good you are at shooting, hmm?"

Yoram nodded proudly and ran to get it, returning a short time later with miniature versions of what his father used on the battlefield. Seeing this, Zyah ran to fetch his own, and soon all the boys were practicing with bows and arrows under Akhab's tutelage, while my brother and I sat back to visit. In truth, Yoram was a terrible shot, but he was young and had only just begun learning. We knew he would improve with enough practice and his father's guidance.

"Your husband is an attentive father," said Esar, leaning closer to me. "I have never seen anything like it – at least, not from among our ranks. It is impressive if a bit unusual. And you seem to enjoy motherhood a great deal – certainly more than our own Ama did."

I chuckled.

"How many children will you give your husband before you tire of it?"

Rubbing my belly, I said, "Only the gods know for certain, but I am thinking this will be the last one." I paused, and then asked, "How is Ama, by the way?"

"Enamored with a new woman, as always. She spends little time with Abbu. He, meanwhile, spends most of his time on the battlefield or with his priestesses and concubines."

"Sounds as though nothing has changed," I mused.

"Not one bit," he replied. "They have mutual respect but lead entirely separate lives. Nothing like you and your husband."

"I cannot imagine living apart from Akhab," I said, smiling as I watched him directing the boys. "Whenever we are apart, I am disconsolate. Other than my writing and religious duties, I find little joy in anything but my husband and my children." When one of the peacocks called out as if in protest, I added, "And my peafowl."

"No joy in being a great queen?"

I permitted a wry half-smile and lifted my eyes. "Hardly. It is a burden I must bear, like much in life."

"I am surprised that your husband permits you to take an equal role in managing his kingdom – unheard of in Yisrael. When Abbu made the terms of your marriage agreement, he thought your husband would only allow you to be his equal in name, not in reality. He is quite pleased. Dare I say, he may even be proud of you."

"Yes, well, I am sure you have also heard of the trouble it has caused for us – with the king's ministers, especially. They are not accustomed to being commanded by a woman."

"I have heard, yes. But I have also heard that you manage it with grace and tact when you are able – and a firm hand, when necessary. Did you ever find that wayward prophet, by the way? The zealot – what was he called?"

"Eliyahu the Tishbite." I practically spit the name from my mouth and for a moment burned with a hatred I had not felt in years. It seemed a few embers of that hatred remained underneath the ashes I thought had cooled but could be stirred up at any moment. A kick from the child in my womb brought me back to the present. With a deep exhale, I moved my hand over the place on my belly where his tiny foot protruded, thanking him silently for the reminder not to brood over things that were out of my control.

253

Esar was about to speak, when we heard Tala asking, "Abbu, why can I not learn to shoot a bow and arrows with the boys? I am just as capable as they are!"

"Of course, you are capable, Tala," Akhab replied. "And if you want to learn, I will let you. Here," he reached for Zyah's bow and handed it to her.

Zyah objected. "Abbu, why do you take my bow? Take Yoram's bow – he is younger and does not need it!"

"Yoram will likely be your Minister of War one day," Akhab replied, "so you should want him to be at least as good as you – if not better."

Meanwhile, Tala stuck out her tongue at Zyah, while Yoram said, "Zyah, just because you are older does not make you more important than me."

"Yes, it does," Zyah replied. "Because one day I will be king."

"Zyah!" I raised my voice to him.

"Keep up that attitude, Zyah," Akhab calmly rebuked him, "and I will name Tala my successor in your stead."

"You cannot do that!" Zyah protested.

"I am king," said Akhab, in a playful tone. "I can do whatever I want."

"That's where he gets it from," I said, causing my brother to laugh.

Akhab smiled at me with twinkling eyes. "He gets it from both of us, wife."

I had nothing to say to that, for it was true. Then Zyah stalked off while Yoram took his place. With a sigh, I turned to my brother. "I better go speak with him. Forgive me, *akhu*."

"Of course, *akhatu*."

I got up and went to find my eldest son. Zyah had gone to his usual place in the women's garden at Megiddu, behind a pool near the outer wall, hidden within the tangled branches of the pomegranate trees that grew nearby. He sat on the ground with his knees pulled up, crying silently while a peahen pecked at the dirt by his feet. He reached out to stroke her feathers, which she permitted until I came through the brush. That's when Zyah noticed me and buried his face in his knees.

"Zyah? Why are you crying, love?"

His reply was muffled. "I'm not crying."

254

With great effort, I eased myself onto my knees with a slight groan, attempting to sit beside him on the ground.

Suddenly, his concern for me overcame his pride. He got up to help me, as I knew he would. "You must be careful, Ama!"

Once I was seated, I smiled and reached up to wipe the tears from his cheeks. Then I touched the tip of his nose and he chuckled. "There's that smile I so love. Do not worry – I will not tell anyone you were crying. But there is no shame in it. Even your Abbu is not too proud to cry."

"Abbu cries?"

I nodded solemnly.

Sitting once again, he folded his knees and looked at me in wonder. "What does Abbu cry about?"

"A great many things. He cries whenever someone he loves is hurting, or when his people are suffering, and he does not know how to help them." Then I looked at him knowingly. "And whenever he feels there has been an injustice."

He seemed to understand and lowered his face.

"Zyah, do you feel there has been an injustice committed against you?"

He nodded. Then he asked, "Why does Abbu favor Yoram and Tala?"

"He does not favor them, Zyah."

"Yoram gets to have everything, and so does Tala! Abbu always plays and makes jokes with them, but with me he is always serious!"

"I know it seems hard to believe, but *you* are his favorite son. That is why he has chosen you to be his successor – and why he expects more of you."

"I thought he chose me because I am the eldest son."

"He has many sons older than you."

"But I am the son of his Melkah," he answered proudly. "That means I am greater than them, even if they're older."

I was silent for a moment, as I considered how best to say what I knew must be said. "It was selfish of you not to share with your sister, and to pull rank as you often do. Your Abbu wanted to teach you a lesson in humility – that is why he took your bow and not Yoram's. And I must say, I agree with him. Pride is a good thing for a man to have in moderation. Too much pride makes a man arrogant. And an arrogant king is not one who takes good care of his people."

My son's face turned red, his jaw set, and he sighed heavily. Nevertheless, I could see him pondering. I remained quiet, giving him time to think. Then at last, he said, "I do not want to be an arrogant king. I want to take good care of my people."

I smiled and reached to embrace him. He got up on his knees and threw his arms around me with his head on my breast. We stayed like this for some time before he finally pulled away.

"You will be a good king, Zyah. You have a good heart and keen mind. Abbu sees that as well as I do. But you must always temper your pride with humility, and any selfish tendencies with compassion for others – as we all must do from time to time."

"You are never selfish, Ama."

I sniffed. "You are not paying attention then. I can be as selfish as any man, but I try not to be. How do you think I know so much about these things? I battle my own worst tendencies daily; some days better than others."

Zyah fell silent and observed a butterfly flitting around the flowering pomegranate trees, going from blossom to blossom. I watched him, meanwhile, admiring the way the sunlight caught in his eye, illuminating faint green flecks that cut through the brown like flames. Atalaya had similar green flecks, although hers were more pronounced and visible even without the light catching them. It had always amazed me to see their eyes change as they grew, once having been as dark as mine.

Seeming to sense me watching him, suddenly he turned to meet my gaze, and my heart swelled with love. Then he said, "I love you, Ama. More than anything in the world."

I reached out to stroke his cheek, and then I brought my hand up to tussle his hair. He giggled and then jumped up and took my hands. "Come. Let me help you up. I want to show you something I found. Nobody else knows about it."

He led me by hand into some thick brush by a sharp curve in the wall near a grate where the channel that fed water to the gardens flowed out. There, obscured by the overgrowth, was a nest of eggs resting in the dirt. There were eight of them in total. The peahen who had dug the nest was the same one he had been petting earlier. She came over as we approached, having been drinking from the channel nearby.

As the expectant mother settled over the nest, Zyah said quietly, "I wonder if they'll hatch when my brother or sister is born."

I chuckled at the thought, and then I put my arm around my son and pulled him to me. He placed his hands on my belly to feel the baby moving inside. Then he put his face near, and said, "Shalom, little *akhu* or *akhatu*. I cannot wait to meet you." He giggled when the baby kicked at his hands. "I hope they will like me."

"They will adore you, my son. As we all do. Never doubt it, not even for a moment."

His smiling gaze cast a reflection of love at me. "I'll try not to forget, Ama. But if I do, please remind me."

"I always will," I said, bending to kiss the top of his head and tightening my arm around him. Then we stayed watching the peahen cooing over her eggs for only a moment longer before we returned to the rest of our family. Yoram and Tala both came to embrace Zyah and apologized. He admitted he was the one who needed to apologize, and then they ran off to play with their cousin, while I sat down to visit with my husband and brother once again. The labor pains began a few hours later, and by dawn of the next day I had provided my husband with another son. He was named for my brother, who was there to witness his presentation to the king.

When Zyah came to meet his new brother that evening, he whispered into my ear, "The eggs hatched last night!"

I gasped, and whispered, "Then you were right. It seems you have the gift of prophecy – a good thing for a king to have."

He threw his arms around my neck and kissed my cheek, and then we smiled together over our little secret.

Two more years passed, and our children and kingdom were thriving: perhaps too much, for a strong kingdom and fruitful wives bring not only admiration but also covetousness. This seemed to be the case when Hadedesar, King of Aram, brought a large army into Yisrael. We were at Shomron for the celebration of the Feast of Ashtarti in the spring. All our children came with us that year, even Ba'alesar, for he had reached the age of two, when it was permissible for them to travel to Shomron for the Ba'alim feasts. I was in the nursery, observing the religious education of my three eldest children, when Kora came to me with the news that Hadadesar had brought an army to lay siege to our city.

"Ama, what is a siege?" asked Yoram, now eight.

My eldest son, soon-to-be twelve, was quick to answer. "It is a battle, you idiot."

"Zyah, for Ashtarti's sake, stop tormenting your brother," I snapped.

I would have explained that a siege was not a battle, but I was eager now to be at my husband's side. Thankfully, Tala moved to sit by Yoram and calmly explained to him what it meant. She would soon be ordained as a priestess of Ashtarti, as I had been when I was twelve, and I was proud of how much she had grown and matured. I gave her an appreciative smile then nodded to the priestess in charge of their instruction before I followed Kora out of the nursery at a quickened pace. I arrived at the king's study as he was leaving on his way to the Great Hall, followed by his generals and ministers. Seeing me, the men bowed their heads and parted to let me pass.

"The King of Aram has sent messengers into the city to speak with me," Akhab explained as I came to him in the corridor. "Is he not your kin?"

"Our mothers are sisters," I said, as I walked with him toward the Great Hall. "But you know family ties mean little where greed and envy arise. Is it true that he is here with an army? That he intends to make war with us?"

"That appears to be the case," Akhab answered with a weary sigh. "They have made camp outside the city. They have us surrounded – more than thirty kings with their armies, soldiers watching the gates to prevent anyone from entering or leaving the city."

"Let me go to him."

"Out of the question."

"He is my cousin. Perhaps I can reason with him."

Akhab stopped abruptly and turned to me. "I am not sending my wife into an enemy camp! Now, you may come with me to the Great Hall and be privy to these meetings, but you will not leave the safety of the palace."

258

I fell silent and, as we were outside the Hall, we composed ourselves before the doors were opened for us. Then we walked together in a stately manner toward our thrones, followed by our bodyguards, and the generals and ministers. Aharon was standing midway up the dais and seemed relieved when we appeared to take over. He bowed to us and stepped aside, while we took our places on the thrones.

The lead messenger was typical: an adolescent boy with an air of importance that melted once he faced us. He looked at me with a particular curiosity, perhaps because I was dressed modestly. I did not even wear kohl around my eyes, for I did not need the splendor of a queen when I was with my children in the nursery.

My husband raised his voice impatiently, "Well, boy, speak up. What message do you bring me from the King of Aram?"

The boy glanced at his comrades and then stood to attention. "Melekh Hadadesar says, 'Your gold and silver are mine, as are your wives and children, even the best of them.' He also says that if you do not give them up to him by the end of this day, he will burn down your city and take it by force."

Akhab bristled at this and looked to me, while I placed a gentle hand on his knee and leaned toward him, to whisper: "Tell him you will do it."

"What? Have you gone mad? Why in the name of Ba'al would I give into these demands?"

"Because you do not wish to bring war into your city." He was fuming, but I calmly went on, "It is a ruse, Akhab. Tell him you will do it, and then let me go to him, and I will convince him otherwise."

He sighed heavily and shook his head. "No, Yezeba'al. I will not put you in danger."

"I will not be in danger. He is my cousin. We played together as children. He will not harm me."

"Possibly, he is not the same as he was then. What was it you said not so long ago about family ties? If he believes you are his, he will try to make love to you."

"Then I will cut off his head."

Akhab could not help but smile at this. "Which one?"

"The better one," I said with a smirk.

"I believe you would," he replied. "But no, I will not take that chance."

259

"Am I your equal, as you have so often said, or am I not?"

"It is…!" He stopped, and reconsidered whatever he was going to say, speaking more calmly than he first began. "Yezeba'al, you are my equal in intellect and spirit, and greater in wisdom, but this is war, and it is a man's place."

"It is not war yet."

"Hadadesar has made a threat against me and my kingdom."

"Do not be so fragile, Akhab. Must everything be an affront to men? It is no wonder you are always going off to war with each other."

"It is about honor."

"It is about conceit," came my retort.

He sighed and laid his head back against the throne. Then he looked at me, his brown eyes pleading. "What will you have me do?"

"Tell him you agree to his terms and let me go to him. Perhaps we can avert a war with diplomacy."

He groaned. "Fine, you will have your way, as always."

"Did you not say I was the wisest of us two?" I said with a playful smile.

"Remind me later to cut out my tongue."

"I would never have that organ removed, for it brings me too much satisfaction."

He smiled devilishly and I knew what he was thinking then, but he had to cut his imagining short in order to deal with the more urgent matter. He looked at the lead messenger, and said, "Return to your king, and tell him I have said: 'Let it be according to your will, Melekh. I and all that I have are yours.' Tell him that before the evening star appears, I will send to him my Queen. Let him be satisfied with her, for she is worth more than all my other wives combined."

The boy looked surprised at this response, glanced once again at his comrades, then bowed, and answered, "I will tell my lord what you have said."

As the messengers walked away, the ministers and court began twittering. Once the boys were gone and the doors closed, Abram came forward and knelt before us. "*Akhu*, surely you do not mean to send the queen to play the harlot for this treacherous king?"

"Of course not," Akhab replied. "The King of Aram is a cousin to the queen. She will only speak with him and convince him to leave without further provocation."

"How will she do that, when he will expect her to lie with him and be the symbol of his conquest?"

Akhab looked to me, apparently wondering the same. Taking a deep breath, I rose to address the ministers' concerns. "My lords, my brother: have I not shown you that a woman is as capable as any man of speaking without employing seduction as a means of being heard? For seventeen years I have been your queen. In that time, I have dealt with some of the hardest of men, having managed to soften many, and not one of them have I convinced or encouraged through harlotry."

Some murmurings of agreement rose from among them, and I continued, "Hadadesar is my cousin. Our mothers were sisters, raised together at the court in Assyria where their father was king. When our fathers went to war against their mutual enemies, we laughed and played together, as children often do. And I am certain that our mutual affection has not waned over the years. If any in this kingdom may convince him to leave without making war against us, I have the greatest chance of succeeding at that, and so I must try."

After my speech, only a few continued to raise any objections, but my husband commanded them to be silent. Then we departed together, so that I could be prepared for my diplomatic mission. While Kora and the others gathered my finest robes and richest jewels, the king sat in my chamber and watched the whole procedure. "You are like a soldier being prepared for battle," he remarked, watching the women fix my gold headdress in place.

Although I had to keep my head still, I smiled and met his gaze.

"The kohl around your eyes and your crimson lips," he continued. "They are your war paint. Your headdress is your helmet; your jewels and your garments, the armor that fortifies you when you face the enemy."

The women, having finishing with my headdress, released me and I was able to respond with a chuckle. "Why do you think I always dress this way holding court? For all the public functions, for that matter." I turned toward the mirror to inspect. "Every time I must face the people, I am fortified in this way."

"You see the people as your enemies?"

"No," I answered, meeting his gaze in the reflection in the mirror. Then I turned to face him directly. "But I never know when one might appear, so I must always be prepared."

A sad smile turned up the corners of his mouth and I could see by the way he leaned with his cheek upon his hand and gazed at me, that he was fearful of my mission. Perhaps, too, he was wondering how I would be protected if my cousin attempted to force himself upon me. I, meanwhile, was putting on my rings and bracelets and thinking of all the same and how I might reassure my husband before I left the safety of the palace.

Once fully dressed in all my splendor, he came to take me in his arms. "I hope you know what you are doing, Yezeba'al. Promise me, you will not let him take you."

"I will not let him take me, love. I will have the best of my eunuchs, and I will take Kora with me into the king's tent."

"What can Kora do to protect you?"

"You underestimate us, my love," I replied, casting Kora a playful smile, which she returned as she carried away my former robes.

Akhab looked at me curiously and, when she had gone away, asked in a whisper, "Will you give her to him instead?"

"Of course not. I would never ask such a thing of any woman, least of all Kora. Besides, he would know the difference. Surely, he will recognize me. I have not changed so much since last I met him."

"You were merely a girl then. So much has changed. You are a woman now, and a queen, and you are more beautiful than you were the day I married you. Already he covets you; once he has seen you, he will be overcome by his lust and his desire for conquest."

I placed a hand to his cheek and looked at him fondly. "Trust me, husband. I will not fail. And if he will not listen, then you will have this war you so desperately crave."

"I do not crave a war, Yezeba'al. He is the one who has come seeking a war with me by threatening to take that which I love best."

He drew me into a kiss. When he pulled away, I laughed and used the inside of my sleeve to wipe the red paint from his lips. I went to my mirror to touch it up, and then I turned back to my husband. "You see now that the paint upon my lips is untouched. It will be the same when I return. I will be true to you, husband."

"I know you will be, Yezeba'al," he replied. "It is him that I worry about."

I let him slide his arms around my waist once again and took his jaw in my hand as I gazed into his eyes. Then I pulled away and beckoned to Kora, and she followed me out with four of my eunuchs in tow. For all my outward confidence, I was secretly terrified to face this man, for I, too, knew he was in love with me even when we were children, and I did not want my husband's fears to become true.

Walking with courage and dignity, I arrived at the camp outside the city with Kora and my four eunuchs just as the evening star appeared over the horizon. I took it as a sign of Ashtarti's protection and I smiled up at the star, bringing my hand to hover above my lips and tipping my head in gratitude. Even before we reached the camp, Hazael, the servant of Hadadesar came to meet us with a bow.

"Are you truly Ba'alah Yezeba'al?"

I pulled at the beads around my neck and turned the opal scarab to show him my seal underneath. He leaned in to scrutinize the inscriptions. Satisfied, he said, "The king awaits, Ba'alah. I shall take you to him."

I gave a single nod and glanced at Kora, and then we followed the steward through the growing throng of curious soldiers and generals who gathered to observe our walk to the king's pavilion. Outside, Hazael stopped and turned to us, holding out his hands. "Wait here, if you please, Ba'alah. I will tell him you have come."

The guards outside the tent looked at me curiously. I kept my head high and my gaze fixed on the entryway between them. I did not deign to give them any sign of benevolence. At last, Hazael appeared again, beckoning to me from between the curtains. "My lord is eager to see you, Ba'alah."

I stepped forward and Kora moved to come with me, but then the steward said, "Forgive me, Ba'alah, but my lord has said that your lady must remain outside with the eunuchs. He wishes to speak with you alone."

My apprehension rose, but I forced a smile and gave a nod of assent. Then I gave the same to Kora, hoping to alleviate any fear she might have at letting me go alone. I took her by the wrist, and she clutched my arm as I whispered, "It will be all right, Kora."

263

Then I pulled away and at last she released my arm so I could step into the pavilion to face the King of Aram. He was bent over a map on a high table with some of the lesser kings who had come with him as allies. Although he was still a youth when last we met, I recognized my cousin immediately. Dressed in a richly embroidered tunic and with a belt around his waist holding a sword, he was tall and broad-shouldered, his dark hair cut short, with kohl around his eyes. His full lips, surrounded by a well-trimmed goatee, turned up in a grin and I noticed the familiar glint in his black eyes when I appeared.

"Yeza! It really is you. I thought Akhab would try to pass off one of his concubines as his queen. I was truly surprised he had agreed to at least some of my terms."

"Hadi, if you wanted to visit, you could have just asked. Why all this blustering?"

He turned to the other kings. "My lords, leave us. It has been a long time since I had the pleasure of my dearest cousin."

The other kings, many of them old and grey, smirked as they left, and some of them leered at me as they passed. I looked away and pretended not to notice, waiting for them all to be gone before I looked once again to Hadi. He held out his arms, but instead of embracing him I walked up to slap him across the face. Then, as he held his jaw, I tore into him. "What is wrong with you? Bringing an army to my husband's kingdom and making these demands, strutting around like an all-important—"

"Peacock?" He knew well of my love for them. "My, my, Yezaba'al; you have not changed a bit. Well, you have aged I suppose, but only in the best of ways." He smelled of alcohol as he circled me like a vulture, examining my form. I slapped his hand away when he tried to touch me as he went. Then he stopped when he reached the front of me again, and said, "Is it true you have given six children to the king? You do not look as though you have had so many."

"Stop trying to play nice with me, Hadi. I am not here to play with you."

"Pity. I had hoped to make love to the Queen of Yisrael before the night was over. I might have known Akhab was the one playing games, agreeing so readily to my terms."

"This is not a game, Hadi. This is a very serious matter, yet here you stand, acting like a boy in the nursery playing at battle."

He smiled. "I remember all the times we played war together. How many times did you slay me from the back of a wooden horse? I would die ten thousand deaths just to make you happy, Yeza." While he slithered closer, I sighed impatiently and looked away. "I remember, too, the time when we slipped into the tent in the nursery."

We were older then. I was thirteen, he was fifteen. It was the last time I had seen him. Our fathers and the other Canaanite kings went to war against the Assyrians that year and lost. While they went to battle, Hadi and I played a different sort of game in the children's play tent, a miniature version of the one we were in now. His breath was hot in my ear, as he leaned in and whispered, "The way we learned to explore each other's bodies when they began to change..."

He brought his hand up to stroke my breast through my robe, but the moment his fingers slid across my nipple, my hands shot up and snatched his wrist and I twisted his arm behind his back. He cried out, and then I released him, and he stumbled forward. He managed to catch himself on the high table, and I said, "Touch me again, Hadi, and I will make it so you can never make love to a woman again."

Turning to me with a sigh, and leaning back against the table, he rubbed his wrist and looked like a dog who had been kicked. "If you did not come to pick up where we left off, Yeza, then why are you here?"

"I came to tell you to leave. Take up your arms, get in your chariot, and return to Aram where you belong. This is my husband's kingdom, and mine, and we will not let you have it."

He appeared not to be listening as he toyed with the beak of a bird skull on the table. I realized it was the skull of a peacock, and I wondered if he had chosen it when he knew I was coming or if it was only a coincidence. Then he sighed and looked up at me. "I will leave Yisrael under one condition: that you leave with me. Denounce your husband, give up your title, and be my queen instead."

"You already have a queen."

"I am tired of her, Yeza. She is not half the woman you are. None of my wives are."

"Do not stoop to flattery, Hadi. It does not suit you."

"Is it flattery if it is true?"

265

"How would you know if it is true? You have never had me."

He winced. The truth seemed to sting, but he quickly recovered. "I do not need to make love to you to know that you would far surpass them in every way. Ever since that day in my tent, I have longed to finish with you what was begun. We were so close, Yeza – why did you stop me? I know you wanted it as much as I did."

"I was betrothed to Akhab. I had a duty to maintain my virtue."

He scoffed. "What is the point of virtue? It is a dull thing, that. It keeps one from seeking pleasure wherever it may be found. So much misery is born from virtue, but pleasure brings such happiness."

"I need not seek pleasure, for I have plenty with my husband."

He almost laughed. "Come now, Yeza; after all these years? Surely, he has grown tired of you and you of him. No man or woman can tolerate one another after so many years of marriage, let alone still find pleasure in the act."

"I can assure you that we do. It is why we have so many children together: more than he has with any of his other wives."

Hadi twisted his mouth to the side. "So, I have heard. He cannot keep his hands off you. Is it true that you have made love to him while holding court?"

"No," I said with contempt. "And you are foolish to believe these rumors, let alone repeat them." I realized that our conduct at the Ba'alim feasts must have been the cause of this rumor, but I was disgusted that it had morphed into such an outlandish report.

Finally, I asked point-blank: "So, you will not leave?"

"Not unless I get what I have come for – and apparently she will not have me, so I will have to take her by force." He began toying with the peacock skull again; now it was in his hand. Looking at me, he smiled wickedly. "That could be equally appealing, wrestling you to the floor and ravishing you. I could, you know. I am a king: who would dare stop me?"

"Akhab was right: you have changed, Hadi. You are not the boy I once knew. I cannot find what I ever liked in you."

His countenance darkened and he crushed the skull in his fist. I started at the sound of it cracking to pieces. Then he wiped the fragments and dust from his hands and came toward me. Even though I was afraid, I stood my ground. "One last chance, Yeza: give yourself to me now, or I will make war on this city. Hundreds, possibly even thousands will die; the city will burn, all so you can maintain your precious virtue? Is one night of passion worth so much destruction?"

"Apparently, you think it is since you are the one threatening to raze my husband's city over me. He will not take kindly to that."

He sniffed. "I do not fear your husband, you know. But you — you I do fear, for I know what you are capable of."

"You should fear my husband. His anger is far worse than mine, and he is skilled in his chariot. You would be a fool to make war with him. Better to have him as your ally than your enemy, Hadi."

"So, you will not give yourself to me?"

"No. And if you force me, I will kill you afterward."

He smiled. "Afterward... I told you I would die ten thousand deaths for you."

"This one would be real. I told you, Hadi: this is not a game, and I am not playing. Leave Shomron. Leave Yisrael. Or suffer the consequences."

I turned then and left his tent. I found Kora and my eunuchs right outside, waiting for me. Kora looked to me, and I gave her a nod, although I was still too nervous to smile. I started to lead them away when Hadi came out and called to me. "Yeza, wait!"

I stopped, lifted my eyes toward the night sky, and sighed heavily. Then I turned around to face him. "What, Hadi?"

"You do not want to walk away from here, or the next time you see me, I will not be charitable."

Now, I smiled. "I do not need your charity, cousin. But you will need mine when my husband hears how you threatened me. Shalom, Hadi."

With that, I walked away and was relieved that he did not try to stop me.

When I returned to the palace, my husband had heard that I was coming and was waiting with some of the ministers and his bodyguards when I entered. The moment I reached him, he took me into his arms and held me tight, and then he kissed me fervently. When he drew back and wiped the red smear from his lips, I gasped.

"But my love, you did not look to see the paint on my lips was still intact."

There were tears in his eyes and he smiled at me. "I did not need to, Yezeba'al. You are a faithful woman." Then he paused, and asked, "He did not try to hurt you?"

I shook my head. "He blustered, of course, and made many threats. But he is still only a boy who thinks himself a man. It is not surprising that his first act as king would be to start a war."

We walked together into the Great Hall, where the rest of our court awaited our return. They all prostrated themselves when we entered and remained that way until we were seated on our thrones and my husband bade them to rise. When they did, he said, "The Queen of Yisrael has returned to us. My love, tell us what you have uncovered on your diplomatic mission."

With a nod to my husband, I rose from my throne and addressed the court: "The King of Aram is a petulant child who thinks of war as if it were still a game in his nursery." There was some laughter from the court, and I continued, "But that does not mean the threat he and his army pose should be taken lightly. I believe he does intend to make war on us; I was unable to convince him to do otherwise. He has many kings and their armies also with him, and while he is inexperienced in battle, some of those with him are not. I recognized there many kings I know of who fought beside my father, the King of Tzidon. They are seasoned warriors and capable leaders, and although many of them and the soldiers were drunk as I walked through their camp, I believe we should prepare for battle – and that we should take the battle to them while they are ill-prepared."

One of the elder ministers came forward now. "Melkah, forgive me, but I do not believe that a woman is capable of making decisions about war and battles. Not even a queen as glorious as yourself," he bowed, "is capable of leading an army."

"I am not going to lead my husband's army, my lord. I am only saying that, as I was in the enemy's camp and saw the condition of his army, now would be the time for us to strike."

"We do not have the men here to engage such a multitude in battle, Ba'alah," said Abram. "It would be foolish to attempt it."

"That is why I say we should go now, when they are not in their battle-gear, and they are too drunk even to defend themselves. A stealth-attack in the dark of night."

"War is not made in the dark of night, Melkah," said another of the ministers, with amusement in his voice, like that of a father speaking to one of his children after they said something silly. I resented it, but many of the other men followed with laughter as he continued, "Night is a time for ghosts and spirits to roam about, not for armed men."

Despite their patronizing attitudes, I remained adamant. "Which is precisely why we should strike now when they would least expect it. When I approached the enemy camp, the star of Ashtarti was before me as a sign of her blessing. And as I returned to the city, the star was rising in its path – a sign of good fortune in this matter. If we attack in the dark, while he and his men are drunk and unarmed, we will be victorious."

"And we will make of ourselves dishonorable men," said another of the elder ministers.

"War itself is dishonorable, when it is waged for no other reason than to fill coffers and expand borders. How many times have you urged the king to go to war for these reasons?"

He waved his hands dismissively at me. "This is why women do not make decisions about war. They do not understand the way of these things."

Murmurs of agreement arose from the other ministers, and I sighed heavily and sat back on my throne. I did manage to convince a few, but the majority remained in opposition and the bickering lasted a couple of hours before my husband finally brought an end to it. He had listened carefully to every side, putting in his own thoughts from time to time, but he relied too much on the counsel of his ministers. When he rose from his throne and dismissed the court for the night, I thought to myself, *Men are hopeless when it comes to war.* That was the one thing about which I could never convince them, although I could often persuade my husband when I was alone with him. Of course, that would not make a difference tonight, for it was too late to take the course that I suggested, and the court would not meet again until morning.

When the court gathered in the Great Hall early the next morning, the messengers from the King of Aram returned with a new message and greater threats. "Melekh Hadadesar says, 'I sent to you saying that you shall deliver to me your silver, and your gold, and your wives, and your children. And you sent me the greatest of these, your Queen: yet she refused me. Now, not only will I take all that you have promised me, but I will send my soldiers to you this time tomorrow, and they will search your house, and the houses of your servants, and whatever is pleasant in your eyes, they will put it in their hand and take it away.' That is what my lord, the King of Aram says."

Akhab had listened patiently, but now he almost laughed. He called to his ministers, "Do you see how this man seeks to cause trouble? For he sent to me for my family and riches, and I did not deny him. Now, he commands not only these things but all that I have and all that you have, as well. What would you advise? As you had so much to say on these matters last night when the Queen returned to us, tell us now, what you think I should do."

The ministers shifted uncomfortably. The messengers looked between us, unaware of what he meant by what he said, for they had not been privy to our deliberations the previous night. While I was not pleased that my advice had gone unheeded, I was satisfied by the king's tacit reproachment of his ministers.

"Well?" the king's voice boomed. "What should I do? Shall I open your houses to him first when he sends his soldiers to murder and pillage and rape our city? Shall I send him your wives and children as well as my own? Tell me what you think I should do, for you have never been so timid and quiet before now."

"Do not listen to him, Melekh," one of them finally said. "Do not give your consent."

I remained still, lifting only my eyes to the ceiling. Meanwhile, my husband said, "Thank you. I could not possibly have made that decision without you."

I had to look away and pretended to cough behind my hand to hide my amusement. In doing so, I noticed Aharon looked confused: sarcasm was always lost on him. Then my husband addressed the messengers. "Tell my lord the king, 'All that you sent for to me, your servant, at the first I will provide; but this thing I cannot do.'"

When the boys continued to stand dumbfounded, he waved his hands impatiently, and said, "Go on; tell your master what I have said."

They seemed to recover their senses then, and the leader of them bowed. "It will be done, Melekh."

Then the boys went away, and the king dismissed the court for a break, during which we returned to our private quarters to eat and spend time with our children. Akhab was holding Ba'alesar upon his lap, while I was speaking with Tala, and our two eldest boys laid across the floor playing a game, when Aharon came to inform us that the messengers had returned. I looked to my husband, who sighed heavily and lifted our youngest from his lap. Ba'alesar ran to throw his arms around my legs, not wanting me to leave, but I moved him aside and Tala took to comforting him instead, while I joined my husband.

Back in the Great Hall, once again seated on our thrones, we listened to my cousin's latest message, this time read from a sheaf of papyrus from which one of the older boys read. "The King of Aram says, 'You mock and play games with me, Melekh Akhab, but I tell you that my army is great and mighty. Let it be done to me and worse, by the will of the gods, if the dust of Shomron will be enough for handfuls for all the warriors who follow me.'" Rolling up the papyrus, the boy said, "The King of Aram awaits your reply, Melekh."

Akhab looked to me with a mischievous gleam in his eye, and then he said, "Tell him, 'A man who puts on his armor should not boast as one who takes it off.'"

This brought some chuckles from the ministers who understood his quip, while I smiled and shook my head, looking down at my lap. Then the boys left once again to deliver their message, as my husband reached for my hand and brought it to his lips. "Let us see what he has to say to this. I do tire of his games." Then he kissed my fingers, and I chuckled.

"He will understand your meaning and will not take kindly to it. My cousin is anything but humble."

"You think it will provoke him to attack?"

His hopeful eagerness angered me, but I pushed it back and nodded solemnly. "I hope we will be ready for it. I do not look forward to you leaving me again for another war."

"You know that I do try to avoid it, my love. But diplomacy can only take us so far. You know that."

"Just promise you will return to me."

"Do you see victory for us?"

271

"I do not see anything. I saw victory for us the other night, had you gone when I said, but now…" I shook my head. "Now, it is out of Ashtarti's hands. Perhaps you may find the aid of Yahowah in this matter, for the Ba'alim have gone silent."

With that, I rose and, with a bow of my head, left my husband to return to my private quarters. Akhab quickly dismissed the court and came after me. Walking alongside me, he asked, "Will you allow me to make love to you, for it may be the last time before I go to war."

"Should I allow it, when you have brought this war upon yourself?"

"Surely, you are not still angry with me for not heeding your advice?"

I stopped walking and turned on him. "You think I like the idea of you going off to war? You are not a young man anymore, Akhab – look, there is grey in your beard." I tugged at it when I said this. Then I started walking again, while he continued pleading his case.

"I am still strong enough for battle. Besides, I only ever lead my men and command them, mostly. I am not ever really in the thick of it."

I scoffed. "I know you have done it before when I have asked you not to – that you have put on a disguise and battled alongside them, as if you were one of them."

"Yezeba'al, I am a king."

"Yes, you are a king, and your duty is to survive and to lead your people, not to die alongside them!"

"I will not die."

"You do not know that!"

"A king must be a good warrior as well as a diplomat." When I did not answer, he took my hands and moved to stand in front of me so I would stop. "Yezeba'al, please – you must know that it was not an easy decision for me to make. It was true, what the other men were saying, but I know I should have listened to you."

"I may not always be right, Akhab, but when I am speaking with the will of the Ba'alim, you should trust it."

"Have they abandoned us because I did not listen?"

"They certainly will not help us; not in this. Our chance came and went, and now they cannot help us."

272

"So, you really think that I should summon a prophet of Yahowah to ask for his aid?"

I shrugged. "It cannot hurt. Perhaps Yahowah will aid you in victory, for my cousin is worse than I am – unless, of course, he cannot be worse because he is not a woman?"

Akhab sighed, while I stepped around him and continued toward our private quarters. Then he caught up to me, and said, "Please, my love. Be frank with me: if I ask for Yahowah's help, will you hold it against me?"

When I met his gaze, my anger vanished. "No, my love; I will not hold it against you. Unlike the zealots, I do not believe it is wrong to seek the aid of other gods, for they all have something to offer if it is worth the price."

He paused to consider. "And if he asks of me to abandon the Ba'alim, to give victory?"

"Do what you must," I said with a wave, starting up the stairs. "I do not care anymore." Then I paused in the middle of the staircase, and turned back to my husband, "As long as he will not take our children from us, worship him alone, worship the Ba'alim, or worship no one."

He stopped in the stairwell beside me. It was narrow, so we were pressed together. He took advantage of this, slipping his arms around me, and saying, "I worship you."

I met his gaze and, despite my desire not to be moved, I knowingly fell into his trap. When he moved to kiss me, I gave into him. Then, as if he was a young man again, he lifted me in his arms to carry me up the rest of the stairwell and to my chamber. And there, we cloistered ourselves together for our own kind of worship.

11

Arsenals of Women

Early the next morning, my husband planned to summon from within the city a known prophet of Yahowah. Before this could happen, however, another prophet appeared before us, having come of his own accord. This was an ancient man who walked with a stick to aid his limp. He stood as straight as he could manage, after offering a feeble bow with the help of one of his young disciples. The man truly appeared to me as if he were a walking corpse. *Has he crawled out of the grave to come here now?* I thought with some amusement, as I looked upon his ancient form.

This prophet, who called himself Zechariah, reported that the army of kings camped outside the city walls was not even dressed for battle, and that the majority of the men in the camp had appeared to be drunk. I was not surprised at this report, as I had seen much the same when I had been there on that first night. He, being an old man of little notice, claimed to have taken a walk outside the city to observe the enemy encampment. Coming near enough to see the state of things, he had pretended to be an idiot who had wandered too far from the city and, as a result, had endured mocking and jeers from some of the drunken soldiers who chased him away when he came too near. Thankfully, they had not suspected him of being a spy. Thus, he was able to bring this information to us.

"You have my thanks for taking it upon yourself to do this, Zechariah," my husband offered.

"It was not my own will but the will of Yahowah that led me to do this thing, Melekh, who also urged me to come to you today." The old man was so feeble, I feared he might drop dead in the middle of our Hall. I could not imagine him being able to take a walk outside the city in the first place. If he had done as he claimed, it was no wonder he was able to get away with playing the village idiot without drawing suspicion from the drunken fools my cousin called his warriors.

My husband, meanwhile, smiled at the prophet. "Yahowah has not abandoned us, then?"

I believe Zechariah meant to laugh, though no sound came out. I noticed that he had no teeth in his mouth and, without thought, I ran my tongue over my own teeth in gratitude. Getting old seemed a terrible thing, and for a moment I was struck with the realization that I was not a young woman anymore. I shuddered and tried not to think about these things, though. They were hardly important when we were on the brink of war.

In answer to my husband's question, the prophet said, "Yahowah has spoken to me regarding this, Melekh."

My husband sat up on the edge of his throne. I turned my head and looked at him, surprised by his enthusiastic interest. "You hear him then?" The old man nodded. "You hear his voice, as clear as you hear mine now?"

"I hear it, Melekh; as clear as I hear you now."

"And what does he say?"

I pressed my lips firmly together and exhaled quietly, turning my gaze off to the side.

"Yahowah says, 'Have you seen this great multitude that has gathered outside your city gates? Behold, I will deliver it into your hand, so you will know that I am God.'"

"By whom shall he deliver it?" my husband wanted to know. I could not tell if he was serious or if he said this in jest. Perhaps he was truly hoping for a miracle that would take it out of his hands that day. Later, he confided to me that it was all these things at once.

The man closed his eyes and stood so still that I wondered if he had died standing up, because he did not appear to even breathe in that moment. I watched him curiously, wondering if he was truly listening to someone speaking to him that the rest of us could not hear, or if he was yet another charlatan who claimed to hear the voice of a god in his head. I had seen many of the latter, but none of the former. Suddenly, he inhaled deeply, and his eyes shot open, as he reached out his hand. "Yahowah says, 'By the soldiers of provincial princes, you shall have it.'"

Some of those provincial princes would be the king's brothers and uncles, who maintained their own armies on their estates spread throughout the kingdom. Most of them were here with us now, though, being active members of our court. Their armies were not with them in Shomron, for it was their duty to guard the estates. I beckoned to my husband and leaned in, to whisper, "How shall that happen? There is no way to send messengers out of the city to summon them from the provinces."

My husband shook his head and held up his hand with a shrug, as if wondering the same. While I began thinking more deeply on this matter of getting messengers out of the city, he remained keenly interested in what the prophet had to say, and asked, "Who shall be the first to strike the other?"

"You, Melekh," the prophet answered without hesitation. His eyes remained closed.

Akhab rubbed his beard and nodded slowly, and I could see that he was deep in thought. Then he dismissed the prophet and called forward the ministers of his court who had estates in the provinces.

He said to them, "My lords, I wonder at what this prophet has claimed. Is it possible, do you think, for you to summon your armies from the provinces to come here in time to end this siege? I do not have enough men mustered here in the city to defeat this army, but if we may summon the provincial armies, and the rest of my army at Yezreel, we might stand a chance."

"If what the prophet says is true, that you will be the first to strike," said his brother, Akhaz, "then there may be time." Then his enthusiasm dropped, and he said, "Only, I do not know how we could get messengers out of the city without being captured. They are not letting anyone into or out of the city, not even farmers or merchants."

"They allowed me to pass," I spoke up.

Akhaz smiled, as if amused. "*Akhatu*, are you suggesting you will go out and deliver these messages to the provinces yourself?"

The other men laughed at this, but I rolled my eyes. Then I answered, "Not at all, *Akhimelekh*. But I have an idea, and it may work."

I looked to my husband, who made a gesture with his hand for me to go on. He watched me with a faint smile, as he always did when he knew I had come up with a solution that neither he nor any of his best advisors and ministers could devise.

Addressing the court, I said, "Several of the king's women are at various stages of pregnancy, yet there is only one fledgling midwife stationed with us at Shomron."

"What does this have to do with anything?" one of the elders asked impatiently. Men understood little in the way of these things, so of course he would think this was little more than silly women's talk. When I was younger, I would have been frustrated by his misinterpretation, but now I understood and would not be dismayed.

"If one of the women went into labor prematurely, or was having complications with her pregnancy," I patiently explained, "we would need to get her to Megiddu to the care of the more experienced midwives. Perhaps the King of Aram, taking pity, would permit us to leave the city for this purpose – especially being that he wants to take possession of the king's wives, and should not like for one of them to be lost when she could be saved. Then, instead of going to Megiddu, we go to Yezreel where I can rally the armies from there."

The men looked to each other, murmuring in consideration. I was pleased that they were not immediately dismissive of my idea. Akhab at once clapped his hands together in agreement. "My love, that is brilliant! I believe it may actually work. This is indeed why you are my Queen. As it is your idea, and you know a great deal more about these things than any of us, may I leave you in charge of working out the details of how this might be carried out?"

"Certainly, Melekh," I replied with a gracious nod.

Then my husband gestured to me with his finger, and I leaned closer to listen as he whispered, "Remind me to thank you for this later."

I smiled and looked at him from the corners of my eyes. "You can thank me in bed."

"I expected no less," he replied, bringing my hand once again to his lips.

It took some time for us to mete out all the details of my plan, but once it was complete and the men satisfied that it might work, I went forth to set it all in motion. Zubira was the wife I chose to execute my plan, and I had little doubt that she would agree to it. She was at this time about six months pregnant with her third child. Because she was one of the most beautiful of Akhab's wives, I was certain that my cousin would greatly desire her and not wish to see her lost. She was afraid but showed great courage by agreeing to come with me on this mission.

The blood of a calf sacrificed to Ba'al for the success of our mission was smeared in her nether region and allowed to drip down

277

from between her legs, to make it appear that she was going into early labor. We dressed for travel, although I had her dressed somewhat more elegantly, to ensure it was clear she was a wife of Akhab. She pretended to be in distress, as she was carried on a litter from the palace. I rode on the back of a horse alongside her, holding her hand and reassuring her all would be well, that her child would not be lost. Kora was with us on the back of a donkey, and we were accompanied by twenty of our eunuchs, who had all been debriefed on the plan and how they were to respond. As I knew would happen, we were stopped on our way out of the city by a group of soldiers belonging to the King of Aram. They were ten in number, but I quickly recognized the most important and sensible among them. Addressing two of them, I demanded to be taken to their king. When they passed each other doubtful gazes, I added, "Tell him I am Yezeba'al, Melkah Yisrael, and that I have brought one of Akhab's wives to meet him."

The two spoke with each other quietly and seemed to be arguing, but then they finally agreed to take us to Hadadesar. I dismounted from my horse, leaving it in the hands of Kora and the eunuchs who were expected to stay behind, and I helped Zubira from her litter when it was lowered to the ground. Then we were led through the camp to the king's pavilion. As expected, my cousin agreed to see us, and we were taken inside where we found him again drinking and cajoling with the other kings. This time, the other kings remained there with us while I brought Zubira forward, directing her from behind with my hands on her shoulders. She performed magnificently, weeping real tears and trembling convincingly. For a moment, I wondered if she was truly acting or if it was her fear of what this king might do if he realized what we were up to.

My cousin was reclined casually in his chair, and he examined us curiously as we approached. As I had expected, he watched Zubira with great interest. "What is wrong with her? Is she truly one of Akhab's wives?"

"She is," I answered. "She is Zubira the Kushite, one of Akhab's favorite wives. As you can see, she is heavy with child but there is something wrong, and we fear she may be losing the child and that her life too may be at risk."

"So? Why have you brought her to me? What can I possibly do for her?"

"I had not intended to bring her to you, but as your men have attempted to arrest us, I had no choice but to come to you, even at the risk that you might be uncharitable toward me."

He sniffed, perhaps remembering his last words to me when I left him before. Then, after taking a drink from his cup, he asked, "If you were not coming to me, why were you leaving the city? Should she not be in bed, attended to by midwives?"

"There are no experienced midwives stationed at Shomron, unfortunately," I explained. "I must take her to Megiddu, so she can be attended to as soon as possible."

"Truly? You brought a pregnant woman to Shomron and did not bother to bring even a single midwife to tend to her?"

"There is one," I admitted, thinking quickly of a believable solution, "but she has fallen ill after eating rotten food – since you will not permit any merchants to enter our city to replenish our food stores."

"My army has only been here a few weeks, Yeza. Surely, the palace is well-stocked, for a few months at least. She could not have been starving."

With a smile, I answered calmly, "She is a simple woman, prone to panic. As she has never lived through a siege before, she was afraid to let any food go to waste, for fear that we might run out. After all, we cannot know how long the siege will last. At any rate, we need to get to Megiddu. We must seek the aid of one of the other midwives stationed there, if there is any chance to save the child and preserve Zubira's life. As you know, childbirth is a dangerous activity, and very messy."

With her permission, I lifted Zubira's robes just enough so that my cousin could see some of the blood that had run down to her ankles. The blood was thick and had started to congeal now, and the men groaned and grimaced at the sight of it. My cousin wrinkled his face and turned away.

"As you can see," I continued, dropping her robes, "she is in grave need of our more experienced midwives. I fear if we do not reach Megiddu by midnight, it will be too late."

"I do not have a midwife on hand, for obvious reasons, but I do have my field surgeons. Perhaps they could help her?"

"Are battlefield surgeons familiar with the nuances of the female body, especially concerning the particularities of childbirth?"

279

"Well, no I suppose they are most likely not familiar with it. But you cannot travel such a distance with a woman who is in labor. I may only be a man, but I know that this is not safe for either of you. I am surprised Akhab would permit you to leave under these circumstances."

He looked at me suspiciously and I nearly lost my composure, but then I used it to my advantage. "He does not know we are leaving, Melekh. It was my decision, made in haste the moment I was made aware of Zubira's distress." Then, doing what I knew might be the only thing to move him, I stepped closer to him and placed a hand upon his knee. "Hadi, please. She is one of Akhab's favorite wives, for she is beautiful and knows well how to please a man. It would be terrible for him to lose her."

His gaze fell upon my hand, and he shifted in his chair. Then he rose and began pacing, rubbing his cheeks and beard with both hands. When he turned back toward me, he grabbed my wrist and pulled me against his body, gripping my arms so I could not pull away. The other kings sat up, suddenly made sober and keenly interested to watch what might happen next. No doubt, they were hoping for a show and perhaps even the chance to take part in its production. I swallowed hard and forced myself to look up at him. His gaze burned with lust, and for the first time I truly was afraid of him.

"If you make love to me, Yeza – here, tonight – I will let her go with your men and servants to look after her."

My lips parted and I desperately considered my options. How had I not anticipated this? How was I to avoid it? I looked to Zubira, who met my gaze with widened eyes and discreetly shook her head. We had to maintain the ruse, or things could be far worse for us – for her, especially, given her condition. Yet, if I agreed... No, I could not be unfaithful to my husband, not even to save his city. Then I thought of what my cousin had said to me, the first time I had come to speak with him: *Hundreds, possibly even thousands will die; the city will burn... Is one night of passion worth so much destruction?*

Closing my eyes and breathing carefully, I began to fortify myself to do what was needed to put an end to this. I swallowed, took one last breath, and opened my eyes. My lips parted as I was about to speak, when suddenly Zubira shrieked and fell to her knees, clutching at her abdomen. Hadi released his grip on my arms and some of the other men jumped from their chairs. All attention was

280

drawn to her as she fell to the floor writhing and moaning, and for a moment, I feared she was truly dying.

Hadi looked at her in horror. "What is wrong with her? What is happening?"

"I am losing my baby!" she cried. "Help me, Yezeba'al! I am afraid! I do not want to die!"

I went to kneel over her and calmed her and placed my hands on her abdomen as if to feel the position of the baby. Not that the men would know what I was doing, but it would make the whole act more convincing – and I wanted to be sure it was only an act. Zubira met my gaze to let me know that she was only pretending, and so I held her hands and caressed her face, and then I turned back to my cousin. "Please, Hadi! If you let us go now, I promise I will come back to you and I will do whatever you want. But she needs to get to Megiddu, before it is too late, and I must go with her to ensure her safety."

"How will you even get her there in time? It looks as though she is already lost."

"The baby will surely be lost, but if I can get her to Megiddu by midnight, there is still a chance that she may yet survive."

"Well, you cannot go alone with only a small contingent of eunuchs to guard you along the way. How many do you have with you?"

"Twenty, but I cannot send to the king, my husband, for more of his men. He cannot know that we have left the palace until we are too far for him to stop us. Some of my ladies remain to tell him where we have gone, but he will be angry with me for taking this risk." Then, looking up at him from beneath my lashes, I whispered, "In fact, I am afraid to return to him, for fear of what he might do to me."

"You may return to me – I will keep you safe, Yeza. Just…take some of my men."

The other kings began to moan and grumble, and one of them sputtered angrily. "This is ridiculous! You cannot send some of your own soldiers to guard these foolish women, Hadi!"

Another said, "Are you truly so blinded by your lust for this woman that you cannot see she is trying to weaken us by taking some of your men on this…reckless errand!"

I shook my head and insisted, "I do not need your men, Hadi. I just need you to let us go, now, before it is too late."

Then one of the kings, the eldest among them, said, "How do we know you do not have a message tucked into your robes? They should be searched, Hadadesar, would you not agree?"

I knew this king – lecherous old man. He had fought beside my father many times and was known for his rude handling of women. I was not surprised by his suggestion. My cousin, naturally, agreed. They searched Zubira first and, of course, found nothing. We would not have been so stupid as to write down a message that could be intercepted, and they likely knew it, but they were gratified in their search of her body – although they avoided that bloody place between her legs, and I was grateful she was spared from that at least.

After searching Zubira, I was grabbed by the arms and pulled to my feet by two of the men. They held me in place while Hadi and the lecherous old king slipped their hands within and beneath my robes, grabbing at places where their hands should not have gone, just as they had done to Zubira. But then Hadi lifted my robes, slid his hands up my thighs, and shoved two of his fingers inside me with a grin. He was rough in his manner and his fingernails scraped and pinched at my tender flesh. I bore this with as much dignity as possible; only a single tear managed to break loose and slide down my cheek.

When he removed his fingers, he held them up and announced, "Look how Akhab's queen desires me."

I held back the urge to spit in his face, knowing that it would not have helped, and looked away when he stuck his fingers in his mouth. My face burned with anger and shame.

When they had finished searching my robes for any signs of a hidden message, I was released. Then Hadi looked at me suspiciously. "Megiddu is...not far from Yezreel, which is closer to Shomron. Yezreel is where the King of Yisrael keeps most of his horses and chariots, is it not?"

Straightening my robes and adjusting my mantle, I claimed, "I do not know. I am a woman – I do not pay attention to these things. Megiddu is our family home. It is where we keep most of the king's children, as it is safer for them than in Shomron." I wondered only later if I had made an error in telling him this. "That is why we also keep the nurses and midwives there, and any of the king's women who are in an advanced stage of pregnancy, such that they must be

282

laid up in their beds. Zubira is not far enough along for us to have thought she would have need of a midwife, which is why we did not bring more than one."

The lecherous old king who had, only moments ago, taken great pleasure in handling my breasts, now scoffed. "Can you not seek a midwife from within your city? Surely, there are midwives for the common people."

"You think that a common midwife would be suitable to tend to the wife of a king, Melekh? Would you have a commoner tend to your wives?"

Hadi sighed, and then he waved carelessly. "Fine, Yeza; go. But I expect you to return to me, as you have promised. I *will* have you in my bed. I will not be made out a fool for believing in a treacherous woman."

"There is no treachery in me, Hadi," I insisted. Then, to be more convincing, I went to him, pressed my body to his, and brought my hand to the swollen place between his thighs. I grabbed tightly, even stroking a bit through his robes as I held his gaze. His breath quivered and he grabbed my hand to not let me pull it away. I squeezed tightly and he moved to me, pulling up his robes and forcing me to take it bare in my hand. I did not want to be unfaithful, but I knew that I must do this least bit, so that my cousin would be convinced. I grasped firmly, and then I gave him pleasure until he was satisfied.

The other men watched eagerly, but Zubira looked away. I hoped she did not think me untrue, for I had done it for my husband's kingdom, and for his wives, and for his children.

I wiped my hand on his robes and let them fall. Then, to be wholly convincing, I took his face in my other hand, and kissed him ardently. When I pulled away, I met his gaze, and said, "A promise, sealed with a kiss: I will not be untrue to my lord, Hadi."

Of course, in his arrogance, he would think that I meant him. Then Hadi grabbed me and kissed me hungrily before releasing me. "Go, get her to Megiddo. And when she has been deposited safely there, you will return to me here."

"It may take a few days..."

"Why?"

"I will want to stay with her throughout the ordeal, to give her comfort and reassurance and to make sure she lives through it.

283

Please, give us that, at least. It is my duty, as chief wife, to look after her wellbeing." Then, placing a hand on his, "I would do the same if we were your wives, Melekh."

He smiled at the thought, surely believing it would come to pass. Then he assented with a nod, and I helped Zubira to her feet. She continued to act as though suffering gravely, maintaining the act even as we left the pavilion. The king, stepping out with us, announced to two of his men, the same ones who had brought us to him, "Follow them to the edge of camp. See that no one accosts them along the way. They have been granted permission to leave."

The men did their duty, escorting us from the camp to where our small entourage awaited us. Then we were on our way, and I breathed a sigh of relief as we traveled further away from the city, moving as quickly as our animals and the men on their feet would allow us to go. Once we were far enough away and sure that we had not been followed, Zubira ceased with her moaning. When we stopped at a wayside along the road, she went into the miqwah. Kora waited outside while I went in with her to wash the taint from myself, as well.

As Zubira cleansed the calf's blood from her lap, she looked at me with a smile. "That was horrible. Remind me again, why did I let you do this to me, Yezeba'al?"

"To save our husband's kingdom."

"Yes, of course. Although, I still cannot believe it worked. Those men were drunken fools."

I gave a single nod of agreement but said nothing. I was still struggling with what had happened in the tent, grateful that I had not been made to do more and that it had worked as I had hoped. I would still have to confess what I had done to my husband, for I could not be untrue, but I hoped he would forgive me.

Finally unable to sit with it in silence, I asked Zubira, "Do you think it was wrong, what I did?"

She thought about it for only a moment. "You did it for a noble cause. So, no; I do not believe it was wrong. Besides, it was only your hand that touched his member."

I offered a meager smile in thanks. Then she moved closer to me and put her arms around my shoulders in a wet embrace. When she pulled away, she asked, "Why do you blame yourself for any of this?"

284

"It is my fault he is here."

"How so?"

"Hadi is obsessed with me; he has been ever since we were children."

"That sounds like it is *his* flaw. You are not to blame, Melkah."

I splashed her with water. "Do not be so formal with me. You know better." She shielded herself and laughed, and I splashed one more time just to make a point. Then I became serious again, and explained, "Back then, I encouraged him, you see. Perhaps if I had not, none of this would have happened."

"Yezeba'al," she said matter-of-factly, "you cannot blame yourself for the actions of men. How many times have you told us that? They are the masters of their own being. They have their own agency, just as we do – only they have more of it, so if anyone is to blame for their failings, it is only themselves that they should blame and no one else. Certainly not we of the 'weaker sex'. They cannot make us powerless and then blame us when things go wrong."

She placed a hand on my shoulder. Water ran from her fingertips, merging with the droplets that were already on my flesh and forming new streams that flowed back into the pool. "You did what you had to do. And when you were a girl, you did not know it would lead to this. How could you have understood it then? I think you expect too much from yourself sometimes. You may be the goddess incarnate, but you are still only a woman. You cannot know everything. We must all simply do the best we can, with our own understanding."

I looked at her, and now I smiled more easily. "You have grown into a fine young woman, Zubira. I am proud of you."

"Thank you," she answered with a gracious nod. Then she raised her chin, and looked to me, "But I learned from the best."

We laughed together and embraced once again. Then I climbed out of the pool and sat on the ledge with my knees up to my chin, while she leaned back against one of the walls and closed her eyes, letting the water settle as it surrounded her with its healing presence. When she opened her eyes, she met my gaze. "It will be good to see my son again. And my daughter."

"They will be glad to see you, too."

I thought of my own children – all of them were at Shomron, and I wished we had not taken them there. It was then that I thought

285

of what I had told Hadi, about Megiddu, and I began to worry I had revealed too much.

Unaware of what I was thinking, Zubira touched her swollen abdomen. "I wonder what this one will be."

"What are you hoping for?"

"Honestly?" she asked, looking at me with a guilty smile.

"Yes, honestly."

"I am hoping for another daughter. The king has many sons after all. I want my daughter to have a sister, because I want them to be close as I was to mine. A full-blooded sister, I mean."

"You never told me about your sisters. How many did you have?"

"Too many," she answered. "But there was one in particular to whom I was very close. We were almost of the same age – only a year between us."

"And who did your brother marry her off to when he became king?"

Her expression changed and she looked down at the water. "She never married. She died before my brother became king."

"Oh. I am sorry."

"It is all right. These things happen, after all. She is with our ancestors now. And with our mother." She smiled faintly and touched the necklace she always wore. "I long to be with them again one day."

"Not too soon," I said as I brought my legs down, letting them dangle over the edge of the pool. I watched the sunlight from the opening in the ceiling, as it danced on the surface of the water. Then I sighed and got up, rising as the water pulled against my robes and dribbled on the ground at my feet. "We should go. We do not have much time."

She nodded and then I helped her climb out. We continued our journey and arrived at Yezreel after the sun had set below the hills. Sending Zubira to rest in the women's quarters, I immediately went to work, first rallying my husband's men and telling them to prepare for battle. Then I went to the king's study and summoned the scribes. Standing by the window and looking out, I dictated letters to be sent out to all the provinces, informing them of our plight and the need for them to muster their men at arms immediately and send them to aid the king. I closed each letter with a cord and my personal seal, pressed into clay to assure their recipients that it came from me.

286

Then I handed them back to the scribes, charging them to go out immediately in all directions and bring them to the provinces.

The prophet of Yahowah had said that these provincial armies would help and that my husband would be the first to strike. I hoped that was true. Although we were likely still not on good terms, I said a silent prayer to Yahowah, asking him to bring victory to my husband and his men, as Zechariah claimed he had promised. While I had said it derisively to my husband the other day, I had also meant it, and now I communicated the same to Yahowah: *if I am wicked in your sight, my cousin Hadadesar is far worse than me, for he bears no shame in doing evil things. You must not let him take Yisrael from my husband, or he will bring true iniquity into this land, the likes of which it has never seen.*

After this, I closed myself in my chamber and fell asleep from exhaustion just as the morning light cut through the sky.

By the grace of the gods, Yahowah included, my plan worked. I had used all the weapons in my arsenal. Now, from the safety of the fortress at Yezreel, I could sit back and watch as the results of my various efforts unfolded, although I would not hear the full details until later. My husband told me, when it was over, what had happened at Shomron after I left. He and my cousin continued sending messengers back and forth. It began when Akhab – knowing the truth of where I was – sent a messenger to Hadadesar, accusing him of stealing me and another of his wives. My cousin sent back that he had not done so, and indeed that he could not have stolen us, for he had been promised all the wives and children of my husband. Therefore, if he had taken us – which he did not – we would have rightfully been his. However, he said, "you may send ten of your men into my camp and search it, even my pavilion, and you will not find these treacherous women, for I do not have them. They left of their own will and came to me, claiming the Kushite woman was in need of a midwife, and that they were all at Megiddu for the one at Shomron was ill and could not tend to her."

My husband sent back to him, confirming that was true about the midwives, and even apologized to Hadadesar for accusing him of stealing us, for it had since been revealed by the women of my chamber who had been questioned, and by the other wives, that I had taken Zubira to Megiddu to be tended to by the midwives there. Then my cousin and all the other kings and soldiers at his camp continued drinking themselves to a stupor, thinking they had won before the battle had even begun. No doubt, my cousin consoled himself with the belief that I and Zubira and all Akhab's other women and daughters would soon be his to claim or to distribute to the other kings that followed him. The promise of riches and women was enough to spur many men onto foolish errands, and no doubt it was that above all else which had inspired the other kings to follow Hadadesar.

Three days had passed since I left for Yezreel and, when Hadi had likely expected my return to fulfil my end of the bargain, he was instead overtaken by our armies from the provinces. They had gathered first at Yezreel before moving on to overtake Shomron at my command. Sitting astride my horse that morning, I thanked them for heeding my call to arms and promised that those who survived would be rewarded handsomely for their service to my husband's kingdom. I gave a rallying speech, speaking of the evils for which my cousin, Hadadesar, was known even in his own kingdom. I promised that the Ba'alim and Yahowah would all be behind them, for our gods had set their own petty jealousies aside and had come together for this purpose just as all the provincial armies had done. Then I kissed the fingers of my left hand and raised it before them all in the blessing of Ba'al.

Those who followed my Ba'al returned the blessing, while the Yahwists among them made their own signs of blessing, and then I nodded to the generals, whose horses and chariots were lined up behind me. Under the leadership of the general of my husband's army at Yezreel, they took over the command of the soldiers, and I watched them depart. Then I dismounted and returned to the palace, where I would don a simple robe, wash the cosmetics from my face, and spend my time secluded in prayer and meditation with the Ba'alim.

I later learned that they came upon the enemy's camp when the sun was highest in the sky. They made sudden and terrible war upon the armies of Hadadesar and the other kings, taking them by surprise and slaughtering many. Meanwhile, my husband's men had been waiting inside the city for the signal that would tell them the reinforcements had arrived. When that signal came, Akhab rejoiced, for he knew it meant I was safe at Yezreel and that I had been successful. Then he rallied his men for battle and led them out to join the fray. By the time Akhab and his forces arrived, however, my spineless cousin had already fled on the back of a horse, leaving the other kings and their armies to the slaughter.

Once the battle was finished, with the armies of Yisrael victorious, the ancient Zechariah appeared again before my husband. He commanded him to go and strengthen himself and his army, warning that the King of Aram would come against him again at the return of the year. My husband decided it best to be prepared and to obey the direction of Yahowah in this matter – but first, we would celebrate our victory.

He trembled when I placed my hand upon his bare abdomen, gently pressing my fingers to his warm bronze flesh. It was smooth beneath the sprinkling of course dark hairs that tangled and pulled at my fingers as I slowly moved them toward his chest. I pressed my lips upon the two long, thin scars that were there – reminders of having cut too deep during some of the awakening rituals at the Feasts of Ba'al. I flattened my hand to let it rest over his heart. I could feel it pounding beneath his ribcage. I closed my eyes to enjoy the tingling sensation, rising slowly from the tips of my fingers, of our souls coming together even before our bodies were united.

When I felt his hand on mine, I opened my eyes and saw him gazing at me. I smiled and my eyes stung with tears, brought forward by the depth and intensity of all I felt in that moment. He was here with me, and I with him. We were alive, together in these bodies that could experience the pleasures of sensation. Although he might have been taken from me, or I from him, the gods had instead preserved our lives, that we could now share this moment in the privacy of my chamber at Yezreel.

I bent forward and pressed my lips to his naked flesh, paying homage to my husband and king. His abdominal muscles tensed as my lips brushed against his soft flesh. He reached for me and beckoned me toward him. When I came to him, he took my face in his hand, and we shared one breath. Then I climbed over him, he clung to me, and we shared one flesh.

It was after the battle. Instead of sending messengers to inform me of his victory, Akhab arrived at the head of his chariots to the fortress and, leaving them, found me collapsed on the floor in my prayer chamber. I had fallen asleep in front of my private altar from having gone so deep in meditation. The incense I burned to aid in my prayers had long since gone out, although the aroma still lingered with the smoke that hung in the air within the small, closed chamber. I awakened to him shaking me to be sure I was alive, and then lifting me from the rug and carrying me to the bed, where he was going to lay me down to sleep in a more comfortable location. Instead, we made love.

Lying in bed after our passions were spent, my head resting upon his shoulder, we settled into a more peaceful state. It was only then that I began to think about all that had transpired since the last time we had seen each other. I had not yet told him about what I had to do to convince my cousin to let me pass, but it was eating at me and so I finally resolved to make my confession.

After I told him what I had done, he looked at me thoughtfully and at first said nothing. I turned my gaze away from him, my cheeks burning with shame. Then he sat up to take my face in his hand and draw me into a kiss.

Afterward, I met his gaze, surprised to see him smiling.

"Is that all? I knew you were troubled. I did not want to ask what it took to gain safe passage from the city."

"You are not angry with me?"

Lying back on the cushions and looking up at me, he asked, "Why should I be? I thought you might have had to do worse than that, in fact. I am relieved he did not force himself upon you. But I am sorry that you had to do even that much. No woman should ever be forced to pleasure a man." He sighed heavily and turned his gaze from me. His features tensed. "It makes me all the angrier that he escaped without punishment."

I placed my hand on his chest and began absentmindedly playing with the hairs. Most of them were still dark, but a couple of them had gone grey, like some of the hairs on his head and in his beard. He was near forty by now. Observing all this silently, I said aloud, "Well, if what that prophet Zechariah had to say is true, you will have another chance, my love. And for once, I hope it does come to pass, for I would like nothing more than to see my miserable cousin get what he deserves. I only wish that I could be the one to give it to him."

Akhab smiled up at me, his arms resting on the cushion beneath his head. "I believe you would, too. But tell me, how would you do it?"

I thought for a moment, a wicked smile on my lips. "I would have him alone and pretend to seduce him, so that he would be naked before me and desirous. Then I would pull a dagger, hidden beneath my robes – the one strapped to my thigh for the Ba'alim rituals – and I would cut off his member. Then, to smother his screams, I would shove it in his mouth and stab him in the heart over and over until he lay dead."

My husband raised his brows and grimaced. "They say brutality belongs to men, but I think what you have imagined is far more savage than anything a man would invent."

I turned my eyes to meet his. "Does this disturb you, my love?"

He inhaled deeply. "Only insofar as much that I am a man, and I do not care for the thought of having that done to me."

"Well, I would never do such a thing to you, for you have done nothing to warrant it."

"I did not realize that your hatred for your cousin ran so deep. I thought you were close once."

"That was before he betrayed us."

I thought back to the way he had put his hands on my body in the tent allowing the old king to touch me, and I burned with rage beneath the surface. "After what he has done, and what he tried to do to you, there is nothing I desire more fervently than to watch him suffer a very painful death. I hope that, for my sake, you will give it to him."

Akhab swallowed hard and cleared his throat. "Well, not in the way you have described. I am afraid I could not bring myself to execute another man by this method."

I chuckled and raised myself onto my knees, moving to run my hands over his body. "You may use whatever method you desire to annihilate him, as long as the result is the same."

I began to kiss and fondle him until he was aroused again – I enjoyed the power I had over his body – and then I gave him pleasure.

Zechariah had been correct in his prophecy, and my cousin did return to Yisrael at the end of summer while we were at Shomron for the Feast of Ba'al. He laid siege to Apiq, a walled city in the Plain of Sharon, alarmingly close to Megiddu. He brought thousands of men to fight for him, more than the last time. Two men of Apiq, having been allowed to escape, came to inform us that the King of Aram had taken the city and was holding it for ransom, threatening to strike next at Megiddu if Akhab did not send his queen in exchange. The messengers were brought to us while we were dining with our two eldest children in one of the outer rooms of my private quarters; it was too urgent to wait.

"He is obsessed with me," I said bitterly, turning my face in disgust while Akhab spoke with the messengers.

"Does he want you to return with a message from me?" he asked them.

"No, Melekh," said the elder of the two. They were both sons of the Lord of Apiq. Their father had been killed defending the city. Hadi held their mother and sisters for ransom, threatening to rape and murder them, even the youngest, if the two sons did not deliver their message. "He said not to return unless we brought him the queen." The boy, still barely a man, looked at me and then bowed his head. "Forgive me, Melkah."

I gave him a stiff nod in response and then looked away. Akhab, meanwhile, said, "Then you will stay here in Shomron at my palace. The queen will look after you – you will be our guests until you are able to safely return to your city – and I will go to Yezreel and prepare my chariots to meet Hadadesar in the plains. If he wants to do battle and will not flee like a dog with its tail between its legs, as he did the last time, I will bring him this battle he craves."

The boys thanked the king for generously receiving them, and then they were escorted to their lodging for as long as they remained in Shomron as our guests. After they left, I looked to my husband with worry. "He is going after the children. I should not have told him that was where they were kept."

This time we had only brought Zyah and Tala with us from Megiddu, so our two youngest were still there, as were most of the

292

king's youngest children and many of his women. Akhab reached across the table and took my hand. "You must not blame yourself, my love. He will not harm them. He is trying to provoke me into battle. But his army, though great, cannot overtake mine."

"Do not be so sure of yourself," I gently chastened. "Hubris has lost many battles."

"Yahowah has promised this battle to me, remember? And you have told me the same promise comes from the Ba'alim – for once they agree on something." He got up and came to me and bent to kiss my cheek. "The gods have prepared me for this, and I am ready. Do not worry, my love, for all will go as planned." He touched my cheek, gently caressing with his thumb. While I gazed up at him tearfully, he said, "You are safe here and the children are safe at Megiddu, but now I must go to meet him. I leave you in charge of the court here, as always, and pray the men will not give you too much trouble."

"Highly unlikely," I answered with a bitter smile.

He chuckled. "And when they do, no doubt you will whip them into shape. I almost regret that I will not be here to see it."

"I can always provide a demonstration for you upon your return," I offered playfully.

"Please do," he purred.

After pressing my hand to his lips, he stepped away and Tala jumped up from the table to throw her arms around his waist. "Abbu, don't go!"

He embraced her tightly and then held her chin, saying, "My little cub, I must go. But gods willing, I will return to you."

Next, Zyah rose from his cushion at the table and went to stand before his father. "Abbu, let me come with you."

"Zyah!" I chastised. "Sit down at once."

"No, Ama. I am thirteen. I am a man now, and I am ready for battle."

Akhab put his hand on Zyah's cheek. "My son, you must stay here. Listen to your mother. If I do not return from battle, the kingdom and your mother will need you. Be strong for them."

Zyah's head dropped and his shoulders slumped forward, but he answered, "Yes, Abbu." My husband embraced him and kissed the top of his head.

I came to him now, and our son stepped aside so that we could embrace. Taking my face in his hands, Akhab gazed into my eyes, and then he kissed me firmly. When he pulled away, my eyes were blurred with tears, and I reached up to touch his face. "Return to me, beloved."

"I will return to you. I will not let Hadadesar have his way with you." He stopped then, the weight of his promise bearing down on him when perhaps he realized he could not make such a promise. Then he began, "But...if the gods are wrong..."

I shook my head. "No, Akhab."

"Listen, Yezeba'al," he continued. "If he should win, I will have messengers ready to come to you at once. And if they come, you must take Zyah and Tala, and you must go into hiding. Take them south to Yerushalayim."

"Yerushalayim? Why not go to Yapo. I can have my father send ships."

"No. That is what your cousin would expect of you, so you must go to Yerushalyim. Ask the king, my brother, for sanctuary there. As my sister is his wife and our daughter is betrothed to his successor, you will be welcome at the court of Yehoshapat." He paused, saying firmly, "Do not go anywhere near Megiddu, not for the other wives, and not for the other children – not even Yoram and Ba'alesar."

Although the thought of losing Akhab and abandoning my younger children pained me, I knew my duty would be to protect the most important of Akhab's heirs. I nodded to confirm my understanding. He kissed me once more before pulling away. And then he was gone in haste to prepare for battle.

Kora, who had been standing nearby, came to me and placed a comforting hand on my shoulder. I threw my arms around her and she embraced me, much as Daneyah did when she was still with us. The older we became the more Kora reminded me of her mother. Her own daughter, Ruta, was also there to serve my daughter as her handmaiden. When I saw the two of them embracing in the same way, I urged Kora to look, and we admired our daughters' friendship. They had grown up together, the same as Kora and me, and we were pleased that they loved each other in the same way.

Zyah, in the meantime, had gone to the window. At the northern end of the palace, the window in the chamber where we dined looked not toward the garden but instead faced the hills and looked over the road that my husband would soon take to Yezreel. I went to stand beside my son and placed a hand on his shoulder. He wanted to be strong, as men were expected to be, but I knew he worried for his father as I did. He turned to me and offered a meager smile.

"Your father will return to us, Zyah."

"I am a man, Ama."

"I know," I said with a nod.

"But...I am not ready to be a king."

At thirteen, by law he was considered a man, but I knew that he still needed the comfort of his mother to soothe his aching heart. I pulled him into my arms and, once he relented, he laid his head on my breast. His arms around my waist, he squeezed tightly, as he did when he was a boy, only now he was beginning to develop the strength of a man. It stunned me to notice the difference, but then I held him tighter, too, and whispered, "Do not worry, my son. It is not your time yet to be king." And I said a silent prayer to the gods in the hope that I was right.

While my husband went to battle against my cousin for the second time, I again spent much of my time in meditation and prayer with the Ba'alim when I was not holding court. Since turning thirteen, Zyah had begun to join us while holding court. He sat in his own chair to the left of his father's throne, so he could observe and come to understand what would be expected of him when he was king. While Akhab was away, I occupied his throne and could more easily see how closely my son watched and listened to all that was happening around him. I was proud to see him taking a true interest in the matters of our kingdom, and pleased whenever he leaned over to ask a question or make a suggestion. If his suggestions were plausible, I took them into consideration.

On the days when court was not in session, and when I had enough of my solitude and craved the company of others, I went to spend time in the women's garden with those of the wives and children who were there. While I tried to hide that I was worried, Zyah always sensed it. As was his custom, he picked flowers and presented them to me with a kiss on the cheek. I embraced and thanked him for always looking after me. Then I assured him I was all right. Holding my hand, he met my gaze a moment longer to be sure. Then he smiled, and said, "I love you, Ama."

"I love you, my son. Now, go and play with your brothers."
Many of the king's young sons ran around in mock battle, shouting
and holding their hands up to their mouths to imitate the blowing of
shofars. I pointed to them, saying, "There appears to be a great battle.
They could use your leadership."

He smiled and looked at the other boys. Then he pressed my
hand to his lips before running off to join those brothers. Zyah was a
natural leader, and the other boys eagerly followed him. It was good
to see, knowing he would one day need to draw on that natural
charisma when he was king. Meanwhile, those of Akhab's sons who
were too old for play but not yet old enough for battle sat comforting
their mothers and sisters until growing restless, and then they went
off to brawl or to find solace in the arms of courtesans. I was grateful
that my eldest son was not yet at that age; I knew it would come soon
enough, and when it came, I would send him to the Temple of
Ashtarti. I did not want my sons drawn to courtesans, who were
prone to scheming and debasing the sex act in an attempt to subvert
the natural order.

Akhab's oldest sons had gone with him; some had already seen
battle. For us women, the thought of our sons going off to war only
filled us with dread, for we were keenly aware of the temporality of
life. Most of us maintained our dignity and composure, sharing
moments of silent understanding in glimpses and discreet nods, but
Tamar was visibly anxious. She had two sons by the king, both of
whom had gone with him to take part in their first battle. As it was
my duty and nature, I sat with Tamar, assuring her that all would
be well, that the king would do his best to protect their sons.

A few of the women – most of them concubines – wept openly.
For us wives, even if the king did not return, our home in the palace
was secure; for the concubines, however, it all depended on the
benevolence of the new king and his mother. While it should be my
son, in which case I would not make any of the women or their
children leave, I looked around at some of the king's older sons,
wondering, if their father died would they attempt a coup? Or would
they respect his chosen successor, who was not yet a man? And their
mothers, many of whom I considered my friends – did any of them
secretly harbor jealousy toward me, coveting the position of gebirah
that I would hold when my son became king? I had been good to all
the king's women and children and believed they respected me,

perhaps even loved me. But the realities of life had taught me that not all who appear to be grateful and loving are true, and wars of succession were often bloody.

Then there was the even greater fear that, if my husband fell in battle, my cousin would become the victor. Akhab told me I should go into hiding if that came to pass, but I had decided I could not leave the other wives and children to Hadi's whims. If it came to that, I would send Tala and Zyah with Kora and their nurses to seek protection at the court of Yehoshapat in Yerushalayim, where they would be safely out of Hadi's reach. Then I would surrender to Hadi and beg him for mercy. I would give myself to him willingly, fulfil his every desire, promise to be true to him...and then I would kill him.

These and many other things ran through my head, even as I sat still and silent, admiring the green leaves of an olive tree set against the deep blue of the sky. The devastation of losing my husband would be bad enough, but there were so many things beyond my own feelings that needed consideration. Protecting my sons' right and the safety of the other women were always at the forefront of my mind whenever war and rebellion took my husband away from us. Now, there was also my burning desire for justice to be served.

When my husband returned, nearly a fortnight had passed. He was still weary from battle and, although victorious, he was bitter and sullen. I wondered at this, as he draped himself in misery across his bed, laying on his stomach while one of his concubines whom I had summoned massaged the soreness from his muscles. As he had not told me anything other than Hadadesar had been defeated, I asked him what had happened at Apiq. At first, he did not wish to speak of it and waved off my questioning, turning his face the other way.

I walked around the bed and stood over him, looking down at him with my hands on my hips. "Akhab, at least tell me this much: is my cousin dead?"

Now, he groaned and, waving the concubine away impatiently, sat up on the edge of the bed with his feet on the floor. "You may leave me, Shoshanna," he said to the concubine, who bowed respectfully and went away.

297

I watched her leave and, when at last I was alone with my husband, knelt before him and placed my hands upon his knees. "Akhab, tell me Hadadesar lies dead. Tell me he did not flee once again."

"He did not flee, Yezeba'al," Akhab sighed, rubbing the weariness from his face.

"So, you killed him. He lies dead in the Plain of Sharon?"

I must have realized by now that was not the case, but I could not fathom how this could be when my husband had won a crushing victory. When he did not answer, I rose and stood over him again, although cannot quite explain what I felt in that moment. I loved my husband. I worshipped him just as he worshipped me. And yet, as I stood looking down at his hunched form, his spirit broken, I felt a seething rage rise from within. I wanted to annihilate him.

He looked up as if afraid to face me, perhaps sensing my wrath in the face of his guilt. Then he confessed, "Hadadesar came to me after the battle, having sent his servants in sackcloth to beg for his life. I took him up into my chariot and spoke to him as my brother. He promised to restore to me the lands that his father took from my father, and I agreed to this covenant. Then I let him return to his kingdom with what few of his men remained."

While I listened, my eyes stung with tears. My head ached. My flesh tingled. I clenched my fists, and my husband continued, "When he was gone, a man came to me. He appeared to be injured with a bandage over his eye, as though he had been in battle, although not dressed as a soldier. I did not recognize him in this guise, and I thought he must have been injured when Hadadesar's men took the city. Many of the people of Apiq had been injured then, or afterward when the wall fell and took many of the soldiers of Hadadesar who had sought shelter there..."

"What of this man? What has he to do with my cousin?"

"Yes, the man," said Akhab, remembering his train of thought. "When he spoke to me, he told me a story: he had been entrusted with protecting another man but lost track of him in battle. The punishment for having failed to protect him should therefore be the forfeiture of his own life. I told him he himself had decided on his judgment, for having allowed the man to be lost. That is when the man removed his bandage, and I recognized him."

298

"Who was he?" I demanded, losing my patience. "Why does any of this matter, Akhab?"

"It matters because he was a prophet of Yahowah! He was one of the disciples of Zechariah, the old man who had promised Hadadesar would be delivered to me by the hand of Yahowah! Ancient Zechariah is dead, but this man was his successor. He told me Yahowah said I had decided my own judgment: that as he had delivered Hadadesar to me for destruction, since I let him go, my life would take the place of his, and my people's lives would take the place of his people's lives. He said that I have brought this judgment upon myself and my people for having shown mercy!"

He wept bitterly and pulled at his hair. I brought my hands to my face and found that I, too, had begun weeping, for my fingers were wet with tears. Then I looked at him in disbelief, my anger again beginning to swell. "Akhab, how could you? How could you let him live after all he has done to us!"

"He is your cousin and a king."

"What difference does that make? Would it have made a difference to him if he had defeated you?"

"How many times have you counseled me to be merciful against our enemies?"

I scoffed. "Do not use my words against me! He would not have shown you such mercy, I can tell you that!"

"So, you make yourself a hypocrite?" he asked, rising from the bed and waving a hand at me as he walked away.

I followed after him. "There is a time and place for all things I have counseled, but this was not a time for mercy, Akhab! Hadadesar cannot be trusted! I have told you that over and over. Why did you not listen?"

Turning back to me, he said, "The man I spoke to in my chariot was not the same man as the one you have described. He was a broken man. I have reduced his army to dust, and he will not make war on us again. He will be our ally instead!"

"He would say anything, swear to anything to preserve his own life," I insisted. "And in the end, he will continue to do what he has always done! What he has done since we were children together. He will not keep his word – he will betray you! How could you be so foolish? It is as the prophet said: in preserving his life, you have handed him your own!"

"Damn it, woman, you think I do not know that by now?" He grabbed me by the arms, his fingers now digging into my flesh.

"Do not touch me!" I shouted as I lifted my hands, bringing them together between his arms and then thrusting them out to break free of his grasp. When he tried to grab me again, I slapped him hard across the face.

We fought; it was brutal. We'd had many battles over the years, but of them this was by far the worst. By the end of it, jars of ointment from his nightstand and decorative vases had been thrown and smashed to pieces; lamps had been broken and dented, their contents spilled to the floor when their tables were overturned or their stands knocked over; thankfully none of those had been lit at the time or we might have burned the palace to the ground in our fury. Both of us ended up bruised, scratched, our hair pulled, robes torn, and bleeding. Then I left him.

We barely spoke a word to each other for days, and he spent several nights in his own bed – a rarity in all the years of our marriage. Whenever he came to me, the fight would start over again, until at last he came down on his knees and wept many apologies. Believing him sincere and desperate to repair what had been broken, I forgave him and he at last returned to my bed. The war was over, the truce made, and we both had won.

12

Sign of Our Covenant

Another daughter was born to us at the end of the following summer. We called her Azba'alah, meaning "strength of Ba'alah," in my father's tongue. She was a welcome surprise and came at the right time: only two months after her birth I was losing my eldest daughter to marriage. Tala was thirteen when we brought her to Yerushalayim to be wed – I had tried to negotiate one more year, so at least she would be fourteen when she married, as I had been, but the King of Yehudah was insistent. He accused us of backtracking on the original treaty and threatened to withdraw from it if we did not uphold its terms. He was a strong ally; withdrawing from the treaty could have disastrous implications, especially for those kingdoms around Yehudah that were under our protection.

Although only fifteen years of age, Yehoram, the bridegroom and his chosen successor, was ready to take a wife. Yehoshapat was eager for it to be concluded. They were supposed to have been wed upon Tala reaching womanhood at the age of twelve, but the war against Hadadesar had interfered. Then, when I found that I was with child once again, we begged an extension for our eldest daughter until after the child was born so that I could attend the wedding. The extension was granted but, upon hearing of the birth of Azba'alah, Yehoshapat sent messengers to remind us of our promise. Thus, the date was set for us to renew our covenant with Yehudah. As soon as I had recovered enough from the delivery to travel, we assembled our entourage and left for Yerushalayim.

Zyah and Yoram, being thirteen and nine now, were old enough to come with us but Ba'alesar and Azba'alah had to be left behind at Megiddu. After my cousin's previous attacks, I was hesitant to leave our two youngest children there when we would be so far away, although Akhab reminded me that it was the safest place for them. When I brought it up again during our travels, he said that even if Hadadesar wanted to break the covenant and attack us again,

301

he would not have been able to rebuild his army so quickly. "It could take years for him to recover," he said with a proud smirk, as he rode on his horse beside my litter on the road to Yerushalayim.

I reached out my hand to him and he held it for a while before riding off to take his place at the head of our entourage. We were only a short distance out from arriving at Yerushalayim by now, and the closer we came the more travelers we passed on the road. Those we encountered, of course, had to move aside to let the long train of our entourage pass. I kept the curtains of my litter drawn but could still see through the sheer fabric. I noticed that some of them bowed, some of them blessed us, and some of them cursed and spat on the ground at our passing.

Zealots, I thought bitterly, grateful that they could not see me through the curtains.

It occurred to me then that we were moving deeper into Yahowah's territory for the first time since my husband had converted to my religion. No matter how much the people of Yisrael had begun to respect, if not wholly venerate our gods, the people of Yehudah remained staunchly opposed and made no secret of their disdain for the Ba'alim. Their main city, Yerushalayim, was the seat of Shelomoh's temple. The zealots increasingly insisted it was the only true Temple of Yahowah: since they believed that there could only be one god, there could be only one temple devoted to him. It seemed strange to me that a god who claimed to have created all things in the universe could not be in more than one place at a time. Nonetheless, his people were expected to make pilgrimage to his temple at least once per year to make offerings and atone for their sins, and the zealots insisted that the temple on Mount Gerizim was not legitimate for this purpose. Hardly surprising, since Yahwist zealotry had its origins in Yerushalayim.

My husband, having never been drawn to zealotry, had gone to the temple on Mount Gerizim but stopped making those pilgrimages many years ago. No doubt word had spread far and wide of his conversion to my religion. No wonder some of the people were spitting as we passed. The fact that they spat on the ground specifically when my litter passed, just so that I could see them do this, suggested they blamed me for his conversion. They could not imagine that a king would choose to worship other gods because those gods had revealed themselves to him through their works. As the first woman was blamed for bringing sin into the world, so I was blamed for bringing my religion to my husband and our people. Nevertheless, we were still welcomed to Yerushalayim by those who mattered.

The King of Yehudah's steward met us upon our arrival. Our family and personal servants were given temporary lodging inside the walls, not too far from the palace, while the rest of our entourage camped with the animals outside the city. It occurred to me that night, as I gazed out a window in the chamber shared with my husband, that so much of this journey was reminiscent of that which brought me to him so many years before.

"Now, it is our daughter's journey," said Akhab. He pulled me into his arms before the open window that looked out across the city. The view was different, but the feeling much the same. Perhaps my daughter and Ruta were now looking out her window as Kora and I had done on my last night of maidenhood.

I sighed wistfully and turned to gaze at my husband, still in his arms. "I can only hope that she might find such happiness with her husband as I have found with mine."

We kissed. Then I turned and wrapped my legs around him as he lifted me and carried me toward the bed.

Going out to arrange for the procession to the palace the next day, I noticed Akhab wincing and rubbing his lower back after climbing into his chariot. "Husband, are you unwell?" I asked as I came to stand beside him in the chariot.

He looked over at me sheepishly and shrugged uncomfortably. "It is nothing."

I chuckled lightly. "Perhaps you should not have carried me to bed last night. You are not a young man anymore. I shall have to go easier on you."

Taking the diadem offered to him by his attendant, he pressed his lips together and looked at me from the side before setting the diadem on his head. "At least I still have the passions of one."

"Thank the Ba'alah for that," I agreed.

He took my hand and pulled me to his side with a grin. "I thank *my* Ba'alah for that. You keep me young, wife. Never go easy on me." He kissed me and then took up the reins, for it was time for the procession to begin.

We rode through Yerushalayim side-by-side in his chariot, presenting ourselves to the people of Yehudah as equals. Even my mother had not been presented in this way at my wedding procession; for a queen to ride in a chariot beside her king was almost unheard of, even in the most egalitarian kingdoms. We caused quite a stir, but most of the people who had lined up to watch the procession continued to wave and cheer once the moment of slack-jawed wonderment passed. We were even pleased to see some devoted followers of the Ba'alim among them, revealing themselves as they gave the sign of blessing to us. Seeing this, we returned the blessing and kept our hands raised even as it caused some of the crowd to hiss and hurl insults against the "faithless idolators." While they cursed us, we blessed them.

When we passed the temple, where many priests had gathered outside to watch with disdain as we passed, the jeers of the people became more intense. They seemed to be putting on a show in view of the priests, perhaps hoping to be rewarded in some way by their faithful rejection of our idolatry. They were especially boisterous as we passed by a large group of Ba'alim devotees who had gathered across the street from the temple and were eager to see us up close. Some of them prostrated themselves, while others blessed us, and many shouted, "Ba'alah, please bless us! Ba'al, bless us!" and, "Hail Ba'al! Hail Asherah!"

This caused the temple priests to grow restless and angry, stirring up their people to even more displays of their rejection of us. But we doubled down and continued to support our faithful. My left hand still raised in the sign of blessing, I placed my right hand over my heart and bowed my head to them in thanks. Once we had passed, however, I lowered my arm to let it rest and turned to Akhab with concern. "Will our daughter be safe in this kingdom?"

"She will be safe," he answered, looking ahead as he steered the chariot. "The Ba'alim will protect her, for she is their emissary." Without moving his head, he turned his gaze on me with a smile. "Just as you were when you came to my kingdom."

"Have I done well?" I wondered aloud, more to myself than anyone else.

"You have done the best you can, and continue to, for your work is not finished. The people have a long way to go, but they have come far. Trust me, Yezeba'al. You remember what they were like when you first came; think of that, to see how much you have done for our people. Our kingdom prospers under the Ba'alim. Yahowah may not like it, and his followers will continue to stir up trouble wherever they can, but they have not been as effective as you, or as they once were. Surely, you have noticed how infrequent the rebellions are now that the people have seen and understand the value of peace?"

I nodded and then we fell silent as we approached the palace. I turned to look at the procession – it was so different being at the front instead of all the way at the back. I could just see the top of my daughter's litter far behind us, and I wondered how she was faring. Hopefully the people would not look unkindly on her, since she was young and innocent as I had once been. At least she was not coming in as the wife of a reigning king. As the wife of his successor, she would have time to get acclimated to her new home and husband before the burden of rulership fell upon them.

I turned forward again and breathed deeply as the shadow of the palace came over us. *Ba'alah, be with us this day.*

It had been many years since the last time we had seen the King and Queen of Yehudah, and it was the first time our children met their cousins. Tala took well to her new husband and he to her. During the ten days of feasting that followed the presentation of the bride, two kings and two queens watched proudly as our newly wed children talked and laughed together, growing less timid with each day of the celebration. Already on the first day after their wedding night, we noticed a distinct change in them.

"Yehoram is not normally so animated," Aya remarked, as we sat together with our husbands at the table nearby, sipping spiced wine and discreetly watching them. He appeared to be telling a story and my daughter was watching him with great interest, cutting in occasionally and speaking rapidly. Whatever she had said made him laugh aloud, such that we could hear him from our table.

I smiled. "Neither is Tala – well, not when she is surrounded by so many people, at least. They seem to be a good match."

"Indeed," said my husband, raising his cup. We all followed and sipped together. Then Akhab, returning his cup to the table, said, "I am glad their first night went well."

At that point, Yehoshapat, who had a fondness for drink and had already imbibed thrice as much as the rest of us, laughed heartily and slurred, "Yehoram is a lusty youth, but timid. I had to force the boy to make love to one of the serving girls so he would have practice before his first night as a husband. It was not that he did not want them, of course – he has my vigor and taste in beautiful women, such as your lovely queen, Akhab…"

He raised his cup and drank without waiting for anyone else to raise theirs. Akhab raised his politely, but looked at me and did not drink. He seemed apologetic in his gaze, as though I might be offended by the lecherous old king's loose-lipped admiration.

"Truly, Yezeba'al," continued Yehoshapat, "Akhab speaks very highly of you – and what he does not say with his lips, he says with his eyes. But now I can see for myself why a king who can have any woman he desires would still be pleased with only one. I too have eyes." He tapped the side of his eye socket.

"Honestly, Hosha," my husband interrupted. "I do not think this is an appropriate topic for our wives to hear."

"No," the stubborn king replied. "Let me tell this – it is good."

While awkward, I was suddenly and keenly interested. I knew men had a way of divulging the secrets of their women to enhance their own sense of prowess when conversing with other men, so I said, "Akhab, let us hear what he has to say. I want to know what sort of things you have been saying of me to other men, O Melekh."

Hosha snickered and went on, "I asked him once, when we rode out to war together against the Moabites…" He paused to reconsider. "Was it the Moabites?"

Akhab sighed and lifted his drink to his mouth. "Yes, it was the Moabites," he answered grimly, before finishing his cup.

"I thought so," Hosha replied. "Anyway, I asked him which of his women would he choose, if he could only have one of them for the rest of his life. Most men struggle to answer, but he answered immediately and without hesitation. Can you guess which one he would choose, Yezeba'al?"

"Which one would *you* choose?" I asked.

"Of Akhab's women?"

"No, of yours," I said with a smile, trying not to laugh. I couldn't yet decide if I was annoyed or amused by his drunkenness. Perhaps a bit of both. His queen, however, was clearly frustrated and I was hoping he might soothe some of her frustration by saying he would choose her. Instead, he blundered his chance to redeem himself.

"Oh, well...I am not sure that I could choose only one, but if I had to..." He paused to think on it and now I regretted asking, because I thought the man had more tact.

"I hope," said Akhab, "you were going to say my sister, your Melkah."

"Oh, yes, of course! Of course, I would choose Atalaya – not to be confused with your Atalaya. I mean *my* Atalaya – Aya – Atalaya the elder?"

"Please, do not call me that," she said, lifting her drink to take a sip. Then, setting it back on the table, "I do not like to think of myself as an elder."

"We are all getting to be elders, wife," he answered with a laugh. Then, slapping Akhab on the back the way men do, he said, "Right, Akhab?"

"Speak for yourself, old man," Akhab answered. "How old are you now, anyway?"

"Fifty years, or thereabout," answered Hosha.

"I am only in my thirty-ninth year," said Akhab.

"That is still old, my friend," said Hosha, placing a hand on Akhab's shoulder.

My husband raised his cup. "To old age, then."

Hosha broke into a hearty laugh, raised his cup, and they drank together. Then he asked, "So, what is it with you and the King of Aram? Is he your ally now, or are you merely in a truce? Who started the conflict, and is it over between you?"

Much to my irritation, they began discussing Hadadesar, who had consumed so much of the past year and a half. I knew my husband had wanted to discuss it with the King of Yehudah, however, because he was hoping to secure reassurances from him as an ally.

After hearing only the most important details, Hosha asked, "Do you believe he will keep to the terms?"

Before my husband could reply, I cut in, "No, he will certainly not keep to it. Akhab hopes that he will, but I know my cousin. He is less honest than the serpent in the Garden of Eden." Of course, I had my own ideas about the serpent and what it represented in the story, but this was not the time or place to discuss such matters and I had only mentioned it because I knew the King of Yehudah would understand the analogy.

Hosha raised his brows. "That bad?"

Akhab said, "Yes, so that is why I was hoping to ask if I could count on you to stand by me, should we ever come to conflict with him again."

"Of course, I will, Akhab," Hosha answered, clapping him on the shoulder. "That is what allies are for – you say the word, and I will come to your aid against that filthy idolator. Erm, no offence, Yezeba'al."

I answered with a nod and a raised palm, and he seemed to be satisfied with that.

"Thank you, my friend," said Akhab. "I am hoping the need will not arise, but if it does it is good to know I can count on you."

"I shall have to come to your kingdom again soon, so we can make it official," he replied. "What lands has his father taken that he has promised to return?"

"There are some lands to the east of the Yarden, in Gilad. I should like the return of Ramot in particular."

"Ah yes, that is a fine city. Located in a strategic position."

I said, "You shall never have it back if you do not take it. But I do not advise that."

"You seldom advise going to war, my love," said Akhab.

"Why would she, *akhu*?" asked Aya. "It is a wife's prerogative to want her husband to stay out of trouble, especially the sort of trouble that may get him killed."

"It is a man's place to go to war," said Hosha. "Of course, women do not understand these things, which is why they are so often against it."

"We understand perfectly," I replied. "We simply abhor anything that would take our husbands' and sons' lives, especially when it is not necessary. Anyway, I am not against war – I know that sometimes it is a necessity. Only I believe it should be avoided, whenever possible."

While the men continued discussing the costs and benefits of war, Aya turned to me and said, "Look at our youngest boys together. What mischief are they up to?"

I looked and saw Yoram sneaking around one of the banquet tables with his cousin, Yehiel. They were about the same age and had been getting along perfectly, seeming to be of like mind in all things. I smiled as we continued watching them stealing sips of the strong liquor that only the men were supposed to drink. They took turns with the cup, grimacing and spitting it out before trying it again with the same effect. Then I shook my head and smiled. "Do you suppose we should let them get away with it this once?"

"What could it hurt? Anyway, their nurses will likely soon find them and give them a proper tongue lashing."

I chuckled, and then said, "Yoram is not my youngest, though. I have another son, Ba'alesar, as you recall."

"Ah yes, of course." Did I sense a bit of envy? She had only had two sons and no daughters. The King of Yehudah spent little time with his wives, preferring instead the company of his concubines, from what I had heard. "How old is he now?"

"Four years," I replied. "And growing faster than his elder brothers did. Zyah, especially. Speaking of Zyah, I wonder where he has gone off to?"

Aya pointed and I saw him then, standing off to the side, watching Yoram and Yehiel in their mischief. After sampling it themselves, they stole one of the cups from the table and returned to him with it. Now he was sipping it with a grimace while the younger boys laughed. Unlike them, however, he did not spit it out. I shook my head and rolled my eyes. "They will all learn when they wake up ill in the morning."

"Yet another reason to let them do it now and learn the hard way," she replied with a laugh. Then she lifted her cup for one of the passing servants to fill, and I did the same with mine. After sipping, she asked, "Your newest child – I forget what you named her?"

"Azba'alah," I replied, watching my husband rise after excusing himself. He walked toward the exit to the courtyard, and I assumed he was going to relieve himself.

Meanwhile, the Queen of Yehudah said, "Yes, a lovely name."

I doubted she thought so, being devoted to Yahowah as she had always been. Nevertheless, I nodded graciously.

309

"I am sorry you could not bring her to Yerushalayim. You must miss her terribly."

"I do," came my honest answer.

Suddenly Hosha cut in, swaying a bit with his drink in hand, "Is it true that you suckled all your children at your own breast, Yezeba'al?"

Shocked, Aya rebuked him. "Hosha! That is entirely inappropriate! You forget you are speaking to another king's wife."

"What? It is only that it is strange for a king's wife to nurse her own infants when there are women better suited for such tasks." His glance at my bosom, currently swollen with milk from not having nursed in days — the pain from which I was doing my best to ignore — suggested the cause for his interest. Now I understood why my husband had suggested I wear a different gown; one that did not have such a low neckline.

"It is not your concern," his wife said more firmly. She turned to me then. "Forgive my husband. He has had too much drink and forgets he is in the company of *ladies*, not in a tent on the battlefield."

Yehoshapat held up his palms as if to surrender, and it was then that Akhab returned. He removed his sandals to sit on the cushion. "What did I miss?"

"Nothing important," I answered.

"We were talking about your new daughter," said Aya, "and how much of a delight she must truly be."

"She is a quiet infant," said Akhab, reaching for a bowl of dried figs. "Mild, hardly puts up a fuss. You would love her, my dear sister. You will have to join your husband the next time he comes to Yisrael, so you can meet her. Hopefully while she is still in infancy."

"I do love infants," she said with a sad smile. "They have such purity and innocence."

"Until they fall into sin," her husband replied. "The moment they are old enough to reason, they begin to follow in the footsteps of Hawwa."

"And Adam," I reminded him, smiling gently.

Yehoshapat cleared his throat. "Yes, of course." Then, meeting my gaze, "But in the fable, it was Hawwa who sinned first and bade her husband to sin after her, and then their sons followed the evil *she* brought into the world, and it has continued ever since. That, I believe, is the meaning behind the tale."

310

"Surely, men are capable of making their own decisions," I answered, continuing to smile. "No one forced Adam to follow Hawwa."

"No one forced him, but his wife led him astray and brought sin to their people."

Now, I knew we were no longer talking about the allegory of Adam and Hawwa, as I had already suspected. Keeping my tone firm yet pleasant, I said, "If he truly believed it was wrong, he would not have followed her; neither would she have followed the serpent. They were both acting in accordance with what they believed to be right."

"As do we all," Aya replied quickly, putting an end to our debate before it turned hostile. While I did not wish for hostility, I regretted not being able to continue in this vein, but she was probably right to end it.

King Yehoshapat fell silent and began looking into his drink, while Akhab leaned over to me. "What was that about?" he whispered. "Are you sure it was nothing, what I missed?"

I shook my head discreetly. "I shall tell you about it later, my love."

While walking together later that night, he remarked, "The tension between you and Hosha could cut iron."

After our daughter and her husband had departed from the feast, before which our own departure would have been taken as a slight, we had quickly dismissed ourselves. Now we were on our way back to our chamber, exhausted from the day's festivities and eager for our bed. Akhab had removed his crown and given it into the hands of his servant, who followed close behind, walking alongside Kora to whom I was handing my headdress and earrings. We had just reached the corridor outside our guest lodging and had begun the undressing procedure the moment we were away from prying eyes.

Akhab lifted an amulet from around his neck and handed it to his attendant, saying to me, "I believe he wants to have a love affair with you, my Queen."

"Hosha wants to have a love affair with every woman he sees," I replied, waving my hand dismissively after handing my bracelets and rings to Kora. She wore the bracelets on her own wrists to make it easier to carry them and clutched the rings in one hand with the earrings in another. I soon added my jeweled collar to the mix, draping it over her arm. In the end, the only piece of jewelry I still wore was my opal scarab pendant, which I would remove and put away myself once in my chamber. I clutched it now, as I often did, and gave Kora a look of thanks. Then she left to put everything else away. Akhab's man did likewise with all his jewelry, and then we slipped into my chamber and closed the door behind us.

My husband pulled me into his embrace. Kissing me tenderly, we fell back against the door with a laugh. Then he kissed me again, looked at me, and yawned tearfully. Afterward, he shook his head. "Oh, Yezeba'al. I fear you were right, what you said the other day. I am not a young man anymore."

I smiled sadly and leaned into his embrace again, resting my head on his shoulder. "I am tired too, my love."

"Then let us go to sleep," he said, taking my hand and leading me toward the bed. We slipped off our robes and draped them on a chest at the foot of the bed. Then he put out the flames on the oil lamps, leaving only the few by the doors, while I removed my scarab and locked it away. Then, at last, we climbed under the thin blankets and huddled together. It was a cool night.

The few remaining lamps cast dramatic shadows across the room; the shadows danced across Akhab's face as I gazed up at him. It struck me then how many years had gone by and how much older he looked – how much older we both looked. Thinking of this, I shuddered and looked away. Then I nestled into his embrace and stared absently at one of the flames flickering on the lamp. "What will it be like, returning to Yisrael without our daughter?" Although my voice was quiet, it seemed loud when it broke through the silence.

There came no answer. Beneath my hand, his chest was rising and falling at a steady pace. Then he started snoring. I sighed heavily, turned over with my back to him, and tried to join him in sleep.

❧ ❦ ☙

After ten days of feasting and two days of quiet, we left for Yisrael, our entourage smaller and our hearts feeling the emptiness. Although he had enjoyed the company of his cousins and their brothers and friends, once we left Tala behind, Zyah became sullen and would not talk to any of us for the first day of travel. When we stopped for the night, I went to the tent that he shared with his

312

brother. Yoram was fast asleep, exhausted from travel, but Zyah was awake and lying on his bed, whittling away at a small block of wood. He barely paused to look up when I entered, and he looked away when I came to sit on the bed. When I reached out to stroke his forehead, he jerked his head away and continued whittling. I placed my hands in my lap and watched him in silence for a while, wondering what he was trying to make until I realized he was not trying to make anything.

Finally, I said, "Is it a good idea to whittle while lying on your back? You are getting slivers and shavings all over your bed."

He paused and I knew he heard me, but still, he did not speak or look at me. Then he shrugged and continued in gloomy silence.

"Would you like to talk about anything?"

Now he looked at me, his eyes seeming darker in the dim lighting. Or was it his dark mood that blackened them? Then he looked away and mumbled, "I don't want to talk." He paused, and then added, "But…you can talk if it pleases you."

I sighed and looked across the tent to Yoram. He was lying on his stomach with his arm draped over the side of his bed. His lips were parted, and a dark spot had formed on the cushion beneath his head. I would have gotten up to close his lips and wipe the drool from his face, if not for my eldest son's need being more pressing. Despite his reluctance to speak to me, I turned back to Zyah and searched his features – sharper, more defined, and even the hint of hair on his upper lip although it would be some years before he had a full beard like his father. His voice had deepened, but it still cracked every now and then. There was little left in him of the boy he once was, and it saddened me a little, for I felt I was losing him, too.

"You miss her," I said finally.

He shrugged and stared at the wood as he continued to cut it to pieces in his hand.

"It is all right to admit it, Zyah."

"I am a man now, Ama. I must be strong, like Abbu."

"Your father feels sorrow, like anyone else. He weeps, too, sometimes. He wept just the other day, and I comforted him. There is no shame in it. I have told you this before."

After a moment, he turned his eyes toward me. His gaze softened, and then he set the wood and knife aside and sat up with his hands in his lap. I waited for him to speak, for I knew he was thinking. Finally, he said, "She will be safe in that kingdom, surrounded by zealots?"

I nodded, despite my own fears for her. Then he shifted and, when I opened my arms to him, he leaned into me with his head on my shoulder. I moved the curls from his forehead and kissed him there. He closed his eyes and seemed to be listening to my heart. Then I broke the silence, "Yisrael was much like Yehudah, before I came and brought the Ba'alim with me to our kingdom."

He sat up and looked at me. "Was it really that bad, Ama?"

I smiled faintly and nodded. "It was, although not quite as openly."

"What do you mean?"

"When I came to Yisrael, the people did not know what to think of me at first. Some were hopeful that I would recover the old ways, which is what I came to do. But the Yahwists assumed I would come to be more like them in their way of thinking – they had hope that I would abandon my gods and worship theirs instead."

"But you did not. You remained true to the Ba'alim. To the old ways?"

I gave a nod. "And so will she."

He thought for a moment. "But will that cause more trouble for her, like it did for you and Abbu?"

I inhaled deeply. "It might, yes. I am sure that it will, in fact. But your sister is strong – stronger than even I am, I think. She will be able to handle whatever she faces, and she will be a wife and mother long before she must become queen. That will give her more of an advantage than what I had coming from Tzidon."

"But when she does not convert to their religion, will the zealots hate her and rebel?"

"I do not think so. It was only when your father converted and became the High Priest of Ba'al, that the zealots began to give us any real trouble."

"Then it is true, what Aharon has said?"

I squinted my eyes at him. "What do you mean? What has he said?"

"He said there was peace in Yisrael before my father prostrated himself at the temple of Ba'al. That it was only when he converted that the rebellions against him began."

314

"That is...somewhat true," I agreed reluctantly, "but only on the surface. The rebellions were the result not of what he did, nor of my being there: they were the result of disagreements that had been building within our kingdom long before any of us were even born. Even before the time of King Dawid, all the way back to Moshe, there have been disagreements about which gods should be worshipped. I did not create division in Yisrael; I merely illuminated it."

His lips parted and his eyes sparked with sudden understanding. Then he asked, "So, that is what you mean when you talk of the old ways? The Ba'alim were already worshipped here?"

"Yes, only not as openly and not in such great number. Your father had always permitted them to worship freely, as did his father before him, but it was only when he converted and became the High Priest that followers of the Ba'alim began to outnumber the followers of Yahowah."

"And that was when you and Abbu began to kill the prophets of Yahowah?"

"Yes, but it was not because of the Ba'alim that we had them killed – it was because they were speaking against us, stirring up the people to rebellion."

"Sedition?"

I nodded. "It was the Yahwist zealots who caused the trouble of those years, and we had no choice but to eliminate them so that peace could be restored in our kingdom. You know we did not punish all Yahwists and have continued to welcome prophets of Yahowah at our court. Religious belief is not a crime in our kingdom, but sedition is, and it is only that which we punished."

"So, what Abbu did was not wrong?"

I tilted my head and asked him, "Do you think what he did was wrong?"

"No," he answered firmly. "They committed acts of sedition in speaking against the king. The people do not have the right to tell a king which gods he should worship. And I believe he was right to convert, even if it angered the zealots. Aharon said that it was only after he converted that me and my sister were born; that before that, you could not have any children, and that is why my father abandoned Yahowah."

"He did not abandon Yahowah. He accepted the favor of the Ba'alim, allowing them to bless us. He still looks to Yahowah for the

315

things he may do to help us, as we may look to any of the gods in our times of need." Then I asked, "What else does Aharon say when we are not around to hear him?"

Zyah shrugged. "Not much. He only answers my questions when I go to his house to see Shmuel and Ezra."

Ezra was Kora's youngest, only a year younger than Shmuel. Both boys had grown up playing with my sons and were as brothers to them. Shmuel was scholarly minded like his father and seemed poised to follow in his footsteps, but Ezra had a warrior's heart and often neglected his studies in favor of playing at war games with the king's sons.

"You should not pester him when he is at home with his family, Zyah."

"He likes that I have so many questions. He says I will make a great king one day."

"I am sure he is right, for you are smart and strong and wise like your father. And I am glad you are taking an interest in these matters. But now, it is late, and you must sleep. We have a long day ahead of us." I brushed my fingers through his curls and kissed his forehead as he settled back into the cushions. Then I lifted the blanket and shook all the wood shavings away from the bed before I tucked it around him again, grateful for what could be the last time he let me do it. "Sleep well, my son."

I went to Yoram and lifted his head to move the dampened cushion from under him, closing his jaw. He was so deep in sleep that he did not awaken. While I readjusted the dry part of the cushion beneath his head and bent to kiss his cheek, Zyah called, "I love you, Ama."

I smiled and turned back to him. "I love you, Akhazyah. Shalom, my son."

"Shalom, shalom," he replied with a yawn, watching me depart.

While I left my sons' tent, the eunuchs standing guard outside moved to let me pass. Those who were off duty were standing around a fire nearby, drinking and singing. They stopped to bow to me as I passed, looking surprised to see me and perhaps a bit embarrassed. I laughed and waved to them, "Carry on, carry on. Do not let me interrupt your beautiful singing." It was only partly in jest; they may not have been professional singers, but they were not bad singers.

316

After this, I came upon Kora standing outside her tent and speaking with one of the other women. They both stopped to pay homage while I greeted them. Then I asked Kora to accompany me to my tent. She gave a nod and immediately followed. As we walked together, I asked, "How are you getting on without Ruta?"

"I miss her, of course, but I know she is happy to be with Tala and to serve her as I serve you."

She followed me into my tent where Akhab was already fast asleep in our bed, snoring loudly. Not afraid that our voices would wake him, I did not bother to whisper when I said, "Still, you had your mother with you, since she also served me."

"I know, Yezeba'al." We both paused to say a silent prayer for Daneyah's soul. Then she continued, "Ruta and I have had many talks about this, and she decided for herself that it was right for her to stay in Yehudah with Tala. She wants to look after her, and when she made her vow of service, she meant it just as I did when I made mine. Our lives will never be the same, but we will get used to it, as we must."

I gazed at her fondly and reached out to hold her cheek. She placed a hand over mine and closed her eyes to my touch, smiling faintly. Then I pulled my hand away and turned my back toward her, and she began helping me undress for bed. We talked as we always did during the undressing procedure, and then she left me, and I climbed into the bed beside my husband. Akhab stirred when I pressed up against him, and without waking pulled me into his embrace. I laid with my head on his shoulder and closed my eyes, listening to the muffled voices in our camp until I drifted off to sleep.

13

By the Laws of this Land

Kora had said that our lives would never be the same and it was true, but we did indeed get used to the changes in our family. Tala wrote to all of us regularly, and we to her, just as Kora and Ruta exchanged their own communications, and soon there was much for us to share and discuss. In her first letter to us, Tala had decided she no longer cared for her childhood nickname and that, from now on, we had to call her Atalaya. I wrote back to her, concerned about the confusion it may cause, to which she explained that at Yehoshapat's court, she was Atalaya or Lady Atalaya, while her aunt was referred to as Aya, Melkah, or Atalaya the elder. I shook my head while reading this, thinking Hosha had his way after all. Poor Atalaya the elder. The nickname was only fitting, however, for she would soon be a grandmother: by the time we were preparing for the Feast of Ba'al the following autumn, my daughter had written to tell us that she was expecting her first child.

I was overjoyed at the news and wept when I read her letter, but I was still adjusting to the idea when we returned to Yezreel after the conclusion of the feast. Akhab found my conflicted reactions amusing. We were in his study and, while he sat pouring over official documents at his desk, I spoke excitedly about our plans to go to Yerushalayim to be present for the birth of our first grandchild; provided I was well enough to travel when her time was near. He chuckled and interrupted me, "*You* will be a grandmother for the first time, Yezeba'al, but I have been a grandfather already for many years."

His eldest daughters had already made good marriages, most of them within our kingdom, and even some of his eldest sons had begun to take their first wives and have children, both legitimate and illegitimate. I had forgotten about them in my excitement, but now I said, "Yes, of course. But this will be *our* first grandchild together, Akhab." Then I sighed and came to stand beside him, resting my arm

318

across his shoulder while holding my swollen abdomen. Although Azba'alah was less than a year old, I was pregnant once again and would give birth only a month or so before Atalaya. "It is hard to believe I am going to be a grandmother when I am still bearing children of my own. I do not feel old enough to be a grandmother yet."

He sniffed and looked up at me over his shoulder with a gleam in his eye. "You are thirty-two. We have been married now for nearly two decades."

"It will be nineteen years in a few months."

He raised his hand. "See? As you always remind me, we are not young anymore."

"*You* are not young," I said playfully, tickling behind his ear. "I still have plenty of youth left in me – and another child on the way." Then I bent to kiss him over his shoulder and tugged at his beard. "I do hope this will be the last, though."

"You have been most fruitful, wife," he replied, setting the document he had been reading on the desk then sitting back in his chair and gazing up at me. Leaning over his shoulder, I began kissing him more fervently. In between kisses, he said, "See, this is why... You cannot keep your hands off me."

"Can you blame me?" I asked, pausing with my hand on his chest and meeting his gaze. "It has been more than a week since the last time we had each other."

Looking back at me over his shoulder, he grinned roguishly. "I am glad you still want me, even if I am an old man."

"You grow handsomer and wiser with age," I replied. Then I brought my lips to his.

"Mmm, I do not know about wiser," he joked, as I pulled away and came around to stand in front of him. I took his hands and urged him to stand, as I climbed back onto his desk. He helped me to lie back and, while I loosened the front of my robe, he slid his hands up my thighs and bent over me to kiss my breasts. Enflamed by passion, I pulled up his robes and, finding him aroused, urged him to take me.

Once we had satisfied our craving, he straightened his desk and went back to his work while I looked through the scrolls on his shelves for something to study. Suddenly hearing a commotion outside, I stopped and moved to peer out the window overlooking the city. Although we were high above the streets, I saw in an alleyway a pack of dogs fighting over and tearing apart the corpse of one of their own kind. I shuddered and turned away, unable to watch.

"Dogs are such horrid beasts," I said, returning to the shelves. "To eat their own kind... I do not know how anyone can bear to keep them in their homes."

"The dogs that roam the streets are wild. They are not well fed like those men keep in their houses, Yezeba'al. They will eat anything they can find."

"They are dirty, thieving animals," I said with a grimace, taking one of the scrolls I had set aside and sitting next to him. He made room for me at the desk and, clearing his throat, held the scroll up to the light so he could see better.

While he kept reading, I went on, "That is another reason I do not care much for Hosha. You know, I saw one of his dogs steal meat from his plate – right in front of him! He saw this and he let it happen!"

"It is his plate," Akhab said with a shrug.

"It was not only his – they did it to some of his courtiers, too. I heard many complaints, but they are all afraid to put a stop to it, for fear the king will side with the dogs. I tell you, if it tried to do that with me, I would beat it with my sandal."

"I am sure you would," he replied with a hint of amusement, although he kept reading.

"I am surprised Aya puts up with it – although, I can tell she does not like it." I paused and thought about how much she had changed since the last time I had seen her. Life had not been kind to her. "She does not seem happy in her marriage. Of course, with a husband like Hosha, who would be? He is not a faithful man and seems not to care for her at all. I am sorry for her."

He hummed in response. I could tell he was not really listening. Heaving a sigh, I sat back with my feet up on a stabilizing rod between the legs of the desk, loosened the ties on the scroll and opened it.

Suddenly, Akhab lowered his scroll and looked up. "You know, I've been thinking..."

"Hmm? What about?" I asked, hiding my annoyance at having been ignored only to now be interrupted the moment I began reading.

"I want to expand our property here – put in a vegetable garden, like the ones we have at Megiddu and Shomron, so the

320

kitchen staff do not need to go to the market every day. It will save them time and save on our long-term expenses, not having to buy all the herbs and vegetables they need – they can go out to the garden to harvest it themselves instead."

Akhab was always coming up with ideas for building and improving our properties as well as the cities. I admired him for it but sometimes it became overwhelming to keep up with him, especially when his ideas became grander than I thought capable of being achieved. I sighed. "Where will we put it? There is not much room in the gardens we already have. I would not want the women and children to lose the only place they have to relax outdoors, and for the children to play. And what of my peafowl? They cannot live in a vegetable garden – it is hard enough for them here as it is."

"Hmm. Perhaps you are right." His eyes took on a faraway gaze. Then he snapped out of it and fixed me with a pithy smile. "It was only an idea."

While he exchanged one document for another, I watched him momentarily, thinking perhaps I should not have shut down his idea so immediately. I knew he was bored with his duties and needed something new and exciting to pull him out of the mundane before he fell into one of his despairs. They seemed to be coming more frequently.

"We'll think of something," I offered sympathetically. He glanced up at me with a weak smile, but his eyes held much sadness before he looked away and returned to his work. I decided it best to return to my studies rather than attempt to continue the discussion.

We continued in this manner for some time, during which he kept shifting in his chair and sighing heavily. It made it difficult for me to concentrate on my studies, him being so restless, and many times I thought about saying something. Finally, when he groaned, I looked up from my scroll and asked in a measured tone, "Is something wrong?"

"More complaints about Nabot…" He laid the document on the desk before me.

I sat up and put my feet on the ground as I lifted the papyrus to look at the latest complaint. Far from being the only neighbors he had trouble with, Nabot was constantly antagonizing the people of the city whose lands bordered his or with whom he did business. This had gone on for many years. He seemed only to grow bolder in the past decade, since we began paying him an annual dividend just to keep him appeased while allowing my peafowl to come into his vineyard to graze every now and then. They had all but died off in the drought, but I managed to keep a few of them alive and had since acquired more through trade, to bolster my flock. They were now doing better than they had been before the drought, and the only way to stop Nabot from finding his own methods of dealing with them was to pay him.

"He is a cheat," I said bitterly, as I continued examining the complaint. "You know, I heard recently that he boasts of the fortune he makes from us and our peafowl. The supposed damages are minimal – the annual sum far exceeds any losses he sustains."

"I have heard the same. But, as in this case," he tapped the corner of the papyrus in my hands, "there is nothing I can do about it. Everything he does is well within the boundaries of the law. I could stop paying him, of course, but then we'll have to listen to even more of his complaints."

"He is clever, I'll give him that," I answered, laying the document on the desk again. "But surely, something can be done about him. The man is a public nuisance."

"Of course, he is – that is why he is so hated. But as I said, he is not breaking any laws."

"Everybody breaks laws – he is not so holy. Just because he has not been caught does not mean he has done nothing wrong."

"He should have been a scribe, had he not been born to be a vintner like his father. He has studied the law more keenly than half my ministers. He knows it as well as I do – sometimes, I think, even better. He uses it to bolster his schemes."

"I wish he would just go away." I sighed heavily.

Akhab was silent and thoughtful. Suddenly, he said, "I could buy Nabot's vineyard."

I lifted my head and sat back in my chair. This was an unexpected idea. I smiled at the thought, understanding where he was going with it before he elaborated.

Tapping his chin with the stylus, he continued, "We could knock down that wall and that is how I'll expand the garden—"

"But leave some of the vines for the peafowl," I suggested.

Akhab agreed. "Yes, of course. They could claim a few vines for their grazing, while the rest of the land would be converted to our

322

needs. We will expand our property and be rid of your old nemesis all at once, Yezeba'al."

"I think it's brilliant, Akhab. Then we will not have to listen to any further complaints from him or the people of the city against him." I rolled my eyes.

"Exactly," he said, pointing to me with his stylus for emphasis.

I gasped with excitement as an idea struck me. "You could even add one of our vineyards as a trade, to sweeten the offer and make him leave sooner. That way he will not lose any time seeking new property and converting it, for it will already be prepared for him."

My enthusiasm for the project fed Akhab's excitement. "He can move to his new land and set up his business there by the end of the week!"

"The people of Yezreel will be rejoicing in the streets!"

"And we shall join them, if he'll agree to it!"

I chuckled, and put my feet up again, straightening the scroll on my lap. "I do not see why he would refuse such a generous offer."

Akhab nodded. "Yes, I shall go and speak with him tomorrow and the matter will be settled to everyone's satisfaction."

It was not settled, however, for Nabot was not so easily bargained with. After going to meet with him in the morning, Akhab returned to the palace and went to his chamber without coming to see me. I was not even aware he had returned, however, for I was busy tending to matters in the women's household. That afternoon, I was summoned to the garden because of an issue the Lord Treasurer and the stewards of the women's household were having with the mason responsible for repairs to one of the cisterns.

Of the king's women, only I was allowed into the presence of all these men, escorted as always by my eunuchs; due to the presence of the mason and his workmen, the other women and children were shut away inside. No doubt they were eager to return to their garden when the work was finished, for the afternoon was hot and, even with all the doors and windows open, it was stifling inside the nursery and the women's quarters.

Some of the women and children watched from the windows that looked down into the garden from above, but they rushed away and drew the curtains the moment I appeared, perhaps fearing they would be reprimanded. I would say nothing, of course – even I appreciated their shirtless, muscular forms glistening in the afternoon sun. The difference between me and some of the king's other women was that I could not be tempted from my devotion to the king. Neither could I be accused, for I was surrounded by trusted men and eunuchs, all of whom would vouch for me if anyone dared to accuse me. Besides, I was there on official matters, and they themselves had summoned me.

The Lord Treasurer and the stewards had already spent the better part of the day arguing with the mason trying to cheat us over the cost of materials. When they reached an impasse, I was brought in to give the final word, but he did not accept my decision with ease. We were still negotiating with him when Aharon came to me, escorted by his wife.

After bowing to me, the Lord Steward said, "Melkah, forgive the intrusion."

"What is it, Aharon?" I asked impatiently.

"I have come on the king's behalf, Melkah. It is a matter of great urgency."

I turned to the mason and the Lord Treasurer. "We shall continue discussing this momentarily." They nodded and went off to continue the negotiation, while I stepped aside to speak with Aharon. "What of the king? Where is he?"

"He is in his chamber, Melkah."

I was already in a foul mood from having to be bothered with these petty household matters while the king was busy tending to the kingdom's affairs, so this news was another barb in my side. Having maintained my composure throughout the tense negotiations with the stubborn mason, I finally lost my patience. "What is he doing in his chamber when there is much to be done?"

"He has taken to his bed, Melkah."

"Is he ill?"

"Not in body," he stammered. "He is...ill in spirit." I pinched the space between my eyes and sighed heavily, while he continued, "He will not rise from his bed to tend to affairs of the kingdom, neither will he speak, nor will he even eat his bread."

Raising my eyes to the heavens, I thought, *why now?* Then I asked, "When did this start?"

"When he returned from his business with Lord Nabot. Please, Melkah, will you go to him? You are the only one who can help him when he falls into despair."

"Yes, of course," I said. "I will be with him presently. But you must take over here. The Lord Treasurer will explain the issue to you."

"Yes, Melkah," he answered with a bow.

I beckoned to the Lord Treasurer, who was standing with the other stewards while the mason had gone off to yell at one of his workmen. He came to me and bowed, "Ba'alah, I am at your service."

Meanwhile, the mason returned and interrupted us. "I would like to see the king to make the deal."

"Mason, as I said before, we know the cost of these materials and we will not pay that much. Now the king is indisposed, and I must tend to him, so you may continue discussing this matter with the Lord Steward. He will tell you the same. Shalom."

With that, I walked away and happily left Aharon and the Lord Treasurer to deal with the stubborn man. Kora followed me, and as we walked through the palace, I asked, "Do you know anything about the king? What has caused his spirit to sink?"

She shook her head, "No, Ba'alah. My lord husband did not say, only that he was desperate and needed you to go to the king and find out what has come over him. It seems so sudden," she lowered her voice, "and he said it is worse than the last time."

I nodded in understanding and dismissed her, as I continued toward the king's chamber. It was not so sudden, for I was aware it had been building for quite some time and had done what I could to alleviate his misery. It was unusual for him to go to his chamber and shut himself away, but whenever it happened, I had always been the only one who could reach him and pull him free from whatever dark spirit had possessed him.

When I went through the door, leaving my eunuchs outside, I found the king collapsed across his bed on his stomach, staring idly toward the wall. He saw me approaching and turned his face the other way. I asked, "What is this? Akhab? Why are you so low that you will not eat?"

He groaned. I sat on the side of the bed and placed a hand on his back. He sighed heavily. I moved my hand up to slide my fingers in his hair at the back of his head, massaging gently. I could see the tension begin to ease from his limbs.

"Where is my Prince?" I asked gently. "My love, speak to me. Tell me what ails you?"

Another sigh, and then he moved to sit up, although his shoulders drooped, and he hung his head and would not hold my gaze. I took the tray off the table beside his bed and set it on the cushion between us. The bread had lost its warmth, but I tore a piece and offered it to him. He took it and held it in his hand, but his hand remained in his lap. I beckoned to one of the slaves who stood by the wall, waiting to be called upon. The boy came to me and bowed.

I held out the plate of bread. "Take this and have it warmed again, so the king can eat of it. And bring him a bowl of olives and some figs to go with it. And have a wineskin brought to him, as well."

"Ba'alah, it will be done." The boy took the plate with a bow and hurried away.

As the boy left, Aharon slipped into the chamber and came to me with a bow, as well, saying that the matter had been dealt with and the mason appeased. I thanked him and then I turned back to Akhab, "Husband, you must pull yourself together. The kingdom needs you."

He fell upon the cushions again and lamented, "I do not wish to be a king any longer."

I raised my eyes to the ceiling and sighed. "I know you feel this way, and I understand, but you *are* a king, and you must do what kings do – rise up and manage your kingdom."

When he still did not speak, seeing it was useless, I placed a hand on his shoulder and caressed him gently until the boy returned with the victuals I had requested. I directed him to place it on the table. He did so and then returned to his station, as I rose from the bed and looked over my husband. "Arise; eat your bread while it is warm."

He sighed and sat up, reaching for the bread. Taking a piece, he tore it and began eating slowly. I waited for him to swallow. Then I said, "Now, tell me what happened."

Staring at nothing, he mumbled, "I went to see Nabot this morning."

"Yes, you said you were going to do that. So, what happened? What did he say?"

326

"He said he will not give me the vineyard."

"Did you offer him a better vineyard, as we discussed?"

"Yes, of course, but he said he could not do it. So, I offered him money instead." He picked at the olives, and went on, "I offered him three times its worth, and still he refused. Ask Aharon; he will tell you."

He gestured to the steward who stood by waiting to be given a command. When I looked at Aharon, he gave a shrug and nodded then turned his gaze to the floor. Meanwhile, Akhab placed the olives in his mouth and spoke while chewing. "The man is stubborn and unyielding."

I put my hands on my waist, and said, "You are the king. Why not just take it?"

He swallowed, and answered, "I cannot just take it, Yezeba'al."

"Of course, you can."

"That is not the way things work in this land." He tore his bread again.

"Then how do things work? Explain this to me, because I do not understand why the King of Yisrael cannot command one of his people to give up his land."

Akhab sighed and waved at the Lord Steward. "Aharon, explain this to the Queen."

The steward bowed, and said, "Melkah, by the laws of Yisrael, property must remain within the family to whom it was originally bequeathed, for it is Yahowah's land, not the king's and not Lord Nabot's. It is his children's inheritance, you see. By the laws of Yahowah, Nabot does not have the right to sell it and prevent his children from taking it, as he took it from his father, and his father before him, all the way back to the time of Moshe when he brought the people to the promised land."

It was so complicated that I no longer wished to hear it. I wrinkled my face and raised my hand to silence him, and then said to my husband, "What difference does it make? You offered him better. They can inherit that instead."

"It is the law of this land, Yezeba'al."

"And you are the king. You govern this land. You have the power to change the law."

"I do not have the power to change *this* law!" he shouted.

"You have the power to change any law you see fit! You do it all the time. Why is this one different from the other laws you have changed?"

"Because it is God's law!" he roared. When I fell silent, he continued, "Inheritance laws supersede the king's power, because he is bound by them as anyone else. It is how the governance of the kingdom itself is passed down by right – just as I cannot sell the kingdom to another man, Nabot cannot sell his vineyard. The sale of land is forbidden in the laws of Moshe. It is just the way it is."

"But people sell their lands all the time here, just as anywhere else!"

Akhab waved to Aharon, and the Lord Steward bowed once again before he explained, "They do, Melkah, but they are not supposed to do it. Any man who does so is technically breaking the law. Nobody enforces it anymore, but any man is well within his right to follow the law and refuse to sell his land to another, even to a king, Melkah."

"Confound the laws of this wretched kingdom!" I took up a handful of olives and ate them one at a time, wondering how we could get around this. There had to be a way. Suddenly, an idea came to me. I placed the olives I had not yet eaten back into the bowl and turned to my husband with a grin. "Let your heart be light – I will procure this vineyard for you."

"How will you do it?"

"By following the laws of this land."

I took his face gently in my hand and bent to kiss him. He smiled and dropped his bread and, when I rose, put his hands on my waist to kiss my abdomen. I felt the child move within me and smiled, taking my husband's hand and placing it there so he could feel it. He smiled up at me with tears in his sad eyes. "No matter how many times, it always seems a miracle."

"It is a miracle. And a sign of good fortune." He rose and kissed me, and I brushed some curls from his forehead, gazing at him fondly. Then I instructed, "You need to sleep. I know you have not been sleeping well, of late. Take the rest of the day and the next; I will manage the kingdom for you, so that you may rest."

He nodded and turned over in his bed. I bent over him, stroked the hair on the side of his face and kissed his cheek, and then I left him and got to work on my scheme.

As his Melkah, like any man acting as regent, Akhab had long ago given me permission to sign letters and documents in his name and to use his seal whenever he took leave of his duties for war, travel, or illness. I had my own seal, of course, which was technically equal to his but most of those we dealt with still considered his seal greater and respected the commands that were issued under it without question. He often commended me for my wisdom and intelligence in managing the kingdom on his behalf, and whatever I did in his name had always pleased him. I had every reason to believe that this time would be no different, for I had devised a solution that would benefit everyone who had trouble with Nabot in Yezreel.

If Nabot could use the law against others to get what he wanted, it seemed fitting that the same should be done to him. After leaving, followed by Aharon and my eunuchs, I went to the king's study and sat at his desk. I then wrote a letter to all the nobles and elders of the city, telling them to declare a day-long fast. To those who could be trusted, those who filed numerous complaints against Nabot, I wrote the following:

Declare a fast, and when the day of fasting is over, when the people come together, give Nabot the honor of being seated at the head of one of the tables. Fill the pitchers at his table with undiluted wine that has been sweetened and bid the servants there to keep filling his cup so that he continues to drink of it without pause. Place there also at his table two men who are known to take bribes. Have them converse with Nabot and accuse him before all the people of blaspheming against God and the king. Then, by the laws of this land, he should be taken out and stoned to death. Send word to me when this command has been carried out in full.

So, it was done. I handed the letter to Aharon and told him to make copies enough for all who were to receive one, but to keep the original. Just as I had the right, so it was extended to him to sign the letters in the king's name and to use his seal. He glanced at the contents of the letter with a troubled expression on his face but bowed obediently and got to work. I left him to take over and then returned to the king.

Two days passed from the time when the letters were sent: one day for the fast, the second day for the feast that would culminate in the stoning. In those two days, while I waited for my plan to unfold, I kept myself busy managing the affairs of our kingdom and our household. When I was not holding court, I went to my youngest children in the nursery, oversaw Yoram's education, and continued to train my eldest son for his future role as king.

Meanwhile, my husband suffered in his depressed state. He would permit no one to his chamber except for me and the servants who attended to him. He would not even eat unless I was there with him. I assured him that the issue with Nabot would soon be over, but he groaned at the sound of that name and said not to speak to him about that man, nor about any of the other things which were happening in the kingdom, for he could not bear to hear it. He would not even allow Aharon to see him – if he had business related to the kingdom, he was to bring it only to me.

"I do not wish to be a king," he grumbled as we sat at the table in his chamber, eating cheese and bread and dried fruit. "I never wanted to be a king. I was born to it, but I have always loathed it. I would rather be a simple man – a farmer or even a vintner like…like…"

"Like Nabot?"

He groaned. "Yes, like him, although I hate the man and everything about him."

Reaching for a bowl of chopped dates, I said, "I am glad you are not like him." I sprinkled the dates into my mouth and chewed, smiling at the thought of being rid of him.

"I do not wish to be like him in character, Yezeba'al. Only in bearing."

"Why?" I asked, while still chewing the dates. I swallowed, and then said, "You are the highest in this land; life is hard enough. Why would you want to be any less?"

"I do not wish to be troubled with the worries of an entire kingdom and its people. It is enough to be worried about simple

330

matters, such as running an estate and caring for my family. That is all a man needs in life. If I have you and our children, I have the world."

"Only, you would not have me if you had not been born to be a king. I might never have met you. Or, worse, I might have been married to another man who was king, only to meet you and not be allowed to have you. That would be a torture I could not bear."

"No, but if you were born a simple woman."

"I am not a simple woman."

"I know, but I mean if you were born into a simple life, and we could still be together. That is all I want, to be married to you – only to you – and to have our family. All else is a meaningless distraction."

It was not that I did not understand what he meant; I simply did not see the need to imagine a life we could not have together, when we had this life and all its responsibilities. So, I said, "You are in a unique position to do many great things in this life – and you have done many great things for the people of Yisrael as king. There is much you have accomplished, and will continue to do, which you could not have done were you born a simple man."

He sighed heavily and fell back onto the cushions that had been piled against the wall by the table. Wiping the vestiges of food from my fingertips, I got up and went to lay beside him. He placed an arm around me, and I laid my head upon his shoulder with my hand over his heart, but he continued to stare at the ceiling. I reached up to wipe some breadcrumbs from his beard and smoothed the coarse hair on his jawline, enjoying the way it was both soft and prickly against my fingertips. While he began to relax, I studied his face.

"I know you have been unhappy with your lot in life, Akhab. But think of all you have because of it. There is much to be grateful for, and so many troubles we do not have because we have instead the troubles of a kingdom. It is heavy upon our shoulders, but the burden is light compared to many other things which we would not know how or care to do. And I am happy to have shared this life, with all its troubles, with you at my side to lessen the burden."

He turned his gaze toward me, and I smiled when our eyes met. Then I placed a hand on his cheek and pulled myself up to kiss his lips. Being thus comforted, we settled into the cushions and were soon lulled to sleep by the afternoon heat.

Early the next morning, I received the message that Nabot was dead. The nobles and elders sent word that it had been done as I commanded. During the feast the previous night, Nabot had been seated at the high table with two men who, having been paid, filled him with wine to loosen his lips. After a day of fasting, the undiluted wine hit him harder and faster, and he was soon inebriated. They coaxed him into a conversation about the king, leading him with a claim that Akhab was raising taxes on landownership, especially land that was used in agriculture. It was a brilliant falsehood; Nabot fell into the trap as surely as my peafowl had fallen for the sweetest grapes that he had used to bait them, and soon he was drunkenly spewing his anger against the king.

Some of those nearest to him, aware that he was treading dangerously close to seditious speech, attempted to urge him toward silence but the bribed men continued baiting him until he had said enough for them to accuse him. It was true that Nabot had blasphemed against the king, but they embellished the accusation to include curses against Yahowah. Although he denied it, the men continued to speak out against him, and the others at the table also agreed they had heard him speak against the king, although they regretted accusing him. Nabot was then taken out of the city and stoned to death, according to the laws of this land.

After reading the message, I sat back in the chair at my husband's desk and breathed a sigh of relief as I gazed out the window at the golden sky. It was a beautiful morning, indeed. Then I wrote a brief message to thank them, including a small gift as a token of our gratitude for their loyalty. It would also cover any expenses they accumulated in the carrying out of our orders. To prevent theft by the messengers, I wrote in the letter what was included and sent it to be delivered. Then I went to bring my husband the good news.

Akhab was just waking when I entered. Seeing me, he smiled and sat up and held out his arm to me. I came to him and placed my hands upon his shoulders and stood before him. He held my waist and pressed his lips to my belly. Then he looked up at me, and said, "I had a dream of you."

"A good dream, I hope?"

332

He touched my abdomen and kissed there again, where our unborn child was safely nestled and growing with each passing day. Then he answered, "It was a glorious dream, and waking from it to see your face tells me it will be a good day."

Running my fingers through his peppered curls, I said, "Indeed, it will be, for I have news: Nabot's vineyard is yours for the taking, for he is dead."

His lips parted and, for a moment, the light in his eyes dulled to confusion, but then it reignited, and he was himself again for the first time in days. He jumped up from the bed as if he was a young man again, pulled me into his arms, and kissed me firmly on the mouth. His fingers stroked a loose lock of my hair that fell upon my bare shoulder, and he asked, "How did you manage this? What happened to him? – No, I do not want to know. Is it true that he is dead?"

"I had him followed," I said with a shrug. "I knew eventually he would be found guilty of some crime or other."

"What did he do?"

"He was heard speaking blasphemies against you and Yahowah, and so they took him out and stoned him. As you well know, treason makes his property forfeit to the king, by law, if you choose to take it. So, take it."

Akhab looked at me with uncertainty. "Is it true that he spoke against me and Yahowah?"

"He spoke against you; the part about Yahowah was an embellishment that sealed his fate so that even the Yahwists who are his friends could not complain." I shrugged. "At any rate, it has been done. The man is dead; Yezreel is rejoicing this day."

He breathed deeply and rested his forehead to mine, placing his hands upon my hips and drawing me to him. The orange glow of the morning sun reflected in his eyes. "You have worked a miracle this day."

"It was no miracle…" I began, but he placed his forefinger to my lips and pushed air through his teeth to shush me.

"Just take the compliment," he whispered. Then he brought his lips to mine and took me in his bed.

Having acquired Nabot's estate gave my husband something new and exciting to throw himself into, and whenever he was not managing the affairs of our kingdom, he was working on his project. As always when there was a new project with which to occupy himself, he became heavily involved in the planning and went frequently to oversee the work. Sometimes, he even helped with what he could, for he enjoyed working with his hands. When I was not busy managing the affairs of the household, which were as numerous as the affairs of our kingdom, I went with him to observe the progress.

Already, after only a week had passed, much had been changed and improved since the day we had sent our agents to take possession of the estate in the name of the king. At first, some of Nabot's sons and nephews accused the king of murdering their patriarch and raised swords against the king's men. After they were struck down, the eldest of his sons, and those of his kinsmen who also lived and worked on the estate, begged for clemency. Because they had not themselves raised swords against the king's men, it was granted, and they were summoned before the king.

When they came to us at court and swore fealty to us, openly denouncing their father and fallen kinsmen for their crimes against the king and his realm, we gave them an offer that would make the change amenable. By law, we could have just taken Nabot's land and cast his family out with nothing, but we offered to let them stay in the house, provided they were willing to work the land and help us convert the vineyard into the garden Akhab had envisioned. They did not accept the offer.

"We are vintners, not farmers, Melekh," said the eldest of Nabot's sons, who was now the head of his clan even over his uncles. "We would be of no use to you."

Akhab sighed thoughtfully. "Then I shall grant you one of my vineyards in the Yezreel valley – the one I was going to give your father in exchange."

The man, who was about our age and easier to deal with than his father had been, seemed amazed, perhaps even relieved. "Melekh, that is a generous offer...more than we could ever expect, given the circumstances."

"Your whole clan should not be punished for the sins of one man. Will you accept this?"

The surviving sons of Nabot looked to each other, and the eldest son to his uncles. They all seemed to agree, even without speaking. Then the eldest son turned back Akhab, and said, "We will accept."

The documents of ownership were drawn up the same day and the family of Nabot was gone by the end of the week to claim their new lands. There they would surely prosper, for it was true that the vineyard we gave them was better for bearing fruit of the vine than the one we took. Now, our men were hard at work, digging up the roots of the grapevines that had already been removed when Akhab brought me there to see all that had been done. He was excited to show me.

Shaded by the canopy some of my eunuchs held over me, I followed along and listened to my husband's explanations of the conversion process. The gardeners paused long enough from mixing the soil to pay homage as we passed. They were not bothered by the peafowl, who wandered freely where once they were unwelcome, and hunted insects that were exposed in the upturned soil. I smiled at their newfound freedom and stroked their smooth, silky feathers when they came near. Meanwhile, Akhab was explaining how new soil had to be laid so that it had the correct nutrients for the different plants that would soon be growing there once the seeds were sewn. That was the next phase, which would begin with the new planting season that was fast approaching.

I smiled at his excitement over this seemingly mundane thing, and commented, "You were right – you should have been born a farmer and not a king. I have never seen you this enthusiastic about official documents and meeting foreign dignitaries. I did not know there were so many different types of soil."

He laughed and came to put his arm around my waist. His face glowed, in part because of the heat but also because he was happy. "You could farm with me, wife."

"You want to see me bending over and pulling up weeds?" I asked playfully.

"Mmm, when you say it like that, you make it sound exciting." He turned my hips and pressed himself against me from behind, whispering a naughty idea into my ear. I laughed and my cheeks grew warm at the thought, but then our playful banter was interrupted when Aharon approached with a message. As always, he had perfectly imperfect timing.

"Melekh," he said with a bow. Then to me, "Melkah."

Akhab released my hips with a sigh, and asked, "What is it, Aharon?"

The Lord Steward cleared his throat uncomfortably and bowed again, stammering, "Melekh, the zealot Eliyah the Tishbite has appeared. He has a message... He wishes to speak with you concerning a prophecy."

My husband groaned and raised his eyes toward the heavens. "Why does this man plague me so?" Then, with a careless wave, he said to the steward: "Go; bring him to me."

While Aharon walked away, cutting across the garden and stumbling uneasily upon the freshly churned soil, I looked at the king, who pondered, "Is what he has to say so important that he would risk death coming to me now?"

With a grimace, I said, "I am surprised he is still alive. I thought for sure he would be dead by now. He is so old."

"Old and tenacious," grumbled Akhab. "This Eliyah is a gnat, buzzing around my ear: no matter how many times I swat at him, he always manages to evade me, and then he is back and will not go away. How many times have we condemned him; how many years have we been searching for him, the best of our men unable to find his whereabouts." He pressed his fingers between his eyes and sighed heavily. "What if he is right?"

I wrinkled my face. "Of course, he is not right. He is the one causing trouble. We do nothing to provoke him or bring him to us."

"No, but what if Yahowah truly is protecting him?"

"It is not Yahowah that hides him from us, Akhab. He has a network of zealots and sympathizers protecting and aiding him. Those who believe his message will do anything to preserve his life."

"And he always knows where to find us."

"He still has someone watching us from inside the palace. It is obvious."

"I know, but who?" he asked, with an impatient wave. "Who could possibly be working against us, without our knowing? Who would dare? I thought we had already exposed and dealt with them."

I cast my gaze toward the Lord Steward, for a moment thinking...but no, it could not be him. The man was a Yahwist, but he cursed the zealots and exposed them whenever they appeared among our ranks. He was a loyal and obedient servant. Intelligent, yes; but not shrewd enough to fool us for all these years. He was too tolerant of our ways to work against us, and he was married to my closest confidant. So, I put the thought out of my mind as quickly as it had come to me.

Akhab's back faced the zealot leader as he approached, but he no doubt heard his footsteps. The moment he was close enough to hear, my husband said, "I have searched high and low, to the ends of my kingdom." Then he turned to face the zealot with a hard gaze. "And you come to find me, my enemy?"

"I might have stayed away forever, Melekh, to the end of my days," the Tishbite replied. "But Yahowah has sent me, and I must obey."

"Why in Yahowah's name did he send you?"

"Because you have sold yourself to do evil in his sight once again."

I came to stand at my husband's side, to stare the zealot down. The man averted his gaze, so I studied him instead. Although older, he looked healthier than he was the last time we had seen him: he had put on some weight. He still dressed in his typical animal skins and, being this close to him for the first time, I was revolted by his stench. His sun-burnt flesh looked clean enough for one having traveled, but the animal skins had likely never been washed. I grimaced and took a step backward, turning my attention then to the man who was with him, for he looked familiar. I realized then that it was Elisha, who was now a grown man and as handsome as I once envisioned, except that his hair was thinning. I raised a brow in surprise and looked at my husband, who still had a full head of hair and was as handsome as the day I married him.

"What evil?" Akhab demanded of the zealot leader.

"Yahowah says you add thievery to murder. Is this not the property of a murdered man?"

"Murder?" Akhab was taken aback. "There was no murder committed here."

"Was there not, Melekh? For I have heard it said that the man who owned these lands was killed by your command."

337

"He was killed by the laws of this land, and by that law his property is forfeit. It was not I who drove him to speak against me and even against Yahowah."

The prophet pulled something from his cloak and offered it to the king. At first, I could not see it, but I knew what it was when he said, "Is this not your seal, Melekh?"

"What is this?" asked Akhab, snatching the letter from his hands. He looked down at the letter and glanced at me before reading it. Then he held it up to me, and demanded, "Yezeba'al? Is this not your hand?"

I turned my gaze from the letter, and said casually, "I was acting on your behalf, Melekh, for you were indisposed."

He clenched his jaw and breathed through his nose, while his fist closed around the letter. The papyrus crumpled in his hand. Then his voice growled suddenly, "I did not permit this!" I jumped at the suddenness, fearing for a moment he would strike me, but his hand remained at his side, as he turned back to Eliyah. "You have found me guilty by this letter, but there were others who swore they heard Nabot speak against me. If two were paid to coax him and bear false witness, so be it, but there were others who heard him and were not paid."

"Intent to commit murder is the same as committing it, Melekh," said Eliyah, now fixing me with his burning gaze. "Commanding it to be done is an even greater sin. For this offense, Yahowah says, 'Behold, I will bring evil upon you, Akhab ben Omri. Dogs will lick your blood – yes, even yours – in the place where they licked the blood of this murdered man! After this, they will eat the flesh of Yezebel in the city of Yezreel, and the flesh of those of your house who die in the city; and of those who die in the field, birds of prey shall eat their flesh!'"

Suddenly, I was gripped by the sensation of a cold hand upon my throat, as I remembered watching the dogs ripping apart the corpse of one of their own. For the first time, fear struck my heart, and I realized it was an omen that I had overlooked. Had I recognized it for what it was at the time, I might not have acted so brashly in my dealing with Nabot. Eagerness to be rid of him had clouded my judgment. I should have consulted the Ba'alim before acting on impulse.

Meanwhile, Eliyah went on, still quoting his god: "'I will sweep you away and cut off all the males of your house, both slave and free. I will make your house like that of Yeroboam ben Nebat, and like that of Ba'asha ben Akhiyah, for provoking me to anger in your wickedness, by which you have also caused Yisrael to sin.' For, Yahowah says, 'There are none so evil in his sight as you, Akhab ben Omri – you, who have allowed yourself to be manipulated by this woman Yezebel, as Adam was manipulated by his woman in the Garden of Eden!'"

Hearing this, Akhab yelled and tore his robes. He dropped to his knees and wept with his face in his hands. I knelt by his side to comfort him, but he shoved me away and shouted, "Away from me, woman! You are the cause of all these things!"

I fell back in the dirt, catching myself on the palms of my hands. Then I pulled myself up and, wiping the soil from my hands, watched the prophet and his follower hurrying away. Aharon was running after him and speaking to him with his arms out, desperate and pleading. Whatever he was saying or asking for, the prophet waved him off and kept going, leaving the Lord Steward to stand by the open gate with his mouth agape and a horrified look upon his face. Was it guilt and regret I espied in his look?

My husband did not speak to me on our way back to the palace, but when we were alone in my chamber and I asked why he was angry with me, he turned on me again.

"I committed murder because of you! *You*, Yezeba'al! The blood of Nabot is on your hands, but the blood of his sons is on mine."

"Just because the zealot calls it murder, that does not make it murder," I replied dismissively. "The old man had it coming, and his sons should not have rebelled against you, or they would still be alive. Their blood is on their own hands, not ours."

"You said he spoke blasphemy against me!"

"He did!"

"You lied to me!"

"I did not lie, Akhab!"

"You set him up!"

"I gave him the opportunity to hang himself!"

"You had him killed, by your own hatred of him!"

"Everybody hated him!" I cried, balling up my fists at my sides. "I was not the only one who had a hand in this! But I did not put the words upon his lips, or the swords in his sons' hands!"

"You did not have to – your accomplices did your dirty work."

"We were following the law!"

"You were following your own wickedness!"

This, at last, brought me to silence and I fell back against the wall to steady myself. Then I sank to the floor with my knees up and my arms helpless at my sides. I was too stunned even to weep. I was aware of my child stirring within my womb, but even that could not bring me any peace.

Akhab, meanwhile, sat on the bed and held his face in misery. "I should have seen it, but I was blinded by my love for you. All these years, I should have seen it. Eliyah was right – you bewitched me..." He turned his gaze on me then – fierce and unloving, as I had never seen before no matter what I had done – and got up, saying, "But no more."

Then he walked away, commanding my eunuchs not to allow me to leave my quarters. I was suddenly alone, with only my ladies to tend to me. Overcome, I laid my face in my lap and wept, while Kora and the others moved around and tried in vain to comfort me. I wanted to die but even death had abandoned me.

14

Dark Night of the Soul

The king banished me from court and refused to see me; neither was I allowed to see my children in my fall from grace, for fear my wickedness would be passed onto them. By the king's command, I remained locked away in my quarters with only Kora and my handmaidens permitted entry each day to tend to my needs, and servants or slaves to bring me food and drink. Akhab, meanwhile, took to his quarters and would permit no woman into his sight, not even his lesser wives, nor his concubines.

Kora told me of my children's wellbeing and of the king's state, after hearing it from Aharon. The king was adhering to a penitential fast and went about in sackcloth, even while holding court. It was said that he even slept in it, although he was not sleeping well, for guilt weighed heavily upon his conscience. There was even talk he was planning on going to Yerushalayim to seek atonement for Yom Kippur, which was around the time Atalayah was due to give birth. We had planned to go together for the birth of my first grandchild, but now my husband would not even acknowledge me. I knew I would not be allowed to join him.

Cast off from the only people who gave my life meaning, I grew desperate. I begged Kora daily to speak to Aharon on my behalf: "Implore him to speak to the king – tell him that I am sorry and that I wish to be reconciled to him. Or, if he will not forgive me, at least permit me to see our children."

She did what I asked, and Aharon went to the king, but Akhab had hardened his heart and remained deaf to my pleas. He would not even bless me with a reply. The steward reported to his wife, who reported to me, that the king ignored every mention of my name and each time moved onto other matters as though he had not heard what Aharon had said concerning me. Were he any other man, I might not have cared so much. I might have cursed him and sworn to do evil against him for the rest of my days, no matter the cost. But it was

Akhab: my Ba'al, my divine counterpart made flesh. Without him, all balance and harmony were lost. I felt myself slipping ever closer to the edge of some great abyss. If I fell, I would be plunged into an infernal chaos from which there was no escape.

After nearly three weeks of this, Kora watched me rise from my bed and go out onto the terrace – my only connection to the outside world. It was a bright, moonlit night in contrast to the ever-growing darkness within me. I stood by the edge, my hand resting lightly on the balustrade. I contemplated what it would be like to fall from that height into the garden below: would the fall be enough to kill me? Perhaps if I landed just right...

My unborn child began to stir in my womb, and fresh tears welled in my eyes. Even death continued to evade me, for I could not punish my child for my own sins: I would have to wait until he was born and then I would do it. I closed my eyes while a warm tear slipped down my cheek. *I brought this on myself, and now I am trapped...*

"Yezeba'al...?"

Startled at the sound of my name, I turned to find Kora standing directly behind me. She looked at me, her eyes wide and arm outstretched, reaching toward me but not daring to touch. "I feared you might have jumped."

At first, I was silent. Then I looked into her eyes, and admitted, "I fear I almost did, if not for this child." I placed a hand upon my womb.

"Forgive me; I would have laid my hands on you. I was not going to let you."

"You would have done right in stopping me. It was I who was wrong." I closed my burning eyes and brought my fingers to my forehead, fighting the ache in my head. "I have been so wrong, in so many things, of late."

"The king loves you, even still."

"He cannot love me, for his love has turned to hate."

"It can turn back. It must turn back."

I shook my head. "I have cost him Yahowah's favor, which he needs in order to govern his kingdom. If he is to regain it, I am the price he must pay. I am the sacrifice."

"He wishes to be reconciled to Yahowah," Kora agreed, "but his soul cries out to you in mourning. Ahru believes his suffering

342

comes more from his separation from you than from his own guilt. And you know my husband: he does not say a thing he does not believe is true."

"Aharon," I said contemplatively. "You know, Kora, I do believe he is the one who summoned the Tishbite back to Yisrael after all these years."

Her lips parted with a sharp intake of air, and she looked at me, eyes wide with fear. And recognition. She knew.

I went on. "It was the letter that gave him away; no one else had access to the original that was written in my hand. Who else but Aharon could have given it to the zealot?"

"He does not mean to cause trouble, Ba'alah. He is not a zealot. He loves you and the king. Only, he fears his god. He wants what he believes is best for the kingdom. That is all. He is not against you."

I closed my eyes and nodded stiffly. "I know."

She dropped to her knees, bowing her head and clutching my hand. "Please, Ba'alah. Please, forgive him. And forgive me for saying nothing, for I feared for my husband. If you punish him, I beg you to punish me also; only do not punish our children for our sins."

I placed my hand on hers, and then I took her by the arms and bade her to rise. "Do not be so foolish, Kora. That is not the way of our gods to punish children for the sins of their fathers. Besides, you and Aharon have served me and my husband well. I told you once, many years ago, I do not know how the king would get on without him. He is smarter than I gave him credit for, but I still believe he is above reproach. I know he never meant for any of this to happen; it is why he has tried so desperately to reconcile me to the king."

"It is true. He blames himself for bringing Eliyah into this. He did not mean to betray your confidence or for the king to turn against you. He only wanted to frighten the king into seeking redemption. He weeps dreadfully when I tell him how you are suffering, and when he sees how the king is also suffering because of it. He only wishes he could undo the damage he has wrought upon you both."

"Tell him I forgive him, and may it bring peace unto his heart."

She looked at me, her lip quivering and eyes now brimming with tears. Without waiting for me to invite her, she threw her arms around me and laid her head upon my shoulder. "Thank you,

343

Yezeba'al!" I returned the embrace, and when she pulled away, she placed her hands upon my belly. "This child is a blessing to all of us."

"This child is my keeper, and I, his prisoner." I removed her hands and returned to my chamber, pausing in the archway long enough to say, "Tell your husband to tell the king that I am desperate. If the king will not permit me to his presence, the moment I am delivered of this child I will find a way to perish."

The joy in her expression faded, and then I turned away and went to my bed. While I pretended to sleep, I heard Kora whispering to the handmaidens not to let me out of their sight, for fear that I might bring harm to myself. They gave her their assurances, and then she returned to her family for the night.

The next morning, while my eunuchs stood their guard and my ladies moved about the chamber at their work, I sat alone at my table reading a letter from Atalaya that had been delivered while I was eating. She was eager to have her child and could not wait to see me again. How would I tell her I had lost the king's favor and would not be allowed to make the journey, as I had planned? My chest ached at the thought of disappointing her. I sighed heavily and dropped the scroll on the table as I turned away from it and closed my eyes.

Then Kora entered with excitement. "Yezeba'al, you have been granted an audience with the king!"

I inhaled sharply, suddenly filled with hope, although I remained outwardly calm and even a bit incensed. "An audience?"

"Under the condition that you are willing to humble yourself before him and his court in a public act of contrition."

"So, he wants to put me on display," I said bitterly, "the better to punish me for my sins." I paused for a deep breath. "So be it."

Then I rose from my cushion and instructed her in my preparation for the public humiliation my husband was determined to impose upon me. I would do it, if that was his wish; but I would do it my way. I bathed. Kora combed out my hair until it shone like polished ebony streaked, though it was, with the first threads of silver – there seemed more since my husband had turned from me. Then she began to braid and twist and pin it up, with the help of one of the ladies, while the others prepared my finest robes.

I dressed as gloriously as I would for any high court function, choosing the form-fitting Canaanite fashion because it accentuated my curves and emphasized my bosom. Akhab had always liked me in that fashion best. My jewels sparkled in the lantern light as I examined my face, admiring the perfect lines of kohl around my eyes. My husband commanded a spectacle to entertain his court. To prove my remorse, I would bear it; but I would perform with all the pride of my station intact.

I entered the Great Hall, accompanied by Kora and another of my ladies, but was now escorted through the main entryway as if a commoner having been granted an audience with the king. Nevertheless, I walked with dignity down the central aisle, led by Aharon and ignoring the stares of the courtiers. To preserve my sanity, I could not look upon them: I did not want to see their expressions, lest they despise me, or pity me, or find amusement in my fall from grace. Instead, I kept my gaze focused on the king ahead and my son seated to his left. Zyah was dressed in his usual courtly attire, but my husband was wearing simple rough garments, with no sandals on his feet and no jewels to adorn him; it was as Kora had said. At least, my chair was empty; I had not been replaced.

Seeing my husband again for the first time in so long, my heart leaped, and my soul yearned for him. Even in rags, he was beautiful to me. I hoped he would be moved to see me, too; instead, he regarded my court finery with a disapproving gaze. Our son, meanwhile, watched me with interest and looked to his father to see what he would do. I could see by his expression that he wanted his father to forgive me and for us to be united once again as a family.

When I knelt before the dais, the king raised his voice in anger. "You come before me as a queen, Yezeba'al?"

Holding out my arms, I said, "I come before you as a worthy sacrifice, Melekh."

He scoffed. "I see now your arrogance knows no bounds."

"Is that not what I am to you, Melekh? A sacrifice to your god, for his mercy."

"Yahowah does not accept a human sacrifice."

"I beg to disagree, for he commands many human sacrifices: cutting apart brother from brother, father from son, *man from wife...* There is to be no love between his people and those he deems unworthy, by his command. What am I if not the sacrifice you must make to prove your worthiness to him? Give to him that which you loved best, that he will at last forgive you for your sins? Cast me aside, if it will give you back that which you have lost for me. I give myself wholly to you, Melekh, to do with as you please."

"I asked you to humble yourself before me. You did not obey. You think I will be persuaded by your beauty to forgive the wickedness it hides, but I will not be moved by this display. Do not return to me until you come in true repentance." He turned his face from me and dismissed me with a wave.

My lips parted and I looked at him in disbelief, while my ladies helped me to rise. Aharon stepped forward with an apologetic gaze and moved to escort me out, but I raised my hand and shook my head, fixing my gaze upon the king. I moved forward with the intent to mount the steps of the dais – if I could just be close enough to him, if I could only look into his eyes so that he could see my pain and the genuineness of my sorrow – but the king's guard blocked me with their spears crossed and would not let me pass. This had never happened before, and I was horrified by the clear sign of his rejection.

"Akhab! Please!" My voice trembled.

"Do not speak my name, woman, for you are not in my sight." He said this without looking at me, his tone firm, but I could hear the tightness in his throat. My own pain was hard enough to bear, but hearing the pain he tried so hard to hide in his voice, I knew that this rift needed to be healed. We could not go on like this, or it would destroy us both.

At last, any remaining defiance in me was broken. Forgetting all decorum, I dropped to my knees and cried out in despair, tearing at my cloak. "My Ba'al, forgive me! I was wrong, I admit it! I was wrong. I was arrogant. Yes, even cruel and selfish. I lied to you because I knew... I knew it was wrong, though I had convinced myself it was right. But I was wrong. I let hatred into my heart and acted upon it. I see that now, and I understand why you are angry with me." My vision blurred. "But truly...I did not mean to do evil, Akhab." I paused, inhaled sharply. "I am not always right. And in this I was wrong." Warm, wet tears at last began to slide down my cheeks. "But you know me...you know my heart better than anyone. And if you cannot forgive me... If you abandon me then I am lost forever. I beseech you, cast me not from your sight!"

346

I prostrated myself then, much like I did on the day we were married, only this time when the medallion hanging from my headdress clanked against the floor, I kept lowering myself until my forehead and the tip of my nose touched the cold stone. Were it not for the child growing in my womb, for which I had to spread my knees to accommodate as I lowered myself, I would have flattened my body across the stone, as well.

The Great Hall, filled with people though it was, fell eerily silent. Although I could not see any of the people around me, I could feel hundreds of eyes on me. Then I heard movement, followed by some gasps and whispers, and my heart quickened as the king approached. I did not know until he was standing over me, when I dared to raise my face enough to look and saw his bare feet on the stone floor ahead of me.

He knelt, placed his hands on my shoulders, and whispered, "Yezeba'al, my queen. Arise and take your place at my side. You are forgiven." Then, as he helped me to rise, his voice choked when he announced to the assembly, "She is forgiven."

When our eyes met, his were brimming with tears. He reached out to take my face in his hands and used his thumbs to wipe my cheeks. They came away blackened with kohl. I could only imagine how wretched I must have looked. Aharon came forward and offered a small linen cloth without being summoned. The king took it while the steward beckoned to one of the slaves. The young boy came quickly to us, bearing a small bowl of water, in which the king dipped the cloth and used it to gently clean my face. Grateful beyond measure, I closed my eyes and allowed him this courtesy. I trembled at his touch.

When my face was clean – I would have to trust his judgment – he left the cloth in the bowl and the slave carried it away. Then he kissed my cheeks, one after the other, took my hand, and bade me to turn and face the assembly. I was embarrassed by the display I had put on, and somewhat terrified to face them, but when I lifted my gaze as the king raised my hand before them all, the people rejoiced at our reconciliation. Only a few balked at his forgiveness, but at least they had the sense to remain silent on the matter.

Then we turned and ascended the dais side-by-side and my son leapt from his chair to embrace me. He then embraced his father, who permitted it for only a moment before sending him back to his

347

chair. Order was restored, and the three of us took our places before the people to resume the day's appointments. Gradually, as normalcy returned, my trembling faded and a sense of peace was restored to my heart.

After dismissing the court for the afternoon, we went together to my quarters and had all our children brought to dine with us there. It was a joy to see them again, and they embraced me tightly when finally allowed to reunite. Azba'alah, who was just learning to walk, was keenly interested in my courtly attire, for I had not yet changed when the nurses brought her and Ba'alesar to us from the nursery. It was the first time I had ever appeared before my two youngest children dressed in such a way. She stared at me in wonder from the arms of her nurse, while I assured her, "It is me. It is Ama."

She looked to her nurse, who reassured her as well. Then she looked to me with a great smile and laughed, "Ama!"

As I took her in my arms, she immediately began touching my jeweled collar and earrings and headdress. Her manner was gentle and curious, so I let her examine these rich things which she had never seen while I sat in a chair with her on my lap.

Yoram came to kiss her cheek, and said, "Azba'alah, Ama is Melkah Yisrael. Someday, you may be a queen, too."

I reached out to stroke my son's hair and gently pinched his cheek. He reached up to push my hand away, though, and said, "Ama, please! I am almost a man."

"You are ten," I reminded him.

"It is only three years away!"

Akhab chuckled and placed a hand on top of Yoram's head, playfully tussling his hair and moving him about. "He is right, wife."

Smiling, I met his gaze – filled with love once again – and my eyes began to sting. He bent to kiss me on the mouth and paused afterward to look at me with tearful gaze, gently stroking my cheek. He kissed me once more, before he kissed Azba'alah on the forehead. Then he stroked her hair as she laid her head upon my breast, and I could feel her relief at being reunited with me after so long a separation.

Then Ba'alesar came to pull at his father's arm, saying, "Abbu, why are you and Ama dressed like that?"

"Abbu wanted to play the pauper," I teased.

"And Ama wanted to slay me with her beauty," he replied. Then he imitated being shot through the heart with an arrow, causing Yoram and Azba'alah to giggle, and even getting a grin out of Zyah.

"What is 'slay'?" asked Ba'alesar.

Zyah came to lead him away, saying gently, "Do not worry about it now, Esar. You are not old enough to understand."

After eating with our children, their nurses and caretakers led them away. Zyah was the only one who did not have a nurse anymore, but he still had his guardian and teacher who waited by the door to escort him to his quarters. Then Akhab reclined on my bed in his sackcloth robe, gazing at me while the ladies dressed me for bed. Despite our joyful reunion, I could still see the sadness and regret in his eyes, and I longed to comfort him.

When at last we were left alone, I went to him and coaxed him out of his sackcloth. "Truly, my love, how can you sleep in that? It must itch terribly!"

"It does," he answered, reclining once again, wearing only his loincloth – at least that was his usual silk. "That is why it is part of my atonement. But for you, I will remove it."

I sat beside him. "How long are you going to wear it?"

"Until we leave for Yerushalayim."

"That long? That is still nearly two months away! Surely, you have atoned enough by now. Are you still fasting?"

"Yes, but only every three days."

I stopped and looked at him worriedly. "Will you no longer be my High Priest?"

He touched my rounded belly and looked up at me. "I am still your High Priest. I have not forgotten what the Ba'alim have done for us. But I must also keep Yahowah's favor, for he made me the steward of his kingdom."

I lowered my gaze but nodded in understanding. I did not agree with it, but I knew what it meant to him. He held my chin and brought his thumb to my bottom lip. Then he sat up and kissed me. At last, I could relax. He brought me down to lay beside him in his arms. We listened silently to each other's bodies and the sounds of the night. There was no passion between us, for we needed gentleness

349

in that moment. The passion would return to us when we had healed enough for the fire in our souls to reignite.

"For the first time in weeks, I feel at peace," I said. "This is all I want, in all the world – to be in your arms here in this bed. There is nowhere else I feel truly safe."

His chest rose beneath my hand, and I felt his body shift. He reached to stroke my hair, and said, "Forgive me, wife. I was a fool to doubt your sincerity. I was cold and unfeeling."

"You were afraid," I replied, lifting my head to look at him. My hair draped as a curtain, and he reached out to touch it, gently sliding his fingers into the locks. Then I rested with my chin on my hand, still on his chest. "And I was wrong. I thought I was right... I thought I was acting in our best interests, but you were right when you said I was blinded by my hate."

"I still should not have turned away from you as I did."

"Perhaps you needed to," I said. "It gave me time to think on my error, and to realize I was wrong. Or I might have continued forever to assert the rightness of my actions and deceive myself."

"Even so, I should have come to you. I should have spoken to you in privacy, not argued with you in court. I should not have asked for a spectacle. I realized as I watched you today...I should not have asked that of you. It was a cruelty."

"And I deserved it, for the cruelty of what I did." I paused, and then confessed, "Perhaps I am wicked."

"You are not wicked."

"I am not sorry that he is dead...only for my part in it, and for deceiving you."

"I am certain there are many who feel that way," he admitted with a sad smile. "I may not have told you to do it...I may not have participated directly in what happened...but I had a hand in it, nonetheless. I allowed it to happen, and I took the spoils for myself without a second thought. If you are wicked, then I am wicked, too."

"What will happen to the garden?"

"I have thought about it a great deal. What is done has been done. I cannot undo it, and there is nothing left of the vineyard to be reclaimed by the family. Even if I returned it to them, it would take so much time to convert it back into a vineyard – years before it would be productive. They are already settled and working their new land, and it is better land. They will prosper there."

He heaved a sigh, and I knew he was thinking of Nabot.

"It is only a shame he did not accept the offer when I made it, but I think he could not let go of the power he had over us – his greed for the money he made – and in that was his downfall. We enabled it, and I think we were all wrong in this – even he. But wrongness does not necessarily equate to wickedness. Who is more wicked: the man who connives to steal from his neighbors, causing trouble to them every chance he can, or the one who takes extreme measures to put a stop to his mischief? I am the king, but even I do not know all the answers. None of us do, for we are only the sons of Adam."

We fell silent, perhaps both of us thinking through the complexities of all that had happened, and his question, which was the last we would speak on that matter, although we would never answer it. Instead, exhausted by it all, I sighed and laid my head upon his shoulder, closed my eyes, and cozied up to him. Now, everything felt right again, and soon enough we were both asleep.

The birth of our last child was a difficult labor and lasted nearly two days. Even with all my meditations and the chanting of the priestesses to soothe me, I had suffered a great deal. When it was over, I swore I would not do it again and consulted the priestesses of Ashtarti for the means to prevent further pregnancies. Despite these challenges, we were delighted with our new son. We named him Abshalom: "his father's peace."

Akhab continued to walk about in sackcloth, but a new peace had indeed overcome him. It was only when it came time for us to travel to Yerushalayim, a few weeks later, that he exchanged his sackcloth for garments that were suitable for travel. I was relieved to see him looking like a king once again, but as soon as we reached Yerushalayim, he returned to his sackcloth. He remained this way until he had gone to the temple for his atonement on Yom Kippur. I stayed at the palace, uninterested in the Yahwist feast, although I enjoyed the festivities the following night and was glad to see my husband smiling so freely once again.

Atalaya was a wonder to see, being so heavy with child, but she looked healthy and strong. When we first came together upon our arrival at the palace, we embraced heartily and kissed on the cheeks.

351

Then I touched her swollen abdomen and we marveled together at this gift of new life. She assured me she was handling the pregnancy well, but that she was eager to deliver the child and be done with it.

Akhab looked at her with a mixture of fatherly pride and sorrow at seeing she was no longer his little girl anymore, and then he embraced her with one arm and firmly kissed the top of her head. "How are you?" he whispered.

"I am well, Abbu," she assured him.

"Do they treat you well here?"

She gave a nod. "The king and queen are good to me, as is my husband. I am happy here, although a part of me will always long for the land of my birth. I miss Ama's peafowl, and all my brothers and sisters."

"You will always have a home with us," he said. "Should you ever need it."

She shook her head. "This is my home now, and it is a good home. But I should like to come and visit you and Ama and the rest of the brood – I hear I have a new brother."

"Abshalom," Akhab confirmed. "A strong and healthy boy with a strong set of lungs."

"Oh, Abbu, I do hope you will let Ama rest from having so many children," she teased.

He looked over at me with a mischievous grin. "Let us see if she will give *me* rest from making them."

I chuckled and playfully punched his bicep. He rubbed it and then, as we followed our hosts inside from the courtyard, discreetly pinched my behind.

Tired and hungry from our travels, we all went to sit together for a small private feast that had been set up in Atalaya's chamber. Hosha, sitting at the head of the table, opened the feast with the usual toast: "*L'khayim tobim ul'shalom*," meaning "for good life and for peace." The rest of us raised our cups and repeated the blessing, and then drank to it. Then we broke bread and feasted on dried fruits and roasted meats, and it was a lively yet peaceful supper between our two united families.

I sat to the left of Hosha and to Aya's right. Yoram sat on the other side of his aunt, with her younger son Yehiel beside him. Akhab sat across from his sister, between our daughter and her husband.

Yehoram sat to the right of Hosha, and Zyah on the other side of Atalaya. The other end of the table was left empty.

As I sipped my wine, I watched Atalaya and her twin talking and teasing and laughing together as if no time had passed. It was strange to see the two of them together again after more than a year apart. She was a woman with a husband and a child on the way, but he was still developing into a man and seemed so far behind her in many ways.

Yoram occasionally jumped into their conversation, but mostly sat by himself picking at the food on his plate. Yehiel occasionally tried to engage him in conversation, but Yoram had little interest in conversation that night. I could tell he was exhausted and bored of the gathering; he preferred those that were more boisterous in nature.

Meanwhile, Akhab talked with Yehoram and Hosha, while the queen and I visited quietly. In excited whispers, she told me about the changes that had taken place in the women's quarters in the last year. "It is such a relief that the old woman is dead. I mean, I know it is heartless to say – Hosha misses his mother dreadfully – but you really have no idea how miserable she made life for all of us here."

"I have heard," I answered, not telling her of the endless complaints that my daughter had written to me about the now deceased Gebirah of Yehudah.

"You are lucky, Yezaba'al," Aya insisted, "You have not had to live with a gebirah over you all these years."

I did not disagree, although there had been many times when I wished to have an older queen to guide and instruct me, and to take on some of the duties that were hard for a melkah to undertake: discipline of the king's women and preparing the king's new wives, for instance. The only objection I voiced was in saying, "But your mother would surely not have been so unkind toward the rest of us."

Aya grimaced. "My mother was worse than Hosha's! You are lucky she passed before you came; trust me on that."

"Truly?" I asked in disbelief.

"Oh yes. She would have made you miserable, especially seeing how close you and my brother are – she would have felt threatened by your importance to him and would have sewn seeds of contention between you every chance she got. She was in perpetual competition with every woman who was more beautiful and cunning

353

than she." Seeing my look of surprise, she laughed. "Trust me; she would have seen you as the ultimate rival. She could barely even tolerate me, and I was her own daughter!"

"All right," I conceded. "I shall take your word for it." Then I raised my cup. "To our dear deceased mothers-in-law."

She raised her cup and then we drank, while our husbands looked at us curiously, having not been privy to our conversation. Then they too shared the toast, and the meal continued in this manner for another hour at least, before we all retired for the night.

Much to Yoram's delight, the festivities for Yom Kippur were more exciting than our private supper had been. He got into his usual mischief with the many sons of Yehoshapat, but this time Zyah stayed close to his sister, her husband, and their friends at court.

It was clear that Atalaya enjoyed being the mistress of her own miniature court. Surrounded by young men and women her own age, she was in her element. Not only those she brought with her, but even the new friends she had made in Yerushalayim had all molded themselves to her every need and desire. She entertained and was entertained by them, and with Zyah being added to the group, their antics became even more wild and absurd. Zyah especially liked making people laugh and was always carrying on in some manner to that effect: strutting around like the peafowl, or imitating other animals in their movements and sounds, or speaking in an unnatural voice while making faces. No one could make Atalaya laugh with quite as much glee as her twin brother, and my eyes teared up as I watched them together once again.

Like me, all my children enjoyed the festivities but refrained from participating in the religious observances. While Akhab joined everyone else at the temple, I stayed at the palace and simply enjoyed being united with my eldest daughter. It was also at that time when I congratulated her recent success at converting her husband but urged her not to make enemies in Hosha's court by pushing too hard for change, reminding her that it had to be done gradually and with care. The King of Yehudah permitted followers of the Ba'alim to worship covertly, but he was not yet aware of his successor's conversion to our religion.

Only two days after the feast, my daughter was taken to the birthing chamber at the palace, with me and Aya and many of Yehoshapat's wives and daughters in attendance. Ruta and Kora were also in attendance, as were several priestesses of Ashtarti who were the only midwives my daughter allowed to tend to her. Thankfully, it was an easy labor and when it was over, Atalaya had a son. I was the first to hold my grandson but brought him immediately to Aya, and we admired our grandson together while Ruta and the other women of Hosha's court helped Atalaya recover from the labor.

Despite it having been a relatively short and easy labor, she was exhausted and had suffered a great deal. I often teased her for her sensitivity to pain; this time, I refrained, for I was proud of her accomplishment. When she was ready, I brought the baby to her, and she wept joyfully as she took her son and gazed upon him for the first time. When the men were finally permitted entry, in came Yehoram the proud father, followed by grandfathers Hosha and Akhab, and many uncles, including Zyah and Yoram.

She named her son Akhazyah in honor of her twin. Zyah was a proud uncle and delighted that his first full nephew was given his name. He would boast about this for many weeks afterward, and I hoped that my grandson would come to emulate his namesake.

We stayed in Yerushalayim until our grandson's circumcision and presentation at the temple. When we left, it was a difficult parting, but we had secured promises that the family would come to visit us in Yisrael sometime in the following year. Their plans to visit us were delayed, however, thanks to an interruption once again caused by my cousin, the King of Aram. Only, this time, Hadadesar approached us as an ally.

Invoking the covenant my husband had made with him, and promising to uphold it, he invited us to his court at Damaseq, where he was currently hosting Irhulani, the King of Hamat. Irhulani was in exile after Shalmaneser of Assyria had taken his kingdom. The King of Assyria was currently enjoying himself at Qarqar, the King of Hamat's favorite residence. He had allowed Irhulani to leave with his queen and their children but had forced the exiled king to leave the rest of his wives and children behind.

According to some reports, the King of Assyria had ravaged some of Irhulani's wives and daughters. When I heard this, I wept for them and prayed they would be delivered from Shalmaneser's hand. I was ashamed that he was another relative of mine: the King of Assyria was a cousin to me and Hadi. His father, Ashurnasirpal, had been a half-brother to our mothers, but we had never met due to his father's subjugation of our families' kingdoms. Now that he was king, Shalmaneser was following in his father's footsteps, bent on conquest and hoping to make a name for himself that was equal at least to that of the scourge of the Levant.

We were aware of this tense political situation, but Yisrael was far enough to the south that we had little to worry about from the King of Assyria. Nevertheless, as tentative allies, we agreed to visit my cousin at Damaseq, and to meet the exiled King of Hamat. At Hadi's request, we brought our two eldest sons with the thought that we might strengthen our alliances by arranging marriages for them from among his daughters, or from among the few daughters of Irhulani who remained with him in exile.

Hadi welcomed us to his court with great pomp and ceremony. I was not pleased to see him, but I withheld my fury toward him for the sake of peace. Of course, he could not help himself – one of the first things he did after we arrived was take us all to the nursery, under the guise of meeting his many children, while his true intention was to point out the old pavilion in the playroom.

"Do you remember, Yeza? How much fun we had in that tent!"

My husband, having no idea what my cousin meant, admired it and suggested we should have one installed in the nursery at Megiddu. At fifteen, Zyah had lost all interest in play, but eleven-year-old Yoram was excited by the thought of having his own battle tent. I merely smiled as I fixed my cousin with a venomous gaze, and said, "What a charming idea. Thank you, Hadi, for inspiring it."

He met my venom with vindictive glee and held up his hand to whisper in Irhulani's ear. The King of Hamat's brows raised and his gaze shot to me, while Hadi chuckled, and said aloud, "To this day, those are some of my fondest memories."

My husband looked to me, at last figuring out what sort of memories they were. When he asked for clarification later, I finally had to confess the extent of my relationship with Hadi. He admitted that he knew I must have had some sort of experience before I married him, because I was not as timid as were most of the virgins

he had taken. Then he looked to me with a questioning gaze, and I
knew what he was thinking.

"I was a virgin when we married, Akhab. I never allowed Hadi
– or anyone else – to take it so far with me. I had dalliances, yes, but
I was not compromised. You remember how much I bled the first
time."

He nodded in understanding and confirmed the memory. He
feared he had been too rough with me, but I assured him he had not
and that, once the pain wore off, I had enjoyed it a great deal. It took
some time for my body to adjust to how frequently and passionately
we made love, however, and my thighs were bruised and sore for
weeks after our first night together. Still, it was not enough to stop
me from wanting more from him, and he had been more than happy
to oblige.

We were not at Damaseq for reminiscing, however. Once the
pleasantries were out of the way and the welcoming feast had been
enjoyed, Hadi revealed the true reason for his invitation to us, which
had not been stated outright until we were there.

Seated at the head table on our second night at Damaseq, the
three kings spoke together of going to war against the Assyrians,
along with the aid of several other kings who had already agreed to
my cousin's plan. They were expected to arrive with their armies over
the course of the following days. One of these was Basa of Ammon, a
sworn enemy to Yisrael who had been one of the kings to follow Hadi
in his first assault against us. Hadi assured us, however, that Basa
was willing to set aside all enmity and declare a truce if we supported
their campaign against Assyria.

Shalmaneser had only been king for about six years, but was
already proving to be as ruthless – if not as cunning – as his father.
He demanded a higher tribute from the kingdoms he subjugated,
threatening an assault if they refused to pay. So far, they had all
agreed to his terms, but many had grown tired of Assyrian
subjugation. Irhulani had been the first to cease his payments and
had suffered greatly for his disobedience.

When he appeared with his entourage and what was left of his
army, having sent ahead to request protection from Damaseq, Hadi
was enraged by Irhulani's report. He had written to my father the
King of Tzidon, thinking he would join them, but my father was old
and tired and said he had no interest in losing another rebellion

357

against the Assyrians. He would not join the campaign, not even send troops to support the campaign, and had chosen instead to stay out of it entirely. It was my father's rejection which led Hadi to consider my husband as an ally instead.

"You are a younger, better leader than my uncle, Akhab," said Hadi, dripping with flattery. "I would rather have you and your armies with us any day."

Listening carefully as I sipped my wine, I withheld the urge to say what I was thinking: that my cousin would not be satisfied until he had assaulted all our relatives and their kingdoms. I would say that only to my husband when we were getting ready for bed later that night, while Kora and my other attendants carried away my jewels and regalia. I thought for sure Akhab would laugh at my comment, but instead he remained silent, watching me as I sat brushing out my hair after it had been taken down for the night.

When he did not say anything, I stopped brushing and turned to look at him, asking if he was listening. He then revealed that he was going to join the other kings in their campaign. This sparked a bitter argument between us. It began while I was still seated at the dressing table but soon poured out onto the private terrace attached to our guest quarters. Even though I knew my cousin was likely watching us from his own quarters, the terrace of which we could see from ours, and that he could hear our voices raised in anger, I knew he could not hear the specifics of what we said.

"You cannot go to war against the Assyrians," I insisted vehemently, getting up and walking toward the window. "You do not want to make an enemy of Shalmaneser."

"The prophets speak favorably of this campaign."

"The prophets my cousin has consulted?" I asked, turning back to him. He answered with a nod. I scoffed. "They are false prophets – they only tell the king what he wants to hear, so he will continue to favor them."

"They are prophets of Ba'al," he said, following me out onto the terrace. "I would think you would approve."

"Every god has his false prophets! Even the Ba'alim! You should not listen to every man or woman who claims to see the future or speak in the name of their god. This is not our war – we should return to Yisrael and stay out of this. Let them kill themselves if that is their wish. We have no business being a part of it."

"There will be eleven kings, all of us together leading our armies against Shalmanesar, who is holed up at Qarqar with only a portion of his army. They plan to continue moving further into these lands, taking more cities and kingdoms along the way, but we will be taking them by surprise. They will not stand a chance."

"They will crush you – no doubt that is my cousin's hope that you should die, and he would lay claim to what is yours!"

"If that was his aim," he said with an ironic laugh, "he would poison my cup or send his men to slay me while we are asleep in his palace, and we should not have come here at all."

"You are right, we should not have come! I said so in the first place!"

Ignoring my comments, he continued, "He would not risk his own army, nor would the others. They have all sworn a truce and will uphold it for as long as I am their ally in this."

"So, you will make a newer, greater enemy for a truce with these lesser kings?"

"It is better to have one great enemy than ten others."

I tensed my jaw and narrowed my gaze. "Assyria does not forget their enemies."

He took me by the arms, gazed at me fondly, and kissed my forehead. "I love you, wife, and I appreciate your concern, but I have already decided."

"Damn it, Akhab!" I cried. "Will you not listen? Are you truly so eager for war that you will so readily agree to side with one who was not so long ago our enemy? If you die in this reckless campaign, do you believe they will extend their truce to me and our sons? You will leave us to Hadi's mercy, and he will not be merciful. He is not a good man like you!"

"I will not die, Yezeba'al. And even if I did, the kingdom would pass to Zyah, by right."

"You think Hadi would not attempt to take it out from under him, with you out of his way? Zyah is still only a boy! He cannot be expected to lead our kingdom and defend it from those who covet what is yours! And if you lose the better part of our army in this folly, you will leave us defenseless!"

"I will not summon the better part of our army. I will bring only a portion of my chariots, and the rest will be foot-soldiers. Our best soldiers and the majority of our chariots will remain in Yisrael, and our kingdom will be safe."

"You should not even consider joining forces with our enemies."

"Hadadesar is not our enemy," he argued.

"He is not our friend! After what he tried to do to us, I cannot believe that you would trust him! I feel you must have gone mad!"

He sighed with exhaustion. "I am not mad, Yeza…"

"Ugh! Do not call me that!" I said, pushing him away when he tried to take me in his arms. "I have told you before, never to call me that! It is what *he* calls me, and I will not stand for it from you."

Now, he ran his fingers through his hair. "What is it with you two? You hate him, he loves you, I do not understand it."

"He does not love me, Akhab; he is obsessed with me. In his mind, you are all that stands in his way of possessing me. You think he sees you as an ally in his bid against the Assyrians? In his mind, you are a rival, and he will stop at nothing to be rid of you! Why can you not see it? That is why he wants me here, while you go to war with him – that if you die, he will already have me in his possession! He will not even need to march on Yisrael to seize me for his conquest!"

Taking me by the arms to stop me from pacing or walking away from him, he looked at me with a fond gaze and a wry smile. "Yezeba'al, for once this is not about you. This is about a covenant I made with Hadadesar. This is about Assyria growing stronger than they should be and posing a greater threat to everyone around them."

"They are no threat to us, *if* we stay out of it."

"You think Shalmaneser does not covet Yisrael and all the other kingdoms, all the way to Egypt? Assyria will continue to grow if we do not put a stop to it."

"You do not know that."

"I do know, Yezeba'al – it is clear for everyone to see! Already, Shalmaneser and his father before him have taken many lands that do not belong to Assyria and forced their kings to pay tribute to them – your own father is one of them!"

"Yes, but even he chooses to stay out of it because he knows it is a fight he cannot win! He already tried. It nearly destroyed him!"

"That is because his strength lies more in naval warfare than it does in the plains." At this, I scoffed, but he continued, "I have a

360

far better chance against the Assyrians with my army than he ever had with his. That is why the other kings want me to be their ally – I have the largest and strongest army of them all."

"It does not matter that we have the largest army, or the strongest, when there is no reason for us to be a part of this war! There is nothing to gain from it!"

Taking me by the arms once again, he spoke slowly as if explaining to a child. "Once we take back Hamat, Irhulani has promised the best of his daughters for our sons to wed, and we will enter a covenant of peace between our kingdoms."

"Irhulani is a weak king. We do not need him as our ally when he cannot even keep his own kingdom from being overtaken!"

"He will rebuild, with our help. And Hadadesar has promised he will return the lands of Gilad to our kingdom when this is over."

"He should return these lands without asking anything of you! They are rightfully yours," I hit his chest with the tips of my fingers, "and he promised to return them for his life, which you gave to him when you should have taken it."

"The generals and the other kings are in favor of this campaign, as are our ministers. They want it as much as your cousin."

"Of course, they do! You are all mad with boredom and seeking a war to entertain yourselves, not thinking of the deaths and destruction it will bring to your midst, and for no good reason!"

"At the very least, it will bring suitable wives to our sons, which they will need soon enough."

"They can take other wives!"

"And it will open new opportunities for trade and agriculture, which can only benefit our people."

"This is folly!" I cried, as angry with him and all these men as I was with myself for losing my battle with the tears threatening my composure. Trembling as I managed to keep them back a moment longer, I said, "Do not let greed get the better of you, or you will lose all you hope to gain and more."

Not wanting him to see me weep now, I turned and walked away, but he followed me inside.

361

15

The Arts of Love and War

The King of Yisrael pledged his aid to the kings of Hamat and Aram in their campaign against Assyria. As part of the new covenant, Hadi pledged his favorite daughter to Zyah when old enough to wed, and Irhulani pledged both of his queen's daughters who were with him in exile. So that Zyah and his future wives would have time to get to know each other, it was agreed that my sons and I would remain in Damaseq with the wives and children of Hadi and Irhulani while the men went to war. Akhab sent to Yezreel for a small contingent of chariots and a division of foot-soldiers, while the other kings involved sent for the best of their men. When they arrived, the soldiers camped outside the city as the final preparations were made.

Before the men and their armies set out, we spent a day in fasting and prayer for a successful campaign. The kings, of which there were twelve including Akhab, each made an offering at the temple of Ba'al Rimmon, the god of Aram. Afterward, they returned to the palace where we ended our fast with a banquet.

We were seated in our places of honor at the head table with Hadi, Irhulani, and the other kings: as the only royal woman welcome at the feast, I was in the central place of honor, Hadi to my right, Akhab to my left. Dancers and courtesans moved freely about, catching the eye of so many wealthy and powerful men. My cousin, not surprisingly, passed around smoking bowls of qaneh-bosem and gave us the best of his wine, perhaps hoping we would lose our senses so that he could have his way with me. He certainly tried a couple of times. Of course, I spurned his advances and stayed close to my husband, who intervened when Hadi refused to take no for an answer.

While I was inhaling smoke from the bowl which he had just handed to me, Hadi leaned over and once again attempted to put his hands on me. Quickly handing the bowl to Akhab, who passed it along, I slapped Hadi's hands away and blew out the smoke in his face. He looked away with a smirk. "Are you ill, Yeza?" he asked. "I have hardly seen you eat anything this whole night."

Akhab laughed and put his arm around me. "My Queen subsists on chickpeas, lentils, and a few fruits and vegetables. She eats lamb occasionally, quail frequently, and camel," he lifted the hunk of roasted meat off his plate, "never. And as for desserts and sweets – she seldom indulges such things, although I quite enjoy them."

While my husband took a bite from one of the sweet cakes he so loved, Hadi laughed. "Qaneh-bosem makes me eat more, not less."

"Unlike you, Hadi," I said without looking at him, "I have learned to control my urges." Some of the others around us grinned, while I continued, "I eat only what I need, and no more." Then I tilted my head to look at him with a smile.

"It is no wonder you are so small, Yeza," he said, as he looked me over with a wandering gaze. "At least you have shape where it matters most."

When my cousin reached out again, this time to touch my breast, Akhab intercepted his hand. I leaned back, as he warned, "Touch my wife again, Hadi, and I will break the hand that offends her."

Akhab's grip was so tight that Hadi could not pull away. Although Hadi was younger, Akhab was a true warrior and in far better shape. He could easily have snapped my cousin's fingers with one hand. Hadi seemed to recognize this and immediately apologized. Akhab finally released him with a stern gaze. Then Hadi went off to flirt with one his courtesans instead. I looked at my husband with thanks and smiled faintly. He gave me a nod and then drew me into a tender kiss, which was interrupted when Zyah came over and plopped down on the cushions beside us.

"This is quite the party!" he said with knees up and arms draped across them. I turned to look at my eldest son, who was beginning to look more like his father each day. He even had the hint of stubble sprouting on his upper lip and chin.

"It is," I agreed. "But I think it is time for you to return to your quarters for the night." Being fifteen and considered a man, he was permitted to join us, but I had forgotten he was even there. Now, the party was growing too raucous for him to stay.

363

He sighed heavily and dropped his hands from his knees. "Come on, Ama! It is not fair! I am a man now."

Akhab looked at his son. "Zyah, your mother is right. You are not so much a man that you should be here for the entire banquet. Some of the things that are happening late in the evening you should not see."

Zyah continued to protest, but Akhab beckoned to his guardians who came at once and bowed to their king, who commanded, "Take the prince back to his quarters, and be sure he does not stray."

They bowed again, and the chief eunuch responded, "Yes, Melekh." Then Zyah, rolling his eyes and heaving another sigh, got up and followed them.

It seemed that we sent him away just in time before the feast became wilder than even the wildest of our Ba'alim feasts. Here, the men and women began to make love while still at the table and while others dined. At first, Akhab found it amusing, but we soon lost our appetites. Looking forward to returning to our guest quarters now, we could not depart until Hadi retired for the night. As our host, it would be considered a snub, a rejection of his hospitality for us to leave before him.

So, while the other kings had their way with some of the dancers and courtesans, and a few of them fell into drug-induced orgies, my husband and I restrained ourselves even from each other and slowed our intake of Hadi's gracious offerings. We had no intention of losing our senses. As the night wore on and my cousin could neither seduce me nor persuade us to join him for a threesome, he finally retired for the night. He even went without his favorite courtesan, a young dancer called Naveen, who stayed behind with the other dancers.

Eager to get away from the revelry now, Akhab and I returned to our guest quarters, commanding some of the servants to deliver a couple of wineskins. At least we could continue with our own private revelry. After sharing half a wineskin between ourselves, I coaxed my husband out onto our private terrace and, laughing, told him that I had seen Hadi spying on us from his own quarters every night. He was there now, in fact, and I discreetly pointed him out, shrouded in darkness but still visible to an observant eye.

Akhab started to turn his head, so I grabbed his beard, kissed him to make it look like it was just part of our love play, and hissed, "Do not be so conspicuous!"

Freezing in place, while I got down on my knees and lifted his robe to give him pleasure, he was able to turn his head to scan the area where I had told him to look. It would have appeared as if he was only looking to be sure no one saw what I was doing to him. Then, as I took him into my mouth, he gasped aloud, and said, "That perverted dog!"

Pausing, I whispered, "Hush." Then I began again, and he let me continue.

Suddenly, I stopped before he had finished and rose to my feet, wiping my mouth with the edge of my sleeve. Then he glanced about again, and asked, "What was that all about? You start and do not finish?"

Giggling impishly, I stripped off my robes and let them fall to the ground.

He gasped, and said, "What are you doing? Yezeba'al, he will look upon you!"

Ignoring his protests, I stepped out of the robes and moved toward him with a determined gaze. I pressed myself against him to feel the bulge in his robes, which I was craving, and breathed, "Show him I am yours."

Now that he understood my meaning, he grinned and turned me around, grabbed me by the waist, and bent me over the edge of the terrace to enter from behind. We rutted like a pair of jackals while I clung to the wall, crying out in ecstasy until my husband had finished.

Invigorated and still craving him, I coaxed him toward our chamber and teased him back into arousal. In the entryway, he seized me and pressed me back against the doorframe with his hands around my wrists, holding them above my head. I bared my teeth to him, and he grinned. Then he bent to kiss and suck my breasts. I leaned my head back against the doorframe with eyes closed and released a sigh. When he stopped and straightened himself to look at me, I opened my eyes and inclined my head toward him, eager to unite our souls in a kiss. He released my wrists and we kissed hungrily, and then he took me again while still standing in the entryway.

365

We had not made love like that in years, and no doubt our bodies would be aching in the morning, but it was worth it. I wanted Hadi to know that I enjoyed my husband thoroughly. I wanted him to burn in his jealousy; to see what he coveted and know that he could never have it. I wanted it to drive him to madness, for I hated him with every fiber of my being and wanted to punish him for all the trouble he had caused us. Hadi stayed in the shadows, watching and waiting until he thought he would not be noticed before storming away. Breathing heavily, as Akhab took my hand and drew me into the chamber, I glanced back over my shoulder and saw him go. Satisfied in every way, I smiled.

The next morning, as twelve kings gathered and prepared to meet up with their armies camped outside Damaseq, contrary to my dignity, I allowed myself to demonstrate how greatly I would miss my husband and how much I feared for him to leave. Standing beside him in the chariot, I clung to the front of his robes, while he held me with his fingers tangled in my loose-hanging hair and pressed his forehead to mine. We kissed and I allowed a few tears to fall as we held each other for what we both knew could be the last time. Each time he went to battle, our parting became more difficult and painful.

"By the gods, I shall miss you," he whispered. Then he kissed me ardently.

"Come back to me," I answered, meeting his gaze, and holding his beard. Then, lowering my voice, I said into his ear, "And keep watch, lest your enemies take you unaware."

As I pulled back my head, I turned my eyes to indicate Hadi, who sat on the back of his horse, brooding, and averting his gaze. My cousin was in a sour mood and could hardly bring himself to look at us. I was pleased to have successfully put him in his place by our little show the night before, but now, sober, I wondered if we had made a mistake by further inciting his jealousy. Akhab nodded in understanding and pressed his lips to mine. We had already discussed that, should something happen to him, his messengers would come and alert me. If this came to pass, my sons and I would flee with our protectors to the fortress of Yezreel before Hadi and the other kings returned at the heads of their armies.

I stepped down from his chariot with the help of Kora and another of my ladies. Then I headed toward the other queens and their children who had also come to see their men off, while the driver of Akhab's chariot climbed up to stand beside him.

Meanwhile, the King of Hamat remarked, "Oh, to have a woman like that…it is a lucky man, indeed."

"There is no luck in it," Akhab declared, while his attendant handed him his helmet. Directing his gaze to me, Akhab continued, "She is a blessing from the Ba'alim."

"You must truly be in their favor, Akhab," said Hadi, patting his horse. There was a hint of bitterness in his otherwise wistful tone.

Placing his helmet over his head, my husband replied, "I am grateful for the gifts they have bestowed upon me. Do not think I take anything for granted, least of all the best of my wives."

Pretending not to hear their talk, which annoyed rather than flattered me, I stood behind Yoram with my hands over his chest. He leaned back against me and watched the men with excitement. Beside us, my eldest son stood sullenly watching the father he idolized but could not join in battle. Seeing his expression, I said to him quietly, "Your time will come soon enough, my son. Do not be in such a hurry to leave your youth behind."

Without turning to look at me, Zyah answered, "I am not, Ama."

Yoram, meanwhile, leaned his head back to look up at me. I smiled and moved my hands to his shoulders, bending to kiss his forehead and tickling him. He quickly pulled away and wiped his forehead, saying, "Ama!"

I chuckled and touched the tip of his nose with my forefinger, then I held him in place while I said to Zyah, "I know you are eager to join your father in battle. Just because you are good at hiding it now does not mean I cannot see it. I am your mother – I know you well and I see everything."

The horns sounded and the noise of horses and chariots rose as the men began to move. Akhab took the lead with Hadi, Irhulani, and Basa. We paused to see them off, holding up our fingers in Ba'al's blessing. When the last of them had gone and Akhab was no longer in our sight, Yoram turned to me. "Ama, what if he does not return to us?"

367

I covered his mouth with my hand and shushed him gently. "Do not say such things. Of course, he will. You must never give voice to your fears when men have gone to battle."

"Why?"

"It will draw malicious spirits into their midst. Instead, we must pray for them. Pray for the favor of the Ba'alim and to draw the benevolent spirits of the land near to aid and protect them from those that would do them harm."

He nodded in understanding, and then we went into the palace to begin our prayers.

While the men went to war and we stayed behind at Damaseq, Zyah was supposed to be getting to know his future wives. They were all sweet girls and would certainly grow to be beauties, but they were still too young to wed. Hadi's daughter was twelve but looked and acted younger, while Irhulani's daughters were eight and eleven, so he had no interest in any of them. Instead, Zyah seemed to be infatuated with the courtesan Naveen, a girl who appeared to be only slightly older than him but certainly experienced in the art of love.

Although not raised to the level of an official concubine, the king's courtesans were still off-limits to the other men at court while they had his patronage. Nevertheless, Naveen discreetly encouraged Zyah's interest. I noticed, and pulled him aside to rebuke him, even suggesting he take an interest in one of the dancers or serving girls that loitered around waiting for the attentions of the men at court. The courtesans had once been among their ranks; these girls were hoping to secure the same position so they could rise above their current station. Those that pleased the king could hope to secure patronage of another nobleman or decent marriages once the king had tired of them; some courtesans had even risen high enough to become the concubines or wives of lesser nobles, although it was rare and generally looked down upon.

"There are plenty of them," I whispered to my son, "and they are all available to any man with an interest, so if you insist on becoming a man tonight, take one of them."

"Ama! You are a queen – you should not speak of these things." Nevertheless, it was his cheeks that were red with shame and embarrassment.

I huffed in amusement. "I know a great deal more about these things than you, Zyah. How do you think you were conceived? You should take my advice on these matters."

"Abbu would..." he began.

"Your father would counsel you the same," I cut him off. "You cannot involve yourself with another man's woman. Hadadesar lays claim to her – you will only make an enemy of him if you take what is his, and he is already barely an ally."

Zyah sighed heavily. "Fine. Have your way." Then he stormed off.

His chief guardian, who had witnessed the exchange, met my gaze and I indicated with my eyes for him to follow Zyah. The eunuch hurried after my wayward son, and I hoped he would be diligent in preventing any trouble from arising. I noticed the courtesan watching my son disappear, and soon she whispered something to one of the others and followed in the same direction.

Tensing my jaw, I immediately went after her and managed to intercept her in the corridor. She did not at first realize who I was, so when I came up beside her and slipped my hand around her upper arm to stop her, she began to pull away and whirled toward me with fury in her gaze. Her lips parted as if she was about to condemn whoever had laid a hand upon her. When she saw who it was, however, she went pale, and her eyes grew wide. Then she quickly bowed. "Forgive me, Ba'alah."

"Where are you off to?" I asked with a sweet smile.

"Ah...the women's quarters, Ba'alah."

"If I am not mistaken, the women's quarters are *that* way, are they not? Unless it has changed since the last time I visited my cousin here."

"Oh! Yes, I...see you are right. I must have been confused."

"Too much wine, perhaps?"

"Oh, yes! I forget that the feast wine is not diluted as much."

I hummed in agreement. Then I lowered my voice, glanced around to be sure there was no one in earshot, and said, "Do not take an interest in my son. He is young and foolish, and I will not allow

369

him to compromise his reputation by carrying on with a woman who belongs to the King of Aram."

She inhaled sharply, and her eyes grew worried.

"If you are caught with him, you will fall by your own doing. My son will not fall with you. Bear that in mind."

She bowed to me in obedience, and then I indicated for her to return the other way. She did so but did not stay long at the feast before going toward the women's quarters with some of the others. I hated courtesans and was glad that at least my husband did not keep any for himself, although there were plenty at our court who had patrons of the other men. Not bound by the same laws that kept wives and concubines sheltered from temptation, courtesans moved freely about and posed a threat to the relations between the men at court, often positioning themselves between them and then watching the men fight for the right of patron. They seemed to forget, however, that in the end the greatest danger was only to themselves.

Thankfully, we were not at Damaseq for a long time before my husband and the other kings returned, battle-worn, and with only a partial victory. All the armies involved had sustained heavy casualties but had managed to push Shalmeneser's army back toward Assyria to recover from their own losses. Before fleeing, Shalmeneser had managed to capture some of their horses and chariots, but he would later claim a great victory on his part. In the end, only the King of Hamat truly got anything out of the campaign, but Qarqar had been sacked and would take much to rebuild. Akhab promised, as part of their alliance, to provide aid in this endeavor and Irhulani was grateful.

During the battle, Akhab sustained a minor injury, but as he laid down to rest in our guest quarters at Damaseq on the night of his return, he laughed it off. I did not find it amusing, because he had sustained the injury while fighting alongside his men in disguise, which he was wont to do from time to time.

I stood before the bed where he lay with my hands on my hips, while the healers moved about with their ointments and bandages to tend to his injury. There was a long cut on his abdomen just below his ribs on the left side, caused by a sword that pierced his armor. It had been tended to on the battlefield but needed to be cleaned and

370

dressed anew. When he admitted he had been disguised as a foot soldier in battle, I was angry and had tears in my eyes while I rebuked him. "You could have been killed!"

"But I was not," he said with a charming smile.

"You are not a young man anymore!"

"So, you keep telling me, wife," he said, while the healers tended to the wound. They poured wine upon the injury to cleanse it. He groaned when the alcohol touched the open flesh. Thankfully, it had not gone deep enough to cause a serious injury, but it was an awful sight and I had to look away until they had covered it again.

When the healers left us alone together, I came to sit with him. Bidding him to turn his back to me, I massaged his aching shoulders. Afterward, he leaned back against me as I leaned against the cushions and the headboard. Gazing down at him while I brushed my fingers through his peppered curls, I said, "Akhab, please stop putting yourself at risk in these campaigns. I fear the next time you do it will be your last." He sighed heavily, and I continued to implore him, "Please, my love. I know you enjoy the thrill of it, but you must take caution."

"I know, I know."

He leaned his head to the side, resting against my arm, as he turned to look up at me. I brought my hand to his chin, hooking his beard between my thumb and forefinger and holding him still as I brought my lips down to meet his. When I sat back again, I stroked his face as we held each other's gaze.

At last, he admitted, "I know I am getting old."

"You have forty-one years on you," I reminded him, my forehead tight with worry.

He nodded. "I suppose it is my way of proving to myself that I am still a capable warrior. I do not yearn for the days when I must sit upon a hill to watch my men fight for me, never taking part in the battle myself."

"You are a king," I said with a gentle tug on his beard. "It is your duty to sit back and watch. Let your generals fight for you, that you may come home to me."

He sighed again and turned so that his head was resting upon my belly. I laid my head back against the cushions, closed my eyes, slid my fingers through his hair, and massaged his scalp. We sat like this for a long time, until it became uncomfortable. My legs were

371

tingling when I moved to lie beside him, careful not to press or rub against his bandaged waist. I began kissing his chest and abdomen, avoiding the bandages that were wrapped around his waist, and made my way down further. Looking up at him, I paused to ask, "May I?"

His parts suggested the answer was yes, but I wanted to be sure. He gave a nod and settled in to watch as I began. When he was satisfied, I dabbed at my mouth with the sleeve of my robe before I peeled it off and came to lie at his side. He slipped his fingers through my hair, and whispered, "Thank you, Yezeba'al. I needed that."

"I know," I answered, looking up at him with my head still on his shoulder. I smiled. "That's why I did it."

"What about you?" he asked.

"I am all right, husband. You need to recover before you can even think about doing anything like that."

"I have a hand, you know."

I chuckled. "I am unclean."

"Ah, I see," he said with a nod. "I did not realize it was that time already."

"Why would you?" I asked with amusement. "Men do not pay attention to these things."

"No, but you are my wife, and I should know anyway."

"Should you know about all your other wives, as well?" He had acquired many over the years, most of whom he never even bothered to consummate with. "And your concubines?"

He laughed, but that was followed by a grimace and his hand went to his abdomen, hovering over the injury without touching that place. Then he said, "All right, I suppose you have a point."

I raised myself up to kiss him once more before we settled into sleep. It would be a few days before he was well enough to travel. Still hardly able to meet my gaze since the night he saw me on the terrace with my husband, Hadi told us we could stay for as long as we liked. I thanked him, although I was eager to return to Yisrael, especially with that courtesan still making eyes at my eldest son. I was on the terrace, looking down into the garden one day, when I spied him talking to her in the shade of a fig tree. I tensed my jaw and turned to go back into the chamber when Akhab appeared. He still could not stand to his full height because his side ached from the injury, but he

372

could walk without aid. He came to stand by me, and I pointed out our son and his paramour.

"That woman is shameless. They have been like this the whole time you were away. I thought she would stop the moment Hadi returned, but I suppose while he is holding court, she thinks he will not notice."

"I think he has grown tired of her, anyway," suggested Akhab. He watched them for a moment, and then asked, "Have they...?"

"I do not know for certain, but I think so, yes. I tried to intervene."

"But our son is as stubborn as his mother."

"And his father."

"Yes, that is true," he answered with a faint smile. Then we watched the two lovers together in silence. When I saw my son reach out to stroke the courtesan's cheek, fury burned within me. Then I saw him take her by the hand and start to lead her away. I gasped and might have gone to stop them, but Akhab placed his hand upon mine. "Let it be, Yezeba'al. He will only resent you if you try to intervene. What's done is done. All we can do is pray Hadi does not find out, or if he does that he will not care so much. He has brought several new concubines from our campaign with which to amuse himself, after all."

"He is only a boy."

"He is a man," came his reply. I was about to object, but he raised a firm voice, "Yezeba'al. Let it be. It is too late. I knew when I saw him the other day, something had changed in him."

"He is my son." I was suddenly trembling.

"You cannot keep him a boy forever."

"I know that, Akhab," I answered, as a tear broke free. He cradled my face in his hand and wiped the tear with his thumb. Then I pulled back and wiped my eyes for myself, grumbling, "She has bewitched him."

My husband continued looking at me with a knowing smile. "Is that not what they once said of you? Some of them still do, I believe."

"This is different."

"Not so much," he replied. "Is it sorcery for a young man to become infatuated with a beautiful woman? Or for a woman to become infatuated with a good-looking man?"

373

"Infatuation is not love," I said firmly.

"You are right. And as such, he will tire of her eventually."

"You do not know that."

"I do – I was once that young man. My first concubine was a woman much older than me, and she taught me so much that has allowed me to be a good lover to you. Let our son learn, so that he too will be good to his wives."

"I do not understand men," I said finally. "I thought I did, but these things... It is different when it is my own son, and he puts himself at risk in such a way."

"Let me speak to Hadi."

"No! Akhab, are you out of your mind? He cannot know if he does not know already!"

"What can he do? Our son is not some servant boy; he is a prince. I will see about procuring this girl, taking her back to Yisrael with us."

"Hadi will never allow it."

"He will – I will compensate him for his loss."

"I do not want her with us. I do not trust her."

"You do not have to trust her, wife. Trust me."

I thought about it with a sigh and then finally relented. To my surprise, Akhab was indeed able to work out an arrangement with my cousin, allowing our son to take his courtesan to Shomron. Hadi, meanwhile, could choose from any of the women of equal rank within our entourage who were willing to stay and become a courtesan. He made a joke about taking me instead, but neither Akhab nor I laughed, so he fell silent and got about choosing the prettiest among those we offered to him. Those he chose from were all hopeful that she would be the one, having been seduced by the idea of becoming the mistress of a king. Hadi was an attractive man, at least; not as handsome as Akhab, but enough to make him quite appealing to them. In fact, when he chose a girl, the others did not hide their disappointment at losing the opportunity to rise above their station in life.

Zyah's newly acquired mistress was pleased with the exchange. As we made our way south, every time we stopped to rest the animals along the way the two of them were entangled, flirting and spooning, their hands constantly all over each other. Resting in my litter, I grimaced and turned away, while Akhab chuckled and pressed my hand to his lips. "You remind me of so many mothers, Yezeba'al."

"Was your own mother this way?"

"No, actually. She encouraged me and my brothers to take as many women as we desired. I believe she was not happy in her marriage to my father, so she wanted us to be good husbands."

"Your sister told me that your mother did not like to compete for your affections – that she was in competition with all those who were prettier than she."

"That is true, but not when it came to courtesans. She knew they could never take her place in my affections, never rise so high in rank, and that the infatuation would fade soon enough. It was a good education. Therefore, let Zyah learn all he can before it is time for him to take a wife. At least she is close to him in age."

"They are both lucky Hadi did not have her killed and swear to make our son his enemy. I still do not know how you managed to convince him to make the exchange."

"I can see when a man is beginning to lose interest in a woman. He was in the rut, looking for something new and exciting to take to his bed."

"Men like Hadi are disgusting," I said, turning away to watch the horses and oxen drink from the nearby stream. "No loyalty and no honor. I wish you had killed him when you had the chance."

Fearing my foul mood would lead me to pick a fight with my husband, I climbed down from my litter, which rested upon wooden blocks when not being carried, and walked toward the horses. I went up to the one I was fond of and often rode when I was out in the field with my husband. She was a gentle beast, and when she saw me approaching, she came to meet me, blowing air from her nostrils and nodding in the hope that I had brought her a treat.

I reached up to touch her smooth, velvet nose. "I am sorry, Rimah. I do not have anything for you today. But I promise to bring you some figs when we are back in Yezreel."

She nodded in appreciation. Then I took her face in my hands and brought my forehead to hers. I chuckled when she raised her head and nuzzled me but, when I heard twigs crunching underfoot, turned to see Naveen approaching. Zyah was speaking with Akhab. No wonder she was not with my son, but why was she coming to me? I wanted to be angry – what right did she have to approach the Queen

375

of Yisrael? – but her penitential gaze and uncertainty softened me somewhat.

She stopped and bowed low, staying like that as she waited for me to address her. I did not know what to say. When I saw my husband and Zyah watching to see what I would do, I wanted to be angry with them for putting me in this position. At least my son could have brought her to me himself. If he wanted me to bond with her...

Rimah snorted and pushed her nose against my shoulder. When I looked at her, she nodded toward Naveen and stomped her foot three times. I sighed heavily and raised my eyes toward the heavens. I was being guilt-tripped by a horse!

I sighed and decided to at least make an effort to be kind to her. "Naveen: is that what you are called?"

She looked at me fearfully and nodded in response. Her cheeks reddened a bit and I looked away, still mildly annoyed while telling myself to give her a chance.

"Do you like horses, Naveen?"

She looked up in surprise and then turned an uncertain gaze toward Rimah. "I...do not know, Ba'alah. I have never been this close to one before."

"Truly?"

She nodded.

"Well, come. Do not be afraid. If you are going to be with us, you will need to know horses. The king and my sons are all obsessed with them. I am fond of a few myself. They are good animals."

She stepped forward, cautiously. I stroked Rimah's nose to show her it was safe. She followed my example, and when Rimah lifted her nose to meet Naveen's hand, the girl broke into a broad smile and sighed in relief.

"This is Rimah," I told her. "Hold out your hands, as if you are offering something."

She did so and, when Rimah licked her open palms and nuzzled them in search of a treat, Naveen squealed and giggled. Much to my surprise, she did not pull away. "It tickles."

Despite myself, I even chuckled a bit. "When we get back to Yezreel, you will find that the horses' favorite treats are figs. You can never feed them too many, and you will give it to them just like that. They will love you all the more for it."

She met my gaze and smiled, for a moment forgetting that I was a queen and looking at me as she might look at any other woman. Then she seemed to realize herself and looked away, perhaps fearful of reproach. I decided to let it pass. It would do no good to have her completely afraid of me – a bit of fear was important, but I preferred the women at court to trust me even when I did not trust them.

"Are you literate?"

"Literate?" She repeated it slowly, as if she had never heard the word before. I knew the answer then but did not want to embarrass her.

"Can you read and write? In any language?"

She shook her head.

"Would you like to learn? There is a...school of sorts in the women's quarters. I used to teach the women myself, but now I have appointed some of the other women, as there are so many."

"How many?"

"Two hundred, at least. Akhab has many wives and concubines, and his daughters and granddaughters who are not yet married still live there. Many of them also learn how to read and write if they have an interest. No one is forced to learn if they do not care for it."

"I would like to learn."

"Good. I prefer the women at court to be educated. You shall begin your lessons once you are settled. I think I shall have Tamar oversee your education. She is one of the most senior wives and easy to get along with, even if she is a horrible gossip. She is good-natured, though, and patient."

"Thank you, Ba'alah," she said with a bow. When she straightened, she seemed hesitant. "Ba'alah, if I may...?"

"Ask."

She gave it some thought, perhaps trying to discern how to word her question. "Zyah said you and the king are in love, that of all his wives you are the one who is most dear to him."

I winced at first, hearing her speak my son's informal name. It was used only by those close to him – typically his family and no one else. But I closed my eyes and let it go with a sigh and nodded before I managed to speak. "The king and I are well matched. The Ba'alim have blessed us." I looked toward the heavens and touched my fingers to my lips in thanks.

377

Naveen smiled sweetly. "I think that is really beautiful. I have never heard of such a thing, except in tales and legends. Like Ashtarti and Hadad."

I knew she must have been familiar with our gods for they were also worshipped in Aram, by different names, but could not help wondering if my son had coached her to make this comparison in the hope it would endear her to me. Nevertheless, I appreciated the sentiment. "Yes, we have long been compared to them."

"Zyah says you are the goddess incarnate. That you are the living embodiment of the Queen of Heaven herself, and that the king is that of her consort, which is why you are so in love. Astharti and Hadad united once again in the flesh." If she had been coached, she certainly seemed convincing, for her excitement at the possibility was sincere and apparent.

"My husband's people know her as Asherah. As for Hadad, they simply know him by his title, Ba'al."

She gave a nod, understanding. "Thank you, Ba'alah."

I examined her in silence for a moment, while she cast her gaze toward the ground and her cheeks reddened once again. Then I said, "As for being a living goddess, do not make too much of it. I am still only a woman. I must pray to the gods, as would anyone else."

With that, I left her and returned to my husband. I did not bother to turn back, but I could see my son gazing at Naveen with a smile. He started toward her but, as we passed each other, paused to say, "Thank you, Ama. You do not know what this means to me."

I placed a hand upon my son's shoulder and gave a single nod, and then we parted ways and I returned to my litter. Once I was settled, Akhab bent over to kiss my lips, and then gazed at me with a smile. "You are a good woman, Yezeba'al. No matter what anyone says, you are a great woman."

"I could have annihilated her for approaching me like that."

"Yet you did not." He brought my hand to his lips. He seemed proud of me, but that only further annoyed me. Before I could say anything, he asked, "Well, and what did you think of her? Is she worthy of our son?"

"Only time will tell. At any rate, she can only ever be his concubine, at best. He cannot make her his wife."

Akhab chuckled, and then he went to mount his chariot so we could continue our journey back to Yezreel.

378

Naveen was introduced into the women's quarters as Zyah's concubine; her former status as a courtesan at the court of the King of Aram in Damaseq was not mentioned. I put her under the care of Tamar, who eagerly took the girl under her wing, and I rarely saw her except when I went to the women's quarters or rested in the women's garden. I was often so busy, my time split between my children, my husband, my duties as High Priestess, and my duties as Queen, that I spent little time with the other women these days. When I was not busy, I was usually resting in my quarters or enjoying the peace and solitude of one of the other gardens in the palace complex. Nevertheless, Tamar kept me updated in all things. I could always count on her to pay attention and, when Maryam had passed away some years ago, I had appointed Tamar in her place.

When I summoned Tamar to my quarters to ask how Naveen was fitting in, she told me the girl was doing well and seemed to take to her lessons eagerly. "She is a sweet girl, not like some of the others, Melkah, but..." She looked around and, seeing Kora and my handmaids at work, lowered her voice. "I wonder at some of her customs and habits. Her table manners, in particular, are strange."

"What do you mean, Tamar? What does she do?"

"Well, first she must be reminded to remove her sandals and wash her hands before she eats. I have never seen this before, so it is difficult even to remember to remind her to do it! And she reaches across the table to take things instead of asking for them to be handed to her. Once, I saw her take something off one of the other women's plates without even asking! It is as though she has never dined in a proper setting or learned how to eat with others. And that is not all, Melkah. You should see the way she eats olives! She puts a whole olive into her mouth, eats the fruit, and *spits out the seed* – just lets it drop onto her plate with a clang, one right after the other!"

My lips parted in surprise, but I said nothing. Tamar could carry on a monologue for hours without interruption, and continued, "And her speech! Well, sometimes it is as if she does not know how to speak within the company of other women, I will just say it that way. Where did you say the prince found her?"

379

"At the court in Damaseq," I said vaguely. "Her father worked for the King of Aram."

He had been a member of the kitchen staff, as I discovered while making inquiries during my son's courtship, but I preferred not to mention her low bearing. I was grateful when Tamar did not persist further in her line of questioning. She simply nodded, and said, "Well, things must be done very differently in Aram than they are here."

"It is true," I said with a nod. "Thank you for guiding her toward right behavior and speech. I am relieved she has not given you any trouble, beyond that."

"She has not, Melkah. Only, she complains about not being allowed out of the women's quarters – strange, is it not? One would think that custom was no different in Aram than it is here."

I forced a smile. "It is the same there for married women. Unmarried women, however, move about rather freely in the care of their guardians, much as it was for me in Tzidon."

"Ah, yes," she said with a nod. "That explains it. She does not like having to wait for the prince to summon her and dislikes being escorted to his quarters by the eunuchs. At least, he summons her a great deal."

"Does he?" I asked, cringing a little. "That explains why I see him so infrequently. When we are not holding court, he is never around. The king said he is not even spending much time in the field practicing with weapons and his chariot, which is unusual for the prince."

"You know how it is with young men, Melkah. Once they have discovered women..."

"Yes, of course." I cleared my throat and then I was quiet for a moment. "You know, I will suggest to him that he take Naveen out of the palace from time to time, so she does not grow restless. Perhaps she would like to see the stables. Remind her that, if she is with the prince, she may travel freely about."

Tamar gave a nod and curtsied. "It will be done as you wish, Melkah."

My advice was taken. The next time I went to the stables, Zyah was there with Naveen. Akhab had been at the stables all morning and had sent a message asking me to ride with him, but I did not see him when I arrived. I knew he was around somewhere, so I stopped and waited, watching Naveen feed the horses, just as I had shown her. Now there were three of them gathered to partake in the offerings. She was timid, but Zyah stood over her protectively while encouraging her not to be afraid. She giggled as the horses lifted their lips and ate from her hands. They snorted for more figs when the handfuls she offered had run out.

Suddenly, Akhab came up behind me and slipped his hands around my waist, taking me somewhat by surprise. Relieved that it was him, I placed my hands over his, and rested against his strong body as we watched the young couple together. He kissed the top of my head, and remarked, "She reminds me a little of you, when you first came here."

I turned my head to look at him. "I was not afraid of horses."

"No, but you were shy and sweet and sometimes tremulous."

"I was not tremulous!" I protested.

He took my chin and tilted back my head for a kiss. Then he nuzzled my nose, kissed me once more, and said, "You were tremulous."

"I thought I was courageous."

"You were that, too. It is possible to be both, you know – that is one of the things that I love most about you, my wife. You are everything a woman is capable of being, all at once."

He brought his lips to mine again and our souls were united once more. Afterward, I paused to meet his gaze and thought how much I loved him and how grateful I was for all these years together. Even then, I often wondered how we could have been so blessed.

When we were able to pull ourselves free from our shared gaze, despite the pain that always came with detaching our souls, we turned back to look at the young lovers. Zyah was petting one of the horses and talking to it, but I saw that Naveen had been watching us. She quickly averted her gaze when our eyes met. Then as the king and I approached, Zyah turned to greet us, but Naveen kept her head down.

First, my son embraced me. Then he and Akhab took each other by the arm and patted each other on the back. Afterward, my husband said, "The Queen and I are going out for a ride. Will you join us?"

At first, I was somewhat perturbed by his offer, because I had been looking forward to being alone with my husband. When we rode together, it almost always ended with us making love in a secluded grotto, or hidden within the weeds, while the horses rested nearby.

Thankfully, our son was not eager to intrude on our time together. He met my gaze briefly, as if to acknowledge our shared reluctance, and then said, "Naveen does not know how to ride, Abbu."

"Well, then it is time she learns how. My Queen, will you assist Naveen in this endeavor?" My lips parted in surprise, but before I could respond, he had turned to Naveen to say, "The Queen is a skilled equestrian, although she does not like to boast. She taught our daughters to ride."

"Daughters?" I asked. "You mean Atalaya – Azba'alah is barely old enough to sit on the back of a pony."

"She is learning," he said. "The point is that you are a good teacher, my love." He turned back to the others with a grin. "Sometimes the Queen takes everything I say too seriously. I have told her many times she has the mind of a man."

"And I have told you I have the mind of a woman. A woman can have a strong mind of her own, Akhab."

He slipped his arm around my waist, pulled me to him, and growled playfully, "I know, wife." Then he kissed me, and I regretted that we were not yet alone together. I could see by the hunger in his gaze that he felt the same way, perhaps for the first time regretting having extended an invitation to the others.

Zyah looked to Naveen, and said, "See, this is what they're like. Constantly."

She smiled faintly and pressed her lips together, further lowering her head as if to hide a laugh. Glancing up at him, she murmured, "Then that is where you get it from?"

Zyah's lips parted as if he might protest, but no sound came out. Then he chuckled, and admitted, "All right, perhaps I am...somewhat like them. They are my parents after all." Then he cleared his throat uncomfortably, and said, "Anyway, we were just finishing up out here. I was going to take her back to the palace."

Naveen kept her face lowered but I saw her chest heave with a sigh, and decided to step in. "Is that what Naveen wants, Zyah? Or is it only what you want?"

"It is what we both want," he insisted, but I was not convinced.

382

I slipped my arm around the girl and pulled her away from him. "You have been cooped up inside the palace far too long, Naveen. If you want to stay out, you can stay with me, and I will teach you to ride."

Akhab did not look thrilled, but since he had invited them in the first place, he would have to suffer the consequences as much as I. Besides, I did not want to see Naveen forced to do whatever my son wanted all the time. She had looked excited when Akhab first proposed the idea, until Zyah had shot it down so quickly. While I still did not trust her completely, she had gone from having some semblance of freedom to none in only a matter of days. As far as I knew, this was the first time she had been taken out of the palace since she arrived several weeks earlier. After my period of imprisonment in my quarters following the Nabot incident, I could understand what that was like, and I did not want her to suffer unnecessarily.

She met my gaze briefly, and in hers I saw gratitude. But then she looked to my son, and I knew she would ultimately choose what would please him. "Thank you, Ba'alah. I would like to learn how to ride sometime, but for now I would like to return to the palace with Zyah."

Again, hearing her call him by that name stung me a little, but I let it pass. Then, as I watched her go with him, I felt sorry for her. It was clear to me that she would do anything for Zyah – that was the way courtesans were trained, for it was the only way for them to keep their positions – but he took little notice of her interests.

Akhab came to stand beside me, watching them walk toward the palace together. "What are you thinking, my love?"

"I am thinking that our son does not truly love that girl, but I am starting to believe she loves him. And it breaks my heart." I turned to my husband, searched his gaze, and said, "I am so grateful to be loved by you."

"Oh, Yezeba'al," he whispered, pulling me into an embrace when I started to weep.

"I know I have been jealous, and sometimes petty, because of your other wives…but I know I am blessed because I have your heart, body, and soul, while they only have your body. I never want to be used like that."

He took my face in his hands. Wiping my tears with his thumbs, he then drew me into a kiss. Soon we were overcome by our passions and, unable to wait any longer to be united in the flesh, I coaxed him into the stables. After following me inside, he took my hand and led me into one of the empty stalls where straw was stored for the horses' bedding. While the stable boys who had been working inside were hurried out by their master, an older man who had seen us do this before and knew better than to stay, Akhab pressed me back against the cool stone wall and kissed me hungrily as we untied each other's sashes and stripped off our robes. We dropped them onto a heap of straw, and there he laid me gently. We made love until we both reached satisfaction.

Overwhelmed by our love, I wanted my children to have the same but feared they never would. I knew that what we had together was rare and beautiful, and I thanked the gods every day for blessing us with each other.

16

Throughout the Night

Sleepless nights had been plaguing me for years, since around the time of Hadadesar's first assault on our kingdom. At first, they had been an occasional nuisance, but by the time we returned from our state visit to Aram, they were commonplace. Insomnia had become my companion; the exhaustion that haunted my waking hours was more welcome than the dreams that haunted my sleep. Akhab slept loudly beside me; sometimes I resented him for sleeping while I lay there for hours, restless and wide awake. Finally, to combat the bitterness and avoid smothering my snoring husband, I began to rise each night when the sleeplessness could not be conquered. Wrapping myself in robes against the cold, I slid my feet into sandals and went to my study. Lighting a lamp or two, enough that I could see without being assaulted by the stinging glare, I sat pouring through scrolls and examining cuneiform tablets, keeping my mind busy so I would not dwell on those dreams.

As I studied, I meticulously took notes and recorded my thoughts and interpretations of the texts. Having been raised in an environment of structured learning, I had done this since childhood. I kept all the papyri scraps and scrolls in chests, occasionally pulling them out to examine them anew. Anything I had since changed my perspective on by further study was discarded to make room for new and more cohesive writings – the old ones burned in a brasier, their embers floating out the window and disappearing into the night. This purging of old material, alongside the creation of new, became almost a nightly ritual, the purpose of which I could not quite envision.

Then as the morning light began to peer over the hills, I extinguished the lamps and the brazier and returned to my bed. My husband was still sleeping peacefully when I returned, and I stood at the side of the bed, gazing at him and wondering how I could ever have wanted to smother him. He was beautiful when he slept like this, and I was glad he was able to sleep, for he needed his rest. The day would start soon enough, the duties of managing his kingdom would take over, and we would be lost in the flurry of activity that only ceased at the end of each day. For now, there was this sliver of time left for us to rest.

Peeling off my robes, I slipped under the covers beside my husband, warming myself against his body just as he began to stir. He turned, smiled sleepily, and pulled me closer, his strong arms a comfort to my weary bones. Sometimes on these mornings, my return to the bed sparked a passion in him. He rubbed the tip of his nose against the side of my neck as he took in my scent. Our fingers laced together and then came apart as we traced each other's flesh and awakened our bodies.

This morning, however, it was not so. After pulling me into his arms, there was no spooning, no aching that could only be cured by a blissful union of the flesh. When he began snoring again, I turned over and sighed heavily. My arm draped over my forehead, I stared at the ceiling and watched the lighting change gradually with the rising sun. As the cool night air began to dissipate, I let one leg dangle off the side of the bed and threw off the blankets, one layer at a time, until only the thinnest covered my naked form. Then with the blowing of horns, the palace came alive once again.

Soon Kora and my other handmaidens arrived to dress me for the day. Akhab slipped on his robes, kissed me, and departed. Even when he spent the night in my bed, he always dressed in his quarters, as it was time for the day's work to begin. We ate as we dressed, listening to the reports from our stewards on what needed our focus that day. If court was in session, we went immediately from dressing to the Great Hall, meeting each other just outside, husband and wife – now dressed as king and queen – always entering together as a united front against whatever we faced that day.

This was not one of those days, so instead we spent much of it apart: while he managed the kingdom's affairs from his study and met with his counsel or members of the public who requested a private audience, I tended to the domestic sphere. This always involved meeting with household stewards, going over the budget to ensure the kitchens were well-stocked with enough to pay for any repairs that needed to be made within the palace grounds; meeting with the chief cook to select the menu for the day – imperative whenever we held a feast or entertained important guests, which was almost every night that we were at our palace in Shomron; and finally going to the women's quarters.

On this day, Abbigail, a Princess of Ashkelon who married Akhab the same year the twins were born, was the cause of yet another quarrel, this time with another wife with whom she had a long-standing rivalry. Nanaya had been a Princess of Moab before she came to us, a year or two after Abbigail's arrival, and they had been at war from the start. They started out sharing space in one of the many large chambers where the women slept communally – around a dozen per chamber – but had been moved to separate chambers when their squabbles began to interfere with those around them. It helped, but they still crossed paths from time to time, either in the bath, sitting areas, gardens, nursery, or dining hall. Each time they saw one another, it sparked another war that would carry on and continue to escalate until it became so bad that I had to be called in.

Now, whatever had started the latest argument culminated in Abbigail waiting until the darkest hours of the night to slip into Nanaya's chamber with shears from her sewing kit to chop off her rival's hair while she slept. The desecration was discovered when all awoke that morning. The battle erupted when Nanaya, surrounded by her supporters, went to confront Abbigail while the latter was eating in the dining hall.

I was still in the process of being dressed and listening to the steward's report, when one of Tamar's handmaids came to me in distress. She prostrated herself, apologizing profusely, and informed me of the incident which required immediate action. Sighing heavily, I bade my handmaids to bring my outer robe. They wrapped it around me and tied my sash in place, and then I hurried to the women's quarters to break up what had become a violent fight.

When I arrived in the dining hall, the two women were still locked in battle, screaming and tearing each other apart. Many of the other women had gathered around them to gawk or cheer. When they heard my arrival, announced by one of the women's stewards, they parted like the Red Sea and dropped to their hands and knees to bow before me.

"Abbigail, Nanaya; rise!" I commanded. They did so, and as I stepped around the other women, I fixed my gaze on the two who stood trembling at the center, hair and robes disheveled, lowered faces red and streaked with tears. They already knew what was coming.

I approached and circled them with a contemptuous gaze, briefly examining Nanaya's roughly shorn hair, and shook my head. Then I stopped and stood over Abbigail, waiting for her to look up and meet my gaze so I could have a good reason to beat her. My fingers itched for it, but after only a few incidents she had learned never to challenge me. She kept her head down and waited for me to speak.

Leaving her, I turned to Nanaya. "What happened here? You may speak."

Nanaya kept her gaze to the floor, but she spoke with anger in her voice. "Ba'alah, Abbigail came into my chamber and defiled me in the night. I woke up this morning to find the cushions covered in my hair – all of it cut off, and I am left like this!"

Not once did she look up to meet my gaze, but she glared with such hatred at her rival that she might have turned Abbigail into a pillar of salt, had she the power.

I looked at Abbigail, who stood with a smirk as she kept her gaze to the floor. She jumped when I called her name suddenly. "What have you to say to this?"

"I did not do this, Ba'alah. It must have been somebody else."

"Liar!" Nanaya shrieked. "I know it was you! Nobody else would have done this to me!"

"She attacked me, Ba'alah!"

"You deserved it! Look what you've done to me – I am uglier than a man!"

"You were already ugly! Consider it an improvement!"

I sighed heavily as the two of them began bickering again. Then I raised my hands to silence them, commanding in a firm voice, "Enough! You may not speak unless spoken to, and you will only answer what you have been asked and nothing more. You will address your grievances to me only. Speak not to each other, or you will *both* be beaten for your insolence!"

They fell silent and I looked around at the other women, still on their knees with their heads down. I was convinced of Abbigail's guilt – her smirk had betrayed her – but when settling disputes, whether at court or in the household, I always tried to be fair. "Who among you knows anything about this? If one of you saw who cut Nanaya's hair, or if you are the guilty one, speak now."

I waited. A few of them shifted. Some of them coughed. No one spoke.

"She who is guilty among you may have her punishment reduced if she confesses her guilt to me now."

Again, I waited. Again, no one confessed. They seldom do, even when it would be to their benefit, stubbornly holding out in the hope that their guilt would not be uncovered. I looked at Abbigail, took a few steps closer to stand over her and intimidate her. Thankfully, she was shorter than me, so it was more effective than it was when I stood over one of the taller women. Either way, I had learned to project my energy in such a way that they were all terrified of me, even without me laying a hand on them – it was enough that I could.

"Abbigail, I will ask you again." I spoke slowly. "Did you, or someone acting on your behalf, cut Nanaya's hair?"

"No, Ba'alah," she insisted.

"Do you swear by your innocence? And before you speak, think carefully on what you are going to say. You know the gravity of making false oaths in my household."

Her voice trembled, but she insisted, "I swear to it, Ba'alah. On Ba'al's seed, I am innocent."

"Tamar," I called. When she looked up, I wagged my finger at her.

She rose immediately and came to me. "Yes, Melkah?"

"Pick two women whom you trust to search all the women's belongings, starting with Abbigail's. Look for any trace of her guilt – look especially at the sewing shears. If any hair is found attached to the shears, bring them to me and take note of where they were found."

"It will be done as you command, Melkah." She turned to call out, "Sarah! Deborah! Do as the Queen commands."

The two of them jumped up, curtsied, and went off to carry out my orders. It did not take long for them to find what they were looking for – it was in the first place they looked, as I had suspected. They soon returned with shears that had a few strands of brown hair matching the shade of Nanaya's hair stuck between the blades.

"Where were these found?"

389

"Among the Lady Abbigail's belongings, Melkah," answered Deborah.

The evidence of her guilt was not enough to make Abbigail confess, for it was too late now. Even if she were to confess, she had already lied and even sworn a false oath to Ba'al, which I took more seriously than the original crime. She knew this and, in desperation, began to accuse Sarah and Deborah of lying and planting evidence. I knew the two of them had no quarrel with Abbigail or Nanaya, so they had no reason to lie.

Pausing to consider what punishment should be meted out, I sighed. It was tiresome dealing with the women's quarrels. Naturally, being shut up in close quarters together, rivalries and factions often arose between them. My implementation of the system of education did little to stop them from engaging in divisive behavior. Only those with an interest in learning and a natural inclination toward courtesy and modest behavior benefited; the others remained as spiteful and bellicose as their nature inspired them. Quarrels were frequent and often petty – accusations of stealing robes and jewels were one of the most common complaints. Most of the issues were solved by the elder women, those I had appointed as overseers, but they occasionally called for my intervention.

An incident many years before involved a group of women using ink to destroy the rich and expensive robes of one of the other wives, a deed perpetrated out of pure jealousy. It resulted in the ink in the women's quarters being locked in a cabinet. Only a few others and I held a key, and use of ink was heavily monitored there ever since. It certainly saved on expenses, but it was an inconvenience for one of those with a key to have to retrieve the ink and supervise anytime one of the women wanted to write a letter to their family. One of those involved in the ink incident was Abbigail. A frequent instigator of trouble, she had been a thorn in my side for many years. Today, I would reserve the greater penalty for her but, due to the severity of their fight, both women needed to be punished.

At last, I said, "Nanaya, when you discovered what had been done to you, instead of attacking Abbigail you should have come to me. Because you did not, you will be taken to the garden where you will receive ten strikes with the rod."

390

I nodded to Tamar. As my chief overseer in the women's quarters, the only woman given the authority to do so, Tamar had to carry out that task. She understood.

Nanaya began to weep but nodded. "Thank you, Ba'alah."

"Abbigail, because you violated Nanaya then lied to me and swore a false oath on Ba'al, you will receive the same number of strikes after which you will spend three days in solitude, contemplating your guilt."

Then I waved my hand to dismiss them, and Tamar took over, directing the women to the garden. I did not stay to observe. Instead, I went to sit with my husband in his study. Zyah was there, holding a clay tablet while Akhab was teaching him about the importance of thoroughly reading all official correspondence, and taking time to consider before responding to it. Although they acknowledged me, they continued their lesson when I entered. I went to stand beside my husband, placing a hand on his shoulder and observing his instruction of our son. Impressed by Zyah's questions and comments, and his eagerness to learn from his father, I smiled proudly. *He will be a good king one day.*

Abbigail would spend three days in a cell with only a single small window for light. As was the custom, she was made to fast, given only bread and water for those three days, at the end of which she was brought before me and given the chance to confess. No one ever failed to confess after that.

On the day she was brought to me following her three days of solitude, I sat on a chair in the garden beneath the shade of a terebinth, sipping wine and snacking on roasted pine nuts. Two of the lesser wives stood behind me with fans, while another stood beside me holding a tray, when Abbigail was brought to kneel before me. Regarding her coolly, I waited before finally addressing her. "Abbigail, do you have something to say to me?"

"Yes, Ba'alah," she answered meekly.

"Speak."

"I confess to you, O blessed Ba'alah, O merciful Ba'alah, Mother of All Life incarnate," she began, having dropped to her hands where she had begun to kiss the gold rings on my sandaled feet.

I cut her off. "Enough, Abbigail. To what do you confess?"

391

"Ba'alah, I am guilty of the crimes for which I have been punished. I cut Nanaya's hair, I lied to you, and...I took an oath to Ba'al that was false." She dropped to her hands once again, touching my feet and weeping as she kissed the rings on my toes. "And I beg of you, Ba'alah, to have mercy on me for all these things."

I watched her, considering. Then I took another sip of my wine, carefully placed it back on the tray, and said, "I believe in the sincerity of your repentance. You are forgiven. Now, go to the bath and be cleansed of your sins."

"Oh, thank you, Ba'alah!" she said, bowing and scraping until I rose. I pulled my mantle around my shoulders and stepped around her to leave. There is only so much penitential groveling one can take, and I was already tired from the afternoon heat.

From the garden, I went to my own private bath to cool off in the pool while Kora tended to me. I had only just stripped off my robes and stepped naked into the water when Akhab appeared, having been looking for me. Standing in the water, which was just deep enough to cover my breasts, I smiled at him invitingly. "Care to join me?"

"I had not intended to," he answered, although he watched me with a naughty smile. "But...the water does look tempting."

"Only the water?"

He began to strip off his robes and I nodded to Kora. She left us alone. Akhab moved through the water toward me as I backed away with a playful smile. I stopped only when my back touched the ledge on the other side, and waited while he caught up to me. He pulled me into an embrace. I wrapped my legs around him and tasted the salt upon his lips. Then I pulled myself free, turned away from him, and submersed myself completely. As I came up, I saw that he had done the same. It felt good to wash the sweat from our bodies.

He came to me again, but I held him at bay, one hand pressed flat against his chest. I grinned when he looked at me with yearning. "What brings you here, husband?"

"Hmm? Oh, right. I forgot why I came..."

I chuckled. "You better say now, before you forget again."

"I already have – in the face of your beauty, Ba'alah, nothing else matters."

"Surely, it must have been important for you to have come all the way here," I purred, stroking his parts.

"Whatever it was, it can wait," he said with trembling breath. Then he pulled me into his arms, and we came together in bliss.

Afterward, we climbed out of the bath, dried ourselves with the towels Kora had left, and dressed. Now, we were invigorated and refreshed. We climbed the stairs that led to my bedchamber, where I went behind the screen to change into fresh robes while he relieved himself in the chamber pot. Then he sprawled across the bed and waited for me to finish changing. Kora was helping me, and then she took my dirty robes to the laundry while I went to lay beside my husband.

"So, what brought you here? Or have you still forgotten?" I tugged at his beard.

"Oh, yes," he replied, sitting up and reaching for a cluster of grapes from the bowl on my nightstand. It had been placed there that morning, but I had eaten little of it. He popped one of the grapes into his mouth and spoke while still chewing. "I received a letter today from Hosha. He intends to come here to Yisrael for that visit we had planned."

"At last," I replied. It had been nearly three years, and we were starting to wonder if it would ever come to pass. When he offered a grape, I accepted, chewed it completely, and swallowed before saying, "I hope he will bring our daughter and grandson when he comes. Surely, little Akhazyah is old enough to travel by now."

"He will bring both of them," said Akhab, "but there is some news concerning our daughter."

"Good news, I hope?"

He shook his head. "She was with child again, but this time it did not go well."

"May the spirits of the unborn be taken unto you, O Ba'al," I prayed solemnly. I felt great sadness for my daughter then, for I knew her pain. But I also knew that she would soon be blessed with another, to ease the ache in her heart for the one she had lost. Nevertheless, a mother's heart never forgets.

Trying not to dwell on misery, I beckoned to him for another grape, and asked, "Will she be well enough to travel?"

"They believe she will," he answered, handing one to me. Then he placed what remained of the cluster back in the bowl and came to lay over me.

I swallowed the grape and giggled when he began pulling at my sash. "What are you doing? Were you not satisfied before, husband?"

"Entirely," came his reply. "But you were left unsatisfied, and I cannot allow that."

I smiled. "Are you done with your work for the day?"

"I am now," he said with a grin, peeling away my robe. I allowed myself to be swept away by him, for I needed his healing touch to soothe the ache in my heart.

After our second interlude, we dressed, and our children were brought to dine with us on the terrace just before twilight. Azba'alah was now four and Abshalom three, so they had to be watched closely on the terrace. Their nurses were ever vigilant.

Meanwhile, Ba'alesar was in his seventh year and eager to tell us about his day, for he had begun to practice with weapons. "Uncle Abram says I am a true warrior!"

"Uncle Abram says that of all his nephews," Zyah remarked, without humor. He had grown so glum, of late. I had hoped that expecting his first child might cheer him up, but he showed little interest in Naveen or her condition. Perhaps the visit from his twin and his nephew would raise his spirit.

Ba'alesar remained unaffected by his eldest brother's sour mood. "Well, with me he means it. I shot an arrow into the center of the target on my first shot. He said I will become the most skilled bowman in Yisrael if I keep practicing."

Yoram, now thirteen and considered a man, smiled at his brother's excitement. "I remember when I was that age."

I laughed. "That was not so long ago, young man."

"Six years is a very long time, Ama," he said solemnly.

Akhab and I exchanged glances. Then Akhab said, "No wonder I am starting to feel old."

"You *are* old, Abbu!" said Azba'alah, climbing onto his lap. Then she took his face in her hands and kissed him on the lips, afterward turning her head to look at me oddly when I began to laugh.

394

"She said it, not me," I said, looking at my husband with a smile.

He tossed a piece of bread at me, and it just missed. I lifted it off the table and put it in my mouth with a wink, while he said, "I may be an old man, but I am still young and strong enough to handle you, my wife."

I smiled knowingly. Then Zyah sighed heavily and excused himself. As he walked away, I called after him. He stopped and turned back to me. "Yes, Ama?"

"Speak to Naveen. She misses you."

He groaned and waved at me, mumbling inaudibly as he walked away. Frustrated by his neglect of her, I might have gone after him to finally confront him about it, but Abshalom climbed onto my lap and wanted to show me something that he had in his hand. "Look, Ama."

"What have you got for me, darling?"

When he opened his hand, a moth flew at me. I squealed in horror, grateful when it flew away from us. He had never heard me utter such a sound, and he laughed heartily. "Ama is scared of a moth!"

Shaking my head, I smoothed his curls, and said, "Not scared, Abshalom. Merely startled. Please do not do it again." Then I kissed the side of his head.

He threw his arms around me and squeezed with all his might. "I promise, Ama. I will not do it again."

After our supper with the children, Akhab and I spent another hour together on our own before he had to leave. He had an appointment with one of the other wives, for it was her fertile time. When I noticed him hesitate to leave, I said, "Go, Akhab. I shall miss you, but I know you will return to me tomorrow."

"You are the best of women: my rose among the lilies."

He pressed my hand to his lips and gently stroked my fingers, while I reminded him, "Lilies are beautiful, too."

"They are," he agreed. "But they will never be as beautiful as the rose – even if she does have thorns." He winked, pressed my hand to his lips once more, and then pulled away with one last glance from the doorway before he disappeared.

Left alone, I closed myself in my prayer chamber, burnt incense and knelt before the altar with my ritual dagger. In the

395

manner I was taught as a girl, I coated the sharpened blade with oil of myrrh and anointed my flesh with the same. Then I carefully dragged the blade across my forearm to draw just enough blood for an offering. Once I had expressed the blood into the small offering bowl, I dabbed the wound with oil of myrrh, wrapped it with fresh linen, and spent an hour in communion with my gods. Only then would my dreams not disturb me, and for once I could sleep through the night.

Yehoshapat, King of Yehudah, and his entourage arrived in Shomron at the end of spring, just before the Feast of Ashtarti which always highlighted our return from Megiddu. As I had hoped, Atalaya and her son were part of that entourage. When I met my daughter for the first time in three years, we embraced tightly, and then she went to her father who kissed her on the cheek. After greeting us and assuring us she was well, she brought her son forward to meet us. Little Akhazyah was nearly three years old and did not remember us at all, but that did not seem to bother him. He quickly warmed to us, and we soon found he was quite the charmer, just as his uncle and namesake had been before turning into a sullen adolescent. Glancing at Zyah, who knelt to greet his nephew, I had hope he would come out of it soon.

After getting our guests settled in their quarters and allowing them time to rest from their long journey, we held a great feast in the King of Yehudah's honor. Naturally, Hosha became inebriated at the feast, but at least he was in a jovial mood, and I could see that my husband enjoyed his company. The two kings laughed and drank together like brothers, and it was good to see Akhab in such good spirits.

Not long after we received the news that Hosha would be coming to visit, word had come to us at court on another matter. The daughter of Hadadesar, who had been promised to Zyah, was instead married to another king the moment she reached marriageable age. Akhab was deeply offended by the King of Aram's breach of their covenant. He immediately sent a messenger to Damaseq to communicate his displeasure, requesting that another daughter be sent in her stead, if she was deemed suitable upon inspection. Hadi responded with an insult: "As Prince Akhazyah has taken the pleasure of my best courtesan, he has no need of a princess to marry, for a courtesan is a more fitting wife for a son of Akhab."

Akhab reacted in rage, such that the messenger was terrified of him, although my husband had no intention of punishing him for what his master had said. Nevertheless, I quickly sent the trembling youth away and then managed to calm my husband.

Fearing that Irhulani of Hamat would also break his part in the covenant, Akhab next sent a messenger to Qarqar with a gift for the king, "In good faith that our covenant will not be broken." The King of Hamat responded graciously, promising to send his two daughters when they were old enough, "for I have not forgotten the great thing you have done for me, in helping me secure my kingdom against my enemies. Unlike some princes, I do not forget my friends."

This comforted Akhab, and when he told Hosha about the whole ordeal, he said, "I am pleased to have one good ally, at least."

"Only one?" Hosha laughed. "Surely, you have more than that. Do I count for nothing, old friend?"

"You of course are without question, Hosha. I simply meant, of those I fought with in that nasty Assyrian business. My wife was right – I should never have involved myself in it."

I smiled somewhat bitterly. "Next time, you will take my advice, I hope?"

"Of course," came his slurred response. I hated it when he drank with the King of Yehudah, for Hosha always encouraged him to keep drinking well past his limit.

"Good, good," said Hosha, slapping Akhab on the back and laughing. "But if I were you, I would march my army straight to Damaseq and teach that wretched Ben-Hadad a lesson." Ben-Hadad was the name by which Hadi was known in Yisrael and Yehudah.

Before Akhab could speak, I placed a hand over his on the table, and said, "Our relations with Aram may be tense, but we have no intention of poking a wasp's nest. My husband knows that attempting a siege of Damaseq would be a fool's errand."

"Indeed, Melkah," said Hosha, bowing his head with a hand over his heart. His speech was slurred, but at least he was trying to be a gentleman. "Forgive me for even suggesting such an endeavor. It was only in jest, I assure you. I assume, for now, your relations with Aram remain...quiescent?"

"For a time, yes," answered Akhab. "Recently, however, there have been more troubling developments with the return of our stewards from the city of Ramot." He spoke bitterly, looking into his cup. "They were sent into Gilad to collect the annual tribute, which was due – remember, I told you that Ramot and the whole of Gilad, while belonging to Yisrael, has for some time been in the possession of Aram."

"Yes," Hosha nodded, "was it not the father of Ben-Hadad who took it from your father? Or was it Ben-Hadad? Wait, I am confused."

"They are both Ben-Hadad," I explained. "Ben-Hadad, my cousin, is the son of the former Ben-Hadad who was king before him."

"Ah, yes!" said Hosha, raising a roasted goose leg into the air and shaking it for emphasis. "I had forgotten that the same name was shared between father and son."

He took a large bite from the goose leg, tearing most of the meat from the bone. Grease poured down his chin and dripped down his beard as he sucked the rest into his mouth. I had to look away, or I might lose my appetite. For a king, he was so barbaric.

When he had mostly finished his mouthful, he asked, "So, was it the first Ben-Hadad or the current Ben-Hadad that stole Gilad from Omri?"

"It was the first," said Akhab, sighing heavily and lifting his cup to drink the rest of it. When he set the cup on the table, I reached over and took his hand, which now rested on his thigh. He offered a grateful smile and squeezed my hand. All this talk of my hated cousin was quickly sinking his spirit, but now the King of Yehudah was too interested to let it drop.

"So, what happened?" asked Hosha. "When you sent your stewards to Ramot? You never finished telling me what happened."

I squeezed Akhab's hand to let him know I would finish telling the story. He smiled sadly and nodded his approval, and then I began: "Upon reaching the capital city, our stewards were informed that the King of Aram had already sent his men to demand tribute, even though – if you recall – he had promised to return these lands to Yisrael as part of his covenant with Akhab for sparing his life."

"Yes, I remember," said Hosha, taking a handful of chickpeas from the bowl in front of him. I took note not to eat from that bowl after he stuck his greasy hands in it.

Meanwhile, I continued, "He renewed it again before their Assyrian campaign."

"Ah, yes. That I did not know. So, he did not return these lands, as promised?"

I shook my head. "As the elders and nobles of the city refused to pay tribute to two kings, our stewards returned empty-handed."

Hosha grabbed his drink, his eyes lit with excitement. "So, what happened next?"

"Furious by yet another breach of their covenant, my husband sent a messenger to Damaseq to assert his right over the land, demanding a return of the tribute. We have not heard back, but I am certain my cousin will not uphold his end of the covenant." I reached for my cup, waiting while it was refilled. "Just one broken promise after another, but I am not surprised. It is his way." I lifted the cup to my lips.

"You must have felt pretty badly, old friend, to have been so duped," said Hosha, patting Akhab on the back.

My husband grumbled something that even I could not understand. Then he got up and wandered away, going out into the garden. After watching him disappear through the archway, I excused myself and followed him. There were a few others out in the garden, but mostly it was quiet. In the dark and amid their drunkenness, they did not recognize me when I passed, so they did not stop to pay homage. When I found my husband, he was leaning against a tree with his robes pulled up as he relieved himself. I stopped on the path and waited for him to finish, turning my face away to give him privacy. When he finished, he dropped his robes and stumbled toward me.

"Yezeba'al? What are you doing out here?"

"I came to make sure you are all right, husband. You seemed upset."

"Of course, I am upset. Remember, I am the one who was duped, as Hosha would say."

"Hosha is a fool," I said bitterly. "You should not listen to him."

"No, but I should have listened to you, and because I did not, that makes me a fool, too. That's what you are thinking – that I am a fool for not heeding your advice."

I shook my head and sighed heavily, and then I reached up to wipe some crumbs from his beard. I attempted to kiss him, but he

399

would not stoop or lower his head for me to reach his lips, and so I stepped back to look at him. "Akhab, I do not think you a fool. I think what you did was foolish, yes, but that does not make you a fool."

"Fool, foolish – what's the difference?"

"The difference is that a fool is not capable of being wise, but anyone is capable of being foolish. You are not a fool, my love. You made a mistake."

"A couple of mistakes. Several mistakes."

"Yes, but have you learned anything?"

"That I should have killed Hadadesar the first time." He clenched his fists and groaned. "What I would not give to have that man standing in front of me now – I would snap his neck with my own bare hands!"

I put my hands on his arms, attempting to soothe his rage, and he brought them down to his sides. Then I took his face in my hands and rose on my toes to kiss him on the lips. This time, he relaxed into it, and then he leaned his forehead against mine and sighed heavily.

"You are exhausted," I observed. "And you have had too much to drink. Come, let me lead you to bed so you can rest."

"I would rather make love to you."

"Are you in the condition to make love, Akhab?"

"If you will not," he replied moodily, "then I will send for one of my other wives."

This stung, but I refused to be hurt by it. I was grateful for the shade of night to hide the tears in my eyes. "Fine, send for one of them, if you just want any woman to bed."

I turned to walk away, but he grabbed me roughly by the arms, pulled me against him, and growled, "I want you, Yezeba'al! Only you!" His fingers were suddenly digging into my flesh.

"Akhab, you are hurting me," I said, attempting to pull away.

He released me and then sank to his knees, soon weeping into his hands. I looked around to be sure no one was watching us. I saw only the dark shadows of guards at their posts, but nobody else seemed to be around to see the king here on his knees. I put my hands on his head, and he leaned against me as he wept. Then, holding my legs, he looked up at me. "Oh, my love, forgive me. Please, forgive me. I am not worthy of you."

400

I sighed heavily. He rarely drank enough to be this low. "Akhab, people will hear you." I looked around, and commanded him, "Get up. You are making a fool of yourself."

"Then you do think me a fool?"

"Damn it, Akhab!" I hissed. "You are not a fool – you are... Oh, it is no use! Just get up, before someone sees you! You are a king – you must not show weakness."

He exhaled deeply and began to rise, and I helped him to his feet. Then I led him inside through our private entrance into the back of the palace, to avoid being seen by our guests in such a sorry state. Upon reaching my quarters, where Kora and one of the other handmaidens were on standby awaiting my return, I told them to send word to our guests that the king had taken ill, and that we had retired for the night.

Kora and the girl looked at Akhab with concern, as I supported him – which was difficult, because he towered over me at his full height. I assured them all was well. "The king has had a bit too much to drink. He will be well in the morning."

They nodded and then Kora sent the girl to the feast hall with the message. She came to help me get the king to bed, which was a relief for it was still several rooms away. He was barely conscious by the time we helped him onto the bed. Before I had finished removing his outer garments, he fell onto his stomach, laying sideways across the bed, and began snoring. I went to move him, thinking he would be more comfortable on his back, but Kora stopped me.

"It is safer if he remains on his stomach," she reminded me.

"Yes, of course," I said, placing a hand on her shoulder. "Thank you, Kora."

She nodded, and then asked, "May I help you dress for bed?"

"Yes, please. First, I think I could use a bath. Is it safe to leave him, do you think?"

"Yes, he should be fine as long as he remains like this." She looked at him and had to stifle a smile. "I do not think he will be moving around any time soon."

"Neither do I," I said, meeting her gaze. Then we giggled together as if we were young again.

"Shall I heat water?"

"No, I'll just use the main bath. I want to be quick, so I can return to keep an eye on him."

"Do you want me send for someone to watch over him, so you can sleep?"

"I have hardly been sleeping, of late. It is fine. I will sit with him."

She nodded in understanding and then accompanied me to the bath. I stripped off my robes and, still wearing my jewels, stepped into the pool. The water was cold and refreshing, but I did not stay long in it. I was shivering when I got out, but Kora quickly wrapped me in linens and encouraged me to return to my chamber. "I'll send Elisheba to fetch your garments when she returns from delivering your message to the guests."

I thanked her and then hurried up the stairs and returned to my husband. He was snoring when I returned, and for once I was grateful to hear that awful sound. He had not drunk this much in years, and I resented Hosha for bringing it out in him. I knew it was not only a result of his bad influence, however; it was the pressure Akhab had been under these past months. It seemed it had finally broken him, but I hoped he would soon recover.

Still wrapped in my linens, I climbed onto the bed and laid down beside my husband. His mouth hung open, and his cheek and upper lip were distorted from being pressed against the bed, but even then, he was beautiful to me. I closed his jaw so his mouth would not dry out, and then I moved some curls away from his face and gazed at him.

After a while, he awakened enough to sit up and began pulling at his robes. I helped him remove them and got him situated correctly, and he mumbled his thanks. He took my breast in his hand and began kissing and sucking, but just when I began to feel that pleasant ache between my loins, he passed out again. Disappointed, I left him to sleep with his head on my breast until he began drooling.

"Akhab!" I said, attempting to push him off me. He was a dead weight. "Akhab, get up! You are drooling on me!"

He woke up just enough for me to make him lay with his head on the cushion, where he continued snoring while I sat up with my knees to my chin. I kept vigil over him for the rest of the night.

It was customary for kings, when on state visits, to hold court with their hosting monarchs. Although the royal guest did not actually take part in the management of his host's kingdom, he could offer advice and support which was sometimes useful. In the mornings on days when we held court, the King of Yehudah and his queen joined us on the dais. The two kings were seated on thrones in the center, with me seated at my husband's left hand and Aya seated on her husband's right. In the afternoons, however, we took leave of our duties at court, and I went to the women's garden to spend more time with my daughter and grandson while they were there. Aya, who never took on any true role at her husband's court, was happy to join me. While our husbands and elder sons played at sport, I took her to the garden where the children played while their nurses looked on. Abshalom was showing my grandson Akhazyah, whom the family had taken to calling Akhaz, the wooden animals from the ark that had been a favorite among all my children. He favored the tigers and lions, but Akhaz seemed more interested in the giraffes until one of my living peacocks strutted by in all his glory.

"*Amabi!*" he cried out to his paternal grandmother, as he dropped the wooden giraffe and ran to her. He clutched Aya's legs and looked back at the peacock, who had stopped to peck at the ground by Abshalom. My son paused from his play to smile at the large bird, which stood as tall as he sat. It was no wonder Akhaz found it so terrifying, but Abshalom was used to them. He reached out to stroke its feathers, to show his nephew of the same age that it was safe. He even beckoned to him, but Akhaz was uncertain. He looked to Aya and then to me for reassurance.

I rose from my chair and offered my hand to him. Aya encouraged him to take it, and so he did, and then I led him toward the peacock, saying gently, "It is all right, Akhaz. He is a friend, I promise. He will not hurt you." The peacock came to me and purred as I stroked his feathers, and said, "Look at the pretty bird. See, he is a friend."

Akhaz carefully reached out to touch his feathers, and smiled at me when he saw that they were smooth and soft on his fingertips.

"It is a peacock," I explained. "His kind comes from Opir, a faraway land where everything is beautiful and full of color, just like him. So I have heard, at least. Can you say 'peacock'?"

"Peacock," he repeated carefully.

403

"Yes, very good," I said, running my fingers through his curls and thinking he looked so like his mother when she was his age.

He smiled up at me and continued stroking the peacock, repeating its name and growing more confident each time. The peacock, meanwhile, noticed a beetle crawling through the grass and went after it. He missed the first time, and the beetle quickened its pace, but on the second attempt the peacock caught his prize and then moved on in search of more.

"Come, Akhaz. Let me show you all the peafowl." Then I took him around and pointed out the others, some of whom drank from the water sources, some who hunted, and others who rested in trees or on top of the walls. He was enchanted by them, now that he realized they were not so terrifying. I was glad when one of the peacocks called loudly and raised his tail feathers, shaking to lift them higher, and then pranced around with his display. My grandson's eyes lit up, he gasped, and then looked at me and back to the peacock.

"Pretty bird," he said.

"Yes, pretty bird. That is how he attracts a mate," I explained. "The peahens who see his display will decide if he is beautiful enough to father their young. Peachicks."

"Peachicks," he repeated. Then he reached out his hands and was about to chase after the peacock, but I gently caught him by the collar of his robe to stop him.

He began to fuss, but then I lifted him to my hip, and explained, "Do not chase them, Akhaz, or they will no longer be your friends. They will be afraid and attack. It is best to be gentle with them or leave them be."

I brought him back to Aya, who took him on her lap, and said, "Akhaz, will you listen to *Amami* Yezeba'al?"

"Yes, *Amabi*," he replied with his forefinger hung at the corner of his mouth. Aya pulled his hand away, but he fussed and put it back. When she pulled his hand away again, he got down and returned to playing with Abshalom.

Then I sat down once again and reached for my drink to parch my thirst, while Aya said, "You have a way with the children, Yezeba'al. You speak to them as if they are equals – you do not talk down to them, like so many others. I can see now why Atalaya is such a good mother. She gets it from you."

404

With a gracious bow of my head, I thanked her. Then I was surprised when my eldest daughter came up and wrapped her arms around me from behind. She kissed my cheek, and agreed, "I do get it from her. She is a good Ama. But so are you, *Abakhatu*." Then, seeing I was dressed in the form-fitting, low-cut Canaanite fashion that I favored, without a word she folded my mantle across my bosom, as her aunt watched in amusement.

"She has always done this," I explained, while Atalaya went to sit on the rug with her son and her youngest brother, to play with them.

"She is a good daughter – concerned for your modesty," Aya said with a laugh.

"Yes, she is," I chuckled, parting my mantle again. "But I have told her she has no need to be concerned for me. Besides, it is a hot day, and the breeze feels pleasant."

Atalaya looked up at me and shook her head, but she was smiling. Then she began telling Akhaz and Abshalom about the ark and its figures, and how she used to play with it when she was their age. They listened with interest. Then she paused with one of the human figures in her hand, looked up, and chuckled. "I remember throwing Noah at Zyah once."

"I remember, too," I remarked.

"I do not even remember why he angered me, but I remember being satisfied when it left him with a swollen brow for a week." She grinned.

I shook my head. "Perhaps that is not something you should be proud of in front of the children. You will give them ideas."

"They have no reason to fight the way that me and Zyah did, though," she replied. "They are not in competition."

I indicated her abdomen. "No, but they might be. You will have others, you know."

She fell silent and, perhaps, she was thinking about the child she had lost. Before I could comfort her, she said, "I am glad Akhaz is still too young to understand these things. I had told him about it, just before it ended. He seemed excited, at least."

"Zyah was excited, too, until he realized he would have to share me with more brothers and sisters. It was bad enough he had to share me with you. He was incredibly jealous, at least until he was older."

"I remember," she said wryly. Then she sat with her legs crossed and rested her elbows on her thighs. "What's gotten into him, anyway? He has been in such a foul mood, and I've hardly seen him since we arrived. Have I offended him in some way?"

"He is not angry with you, Atalaya."

"I thought he would want to spend more time with me while I'm here," she continued, "but he's nowhere to be found. I asked Yehoram if he has seen him, but he said Zyah has not been at sport with him or the other men. That seems unusual, since Zyah has always enjoyed sporting."

I sighed heavily and raised my eyes toward the heavens. "He has been like this for weeks now, and he will not speak to anyone about what troubles him. Believe me, I have tried, but the more I try the more he shuts me out. Of course, you know he has always been prone to dark moods, but lately it seems as if he may never come out of it."

Aya sat forward in her chair. "You said that his concubine is expecting their first child?"

I nodded. "Yes, she is due in a matter of weeks."

Aya hummed. "He is likely overwhelmed about the reality of becoming a father at such a young age. How old is he?"

"Seventeen years."

She nodded. "I forget he is Atalaya's twin."

Atalaya grinned and held up her hand. "Finally, someone gets it right!"

We all chuckled, and then Aya continued, "Once he sees his child, he will be overwhelmed, not by fear but by love for this tiny person he had a part in creating."

I thanked her for her observation and hoped she was right.

That night, while seated at my dressing table preparing for bed, Akhab entered to find me staring into the mirror and pulling at the skin under and around my eyes. He stopped to watch me, and then chuckled. "What are you doing, wife?"

I turned to him and frowned. "I'm getting old, Akhab."

"Yes," he agreed, coming toward me with a twinkle in his eye. I gasped, but then he slid his arms around me and kissed my cheek. "And you're still beautiful."

Chuckling, I grasped the sides of his robes, and looked up at him. "Will you be spending the night here, or must you lie among the lilies tonight?" That was the euphemism we had developed for nights when he needed to lie with one of his other wives instead of me, his Rose of Shomron.

He placed a hand on my cheek, and said, "I was supposed to lie with Deborah tonight, but...I do not want Deborah. I want you. Only you." He took my hands then pulled me to stand, and when I leaned into his embrace, he kissed my cheek. He began to move his lips down the side of my neck, and I shivered. Then I opened my eyes to meet his gaze, took him by the hand, and led him to my bed.

After we made love, we fell asleep but, as usual, I did not stay asleep. I slipped on my robes and went to my study, lit a lamp, and sat down at my desk to work. Sometime later, Akhab shuffled in, leaned on the doorframe with a yawn, and rubbed his face. "Yezeba'al?"

"I am here, Akhab."

He came to look over my shoulder. "What is it that you are writing?"

I sat back with my arms draped over the sides of the chair, a stylus between my fingers. "I do not know, really. An account of things, I suppose."

"An account of things?" He crouched beside me with his elbow on the desk, gazing at me, and we shared a smile. Then he took the papyrus to see what I had written. He lifted it to get a better look.

Anxious to have anyone reading my private thoughts, I explained, "It is nothing, really. Merely a chronicle of sorts..." I had been writing about the early years of our marriage, up to the time of Akhab's conversion and the birth of our twins.

He smiled and carefully placed it back on the desk, even straightening it so that it was as he had found it. Then he observed, "It is about us – our kingdom, our family. It is our story."

"You do not think it silly to record all these things?"

"No, I think it's beautiful. You should keep writing it."

I smiled and set the stylus down, as he dropped to his knees and moved to embrace me. Then we shared a kiss, and afterward rested our foreheads together. Then I explained, "I have not been sleeping much, of late. So, I've been coming in here and working to

407

pass the time. Better than lying in bed for hours, turning about, and listening to you snoring." I playfully pinched the tip of his nose.

"No, I do not snore – do I?"

I nodded. Then I added, "Loudly."

"I suppose that is why you cannot sleep."

I shook my head. "It is the same even when you are not with me here and my chamber is silent. I sleep better when you are here, in fact. When you are not, I seldom get any sleep at all, unless I pray before the altar of Ashtarti for relief."

His gaze fell to the thin cuts on my forearm that were still in the process of healing. He never cared for that particular ritual. He gently touched my arm, and asked, "Have you consulted one of the healers?"

I pulled my arm away and hid the cut beneath my mantle, saying, "I have spoken to healers, priests and priestesses, prophets...none of them have been able to find a solution. It's these dreams I've been having."

"Dreams?"

"Yes, terrible dreams. It began around the time of the siege, but they were infrequent at first. Then over the past year or two they have grown more frequent and intense, and they are all the same, even when they are different. It is as though they are pointing to something terrible, but I do not know what. No one has any answers for me – of course, they all offer their predictions and interpretations, but all of it is meaningless. I can tell when they are making it all up, hoping to please me."

"Tell me about them. I am not a dream interpreter, but perhaps I can do better? If not, at least I can listen, and you can share the burden with me."

I met his gaze, trying to discern if I should tell him.

He brought his hands to my waist and rested his arms upon my thighs. "Speak to me, wife. Tell me about these dreams."

I finally gave in to his entreaties. "Most of them involve me being lost without you. In them, we are caught in a flood, and we are desperate to find something to hold onto, but I get swept away from you. Sometimes, I awaken in a strange and foreign place. The flood is gone, there is no sign of it, and you are nowhere to be found. I call out to you, search for you, but the only people I find do not know you. They are strange people, and they look upon me as if I am mad. They all seem to know me, but I do not know them. I have the sense of knowing them, but I have never seen them before in all my life, and they are speaking languages I do not understand. Sometimes, there is no one around at all, and I am completely alone. At least, in those dreams, I am not surrounded by these strange people dressed in strange garments and surrounded by so many things I cannot comprehend."

"What kind of things?"

"I do not know," I answered, closing my eyes and shaking my head. "I cannot describe these things. Most of them I have forgotten – the details fade in time, but everything about them is terrifying. But most terrifying of all is that I cannot find you. I never find you in any of these places. And when I wake from these dreams and you are not next to me in my bed, I feel as if the dreams are starting all over again, and I weep."

He pulled me into his arms, while I continued, "At least, when you are here, I know that all is well...but still I cannot sleep for I am haunted by those dreams. So, instead, I come here, and I write about our life. I write about my memories of you and us and our children, of everything wonderful and everything terrible, because then I know it is all real. *This* is real, and these other things, these floods, these people...they cannot find me, and they cannot take me away from you."

He took my hands in his, brought them to his lips, and then rose onto his knees to draw me into a kiss. Then he said, "I am here now, and no one will take you away from me. I would never allow it. Come, Yezeba'al." He stood up and pulled at my hands. "Come to bed. Let me hold you in my arms, so you can sleep."

I rose and followed him to my bed. There, he helped me out of my robes, and I helped him out of his. Then we lay beneath the blankets, and I rested my head upon his shoulder, and he held me close. He stroked me, whispered reassurances, kissed the top of my head, and at last I began to relax enough to sleep. Then, for the first time in several months, I slept fully through the rest of the night.

17

The Last Offence

The messengers we had sent to Damaseq with Akhab's complaint about Hadadesar's possession of Ramot in Gilad returned with his response while we were holding court the following morning. Reading from a clay tablet on which Hadi's message had been etched, the chief messenger said that the King of Aram claimed that these lands were not part of their covenant, although I had been present the second time it was made, when we were visiting Damaseq. Ramot had absolutely been part of the agreement. However, Hadi's message continued, "Send me your Melkah, the best of your wives, and I will return these lands to Yisrael, and more. But if you do not send her, I will not do what you ask of me."

Akhab gripped the arms of his throne, and I heard him exhaling slowly. Then he rose and held out his hand. "Let me see. Bring me the tablet."

He gestured with his hand for the messenger to come forward. Aharon stepped down to meet the messenger, took the tablet, and brought it to my husband. Akhab peered at the tablet as if to read it himself. Then he raised it up for all the court to see, and proclaimed, "This is what I think of the King of Aram's demand." Then he dropped the tablet and it smashed into pieces on the floor.

While the slaves came to clean it up, Akhab returned to his throne. As he prepared to sit, he grumbled to me, "I have had enough of your cousin."

"He is baiting you," I said calmly. "Trying to provoke you to make war against him."

"If that is his wish, he will have it," he said through clenched teeth, as he settled into his throne once again. Hosha was watching us from his throne on the other side of Akhab, and I wished this was not happening while he was present.

Keeping my tone measured, I urged, "Do not let him have his way with you."

410

"Do not tell me what I should or should not do concerning this!" he hissed.

Now Aya looked around her husband from her throne, and it was clear to all who were near us that we were bickering. I was humiliated by Hadi's ongoing obsession and frustrated because it could have ended years ago. "If you had killed him when you had the chance —"

He brought his hand down on the arm of his throne, and raised his voice, "I do not want to hear another word about my mistakes, woman! You will be silent!"

"You speak as if I am the one to blame."

My husband rose from his throne and whirled around to face me in his fury. "Are you not? Is it not *you* that is the object of his obsession? *You* who are the reason he assaults my kingdom and insults me as a king and as a man?"

"I did not bring him here," I said bitterly. Then I rose to face my husband, and declared, "I will not be blamed for his actions! I did *not* ask for this!"

"And neither did I!" he roared.

At this, I turned and walked away. I went through the curtains behind the thrones, followed as always by the captain of my eunuchs and two others. Soon I heard another set of sandals racing up from behind me, and I stopped to see who had followed. It was Aya. She slowed her pace to walk with more dignity, and then stopped before me with a sympathetic gaze.

"Yezeba'al...I am sorry you must go through all this, and that my brother would blame you for what your cousin is doing."

I looked down at the floor and shook my head. "I know he does not truly blame me, Aya. He blames himself, and he takes it out on me because I, too, blame him. For he had a chance to kill Hadadesar and did not take it. I should not have said so to him, though. He does not need me to remind him, and I shall have to apologize."

"Why don't you come back to court and tell him that."

"No," I answered. "I will speak to him when we are alone together. For now, I am going to pray and then I will go to the garden to find peace."

"Shall I join you?"

411

"No, return to court. Keep an eye on things for me. Do not let the men do anything stupid. And if they try to, come to me and I will talk sense into them."

She nodded and stayed to watch as I turned away and continued to my quarters. Once there, I stripped out of my court regalia with the help of my handmaids and dressed in more comfortable attire, while the eunuchs kept watch from their posts by the door and the balcony. Then Kora brought me the juglet in which I kept my sacred oil, and I took it into my prayer chamber, where I closeted myself for an hour of solitary meditation. When I came out, Aya was waiting for me with an anxious expression.

Handing the juglet of oil to Kora, I went to my sister-in-law, and we clutched forearms. "What is it? What has happened?"

"They want to go to war against the King of Aram, Yezeba'al."

I sighed heavily and raised my eyes to the ceiling. "Of course, they do. This is what I feared. Tell me what is being said."

"Akhab asked my husband if he would go with him to take the city of Ramot out of the hand of the King of Aram. My foolish husband, of course, said our people are your people and our horses your horses, in the usual manner of agreeing to these things. Then my husband asked Akhab first to consult a prophet for Yahowah's blessing."

"Did he receive it?"

"I do not know. They have made plans to go out into the city, to the plaza by the gate, to meet with the prophets that have been summoned. They will do this on the last day before the shabbat. I am praying the prophecies are not favorable, for then my husband will refuse, and I know my brother will not be so foolish to make war against Hadadesar on his own."

"I will speak to him. Where is my husband now?"

"When I left the court, they were on their way to his study with some of his ministers."

I clutched her by the arms again. "Thank you, Aya." Then I pressed my lips to her cheek and hurried away.

Akhab and Hosha were in the study with Aharon, Abram, and a few others. They were the usual group of ministers, always eager to talk the king into making war against any number of his wayward vassals and enemies. I had always struggled to hold sway with the king against them when I thought poorly of their plans, often losing

412

the battles, being outmatched in number if not intellect. When the door was opened to me and I appeared, the ministers were gathered around Akhab who was seated at his desk. They all looked at me with sneers, for they knew why I had come. Then Akhab looked up himself and pressed his lips firmly together.

"Yezeba'al, I do not want to hear it."

"You cannot seriously be planning a war over an insult, Akhab."

"I am not planning a war over an insult," he said icily. "I am planning to take Ramot and that is all. I have grown tired of doing nothing while Hadadesar continues to take what is rightfully ours."

I pressed my fingers to my forehead and sighed. "Why can you not see that this is what he wants of you? If you go to Ramot to do battle, he will be there waiting. He will be expecting you, and you will walk right into a trap."

"You give him too much credit, Yezeba'al – and to me, not enough. Hadadesar is a fool."

"A fool, yes; but a clever one. I know him better than you, Akhab. He wants you out of the way, so he can play the conqueror."

Akhab looked down at the letter he had been writing and waved me away. "Go. I am done talking about this."

I looked at Hosha. I could see that he was as eager for war as the others. Only Aharon seemed sympathetic, but he was the least among them. I knew when I was defeated; my husband's mind was already made up before I came. He wanted this war as much as Hadi, if not for the same reasons, and would find any excuse to make it happen. Before leaving, I said, "I pray these prophets you have sent for speak truthfully and tell you what you need to hear. Unlike you, I do not need prophecy to know that this action will lead you to ruin."

Unwilling to waste my energy further, I returned to my chamber and laid down to rest, for I had developed a headache and an ill feeling in my stomach. I told Kora to turn anyone away who came to see me, save for the king, but he did not come to me that night.

On the day before the shabbat, two thrones were set upon a platform in the plaza by the city gates, and all the prophets of Yahowah came before the two kings. I heard about the affair only after the final

413

decision had been made, based upon the prophecies, which were unanimously in favor of the campaign. When Akhab and Hosha returned to the palace, I was in the garden with my children. Aya and Yehoram were also there with us, while we awaited the news of their return. When it came, I was informed that Akhab was coming there to speak with me concerning the decision that was made.

"What is the decision?" I asked of the servant who had come to me with the news.

He bowed his head, and answered, "The king will go to Ramot, Melkah."

I clenched my jaw and inhaled deeply, closing my eyes and willing myself not to cry. It was as expected, although I had hoped for a different outcome and prayed for it fervently. I thanked the messenger, sent him away, and then rose and told the nurses to take the children back to the nursery. Only Zyah and Yoram remained with the rest of us. I had thought about sending Yoram away, but now that he was considered a man, I decided to let him stay, for he had an interest in these things and might one day replace his uncle Abram as Minister of War.

When Akhab and Hosha appeared with their attendants, they came with enthusiastic spirits, talking and laughing together. I went up and met them on the veranda, and when my husband saw me, he stopped abruptly. His expression became sheepish. He held out his hands, and said, "My love, forgive me. I know this is not what you want."

"This is not about what I want, Akhab." Then I cast a fierce gaze on Hosha, who slunk away to stand with his wife and the others. Hosha began to explain to them what happened, but soon their attentions were drawn back to me and Akhab. They watched helplessly as we locked horns in a bitter argument.

"My love, the prophets have all said the same thing: 'Go up to Ramot in Gilad and prosper; for Yahowah will deliver it into the hand of the king.'" Akhab smiled proudly.

"Which king?" I asked skeptically. "I suppose he was not specific on that matter?"

"What do you mean, which king? What other king would he mean?"

"There will be at least three of you involved in this battle, and more if Hadi brings his allies into the fray."

414

"They said *I* am to go up to Ramot and prosper. That is pretty specific, Yezeba'al."

"If they said that, then they are all liars and false prophets, for I have seen otherwise."

"What do you mean? What have you seen?"

"I have told you of the dreams I have been having, ever since these conflicts with Hadi began – in all of them I am without you."

"What of these dreams? They mean nothing to me – they are about floods and strange people, not battles."

"They are messages from the Ba'alim! Warning me that I am going to lose you to some terrible thing that is beyond my control!"

"If it is beyond your control, then why are you trying so hard to fight it?"

"I am trying to preserve your life!"

"I am not the one being swept away in a flood! These are your dreams, and you are the one being swept away, so perhaps *you* need to be careful, not me!"

"Last night, I saw you lying dead in a tomb!" I shrieked, my eyes stinging as it flashed in my memory. "It cannot be more specific! Until last night, I could not be sure what any of those dreams meant, but now I know they are messages from the gods. They are trying to warn me, Akhab! To warn *you* against this campaign."

"You try to warn me against every campaign!"

"Not every campaign!"

"Yes, *every* campaign!"

"There have been a few that I truly believed in, and I supported you then," I reminded him. "And you made great victory. But in this one there can be no victory!"

"There will be victory! The prophets have spoken!"

I stopped and breathed deeply, and then said as calmly as I could, "No, Akhab; this one is different. I have a bad feeling about it."

"You have a bad feeling every time I go to war!"

"But this time, I've had dreams..."

"These dreams you've had – it is your mind conjuring your worst fears. It is not the gods trying to warn us, but some mischievous spirit, hoping to frighten me into inaction! But now I need to take action! I am done waiting for Hadadesar to uphold our covenant!"

"Damn your covenant, Akhab! You should never have put your faith in it!"

415

"And you should not put your faith in dreams!"

"Like you put yours in the word of these prophets?"

"I do put my faith in the word of these prophets, just as you would do if all of them spoke favorably of something you desire!"

"I would not put my faith in them if they spoke against what I know to be true, and I know what I have seen."

He scoffed. "Yezeba'al, I love and respect you, but I do not believe that all these prophets were lying to me. Every one of them spoke of prosperity."

"You are telling me not one of them spoke of doom?"

"Not one – well, except for that wretched Mikhayah ben Yimlah." He grimaced. "But he never has anything good to say of me, and he has been wrong so many times, so why should I listen to him?"

"I am not asking you to listen to this prophet." I took his hands between mine and implored him with my gaze. "Listen to me, Akhab. Do not go. Do not make war against my cousin for these or any lands. Not now. The time is not right."

He pulled his hands from mine and crossed his arms over his chest. "If it is the Ba'alim that have sent this dream to you, when do they say it will be right, then?"

"I do not know. Perhaps never."

He scoffed.

I took his hand again and pressed my body to his, tilting my head to the side. "Let Hadi have Ramot. Let him keep Gilad. He has had it all this time. It is of no consequence to us, my love, for we have each other."

For a moment, as I touched his brow and met his gaze, I thought he would capitulate. Then he pulled away, and said, "It would be good for us to have these lands in our possession. They belong to us and will bring prosperity to our kingdom."

"I would rather have you!" I shouted, as fresh tears began to blur my vision. "Don't you understand? I do not want you to go because if you go, I know this time you will not come back to me!"

He softened then and came to take my face in his hands. "I will come back to you," he swore. When I tried to look away, he held my head in place. "Look at me. I will come back to you, my love. I promise."

Giving up the fight, I spoke with calm authority. "You will come back to me a corpse." Then I pulled away and left him there

416

with all the others. Only my daughter came after me. She caught up to me when I was on the staircase leading to my quarters.

"Ama!" she called from the bottom of the stairs. I stopped, turned, and came down to her. She met me with sorrowful gaze, and asked, "Is it true, what you have seen?"

I nodded slowly. "I have seen this, and I am certain of what it means. I wish I could say it was not true, Atalaya. I wish I could believe that it is all nothing, that it means nothing, for your father is determined and nothing will dissuade him from this course."

She looked as if she might burst into tears but managed to hold them back. "Then we must pray that the Ba'alim will alter his fate and keep him safe, or that he will still change his mind before it is too late."

We embraced tightly, and then she escorted me to my chamber where I lay down to rest. She sat with me, stroking my hair and holding my hand, while Kora and the others went about their work and tended to my needs. I was grateful to my daughter for her love and support; I would surely need it in the days to come.

Yehoshapat and the others had planned to stay with us at Shomron until the Serpent's Feast, one of the minor Ba'alim feasts commemorating Ba'al's defeat of the sea-god Yam – represented by a serpent. It was celebrated each year at midsummer, when the real battle was believed to have taken place between the divine brothers, after their father El had held a banquet at which he chose Yam over Ba'al to rule his kingdom. Instead of preparing for the feast, however, Akhab sent word to Yezreel for his generals to prepare the best of his chariots and foot soldiers for battle and bring them to Shomron. Then the King of Yehudah sent word to Yerushalayim, summoning the best of his horses and men. When they arrived, the day was set when the men would leave for Ramot: the day after the Serpent's Feast.

After making the customary sacrifice at the temple and praying for the safety of the kings and their men, on the last night before Akhab and Yehoshapat led their armies to Gilad, we held the Serpent's Feast at Shomron in their honor. It was a solemn feast – not like the raucous affair at Damaseq. After serving the customary dessert of curdled milk sweetened with honey and bits of dried fruit

417

to our guests – just as El had done at the first banquet – Akhab and I departed early so that we could be alone together for what could be our last time.

My husband took me to my chamber, where I dismissed my handmaids for the night. Then, as I always did before he left on a journey or went to battle, I washed his hands and feet before anointing him. Carefully pouring drops of sacred oil, I anointed his hands and feet and forehead and breast, kissing and gently caressing where it touched his flesh. I lit incense and carried the censer around him, bringing it up and down as I circled him, chanting prayers and blessings and incantations of protection over him. Their purpose was for the Ba'alim to safeguard his return to me – and if he fell in battle, then they would receive him unto them, and bless him in the underworld.

After it was finished, I placed the censer on the table beside the juglet of oil. My duty done, I was overcome by a wave of heaviness, unable to move from where I stood. I was near to tears. Akhab came to me then, gently lifted my chin, and silently urged me to look into his eyes. Then he touched his thumb to my bottom lip and drew me into a tender kiss.

Tears fell as we undressed each other carefully, taking our time and feeling each moment, savoring each sensation. I ran my hands over every part of him, feeling the strength of each muscle, curving with every joint. I pressed my lips to his naked flesh and breathed in that familiar smell of sweat and sacred oils which blended to create the perfect aroma – the scent of him. He did all the same with me, and my flesh tingled with the warmth of his breath. He knelt and brought his mouth to my breast. I gasped and held my breath and tangled my fingers through his curls.

When I began to tremble, he knew my body was ready to receive him. He rose and met my gaze, and in that moment took my soul from my body as surely as he took my breath away. Then he led me to bed, and we spent our last night together in love's passionate embrace.

We gathered outside the palace the next morning to see the men off: two kings, two queens, two successors, and all my children

418

with their nurses and guardians. While Hosha bid farewell to his wife, son, and grandson, Akhab bid farewell first to Atalaya and her son, and then to all our other children. He came to me last and looked into my eyes with sadness and regret. Perhaps it was only a reflection of my own, for I could see that he was confident, hopeful, and excited to be going off to battle.

"My only regret," he said, taking my hand, "is leaving you behind to wait for my return."

I looked down, attempting to compose myself, but was unable to speak.

"I know you fear for me," he continued, "but do not fear – for the Ba'alim are with us. They are always with us, even at our darkest hour."

He paused. I looked up, as he continued, "I have never told you this, but whenever I am going into battle, I take comfort in a song of King Dawid: 'Yea, though I walk through the valley of the shadow of death, I will fear no evil: for you are with me; your rod and your staff they comfort me.' I know every time I go into battle, that death follows me. Death follows us all from the moment we are born to the moment when it succeeds in taking us to the grave. But while we are alive, we must live, Yezeba'al; for as long as the gods have granted us life, we must live, and we must do whatever they have compelled us to do."

He slipped his arms around my waist and pulled me to his body. I closed my eyes, to feel the strength in his arms; rested my head upon his chest, listened to his heart beating, and inhaled his scent. It took all my strength not to weep.

When at last, I pulled away and opened my eyes, he was watching me with an odd smile. "What are you doing, wife?"

"Savoring your arms around me for the last time," I answered, searching his gaze for any glint of hesitation. Seeing none, I inhaled sharply – it hurt to breathe – for I knew that I had to let him go.

He touched my chin, drew me into a kiss, and then he looked into my eyes again. "Pray for me, that the gods will bring victory – as Ba'al had victory over Yam at this time – and that I will return to you."

"I would feel more certain if you were going to do battle with the sea-god than with Hadi," I replied truthfully. "But I will pray for you every day, as I always have, from the moment I first laid eyes

419

upon you." I looked down as a tear broke free, and then said, "My spirit will be with you every moment; if only my body could be with you, too."

"Your place is here, my love. With our kingdom and our children." He looked down and then he brought my hands to his lips. He inhaled the scent of the oil with which I had anointed my hands when I rose that morning. I could feel that he was about to pull away, but then he hesitated.

I looked up to see him gazing at me with a playful smile. "What is it?" I asked, hoping he might still change his mind.

"I was thinking about the first time I looked into your eyes – how intense they were, how deep and intelligent, yet gentle. I loved you from that very moment." He paused, and then he said, "Keep writing your story."

"Our story," I reminded him.

He cocked his head and looked at me oddly. "That's what I said: our story. Keep writing it. I would like to read it when I return to you if it is finished."

He pressed my hand to his lips once more and then pulled away. I let my hand fall to my side. As he walked to take his place in his chariot where the driver was already waiting, I closed my eyes and prayed silently that what he said was not an omen.

When I opened my eyes, Azba'alah had come to me. She tugged at my robes, and asked, "Where is Abbu going, Ama?"

As she turned and leaned back against me, I put my hand over her heart, and looked up to watch my husband mounting his chariot and talking with Yehoshapat, who was on the back of a horse. I did not know how to answer her simple question, for it held so many answers, none of them satisfying.

"Ama?" She turned her head and looked up at me.

"He is going to Ramot, Azba," I said at last.

"What is Ramot?"

"It is a city in Gilad."

"What is Gilad?"

"It is a land that belongs to us."

She fell silent for a moment, for which I was grateful. Then she asked, "When will he return to us?"

Finally, unable to take any more of her questioning, I covered her mouth with my hand. I was struggling to hold back my tears.

420

When I had composed myself, I answered, "He will return to us when the Ba'alim allow." I looked up at the cloudless sky. "I pray it will be soon."

Hosha was smiling and playful in his manner as he spoke to Akhab, who looked more reserved now than usual. I could not hear what was being said between them, but the driver of my husband's chariot smirked while Akhab looked toward me with longing in his gaze. Then Hosha laughed and elbowed him and continued speaking, and they exchanged words. When they fell silent, Akhab raised his hand. Two kings nodded to their generals and, as the trumpeters blew their horns, waved back at us as they set off.

As they disappeared through the palace gate, I closed my eyes and prayed silently in my heart: *Come back to me, Akhab, my love.*

18

Under the Setting Sun

The campaign to reclaim Ramot in Gilad was not a quick affair, but I never expected it to be. First, it took time to travel with an army of horses and chariots across the mountains and plains, and they also had to cross the Yarden along the way. Then there came the siege and the clash of armies and kings. This could be over quickly or drag on indefinitely. It could be weeks or even months before we heard anything from our men, so we had to remain calm and go about our affairs as usual. With Akhab gone, I assumed my role as regent. The presence of our guests, which might have put more pressure on me in other circumstances, eased some of the burden when Aya and Atalaya stepped in to handle the daily household affairs. This allowed me to focus on managing the kingdom alongside my duties at the temple, which were many. I was grateful to have such capable women at my side.

The only time I was called away from duties to the kingdom was to attend the birth of my second grandchild. I was holding court when Aya herself came to inform me that the midwives confirmed Naveen's labor had begun. Zyah, the expectant father, was sitting in his usual place beside Akhab's throne, which I now occupied. His aunt gave him a warm smile when she delivered the news. I looked at my son, whose face was flushed with a panicked expression. He gripped the arms of his chair, knuckles white.

"Is she...going to be safe? What can I do to help her?"

I placed a hand upon his and spoke calmly. "Do not worry a thing about this. It is women's work. But I must go – can you manage without me here?"

He met my gaze with alarm. Once so eager to take on more responsibility, he now seemed terrified by the reality of managing the kingdom on his own. Seeing this, I reassured him, "It will be all right, my son. Aharon is here. He will advise you. Anything that you are unsure of can be put aside for me to handle when I return to court.

Understand, nothing is urgent. No decisions must be made immediately: they would not bother bringing their issues and complaints before the court and waiting for an audience."

He nodded slowly, but his eyes remained panic-stricken when Aharon announced my departure. I rose from the king's throne but, before leaving, paused once more to give my son a reassuring nod. He returned the nod, inhaled deeply, and straightened his back to appear more regal now that he was left in charge. I proudly walked away from my first-born son, leaving him to manage the kingdom as I went to aid in the birth of his first-born child. I felt excitement now as I followed Aya to the women's quarters.

"The midwives are in agreement that everything is going well," Aya informed me on the way. "They anticipate a smooth labor with no complications."

Naveen was in agony, meanwhile, but my arrival seemed to bring some comfort. As was the custom, I chanted the blessing of childbirth and held up a juglet of sacred oil for her to smell. She was not royal or a priestess, so I could not anoint her with it, but the fragrance was pleasant and stimulating. Afterward, I handed it to one of the attendants and spoke words of encouragement while gently stroking her hair. "You are all right, Naveen. You can do this. Your body is made to do this." Then I reminded her, "You are bearing a child of the future king. Take great pride in what you accomplish this day."

She nodded and, as I stepped back to observe, her resolve seemed strengthened. It was evening, near sundown, when a son was born to Naveen. As the son of a concubine, he could never inherit the throne, but none of that mattered because there was plenty of time for Zyah to take wives to bear his direct heirs. This was a child to love and cherish without all the duties and expectations of succession to interfere with a father's natural affection.

When Zyah was brought in to see his son for the first time, he wept tears of great joy and exalted Ba'al for this gift of life. For the first time since the discovery that he was going to be a father, Zyah became himself again – smiling and laughing, kissing Naveen and caressing her hair as he praised her for delivering the greatest of all gifts.

This pleased me, as well, to witness. I stood by my son and smiled with him as we gazed down at the newborn in his arms. Zyah was seated in a chair beside the bed Naveen occupied, and he laid his head against me while still gazing at his son. I put my arm around his shoulders, and everything seemed perfect. I found myself thinking, *if only Akhab was here to see this.* Yet suddenly, I felt in that moment that he actually was standing beside me. I even turned to speak to him, only to stop suddenly.

"Ama, are you all right?" asked Zyah.

"Yes, I am fine," I answered, slightly unnerved. Then I chuckled. "I thought for a moment your father was here, and I was going to speak to him, but then I remembered he is still at Ramot."

Thinking nothing of it, Zyah hummed and returned his attention to his son, while I on the other hand closed my eyes to strengthen myself against a great sorrow that suddenly possessed me. My soul ached for my husband. I felt his absence in a way that I never had before, and hoped to have word from him soon that all was well.

Word came the next day, while I was at my morning prayers. I was on my knees, prostrated before the private altar in my chamber and enveloped in the smoke of incense, when the door slowly creaked open. Kora's voice came softly to me, "Ba'alah, forgive me…"

Still prostrated, my arms stretched above my head and reaching toward the altar, I said firmly, "What reason do you have for interrupting my communion with Ashtarti?"

She inhaled sharply behind me, and her voice faltered when she tried again to speak. Still annoyed but realizing it was truly important, I broke posture, sat upon my knees, and turned halfway to look at her. She seemed paler than normal. Her lips opened and closed, but no sound came out.

"Kora?"

I pulled myself up now, as she finally found her speech. "Yezeba'al, a messenger has come. From Ramot. He said it is urgent." Then, barely above a whisper, "He must speak with you."

All at once, everything seemed to stop. She could not have known with any certainty why the messenger was here, but I could see the fear in her gaze. I nodded and removed my prayer shroud, handing it to her as I went out of the chamber. I prepared myself now

424

to receive the message, trying to remain calm and hopeful. But in my heart I knew.

The messenger was waiting in my private audience chamber. When the door was opened for me to enter, he appeared to have been pacing, helmet in hand. He whirled around immediately, and I recognized him as the King of Yehudah's chief messenger. In an instant, I saw the beads of sweat on his forehead, his expression grave. He dropped to one knee, bowed his head, and addressed me: "*Gebirah.*"

I inhaled sharply and the tears I had been fighting rushed forward to sting in my eyes. That one word was like an arrow through my heart, for I knew in that moment: the king, my husband, was dead.

The armies of Yehudah and Yisrael were on their way back to Shomron with the body of the king when Yehoshapat's messenger informed me of all that had happened. Hosha later confirmed what his messenger had said: Akhab had thought it safer to disguise himself and go into battle as a low-ranking charioteer, after his scouts informed him that the King of Aram was indeed waiting at Ramot with his army. This time, rather than being a drunken, unruly bunch, they were prepared to meet the King of Yisrael when he arrived.

"He must have told his men to attack Akhab with all their might," said Hosha, "for when they saw me, they surrounded me and cried out against the King of Yisrael whom they had been charged to destroy. I thought, surely, I am going to die this day. Then the captains of the King of Aram's chariots saw me and knew I was not Akhab, and they turned back their men.

"I looked for Akhab," he continued, "and I knew his chariot by the strip of red cloth he had tied to the end of a spear. He was fighting alongside his other men. The battle was going well but raged on without pause. It was only toward the end of it, when the cry was made that the sun was going down, that I found he had been struck by an arrow between the joints of his armor. He had told the driver of the chariot that he was severely wounded, but they were in the thick of it and could not retreat to safety for his wound to be tended."

Hosha paused, shaking his head with his hands up to the sides of his face. "He stayed fighting until he could no longer stand, for he had lost too much blood. I saw myself the blood of Akhab, spilled upon the floor of his chariot. He was still alive when the battle ended, and the driver called out to us, but by the time the surgeons made their way to him it was too late. He had already drawn his last breath. He died at sundown."

There was a tomb beneath the ground floor of the palace at Shomron that Akhab had told me was meant to be used for him one day. "My father had it built, alongside his own, when I was named his successor."

"Akhab, I do not want to think about your death," I had answered, pulling away.

It was the first time he was taken away from me, in the early years of our marriage, when the Moabites rebelled against his dominion over them. Lying on my side in bed with my hands beneath my cheek, I turned my back to him and refused to listen to his talk of tombs and death.

He moved to lay alongside me, placed a hand on my shoulder, and said, "Yezeba'al, it is important for you to know this. If I do not return…"

"I do not wish to think about it," I said sharply. I did not want him to see my tears. I closed my eyes and breathed deeply, and then said, "You will return to me."

"I pray to the god of my fathers that is true, my love. But if I don't…"

"*You will*," I insisted, finally turning to face him.

He saw that I had been crying, but when he moved to comfort me, I got up and slipped on a robe. Then I went to collect the sacred oil and some incense. He watched from the bed, his face ablaze in the dancing light of the lamps.

"Come," I beckoned to him. Then, while he stood naked before me, I anointed and blessed my husband for the first time. When it was finished, he tried again to speak of the tomb beneath the palace, but I placed my fingers to his lips and, with my other hand, pulled the sash from my robe so that it fell open before him.

"You will return to me," I commanded, taking his hand, and bringing it to my breast. I brought his other hand to my waist and let the robe slip from my shoulders while I pressed myself against him so that his body came to life. "You will return to me."

"Yes," he answered breathlessly.

When I moved away from him, he attempted to take hold of me, but I grabbed his wrist to stop him and looked him in the eye. "You must promise me."

"I promise...I will return to you."

Again, he tried to take me, but I was still not satisfied. Now, I held both his wrists. I brushed my lips against his, refusing to give him complete satisfaction. Then, meeting his gaze, I said, "Promise you will never leave me."

"I promise, Yezeba'al: I will never leave you."

I released his wrists and smiled. "Then I am yours."

He never spoke of the tomb again, but I never forgot. I simply chose not to dwell on it. Now, as I walked – shrouded in mourning clothes, supported by my son the new king, at the head of my husband's funeral procession from the temple to the tomb – I wished I had let him speak. What I would not give to hear him speak to me, of anything and everything and nothing at all. It would not matter to me what he had to say, if I could only hear his voice once again.

I clung to my mantle, while the sounds of flutes and the mournful wailing of women assaulted me, worsening the ache in my head. My cheeks were dry, but they were raw from all the tears I had already shed. I closed my eyes against the endless wailing, the sound of which could not come close to expressing the emptiness I felt within my soul. Did any of them know the sorrow in my heart? Could they imagine? Their cries were nothing compared to the silence with which I bore my own grief. No sound could express the depths of my torment.

After the Yahwist rites had been concluded, as had been my husband's wish, the Ba'alist funerary rites were to be observed after the body of the king was placed within the tomb and all mourners departed. Once the body was delivered into the tomb and placed upon its place of final rest, while everyone who had come with us into that cold underworld had begun to file out, I stood staring at my husband. There was only myself and the priests of Ba'al, waiting respectfully for me to leave so they could perform the rite of passage to the

427

underworld. This was the vision from my dream, the one I had dreaded and tried so hard to warn him against.

While waiting for me to leave, some of the priests chanted quietly while others lit offerings of incense and arranged them among the grave goods. A pair of elder priests began to cover Akhab with his burial shroud, but I held up my hand and they backed away. He was lying so still, dressed in a rich loincloth and jewels, and holding the ankh and the ceremonial axe he had used for so many Feasts of Ba'al. I could almost believe he was only sleeping, waiting for me to enact the ritual we had performed every year since he became High Priest.

I looked up at the priests, who stood watching with uncertainty, until I commanded, "Leave us."

"Ba'alah," the chief priest began, apologetically.

My voice rose sharply, "I said, leave us."

They bowed and held out their arms and, prompting the others to follow, backed out of the tomb. I looked at the statue of Ba'al that stood upon a low altar that was placed against the rear wall. The statue held up a brazier, on which a fire burned. There were other, simple braziers lit throughout the chamber. My gaze drifted from one dancing flame to the next, examined the richly painted carvings and bas-reliefs that decorated the walls, and fell upon the furniture, statues of gold and ivory, amphorae of wine, food stuffs, and other grave goods that had been placed within before the body of the king was delivered to its final resting place. Would he be comfortable here in this cold, dark, lonely chamber, after a lifetime of freedom and activity?

A tear slipped down my cheek as I returned my gaze to the face of the statue. "Please...send him back to me." My voice broke as I knelt before the statue and addressed the god of death: "Motu, send him back to me." Then, "Ba'al, come back to me." I wept at the feet of the statue, kissing and caressing, hoping that my god could feel my touch through the cold and lifeless stone.

When no answer came, I rose and went to stand over my husband's body. I inhaled the fragrant oils, those same ones with which he was anointed every day while he lived. But the scent was wrong now. It did not smell like him. I touched his cheek, but recoiled when I felt no warmth – it was as cold as stone.

A cry escaped from my throat; my voice echoed in the chamber. I looked around, waited to see if anyone outside heard me.

Grateful when no one came, I summoned my strength. Then I climbed over my husband's cold and lifeless form, drew the dagger from my belt, and began whispering the prayers and incantations of the awakening ritual. It must work. It had to work. But when I slashed the blade across his chest, the wound did not bleed. Without blood, the ritual could not work. I stared at the cut in shock. Then I tried again, waited, and still no blood came forth. It was then that I began to fill with dread. I climbed down and stepped back, staring at the body, and realizing for the first time it barely looked like Akhab anymore.

Recovering from the shock, an idea came to me, and I returned to stand next to his body. In desperation, I held out my arm, closed my eyes, and prayed, "O Ba'al, Conqueror of Death and Giver of Life, accept this sacrifice." Then I dragged the blade across my flesh. Life-giving blood seeped from my arm and dripped upon the bloodless wounds on my husband's chest, directly over his heart. I held my breath. Nothing happened.

I cried out and attempted again, repeating my prayer and cutting my flesh once more, this time slicing deeper. The blood spilled out upon his chest, and again I waited. When no sign of life came to my husband, I wailed in agony and threw myself over his corpse. "Akhab, please, come back to me!"

His body remained cold and stiff. No arms wrapped around to comfort me. Suddenly, my anger flared, and I began beating my fists upon his chest as blood that had dripped from the cuts on my arm spattered. "I hate you! I hate you, Akhab! Why did you not listen to me? You promised! You promised you would never leave me!" Then, my anger spent, I clung to him and wept. "Why did you leave me?"

I began to grow faint and sank to the floor. I had never felt as alone as I did in that moment. I looked up at the statue of Ba'al, and yelled, "I've done all you asked! Why have you forsaken me?" I held myself and sank once again over my knees, weeping. My lips were dry, as I whispered through my tears, "Why have you forsaken me...?"

"Ama?" Atalaya's voice echoed down the narrow passageway. She soon found me crumpled on the floor, covered in fresh blood from the cuts on my arm. "Ama! What have you done to yourself?"

She pulled off her mantle and wiped the blood from my face and neck, and when she found the wounds on my arm, gasped, and

429

pressed the cloth against them to stop the bleeding. Inconsolable, I tried to push her away. "No, let me bleed to death! Let me go to him!"

"Ama!" she pleaded, fighting to keep the mantle pressed against my wounded arm.

"He promised he would never leave!"

She grabbed my shoulders and shook me. "Ama!"

"I promised I would follow him anywhere! I must go to him!"

"Ama, stop!"

This time, she shook me violently. I fell still and silent.

Again, she pressed the cloth against my wounds. When I did not pull away, she placed her other hand upon my shoulder, and admonished, "You must be strong! You must go on to live. It is what Abbu would have wanted."

"He needs me," I whined pitifully, at last defeated.

"Abbu is dead, Ama," she said firmly. "He does not need you. Zyah needs you. I need you. And your other children, and your grandchildren." Then she placed my hand upon her abdomen, and continued, "We *all* need you to be strong."

I looked at her in wonder, while a tear slipped down her cheek. "Yes, Ama. It was confirmed just this morning, by the midwives..."

My ears were ringing, and I could not hear all that she said over the piercing noise. My vision began to fade somewhat. Little bursts of light, a field of stars, appeared and then disappeared, overlaid upon the tomb. Feeling myself growing weak, I began to sink forward. My head was pounding.

Perhaps thinking it was my sorrow that began to consume me again, Atalaya lifted me and held me firmly by the chin, reminding me, "You were the wife of a king. The daughter of a king. Now, you are the mother of a king, and he needs you. He needs you now more than ever, and you cannot abandon him!" She shook me again, and said, "I will not allow it! Do you understand me, Ama? I will not allow you to abandon us!"

"At'la," I tried to say her name. I was trying to ask for help and tell her what was happening to me, but I could not quite speak. It was like being drunk, only far worse than I had ever been. I fell into my daughter's arms, and she realized then that something was terribly wrong. She held me in her arms and called for help. The eunuchs and priests and a few others, including Zyah, came rushing

430

to us from the narrow passage. My consciousness came in waves, one moment almost gone and the next alert.

"She has cut herself," I heard Atalaya explain to the others when they arrived. "She has lost too much blood. She needs a healer, immediately."

Eliezar, who was now my chief eunuch, knelt beside us and took my daughter's mantle. "Forgive me, Princess." Then he tore the rich cloth and tied a strip of it tightly around my arm, above the elbow. It hurt, but the bleeding slowed and eventually stopped.

Then he said to me, "Forgive me, Gebirah," and scooped me off the floor to lift me in his immense arms. I could not find the words to thank him, but I laid my head upon his shoulder. Then, while the priests tended to the body of my husband, I was carried out of the tomb and into the palace, where the priestesses could tend to my injuries.

The cuts on my arm were stitched together, treated with balms to keep away infection, and tightly bandaged. I had lost so much blood that I fell very ill and had to stay in bed for days. Kora, Atalaya, and some of the other women took turns sitting with me, feeding me broth, and telling me stories about the children or the animals that roamed the palace grounds. One of the cats who frequently wandered around the palace catching vermin slipped into my chamber and had taken to lying on me and purring while I was indisposed. Atalaya suggested it was being used by the Ba'alim to comfort and look after me. Zubira, who came to me often, said it was Bastet who sent the cat. Whichever god had sent the cat did not matter – I appreciated its warming presence either way. Even after I recovered, I allowed the cat to stay with me, noticing that it often curled up on the cushions beside me where Akhab used to lay.

It would be some time before I recovered, however, because the worst of the two wounds became badly infected. When our own healers were unable to keep the infection away, Tamar suggested Zyah summon a priest of Ba'al Zebul, the god of Ekron, whose priests were highly trained in the healing arts. He came immediately to Shomron to tend to me and appeal to his god on my behalf. Under his guidance, my priestesses and eunuchs tended to my wounds, frequently changing the bandage and applying fresh ointments. They spent hours chanting and praying over me with incense when I became consumed with fever. And every day, Zyah made sacrifices at the temple for the restoration of my strength.

Once I was able to get out of bed, my arm had to be wrapped in a sling to stay elevated until the wounds closed enough for the sutures to be removed and the swelling stopped. I was told that I was blessed, for the Ba'alim had protected me from causing any permanent damage: had I cut any deeper, I might have severed the tendons and lost the use of my left hand. When the wounds had fully healed, two thin white lines, with parallel dots running alongside them, were all that remained. While the rest of my skin tanned in the summer sun, the scars stayed as white as a paschal lamb. They served as reminders of all I had lost.

After the funeral, once the initial period of mourning was past and I was well enough to return to my duties, Yehoshapat and his entourage departed for Yerushalayim. Although I would miss my daughter and grandson, and appreciated the help Yehoshapat provided to my son while I was indisposed, I was relieved when he and the others left. I could not bear the whispers and pity, all of which put me in a foul mood. It was an unnecessary distraction when there was so much work to be done.

Atalaya would have stayed with me longer, but in her condition, it was necessary for her to return to Yerushalayim while she was still able to travel. She was concerned for me, but I insisted that she not worry. The return to a steady routine, the daily activities of managing the kingdom and household and serving the Ba'alim would provide more relief than moaning about my sorrows ever could. The pain of Akhab's loss would never heal completely, of course, but I supposed it would fade and grow easier to manage with time. I could still feel him with me, especially in those quiet moments when I was at prayer or tending to the needs of our children.

My children and my newest grandson, Zyah's son who was named after Akhab, kept me anchored to this world. Of all my children, Yoram was most grievously affected by his father's death, for he did not have the same sense of connection with the spirit world that I and my two elder children shared. Although his body was gone, we could still feel Akhab with us. That sense of his ever-loving

432

presence helped us recover more quickly. Of course, each of our children noticed his absence and grieved in their own way, but Yoram had practically worshipped Akhab and had been closest to him of all our children. Comforting their sorrows, and the sorrows of Akhab's other women and children, helped me to stop dwelling on my own.

Many of the other wives and concubines left the confines of the women's quarters after Akhab's death; those whose children were married and had households and families of their own took them into their care. Only those who were still with child by the king, of which there were three, or whose children were still too young to take spouses remained at court, for until they were wed, the children of Akhab were under my care and the protection of their half-brother, now known as Melekh Akhazyah.

Zyah had been training to become king since his thirteenth year, when Akhab officially declared him his successor. Even with four years of practice, however, he still depended upon me a great deal to help him manage the kingdom and deal with the stubbornness of his ministers. As was common with a change in leadership, the older and more experienced ministers often tried to push their way with the new king. My experience and wisdom were critical for ensuring they did not get away with their attempts to mislead or tyrannize the king. I handled them with the same finesse and occasional firmness I had developed over many years of working alongside my husband. My son was grateful and trusted my advice above that of his ministers, for he had been taught well not to trust men who made a living by flattery and deception, especially if they were kin.

A few of the ministers were removed upon Zyah's rise to the throne: Abram, the Minister of War, was the first to be replaced. Some were replaced by my advice, but Zyah himself replaced those who had been most in favor of Akhab's campaign to take Ramot from the King of Aram, who pressured Akhab to make poor decisions. Zyah accepted my advice on their replacements, and I chose men based on merit above all other considerations.

Several of Akhab's elder sons had expected to be given these roles, but I overlooked any whom I knew to be deficient in knowledge and experience, or those who had shown any signs of envy or disloyalty to their father or myself and my children. Most of Akhab's eldest sons had been granted estates, or positions of leadership in the military, or lordship over the other cities in the kingdom when their father was still king, so they wanted for nothing even without being granted an official position at Zyah's court.

In the end, only two of Akhab's sons were appointed as their half-brother's ministers: Natan, son of Tamar, became our Minister of Commerce; and Ishaq, son of Fang-Hua, became our new Minister of War. Pleased with her son's appointment, Tamar remained at court to continue in her role as the head of the women's household and to be close to her only surviving son. Since Fang-Hua had died when Ishaq was only ten, at the time the fever took Hannah from us, I had tried to be a mother to him. He had taken to calling me Ama, but as he grew into an adolescent his feelings developed into something different.

I brushed it off – boyhood infatuations were common among adolescents of a certain age. Akhab, who found it amusing, took his son to the Ba'alim temple to receive the blessing of Ashtarti and then introduced him to courtesans in order to steer his affections elsewhere. Ishaq had been closer to his father than most of his sons, apart from my own. He was Akhab's first legitimate son and, therefore, had the greatest claim to the throne after my own sons; yet he was loyal to them, especially Zyah, who was only four years his junior. Both men had honored Akhab during his lifetime, loved me as a second mother, and, most important, were devoted to the Ba'alim.

Any man who was not devoted to the Ba'alim would not be considered, for I continued to harbor a resentment against the followers of Yahowah for all the trouble they had caused me and my husband throughout his reign. Those with sympathy for the zealots especially were overlooked, for I could not risk disloyalty of any kind from those closest to the king. Once I had ruled out the rest of Akhab's sons for vacant positions, I chose from among the nobles of the realm and his other kin.

Apart from the ministers, the rest of the court and household remained the same. Aharon maintained his position as Lord Steward: the only Yahwist allowed to remain in a lofty position at my son's court, due more to his marriage to Kora than anything else. I had never quite trusted him fully after discovering his disobedience regarding the prophet Eliyah, but he went out of his way to repent for his transgression and had proven his sincerity. Besides, no one else could sufficiently perform his duties. For all his faults, he was the best suited for his position, knowing everything about the way the kingdom functioned at all levels, from the highest to the lowest.

It was Aharon, in fact, who reminded me of the covenant that Akhab had made with the King of Hamat, concerning the betrothal of his two daughters to Zyah. The Lord Steward urged me to send a message to Irhulani, asking if he would still honor this covenant with the widow of Akhab instead. Irhulani sent the messenger back to us with a new promise: "Blessed Gebirah, beloved of Akhab the great warrior king to whom I owe all that I possess: I will honor my covenant and send my daughters to be wed to the new King of Yisrael as soon as you are ready to receive them into your house."

This was better than I had expected. I sent word back to him, saying, "We are honored to receive them when we return to Shomron for the Feast of Ashtarti."

So it came to pass that when we returned from Megiddu in late spring, the two princesses of Hamat – Be'ulah, who was then in her thirteenth year; and Shalima, who was ten – came with their uncle and a great entourage to Shomron. The two princesses were received with much fanfare, brought about by the joyfulness of having something to celebrate after so much sorrow in the Kingdom of Yisrael.

Be'ulah and Shalima were presented to Zyah at court, who stiffly accepted them, and then they were taken to be housed in the women's quarters. My son was not pleased about accepting them, and a week passed before I finally went to speak with him about his noticeable neglect. He was at the stables, tending to one of his horses, when he saw me approaching. He made no attempt to hide his annoyance with me.

"What do you want, Ama?"

"Is that how you greet your mother?"

He turned away and said nothing.

"I have come to speak to you about your wives. You must go to them in the women's quarters. You cannot ignore their presence here."

"I do not want to lie with little girls," he growled.

"You do not have to lie with them," I said, annoyed that he would even think that was what I was suggesting. "I would not allow it, even if you wanted to. They are too young to be known by a man."

"Then why must I go to them?"

435

"Speak with them. Learn about them. Find what there is to like about them."

"What if there is nothing to like about them?"

I slapped the back of his head. "Do not be such an Elihu," I said, in reference to his youthful arrogance. "There is always something to like about anyone."

"Except for Elihu," he retorted.

Attempting to hide my amusement at his bad joke, I sighed heavily and rolled my eyes. "Even Elihu had good qualities, I am certain."

He snickered. "You've met Elihu? I did not think you were that old, Ama."

Again, I slapped the back of his head. "Enough of your foolishness. Can you be serious when I am speaking to you?"

"Fine," he sighed. "Ama, I'm sorry."

"Speak to your wives. Listen to what they have to say. You need to give them a chance, so that when they are mature enough for you to consummate your marriage with them, it will be pleasant for them as well as you."

"And what of Naveen?"

"What of Naveen?" I asked with a shrug. "She is your concubine, not your wife."

"She is the mother of my child."

"And he is a wonderful child – I love him dearly – but he can never be king. Do not forget that." I paused and watched some of the horses frolicking with each other. I missed Akhab most when at the stables.

After a moment, I turned back to my son. "I do not mean to be hard on you. There is no hurry – you are only eighteen and in good health, praise the Ba'alim. But you will need to lie with them eventually, and it will be easier for you and them if you build a rapport first. That is all I am asking."

"Fine. I'll go to them tomorrow after dismissing court for the day."

I nodded my approval, and then left him to his horses.

Atalaya wrote frequently from Yerushalayim, asking after me and her siblings, sharing little stories about Akhaz, and providing updates on the progress of her pregnancy. When the time came for her to enter confinement, she begged me to come to Yerushalayim to attend the birth.

She wrote: "I know you will say that you cannot make such a journey while you are in mourning, and that Zyah needs you to be there for him, but I also need you. I insist you come. It will take your mind off Abbu's death, to see your grandson who grows stronger each day, and to give Zyah a chance to manage the kingdom without you. He depends too much upon you. You need to take a break from all these things that weigh so heavily upon your shoulders. Besides, Abbu would not want you to prolong your grieving. He would want you to live your life in memory of him, not to stop living because he is gone."

"Of course, she is right," I said to myself, sitting back after reading the letter.

I thought about Zyah and wondered if he would be able to manage the kingdom without me for a few weeks. Surely, enough time had passed, and his new court was firmly established with loyal and capable men. So, I sent a message, summoning him to my quarters to discuss the matter. He came in from the field, where he had been practicing with his chariot. Ishaq was with him, for apart from being his half-brother, Fang-Hua's son was his closest friend and the driver of his chariot.

When the two young men appeared, I was seated in a chair on my terrace, watching the children play and the peafowl roam about in the garden below. A terrible storm had blown through the kingdom, which lasted two days even after it made landfall. Now that the torrent had passed, we were all eager to be out in the sun. I had taken my veil down, but when my son and his half-brother appeared, I lifted it to cover my hair and shoulders as they stopped and knelt before me.

First Zyah took my hand and pressed it to his lips, bowing his head with his greeting. Ishaq did the same, taking my other hand and pressing it to his lips; only instead of 'Ama', he addressed me as 'Ba'alah', which surprised me because we were not in a formal situation. Brushing it off, I said, "My sons, thank you for coming to me."

437

Zyah, still kneeling and holding my hand, said, "Ama, you sent for me. Is everything all right?"

"Yes, I am well, Zyah."

Now, he released my hand and rose, and Ishaq did the same. Together, they waited for me to gather my thoughts. I smiled at Ishaq when I saw him watching me with a curious gaze. He had his mother's eyes but Akhab's face – an appealing combination, especially now that he had grown into a fine young man.

Clearing my throat, I looked away and lifted the papyrus off the table beside me, saying, "I had a letter from your sister in Yerushalayim." I handed it to him, and explained, "She wants me to come for the birth of her second child. Can you manage the kingdom without me?"

"For how long?" he asked quickly, looking at me instead of the letter. He handed it back to me without bothering to read it.

"A month or two, I should think," I answered, setting it on the table again. "More, if she is not delivered soon enough, or if she has a daughter instead of a son – you know how Hosha's people are. I would like to stay with her until after she is cleansed, and to help her with the new baby for as long as she needs me there. You understand, of course?"

"Of course, Ama."

"Are you prepared to be on your own for so long?"

He looked at Ishaq and considered. "Well, I have Aharon and my ministers..." He grinned suddenly. "I think I can manage with them."

"Do not burn down the kingdom while I am away," I said with the hint of a smile.

He bent to kiss me on the cheek. "That's the first I've seen you smile in weeks. I like to think I brought it out of you."

"You have always managed to make me smile when no one else could. You are a good son to your old Ama."

He chuckled. "You are not old, Ama. Tell her she's not old, Ishaq."

"You are not old," Ishaq answered, sincerely.

"You are only thirty-six," Zyah insisted.

"Speak to me again when you are thirty-six, and tell me you do not feel old," I said with a laugh.

438

"If I may," said Ishaq, "you may feel old, Ba'alah, but you certainly do not look it."

I met his gaze from the side and, in spite of myself, my lips parted into a smile. Then I said, "I have two grandchildren and a third on the way."

Zyah suddenly cleared his throat. "Actually..."

I raised my brows and noticed the two of them exchanging a knowing glance.

Then Zyah explained, "Naveen is with child again."

"One of the women of my household is with child, and how is it you are the first to know?"

"She told me herself, just this morning. She thought, as the father, I should be the first to know. She has not told anyone else yet – not even Tamar."

"Of course, she has not told Tamar, or I would have been told."

"If she had told Tamar," Ishaq laughed, "the entire kingdom would have been told."

I chuckled and shook my head. "You are too hard on her, both of you."

"Come, Ama," said Zyah. "You know it is true. She is a good woman, but a terrible gossip."

"I know. Why do you think I appointed her to manage the women's household? Nothing happens there that I do not hear about." I paused to take a drink. Then I said, "So, do I have leave to go to Yerushalayim?"

"Yes, Ama. We will manage."

"Good, then I will send word to your sister that I shall arrive within the following week. Now, return to your chariot races and whatever else you boys are up to."

They knelt again, and each took a hand again to press to his lips. Before he rose to follow the king, Ishaq looked up and boldly held my gaze with hunger. Taken aback, I held my breath and looked away. I did not look up again until their backs were turned to me as they left. Then I watched the two of them walking away together, talking and laughing, and exhaled slowly as my gaze followed Ishaq until he had disappeared.

439

19

Good King Yehoshapat

In the days leading up to my journey to Yerushalayim, news came that a fleet of ships, intended to sail to Opir to acquire more gold for Yehoshapat's kingdom, had been wrecked in a storm that came off the sea before they left the harbor. We had sent some of our stewards to acquire more peafowl for my flocks. It was my idea to send our men with Hosha's, and Zyah had readily agreed to it, for he was eager to acquire more gold for our kingdom, as well. Hearing of the fleet's destruction was a great disappointment, but we knew Yehoshapat would try again once his ships were rebuilt. However, it was soon said that the ships were wrecked because Yahowah disapproved of Hosha's alliance with us.

"Will you ask him to allow us to send our stewards again?" Zyah pestered me. Settling into my litter the morning of my departure, I did not reply. He persisted, "Ama. Will you ask him? Convince him that it was not Yahowah who caused the storms to come."

"I will try, Zyah," I answered with a heavy sigh, "but you know how stubborn Hosha can be, especially where talk of his god is concerned. If he has heard the same rumors, he will not be moved by anything I say."

"But you will try?"

"Yes, I will try."

"Is there...anything more you can do to convince him to be on our side?"

I squinted my eyes at him. "What are you implying, my son?"

He became sheepish then and answered, "I am not implying anything. Not exactly. Only, I know the King of Yehudah has...admired you for quite some time."

I scoffed. "Do not even suggest such a thing! I cannot believe you would expect me, your own mother, to be used in such a manner.

What kind of son have I raised? Your father would be disgusted by this, as am I."

"Ama, I did not mean it that way!" he insisted. "I meant only that...if something should arise naturally between you and he, it could be to our benefit."

"There is *nothing* between me and the King of Yehudah," I said vehemently. "Neither will there ever be. He is a lecherous old man, and a drunkard, and I can barely tolerate to be in his presence. He may be a king, but he is less than a dog to me."

With that, I loosened the curtains and drew them closed. I heard my son's heavy sigh as I tapped the frame of my litter with a rod to give the sign that I was ready to depart. Then the litter was lifted onto the shoulders of eunuchs, a shout went out, horns were blown, and my entourage began its slow procession toward Yerushalayim.

Given the size of my entourage, the rough terrain, and the need to stop along the way for the men and the beasts to rest, it would take a few days to travel from Yezreel to the capital of Yehudah. At the end of the first day, we would stop at Shomron to spend a night at the palace. There, I would offer a sacrifice at the temple for protection on our journey before moving on. The rest of the journey would require us to make camp for at least one night if we could not reach one of the cities along the way before sunset. Daylight was shorter that time of year, making the journey even longer.

When we finally arrived in Yerushalayim we were no worse for the wear, but there was less fanfare than I was accustomed to receiving. The streets were crowded, like always, but my entourage was forced to move slower than usual, since the people were not keen to move aside to let us pass. The energy in the air seemed ripe for unrest. I was certainly used to the scorn and poor manners of Yahwist zealots, who were worse in Yehudah than in Yisrael, but this time it was far more pronounced than it had been in previous years. The King of Yehudah, having anticipated the poor reception I would receive, had sent an armed escort along with his stewards to meet us on the road as we entered his kingdom.

At first, it seemed an unnecessary precaution to me until, as we approached the city gates, the need became apparent. I had hardly expected this to be the most treacherous part of my journey, but as they led us through the commercial district of the city, not only did people hiss and spit and curse me along the way, now they threw rotting vegetables and even stones at my litter.

As the crowds grew larger and more unrestful the closer we came to the palace and the Temple of Shelomoh, the armed eunuchs, my own and the King of Yehudah's alike had to raise their shields. Any projectiles that missed the shields either struck the frame of the litter or bounced off the curtains, which I'd kept drawn. The sound of rocks pelting against wood and iron, always with the angry cries from the crowd, made it feel as if we were suddenly in the midst of a battle. For the first time I was truly frightened of these people.

The eunuchs continued to surround and protect me as we inched forward through the angry masses. They were also shouting at the people, "Get back! Move aside! By order of the King!" and had to strike out against those who refused to move away as we approached.

Wishing Akhab was there to protect me, I felt alone and afraid in a way I had never felt before. Almost in tears, I clutched one of the cushions and flattened myself against the back wall of the litter with my knees up, listening to shouts and accusations hurled all around me: "Whore of Ba'al! Go away! Leave the city of God! May Yahowah strike you down! Death to the idolatress! May the dogs eat your flesh!" I could feel their hatred and knew that some would kill me if they had the chance.

When we made it safely to the palace and the heavy gates were closed to the people of the city, I said a prayer of thanks to the Ba'alim for preserving me. Still shaken when I emerged from the litter, I was quickly escorted to meet Hosha and Aya, as well as Yehoram and Akhaz. Atalaya would be waiting to greet me in her quarters, for she had a difficult pregnancy and was taking all the midwives' precautions seriously. I was glad she was not there to see me immediately after the ordeal.

I knelt at Hosha's feet when I met him, kissed his hand, and thanked him for having had the foresight to send the armed escort. He bade me to rise, and said, "It was my ministers who suggested it, for they had heard talk of a group of zealots that had planned to attack and kill you when you entered my city. I would not let that happen to the widow of my good friend, Akhab. It is not right for a queen to be received in such a way."

Aya stepped forward to embrace me, and said, "I am glad you made it safely to us, Yezeba'al. I was not aware of this danger to you, for my husband did not bother to tell me."

"I had no intention of worrying you, wife," he replied. "I had it under control."

"*Amami*, I missed you!" my grandson shouted, tired of being ignored.

He came to me and wrapped his arms around my legs, and I got down on my knees to embrace and kiss him. I hugged him tightly and began to cry. Then I held him out and said, "Akhaz, let me have a look at you. My, how you've grown these past months!"

He wiped a kohl-black tear from my cheek, and asked, "*Amami*, why are you crying?"

"I am just so happy to see you, my dear boy." Then I kissed him once again on the cheek before rising to greet my son-in-law.

"I am glad you made it safely to us, *Akhatamu* Yezeba'al." An attentive and caring husband to my daughter, Yehoram continued, "Atalaya does not know you were in danger…"

"And I will not say a word to her about it," I assured him. Then Kora came to me with water and a washcloth to wipe the tears from my cheek before we went any further. I assured her I was all right, and when we were alone in my quarters later, I embraced her and expressed my gratitude that she had not been hurt by the terrors we faced in the city. For now, though, we shared only a discreet nod before I was ushered into the palace on the king's right arm.

While Kora and my servants took my things to the guest chambers, the King of Yehudah escorted me to Atalaya's quarters, where she was sitting up in bed and waiting eagerly to see me. She held out her arms and I went straight to her for a long-awaited embrace. Then I placed my hands on her swollen abdomen and gasped. "Look at you – I would not be surprised if you were carrying twins! Would that not be exciting?"

"I hope I am not," she said, revealing the exhaustion in her voice now as she laid back against the cushions. "I am not sure I could handle such a blessing."

"Perhaps we shall soon find out," I suggested.

"Sooner than anticipated," she agreed. "You made it just in time, Ama. The pains have begun, and the midwives believe I will be delivered of this child by this time tomorrow."

The midwives were close in their estimation – I hardly had time to settle in before being summoned to the birthing chamber where my daughter had been taken. True labor began that evening. By morning, Atalaya had delivered a pair of healthy twin daughters, who were identical. They would be named Yezeba'al and Yahosheba. I was pleased.

Atalaya was grateful to have nurses to tend to them. Once she recovered from the delivery, however, she was enchanted by their shared features. She looked on from the bed, where she had eagerly returned as soon as the delivery was over, while the two proud grandmothers held the twins together to compare.

Atalaya said, "I wonder if they are truly identical, or if they will have differences that become more apparent as they grow." She paused to admire them, and then said, "Ama, wasn't your mother also a twin?"

"Yes, she was," I answered. "She and her sister were also identical, but they were as different in character as they were similar in looks, from what I understand."

"Did she get along with her sister?"

"Yes, for the most part. I only met my aunt once when she came with her husband, the King of Elam, to make an alliance with my father at Zour. She and my mother were pleased to see one another, but as I recall my mother was more pleased when her sister returned to Elam, for they were often in disagreement about many things." I looked down at my newborn granddaughters, and said, "Hopefully that will not be the case with these two."

Atalaya laid back and closed her eyes. "I hope they will be close, for I do not want to do this again."

"What do you mean?"

"I mean, I do not want to have any more children," she replied heavily. "I do not know how you could do this so many times."

"Then you will have to encourage your husband to spend more time with his other wives," I said, doubtfully.

"I could do it easily," said Atalaya. "While I have enjoyed his affection, I may enjoy the company of women in his place. It does not matter so much to me whether it be a man or a woman in my bed."

"Then I see you take after your grandmother in that way. It is just as well, if that is your wish," I said, handing my granddaughter off to her mother.

The baby started fussing, and Atalaya quickly offered her back to me. "Take her – she seems happiest with you!"

I caressed her little cheek with my finger. She turned her head and began puckering her lips in an attempt to latch onto it. Then I said, "She is hungry. Will you feed her?"

"No," said Atalaya with a grimace. "That is what nurses are for." Then she beckoned for one of the nurses to come, and I handed my granddaughter off to the nurse with a sigh.

"You should feed them yourself, at least part of the time. It will help your body return to normal. It is also good for the bond between mother and child."

"I do not like it," she frowned. "It hurt the last time, and Yehoram does not like it when I am dripping with milk."

"Perhaps you should feed them then," I suggested. "It will keep him away from you, and he will seek the company of his other wives. Is that not what you want?"

"Yes, but I do not like to be dripping with milk, either."

I sighed and looked down at my other granddaughter, who was still in Aya's arms. "I miss nursing my children. I thought it was a wonderful experience."

"You are welcome to try nursing mine," Atalaya remarked dryly.

"I do not have any milk, or I would happily do it," I quipped, laughing. "Akhab was never bothered by it. He quite enjoyed it himself."

Atalaya made a sound of disgust. "Ama! I do not wish to hear these things about you and Abbu! Honestly, I do not understand the two of you." Then her countenance fell. "I miss him, though. I wish he could be here with you."

"So do I, Atalaya," I answered, as my heart twisted in my chest. My stomach began to ache. "So do I."

After handing the other newborn off to another nurse, Aya placed a hand upon my shoulder and said, "He is still here with us, Yezeba'al. I have felt him around us here. So has Atalaya."

I nodded and attempted to smile. "Yes, I feel him with me always, and I am certain he comes to you, as well. In some ways, he can be with all of us now more than he could before, I suppose."

Aya shook her head. "I fear that if he is here with us, he is not at rest in Sheol awaiting the resurrection, as he should be. Hosha thinks his spirit is restless because he displeased Yahowah."

"Hosha would believe such a thing," I said bitterly. "Akhab's spirit is not any more restless in death than he was in life. You know your brother, Aya: he could never be satisfied sitting around and waiting for something to happen. Besides, he promised he would never leave me. That is why he is still here. He wants to look after all of us, as best as he can from where he is now."

She nodded. "I think you are right, Yezeba'al. Thank you for reminding me of that." Then she chuckled. "Akhab always was on the move. He never could sit still for very long, or stay occupied in one activity, before moving onto the next. That is why it was impressive, his devotion to you."

"Apparently, I used sorcery to keep him that way," I said ironically.

Atalaya sighed, "If you used sorcery on Abbu, Ama, he would have listened to you instead of going off on a fool's errand to his death."

"I saw the way he loved you from the very beginning," Aya countered gently. "You never had to do a thing. He worshipped you. If only his love for you had been enough to keep him in one place, he would still be here with us."

I shook my head and turned away to hide tears that were stabbing at my eyes now. "Please, let us not speak of this. I want to enjoy this glorious occasion – the birth of our beautiful granddaughters – not think of the sadness we have all endured these past months."

The two women agreed, and so we talked of other things while the newborns nursed. When Atalaya became tired, we left her to rest. Aya took me to see Akhaz, who was at play with his half-siblings in the women's garden. It was a beautiful day. As I watched the people and animals, I did indeed feel as though Akhab was there with me, and it brought me peace.

On my second night in Yerushalayim, the King of Yehudah held a feast in my honor. When he opened the feast, he stood at the head of the table, petting his dogs as they sniffed and drooled at the food laid

446

out before us. I was seated to his right, Aya to his left, and Yehoram on the other side of her. When one of his dogs came too near me, I swatted it away and mumbled curses against it in my father's tongue. The good king, as usual, was unbothered by their presence. He rubbed their fur and praised them even as they stole from his plate.

After washing his hands, Hosha raised his cup to praise his god and to bless us all in his name. Then he thanked me for coming to his kingdom as his honored guest. I nodded graciously, aware that not everyone present was a friend to me, but that they would not offend their host with open insults. By this time, he had already imbibed too much un-watered wine, having begun drinking well before the feast. Now, as he continued his blubbering speech, he started reminiscing about one of the last private conversations he had with my husband, on the day they departed for the campaign that had ended Akhab's life.

"Before we left the fortress at Yezreel, while standing in our chariots, I leaned over to him and asked the King of Yisrael: which of his women did he make love to on his last night before going to war?"

Hearing this and seeing how those gathered at the feast all looked at me, I held my breath. I was mortified. Nevertheless, I steeled myself, while he seemed amused by his own reminiscences. "Of course, he did not answer, but I saw...I saw the way he looked over at his Melkah," and he raised his cup to me, "and I knew it was she – Yezeba'al, who sits here with us tonight – that he had spent his last night with. The last woman he ever knew before his death on the battlefield."

Heat spread across my face, and so I looked down to hide my embarrassment, sadness, and anger, while the good king continued: "And so, I said to Akhab, 'She must be an amazing woman to have such a hold over you after all these years.' And he admitted she was indeed an amazing woman, that he had never loved another as he loved her. Being myself a man who loves the company of women, I could not understand how a man could be satisfied with only one woman, but he would not discuss the secrets of his passion for her, and I was displeased at his secrecy surrounding this woman. I must admit, I have never met a man who would keep such secrets to himself, and so I cannot help but think she must truly be an amazing woman, the Gebirah who sits before us this night. To you, beautiful Yezeba'al. Thank you for joining us in Yerushalayim this night."

447

He raised his cup to me, and I felt obliged to raise my cup in response, despite my sheer displeasure at his drunken speech. However, once his household and guests became enrapt in their own conversations, I decided to use this opportunity to broach the subject of our joint expedition to Opir. I began by saying, "Thank you, Hosha, for that...remarkable speech."

"I speak only from the heart, dear Yezeba'al," he said, with a hand at his breast.

"I wonder, my dear friend, if you would allow me to discuss with you the matter of our previous agreement?"

"Which agreement is that?" he asked, meeting my gaze over the rim of his cup.

"The king, my son, has charged me with speaking to you on the matter of Opir. He is hoping, of course, that you will still allow his servants to join yours when the time comes for them to take up their journey, as originally planned."

"Yes," he said, rubbing his bottom lip with meaty fingers. His gaze became shifty now, and he cleared his throat as he readjusted the way he was seated on his cushion.

"You are still planning for your men to take up the expedition, are you not?"

"Well, yes," he answered with a nod. He took another hearty sip of his drink. Then he cleared his throat again, and said, "I...plan to have my ships rebuilt, of course. But...I think it is best if my servants go on their own for this expedition. You understand, I hope, that with the talk of their destruction in the storm being a judgment from Yahowah that I...cannot take such a risk."

Anger immediately began to rise. "Then you will not uphold our original agreement?"

"Well, I...will have to take time to think on it. Of course, I would like to keep my word, but...there is this prophet – I believe you know of him. He is called Eliyah the Tishbite, very well respected among the followers of Yahowah..."

"Eliyah the Tishbite?" A tense smile was frozen on my face, while I gripped my cup so tightly that my hand began to ache. Realizing this, I slowly loosened my grip and set the cup down. Clearing my throat, I rested my hands in my lap, assuming an air of calm. "Yes, I know of him. A zealot. He is their leader. Do you know

448

of his whereabouts? I have some…unfinished business with this Tishbite."

"He lives here, in Yehudah, although he moves around and can be difficult to find," answered Hosha. Then he gave me a stern look. "Zealot or not, I will let no harm come to him while he is here in my kingdom, you understand."

"Of course, Hosha. Just as you extend your protection to me while I am here, so I would expect you to do the same for one as…renowned as the Tishbite."

"Well, good," he said with a nod. Then again, "Good. Yes."

"So, what does the Tishbite have to say about our alliance? As he has so many opinions on things which he knows nothing about."

The king cleared his throat. "Well, he says of course that Yahowah disapproves of our alliance…as you serve other gods in your kingdom…"

"And you believe this is true? That a storm that wrecked your ships was a judgment against our alliance?"

"Well…it does seem rather self-evident."

"I see," I answered, taking a deep breath and letting it out slowly.

"That of course is not to say that you will lose Yehudah as an ally, Yezeba'al – I will not turn against Yisrael or the son of Akhab, who was as a brother to me, or his widow who is also dear to me as the mother of my lovely daughter-in-law."

"But you will not allow us to send our stewards with your own on the ships to Opir."

"Well…I did not say I will not allow it, exactly."

"Then what *did* you say, exactly? You are talking in riddles, Hosha. I do not care for riddles. I find them irritating and tasteless."

"Husband," Aya said firmly to him now, "just say whatever it is you are trying to say."

"What I mean is," stammered Hosha, "that I am not completely closed to the idea of your stewards joining mine but that it may take a…bit of convincing…to reassure me that the expedition will go smoothly."

I forced a smile. "And what, pray tell, might we do to…convince you."

"We can discuss the terms of the agreement another time," he said affably, holding my gaze and lifting his cup to me. I lifted my cup

449

in return but, while he drank, I did not for I suspected what he was alluding to. I did not wish to give him the impression that I wanted any part of it. In truth, I was furious that he and my son were both thinking the same thing. Akhab would never have tolerated such disrespect toward me.

Of course, it was only natural that these men would think in this way. After all, what were we women to them but pawns in the games they played? Akhab himself had behaved in such a way toward other women, but with me he was different. He had been the only man who had not treated me as if I was inferior to him. Even my own father, who believed I was the incarnation of the very goddess he worshipped and devoted his life to, had used me as a bargaining tool in the game of war and peace. Realizing that my own son viewed me in this light, even after his father had shown him a different way, reminded me what it was for a woman to live in a man's world. And it was a cold realization as I sat there at Yehoshapat's table, feeling alone and powerless for the first time since leaving my father's kingdom to become the Queen of Yisrael.

Two weeks after the birth of her daughters, I accompanied Atalaya to the palace miqwah for the ritual cleansing after childbirth. Had she a son, she would only have to wait a week to be cleansed, but because she bore daughters, the time of uncleanliness was doubled. I was not quiet about my disdain for this ridiculous belief, so opposed to that with which I was raised. In my father's kingdom, women were at least thought to be the equals of men – even if it was not the practice.

While my father's people believed that blood, as the source of all life, had power and was not something to be feared, my husband's people – and even more, the people of Yehudah – believed it to be a source of evil and, therefore, unclean. While my daughter believed as I did, she was willing to respect the beliefs of her husband's people, and I respected her for that even if I did not agree. At least, after the ritual cleansing, she was allowed to return to court with the rest of us. That night, the King of Yehudah held another feast, this time in her honor and for the celebration of the two daughters she had given his son.

450

I partook of the spiced wine sweetened with honey and enjoyed the company of the Queen, along with some of the ministers' and nobles' wives who had been permitted by their husbands to attend the feast in support of my daughter. Aya was always a gracious hostess and ensured that my cup never emptied, and Hosha made sure there was plenty of qaneh-bosem for all his guests.

Normally, I limited my intake of feast wine and qaneh-bosem, but with the strain of being at Hosha's court and having to endure his frequent intimations, I allowed myself to indulge in the many offerings at the feast that night. As long as I remained surrounded by the women, I felt safe enough to indulge. It was foolish, though, and that night I suffered a dangerous lapse in judgment.

While we were talking and laughing together about, I do not remember what, Hosha appeared before us in a playful manner. "My apologies, ladies – I am sure you are discussing important matters, but I have not yet had much time to speak with the mother of my son's wife and we still have that issue with the expedition to Opir to discuss. I wonder, Yezeba'al, if you would be so kind as to grace me with a walk in my garden?"

The smell of liquor and qaneh-bosem was strong on him, but I supposed it was also strong on me, so I smiled, extended my hand, and offered a gracious nod. "Thank you, Hosha. It would be my pleasure." I turned to the Queen and other ladies to excuse myself.

Aya nodded, and I walked with the King toward the wide-open archway that led to the enclosed garden. Hosha was excited to show me the alterations he had made to his garden since the last time I visited Yerushalayim. Fruit-bearing trees, vines, and fragrant flowers, which had always been a feature, were now laid out along a stone walkway that led to a central pool fed by a natural spring. It was a lovely garden, if somewhat smaller than my own at Shomron and Megiddu, and Yehoshapat was quite proud of the improvements he had made.

I sensed, however, that it was not the garden itself he wanted to share with me. There was a distinct sense of privacy amid the darkness of a moonless night. Apart from his sentries posted along the walls and by the exits, and the chief of my eunuchs waiting by the door, there was no one else around. It felt eerie. All his guests and courtiers were inside, enjoying the festivities. I suddenly became keenly aware that I was alone with this man, a king, who was obviously drunk and had a long history as a womanizer. As we walked slowly through the garden's winding paths, moving farther from the palace with each step and slipping deeper into the darkness, he nearly stumbled into me several times – by accident or design?

His speech rambled with a faint slur, growing more fervent once we were in the center of the garden, far out of earshot of guards and courtiers alike. His hands continuously swirled and slithered in the air around me. Several times he nearly touched my arm, but I held myself stiff and formal, growing more tense with each passing moment.

"I must confess, Yezeba'al – and I need not tell you how aware I am that what I am about to say would not be well received by many within my kingdom – that, although you are an idolatress and a Canaanite," he chuckled, "I hold you in high esteem. Your...violent designs against the prophets of my god are well known and I do not condone them, just to be clear. But your faithfulness to my good friend, the late Melekh Akhab – may the Lord God of Yehudah give him rest – is to be commended. He spoke highly of you, and often, when he was in my presence. And despite the reports of your...religious activities...when it came to your position as the wife of the king and your devotion to him, my agents and emissaries could speak no ill of you."

I remained silent. It was hard to know what to say to his combined disparagement and praise. Still trying to determine his intentions, and now more uncertain than before, I felt even more vulnerable and wary of our surroundings. I scanned for any sign of danger, any hint of movement that could suggest an assassin lurking in the shadows and waiting for a cue, or for the right moment to strike. The king had promised to protect me while I was in his kingdom, but what if it had all been a ruse, meant to lull me into a false sense of security? How much had he been swayed by the zealots?

My chief eunuch still waited by the doors, keeping a watchful eye on my whereabouts; I had instructed him to wait for me as we left the palace. He would not move from his position unless he thought I was in danger, but he was too far away to reach me in time if something were to happen and, as we were partially obscured in darkness, I was not even sure how well he could see me from his vantage.

452

Seeing no sign of danger yet from within the shadows, I turned my attentions back to the king. I watched his hands and observed the ever-changing expressions on his face to determine whether there was malice or ill-intent. He had designs, to be sure, but his rambling did not seem intended to distract or endanger me. He was simply fighting a battle within himself: a battle he was quickly losing. I stood as silent and unresponsive as the idols and graven images he so disparaged even as he stupidly sought to win my affections through his awkward praise.

Now, he brushed his fingers against my mantle, which I had pulled around my arms and torso to shield myself from both the cool night air and his wandering eyes and hands. Normally, I enjoyed being admired and even desired by men and women alike, especially knowing they would never dare attempt anything unless encouraged and invited; now, perhaps because he was a king and I a widow without my husband's protection, his unwanted advances felt both dirty and vaguely threatening.

"Now that dear Akhab sleeps with his fathers, I would imagine you must struggle with the loneliness of your position, especially as you are not yet old, and you are still...comely. My own dear wives, many of them, cannot boast such a figure after motherhood has taken its toll on their bodies, yet you have had many children... How many did you bear for your husband?"

Although I sensed flattery, motherly pride overtook my sense of caution for a moment. "Eight born alive and strong – five sons and three daughters – although only six remain."

He raised his brows, his eyes yet again scanning my form. "That is impressive to have so many, and so few of them taken by illness or calamity. I had heard of your fruitfulness with your late husband. To have so many children from a single wife is...unusual."

"I have had more than all his others, it is true."

"How many did they give him?"

I gave it a moment of thought. "Two or three each, at most. One of his concubines had four, I believe. I do not keep track of these things; after all, there are so many. If you would like an exact count, I am sure one of the stewards could tell you."

He frowned and his eyes glazed over – he was clearly disinterested, much to my dismay, as I had hoped to move the conversation away from where I feared it was heading. Clearing his throat, he said, "You must have brought him much joy in your company." He swayed closer to me and lifted his hand to push my mantle away from my face. His fingers brushed against my cheek.

Startled, I stepped back, growing more tense and wishing I had not agreed to accompany him. "It is cold... I think it is growing late."

"Yes," he nodded cheerfully, "we should retire."

With a nod, I moved to step away, but suddenly he took hold of me, wrapping his arms around my waist and holding me so that I could not pull away. "Come to my bed. Let us work out an arrangement that will please us both."

In a panic, I was unable to speak and desperate to get away from him. I had never been in such a position before, so I did not know what to say or do. In the struggle to free myself, my veil fell open and hung from where it was pinned beneath my headdress, and my sleeve slipped down to expose my shoulder. Pushing himself against me, Hosha clawed at me and pressed his lips to the exposed flesh. His voice came as a low growl in my ear. "I want you, Yezeba'al. I have not felt like this in years. You have enflamed my flesh with unholy desire!"

"Stop!" I finally managed, continuing to struggle against him. "Hosha, please! Let go of me!"

At last, I managed to extract myself, but again he reached for me. "I must have you! I must know what you did to make Akhab so enamored with you!"

Twisting out of his grip and throwing up my hands to keep them free from his reach, I stepped back. Then I gritted my teeth and slapped him hard across the face when he came toward me again. "You think because I do not worship *your* god that I am a whore? I will remind you that, although I am a widow, I am still a queen and High Priestess."

While he stood in shock, still holding his cheek, I glared at him. "You are not worthy." Then I turned and walked quickly back toward the palace. As I passed in a silent rage, my chief eunuch looked at me and then at the king, his muscles tense. The uncertainty about what actions he could legally take, given Yehoshapat's rank, were clear upon his face. He had seen the whole thing but had not known what to do, forced to watch helplessly as a king attempted to assault a widowed queen.

454

I gave him a nod, and he followed me inside. "Stay close," I ordered, then paused to search the hall and found Atalaya and her husband now seated together. Some of her ladies and his men surrounded them. Fueled by the wine, which was plentiful, everyone was laughing as they engaged in spirited conversation. My daughter was always a great deal more social than I ever was, and I admired her eyes sparkling in the light from the many radiant oil lamps that gave the hall its evening splendor. When she saw me coming, though, her expression changed to one of concern.

Without a word to her companions, she rose and came to meet me. "Ama, are you all right? Are you ill?"

I forced a reassuring smile, and said, "The day's festivities have taken their toll, I'm afraid, but I am well. I think, however, that I must retire. I intend to be on the road early..."

"You're leaving tomorrow?" Her voice rose slightly in disappointment. "I thought you would stay at least a few more days..."

Averting my gaze, unable to face her, I saw Yehoshapat stumble in from the garden and stop to talk to one of the guards posted at the door. I inhaled sharply and turned back to my daughter. "Yes, I am afraid I cannot prolong my stay. I must return to Shomron and see how your brother is getting on without me." I embraced her quickly and pressed a kiss to her cheek.

Seeing the king striding rather unsteadily toward us, I briefly touched my daughter's cheek and gave her one last gaze, then hurried away before Yehoshapat could catch up to me and my eunuch. While exiting the hall, I glanced back to see Hosha, talking now to his son and my daughter, all of them looking after me with a mixture of confusion and concern. Only the king himself was aware of why I hastened from an evening of revelry and merriment. Short of an emergency, for a guest to leave a party before their host retired was considered a grave insult – or a clear sign of contempt. In doing so, I sent a message to the king before all his guests.

Fearing the king would still follow, whether to make another attempt or to berate me for insulting him before his guests, I quickened my pace as we made our way to my lodging. The eunuch said nothing, although he had seen everything; he knew his place.

My steward had been relaxing on a bench with a pitcher of wine when I entered, having no doubt expected me to be gone for most

455

of the night. He jumped up and bowed, mumbling drunken apologies, which I waved off carelessly.

"Prepare the household. We are leaving at sunrise."

His brows raised, but he bowed his head dutifully. "Yes, Gebirah."

Then I carried on toward the inner chamber where Kora would be waiting to help me prepare for bed. There was only one entrance. I stopped there and turned to my chief eunuch. "Let no man pass into my chamber for any reason, be him a servant or even a king."

For once, he broke protocol and briefly met my gaze in a moment of understanding. Realizing himself, he quickly looked down, and said, "Yes, Gebirah."

I stood a moment longer, watching him and wondering if he would tell others about what he had witnessed. I thought to swear him to silence but decided against it. I would not speak of the king's conduct to anyone, not even to Kora, but if Hosha did not wish for others to regard him as a lecher, he should not have acted as such. My conduct had been beyond reproach, for I had done nothing to encourage him. If others heard about what had happened between us, they would understand why I was so affronted, why I would openly insult the King of Yehudah before all who had gathered at his palace that night.

Leaving Yerushalayim was easier than entering had been. It helped that we were not departing when I had originally planned, so the people would not be expecting me or my entourage. We also travelled without our standards raised, drawing the least amount of attention possible.

Although I tried to slip out discreetly that morning, Yehoshapat still met me in the courtyard at sunrise, along with the Queen, Yehoram, my daughter, and grandson, all who came to see me off. I was glad to see the others, for it had pained me not to say a proper goodbye, but with Hosha I remained stiff in manner. Nevertheless, he provided an armed escort for my departure, for which I thanked him. At least, he was a man of his word, for he had promised to let no harm come to me while I was in his kingdom.

456

He did not apologize for his behavior, but I did not expect him to, for I knew it was beneath him. In fact, he made it clear that he was not in the least sorry for his actions. As I settled into my litter, after embracing my daughter and kissing my grandson goodbye, the King of Yehudah came to me with a false smile to hide the coldness of his gaze.

"Concerning the journey to Opir: tell the King of Yisrael that his servants will not be welcome on my ships. I am sorry, but I must honor the will of Yahowah on this and all matters."

I was not surprised. Zyah, on the other hand, would be mortified. I did not see him at first, upon my return to the palace at Shomron. He had taken up residence there while I was still at Yerushalayim. I was preparing for bed, seated at my dressing table and wiping cosmetics from my face, when my son stormed into my chamber. His entrance was so sudden, so unannounced, that Kora and the handmaids jumped when he threw the door open. The girls all stopped what they were doing and dropped to their knees to prostrate themselves before the king, while Kora stood respectfully with her head bowed.

Zyah looked at the maids with annoyance, then commanded, "All of you, out. Even you, Kora. I need to speak with my mother alone."

The handmaids immediately hurried out, bowing as they left. Kora offered me a look of sympathy before bowing to Zyah and departing. She closed the door on her way out. I sat facing my son, my gaze downcast, waiting for him to speak.

"What is this I hear of Yehoshapat refusing to let my servants on his ships? Did he tell you this himself?"

I sighed heavily and turned back toward my dressing table. Wordlessly, I began applying a soothing balm, made up of aloe and other moisturizers, to keep the skin from aging. While I did this, I finally said, "Yes, he told me as I prepared to leave Yerushalayim."

"Why did you not come to me with this right away when you arrived?"

I almost laughed. "When I arrived, I was told you had retired for the night and did not wish to be disturbed."

"That did not apply to you, Ama. You should know that. Especially when it comes to a message I myself asked you to deliver."

"Forgive me for not knowing, Melekh," I answered dryly.

"Do you speak to me that way? I am your king!"

"And I am your mother," I answered, turning to face him. "Do not take that tone with me, Zyah. King or no king, you owe me respect and honor."

He sighed and apologized, while I turned back to my dressing table and began applying the aloe once again. Then he sighed impatiently, and said, "Ama, will you please stop doing...whatever it is you are doing and listen to what I am saying?"

"I am listening, Zyah. I am fully capable of doing two things at once, you know. You are the one who seems to be distracted by what *I* am doing."

He rubbed his face with his hands then ran his fingers through his hair, much like his father used to do. "Yes – yes, it is distracting to *me*, so will you kindly stop doing it?"

"All right, fine," I answered, turning to face him. "What is it you want to say to me? Speak, since you are so eager for me to listen."

"Even before your steward came to inform me of your return, I had heard about the King of Yehudah's decision, but I did not believe it until the steward told me it was true."

"Yes, so? What of it?" Again, I turned back toward my dressing table and continued applying the ointment to my face.

"They are lauding him as a champion of his god for refusing my request!"

"What do I care what they say of him?"

"They are calling him Good King Yehoshapat."

I shrugged. "Let him be praised. I do not care about the opinions of lesser men, and neither should you."

"And shall I tell you next what they are saying of you, Ama? And of Yisrael?" I did not answer, so he continued. "They are saying you insulted him – that you spurned his hospitality!"

Now, I rose and turned to face him with a sneer. "His hospitality indeed!"

"Why would you do that? They are calling it a diplomatic catastrophe!"

"I was not there for diplomacy," I said hotly. "I was there to see my daughter and my grandchildren. That was all."

"You could have at least done something while you were there. Anything to attempt to curry favor with Yehoshapat. Instead, you went out of your way to destroy all hope of good relations with the people of Yehudah."

"Shall I tell you what the people of Yehudah did to me? How I was received when I arrived at Yerushalayim? From the moment I arrived in that godless kingdom, I was under constant threat from Yahowah's zealous followers. And Hosha...!"

I stopped short and covered my mouth, realizing what I was about to say and suddenly remembering how frightened and vulnerable I had been when he accosted me in the garden that night. I turned away and closed my eyes, breathing deeply to steady myself.

"Ama?" he asked gently now. "What did Hosha do to you?"

I turned to face him, letting him see the tears in my eyes and the fury in my gaze. "It is not what Hosha did or did not do that offends me so. It is what you – my own son – would expect me to do. I expect it of Hosha, and of other men, but you...I expected better of you."

Returning to my dressing table, I spoke with my back toward him and pretended to be occupied. "You may leave now. I am exhausted after my journey."

He sighed heavily and walked away, leaving the door wide open. Once he was gone, Kora returned to me, and then I thanked her before dismissing her for the night.

Despite the rumors already spreading, and the praise Yehoshapat received for his decision, I never told anyone about his disgraceful behavior. However, I began to worry about Atalaya, and decided to warn her, lest she also fall prey to his lecherous ways. I sat down to write her a private letter, in which I told her, "Be ever vigilant and guard yourself from the advances of weak men who think their rank gives them the right to take what they want from our sex."

I closed the letter with my own seal, so she would know that nobody else had seen its contents, and sent it by my most trusted advisor – Raman, a priest of Ashtarti who had long served me in this capacity. He was one of the young boys who had been training at the time of Eliyah's massacre of my priests and priestesses. His survival was due only to the fact that he was still too young to be ordained. He had, therefore, stayed behind at the temple with the other acolytes, while Daneyah and the rest of them marched unknowingly

459

toward their slaughter at the high place in the mountains of Kerem-el.

Now, he was a grown man and, after serving for the requisite amount of time at the temple in his youth, Raman served at the palace. Apart from trusting him to deliver my letters unscathed, I valued him as a confidant and gifted musician, also appreciating his wry sense of humor. In the time since Akhab's death, he had cheered me up more than a few times by pointing out some of the handsome men who came to court, suggesting I should take one for a lover. Being of that nature, he had a good eye for attractive men himself and once teased, "If you will not take him for a lover, Ba'alah, then I will."

"You are welcome to take him, if he will have you," came my playful response. Then I became serious, and said, "I do not wish to dishonor my husband."

"Forgive me, but you dishonor yourself, Ba'alah," he replied with a bow. "A woman should not be punished for being alive when her husband rests in Ertsetu. Even a widow has needs."

What he said stuck with me, but I was still in mourning for my husband and thought no man could move me to desire again. I could appreciate and admire them, but unlike Raman I had no intention of seeking their attraction. Thinking back to those days when he came to receive the letter from me, I teased, "Did you ever make love to that man you so admired?"

"Which one, Ba'alah?" he asked with a wink.

"The one who came from Egypt to present my son the king with Pharoah's blessing."

"Oh, that one," he said with a blush and a telling smile.

I chuckled. "I take it you enjoyed him?"

"He was incredible, Ba'alah," Raman answered wistfully. "I am sorry you missed out on what he had to offer – his gifts were many, and he offers them to men and women alike."

Smiling in amusement, I rose from my desk and handed him the letter. "Take this to Yerushalayim. Give it directly into the hand of my daughter, and no one else."

"It will be done, Ba'alah," he said with a bow.

"Thank you." I sat at my desk once again. "Travel undercover through Yehudah, especially when you reach the city – do not let it be openly known you are a priest of Asherah or that you are an agent

460

of mine until you have safely entered the palace, for the people there have gone mad."

"Yes, Ba'alah," he answered uncertainly.

"I mean it, Raman. Your life could be in peril if the wrong people know of you and of whom you represent." He nodded, understanding now, and so with a wave, I said, "That will be all." He began to leave, but then I called, "Raman, one more thing!"

"Yes, Ba'alah?"

I met his gaze with a smile. "When you get to Yerushalayim, at the palace, ask after Elchanan the scribe. You will find him to your liking, for he is inclined toward men such as yourself, and he serves the Ba'alim."

Raman could not hide his smile. He bowed graciously, and said, "Thank you, Ba'alah. You are a benevolent woman. It is an honor to serve you."

I waved him away as he went to carry out my orders. A month passed before he returned, clearly refreshed by his time in Yerushalayim. He came bearing a letter marked with Atalaya's seal. My daughter was discreet, but it was clear that she understood my meaning, for she wrote: "I will not ask to whom you are referring, dear Ama, or what experiences you have borne in grace and silence. However, I assure you that I would sooner cut off a man's parts and feed them to his dogs than allow him to force his way with me, whether he be a pauper or a king."

When I read that part of her letter, I sat back in my chair in amazement. Then I smiled proudly, certain as I was now, that my daughter was quite capable of handling herself at the court of Good King Yehoshapat. As for me, I was content to never travel to the Kingdom of Yehudah again for as long as he reigned.

461

20

The Ba'alah Within

Settling back into my duties at the palace began with a report from Tamar on the happenings in the women's household, most of which were the usual petty squabbles and small triumphs that required nothing from me. There was one report, however, that came as a surprise. It concerned one of the princesses of Hamat, Be'ulah in particular, who was beginning to act out, making trouble for Tamar and the other guardians.

"She is rebellious and headstrong, Gebirah," Tamar reported. "She will not listen to the wisdom of her elders and comports herself immodestly."

"How so?"

"Just the other day, I caught her gazing out the window at one of the men at work in the garden, admiring his form and trying to gain his attention."

"That hardly seems like risky behavior, Tamar," I remarked with a faint smile. "It is not like the gardener can just walk into the women's quarters, past all the eunuchs, and make love to her. Neither can she just walk out."

"It is not only that, Gebirah," Tamar insisted, lowering her voice. "One of the eunuchs had to be summoned before the king and whipped for committing indecent behavior with her."

"A eunuch?"

Tamar nodded. "One of the guards, Gebirah. He was restationed to another part of the palace after the event, but it was clear that they were...attempting to be intimate."

"Attempting? Is he truly a eunuch?"

"Yes, Gebirah, he is, but they still think as men and can sometimes still use their parts – or their hands where their other parts fail them."

After some initial shock, I asked, "How intimate were they?"

462

"It does not appear that they actually consummated the act, but it was clear that they intended to do so. They were caught together at the end of a corridor at night, trying to obscure themselves behind the palms. The midwives examined her after the incident. She does not appear to be compromised, from what they can tell, but I think we misjudged her readiness to be known by her husband. She is now in her fourteenth year, after all."

"The Ba'alah is strong in her," I murmured.

"Gebirah?" she looked at me quizzically.

"Never mind. I will speak to the king on this matter. But now, what of her sister, Shalima? How is she getting on here?"

"Shalima is as pure as a dove, Gebirah," she answered. "The girl has taken to the studies you have outlined for her and behaves herself with grace and modesty in all things. She is the complete opposite of Be'ulah, in every way. Although she is younger, she attempts to steer the older one away from her folly. It was Shalima, in fact, who alerted the other guardians to what was developing between her sister and that faithless eunuch. If not for her, Ba'al knows what might have happened."

"I shall have to thank Shalima for her honesty and wisdom in this. Does Be'ulah know it was she who revealed them?"

"No, she was discreet, and so were we – I pretended to come upon them by accident, to avoid causing trouble between the sisters. They are close, despite their differences, and the occasional quarrels that rise between them."

"Good; we should strive to keep it that way, for the younger princess has already proven her value by remaining in the elder one's confidence."

She nodded in agreement, and I thanked her for her vigilance. Then I went in search of my son, the king. Zyah was out in the courtyard, practicing with his bow when I came upon him. Yoram and Natan were there with him, also practicing, but Yoram noticed me coming and alerted his brother. Zyah glanced at me with displeasure and then returned to aiming his bow. When I reached him, he loosed the arrow and hit his mark.

While Yoram kissed my hand and Natan knelt in homage, my eldest son spoke bitterly. "Thank you, Ama, for providing the means for me to make a perfect shot."

463

"I hope it was not myself you were imagining on that target," I responded sharply. Then to Yoram and Natan, I said, "Carry on. There is no need to let me interrupt you."

They nodded and returned to their archery practice, while I said to Zyah, "No doubt you have heard of the near mishap between your wife and the eunuch."

"Yes, of course," he answered, clearly confused as to why I was bringing it up. "I punished the eunuch myself. He is lucky I did not have him killed, but since Tamar assured me nothing happened between them, I decided to be merciful. Should I not have done so?"

"Of course," I replied. "That is not why I am broaching the subject with you."

"Then what is it?"

I was distracted momentarily by the sound of the arrows striking their wooden targets. It vaguely reminded me of the stones pelting the eunuchs' shields in Yerushalayim, but I quickly brushed it off and returned to my purpose. "Do you not think it is time for your marriage to be consummated?"

He sighed heavily, letting his head fall to the side as he rolled his eyes. "She is still only a girl."

"She is fourteen," I said, watching him adjust his leather wristbands. "I was the same age when I married, and my marriage was consummated the same night."

"*You* told me *not* to consummate the marriage."

"Yes, and at the time it was right. Sometimes it is better to wait, but now things have changed. Her behavior shows that she is ready for it."

"Her behavior shows that she is silly and foolish; a confirmation of my first impressions. I have no interest in her."

"Many girls are like that at her age. The duties of a wife and motherhood quickly correct their behavior."

"Naveen was not like that."

"You did not know her when she was that age. You must remember that Naveen is older than you and came to you already with years of experience."

He rolled his eyes again.

"She needs to be given a purpose, Zyah," I persisted, "more than being locked away inside the palace, with no children to look after, no thoughts of a husband's touch to calm her passions and raise

464

her spirits. She has only herself and her childish fancies with which to amuse herself, but now she is ready to be made a woman."

"She may be ready, Ama, but I am not. Neither is Naveen, and I want only her. She is enough for me."

"It is your duty as king to father as many *legitimate* sons as possible. Even your Abbu knew that – he wanted only me, but he understood his duty to the kingdom. As did I, which is why I agreed to share him with his other wives. You think I do not understand the anguish Naveen feels at the thought of sharing the man she loves? If she is unwilling to do that, she is as selfish as I first judged her to be."

"You have always hated her," he sputtered.

"I do not hate her, Zyah. I never have. In fact, these past years I have gained more respect for her. But that does not change what she is. She is not royal. She can never be your wife."

"I am king! If I want to make her my wife and legitimize my sons with her, I can do that."

"Yes, but you will not have the support of your kingdom, and neither will you have the support of your family or your court. Only those with royal blood can inherit the kingdom. That is the law."

"My son has royal blood – he has *my* blood – and that is all that should matter," Zyah argued. "Besides, was not my grandfather a man who came to the throne through bloodshed and not by the right of his blood? Both of my grandfathers, in fact."

"Omri took the throne when it was offered to him, after the traitor Zimri betrayed their king, but he was descended from the line of kings Dawid and Shelomoh. And my father took the thrones of Zour and Tzidon in a similar fashion, but he also is descended from an ancient royal bloodline – one that was established by the Ba'alim themselves, when they walked this earth as living gods. Shall I pull out the genealogies for you to examine as proof? Not one of us is descended from an impure source. Only royal and noble blood runs through our veins – divine blood – and only the same will be accepted by the people of Yisrael."

He sighed heavily and looked down toward his feet. Then he raised his head to meet my gaze. "I will consummate the marriage when I am ready, but as you said yourself, there is no rush. I am young and there is plenty of time for me to father *legitimate* heirs.

Until the time when it becomes necessary, I will be satisfied *only* with Naveen."

Then he reached for his bow, snatching it from the hand of his attendant with little warning, and returned to his shooting. While he aimed at the target, he said to me, "You are dismissed." Then he loosed the arrow and, once again, struck the mark for which he had aimed. I took the hint, bowed to the king, and went away.

On my way back, I came across Ishaq inside the palace. He stopped to pay homage as I passed. It was the first I had seen of him since my return from Yerushalayim, so I stopped to greet him. He knelt and I gave him my hand, which he pressed to his lips with more fervor than usual. I tried to ignore it, as I had ignored his boyhood infatuation with me, and said with a smile, "Shalom, Ishaq. Are you on your way to join the king at archery?"

"Shalom, Ba'alah," he said, rising to stand. He was tall, like Akhab, and I had to look up to see his face. Then I realized he was still holding my hand, and so I pulled it away, while he continued, "I am on my way there, yes, but I am glad to have met you along the way."

I smiled faintly and looked away to hide the warmth on my cheeks. Then I cleared my throat. "Well then, I shall not keep you."

His eyes betrayed disappointment, but he bowed respectfully. Then, as I passed, he said, "Shalom, Gebirah Yezeba'al."

I stopped and inhaled sharply. The sound of my name upon his lips, the tone of his voice so like Akhab's...it was almost as if Akhab himself had just said my name. "Shalom."

I stole a glance back to see him still standing there, watching me. Then I turned forward and quickened my pace. I was angry with myself. He was barely older than my own sons – so what if he was now a man and the image of his father. It was only my loneliness for Akhab which stirred these impure thoughts and desires within me. Then I thought I should be angry with him, and not myself, for was he not the one to blame? I should have him punished for behaving in this way toward me...only then I would have to confront him.

But then I was disturbed at the thought of punishing him for...what exactly? What had he done wrong? He was a man – it was only natural he should have feelings for a woman. I knew it was not uncommon for young men to become fixated on older and experienced women. After all, it was a common practice for fathers to take their adolescent sons to the temple to receive the blessing of Ashtarti from one of the priestesses to be taught how to be with a woman before discovering it for themselves with the wrong sort. And was I not a priestess of Ashtarti? Not just a priestess, but the High Priestess, and the incarnation of Ashtarti herself? How could he not, having been raised to revere the Ba'alim, be drawn to the Ba'alah within me?

As I entered my bedchamber, Kora was there working. She was about to greet me warmly, until she saw the anger in my bearing. Then she stopped abruptly and stood with her head bowed. I looked at her with irritation. "What is the matter with you?"

"I... Forgive me, Ba'alah, if I have offended you."

I sighed heavily and shook my head. "No, it is I who must ask forgiveness, Kora. I should not have snapped at you. You have done nothing to offend me – you have only ever been a good friend to me. My only friend, sometimes I think."

Then I sat in the chair at my dressing table, and she came to massage my shoulders. I saw her trying to smile at me in the mirror. "If I am your friend, Yezeba'al, then you must tell me what it is that troubles you."

I met her gaze in the mirror then looked away again. "I cannot tell you, for it is shameful."

Her smile faded, but she continued massaging out the tension in my neck and shoulders. Her expression became thoughtful as she worked. Then she said, "If you do not wish to speak of it, of course, I understand. But we have been together our whole lives – we were nursed together at my mother's breast, and you have always been a sister to me. Whatever it is that you have done, or not done, it could never diminish my love and respect for you, my sister, my Gebirah, my Ba'alah. I love you most of all the people I have ever known."

I smiled faintly. Then, at last, I began, "You know Ishaq, Akhab's son with Fang-Hua?"

"Yes, I know of him. Is he not one of Zyah...*the king's* closest friends?"

"Yes, Kora, he is one of Zyah's closest friends. You know you do not have to refer to him as the king when we are alone together – you were like a second mother to him. Or a third, I suppose, considering his nurse."

467

She gave a nod. "Well, what of Ishaq?" Then she stopped massaging, leaving her hands to rest upon my shoulders and leaning over to make a face. I laughed and playfully pushed her away, and then she stood triumphantly. "There, my work is accomplished. Now, what could possibly be shameful about Ishaq?"

I looked at her from the side but could not bring myself to say it.

"Yezeba'al, I know you better than anyone. I am sure I already know, but as you have come this far, you might as well say what you are thinking."

"Oh, Kora," I lamented, laying my face in my arms upon the table now. "I have only seen him a few times these past months, but whenever I do...I find I am drawn to him in ways I should never be. It would not be so difficult if I did not believe...if I did not *know* that he is drawn to me in the same way. I would not even have thought such a thing of him, but every time we meet now, he looks at me in this way...and it has stirred something within me."

She listened patiently, and when I stopped, she remained quiet. I looked at her guiltily, then at last she said gently, "Yezeba'al, he is a man. It is perfectly natural that you would feel these things for a man, even a younger man."

"Yes, but he is Akhab's son! Fang-Hua's son!" I said, rising from the chair.

She took me by the arms. "But he is not *your* son."

"Not of my body, no, but...I tried to raise him as my son after Fang-Hua died. When he was a boy, I looked at him the same way I look at my own sons. Now, they are grown, yet my feelings for them remain pure, unchanged. But with him...I never thought these things would arise in me, and I feel so ashamed." I hid my face with my hands for a moment, and then continued, "I do not know what to do, Kora. When he was a boy, when he first developed an infatuation with me, I was able to laugh it off with Akhab – gods know he is not the first of Akhab's sons to develop an attraction toward me – but now...suddenly with him, I find myself unable to ignore it. Only I do not know what I should do to make it stop."

"What did you do many years ago, when Akhab's brother – what was his name, the one you appointed to plan all the feasts and ceremonies?"

"Asa."

"Yes, Asa. What did you do when his infatuation with you began to cause talk at court?" She gave me a knowing look, and I nodded in understanding. "That is what you must do now, if you want to turn his affections away from you."

"It did not work completely with Asa," I said with a sigh. "He still harbors deep affection for me, to this day, but he is better at hiding it because we are older now and he knows his place."

"Perhaps it did not change his desire for you, but it worked well enough, did it not? He has not caused you any difficulty since."

"This is different, Kora. I was in love with Akhab then. I was happy in my marriage. I would never have even considered...having an affair with Asa."

"But you have considered it with Ishaq?"

"No, I mean...not exactly. I would never...consider it. This is the first time I've even admitted to myself, or to anyone, that I've had these desires. But I cannot have an affair with one of Akhab's sons, even if he is a man and not of my blood!"

"Then you must turn his affections away from you and eliminate the temptation. Send him away or find him a wife, as you did for Asa, and he will know what he must do. He will learn his place, just as Asa did."

I calmed myself at this and took her hand. "Thank you, Kora. I should have known you would have the right things to say, the right ideas. You grow more like your mother with each passing year." I lowered my face when my eyes began to burn. A single tear dropped before I lifted my sleeve to wipe the rest away. "I miss her so..."

"I miss her too," said Kora. Then she squeezed my hand, and I pulled her into an embrace. When I pulled away, she took my hand again and patted it gently. "Now, you will speak with the king about finding a wife for Ishaq, and in the meantime perhaps you should consider taking a lover to distract yourself and fulfill your own needs, as well."

"Raman said much the same thing, although he has no idea of these desires I have had. He has only said it to cheer me up, when he sees that I am lost without Akhab."

"Then you should listen," she replied. "You have had it from two sources now: it may as well be a message from the Ba'alim. You, of all people, cannot spend the rest of your life alone without the comfort of a man. You are the incarnation of Ashtarti herself, Yezeba'al. You must do what comes naturally to you."

I shook my head. "I do not think I am ready to take a lover. It has not even been a full year since..." I stopped short, unable to say it. I could still never quite bring myself to say it.

She placed a hand upon my shoulder. "You will know when it is time."

The challenge of finding a wife for Ishaq was that it had to be done through the king who, unfortunately, was currently harboring resentment toward me for interfering in his own romantic affairs. I could not confess to him what was between Ishaq and me – was there something between us? Yet, I feared that if I went to my son with yet another matchmaking quest, it would only further invoke his anger at me for what he considered meddling. I had to take courage, however, and remind myself and him that if I was meddling, it was my duty to meddle. As Gebirah, it was my responsibility to manage the courtship of princes and princesses of the House of Omri. If Zyah was angry with me for performing my duty, so be it.

He was in the king's study when I was granted an audience the following morning. I had not been in the king's study since Akhab was king, so it was strange to be there and find my son sitting at my husband's desk. I remembered him seated there once as a boy, playing at being king, while Akhab stood reading by the window to get better light. I had alerted my husband to Zyah, who let his legs dangle from the chair, humming. He lifted a stylus and pretended to sign one of the documents, as he had watched Akhab do many times. My husband and I, proud of our son who would one day be king, shared a smile in that moment, unaware of how soon it would all come to pass.

Now, ten years or so later, my son the king looked up from the scroll he was examining with a weary gaze. "Ama, have you come to rebuke me once again? Or do you have good reason for disrupting my work?"

My fondness for him was overshadowed by this. I narrowed my eyes, walked directly up to the desk and snatched the scroll out of his hands. Then I rolled it up and whacked him on the side of the

470

head with it, after which I pointed it at him, and said, "I did not come to rebuke you, Zyah, but if you continue to behave in this manner toward me when I have done nothing wrong, you will continue to earn my rebuke! I am your mother. I will not be mistreated by my own son, who owes me his very life!"

With that, I slammed the scroll down on top of the desk, while he sat there, wordless. Satisfied by his speechlessness, I drew in a short breath, and continued, "Now, for once, as I am sure you will be pleased to hear, it is not about you that I have requested an audience, but Ishaq."

"Ishaq? What has he done to displease you?"

"He has done nothing to displease me. I have simply come to speak with you about seeking a wife for him."

"Why should I seek a wife for Ishaq?"

"No one of the royal House of Omri is allowed to marry without the approval of the king, whether he be a servant or kin. Ishaq is twenty-two now – he needs to take a wife."

At this, Zyah rose and walked to the window. Then he turned to me and asked, "Why should it be any concern of yours? If he wants to take a wife, let him come to me himself and ask for permission."

I looked away, in part to hide my shame. "It is one of the duties of being the mother of the king, to find and arrange suitable marriages not only for my own children, but for all your unwed brothers and sisters. That is, unless they are one of your sisters being given as part of a dynastic marriage contract. Then it would be your duty alone to arrange it with another king or his agents, with my guidance if you need it, of course."

He returned to the desk and began fidgeting with papers that were laid out in a pile, held in place by a miniature ivory sphynx. "Do you have a girl in mind?"

"Not yet, because I must seek your permission to act in this regard."

He waved carelessly. "Then you have my permission." He seated himself again at the king's desk – his desk – when he added, "But I will not force Ishaq to take a wife with whom he is not pleased."

"Of course, and I will take his...desires into consideration before making a decision." I paused. "Is there...a suitable girl in whom he might have taken an interest?"

471

"Ishaq? Not that I am aware of. He has had a few affairs with courtesans, but they were never serious. Mostly, he finds satisfaction from the priestesses at the temple, which you should find more suitable than courtesans anyway. As for a girl he would be allowed to marry...I know of none that interest him. But with your knowledge and familiarity with the wives and daughters of the nobility, I trust you will soon find one that would make a suitable wife, Ama."

Although I had hoped to avoid having to go directly to the source, I said, "I will talk to Ishaq then, and try to determine his opinion on the matter before I begin my search. Like you, I want him to be pleased with whomever I choose; nevertheless, she must be approved by you before a betrothal can be made."

"All right then." Zyah absentmindedly lifted the ivory sphynx and studied it for a moment. When he was a boy, he used to play with it whenever I brought him to visit Akhab while he worked. I closed my eyes against tears, coming back to the present when my son said, "Speak to him on the matter and return to me when you have a girl in mind. Now, if you will excuse me, Ama – I have many important matters with which I must acquaint myself before court tomorrow."

"I am at your service, Melekh," I answered with a bow of my head and then I left him, wondering how in the time I was away, he had grown so used to doing everything without me.

I returned to my quarters heavy hearted and shut myself inside my prayer chamber to seek communion with Ashtarti. Apart from needing to find comfort from my wounded heart that had been ripped open to bleed anew after seeing my son so changed by his succession, I needed to ask the goddess for guidance and strength. I also needed to be fortified when summoning Ishaq to discuss the necessity of his marriage. All of this required a blood offering, of which only the power in my own blood would suffice, and so I brought out my ceremonial dagger and myrrh oil to complete the ritual.

Kneeling before my private altar, from which the small figure of Ashtarti gazed upon me with her ruby eyes, I whispered the incantations while coating the blade. I then made a careful incision between the scars on my arm to draw blood. Long ago, in my training as a priestess, I was taught how to cut just deep enough to draw the necessary amount for blood rituals without leaving a permanent mark behind. It was a specific procedure, performed with clarity of mind and pure intention. The blood could not be tainted with frenzied or negative elements, or it would distort the purpose of the ritual.

Blood is power. Blood is magic. That is what we believed, and why it was so important in a sacrifice, and in our rituals. Blood is life, and in it was believed to be the very essence of our souls. To spill blood was no small matter, just as mixing it with the blood of others through the production of offspring could not be frivolously undertaken.

The offering of royal, divine blood – the blood of a high priestess – was made and the ritual performed. Then I extinguished the incense, cleaned the ritual instruments and altar, and prostrated myself once more before going out to summon Ishaq and perform my duty to the kingdom.

Ishaq came to me when I was sitting in the garden, under the shade of a flowering almond tree. I was alone except for Be'ulah, whom I had appointed my cupbearer that afternoon. It was an honored appointment, for it allowed the chosen lady to be in close confidence with the Queen and a chance to curry favor. Be'ulah was pleased to have been chosen for this position. She listened earnestly whenever I spoke to her, or answered with eager modesty whenever I asked her a question. Meanwhile, her sister Shalima played with the other children around her age, while the remaining widows of Akhab sat together or with their children, sunning themselves.

Other than children or peacocks, the only males about were the eunuchs, those silent sentinels whose presence had never seemed a threat to the sanctity of the women's household. Now, I could not quite look at them the same, knowing that even without the ability to impregnate a woman, they could still hold desire in their parts. Then I thought of the other wives – all of them now widows, except for Be'ulah and Shalima. Some of them found pleasure with each other, and it was accepted because it did not threaten the legitimacy of the king's heirs. Was it then such a terrible thing if one of those wives, uninterested in the other women, sought the same pleasures with a eunuch instead?

My pondering was interrupted when Ishaq appeared. I spotted him coming – the only bee within a garden of lilies, many of them in full bloom. Being a king's son, he was permitted only because most of the women there were his half-sisters, or were considered his mothers, and because I had summoned him. I watched him making his way through the garden toward me, being led by one of the stewards of the women's household, who was also a eunuch. Ishaq paid no attention to the many lilies he passed; they were not of interest. Then he lifted his gaze to meet mine as he drew near. I looked away, ashamed of the pleasure I took from knowing I was the only one he desired among them: a rose among the lilies.

He knelt; I gave him my hand. He pressed it to his lips, soft and tender and worshipful. I took care in each breath, drawing on the strength of the Ba'alah within me not to reveal any sign of unmotherly affection, lest it encourage him. That was part of why I chose this setting in which to have this conversation. Once the steward stepped away, the only person within earshot was Be'ulah, who I had determined was not prone to gossip. Nevertheless, we were surrounded by so many others who could prevent, by their very presence, any weakness from overcoming me.

"Shalom, Ishaq," I greeted with stinted warmth.

"Shalom, Ba'alah." I thought it best to pull my hand away and did so immediately. He looked up at me with an almost injured gaze; it injured me, as well, to see the hurt in his eyes.

"You are in your twenty-second year, are you not?" I asked, reaching for my cup. I held it without taking a drink as I studied him, taking care to remain neutral in bearing and countenance.

"Yes, Ba'alah," he breathed his answer. "I will be twenty-three in less than a month."

I gave a nod then sipped my drink. I noticed Be'ulah watching him closely when I set my cup on the tray. She nearly dropped it but caught herself. Then she lowered her gaze, her cheeks flushed with shame. It was unfortunate she was already married to Zyah, or I might have paired her with Ishaq to solve two issues at once. He showed no interest in her, however. His gaze remained fixed upon me, eager and hopeful. It was a shame that I would have to dash those hopes.

"Twenty-three is a good age for a man to take a wife," I said at last. "I have spoken to the king on this matter, and he agrees that it is time for us to find a suitable wife for you. Before I begin my considerations from among the royal and noble families of the realm, I thought it best to speak with you first, and learn from you, what you may desire."

474

He remained silent, lips pressed together.

"Is there, perhaps, a suitable maiden in whom you are interested?"

"No," he answered quietly. "My interests do not lie with maidens, Ba'alah."

I raised my brows. Had I misjudged his interest in me? Perhaps his obvious admiration was not attraction, but a desire to emulate. "Men?"

"No, Ba'alah."

I looked at him squarely. "Why do you continue to call me that?"

"Ba'alah?"

"Yes."

"Is that not what I should call Ashtarti incarnate?"

"When you were a boy, you called me 'Ama'."

"I am not a boy anymore," he replied.

"You may still call me 'Ama', even when you are a man, Ishaq."

"With all due respect, Ba'alah, you are not my mother. Nor do I want you to be."

Looking away, I reached for my drink. After quenching my thirst, I put it back on the tray, and took the opportunity to gauge how much Be'ulah understood of the game we were playing. She seemed only vaguely interested, her naivete outweighing all other considerations.

I returned my attention to Ishaq. "You said your interests do not lie in maidens…"

"They do not, Ba'alah."

I saw golden flecks in his warm brown eyes when they caught the light and was momentarily taken aback by the depth of his gaze. Why did he have to remind me so much of Akhab? Warmth spread across my cheeks, but I persisted, "Where do they lie?"

"With one I cannot have."

Losing my nerve, I began fidgeting with the hem of my mantle. "Is she a married woman?"

"No, Ba'alah."

"Then why can you not have her?" I asked, somewhat impatiently. "Does she not want you in return?"

He thought about his response before answering. "She is exalted above me in every way, Ba'alah. I could never ask her to love

475

me in return." He paused, and then added, "But if she would have me, I would devote my very life to her and give her all that she desires."

My mouth went dry, and my heart began to race. I needed another drink. This time, when I reached for my cup, I saw Be'ulah watching us with more interest. When I met her gaze, she quickly averted hers. I took another drink. My hand trembled when I returned it to the tray, but I affected a cool air as I turned back to Ishaq.

"Whoever this lady is...perhaps she cannot have you either. If that is the case, then you must be satisfied with one you *can* have. I will begin searching for a suitable candidate. It may take a while, as there are many considerations when finding a wife for a brother of the king. I will give you some time to think if there are certain features or characteristics you desire in a wife. When you have compiled a list of these things, or certain recommendations, have them sent to me and I will begin. That will be all."

He bowed his head as I rose from the chair. He remained on his knees. Looking down at him, I said, "Shalom, Ishaq."

"Shalom, shalom, Ba'alah," he murmured, as I walked away. The steward had been standing at a respectful distance but stepped forward to escort Ishaq out of the garden. It was not appropriate for a bee to remain among the lilies; only I knew it was not the lilies who were threatened by his sting.

"The Ba'alah is strong in her."

This was spoken years ago by Daneyah, in a conversation with my mother in the garden at the palace at Tzidon. I overheard this in the afternoon following my greatest mishap, which might have led me to ruin had it not been interrupted.

Despite all the levels of protocol and prevention, I had been found in a compromising situation with a young man for whom I had taken a fancy. The man in question was a priest of Ba'al who served as a scribe at my father's court. Unlike my sisters and most of the other women at court, I always had more freedom to roam the palace grounds, as long as Daneyah and a pair of eunuchs went with me. I spent a great deal of time in the palace library, where I had first come

476

to notice the handsome young priest. He had also noticed me, and soon we began going to the library every day at the same time.

Making our way through the shelves of tablets and scrolls, we ended up on opposite sides and looked through the diamond-shaped opening where the scrolls were stored. He smiled at me, and when I reached into the opening as if to take one of the scrolls, he dared to reach from the other side, placing his hand upon mine. It was warm and sent chills through my body that delighted me. It did not take long, however, for Daneyah to become aware of our attraction. She became more vigilant and would not let him anywhere near me, nor I him. So, we quickly developed little ways of discreetly communicating with gestures, facial expressions, and our eyes.

Then one day, I left him a note on the table where I had been studying and he found a way to write a reply. We began leaving notes hidden beneath clay tablets or tucked into the shelves where we often gazed upon one another. We always used vague and coded wording so that anyone else who found our messages would think nothing of them and leave them where they were left in place.

After several weeks of this, I devised a way for him to come to me, convincing Kora to help him slip into my chamber one night. Nothing happened at first. We spent many nights talking endlessly about a great many things before he ever dared to lay a hand upon me. Once he did, at my urging, we would not have been able to stop ourselves had Daneyah not heard noise from where she slept and come to investigate. She found him in my bed, naked and lying over me. Her shouting alerted the eunuchs.

He was barely given enough time to dress before being arrested and taken away, while my mother came with one of the midwives. She glared at me in furious disbelief and slapped me across the face. She had never laid a hand upon me in anger before, but the sting on my cheek was nothing compared to the sting of her disappointment. Then she berated me with fury. Although I swore that he had not taken me, I was subjected to an examination to determine if I had been compromised. It was confirmed that my maidenhead was still intact, but it had been a close call; unlike Hadi in the tent at Damaseq a few months earlier, I was not going to stop my priest of Ba'al, for I was eager and thought myself to be in love.

Nevertheless, despite my protests and insistence that it had all been my idea, which was true, the young priest was executed for

477

the offense – an explanation for which was never offered to his grieving family. He had committed treason; that was all the explanation given, and with my marriage to King Akhab fast approaching, it was imperative that my reputation be flawless. While I could not grieve openly, I keenly felt his loss and blamed myself because he would never have dared such a risk without my encouragement. I also learned a valuable lesson that day, which emphasized the dangerous nature of sexual energy if left unchecked.

Kora had nearly been punished too, but I intervened. I claimed she had only left me alone in my chamber because I had commanded her to and that she had been ignorant of my plans. Aware of her daughter's devotion to me, Daneyah knew I was lying but was grateful to me for protecting her. She dealt with Kora on her own terms. The plans for my upcoming marriage were attended to with greater urgency, and the near disaster was never spoken of again, except in the garden the next day between Daneyah and my mother.

Continuing her thought, Daneyah said, "It is no wonder she was drawn to him."

"She is searching for her Ba'al," my mother agreed, "as is her nature."

Having snuck up on them, I peered through a wooden screen covered in fragrant jasmine. Daneyah was nodding when she said, "She must have a strong husband to whom she can direct all her energy. I hope this king will be strong enough to manage her."

"By all accounts, he will be," came my mother's response. "The Ba'al is in him – I am certain of it. He is searching for his mate, just as she is searching for him."

"Is he searching?"

My mother nodded. "He is only in his twenty-first year, but already he has sixteen concubines and treats them all fairly, so I have been informed."

"Truly?" Daneyah's expression was equal parts shocked and impressed.

"No doubt he bores of them quickly, and is in need of a woman like Yezeba'al to give him the healing and satisfaction he so desperately seeks."

"A man such as he would make a suitable High Priest for her," Daneyah suggested, "if she can convince him to turn from Yahowah."

478

Again, my mother nodded. "I believe she will succeed in her mission. If it is true that the Ba'al is in him, they will be well suited for one another. The prophets have all said that theirs will be a true love-match, the like of which is rarely seen."

"That is promising," said Daneyah. "I hope, for her sake, they are right."

Listening to all this, I did not think it was possible to love anyone the way I had loved my young priest of Ba'al. I did not yet understand the difference between love and infatuation. All that changed the moment our eyes met, when my soul recognized his soul, and in time I came to understand what my mother meant when she said the Ba'al was in him.

Now, so many years later, I was without my Ba'al once again. It was a warm and sultry summer night when I remembered that conversation and all that had inspired it. I had not thought about that incident in many years. I locked it away in the deepest corners of my mind, until the day that Tamar spoke to me of Be'ulah and the eunuch with whom she had been infatuated. Now, lying on my back in my bed at Shomron, listening to the calls of owls and other nocturnal birds in the palace garden, I was unable to sleep. It was almost a year since I lost my beloved husband, and I was certain that I could never love another as I loved Akhab. Yet, I was beginning to feel the urge to take a lover, just so I could have a man in my arms and in my bed once again. Both Kora and Raman had urged it; my own body craved a man's touch, so why did I resist?

The Ba'alah *was* strong in me. It had always been, and so it would always be. I realized this as I lay there with my forearm draped across my forehead, breathless and staring up at the ceiling after having satisfied myself. It was why I understood Be'ulah and wanted to protect her from making the same mistake I had almost made. Raised to understand my own sexual energies, I had been instructed to harness their divine power and use them to heal myself and my husband. Yet, even with all the care my mother and Daneyah took to guide and instruct me, those energies had almost destroyed me when they began to build before I had a husband into whom I could safely direct them. Now, without a husband once again, I was reminded of what it was like to be in that position.

The means I had to satisfy my own carnal urges were not enough, because it was not mere lust which prompted these desires.

Sexual energy could not be left unchecked, but neither could it be stifled. I needed a man with whom I could share my sexual energies, a man whom I could heal and bless through them. And while no man could ever compare to the one I truly loved, I knew the time had come for me to find a man in need of what I had to give, one who could provide an outlet for this build-up of energy. Before it became detrimental to my mind, body, and spirit. Before I committed what I thought would be a grievous sin.

While I continued to search for a suitable bride for him, I had to find another with whom I could redirect my own passions. And I knew just such a man who had long desired me but would never dare to express it – only now, I was a widowed queen, and no harm would come to him if I summoned him to me. Besides, I had a reason to summon him for which no one could fault me: it was time to begin making plans for the Serpent's Feast, and it was his duty to arrange the festivities.

21

Craving the Profane

Asa came to me the next evening. I'd summoned him to dine with me and the king in my quarters under the pretext that it was time to begin planning the midsummer feast. However, I made sure my son, the king, would not be present when his uncle arrived, simply by not telling him about the meeting. Kora also made sure none of the other handmaids were around and had the meal prepared in my private dining chamber ahead of the arrival of my guest. Plentiful wineskins, fresh bread, roasted fish, quails, and lamb, along with a variety of fruits, vegetables, and legumes were laid out. Three places were set at the table, so the servants would not suspect a thing. Then Kora dismissed them under the pretext that she alone would tend to our needs, which was always the case when we were discussing plans for the Ba'alim feasts.

When Asa arrived, she escorted him to the dining chamber and then made her exit, leaving us alone together for the night. As he stepped forward, Akhab's brother, who bore the closest likeness to him apart from Ishaq, looked around with uncertainty. "Will the king be joining us later, Gebirah?"

While he dropped to his knee to pay the usual respects, I held out my hand to him and replied, "He is otherwise occupied tonight."

Still kneeling, Asa's gaze shot up to meet mine, with the hint of a smile on his lips as they grazed the back of my hand for a second time. Then, after I bade him to rise, he stood before me as if unsure what to do next. I was not eager to rush to the bedchamber, especially when the servants had gone through the trouble to make such a delectable meal for us. So, I held out my hand to indicate the table with its sumptuous feast. He nodded in understanding, and we went to the table together, sitting on opposite sides where we could face each other while we dined.

Before eating, I led us in prayer and lit a bowl of qaneh-bosem to awaken our appetites. After whispering an incantation, I lifted the

481

smoking bowl, inhaled, and then passed it to Asa who did the same. Soon, we were laughing and eating together as we had when Akhab was still with us, when the three of us would sit together in the same manner to plan the Ba'alim feasts year after year. Initially, we talked about the upcoming feast, and Asa excitedly shared his latest ideas for how it might be conducted.

The most important aspects of the feasts were always the same, but the presentation and entertainments changed each year to keep the people awe-struck and enthusiastic. The element of surprise was especially important, which is why Asa was made the Minister of Ceremonies at such a young age. He was brilliantly creative and well suited to his task. Over the years, he never tired or failed to invent something new and exciting to appease the people's ever-changing tastes.

Sipping my wine and nibbling at the food, as was my custom, I listened to him with rapt attention. Only when he had finally exhausted himself from talking about these things did I begin to reveal my true reasons for inviting him to dinner. Over another bowl of qaneh-bosem, I asked after his wives and children, and teasingly brought up his youthful infatuation with me that had prompted his brother and I to arrange the first of his marriages.

He tilted his head, smiling, and said, "I knew that was the reason for it! I was so angry with Akhab – may his soul know the peace of Ba'al – but when I knew you also desired it, I had to accept his decision." He paused to inhale from the bowl, after I handed it to him. Then he passed it back, and when he exhaled, coughed a few times. Then he continued, "It was not a bad decision: she has been a good wife to me. The best of them all, in fact."

"I hope you had a chance to tell him that, before he left us," I said before lifting the bowl again to inhale deeply of its fumes.

I coughed heavily as I extinguished what was left in the bowl. When I recovered, we laughed together, and he teased, "It feels good, does it not?"

I nodded, wiping the tears from my eyes. "It feels very good."

Then I laid back across the cushions and laughed again, one arm draped across my forehead as I stared up at the ceiling. It felt like the room was spinning. I realized I had not indulged in this way since Akhab was still alive. Even then, it was rare that I allowed myself to become intoxicated.

Then I suddenly remembered what we had been talking about. I sighed and looked across the low table at him. He was still sitting on his cushion with his legs crossed, chin resting in his hand as he watched me thoughtfully. When he stopped tracing the shape of my body with his eyes, I met his gaze and said, "I am glad you are happy in your marriage. It was all Akhab and I ever wanted for you, to be as happy as we were together."

He sniffed then reclined against the cushions, holding his cup with an arm draped across a raised knee. He held my gaze. "I never stopped thinking about you, though. How can a man forget the perfection of a goddess in human form?"

I chuckled and sat up to have a drink. Lifting my cup, I said, "Do not flatter me, Asa." Then I brought my cup to my lips, watching him as I sipped from it and waiting for his next move, wondering if he would take the bait.

"I do not flatter you. I assure you, Ba'alah, every word is true. But I respected my brother – and you – too much to even think I could have you."

"And now?" I tilted my head to the side, smiling faintly: a challenge that I hoped he would accept.

His smile faded and for a moment he seemed lost to me. Then he sat up, pulled at his robes as he adjusted the way he was sitting, and leaned his elbows against the table as he came to terms with what I was suggesting. He took a long drink of his wine and then he held his cup, staring at me with a half-smile. Then he chuckled once or twice and ran his fingers through his hair. At last, he took a deep breath, set down his empty cup, and came to stand over me.

He held out his hand. I took it and he pulled me to stand. Then he reached up to take my face, hesitating for only a moment before at last daring to touch me. I closed my eyes and shivered as he pushed down my veil and slid his fingers through my hair. It was loose and he let his fingers tangle in it as he gazed at me hungrily. I watched him from heavy-lidded eyes, tilting my head to invite him. Suddenly, he grabbed the hair on the back of my head. Tears sprung to my eyes, and I gasped as he brought his lips to mine. His kiss was forceful and possessive, but Akhab had sometimes been that way with me, and I liked it. So, I led him by the hand to my inner sanctum, where I took him to my bed.

483

Asa was not a gentle lover, but I did not want him to be gentle with me. Everything between us was twisted and unholy, in the same way that my love with Akhab had been sacred and pure. It was painful yet gratifying in its own way. Sometimes he terrified me, but I became addicted to the fear, to the comingling of pain and pleasure that he offered. I wanted to be consumed, to be punished for the unholy thoughts I continued to have for Ishaq, and for living while my husband was dead. Asa enjoyed punishing me. He enjoyed having power over me, and I enjoyed letting him have it once he had earned it.

Not that I let him have it all the time. I enjoyed torturing him as much as he enjoyed doing the same to me, although we used different methods. He held me down, wrapped his fingers around my throat, and clenched his teeth down on my flesh while I writhed in agony until I could take no more and lashed out. Barring my teeth, I raked my fingernails across his flesh, even cutting him with my ritual dagger – after which it needed to be cleansed from the profanity for which it had been used and reconsecrated for its sacred purposes.

I wanted to punish him for not being Akhab. I wanted to punish him for the way he punished me. I wanted to destroy him simply because he had the power to seduce me away from the sacred practices that I had spent a lifetime learning and refining. Just as I had learned with Akhab all the ways that sex was sacred, with Asa I learned all the ways it was not. That base part of me, the part that was all lust and animal instinct – which had only come out with Akhab occasionally – was all I had with Asa. And he liked the way I devoured him: ferocious, cruel, and unbending.

He also liked the struggle to overcome me, to force me back into submission when he wanted to be the one on top. And once he had his way with me and was satisfied, whether I was satisfied or not, he fell asleep. He was always gone by morning. I hated him for that, most of all, and I hated myself for wanting more of him, anyway.

At sunrise each morning, no matter how exhausted and aching I was from my nocturnal exertions, I cleansed myself in the bath and then went into my prayer chamber to reconsecrate my body and dagger for their divine purpose. Then I would commune with my Ba'alah before the rest of the palace awakened. Soon I would be swept away in the usual flurry of activity when Kora and the handmaids

484

arrived, followed by the stewards with their daily reports and the servants with victuals to break my fast. After I was dressed, my days were filled with the usual appointments and audiences, broken up by religious duties at the temple on high holy days or private meditations otherwise. Since Akhab's death, once I had recovered enough, I ended each day at Shomron by going down to his tomb to commune with him in the only way I could.

The innermost chamber where his body lay at rest was sealed, but there was an antechamber at the bottom of the stairs. There, an altar had been set up where once there was a doorway, so that anyone who came to leave offerings and commune with him would face where he lay. While many brought him figs, dates, pomegranates, wine, or sprigs of olives and grapes, I always brought him a small plate of his favorite sweet cakes.

I knelt on the rug before the altar, where I moved aside some of the other offerings of the day to make room for the plate. Then I lit incense, pressed my hands together, whispered an incantation, and bowed with my forehead to the floor. I bowed three times, each time pausing to say a prayer, and then sat on my knees with eyes closed, steadying my breathing until I was in a state of calm. I would talk to him as if he was sitting there in the flesh, and I believed he was there listening. Sometimes I paused to listen for him, and sometimes, when not too troubled to hear it, I could perceive his response and feel him with me.

After beginning my affair with Asa, however, I stopped going to commune with my husband for a while, fearing he would be angry with me. When I finally had the courage to return to him, on the eve before the Serpent's Feast, I brought a cup of spiced wine along with my usual offerings. I wept as I bowed and whispered my prayers. Then I sat for a while, weeping in silence, before at last I had courage enough to speak.

"My Ba'al, forgive me for staying away for so long. I was ashamed. I could not face you after what I have done, but now I must confess and pray you can forgive me for it."

I paused to take a deep breath as a fresh wave of tears came forth. Then, when I could speak again, "I have betrayed my love for you in the arms of your brother Asa." I fell forward, touching the feet of the statue of Akhab that stood in the center of the altar. I kissed and caressed as I wept over his bronze feet. Then I sat up once again and continued, "I do not love him. I do not even like him – not now that I have come to know him in this way. I do know why I am drawn to him..."

It was as much a realization as it was a confession, and I paused to consider it. Then I inhaled deeply and said, "Perhaps you already know. Perhaps you have seen my shame with your own eyes. Perhaps you have watched us together and cursed me, and him, for dishonoring you in this way. You are well within your right to curse us for betraying you." I shook my head. "I have no excuse, Akhab. All I can say is that I love you and I am sorry."

I began weeping again and bowed with my forehead to the floor. "I do not mean to dishonor you. I only pray that you can understand. And that you can forgive me for my faithlessness."

Suddenly, I heard the scraping of sandals on stone. I sat up and turned to see Zyah entering the chamber with a cup of wine for an offering. So, it was he who always left the wine for his father. He looked at me, studying me, and asked, "What does Abbu need to forgive? What faithlessness have you ever shown to anyone, least of all to him?"

I looked away to hide my shame. "You were not meant to overhear. I cannot speak to you of what I have done, Zyah."

He shrugged. "So, you have taken a lover."

I was surprised by his perceptiveness. I wondered then, how long had he been in the corridor before revealing himself? How much had he overheard?

He came to sit down beside me. Crossing his legs, he set the cup on the nearby altar and said a prayer, touching his fingers to his lips as he beheld the face of his father's statue. It was a decent likeness, but the face was too thin, the eyes too close together. I could not bear to look at the face, but it did not seem to bother my son. I watched him now, intrigued. His devotion to his father was beautiful to see.

After making his offering, Zyah breathed deeply and turned to face me. I lowered my head, my cheeks burning with shame. I winced when he suddenly stroked my cheek. Then I took his hand and held it there, while a tear broke free from my tightly closed eyes. When he moved to embrace me, I wept on his shoulder, at once feeling safe and relieved and loved. It had been so long since I felt that way.

When he finally pulled away, he asked, "So, who is he? Anyone I know?" He waited, and when I did not answer, he chuckled. "Tell me it is not one of the eunuchs."

At last, I laughed quietly and dropped my hands into my lap. "It is not one of the eunuchs, my son. I am not that lonely and desperate."

Now he laughed aloud, his deep voice resonating in the small chamber. Then he reached out to take my hand, and said, "You should not be ashamed. You are still alive, Ama. If I can understand, surely Abbu can understand, as well."

I whispered, "Thank you."

"So, are you going to tell me who he is, or are you afraid I am going to have him beaten for daring to lay his hands on my mother?"

I laughed through my nostrils, embarrassed. "It is your *Abakhu*, Asa. I hope if you are going to beat him, you will at least wait until after the Serpent's Feast is over. He is too important to its function to be indisposed."

"So, I can still beat him?" he asked with feigned hopefulness. We laughed together, and then he became serious again. "It feels good to sit with you like this here, Abbu with us once again." He looked up at the face of the statue and was almost overcome but managed to steel himself against his grief. "I miss him, Ama."

I reached out to take my son's hand. "I miss him, too." My eyes stung and then I looked up at the face of the statue. Then I shook my head, and said, "It does not look at all like him. The more I look at it, the more I can see its flaws and am disappointed in it."

"It is a close enough likeness."

"You did not know his face like I did." I closed my eyes and imagined his face, focusing on his eyes, at the depth and warmth in his gaze. "I spent over twenty years studying every part of his body."

My son cleared his throat, and said, "Ah...well, I suppose as his wife..."

I chuckled. "Forgive me, I should not have said it that way – although it is true. How do you think you came to be in this world?"

"I know, I know. This is not the first time you have reminded me." He stopped and seemed to be contemplating the flame on one of the altar lamps. Then he grimaced. "*Abakhu* Asa? Truly, Ama, you can do better than that."

"He is a handsome man," I frowned, almost offended. Then I tipped my chin toward the statue, "He is a better likeness than that, anyway."

"Yes, and I love *Abakhu* Asa but...he is nothing like Abbu in character or spirit, even if they did have the same mother and father. Well anyway, I am glad he can...make you happy."

I rolled my eyes and looked away with a sigh. "He does not make me happy, Zyah. It is only a... I do not really know what it is, actually. A necessary evil, I suppose."

"Have you already grown tired of him?"

"We have grown tired of each other, he and I. We will always get on well enough, but..." I shook my head. "He is not your Abbu. He cannot make me happy the way your Abbu could. I suppose no man ever could, but at least it is something for me to entertain myself with from time to time." Then I leaned over to bump him sideways, and said, "But why am I talking with you about this?"

"Because I am here, and I asked about it. But now I think I have heard more than enough." He then looked at me with concern. "What will you do if you become...pregnant?"

I smirked. "I have means of preventing it. There is no need to worry about these things."

"Preventing it? How can you...?"

"I am the High Priestess of Ashtarti. Her normal priestesses are not even allowed to become pregnant. That is why they seldom do."

"Isn't Kora...?"

"The daughter of a priestess of Ashtarti? Yes, Daneyah was a priestess, but she left the temple so she could have Kora. I am glad she did."

"What would have happened if she did not leave the temple?"

"She would have had to terminate the pregnancy and offer the remains up to Ba'al, just as it is done with the remains of all children who die too young."

"What if the pregnancy could not be...terminated? Has it ever happened?"

"I do not know, Zyah. I have never lived at the temple," I said with a sigh. "All I know is that pregnancy can be prevented, and that it must be prevented among the other priestesses. When it is not, they must leave the temple and serve in other ways."

He was quiet for a moment, and I wondered what he was thinking. Then he asked, "Is it true, what our enemies say about the Ba'alim?"

I wrinkled my brow. "What do they say?"

"That we...sacrifice children upon the altars."

That brought a heavy sigh, and I said, "I just told you what is meant by that rumor. Have you ever seen a living child sacrificed in any of our practices?"

"No, but...I have heard that it is done sometimes."

"It has been done, but *not* by true believers," I said sharply. After a pause, I explained, "*Our* Ba'alim do not demand a human sacrifice – in fact, they abhor it – that is why you have never seen one performed at our temple. Those who are burnt upon the altar of our Ba'al are already dead." I placed a hand over my womb, and said, "Many of my own children have been burnt upon the altar in this way, lost before they were born. Their souls are sent to Ba'al, to stop Motu from taking them and preventing their return."

He wrapped his arm around me now, and I leaned into his embrace, resting my head on his shoulder. Then he kissed the top of my head. "If I would die before you..."

"Do not even think it!"

"No, but if I did, I would want you to send me back to Ba'al in the same way. I do not wish to be sealed in a cold, dark tomb like Abbu." He shivered.

"You will not be." I put an arm around him as if to protect him from such a fate. Then I rose onto my knees, kissed the side of his forehead, and stretched to ease the achiness in my body. I patted his shoulder, while he sat still, staring into the flame of a lamp. "Thank you, my son. I have missed you. I do not like it when we are at odds with each other, especially now when we need each other most."

"You are right, Ama. I am glad too." He took my hand and pressed it to his lips. Then he looked up at me with a smile. "I am sorry. I know you have only been trying to help me. I have been a wretched son to you these past months. It has not been easy, adjusting to my role as king, but that is no excuse."

"Your Abbu was around your age when he ascended to the throne, as well. That is why he did his best to prepare you for it, but...one can never truly be prepared for when it comes to pass." I caressed his cheek. "You are doing well, Zyah. Do not be so hard on

489

yourself. Just do the best you can. There is no other way. In the meantime, speak to him," I tipped my head toward the altar and the sealed chamber beyond. "You can always ask him for guidance, and he will always do whatever he can for us, even where he is."

"Thank you, Ama," he said, patting my hand. Then I left my son alone in the tomb, so he could commune with his father in solitude.

We had just arrived at Yezreel, following the conclusion of the Feast of Ba'al at the end of summer, when one of the stewards came to me with a message from a high noble of the city. Lord Haran had been one of my staunchest allies against Nabot, and I had a great deal of respect for him. He was one of the first converts to my religion when I came to this land. Now, his daughter Naomi was ripe for marriage, and he had heard that the king was looking for a suitable wife for his brother. He hoped that when we arrived at Yezreel and were settled, he could have an audience with me regarding Naomi's eligibility. It was customary to present daughters of the nobility to me at court when they reached marriageable age, but whenever the king or one of his brothers or sons looked to acquire a new wife, the number of marriageable daughters seemed to multiply.

Ishaq was currently the most desired man in the kingdom, apart from the king himself. Not only was he the right age for marriage, he was handsome and honorable and, in his position as a minister at court, could provide well for his wives and any children they bore him. Ever since word got out that he was ready for marriage, we suddenly had a great many offers, all of which I had thus far declined without ever speaking to the king – although I used his seal on the letters that went out to inform the unlucky maiden's family of his rejection. It was never personal – that the girl appeared too young or immature for marriage, or offered an unacceptable dowry were the usual excuses – although many had offered more than enough. I simply found that none of the girls were suitable for Ishaq, and I would not bother the king with anyone not worth his time.

The steward read Lord Haran's message while I sat at my dressing table. Kora was arranging my hair, twisting and pinning, braiding and pinning. While he read, I thought about what a waste of time it all was, meeting with these families and interviewing their daughters, only to ultimately turn them away for some minor flaw in their looks or in their characters. But I finally now realized the true reason I found them so unsuitable: I was consumed by a sense of loss and jealousy at the thought of Ishaq being happily married to another. The longer it took to find a suitable bride for him, the harder it became for me to accept my duty.

"Gebirah?" the steward asked suddenly. He had been waiting for my response.

"What?" I asked impatiently, turning my head to him. Kora had not been expecting it and was jerked forward by the motion. She pulled my hair hard in the process, although I hardly noticed, being so used to it from my wild evenings with Asa.

"Shall I tell Lord Haran you will be granting him an audience?"

I sighed heavily. "Yes, I will grant him an audience. Tell him to come this afternoon. I will meet with him when I am finished with my afternoon prayers. And tell him to bring his daughter. I would like to meet her myself to determine her suitability."

The steward nodded and had his scribe make note of it before moving onto the next item on the agenda. Again, I was only half-listening, for I was silently praying to the Ba'alim for the strength and courage to do what I must.

The meeting with Lord Haran and his daughter Naomi went better than I expected. I wanted to despise her, but she was a genuinely sweet girl whose eyes lit up every time she looked at me. No doubt she had been raised hearing about the goddess queen her whole life, and now that she knelt in my presence, I could see the sense of awe and reverence with which she regarded me. Many of the noble daughters presented at court looked at me in that way, and their admiration always endeared them to me more than those who seemed bored or disinterested. Naomi stood out to me more than most however: she bore herself meekly, with a quiet strength. She would do well as a wife to any man of consequence. I knew that if I brought her case before my son, he would surely accept her as a bride for his favorite half-brother. Of course, I knew Zyah would likely accept

491

anyone I brought before him, which was why I did not bring any to him until I myself could accept her.

At the end of the meeting, I thanked Lord Haran. "You have done well and passed through the first gate – me. Now, you must make it through the next gate, which is the king, and then the final gate, which is the bridegroom. I will put in a good word for you and Naomi, but I want you to know that there have been a great many offers. I do not wish to have your hopes raised before it is certain that yours will be accepted."

Haran bowed his head and said graciously, "Thank you, Gebirah. You have always been good to me and my family."

"As you have been to mine," I answered. "I will send word to you, either way, as soon as the king has made his decision."

After dismissing them, I went immediately to find Zyah. He was in the nursery with Naveen and their son, who was now able to walk and chatter incomprehensibly, as if he was some grand Athenian orator, causing everyone to laugh with delight. He was currently regaling his mother and father on some mysterious topic, unaware I was coming. Zyah and Naveen looked up at me, and I held my finger to my lips so as not to reveal my presence. Then I came up behind him, knelt, and scooped him into an embrace.

He giggled when I kissed his nose and tickled his sides, and when I rose to address my son, my grandson stood beside me, clinging to my robes. First, I greeted Naveen, who was now heavy with child, and due to give birth any day. In her condition, she was exempt from kneeling to me when I arrived, but she bowed with her head and shoulders. Then I looked at my son, who rose to embrace me and kissed my cheek. When he returned to his seat, I informed him of the offer we had received. He listened carefully, nodding his approval. When I finished, he said, "Ama, I trust your judgment. If you believe it is an appropriate amount and that the girl is suitable, then I give my assent. What is the next step?"

"Well, now you or one of the scribes – or me, acting on your behalf – will write up the contract and have it delivered to Lord Haran for him to sign, if he is satisfied with the terms."

Zyah seemed slightly surprised. "Which...he should be, if he himself made those terms."

"Yes, it is mostly a formality. However, as king you reserve the right to make any changes to the terms he offered in the form of a counteroffer."

"Should I make changes?"

I shook my head. "Not unless you are unsatisfied, but I assure you there is no reason to be. This is one of the highest offers I have ever seen for a non-dynastic royal marriage, and Lord Haran is one of the only noble elders who could afford to pay it."

"Truly? And with no competition?" He paused as if to reconsider. "Actually, I am surprised it took this long for an offer to be made for Ishaq."

I looked away and gently cleared my throat. "Others have been made, but they were unsatisfactory. Naturally, I would only come to you with a fully suitable offer."

"Ah, yes," he answered, apparently satisfied with my explanation. It was true, after all. Perhaps, in this case, I was more exacting on what I considered satisfactory than I would have been with any other non-dynastic marriage arrangement. If Ishaq was going to be forced to marry, after all, and by my own doing, I wanted him to have the very best.

With Zyah's approval, the arrangement was brought before Ishaq. I instructed Zyah on how he should broach the subject with his brother, and apparently it went well. Although Zyah told me that Ishaq seemed somewhat sad about it, he accepted the king's decision without argument.

The betrothal took place in the king's study soon after the contracts were signed. I was present for the betrothal rites, which were done in the Ba'alist manner since both families were devoted to the Ba'alim. Ishaq was courteous to his intended, while she remained gracious yet reserved; hopefully the two would warm up to each other in time. It was decided that the wedding would take place in early spring when the almond trees were still in bloom.

At the wedding feast, Ishaq and his bride sat in the place of honor at the head table with the king and me as their hosts. They were granted their own houses on the palace grounds, at Shomron, Megiddu, and Yezreel, as a wedding present from the king. Ishaq was also granted an additional allowance to that which he already

493

received as a minister at court, which would afford the couple a comfortable life with a full staff to attend to their needs. They would want for nothing, except perhaps true affection.

I watched the young couple discreetly as the feast went on, noticing that they talked little. Ishaq tried to prompt her into conversation every now and then, but she seemed unreceptive, and the results appeared awkward. Then he gave up and sat staring at his plate without eating, drinking very little of the spiced wine in his cup. Occasionally, I noticed him watching me. Was that yearning in his gaze? I tried to ignore it, moving around the hall to mingle with the guests, but even then, I could still feel him watching me. When I finally turned in his direction and our eyes met, it became almost too much to bear. Soon afterward, I decided to retire for the night.

I went to the head table to congratulate the young couple and give them Ashtarti's blessing before departing. Ishaq looked almost alarmed at my departure; perhaps it reminded him of his duty to consummate his marriage. He met my gaze, almost pleading, and I was inwardly struck by a deep sense of regret at having forced this upon him. I tried to reassure him with my eyes, but in doing so allowed my own true feelings to break through. My face grew warm, and I looked away, but it was too late. He had already caught a glimpse of what I wanted – to be the one in his bed – before I was able to stifle it behind the iron veil that I had draped around myself these past months.

"Shalom, Ishaq," I said quickly. "Shalom, Naomi."

"Shalom, shalom, Ba'alah," Naomi murmured, glancing at me with a gentle smile. When Ishaq said nothing, she glanced at her husband, who continued to stare at me with longing. She looked at me, and then back at him, and then looked down at the hands in her lap helplessly. I should have felt more shame then, but all I felt in that moment was victory. I held his gaze for a long moment before finally turning and walking away without another word.

After returning to my chamber, Kora and the handmaidens helped me out of my regalia and into a thin, light gown of pale green diaphanous silk. I would wear that until I laid down in bed, at which point it would come off. I poured a cup of wine and went to stand in the archway that opened onto the terrace, looking out at the moon and listening to the chorus of insects mating in the lush grasses of early spring.

I breathed in the fragrance of jasmine that hung in the evening air, sipped my wine, and thought about summoning Asa to my bed. No doubt he was still at the feast, waiting and hopeful to receive a summons. After only a moment of consideration, I decided against it, for I had no real desire to be prey to his abuses. I yearned for a gentler touch, which I had not had since my last night with Akhab before he left for Ramot a year and a half ago. I closed my eyes and tried to picture his face and the look in his eyes. But the image was distorted by the look in Ishaq's gaze.

I was just bringing the cup back to my lips when I heard a commotion in the next room. Suddenly, the door to my bed chamber burst open. I spun around to see Ishaq, who had forced his way in. The handmaids who were cleaning up the chamber all stopped and gasped in fright, as he dropped to his knees before me.

"Tell me to leave, and I'll go from here at once and never after return to your sight – for I yearn only ever to please you, my Ba'alah."

The eunuchs who had followed him in were taking hold of him now, but I immediately held up my hand. They stepped back, waiting for further direction.

Meanwhile, Ishaq dropped down onto his hands, his face to the floor. "But if you ask me to stay, I will happily stay always in your sight, which is the only place I long to be."

I met Kora's gaze from across the chamber. She tipped her head and raised her brows. I used my eyes to give her instructions – she knew all my cues, without the need for words – and immediately sent the handmaids away. Their faces fell as they scurried away at their mistress' command. Then I dismissed the eunuchs, assuring them all was well. They, too, seemed almost disappointed to be sent away – certainly they had been eager to take action against this intruder – but I noticed a few eyeing each other and smiling as they went out.

Once everyone had gone, Kora herself slipped away. Before closing the door, she met my gaze with one last smile and nodded her encouragement. Meanwhile, I stood frozen and uncertain, still torn about what to do. Ishaq remained on his knees and seemed to hold his breath. Certain we were alone together, at last he exhaled. Then he cast his gaze around my chamber – my innermost sanctum, which he had never before seen.

For the first time he seemed almost shocked and ashamed by what he had done. We stayed like this for what seemed like a long time – he, gazing at me and looking around, while I looked away in silence, fighting a fierce inner battle that belied the apparent calm of my exterior. At last, I stepped around him and went to stand by the table. Once there, I finished off my drink then refilled my cup. I took another drink, and then another, and at last I found the words to speak.

"You have placed me in a most unnatural predicament." Now, I turned toward him. He still knelt where I left him, but he was watching me from the side and listening. I continued, "Even if I send you away, those who were witnesses to your display will believe that something happened between us. What will they say? What will they do? They are sworn to secrecy regarding me, but that does not mean they will not talk about what they have seen nor swear to what they believe we have done."

He got up slowly and came to stand beside me – close, but still at a respectable distance. I took another long drink and then offered my cup to him. He accepted, finished off what was left, and then refilled it. He offered it back to me. I accepted but then placed it on the table without taking another drink.

"Ba'alah," he at last began, "I apologize for having done this to you. I have nothing to say for myself; only that I was not thinking clearly. I acted on impulse. I did not think about the implications..."

"No, you did not think," I said sharply. "And that is a problem, if you insist on going down this path with me."

"I...do not mean to insist, Ba'alah. I would never do anything to hurt you or to displease you, not intentionally. I..." He stopped and lowered his face. "Forgive me. I thought I had seen something in your gaze before you left the feast. I must have imagined it. I must have seen what I wanted to see, instead of what was really there."

"You did not imagine anything!" I confessed in a sudden outburst. "Only, I cannot have you – do you not understand?" I turned away from him and brought my hands to my mouth, realizing what I said. I leaned forward and then began to weep.

He stood still, likely in a state of shock, and not knowing what to do. Then he stepped up behind me and placed his hands on my arms – lightly at first, as if still afraid to touch me. When I did not flinch or pull away, his touch became firmer and more confident.

Moving slowly, he brought his lips down upon my shoulder. When I did not stop him, he continued brushing them across my flesh until I turned my head to let him kiss the side of my neck.

I shivered and my breath came in shallow. Then I laid my head back against his shoulder and reached to place a hand upon the back of his head, letting my fingers tangle in his curls. He brought his own hands around and cupped my breasts; the thin layer of fabric between our flesh was insignificant. I released a quiet whimper and turned my head to look up at him. Then our lips came together and, at last, we shared one breath.

I moved my body toward him, and he put his arms around my waist, pulling my hips to his while I hooked one leg around him. Again, we kissed and, our hunger growing, began to undress each other as we moved gradually toward the bed.

As he lay over me, holding my cheek and gazing into my eyes, he said, "Naomi is my wife in name, but you – Yezeba'al – I take you as my wife in the flesh, if you will have me."

Trembling as he came over me, I held his gaze, and whispered, "So may it be." Then I closed my eyes, and we came together as one flesh.

22

Cry in the Night

Despite having spent his wedding night with me instead of Naomi, Ishaq did eventually consummate their marriage and, by midsummer, it was announced that she was with child. I was not jealous and, if she knew he was coming to me, she never showed any signs of resentment at court. He would soon take other wives, as expected, and there was no need for competition between us. Although I craved the tenderness and passion with which we made love, I knew that I was not in love with Ishaq any more than I had been in love with the priest of Ba'al from my youth. No matter how much he resembled Akhab, he would never amount to what his father had been to me, although I allowed myself to be infatuated with him to fill the void and warm my bed. He spent many nights with me, coming eagerly whenever I summoned him and, unlike Asa, staying until Kora came to rouse us before dawn.

Devoted and concerned for my reputation, as she had always been, Kora shielded me as much as possible from being discovered, making sure that my lover was secreted away before the other handmaids arrived. However, the eunuchs were always around, always observing; we could only hide so much from them. That is why they took oaths before they were welcomed into the service of kings and were not allowed to live outside the palace: they were aware of the highly confidential things that were discussed between the king and his ministers; they were aware of which princes and nobles were having affairs with other men's wives at court; and they were aware that Kora was admitting men into my chamber late at night.

My love affairs with Ishaq and Asa were conducted with such secrecy that, were it not for Asa bragging about his exploits in my bed, none but the eunuchs might have ever known. His indiscretion came to my attention when I was hosting a small banquet for some of the priests and priestesses of Ashtarti.

I had been perched on the edge of the table after the food had been cleared, sipping wine, and nibbling on pieces of dried fruit. Raman was regaling us with stories about one of the men who had been a regular patron of his when he was still serving at the temple in that capacity. I was at ease, laughing and enjoying the company of my friends, when Ishaq suddenly stormed into the chamber without waiting to be admitted.

"Yezeba'al, I need to speak with you at once!" He stopped suddenly when he saw that I was not alone.

I narrowed my gaze at him, and said, "*Akhimelekh*, you interrupt my banquet, making demands of your queen?"

He tensed his jaw and lowered his face, but his brows were still furrowed with anger. "Ba'alah, I apologize. I was not aware that you were having a banquet."

"What do you want?"

"I... Ba'alah, I humbly request an audience with you. It is an urgent matter."

I sighed heavily, looking at my friends apologetically as I excused myself. Then I turned and went into a side chamber where I expected him to follow. It was a small room where extra wine skins and cups were being stored for the banquet. Bowls of fruit and platters of sweet cakes were laid out on the high table in the center, waiting to be served for dessert. None of that interested us at the moment.

Once the doors were closed behind us, I turned on him. "What are you doing, bursting into my quarters in this manner? What right do you have to come here when you have not been summoned?"

"I remember a time not so long ago when I did, and you welcomed me to your bed!"

"I should never have done that!" I said, and I slapped him across the face. "This is twice now that you have humiliated me, and this time when I am among friends!" I went to slap him again, but this time he grabbed my wrist. When I yanked my arm free from his grasp, rubbing the ache from my wrist, I demanded, "Why have you come here?"

"Zyah had to break up a fight between me and our uncle today."

"What has that to do with me?"

"It was a fight about you."

I wrinkled my brow. "What?"

"The king was having a banquet with his ministers."

"Yes, I know. Why is that important?"

"Because while the other men were bragging about their conquests, Asa said he would put them all to shame: he claims himself as your lover! Even in front of the king, who did nothing, said nothing to defend you, as his own uncle bragged that he had known his mother!"

I was shocked that Asa would be so foolish and indiscreet. I went to pour myself a drink, silently stewing as Ishaq continued ranting.

"I looked to the king, asking him why he did not defend you. He simply sat there drinking and said that he already knew of it and that he did not care what his mother did privately with other men. Other men! What other men?"

"There are no other men," I answered bitterly, bringing my cup to my lips.

"So, what Asa said was not true?"

I sighed heavily and turned my back to him as I finished my drink. Then I went to pour another. He came up behind me and grabbed my hand. Taking the cup by force, he slammed it down and then held my wrists as he turned me around to face him.

"Yezeba'al, is it true, what my uncle said? Do you permit him to your chamber...? Let him lie with you in the same bed where you gave yourself to me?"

Although I was somewhat afraid of him at that moment, I refused to show fear. I raised my chin defiantly. "Yes, it is true. What of it?"

He roared and pushed me away from him. I stumbled back against the table and used it to steady myself, while he pulled at his hair and paced, groaning, and growling like an animal. He shook his head, clenched and unclenched his fists, and then at last stopped to look at me with a mixture of rage and injury. "How...can you?"

"You lie with Naomi," I said, pretending to shrug.

"I am a man! Naomi is my wife! As are you!"

I laughed. "I am not your wife, Ishaq. Nor can I ever be."

"You gave yourself to me."

"I gave myself to Asa long before I gave myself to you. What difference does it make? I am no more your wife than I am his. You

500

have no right to me, except what I choose to give you. I belong to no man."

"You are a whore!"

I sniffed. "Fine. I am a whore. I admit it – in fact, I am proud of it. I enjoy giving myself to different men. Why stop at two? I think it is getting time for me to add a third – maybe even a fourth and a fifth. Soon, I shall have a whole collection of lovers. What do you think? Whom should I choose to lie with next? There are so many men to choose from – I may as well have them all. Why not? I am still youthful enough – I should have every man in Yisrael to my bed before I am old and grey!"

He cried out and turned from me, and I laughed. Then I said, "You are not half the man your father was – is it any wonder I am not satisfied with you?"

It was the wrong thing to say, I admit. The battle that ensued was fierce: shouting, slapping, hitting, scratching, clawing, biting, and throwing things. All the fruit and dessert ended up scattered across the floor. It was so bad that some of the eunuchs came to intervene, but I shouted at them to get out and told them not to return unless I summoned them, as I launched an already dented bowl in their direction. It crashed against the wall beside the door.

Ishaq took advantage of the interruption. He grabbed me around the waist from behind and dragged me toward the table in the center. I pounded my fists against his hands and tried to pry them off me, but he was too strong. Upon reaching the table, he bent me over the surface, held me down, and pulled up the skirts of my dress.

"No!" I growled, my cheek pressed to the table as I struggled against him.

"You are mine!" he insisted, gripping the back of my neck as he pinned me down and pulled out his part. "Only mine!" Then he thrust himself inside me.

The pain of his entry was far worse than the tearing of my maidenhead on my wedding night, but instead of crying out I fell still and closed my eyes to brace against the pain. It seemed to be everywhere all at once. Thankfully, it was over quickly and when he was satisfied, he left me bent over the table, still too shocked and sore to move. I could feel something warm and wet running slowly down my thigh; it turned out to be blood.

501

When I was sure he was gone, at last I began weeping and sank to the floor amidst the chaos. Finally, Kora appeared and helped me up. Shielding me from my guests who stood gaping from the next room, she led me through a side-passage toward my bed chamber, while the eunuchs followed and the slaves went in to clean up the mess that had been left behind.

I could have denounced him. I could have had him arrested and executed for assaulting me. Instead, I withdrew deep into myself and said nothing of what happened when the eunuchs questioned me. They knew what had happened, while they did nothing – after all, I had sent them away when they attempted to intervene. The problem was that I was confused. He was Akhab's son, my own son's closest friend, and a minister of the king's court. Although I outranked him, he was still high enough that to act against him would cause trouble for my son. Besides, I blamed myself more than I blamed him for what he had done to me. So, after admitting to Kora what had happened, I buried it beneath a veneer of nonchalance and went on with my life as usual. The only thing that changed was that I stopped summoning both Ishaq and Asa to my bed.

No one at court had figured out that there was ever anything between me and the handsome young Minister of War. He was a man of high repute, so they assumed his offence at the things Asa had said was due to a sense of honor and nobility, to his respect for me as the goddess incarnate, not a sense of ownership. Neither did I betray my own feelings about him, because I considered managing the kingdom and keeping the peace to be more important than vengeance. At court, I remained detached and cool, as I had always been. I showed neither favoritism nor spite when dealing with the two ministers who were my former lovers, and to their credit neither did they.

If anything, both men seemed to realize they had fallen from grace and accepted their fates without further disruption. Asa must have known word had gotten back to me about his indiscretion. Ishaq was tail-tucked and avoided looking at me altogether, and for that I thought him even more a coward. Only a weak man and a coward would feel the need to force himself upon a woman to prove his dominance. Neither of them was half the man that Akhab had been, and now that I realized it, I wanted nothing to do with them.

I still needed the touch of a man, however; and if I was to be accused of being a whore – while I had been speaking in hyperbole at the time – I decided to make true of it, at least in part. I remained selective in my partners but, if there was a prince or nobleman who caught my fancy, and if I knew he desired me, I summoned him to my bed. Most of them never lied with me more than once. Even those few who could satisfy my carnal needs were incapable of satisfying my spirit. I began to sink further into discontent, hating myself and hating them in equal measure, yet unable to stop.

Perhaps if I had not been so distracted by my unhappy love affairs, I might have seen what was coming and done something to prevent it. Zyah was intelligent and sensitive, but he was still very young to be king and desperate to prove himself to the people of his kingdom, to his ministers, and to me. It was impossible to keep everyone in a divided kingdom happy, and the burden of trying was quickly becoming too much for him to bear.

That summer, Mesha, King of Moab, refused to pay the usual tribute of rams and wool to our kingdom, thinking he could get away with it now that Akhab was dead two years. Zyah went out himself to put the wayward king in his place and prove he was not the boy-king that the Moabites believed him to be. I knew well the character of the Moabite kings, for Akhab had dealt with their unruliness throughout his reign, especially in the beginning. They were loud but they were weak: they only postured when they did not expect retaliation. So, I told Zyah and his ministers to muster the entire army of Yisrael, including the armies of the provinces, and march them into Moab in a show of strength.

At first, everyone was surprised by my advice, for I usually took a more peaceful stance. In this case, however, I did not believe a battle would be necessary: the king simply needed to frighten Mesha into submission. It worked, just as I had expected. The King of Moab was not prepared when my son arrived at the head of his army. He capitulated almost immediately. Apart from providing the tribute he owed to the Kingdom of Yisrael, he offered up the best of his concubines for the young king's delight in the hope that Zyah would be merciful and spare his kingdom and his life.

503

Zyah accepted the tribute and the concubines, thirty-seven in number, and returned to Shomron. On their way back home, he allowed his armies to pillage a small Moabite town on the banks of the Yarden, just to keep his soldiers placated after a warless victory left them restless and dissatisfied. Then he held a banquet for his ministers and generals to celebrate their safe return. There, he paraded the thirty-seven new concubines before his guests and had them line up on the dais while he inspected them and selected his favorites. He chose only seven concubines to keep for himself. The other thirty he sent down from the dais to let the generals and ministers each choose from among them until they had all been claimed.

I found out about the whole thing the next morning, when the stewards reported to me the arrival of seven frightened concubines who were brought to the women's quarters in the middle of the night. After dressing, I went immediately to see what I could do for them. Thankfully, Tamar had mustered several of Akhab's few remaining widows and concubines to comfort and assist them, so that by the time I appeared, they were able to speak without fear. They insisted they had not been forced upon, and that the king had been kind to them, which I expected, but then they recounted what had happened at the banquet.

The king had them stand around his throne, tending to him, while he sat removed from the rest of the women and his guests. They were honored to have been chosen, especially because what he allowed to happen to the rest of the concubines was horrific. Most went willingly to the other men, eager to win their patronage and protection after the king had rejected them, but several were forced upon by the ministers and generals who desired them. Those who refused outright were passed around from man to man, forced to take part in a drunken orgy. Zyah himself did not participate, but he sat on his throne the whole time, drinking, and watching with disinterest. Only after the other thirty women had been passed around did Zyah send his chosen few out to be cloistered in the women's quarters, where they now spoke about it with a mixture of horror, solemnity, and gratitude.

Naveen, who was nursing her daughter at the time, listened to the girls recounting their report in cold silence. Finally, after handing her daughter off to one of the nurses, she got up and shouted,

504

"That is not my king! That is not my Zyah! He would never do such a thing!"

I was caught between comforting the seven new concubines and trying to placate the first one in her heartbreak, all while being reminded of what Ishaq had done to me and feeling the utter devastation of knowing my own son had allowed this to happen. What Naveen said could easily have been my own words, for I had never known my son to behave in this way, either. I had heard of such things happening at other courts of other kings, and even worse things, but never had I imagined it would happen at the court of my own son.

After helping Naveen to calm down, I returned to the other girls and apologized for my son's behavior, although nothing I said seemed sufficient for what they had been subjected to. I was still trying to come to terms with it myself, when I said, "He is my son, and the king. You must understand how difficult it is for me to hear what he has allowed. His father never behaved in such a way, never permitted these things... Ask any of his women who are still here: Akhab was good to all of us.

"Akhazyah...the king is good. He is good. But what he has done is unacceptable, and I will not stand for it." I could barely speak now, as a memory of being pinned facedown against the table flashed before me. I held myself and closed my eyes, trying to shut it out, as I repeated in a whisper, "I will not stand for it."

After departing, I went to see the king at once. Although it was now midday, he was still in bed, hungover from his night of drunken revelry. His personal attendant, Shmuel, the son of Kora and Aharon, attempted to warn me that the king commanded not to be disturbed. I silenced him with a wave of my hand, and he was forced to step aside as I opened the door myself and went in.

The room was dark, the latticed windows shuttered, lamps extinguished. Zyah lay where he had likely collapsed the night before on his stomach on the edge of the bed. He was bare naked, his arm hanging off the side, snoring quietly. I walked up to him, removed my sandal, and smacked him on his buttocks: the leather cracked against his bare flesh. He howled awake, while I returned the sandal to my foot where it belonged and then crossed my arms as I waited for him to acknowledge me.

505

When he saw it was me standing over him, he grabbed the bedlinens to cover himself, and cried, "Ama! What are you doing? I am not even dressed!"

"Relax, I did not see anything – I was not even looking."

After having opened the shutters to let in the daylight, Shmuel brought the king his tunic. I noticed Shmuel struggling not to laugh and attempting to hide it. Sitting on the edge of the bed with his feet on the ground, covering his nakedness with the linens, Zyah narrowed his brows at his friend and yanked the tunic from him. Then he pulled it over his head and got up from the bed, dragging the linens with him to cover his bottom half as he went to use the chamber pot. He stood there a long while, unable to go, until finally he turned to me. "Ama, would you mind at least letting me get dressed before you rebuke me for whatever it is I have done to displease you?"

"Am I making you uncomfortable, Zyah?"

"Yes, that is the point," he said, oblivious to my sarcastic tone.

"Imagine, then, what a woman feels when she is being forced upon by a man. What you are feeling now does not even come close to it."

He sighed heavily and seemed thankful when Shmuel came to hold the linens for him. Obscured, he could at last relieve himself. Once finished, he took the linens and went to stand behind a screen while Shmuel helped him to dress. Then he came out from behind the screen and slumped in a chair, while Shmuel poured him a drink.

"Are you just going to stand there and glare at me all day?"

"Have you nothing to say for yourself?"

"I...do not know what you want me to say, Ama." Then he took a long drink.

"Are you not my son, Zyah? Have you really changed so much? I hardly recognize you."

"Is there a point to all this? Because it is early, and I have a headache."

"It is around midday – it is hardly early. I just spent the morning trying to comfort seven terrified young women, who all witnessed the rape of several other women at *your* banquet last night."

He hung back his head and rubbed his face. Then he said, "I did not do anything to them. It was the other men."

506

"You permitted it. You allowed it to happen. You did *nothing* to stop what was being done to them!"

"What was I to do?"

"You are the king!" I shrieked. "You could have told them to stop!"

"They would not have listened!"

I stood there looking at him in disbelief. My son. Akhab's successor. He was not the man his father and I had raised him to be. Finally, I said, "Then you are a weak king, indeed."

He sat there for a moment, staring at the patterns of light the latticework made in the middle of the floor. I began to wonder if he had heard me, but suddenly he threw his cup and turned over a table as he got up, causing me to jump. Then he began railing, "Yes, I am weak! That is what all the men say of me! 'Poor little Zyah, the boy-king! Run back to your Ama and suckle at her breast!' Oh, that's right – half the generals in my army have already done so! And at least two of my ministers! You make yourself a harlot and tell me how I should be conducting myself as king? I am a laughingstock because of you! They mock me because of *you*, Ama!"

When I finally got over the shock, I said, "Zyah...I did not know. I am sorry. But that still does not excuse what they did – what *you* permitted."

"Is it true that you made love to Ishaq?" he demanded, taking his seat once again. "My own brother, whom you practically raised as your own?" When I did not deny it, he sniffed and looked away with a bitter smile. "I wanted to believe he was lying, but Ishaq never lies."

"Zyah, please," I tried to say, wanting to explain everything, but my voice broke, and I could not go on.

Then he held up his hand. "Do not speak to me. Do not speak my name, Lilitu – for I am not your son." He pinched the bridge of his nose, and said, "*Abakhu* Asa I could handle. The others...they were bad enough. But Ishaq...a son of my father. I am disgusted by you." He paused, and then added, "If I have changed, Ama, then so have you. I suppose we are both corrupted by the death of my father. Nothing has been right since he left..."

Anger gave way to despair in his tone, and he began weeping. Although my heart cried out to him, I did not move to comfort him, for he had wounded me. *He is disgusted. I am disgusting.* If that was true, then he would not want me to comfort him. So, I stood with my hands folded in front, silent and unmoving. It was all I could do to hold myself together – turn myself to stone, cold and unfeeling as the statue of Akhab in the tomb below. While his body lay rotting and decayed beneath the palace, we were rotting along with him. *The entire kingdom may as well rot with us*, I thought bitterly. Then I turned and, without saying another word, walked away to find solace in the arms of a lover. But I wish to the gods that I had stayed.

A cry woke me in the middle of the night, low and mournful. It was followed by a long silence. I lay in bed, breathing heavily and wondering if I had only dreamt the sound. Then another cry and then a shout, and more voices were soon to follow, echoing in the darkness. I assumed it was coming from outside, somewhere in the city near the palace, until the horns were blown from the ramparts, and I knew something was terribly wrong.

I got out of bed and pulled on my robe. Only then did my lover begin to stir. It was the governor of Shomron, Lord Amon, with whom I had recently taken up after being dissatisfied with so many others. He was somewhat heavyset but a lion in bed.

"What's happening?" he asked, his voice deep and heavy with sleep.

"Nothing," I said shortly. "Go back to sleep."

He sat up and watched me go to the arched doorway to look out across the terrace. Now, it was silent again, but for the nocturnal creatures lurking in the garden, yet even they were on alert. One of the peacocks had awakened and was now pacing the rooftop, looking for signs of trouble in case he needed to alert the rest of his flock. If it had not been for the horns that were already blown, I would have thought perhaps it was the cry of the peacock himself that had awakened me.

Suddenly, a knock came at my door – pounding, desperate – followed by the voice of one of the eunuchs calling to me. My lover jumped out of the bed and grabbed his clothes, and I shepherded him into the antechamber where I had my bathing font. He pinched my behind and kissed me as he went. I laughed and shooed him away. Then I closed him inside and returned to my bed, to make it appear as if I had just awakened.

"Enter."

The door opened and the eunuch came in, haggard yet in a state of alarm. He knelt before me, and his voice trembled as he spoke. "Gebirah, there has been as accident... The king... He is greatly injured. Please, you must come, Gebirah."

"Zyah..." I whispered. Then I grabbed a mantle, threw it over my head and followed the steward to the king's quarters – forgetting about my lover and everything else in an instant.

As we came near the king's quarters, we heard many boots shuffling quickly against the stone floor, and we stopped to see who was approaching. Then came the agonized groaning of my son, being carried by the eunuchs to his bed. In the darkened corridor, I could barely see him, but something about the way they carried him seemed wrong. Was there blood on his face?

Once they had passed, we followed behind them into the king's bedchamber, where some of the servants were already waiting after having been alerted to the accident. They began tending to the king, while I stood for a moment uncertain of what I could do. My eyes stung with tears, and I could not understand what was happening. Then I looked toward the window and saw the broken latticework.

A memory flashed before me: Zyah as a little boy, no older than three or four, standing in the window when I entered his chamber. He had climbed up to peer through the lattice, and he turned to smile at me when I called his name in alarm and ran to pull him out of the window. His nurse came running from the next chamber, where she had gone to relieve herself, and began apologizing. I silenced her with a wave as I knelt on the floor, clutching my son and sobbing. He stood rigid in my embrace, and when I sat back to look at his face and brushed his curls to the side, he asked, "Why are you weeping, Ama?"

He reached to wipe the tears from my cheeks, while I answered, "I do not know, Zyah. It is only because I love you so much and could not bear for anything bad to happen to you."

Then he kissed my cheek, and said, "Nothing would happen, Ama."

"You could have fallen through the lattice," I explained, grateful that I had come upon him when I did. "It would have been a terrible fall. Never climb into the windows again. If you want to look out, you must always ask one of your elders to help you do it. Do you understand?"

He nodded, his large brown eyes shining as he met my gaze, and then I pulled him into my embrace once again.

Thrust back to the present when my son's agonized wail rose suddenly, I brought my hand to cover my mouth, and the sting of fresh tears came again. He was covered in blood and writhing in agony as the servants and eunuchs tended to his injuries. One of his legs was clearly broken, the bone jutting through his flesh. The eunuch who was tending to him carefully moved to the king's broken leg and set the bone back to where it belonged. Zyah did not react to this, and the eunuch looked at him in surprise. Then he turned to me.

At last, the shock wore off and I went to my son. I knelt on the floor beside his bed, and he clung to my hand, squeezing terribly and pressing it to his lips. He wept and trembled.

"Ama," he cried. "Ama, please! I'm sorry! Please, forgive me! I am sorry!"

"It is all right, Zyah," I answered, kissing his hand, and trying not to show the horror that I felt as I looked at his bloodied face. "I am here. I forgive you. I love you. It is all right. I am here, my son."

Suddenly, his eyes took on a distant look and his whole body went stiff. I cried out, at first thinking he was dead, for he seemed to have stopped breathing. Then suddenly he began crying and moaning again, foaming at the mouth like one possessed. It sounded as if he was choking, while his body writhed on the bed. The eunuchs rushed forward to hold him down so he would not fall from the bed. I stepped back in horror.

"What is happening?" I cried, my hands to my mouth. My son was dying, it seemed, and there was nothing I could do but stand and watch.

"It is from the fall, Gebirah," the eunuch explained calmly. "It happens sometimes, as a result of the impact."

"Is he dying?"

Now, the eunuch set his jaw and looked away without answering. After a few minutes, the writhing stopped, Zyah's body relaxed, and his breathing returned to normal. He appeared to be sleeping. That's when the eunuch turned back to me, and said, "Gebirah, he should be all right for now, but..." He lowered his face

510

and sighed. Then he looked up, and said, "Forgive me, Gebirah, but I think you should send for a priest of Ba'al."

"No," I said, shaking my head and looking at my son. "No."

Suddenly, Kora came to me and put her arms around me. I do not know when or how she came, but she was there with her husband and their sons together. They must have just arrived, after having been summoned. Shmuel and Ezra went to the king's side, while Aharon spoke with the eunuchs and the others present to get a report. Meanwhile, I wept on Kora's shoulder as she held me the way that her mother used to hold me when I fell into despair.

A few minutes later, Zyah woke up. He cried out for me, and I went to him immediately. I sat on the bed and held his hand and stroked his forehead. His face was bruised and, although the blood had been washed from it by the servants when they tended to him while he slept, I could see broken flesh beneath the swelling. Apart from the broken leg, which he could not feel because he had lost all sensation from the waist down, he had two broken ribs and a fractured elbow. At first, he could not remember what had happened. I had to explain to him that he had fallen from the window.

"I did not fall," he said quietly.

"Of course, you fell, Zyah," I explained. "How else do you think this came to pass, that you are like this?"

"I did not fall," he said again, and he turned his face from me in shame.

It was not an accident. After I left him that afternoon, Zyah had sent for Naveen in the hope that she would comfort him, but she refused to see him. He had spent the rest of the day drinking and wallowing in his grief until deciding in a moment of despair that he was going to end his life. Now, he regretted it and was fearful of death. I blamed myself, for I had not been there to comfort him when he needed me most. For the past year, at least, I had been so distracted that I was hardly a mother to him. And one of the last things I had said to him before he had attempted to end his life, was to call him weak. How I wished that I could take back those words. How I wished I could have done and said so many things differently.

There was no time for self-pity though, or even for self-loathing. All I could do now was tend to my son whenever I could get away from managing the kingdom for him, and pray for a miracle, even as the reality of his situation became more apparent with each passing day. He continued to live in agony. Whenever he fell unconscious and his body again began to seize and writhe about, I sat with him and held his head in my lap, stroking his forehead and singing to him through my tears, as the eunuchs and healers came to support him so he would not fall from the bed and sustain further injury. They turned him onto his side which caused him great pain, but it was necessary so he would not choke while the fit raged on. Meanwhile, I continued to support his head and stroked his hair until it was over.

The healers tended to him the best they could, but after the first two days, they admitted that his condition was beyond their capabilities to heal. They urged me to send for a priest of Ba'al, but I still refused to accept that my son would die. I went to the temple and made an offering, but the smoke turned thick and black as the offering was burnt: a clear sign of rejection. I understood that my Ba'alim would not heal Zyah because he had done it to himself with the intention to commit self-murder, which they abhorred as much as they abhorred a human sacrifice. I wept and went away knowing that I would have to seek the favor of another god to heal my son and preserve his life.

That is when I remembered the priest of Ba'al Zebul who had come to heal me when I was near to death after wounding myself when Akhab died. I dispatched messengers to Ekron, to request the aid of that priest early the next day, but they returned a few hours later, having not made it to Ekron.

"What are you doing back so soon?" my son demanded weakly of his messengers. He was trembling, having been throwing up. His forehead was covered in sweat, his eyes looked hollow, and his face was gaunt. I feared another fit was coming on, for I was starting to notice that he often became ill before those fits began, when he was not himself.

The messengers knelt, prostrated themselves before us and apologized. Then the chief among them explained, "Melekh, a man came to meet us on the road, and said to us, 'Go, return to the king who sent you, and tell him Yahowah asks if it is because there is no God in Yisrael, that you send to inquire of Ba'al Zebul, the god of Ekron? Therefore, you will not come down from the bed where you have gone up, but you will surely die.' That is what the man has said to us, Melekh."

512

I narrowed my gaze, and darkness filled my heart as I recognized the tone of these warnings. Then I whispered to my son and, following my prompt, he asked, "What kind of man was this who came to meet you, and told you these words?"

The messengers looked each to the other, and then the head of them responded, "He was a hairy man, and old. He wore animal skins and ropes and a leather belt around his waist."

While I sneered with recognition, my son said, "It is Eliyah the Tishbite. Is that not how you have described him, Ama?"

"It is he," I said bitterly. Then I shushed him when he tried to speak again, gently placing a hand to cover his lips, and urging him to rest his head once again upon my lap. I looked at the messengers, and commanded, "Go. Send for one of the captains of the king's guard. Tell him this is the king's command: that he should take fifty of his men to find this Eliyah the Tishbite and bring him here to see the king."

The messengers bowed obediently and left to carry out my orders. They left just in time, too, for a short while after, another fit came upon my son. I sat with him the whole time, waiting for it to pass, before I left him to sleep. I then went to meet with the Lord Steward and the ministers of court, telling them about what had happened with the king's messengers. Aharon averted his gaze when I gave him a look, and the ministers were disgusted that the Tishbite had returned to plague us yet again – especially those of whom were old enough to remember when he was most a thorn in our side.

I stood over the king's desk, resting the palms of my hands upon it, when Asa attempted to comfort me. He placed his hand upon my back, but I jerked away from his touch. He sighed heavily while I went to stand by the window instead, looking out at the evening sky. Then I turned back to the men and said, "When he arrives, we will ask what he has to say of this so-called prophecy."

Still wincing from my rejection, Asa asked, "Will you have him killed, Ba'alah?"

I sniffed in amusement. Then I said wistfully, "No. What is the use? If I have him killed, another will only rise to take his place, and the next one could be worse." I narrowed my gaze at a movement in the latticework by the corner of the window and watched a spider working on its web. Then I mused, "They are like spiders, these zealots. The more you exterminate them, the more they seem to

513

appear, and before long you have an infestation that you cannot be rid of." I turned to face the ministers again, who were watching me in confusion. I smiled bitterly, and continued, "You have to find the nest and destroy all the eggs before they are hatched, or they will only continue to grow in number."

"Gebirah?" asked Natan, Tamar's son.

I shook my head. "You are too young, perhaps, to understand metaphors. And the rest of you...?" I held out my hand, but most of them did not understand what I was implying.

"I understand," said Asa. He never wanted to be seen as incompetent. "So, how do we find their nest to exterminate them once and for all?"

"We don't," I said. "One cannot kill a god. Even if you kill all his followers, more will come to know him in time."

"Are you saying you believe in their god, Gebirah?" asked Natan.

"Of course, I believe in him. Just as I believe in my own, and everyone else's. I always have. I simply do not believe he is a righteous god, for he has no honor and refuses to accept that he is not the only one."

With an exhausted sigh, I waved dismissively so they would know that I was done with the meeting. Then as I made my way to the door, they all knelt and watched me depart. I returned to my chamber for a short respite, summoned Amon to me, and took solace from him. Then I went back to sitting with my son.

This time my other children came to sit with us, and Naveen was also there with her two children. The only one missing was Atalaya, who had been informed that her brother was sick and possibly dying, but good King Yehoshapat refused to give her leave to come to us. He feared the displeasure of his god after he, too, had heard that my son's condition was a punishment from Yahowah for his refusal to turn away from the Ba'alim. Yahowah was, indeed, a god of no honor, I thought bitterly, if he would refuse to permit a woman to attend the bedside of her dying brother.

The first of our captains and their fifty men-at-arms were slaughtered by the Tishbite and his people when they found where he was hiding, once again having taken up residence in the

514

mountains of Kerem-el. It was said that fire came down from the sky and consumed all the men, and the messengers who returned to tell us about what had happened were terrified. I remembered that trick of the Tishbite and his followers, using the same Egyptian magic they had used for many years.

Thinking they had not enough time to rig up their traps again, I sent another captain and his fifty, only to have the same thing happen to them. When the messengers came to me with that report, I was outraged, while they were terrified – not of me, but of the Tishbite and his god. They refused to act anymore on my or the king's behalf. Rather than lose my temper with them, I summoned a court magician to come and show them how it was done. He easily performed a similar trick to that which the messengers had witnessed, although it was on a much smaller scale in the courtyard with a nest of wasps as the target.

After seeing how simple and easy it was to replicate the Tishbite's Egyptian magic, the messengers were somewhat put at ease, if not wholly convinced. At least, they were willing to summon another captain and his fifty to go to the mountains and bring the Tishbite back to face us at Shomron. This time, I told them to reassure the Tishbite that the king had promised he would not be harmed while in our presence, which I hoped would prevent another incident.

The trip there from Shomron took a couple days; it was no wonder the zealots were able to rig their traps again before our men arrived the second time. I hoped the third time would be successful, especially because I feared my son's time was running out. Although his wounds and broken bones were healing slowly, the fits were becoming more frequent and severe, and his overall condition was worsening with each passing day. Although it seemed the prophecy of Eliyah was proving true, my hope was that it was still not too late for his god to remove the curse upon us.

On this third attempt, Eliyah was convinced not to murder the captain and his fifty men, and he came willingly with them to Shomron. A messenger had ridden ahead to inform us of their expected arrival, and so when the time came for him to be brought to us, I was dressed for battle: a queen in all her glory. When the prophet was led to the king's chamber, I was there to meet him, seated in a chair beside the king who was propped up with cushions

515

in his bed. Zyah had been washed and dressed for the occasion, but his illness was impossible to obscure no matter how fine his robes, how rich his jewels.

The prophet was old now. He had always been old, it seemed to me, but now he seemed positively ancient. It was clearly him, though. I recognized the fierce obstinance of his gaze, although when he first laid eyes upon the sickly king his countenance softened more than I had expected. This was an old man who had lived a long life, perhaps realizing the unfairness of a young and previously active man being deprived of his health. Then he turned his gaze to me, and his countenance once again hardened. Yet, always there was the sense that he could almost smile: that scornful, satisfied grin that I despised with every fiber of my being.

"Melekh Akhazyah. Gebirah *Yezebel*. Forgive me for not kneeling – I fear if I did, I might not get up again, and then you would be forced to look at me for the rest of your days." He paused and seemed to reconsider his use of that particular phrase.

Zyah looked at the prophet curiously. He had never met Eliyah the Tishbite, never laid eyes upon him, but he had heard a great deal about this prophet who had made himself my greatest nemesis. I could not know what he thought of this ancient man when he first looked upon him; he never had the chance to tell me what he thought. Once he had finished observing the man, all he said was, "Eliyah the Tishbite – my father said you had a wicked wit. I see that this was true. He also said that you were unbelievably stubborn in your unwillingness to show the king proper respect. You may use your old age as an excuse now, but I wonder what excuse you might have had before you were old?"

The prophet seemed about to speak, but Zyah cut him off. "No matter. I do not much care if you bow to me or if you do not. I only want to hear what it is you have to say: what is it that you told my messengers, when you stopped them on the road and prevented them from performing the task set for them."

"Melekh," said Eliyah, "you have sent messengers to inquire of Ba'al Zebul, but in doing so you have shown that you have no faith in Yahowah, the true God of Yisrael. Therefore, Yahowah says that you will not come down from that bed where you have gone up, but you will surely die."

Zyah inhaled sharply and turned to me. I could see that he was exhausted and afraid. I reached out to take his hand, squeezed tightly, and then rose from my chair. "Tishbite, I have spared your life so that you might come here to speak with my son the king."

"Yahowah has spared my life, Gebirah," he said calmly, keeping his head high and his gaze fixed beyond me.

"*I* have spared your life, zealot. So many times, I could have killed you, but you were always given fair warning and had time to flee."

"Yahowah inspired you to warn me, Gebirah."

"If he can inspire me to do his bidding when it comes to sparing your life, why can he not inspire me to follow him?"

"He will not force you to believe in him."

"I do believe in him. I simply do not follow him."

Now, he looked at me – for only a moment – and then returned to staring past me. "Free will is a gift he has given to all of us. He cannot help that you have chosen to squander it, anymore than a father might be able to help what his son does with his inheritance."

"He is a god, not a man. Is he all-powerful, or not?"

"He will not force you to follow him."

"Is that not what he has been trying to do, by cursing me and those I love? Or perhaps it is not your god that has cursed us – perhaps it is you trying to bend us to your will."

"Not my will, but the will of Yahowah be done." He seemed to hesitate, and then he said, "I told you many years ago, that Yahowah would curse you and Akhab, and all the men of Akhab's house, for what you did to the man Nabot."

"Then you are saying that he has done this to my son?"

He met my gaze: a brazen act. "I warned you, Gebirah. I warned you what would come to pass. The sins of the father – and the mother – shall fall on their descendants. It is written in the laws of Moshe."

Finally, my composure cracked. I was desperate, and I began to plead, "If he has done this, then tell him to undo it."

"I cannot command the almighty."

"You have done it before, so they say – you have spoken to him, and he has done what you asked. He has healed those who were believed to have been lost."

"That was different, Gebirah."

517

"It is *not* different! If he is all-powerful, nothing is beyond his doing!" I dropped to my hands and knees now and began to weep openly. "If he listens to your word, tell him to heal my son!" I rose onto my knees with my hands clasped together. "Tell him to heal him, and I will believe!"

Eliyah looked at me with pity. Then he closed his eyes, and it seemed as if he was listening to someone else speak. After a moment, he shook his head and sighed. "It is too late, Gebirah. I am sorry. Truly, I am. Nothing can be done for your son the king."

"No!" I wailed, dropping again with my hands on the floor.

His voice was strained, yet he spoke firmly, "You should have turned away from your idols and your wickedness when you had the chance, but you refused, and now you are paying for your disobedience. I cannot undo what you yourself have done."

I looked up at him, at first in disbelief. Then I hardened my heart, wiped the tears from my cheeks, and pulled myself to stand. "Then I curse your god. I curse him, and you, and all who believe in him. If he will not help me, when I am desperate and in need, he has proven that he does not deserve my worship and obedience. I will not serve a jealous tyrant." Then I spit at the prophet's feet and turned away.

Without facing him, I said, "I promised not to harm you when you came to us. I always keep my word." Now, I turned to him, and continued, "But know this: if you ever come near this city, or any city in this realm and I hear of it, you will be arrested and condemned. You have three days to remove yourself from this kingdom before you are hunted as a fugitive and an enemy of the House of Omri."

Then, with a wave of my hand, I summoned the eunuchs who brought him to me, and commanded, "Take him away. He is free to leave."

They took him, and when the door was closed, the last of my façade crumbled. I began trembling and went to my son and dropped to my knees beside his bed. I took his hand and kissed it and wept, holding onto him for as long as I could. He reached for me, and he also wept, and said, "It is not your fault, Ama. Whatever he has said, it is not your fault. Know that I do not blame you or Abbu for my death, nor even Yahowah. I have only myself to blame."

I shook my head and held his hand to my cheek. "Do not say that, Zyah. It is not a certainty. There is still a chance…" But I knew

518

now that there was no hope, and that it was only a matter of time before the prophet's word came to pass.

Although I still insisted there was hope, I did summon a priest of Ba'al to perform the rites of the dying upon my son in his final hours. Afterward, when I came to sit upon the bed behind him and held his head in my lap once again, he looked up at me and in his gaze was a look I had not seen since he was a small boy. Once, when he was afraid of a thunderstorm, he had run to find safety in my arms and he looked at me with such trust in his gaze, knowing that I would always be there to protect him. As I had done then, I smiled down at him and touched his cheek. Now grown, he closed his eyes and held my hand there. Then he opened them again, and said, "Ama...I am afraid to die."

"You will not die, Zyah," I assured him, not wanting him to be afraid. "You are getting better." I touched his forehead gently. "Your wounds and your broken bones are healing. And soon your body will also be healed. Do not listen to what that so-called prophet said. He is a hateful man, and he has always been against us. Do not be afraid, my son. All will be well – we need only to have faith."

He settled into my arms and looked toward the wall by his bed, where the sunlight created a pattern of bright orange with the latticework, as it always did when evening approached. I stroked his forehead, letting my fingers brush against his curls, and a single tear slipped down my cheek. "Soon, you will be well again – your pain will fade, and your legs will walk, and you will have nothing at all in the world to fear. And I will be with you, my son. I promise, I will never leave you."

He sighed with exhaustion and closed his eyes. And when the next writhing fit came upon him, it was his last. I held him the whole time, and continued to hold him even afterward, when it was confirmed that he was gone. Weeping quietly, I gazed upon my son, remembering the joy I had the first time I held him in my arms.

519

Part III

On Sacrifice

23

What's in a Name?

There you are," I said, stepping out onto the king's private terrace overlooking the courtyard and the palace grounds. We were at Megiddu; it was late afternoon, and the city was rejoicing after the birth of an heir to Yoram and his queen, Be'ulah. My second-born son stood taller than his elder brother had, but from behind I might have thought it was Zyah leaning with his elbows against the terrace wall. When he heard my voice, Yoram stood to his full height, and turned to offer me a gentle smile.

At sixteen, he was only just starting to grow a beard, and his features resembled mine more than his father's, which only made him look even more youthful than Zyah had at his age. In time, Yoram would look more like a man, and then he would resemble my brother Esar. For now, though, I could still see in him the little boy who had always been too busy trying to be a man to cuddle with his Ama.

I stepped up beside him and placed my hands upon the ledge. The sun had dipped below the palace behind us to the west, and the stone was cool to the touch. I looked up at my son and returned his smile. "I wondered where you had gone – as did Be'ulah. Have you tired of the banquet already?"

He hummed and turned back to look out over the courtyard. Three of his half-brothers and several other members of his court were out playing a game: tossing a ball to their partners and then racing across the dry summer grass to see who would reach the other side first. It was a game the men and boys often played, taking turns either standing on the sidelines or participating. Yoram was watching, saying nothing.

One of them, a half-brother, looked up and saw the king. He called out and waved to him, laughing, then making an ass of himself the way young men often do when they are among friends. Yoram permitted himself to chuckle and wave back. Then one of the other men below threw their arms around the half-brother's neck and alerted him to the presence of the queen mother beside the king. His mouth dropped open, and his brows raised, and then he offered a quick reverential bow.

Laughing, I shook my head at his antics and offered him the blessing of Ba'al. He kissed his fingers and returned the blessing, and then went back to the game. Meanwhile, I said to Yoram, "I am surprised you are not down there with them."

"I do not feel like playing, Ama."

After studying my son, I said, "The weight of the kingdom is heavy upon your shoulders. And now with a son of your own to look after... It is a lot for a young man to bear."

He nodded. "You understand my predicament."

"Yoram, just because you are a father and a king now does not mean you cannot make time to enjoy the pleasures of youth. Even your Abbu was not above play. You remember – he was always out sporting with the other men."

"I remember he was always with you," he said, turning to look at me, "and how happy you were together."

Now, I leaned with my elbows on the terrace and looked out across the courtyard, toward the temple that rose higher than the other buildings in the palace complex. "We were happy. Just as I hope you will be with Be'ulah. You seem to be well-matched."

He sighed. "Be'ulah is a good woman. I care for her deeply, but...we will never have what you and Abbu had together." He paused and looked at me again. "How do you manage it? To go on with life, managing the kingdom and the household as if nothing has changed, when everything has changed?"

"Everything has changed," I agreed, breathing deeply to maintain my composure. "But we must remember that all was not lost – even though it feels that way, at times. Your Abbu...I still feel him with us. And Zyah, too. And I know how proud they are of you: as proud as I am."

He shook his head and sighed again. "Zyah did not feel that he could ever live up to the man that Abbu was, and he was raised for this. I was not."

I worried for Yoram, having seen what my eldest son had gone through only after it was too late. With my second son, I wanted to avoid making the same mistakes. "You have done well, taking a throne that was never meant for you – a role that you were never expected to take. It was thrust upon you without any preparation, any training, but you have risen to the challenge. Be proud of what you have accomplished this past year."

"What have I accomplished? If not for you, Ama, I would not even have a throne to sit on. You should be king; I have done nothing but rely on you for everything."

"I cannot be king," I said, chuckling at the thought. "Nor would I want to be. And you have done more than you take credit for."

"On the contrary – I take all the credit, while you do all the work."

"Such is the way of kings and queens," I joked. Then I became serious again. "In time, you will do more, and I will do less. I look forward to that day." I reached up and tussled his hair. He brushed my hand away, but I could see that he was trying not to smile. Then I said, "You are going to be a great king, Yoram. Have patience with yourself while you are learning. You cannot do it all at once."

"Abbu was great without even trying to be great."

"Not at first," I admitted. He turned to look at me in shock, while I shrugged. "It took years for your Abbu and I to adapt to the duties of managing an entire kingdom – one that has grown immensely since the start of his reign."

"But Abbu was a man grown by the time he rose to the throne."

"He was only in his twenty-first year. He still had much to learn."

"The kingdom respected him."

"And it will respect you if you show yourself to be capable and wise."

He seemed overwhelmed at the thought, and asked, "How can I do that?"

Again, I tussled his hair, and teased, "By listening to your Ama. And your ministers: such as they are. But even we are not always right, and then you must learn to fall back on your own judgment."

"And if my own judgment is also wrong?"

I tilted my head and thought about how best to answer. "At times, it will be. And when that happens, you must readjust and learn from your mistakes. Even kings make mistakes, Yoram. The

525

mark of a great king is not that he never makes a mistake, but that he learns from it and tries to do better. To do that, he must be adaptable and fair: he must be firm when he needs to be, and merciful when he can afford to be."

"How will I know?"

"Practice. Experience. And when you are uncertain, you have me and your ministers to guide you. It is not all on your shoulders. Remember that."

"Sometimes it feels as though it is," he answered with a sigh.

"Listen: no kingdom can be managed by one man alone. That is why you have all of us to help you. And the princes of the provinces, and the elders and the governors, and your generals, and even the slaves are here to help you. We all make up this kingdom – every man, woman, and child, slave or free. And together, with each one in his place, we all keep it functioning as best it can."

"Until one of them is unhappy with our rule and rebels. How many times did Abbu have to send one of his armies to strike down a rebellion in one of the provinces?"

"Not often, but it did happen sometimes – especially during the years of the great drought."

"But how many of those rebellions happened because he intervened in a dispute between two princes, and the one he ruled against was angry with his decision."

"More often than you realize," I answered. "Yoram, you made the right decision. Prince Baraq was displeased, yes, but you cannot keep everyone happy. The harder you try, the more it will feel as though everything is falling apart. You must do the best you can, to give concessions and make compromises wherever it can be done, but in the end, you can never make everyone happy. So, you must base your decisions on what is for the highest and best good."

"How will I know what that is?"

"It will benefit the most people at a time, or it will hurt as few as possible."

"As few as possible," he repeated with dissatisfaction. "And for those people whom it will not benefit – do they not matter, Ama?"

"They matter; but you cannot do for them what will harm the majority of your people, or you will lose everything. The kingdom cannot stand if those who do the most to support it are dissatisfied. So, when it comes to pleasing one prince or one group over another, you must please those who have the greatest impact – not necessarily those who have the loudest voice. Prince Baraq had a loud voice, but he was wrong, and the rest of the princes were against him. You made the right decision."

"But should that decision have cost him his life? And his family their estate?"

"Yoram," I said firmly, "*your* decision did not cost him and his family. *His* decision to rebel cost them that. He should have accepted your decision. If he had done so, he would still be alive. You must not feel shame or guilt for doing what was necessary to maintain the wellbeing of your kingdom. And you must let go of this idea that all young people seem to have, that you must find a way to please everyone, for it is not possible and you will drive yourself mad trying."

He was silent, but I could see that he was thinking about everything. Then he nodded, and said, "Thank you, Ama. I will try my best."

I held his shoulders and rose to kiss his cheek. Then, I stepped down and looked up at him with a broad smile. "That is all you can do, my son. And I want you to know that by concerning yourself with these matters and asking these questions – these are the marks of one who has the potential to become a great king. Never stop asking the hard questions."

He chuckled and turned to lean on the wall again, while I changed the subject. "Now, concerning the matter of your newborn son. Have you discussed with Be'ulah what he is going to called? His circumcision is in three days, and you must have his name by then."

"I want to name him Akhab, but she does not think it is appropriate, because Zyah's son was named Akhab. I told her, it does not matter, since my nephew is not in the line of succession. Besides, he is not even here anymore since Naveen returned to Aram."

After the death of Zyah, Naveen had mourned his loss terribly, but she felt she had no place without him here. She had asked for permission to return to her family with her two children, my grandchildren. It had been a hard decision to make, but I had ultimately advised Yoram to let her go. Her children were not legitimate and could never succeed to the throne, so there was no threat from her leaving with them. Yoram had no interest in Naveen, although apart from being married to Be'ulah and taking Shalima as his wife in name only, he had claimed the seven new concubines for

527

his own. Now, five of his concubines were at various stages of pregnancy and he had a son with his queen.

"What does Be'ulah wish to name him?"

He sighed and raised his eyes toward the heavens. "She wishes to name him Hanniba'al."

"What is wrong with that name? It is a good, strong name and it honors our god."

"It does not seem appropriate for a future king of Yisrael, Ama. This is not Hamat or Tzidon – those are kingdoms of the Ba'alim, but the people of Yisrael belong to Yahowah and I feel that my son's name should honor him, if it does not honor my father."

My lips parted in surprise, and I did not at first know what to say. Then I said, "It is customary for the mother to choose the names of her children."

"Yes, but this is not just any child, it is a boy who will likely one day become my successor. He needs a name that belongs to Yisrael, just as he belongs to it."

"I do not disagree – after all, your brother and you, and most of my sons, were given names to honor your father's people and their heritage for that same reason. But this is a different time, Yoram. The people of Yisrael are in favor of the Ba'alim. They have always been, until the foolish belief in one god captivated them. I believe they would accept a king with a strong name such as Hanniba'al to honor the gods who are worshipped here just as they are worshipped in Hamat and Tzidon and elsewhere. Let Yehudah remain as Yahowah's kingdom alone. Yisrael is our kingdom, and our gods are the Ba'alim – *all* of them, not just the one."

I placed a hand over his, while I prepared to leave. "Think on it. If you cannot reconcile yourself to that name, talk with Be'ulah. See if there is a name you may both agree on. And remember what I have said about compromise." I winked at him, and then returned to the banquet.

Three days later, my grandson was given the name Abdiel: "servant of El." It was the closest they could come to an agreement, and seemed a worthy compromise because El was the father of both Yahowah and our Ba'al, and often had to intervene in their disputes. Perhaps a king with that name to honor him would one day manage to bring peace between these two sons of El, who seemed never to be capable of compromise. The name was received with favor by

Yahwists and Ba'alists alike, for Yahwists considered El to be an alternative name for Yahowah instead of recognizing him as the father of the gods. In this name, both factions saw what they wanted to see, and I considered this a good sign for the future of our kingdom.

It was perhaps a week or so after my grandson's circumcision, when the court moved back to Shomron, that the Kingdom of Yisrael faced yet another rebellion by the King of Moab. Early one afternoon, while in bed with Amon, who was by now my predominant lover at Shomron, Kora discreetly entered the chamber. Averting her gaze, tone apologetic, she said, "Ba'alah, forgive me..."

Amon was on top of me and was about to pull away, but I clung to him, and commanded breathlessly, "Don't stop!" Then I shouted at Kora, "Get out!" and continued with my lover.

Kora knew better than to interrupt when I was with a lover, so I knew it must have been important, but in that moment I hardly cared. Whatever it was, it could wait until we finished.

My lover continued, but Kora did not go away. Instead, still averting her gaze, she said, "Ba'alah, one of the king's eunuchs is here."

Desperately close to satisfaction, I held onto Amon, and shouted, "Send him away!" Then I growled and dug my fingernails into Amon's flesh, so he would grow fiercer, because his performance had begun to wane.

"The king has summoned you!"

I howled in frustration.

She continued, "He has called for an assembly of the high council."

"Now?" I asked through gritted teeth, finally lying back on the bed.

Amon groaned and pulled away, grabbing at the bedlinens to cover his nakedness. This time I let him go. It was no use anyway – he had gone flaccid.

"Am I also summoned?" he asked, reaching for his cup on the bedside table.

"No, my lord," she answered. "It is only the queen, ministers, and generals who are summoned, according to the eunuch."

"Praise Ba'al." He set down his cup and went to use the chamber pot. He grabbed his loincloth on the way, holding it over his parts as he walked across the chamber.

Meanwhile, I was still lying on my back, breathing heavily, staring up at the ceiling with hot tears in my eyes and trying to compose myself. I could have killed Kora just then, or the eunuch who was the king's messenger, or even my son the king himself, for this intrusion. *This would never have happened when Akhab was alive,* I thought bitterly. Of course, that is because it would have been Akhab who was with me. A stab of grief struck me in the heart and I had to breathe deeply to ease the sudden ache.

Meanwhile, Kora continued to explain, "The king wants everyone assembled at court in half an hour."

I lifted my head, and cried, "Half an hour?" I let my head drop back against the cushion. "I cannot be ready for court in half an hour. Of course, *he* can because he is a man!" Then I paused. "Has he forgotten the Shabbat?"

"The eunuch says the king said it is urgent, Ba'alah."

I heaved another sigh and rolled my eyes. "Fine. Tell the eunuch to tell the king that I will be there as soon as I am properly dressed. He will have to wait for me or start without me, because I need more time than what he has allotted. Then assemble the handmaidens and come back to help me dress."

She nodded. "It will be done, Ba'alah." Then she pulled the door closed and was gone.

Coming back to bed, carrying his bunched-up loincloth in his hand then dropping it on the foot of the bed, Amon looked at me regrettably. "Should we finish?"

"No, the mood has gone," I said bitterly, getting out of bed.

"Shall I wait for you?" he asked, following me. He slipped his arms around me and pulled my body to his, and I could feel him growing desirous again.

I reached up to brush my fingers through his curls. "It may be a while, if the king has summoned the high council and his generals..."

"I know," he answered, pulling me into a kiss. Then he said playfully, "I do serve in the civil court."

"I know," came my reply. Then I coaxed him into another kiss and bit his bottom lip.

530

He growled and kissed more fiercely, dug his fingers into my bare flesh, and pressed himself to me. "Ba'alah, let me take you. We have time before your ladies return."

"*You* have time," I said, extracting myself and holding him off. "I do not." Then I walked toward my wardrobe, saying, "I do not have long before we are supposed to assemble, Amon. I must prepare."

After pulling out one of my richest robes – which I only ever wore for court or special occasions – I went to the dressing table. Meanwhile, he came and took it from my hands, tossed it on the chair, and held me again. "You could make love to me and then put on that dress you wore earlier."

It was tempting.

Then, cupping my breast, he added in jest, "Or just go as you are – the men would surely appreciate it."

While he bent to bring my breast to his mouth, I laughed. "My son the king would not."

"It would serve him right, for summoning the court on the Shabbat," he said, straightening again and pressing himself to me.

I enjoyed feeling him against me, but then I kissed him once more, stroked his part, and pulled away. I picked up my robe and carefully laid it out the way my ladies would, and said, "You know I cannot go to court looking any less than a queen."

"I remember the time when you did go to court without all that regalia. It was the first time I had ever seen you as you truly are, and only then did I understand why the king was so enchanted by you."

I rolled my eyes, but I was smiling broadly as I returned to the dressing table. "I do not look better like this."

"You do," he insisted.

"Besides, that was a truly urgent matter. We were under siege." I paused to slip on a diaphanous under-gown. "And I was young then."

"You are only thirty-nine," he said, draping himself across the bed.

"*Then* I was thirty-one," I answered, sitting at my dressing table, and starting to put on my face cream, to prepare my skin for the cosmetics that would come next. I paused long enough to turn to him, and said, "Get dressed. The handmaids will be here shortly, and I do not think you want them to look upon your nakedness. Nor do I want them to."

"You want me all to yourself, Ba'alah?" he grinned, getting up.

I turned to smirk at him, glancing at his parts, and said, "That, and I do not want them getting any ideas."

"They already know that you lie with me," he said, pulling on his clothes.

While I began applying the kohl around my eyes, I said, "Yes, but I intend to guard their innocence, as is my duty toward their families for letting them serve me here. I cannot be so irresponsible with their maidenhood."

"What, you think I would deflower a nobleman's daughter?"

"No, but they might seek it elsewhere, if they see the beauty of a man and desire him – as I did when I was their age."

"Did you lose your maidenhood before you were married to Akhab?" he asked, coming to kneel on the floor beside me.

"No, but I wanted to – and nearly did," I admitted. "Thankfully, my nurse came upon us in time, and I was preserved for my husband."

He made a low snicker from his throat, held my legs and began spreading them. He brought his lips to my flesh through the gown, moving them gently up my thighs. I giggled and attempted to continue painting my face, while he lifted my gown, saying, "You gave me pleasure before, my Ba'alah. Now, let me give you pleasure at least, before you must go face the king's council."

I would have let him, but then the door opened, and Kora appeared leading the handmaids. We both sighed in frustration as he lowered my gown and pulled away to the giggles and twittering of the handmaids, which ended the moment Kora shushed them. Amon went out onto the terrace, while the handmaids immediately got to work, two of them combing and putting up my hair, while Kora began pulling out my jewels and handing them to the most trusted of the girls. When all the rest was finished, they helped me into my sumptuous robes, glittering jewels, and golden headdress and I was ready for battle at last.

Dressing for court was a long and tedious process, so by the time I arrived twenty minutes later than the appointed time, I was fuming again and made little effort to hide my displeasure. My son and the rest of the council had already begun without me, but paused when I appeared so that I was given the proper reception. Yoram remained sitting on his throne, pouting while I stopped before the dais with a purposefully casual bow.

"Ama," the king announced, "I am glad you finally deigned to make an appearance after I summoned you."

"I was not dressed for court, Melekh," I explained as I began to slowly make my way up the steps. "I was in the middle of my devotions."

Yoram smiled bitterly. "Your devotions..."

Reaching the top of the dais, I paused and said, "Melekh, you forget that apart from being your Gebirah, I am also the High Priestess. I have many duties related to that function and am not accustomed to being summoned before the court when it is not in session."

"I believe you were informed that it was an urgent matter."

"*It is the Shabbat,*" I snarled, at last taking my seat. "Whatever this is, it could have waited until morning."

"Ama, when have you ever cared about honoring the Shabbat? It is of no consequence to Ba'al or Asherah."

The men of the court who were near enough to have heard our exchange chuckled at his response, but I could see that they had also been forced to dress quickly and were not thrilled to have been summoned, either. Only the Yahwists at court – few though they were – truly cared about the Shabbat, but it was a tradition we had all grown accustomed to and appreciated, especially when it was revoked.

With a nonchalant wave, I said, "Well, I am here now, so you may resume with your urgent matter...Melekh."

"*Abarakkum,*" Yoram summoned Aharon, "illuminate the Gebirah on the matter at hand, so we may continue where we left off."

Aharon was not much older than Akhab had been, but he had aged a great deal faster, especially in these past three years. He stood with a hunch now, and his hair and beard were almost completely white. As he turned to address me, he attempted to straighten his posture, but I could see by the tension in his movements that it pained him to do so. Perhaps, when all this was over, I would talk with Yoram about urging Aharon to retire from his service and allow his son to replace him. For now, of course, it would have to wait for this important matter.

In brief: with annual tributes being due from our vassal states, we had again not received the usual tribute from Moab. Having thus sent some of our men to demand of Mesha his kingdom's tribute, we were met with opposition. As in the previous year, Mesha refused to admit our men to his city, so they sent their messengers to demand tribute in the name of the King of Yisrael. Last time, this provoked an outright refusal to pay, but this time Mesha responded with an attack. Our men were slaughtered, having been caught unaware as they waited in their camp outside the city.

The messengers had just returned to Shomron with their report, and Yoram had assembled the rest of us in order to discuss what action we should take to subdue Moab once again. Ishaq and most of the generals were, naturally, in favor of wiping the Kingdom of Moab off the map entirely. General Dawid, a cousin of Akhab, was the only man of war who opposed that course of action. Instead, he and the rest of the ministers were insistent that Moab needed to be preserved, because much of our trade and commerce depended upon the tributes we received from Mesha's kingdom. The divided council had been arguing their cases vehemently when my arrival was announced.

When Aharon finished his recapitulation of what had previously been discussed, Yoram was about to speak, but I cut him off. "This could have waited until tomorrow."

"They committed an act of rebellion against us!" Yoram protested.

"Yes, and they should be punished, but this does not warrant an immediate response. If you were more experienced, you would understand why it could have waited until the court was assembled *at our usual time* tomorrow."

Much of the assemblage murmured and nodded discreetly, likely having been too afraid to express their feelings on the matter until I said what they were all thinking. While the ministers and I were often at odds, in this case I became their champion. Yoram, of course, did not care to be chastised in front of his ministers and generals – if they had thought Zyah only a boy at nineteen, Yoram certainly had it far worse at sixteen – but in that moment I did not care about petting the fragile ego of an adolescent king who also happened to be my son.

His face turned red as he looked around at the assemblage of his elders. Then he said, "An act of war demands immediate attention!"

Some murmurs of agreement arose, as the men considered the king's stance. Seeing their agreement, he raised his head proudly and crossed his arms over his chest.

Meanwhile, I continued in a firm yet composed manner: "Is Mesha's army marching on Shomron, Melekh?"

I paused for effect.

"Are they ravaging our cities and our people as we speak? No?"

I looked around, and the men who had previously agreed with the king were now shifting uncomfortably where they stood. Only one or two still appeared to side with Yoram, their faces obstinately fixed with resentment.

Nevertheless, I continued, "Then this news, although disappointing and unpleasant, did not require the King of Yisrael to command the high council to assemble as quickly as possible on the Shabbat. Unless there is an immediate threat posed by this meager rebellion, *it could have waited until tomorrow.*"

Now, I sat back and breathed deeply. Then I went on, "But, as you have assembled us and we are here, we may as well proceed."

The ministers and generals were all there before us, ready to do their duty, but their mix of exhausted and bitter expressions betrayed their annoyance at having been summoned when they had been at rest in their homes with their families. Yoram looked out at them. The majority were clearly with me now. At last, he heaved a sigh and rose from his throne.

"The Gebirah has *generously* reminded me of the Shabbat which, although she does not herself feel the need to follow, *I* desire to please Yahowah alongside the other Ba'alim. As such, we may resume our discussion first thing in the morning when the court is assembled at the usual time. You are dismissed."

The men expressed their gratitude and paid homage, and then at once filed out. I sat watching them with a pleased smile. Then Yoram turned to me, furious. "Well, Ama, I hope you are satisfied – now that you have humiliated me in front of the high council and my generals."

Rising from my chair, I said, "Yoram, if there is one thing you must never do as King of Yisrael, it is to deny your ministers the Shabbat, or they will grow to resent you."

"Most of them do not honor Yahowah," he said bitterly as I got up and we began to walk together out of the Great Hall. "What is the Shabbat to Asherah and Ba'al?"

"Nothing to them – but to the rest of us, it is a much-needed day of rest. Even followers of my Ba'alim can appreciate that, Yoram."

"Yet you and the others have advocated for opening the markets and permitting trade on the Shabbat."

I stopped walking and muttered a curse in my father's tongue. Then I turned to him, and said, "Yoram, you must understand the difference between what is necessary and what is good for your kingdom. No one is forced to work or trade on the Shabbat – however, they are *permitted* to do so, and that is to everyone's benefit. Now, if you will excuse me, Melekh, I would like to return to my devotions."

While I began walking away, my son called, "I was not aware Amon was one of the gods you served, Ama."

I stopped. Then I turned back to my son and met his gaze. "Amon is not a god and I do not worship him – he worships me. I am performing a religious duty."

He scoffed. "You call what you do with him a religious duty?"

"I am serving my goddess. And I will not be questioned by you or anyone else about the nature of my devotions."

"I am your son: it is my duty to protect you."

"From what?"

He paused, seemingly not prepared to answer this question. Then he stammered, "From anything I believe could be hurting you."

I laughed. "Amon is *not* hurting me."

"Is he making you happy, though?"

Now, it was my turn to pause, unable to answer the question. Yoram took the opportunity to continue his thought, "I have not seen you truly happy since Abbu died. And since you have begun taking up with these other men, I have seen the light drain from you."

"The light came out of me the night your Abbu died, Yoram. What I am doing is helping me sustain what little of that light is left in me. I do not ask you to understand – only to accept it and stay out of my affairs."

536

I narrowed my gaze at him. "Who have you been talking to, that they have distorted your understanding of these things?"

"No one," he stammered, turning away. "It is just...something I have been thinking. And anyway, you are not a common priestess – it is not part of your religious duty to provide these services..."

"I am Ashtarti incarnate: who better to provide this service to those who are worthy?"

I turned again to walk away, but then he called, "Do you also accept payment for these services, Ama?"

Incensed, I whirled around and walked back to slap him sharply across the face. "It is not your place to question my devotions, nor my relations with other men. You are my son, not my husband."

"I am your king."

"And who raised you to be king?"

"No one, remember?" he snapped at me. "That was Zyah who was raised to be king. I was nothing to you. Abbu gave me more attention than you ever did. You only had time for Zyah and all the others, and finally me when they were not around."

I wrinkled my brow. "Where is all this coming from? I have not been perfect; but I have been here for you every day since you became king, with very few exceptions."

"Since your favorite son died, yes. Now that he is not here, at last you have time for me."

"I have shown love and favor to all my children. If I gave more of myself to Zyah, it was only because he required more time spent with him in training for his succession, not because I favored him over the rest of you. Who has put these thoughts into your head, Yoram?"

"No one."

"This past year, we have worked well together, you and me. I do not understand why, suddenly, you are accusing me of not loving you and even questioning the religion into which you have been raised."

"I am only questioning why my mother, a queen and High Priestess, has chosen to lower herself to the role of a common priestess."

"I have *not* lowered myself. And I am done talking about this with you."

537

Again, I began to walk away, but then he called, "Ama, wait! Please...I'm sorry. Perhaps I have been too harsh... I should not have said anything."

"No, you should not," I agreed. "You may be king, Yoram, but when it comes to our religion, *I* am the authority. You would do well to remember that your place is in the earthly sphere – not the spiritual."

He lowered his face and nodded in understanding. Then he looked up at me again, eyes pleading. "I know you did not want to discuss the Moabite issue now but...I need your advice. Will you at least talk with me about it, privately, before we meet with the rest of the council tomorrow? I am overwhelmed by all the opinions of the other men, and tomorrow will be worse, for they will have had time to think through their arguments."

With a heavy sigh, I thought about Amon waiting for me. Then I remembered how I had let my lovers distract me from being there for Zyah, and so I relented. "All right. I am sorry – yes, I will speak with you. But let us go somewhere more comfortable than standing here in the corridor."

He smiled his gratitude, then together we went to his quarters, which had once been Akhab's and, for a brief time, Zyah's. From there, we decided to go out onto the terrace where we had been the other day. It was more comfortable in the open air because the heat inside was stifling this time of the day. It was so bad, in fact, that I commented on it as we walked through on our way to the terrace, partially in jest: "I am surprised these quarters that were built for the king do not have better flow of air. I am starting to wonder if that is why your Abbu spent so much time with me in mine."

Yoram chuckled. "If that were the reason, Ama, he could have spent more time out in the courtyard or in the field instead. He wanted to spend his time with you."

I reached out to touch his cheek, smiling fondly. "I know, Yoram. I am only teasing."

Then he followed me to the ledge, and we looked out over the courtyard together. It was still now, for the courtiers were at home or in their own small gardens enjoying their day of rest. Only the peafowl, cats, and wildlife roamed about, eager to take advantage of the uninhabited space. One of the cats came too close to one of the peacocks, and we laughed together as we watched it get chased away. The peacock, having secured his territory, called out and strutted about.

"So, that is where they go on the Shabbat," I replied, indicating the peafowl with my hand. "I thought perhaps they had their own devotions that led them to disappear from the gardens on this day."

"They disappear from the gardens on the Shabbat?"

"Have you never noticed?"

"No," he answered with a laugh. Then he narrowed his brows and squinted at me suspiciously. "You are being serious, Ama? You are not teasing me?"

"No, I am serious," I insisted, although I was smiling. "Every Shabbat, there are fewer of them in the gardens than there are on other days. Now, I see they must have been coming here, for there are no wives and children to get in their way as in the gardens."

"Get in the way of what? They do not do anything. They merely strut around all day, pecking at the ground."

"They are hunting for food. You know that – I have told you that."

"Yes, but why do they need to hunt? No animals are better fed than your peafowl, Ama."

I chuckled and we turned our attention back toward the courtyard again, where one of the peacocks was calling out and lifting his tailfeathers, attempting to charm a peahen. Sadly for him, she was not interested in his display, but some of the others came closer to get a better look.

Yoram smiled sadly. "Do you remember the way Zyah used to imitate them? Lifting his arms and strutting around like that, mimicking their calls."

I laughed aloud, but then the sting of tears came to my eyes. I had to wipe them away, careful of the kohl, before I leaned on the wall and sighed. "Zyah had a way of always making me laugh."

"Zyah had a way of making everyone laugh." He leaned on the wall next to me, and his tone became serious. "Do you think that Moab would have rebelled again if Zyah was still king?"

"Not after the way he put them in their place when they tried this last year."

"Then I must do the same thing." He paused to look at me, as if waiting for approval. When I did not say anything, he lifted his chin and stood erect, nodding as his decision was made. "Yes. I will rouse all the armies of Yisrael, and we will go to Moab and show Mesha what Yisrael can do."

"Do you think it is wise to take all the might of Yisrael, even from the provinces?"

"That is what you had Zyah do last time!"

"Yes, but will that work a second time?"

He furrowed his brow, and his shoulders began to slump forward.

"Think about this, Yoram. The other kingdoms around us know what we did last time, leaving our kingdom vulnerable to attack. We cannot risk doing it a second time. This does not call for a show of strength in numbers: Mesha already knows the size of our army. He knows that, under the right leadership, it could lay waste to his kingdom."

"Well, he is testing me, just as he tested Zyah."

"Is he?"

"Yes!" he answered helplessly. "Once he sees that I am willing to do the same thing..."

I cut him off. "He is counting on it. But he has had a full year to lick his wounds and prepare for an assault. Do you think, after seeing the might of Yisrael at his door, he would so readily refuse to pay tribute for a second time? To command his men to slaughter those we sent to collect it? If he is doing this now, it means that he is prepared for us to retaliate – and counting on your youth and inexperience to ensure that you will not think it through before you act."

Now, he rested his elbows on the ledge and buried his face in his hands with a heavy sigh. "This is all so hopeless..."

I placed my hand upon his shoulder. He looked up at me and I smiled, tipping my head to the side. "It is not hopeless, Yoram. It simply requires another, more careful approach."

"I know what the other men want, and I believe I understand both sides, but I do not know how to compromise when they are so divided. Ama, what would you have me do?"

I silently watched the peafowl in the courtyard below. Then I finally said, "You know that I despise war when it is not necessary.

540

In this case, however, I believe it has come to the point where battle must be made against Moab. Last time, we threatened an attack that was never made – we showed mercy, and this is how Mesha has repaid us. He knows our strength, yet he slaughtered our men in the hope of provoking an attack. That suggests he is not alone in this – he has the help, or the promise of help, from other kingdoms."

"Who would help Moab to rebel against us?"

"I would place my bet on Aram and the Ammonites – they have much to gain by distracting us with a war in the south, hoping we will make the mistake of leaving our eastern and northern borders unprotected. And if they have promised aid to Moab, we will need to gather our own allies."

He grimaced at the suggestion, but asked, "Whom should I consult?"

"The King of Yehudah has always been a reliable and trustworthy ally in matters of war. And his kingdom is directly across from Moab on Yam HaMelah."

At the mention of Yehoshapat, my son's expression became bitter and defiant. "Did he not refuse to send my sister to us when Zyah…"

He stopped suddenly and inhaled sharply. I rubbed his back and then placed my arm around him from the side. Then after squeezing him, I leaned against the ledge again, and said, "You will find Yehoshapat to be stubborn at times, and selective in his obedience to his god – especially where his image is concerned. But when it comes to matters of war and state, you can always count on his aid – as long as you can find a prophet of Yahowah to support your campaign. It was a prophet who told him not to allow Atalaya to come to us – he will do nothing without the assurance of prophets."

"Then he is a wise king," said Yoram, his resentment against Hosha fading at once.

I held back the urge to scoff openly, for I placed little faith in the words of those ragged zealots who called themselves prophets of Yahowah. Many of them were lowborn and, more importantly, they were not priests. Only the worthy – those who had been anointed and ordained – had the capacity to commune directly with the divine. That is the way it was in my father's kingdom. The people of Yisrael, however, had a strange fondness for these wandering prophets that my son had apparently inherited from his father. While I did not

541

believe in these prophets, I had learned to hold my tongue and even to use the belief in them to my advantage when necessary.

"Find a prophet of Yahowah who will speak highly of your campaign to Hosha. Send them to Yerushalayim with your messengers. Have them tell the king what they have told you – that the campaign will be successful – and he will agree to raise up his armies and go with you into Moab to clean up this mess."

He sighed heavily with apparent dissatisfaction.

"What is it?" I asked.

"I do not know why we should even bother with allies whose armies will share in the plunder. The might of Yisrael should be enough to subdue Moab."

I held up my hand. "You must not take all the armies of Yisrael to Moab. We must not be left undefended along our eastern and northern borders. If Mesha is indeed receiving support from the kings of Aram and Ammon, they will likely be waiting for the opportunity to strike us from behind."

"But how do you know they are helping him? Were they not our allies when Abbu helped them to defeat Assyria and recover Hamat for Irhulani?"

I nodded, but explained, "That was only a temporary alliance, in support of a mutual ally. Hamat has long been on friendly terms with Yisrael, but Aram and Ammon have been against us more often than not."

"It is all so complicated," he lamented, holding his head.

"I know, but listen, because you must understand this: Aram and Ammon have always gone back and forth with Yisrael. One moment, they are allies, the next moment they are enemies. In this case, you must always think of them as a potential enemy – never trust them, and never let down your guard. That is why, when you raise the armies of Yisrael, you will take them only from the southern and eastern provinces."

"And Yezreel?"

I nodded. "Yes, and Yezreel. But you will leave a portion of the men and chariots at Yezreel behind, just as you will leave the soldiers stationed here at Shomron. Even Zyah did not take every horse, man, and chariot of our army into Moab."

"But it was said that he took the whole army."

"It was said..."

542

His lips parted with an intake of breath. "Ah, I see."

I slipped an arm around him. He permitted it just long enough before he wiggled away, as he always did. Then I said, "When you return victorious, it will be time for us to begin renewing some of our alliances."

"How do we do that?"

I looked at him with a sideways smile. "You will do that by taking more wives, the daughters and granddaughters and sisters and nieces of other kings."

"Oh," he answered, his face and the tips of his ears growing red.

"Once you have a great victory of which to boast, you will become quite a popular king – worthy men will be eager to send you their worthiest maidens to wed. It is a good thing, and it is your duty as king to take as many wives and make as many legitimate heirs as possible."

"I know, Ama." Then he cleared his throat, and asked, "What of my second wife, Shalima? Should I not consummate the marriage with her now?"

I shook my head. "Wait another year, at least. She is only thirteen. She needs more time to mature."

He seemed relieved. Then he turned to me. "Thank you, Ama. For...everything you do for me, for the other women, and for the kingdom. I can see now why Abbu put so much of his trust in you."

"Not enough, or he would still be here," I said dryly. Then I sighed. "Well, if you are satisfied...?"

"Yes, you may return to your...devotions." He looked down and cleared his throat again.

"Thank you, Melekh," I answered with a dip. Then I returned to my quarters, where the Lord Governor was still waiting to resume his communion with the Ba'alah.

24

Consorting With the Unworthy

Yoram took my advice and presented the plan we devised before his ministers at court the next day. The plan was accepted. So, the king sent his request and, when it was received favorably, went down to Yerushalayim with a portion of the armies of Yisrael, taken from the western and southern provinces along the sea and the borders of Yehudah and the Philistine states. I sent ahead to Hosha asking him to safeguard my son, that he not go himself into battle the way his father did, and that his youth and inexperience be taken into account. The King of Yehudah sent back to me that he would do everything to protect Yoram and preserve his life and counseled me not to worry, "for Yahowah is with us."

Trusting not in his word or his god to preserve my son, I began each day at the Ba'alim temple with an offering of sacrifice and prayers for the preservation of Yoram and the armies of Yisrael. Then I went about my days as usual, managing the kingdom and household, communing with Ashtarti, spending time with my children and little Abdiel, and, at the end of it all, summoning Amon to my bed.

I was still having occasional bouts of insomnia, but not as bad as during Akhab's final years. On those nights, or on evenings when I did not summon Amon, I often went to my study to continue working on the chronicle. I had promised Akhab that I would finish it and, while my dedication to the project waxed and waned, I kept an overall steady pace. Sometimes, it seemed a pointless endeavor and I would give up on it entirely for weeks or even months at a time. But then I would return with a renewed sense of zeal when I reflected on the many glorious years of my husband's reign and the challenges we overcame together.

It was on one of those evenings when I was spending the night alone, eager to work on my chronicle, that Kora came to inform me that a messenger had arrived from the king. I put down my stylus

544

and took up my mantle on the way out, reminding myself that all was well and not to worry. The messenger had a grave expression when he saw me, and I suddenly feared the worst.

He knelt when I arrived and, taking my offered hand, said, "Gebirah, the king sends his blessings."

I breathed a sigh of relief. "What news have you from the king?"

"Gebirah, I come bearing news not of the king – who assures you he is well – but of *Akhimelekh* Ishaq. He was wounded in battle at Kir Kharaset and taken back to the camp but did not survive the night. The king asked me to come straight to you with the news first before taking it to his family. He grieves for his brother and asks that you consider who among his generals will make a suitable replacement as his Minister of War. He suggests his cousin, General Yehu, for your consideration, Gebirah."

While I received this news, I brought my hand to my chest and steadied myself on the back of a chair. Then I considered the king's suggestion: Yehu was the son of one of Akhab's favorite cousins. They had a falling out after Yehu's father abandoned his faith in the Ba'alim in favor of the Yahwist cult. He was twenty-one and a capable warrior, though, and had been close to Zyah. My eldest son had raised him to the rank of general, in fact, one of his last acts as king. Despite his misgivings about our religion, Yehu had always shown loyalty to his uncle and cousins. Still, I did not trust him, and the idea made me uneasy.

"Send word to the king that I will consider his suggestion, but that he should not make any decision until there has been time for us to discuss all suitable candidates. In the meantime, you may go and deliver this sad news to *Akhimelekh* Ishaq's family, with my deepest regret as well as the king's. Assure Lady Naomi that her husband will be given a funeral befitting the son and brother of kings, and that she and her son will be protected and provided for even in his absence."

He nodded. "It will be done, Gebirah, as you have instructed."

Then the messenger was dismissed and at last I was able to relax. I fell into the chair, and for some reason began laughing even as I wept. Returning to me after the messenger departed, Kora asked, "What is it? What has happened? Yezeba'al?"

"Ishaq is dead."

Then I began laughing again, laying back my head and closing my eyes, and wondering if his spirit was there watching me rejoice. Thinking that he was, I said aloud, "May you have what you deserve in Ertsetu, and may your father be the one to deliver it." I laughed again, and Kora stood watching. I could not know what she was thinking but neither did I care, for the man who had assaulted me was dead.

Yoram and the armies of Yisrael, together with the armies of Yehudah and its province of Edom, laid waste to the cities of the Kingdom of Moab. Our armies then made their way to Mesha's palace at Dibon, where he fled after being defeated in battle. When he saw all was lost, he did the unthinkable, offering his own son in sacrifice upon the wall to appease his god. Yoram returned to Yisrael in a sad state, having withdrawn with the others after relinquishing all rights to the decimated kingdom. He wept as he recounted the horror of seeing the eldest son of Mesha hanging from the ramparts and set aflame, the scent of his burning flesh assaulting the men as they watched in disbelief.

"How could he do it? To his own son?" Yoram lamented, pacing before me in the king's study. I sat in a chair beside his desk, looking to the side as I envisioned the horrible scene my son had described.

Suddenly, he stopped and turned to me, his youthfulness apparent on his tear-lined face. "Is *this* the god we worship, Ama?"

"Our Ba'al does not accept such sacrifices, Yoram. You should know that."

"It is said that this was an offering to Ba'al!" His voice was tense, as if he was holding back the fullness of his rage.

"It is not the same Ba'al!" I insisted. "There are many Ba'alim, Yoram – not just the ones we worship. It is a title, not a name – you should know that. If he sacrificed his son to one of them, surely it was Khemosh, for that is the Ba'al who is worshiped by the Moabites. Khemosh is hungry for human blood, but that is not our way. That is not the way of our gods."

"Yehoshapat says they are all the same."

"And you believe that when he does not know our gods? You have served the Ba'alim your whole life – when have you ever known us to commit such atrocities in their names? Even during times of great distress, we have not done these things."

"But what of the prophets of Yahowah you had killed at the time of the great drought?" he challenged. "The one that happened after Abbu converted?"

"Those people were not sacrifices," I said with disgust. "They were zealots – seditious dogs, spreading dissent and stirring up rebellions throughout the kingdom in the early years of your father's reign and our marriage. They were doing these things from the moment I arrived in the kingdom as his bride, and it only became worse and worse until we finally had enough. We had to put a stop to it before they tore the whole kingdom down with their zealous insurrections. There was no other way, and by eliminating the worst of them, we brought stability to our kingdom once again."

Tired of talking about this, I got up and began to walk away, but then he said, "Except the Tishbite."

"What?" I asked, turning back to him.

"He was the worst of them, and he got away. Lived a long life, protected by Yahowah until he was taken up by him. That is what they say."

"What do you mean, taken up?"

He shrugged. "On the way to Moab, when we were lost in the desert of Edom, I met a man of God called Elisha. He served Eliyah the Tishbite for much of his life and was chosen by him and anointed to replace him."

"Yes, I know this Elisha," I said impatiently. "What of him?"

Yoram paused and looked down. When he lifted his head again, he met my gaze, and said, "Ama. Eliyah the Tishbite is dead."

My lips parted and I stepped back to lean against one of the beams that held up the ceiling and the floor above. I should have been pleased – and in part, I suppose that I was. But I was also inexplicably sad. My old nemesis was gone. I had hated him; hunted him. I had blamed him for so many of the evils that had befallen my family and our kingdom. But over the years, I began to understand him. He was only doing what *he believed* was right, as were all of us. It was his god who was to blame; Eliyah was only the messenger. So, when I could have killed him – when he stood before me for the last time in the chamber of my dying son and blamed me for it – I did not order him to be slain. Now, he would never return to trouble me

547

again. Why, then, was I not rejoicing as I had when I heard the news of Ishaq's death?

Unaware of the troubled thoughts that consumed me just then, Yoram continued, "It is said that he was taken up in a whirlwind caused by a chariot of fire led by horses of fire. I do not understand this, what it means or how it could be, but it seems it is true: the Tishbite is no more. Elisha wears his mantle. They say the spirit of Eliyah is in him now. He speaks with the same authority."

"You mean arrogance?" I muttered, going to stand by the window. I looked out through the lattice, watching a pair of birds with mottled feathers chase each other through the air. I did not want my son to see the tears that slipped down my cheeks, so I remained looking out until I was able to compose myself again. Then I carefully wiped the tears, hoping no traces of kohl remained to betray me, and turned back to him with a forced smile. "Thank you for telling me of this. It is a joyous day. I would like to commune with Ashtarti, to give her my thanks. May I take my leave, Melekh?"

"There is...one more thing I would like to discuss before you go, Ama," he began. It could have been a command, but it came as a request, as if he were a boy again.

I smiled fondly. "Yes, my son. Whatever you need."

He came to stand beside me at the window and paused to look out. When he turned to me, I offered another smile. The corners of his mouth twitched. Then his lips parted, and he drew in a deep breath, before he asked, "Have you given some thought to the vacant position we now have at court?"

There was tension in his voice again – why did I get the feeling he was angry with me before he even knew what I was going to say? I tilted my head back and inhaled deeply. "You want Yehu to be your new Minister of War."

He nodded.

After a pause, I said, "Do you truly believe he would make a suitable minister?"

"Why would he not? He holds the rank of general, which is the basic requirement."

"The basic requirement – but of all the men who hold that rank, is he the best of them?"

Yoram's mouth opened but he said nothing.

With that, I went on, "If you want my honest opinion, Yoram, I do not think that he is qualified to serve as a minister at court — especially not when there are men who are older and wiser."

"But you let Zyah appoint Ishaq in that position."

My cheeks grew warm, as I thought about how I had allowed my own attraction to color my vision. Then I said, "I did, but looking back, I do not believe it was a wise decision. There were other generals who had more experience and wisdom, who should have been given that position."

"Yehu has plenty of experience, and he is intelligent."

"Intelligent is not the same as wise, Yoram."

"You only hate him because he worships Yahowah instead of our gods."

"That is not true — I do not hate him, and I do not care who he worships."

He cocked his head to the side. "Really? That has nothing whatsoever to do with it?"

"It does not — as long as who he worships does not interfere with his ability to serve us and our kingdom with loyalty and honor. But I do not see him as the right choice for minister. There is more to being minister than having experience in battle, Yoram. And intelligence without wisdom is worth nothing at all. Dawid is the only one of your generals who is both qualified and level-headed enough for the position."

"Dawid is too old and cautious," he said with a grimace.

"Is caution a bad thing? Had you shown some restraint in your dealing with Moab, we might still have that kingdom in our possession."

"There was nothing left of Moab by the time we were done with it," he said with a smirk.

"It was a bold move — and foolish. Our kingdom, our people, benefitted from the share of rams and wool we attained from Moab each year."

"We have our own rams and wool."

Raising my voice just enough to make a point, I continued, "We benefit from keeping our vassals strong."

"Strong enough to rebel against us?" he asked testily.

"Strong enough to support the needs of our people. I am talking about trade and commerce, not armies, Yoram. We keep a strong army and subdue those of our vassals, that they may not rebel against us – but we do not, we *should not* subdue their people and the very things from which we are also strengthened."

"The people themselves rose against us. It was not just soldiers of Moab, but the men from the fields and even women taking anything they could find to use as a weapon against us. It was not the Arameans and the Ammonites, as you suspected – it was the people of Moab. We had no choice but to subdue them. Now Mesha rules over a kingdom of rubble. There is no loss to us – we produce plenty of our own wool and can trade for more with our allies. Yehoshapat said we should destroy Mesha's kingdom and leave it to him as a parting gift, so that any others who consider rebelling against us will think twice."

I sighed in frustration and walked away from the window to stand by the desk, where I looked down at a large map drawn on papyrus that was spread out across the surface. Looking at the place where Moab was drawn, I said, "He will rebuild his kingdom, and be fueled by the anger in his heart. His people and his descendants will be strengthened by what we have done to them – what *you* have done to them. You should not have followed Hosha's advice."

"You said I should take his advice!"

"I said you should *listen* to him as your elder but think for yourself and listen to your heart. Think of what your Abbu would have done in the same position. He would have subdued Moab, but he would have shown enough mercy to hold onto it. Show Mesha what we are capable of doing – but don't actually do it!"

"I did think for myself, Ama," he said, raising his chin. "I am not my father – it was his mercy that led him to make poor decisions regarding the King of Aram. You said that yourself. I will not make the same mistakes that led him to an early grave."

"This is exactly why young men should not be made kings, neither should they become ministers at court: they do not understand the delicate balance between justice and mercy, when to show it and when to withhold it."

"Abbu was not a young man when he made the decision to show mercy to Hadadesar. I love my father – I will always respect the great man he was, but even you have said that he sometimes lacked wisdom in these things. So, do not tell me about my youth, and the youth of Yehu, as if that alone is reason for a man's lack of judgment."

550

"I did not say that is the only reason – but it does not help matters. Your Abbu learned the delicate balance as he aged, and yes sometimes made mistakes – especially when he took the advice of others."

"You mean other than you?" he asked pointedly.

"That is not what I said."

"But it is what you meant."

"That is not what I meant, Yoram," I said firmly.

"It is. You are only angry about the times when Abbu did not follow your advice, and now you are angry at me that I did not follow your advice concerning Moab."

"Yes, I am angry you did not follow my advice, and the advice of your wiser ministers – but it is not about me. It is about what is right."

"Which, apparently, only you know?"

I made a growl of frustration and pounded my fist on the desk, cursing in my father's tongue. "Will you stop with this nonsense and listen for once? Where is all this coming from? Who has put these thoughts in your head?"

"No one," he mumbled, turning away to look out the window again.

I went around the desk to stand by him and waited until I was calm again before speaking. "You have grown closer to Yehu this past year. Is it he who has made you doubt my wisdom and sincerity?"

"Yehu has said nothing against you. He has remained faithful to us, and to the kingdom, yet still you misjudge him. Just as you misjudge me."

"Let me ask you: was Yehu one of the generals who agreed with the course of action you took against Moab?"

Yoram huffed and turned his face from me. "So, what if he was? All the generals agreed with it, even your precious Dawid."

"Then none of them deserve the position they covet."

"You women are all the same," he snapped.

"What did you just say?"

"You heard me," he said, sitting in the king's chair at the desk and looking directly at me. "I do not say it to hurt you, Ama. I love and respect you, but I am also aware of your failings and the failings of my father. I know and understand more than the credit you bestow upon me."

551

"I have many failings, Yoram – I will be the first to admit to my faults – but being a woman is not one of them."

He scoffed. "Women are too sentimental to govern and too gentle for matters of war – they cannot make the necessary decisions. When it comes down to it, they will always grow soft, just as you grew soft about the Tishbite."

He paused and fixed me with a knowing gaze, while I stood speechless.

Looking away to fidget with the things on his desk, he went on, "My father was weakened by his devotion to you, softened by your influence: only for you to turn that against him when he did not do what you wanted. You speak of my youth and inexperience, Ama – but I know better than my father. I know that, as a man, I am still better equipped to make the right decisions about war and rebellion, and so is Yehu."

Collecting myself, I walked over to stand before him, leaning with my hands upon the front of the desk. Fixing him with a stern gaze, I spoke in a cool tone. "You think that because you went to war and came back a victor, you suddenly know more about the world than I do? You think that having a cock between your thighs gives you some sort of special wisdom and knowledge to which I am not privy?"

He sat back, looking at me in shock.

I stood erect and smiled bitterly as I looked down at him. "You think I give you less credit than you deserve, Yoram? If this is what you think and how you will behave going forward, then I have given you *too much* credit. I was proud of you before you went to Moab – I thought perhaps you might make a better king than your father was, and your brother might have been. Now, I am wondering if that was a mistake, for I do not know who you are when you speak to me in this way. You are not my son, but an imposter – a boy who thinks that putting down a woman is what it takes to be a man."

I walked toward the exit, and then turned back to him. He sat with his face in his hand, staring into the flame of an oil lamp on his desk. His expression was unreadable, but I could see that he was thinking. "You are my son, Yoram. I love you, but I will not be spoken down to by you or any man. If you still have any respect for me and wish for my advice, send for me and I will come to you. But if you insist on doing things in this way – if you do not think that I have what it takes to advise you, then do not bother to summon me again. I will not go where I am not wanted."

With that, I walked away. I trembled as I went but managed to hold back my tears until I was safely shut away in the privacy of my chamber, where only Kora was present to see me weep – for only she could truly understand and comfort me.

While Yoram and I remained at odds for a time, he ultimately took my advice and appointed General Dawid as his Minister of War the next day. Most of the court and the rest of the council applauded his choice. I was pleased, but I let him take the credit for making the right choice. We needed a strong, wise council now more than ever. Our relations with the other kingdoms had been strained ever since the death of Akhab and had only become worse since Yoram took the throne. Now, Yoram had established his position as King of Yisrael in an unforgettable way.

The aftermath of Moab, with the horror of Mesha's sacrifice, had far-reaching consequences, some good and some bad. The anger at Yisrael was fierce. We were blamed for having caused the desperation that led to the King of Moab taking such an extreme measure. However, those kingdoms that were beholden to us were fearful of Yoram's wrath and eager to show themselves as loyal and obedient to their overlord. He was pleased with the effect, especially when he acquired several new wives and a considerable number of concubines from our allied and vassal states: gifts made to the fierce young king to bolster relations and attain his favor.

It was a good thing that he received them, for he had grown tired of Be'ulah and his seven concubines. He also kept company with other men; one of them I knew to be Yehu, but theirs was a tumultuous love affair. Yoram did not care if others knew that his affections lay with men and women alike, but Yehu was extremely secretive about it, and that caused tension between them. I learned about the affair when Yoram came to seek my advice during one of their lover's quarrels.

Seated outside on a cushioned bench in his private courtyard one afternoon, Yoram lamented, "I do not understand him, Ama. When we are alone together and it is just the two of us, he is warm and loving and affectionate. I crave his touch, the strength of his body when he wraps me in his arms and pulls me close to him. He knows just how to comfort me when I am down, and I don't mean only by lovemaking...although he is exceptional in that regard. What I mean is that he understands me in a way that no one else does – except you, perhaps, which is why I am coming to you for advice."

He looked up at me almost shyly, as if afraid to admit all this to me. I had long known of the duality of his tastes, but this was the first time we had ever spoken openly about it. He seemed afraid to admit to his relationship with Yehu, but when he saw by my sympathetic expression that I did not hold it against him, he confessed, "I have never felt this way about anyone else, not Be'ulah or any of my wives, nor my concubines."

He paused, and his eyes suddenly filled with tears. He looked away, wiping at his cheeks, and said, "I love him, Ama. And I used to think that he loved me, but now I do not know what to think, for he spurns me whenever anyone else is around. He is not cold, exactly, because I am his king, but stiff and formal. It is as if he is afraid for them to see, and when I confronted him about it, he grew angry and refused to discuss it. He wanted only to make love. Afterward, he wept and when I tried to comfort him, he pushed me away and said that he was wicked in Yahowah's sight. He refused to elaborate when I asked what he meant. He dressed and told me never to summon him again, and then he left and now...here I am, coming to you, when I have been so unkind to you of late. I am the worst son..."

He hung his head and covered his face with his hands. I came to sit beside him on the bench and put my arms around him. He leaned into my embrace, clinging to me and weeping on my shoulder like he always did when he was a boy – the only time I could ever get him to sit still and stay in my arms long enough.

I hated to see him in pain, but once I sensed he had cried it out and I had enough time to gather my thoughts, I said, "Yahowah's followers do not accept the love that sometimes exists between two men or two women, Yoram. When Yehu joined the cult of Yahowah, it must have had a profound effect on the way he relates to you and other men, especially when he has these urges for you. If he believes that he is wicked in Yahowah's sight, then it stands to reason that his stiffness and his fear that you have described come from that belief. He wants to follow his god perfectly, yet his urges for you

554

remind him of what he sees as an imperfection – what his god's laws claim to be an imperfection."

"Is it an imperfection?" he asked, looking up at me with a red-eyed gaze. "What if what we are doing together is wrong, Ama? What if I have harmed him in some way?"

"Is it wrong to love someone, Yoram? Yehu is your peer – you are both men, both fully aware of what you want and need from each other. He may be confused about what is right and wrong because of the laws of his religion. But his affection for you seems quite natural, whereas his beliefs do not. Yahowah's laws curb and deny what is natural between two people and give rise to conflict where none would otherwise exist. The Ba'alim accept love in all its forms, but he has rejected them and so rejects himself. One can only pity him."

"Then it is not me he rejects?"

"No, I do not think so. But if he cannot reconcile himself to what he feels for you – if he must choose between you and his god, he will likely always choose his god, and so you should let him do so and not cling to him. You would be wise to find love elsewhere. Go to the temple: seek a union with Ashtarti through one of the priests. There, you will find healing in her divine embrace."

"You are Asherah incarnate – can I not find healing in your embrace?"

My eyes widened in horror, and I realized he did not understand what I meant. "Not that kind of healing, my son. I am speaking of sexual union."

"Oh!" Looking away suddenly, he was struck with horror, as well. Then he got up and began pacing nervously, avoiding my gaze, as he went on, "I...did not know what you meant. I thought the healing was...something else."

"It is through sexual union with Ashtarti that healing is attained. That is why only men go to the temple for that service."

"Do women not also need healing and the divine love of the goddess?"

"They receive it without sexual union – or by such a union with their husbands, who come to them after receiving it at the temple. The priestesses may teach you how to please your wives and concubines, and they will love you all the more because of it. I recommend you go to the temple for this service frequently, at least once per moon cycle. More, if needed."

555

"Did...Abbu go to the temple for this service?"

I smiled sadly, thinking of my husband. "He did not need to – he had the High Priestess for a wife, remember?"

The color drained from his face, and he looked at me as if seeing me for the first time. "You...offer those services *at* the temple?"

"No," I said with annoyance, getting up and going to stroke the feathers of one of the peahens who was approaching me just then. She was one who always came to me for affection. While petting her, I explained, "The High Priestess does not perform such duties for the public – my duty is to Ba'al alone, through my husband, your father. Without him, I can only unite with Ba'al in spirit."

My chest ached when I thought of how long it had been since I last united with my true consort and mate. The other men I had since lain with were nothing compared to him, and none of them were worthy to unite with me in my rituals at the temple on high holy days. The few women I had lain with – all of them priestesses of Ashtarti – were better than most, but they were still not my Ba'al and could not fully satisfy me in the way that Akhab always did.

Yoram had been silent for quite some time. I did not realize it, though, as I was so lost in my own thoughts, until he spoke once again. "Then perhaps I will go to the temple, as you say. I am at least willing to try to find healing, and to turn from Yehu if my love only causes him pain and uncertainty."

"I believe that is a wise decision, Yoram. And a selfless one. Find satisfaction from the priests of Ashtarti, and then go to your wives and concubines for the rest."

He nodded in understanding, and then I touched his cheek, gazing upon him with motherly affection. He placed a hand over mine and closed his eyes but then pulled away. "I will go to the temple tomorrow – would you mind holding court in my absence?"

I nodded my assent. "The weight of kingship is heavy, I understand well. Take as long as you need, Yoram. I appreciate your trust in me."

"I should never have doubted it," he said, apologetically. "You may take your leave now."

With a bow of my head, I left his presence, having no idea how much he would come to depend on me to govern the kingdom for him.

Having discovered a renewed and robust taste for his newest wives and concubines after his affair with Yehu seemed to end, my son left me to manage the kingdom while he spent most of his time with them. He occasionally came to hold court or meet with his ministers. But most of the time I was acting as regent on his behalf, while he gave himself enthusiastically to the duty of consummating marriages with each of his wives, including Shalima as soon as she reached her fourteenth year. On the one hand, I was somewhat annoyed that he suddenly showed little interest in governing the kingdom; on the other hand, I was relieved that I had no need to encourage him toward his duty to produce heirs.

By the start of his third year as king, there were several new pregnancies within the women's household, the majority from among his wives. This alleviated much of my previous fear that, if something happened to Yoram, he would not leave a legitimate heir as his successor. By the end of that year, however, he would have four legitimate sons from which to choose, and still more on the way. He also had many daughters. I delighted in all of them, but I was so often busy holding the kingdom together that I had little time to spend with my youngest children and my ever-increasing number of grandchildren.

Meanwhile, the already tense relations between Ba'alists and Yahwists throughout the region had reached an all-new high. As feared, rumors began to spread again among Yahwist circles that Ba'al worshippers of every kind not only condoned child sacrifice, but that we encouraged it. While Yoram entertained himself with the delights of both sexes, I spent an exhaustive amount of time at court putting out the fires of Yahwist misconceptions about our religion.

The Yahwists had always considered our practice of cremating children upon the altar to be a form of child sacrifice; now, the zealots claimed that we not only burned our dead children upon the altar, but that we murdered children before placing them on our altars or even burned them alive to appease a blood-thirsty god. In my effort to assure the Yahwist members of our court that we did not take part in child sacrifices – neither during our everyday practices, nor during our religious festivals – I invited them to the temple to observe our

557

practices. I told them they were welcome to come to the Ba'alim temples at any time and encouraged them to do so unannounced so they could see that we were not hiding anything.

This was unheard of, and many Ba'alists did not agree with my decision to allow those who did not worship our gods to enter the sacred ground of our temples. Normally, this was forbidden to outsiders. Only Akhab had been allowed to enter the Ba'alim temples before he was consecrated as High Priest, having been granted a special dispensation as the King of Yisrael. So, they were pleased when the majority of the Yahwists refused my invitation for fear of being provoked or seduced into false worship and incurring their god's wrath.

There were still some Yahwist visitors, however, and instead of finding child sacrifices they found something apparently far worse in their eyes: our sacred sex rites. Performed by the priests and priestesses at the Temple of Ashtarti, these rites drew a few new converts from among the Yahwist visitors, but most were repulsed. They determined it was nothing more than prostitution, not understanding the sacred purpose of these acts. Yoram had been going to the temple regularly, as I had suggested, but when word began to spread that prostitution was being performed at the Temple of Ashtarti, he began to distance himself even from daily worship at the Temple of Ba'al and soon stopped seeking sacred union with Ashtarti entirely.

Instead, he began spending more time than ever with his women, going from one favorite to the next until at last he settled on Shalima. When she was found to be with child by him, he exalted her and promised to make her his Melkah in her sister's place if she bore him a son. I was horrified when I heard of this. It also sparked the wrath of Be'ulah, who was already causing a great deal of trouble in the women's household because of Yoram's inconsistency.

When not holding together his kingdom, I was holding together his household, assuring Be'ulah that she would always be secure in her place as Melkah, no matter whom the king favored at the time. But now that he openly made promises to raise Shalima in her sister's place, my reassurances could no longer keep the peace within the women's quarters. When a physical altercation finally broke out between the two sisters, Tamar sent one of the eunuchs to fetch me.

I was hosting a banquet for the priests and priestesses of Ashtarti when he arrived. Begging the pardon of my guests and informing them that some urgent matter had arisen, I encouraged them to stay and enjoy themselves for as long as they liked. Then I went to the women's quarters to intervene. After the sisters had been separated, I spoke to them separately in an attempt to soothe their quarrel. That was when I was told about Yoram's promise to Shalima, which was naturally received as a threat to Be'ulah. I realized it was time for me to have a talk with my son about his handling of the women.

Before returning to my guests, I sent a message to the king, requesting an audience with him. He was out in the field, at practice with his chariots. When Akhab was king, unless we were quarreling, he would have come at once upon receiving my summons. Yoram, however, was in one of his defiant phases. He was eager to show me that he was a man of his own and would not be told what to do by any woman – least of all, his mother. So, he sent the eunuch back to me with word that he would send for me when he was at leisure. I did not receive his summons until two days later.

I had been returning from the Temple of Ba'al, where I sought spiritual guidance and prayer after receiving sorrowful news, when Shmuel came to me with word that the king was finally prepared to receive me in his study. Shmuel had taken over in his father's place as Lord Steward in the past year, although Aharon occasionally came out of retirement to advise his son on important matters. The young man was doing a fine job in the role, though, and Kora was quite proud of her eldest son.

Although he had been formal in his delivery of the king's message, I responded with the warmth and affection that I had always shown him. I patted his cheek and thanked him. He turned his gaze toward the floor, and said, "It is my duty, Gebirah."

"How is your Abbu?" I asked, beckoning for him to follow me as I changed direction. I had been on my way to my quarters, but now I headed to the king's study.

"He is well, Gebirah," Shmuel stammered as he followed along. "Thank you."

"I hope he is not too bored in his retirement?"

"No, Gebirah. He has taken up writing."

"Writing? What is he writing about?"

559

"He is...writing a chronicle of sorts," he explained. As he went on, his tone became less formal and more animated, the way he used to talk to me when he was a child before he became aware of my rank. "A history of the kings of Yisrael, starting from the very beginning with Saul and Dawid and Shelomoh. He is combing through all the writings and letters and histories of them that he has access to – the king has even agreed to help him in this endeavor. Yoram has written to the King of Yehudah to request copies of the original tablets be made and sent to him here, and when they arrive, he has me take them to my father. He is currently finishing up with the reign of Dawid and preparing to move onto his son before he gets to where the kingdoms divide, and then he will no longer need to depend upon the archives at Yerushalayim, since we have everything needed here to continue."

I smiled and turned to him as we stopped outside the closed door of the king's study. "That sounds like the perfect occupation for Aharon – no one could write it better than he. I look forward to reading it when it is finished, if he will allow me the privilege."

"I'm sure he will be delighted to hear of your interest, Gebirah," he answered with a bow. Then as the door was opened to me, he bowed again, and I went in to see my son.

Yoram was standing by the window reading something from a clay tablet. When I entered, he came and set it on his desk, where he sat to receive me. He held out his hand and I pressed my lips to his signet ring – the gold band had once belonged to his father but was now set with Yoram's seal. Akhab's seal had been carved into brown topaz; Yoram's was onyx, and he always wore it for protection.

"Ama, good of you to come," he said in a lofty tone.

"Melekh," I greeted him, holding back as much bitterness as I could manage. "I have not seen you at temple much of late."

He looked toward the window and sniffed. "I was busy. Managing the kingdom requires a great deal of my time and energy, you know."

"Considering I am the one who does most of it, yes, I do know. I am glad you have found it in you to take it upon yourself once again."

He sighed exhaustively. "You did not request an audience to chide me for not going to temple, Ama. Neither I suspect, did you request it to complain about how hard you must work for me. What is it that you need?"

I fixed him with a burning gaze but managed to hold back the rage that was building in me, for it would not do to quarrel with him. "I have come for two reasons: the first is to inform you of some difficulties that have arisen among your women – most especially between your Melkah and her sister, your new favorite."

"Is it not your responsibility to manage the women? Why are you coming to me with this?"

"It is because of your actions that these issues have arisen. While jealousy and bickering among the king's women is quite normal, in this case *you* have enflamed it unnecessarily."

"How have I done this?"

"Is it true that you promised to replace Be'ulah with Shalima in the position of Melkah?"

He shrugged. "What of it? Do I not have the right as king to determine who among my wives is worthy to be my queen?"

"You do, but you must not make threats and promises to raise and lower them at your whim as you play favorites."

"Abbu knowingly favored you among all his women. It was clear to everyone in the entire kingdom that you were the only woman that he loved of the hundreds from which he had to choose."

"Yes, but he never sought to create competition by pitting us against each other, as you have done. I was his Melkah – he never threatened to take that from me, nor promised it to another, even when his ministers and the court attempted to persuade him to set me aside and raise another in my place."

"Abbu loved you. I do not love Be'ulah. She became my Melkah simply because she was my first wife, not because she is worthy of it."

"How is she not worthy?" I demanded. "She has done her duty by giving you a son. She could give you more sons if you summoned her more often."

"I do not want to summon her. I do not enjoy her company the way that I enjoy the others."

"If you displace her and Abdiel for no good reason, she will resent you for it, and raise him also to resent you and any of his brothers whom you have exalted above him."

"I did not choose Be'ulah to be my wife – you made the decision for us to be married, and I did *my* duty by consummating my marriage with her. But I do not like her the way that I like Shalima and the others. Shalima is the most beautiful, and the most obedient, and that is why I favor her."

"Shalima is of a sweeter disposition, that is true. And Be'ulah is harder to control, but that is all the more reason to keep her satisfied. She may do more damage if you revoke her position than she could ever do as Melkah."

"How would she do that?" he asked, raising his palms.

"You spend so little time with any of your children, that it would be easy for their mothers to turn them against you, especially when you so readily cast them aside at your whim. If you show no consistency in your behavior toward your wives, it will not only affect the women's household – it will affect your heirs, and what affects them affects the entire kingdom. If your sons grow to despise you, they will see little harm in removing you when they decide they are ready to take the throne. And I will not live forever, Yoram – I will do my best to encourage your sons to love their father, but if I am not here to protect you, what then? Abdiel is your eldest son, born of your Melkah; if you lower her rank, you lower his, and he will never forgive you for it."

He sighed and then got up to return to the window, where he stood looking out for quite some time before turning back to me. "Very well. I will retain Be'ulah in her position, but I will not summon her to my bed, for she does not satisfy me."

"It would be wise for you to try to have at least two children by every wife, Yoram. There is more satisfaction to be had in the birth of sons than in fleeting moments of gratification – the former lasts generations."

"If you want me to bed her again, since you are apparently so skilled in these matters, why don't you teach her a thing or two about how to please a man?"

I exhaled in disgust but did not deign to gift his insult with a response. Instead, I changed the subject. "There was a second reason I needed to see you, Melekh, which I only learned of early this morning."

When I paused, although he was not looking in my direction, he held out his hand for me to continue.

562

I took a moment to harden my outward composure, which nearly faltered, then said, "I received word from Tzidon that my father has passed."

"Oh," he answered. "Yes, I...received word of it myself, from my official at court there. I forgot to tell you."

Holding back any anger I might have felt, I continued, "I know you hold him in little regard, for whatever reason, but I would like to seek your permission to take a leave of absence, that I might go to Tzidon to be with my mother and attend my brother's coronation."

He softened somewhat at this news, and then said, "Of course. Take as much time as you need. I'm...sorry, Ama. I know you respected your father a great deal. He was...a good man."

Holding back the urge to cry, I said, "I would like to take your younger brothers and sister, if you will permit them to accompany me?"

With a nod, he answered, "Yes, of course, they may go with you." Then he lifted his stylus, dipped it in ink, and began scratching a letter onto a sheet of papyrus he had already prepared. "Will you go by land or by sea?"

"I would prefer to go by sea. It is faster and safer, considering our relations with Aram. My mother has promised to send ships to meet me at Yapo if I will come."

"How long will you be away?" he asked, pausing to refresh the ink on his stylus.

"I would like to have a fortnight, at least. A month would be preferrable. My mother would benefit from having her only daughter with her in this transition. Will you be able to manage for so long without me?"

He smirked. "Yes, I think I can manage my own kingdom without you for a month, Ama. I am not a boy. If I need anything, I am surrounded by capable and experienced men."

Again, it took all my strength not to say what I was thinking. Instead, I thanked him and offered a courteous bow. Then I took my leave and returned to my study where I would immediately compose a response to my mother's letter, assuring her that I would be coming to her as soon as the arrangements could be made for the ships to meet me at Yapo.

563

Nothing had changed in all these years: I was dreadfully ill for the entire voyage from Yapo to the southern port at Zour. Thankfully, my three youngest children seemed not to inherit my weak constitution at sea. While I remained in my bed in the cabin with Kora, keeping my eyes closed and lying on my back whenever I was not retching into a chamber pot, I could hear their excited voices and laughter drifting in from the deck where they spent most of the voyage in the company of their nurses and guardians. At least the sound of their joy brought me some comfort and peace.

After dumping the contents of the chamber pot out the window into the sea, Kora cleaned her hands and then came to sit beside me on the edge of the bed as I settled back in. She smiled sadly, as she touched my forehead with a damp cloth to wipe away the sweat that had gathered. "My poor Yezeba'al. This has always happened to you."

With a quiet chuckle deep within my throat, I took her hand and looked up at her in gratitude. "It is better now, at least. The sounds of my children enjoying their time at sea gives me a sense of pride and satisfaction I did not have on our first sea voyage. Of course, we had our youth once, so long ago."

She studied my face, while I studied hers. The same sensible yet mischievous gleam alighted in her eyes, but her face was lined with the exhaustion of so many years that had passed, just as mine was when I did not conceal it behind my cosmetics.

"We are quite the pair, are we not?" she asked with a smile. "A goddess who became a girl who became a queen, and...me. What am I, anyway?"

"The most noble and loyal servant and friend there ever was," I replied, squeezing her hand. "I could not have made it through all these years without you, Kora."

"You speak as if you are going to die, Yezeba'al."

"I feel as if I might." I paused as a groan escaped from my throat. "I forgot how wretched I feel when I am at sea."

"It is like the pain of childbirth, is it not?" she teased. "But I remember it well enough not to do it ever again. Thankfully, I do not even believe I can."

"Have you stopped bleeding so soon?"

She nodded proudly.

"Permanently?"

"I believe so," she answered. "It is a relief, not to have to worry about it anymore."

"Are you and Ahru still...?"

She smiled bashfully. "We do, sometimes. I know you have always found it hard to believe, but he can be very affectionate and passionate with me. Not the way Akhab was with you, I suppose – I do not think anyone could be as passionate and affectionate as you were together, to be perfectly honest."

I laughed, but then my ribs and belly ached, and I grimaced. Thankfully it passed, so I did not need Kora to grab the chamber pot. I closed my eyes against the sting of tears. "I miss him."

"I know," she answered, giving my hand a gentle squeeze. "Find strength in the goddess – her essence is within you."

I nodded in understanding and then inhaled deeply before changing the subject. "Shmuel was telling me about Ahru's history of the kings of Yisrael. Why have you not told me about this?"

"Oh... Well, I suppose I thought you would not find it interesting."

"You underestimate me, Kora. I find it very interesting. I thought you knew me better than that." When she met my gaze, I was smiling mischievously.

She chuckled. "I suppose you're right. I should have known that it was something you might enjoy, but he has been very secretive about it."

Thinking of my own chronicle, which only she and Akhab knew about, I said, "I suppose I understand. Tell him I would love to read it, if he is willing to share it when it is completed."

With a nod, she answered, "I will tell him, and I am certain he will be flattered by your interest – although, it may put more pressure on him than he would like."

"In that case, say nothing. I hope Shmuel did not already tell him of my interest." I closed my eyes and was overcome by a yawn from deep within. I had not realized how exhausted I was, even though it was the middle of the day.

"You should try to sleep, Yezeba'al."

"It would be a blessing if I could," I said with a faint smile.

565

Kora stayed with me, as I dozed in and out between fits of violent hurling every time a particularly powerful wave took up the ship and tossed it around with the others. I would be relieved when I could be on steady land once again, where I belonged.

When we arrived at the palace in Zour, my mother and brother greeted us warmly. Azba ran into her grandmother's arms, who held her out and marveled at how much she had grown since the last time she had seen us. As I watched my mother greet her grandchildren, I was amazed at how much she had also aged since the last time we met. Her long hair, which was partially loose, was now mostly grey with only a few streaks of black, while mine was still mostly black with a few streaks of grey. She had aged well, though; in that, at least, I had hope of the same.

She lifted her kohl-lined black eyes to meet my gaze then and smiled warmly, coming to meet me with her arms outstretched. "Yezeba'al, you have been too long from home. We have missed you here – the people have missed the presence of their Ba'alah."

"Ama," I said as we embraced, and she kissed my cheek. Then I said playfully, "You look good, Gebirah."

"I could say the same of you," she answered, and her eyes squinted as she smiled at me before my brother came to pull me into a tight embrace.

"Dear *akhatu*, thank you for coming!" Holding me out to look at me, he said, "I hear your son is keeping you quite busy."

"He is, *akhu*," I confirmed.

"I feared you would not be able to make it, but I am glad you were able to get away – and to bring my favorite niece and nephews!"

After all the greetings and embracing were exchanged, the children were shepherded off to my residence near the Temple of Ba'al, while my mother took me to her own quarters in the palace to rest and catch up. As she led me through the corridor where I had spent so much time looking out at the sea and watching the storms move in when I was a girl, the sheer undyed linen curtains on the great windows danced gently to the tune of a soft breeze. It was nothing like the last night at Zour before I was married, I thought, as I remembered how fiercely the wind had blown through the corridor when the storm came in that night. It was so long ago; it was strange to think about how much had changed since then.

While I sat on a chair bolstered with luxurious cushions, my mother sent the slaves away and poured our drinks herself. "Azba is a dear. Is she taking to her training well?"

"Yes, she takes it all very seriously and learns quickly."

She brought two cups of wine, handing one to me, and then took up her seat. "Sounds like you…"

"I believe she will make a fine replacement for me when I am gone."

"Have you found her a suitable husband?"

"Not yet. She is only a girl, Ama."

"Yes, but in only a few years she will be a woman."

"I am aware of this, and I am considering her options."

"You should send her to me. I can complete her training and find her a suitable husband here."

"Do you have someone in mind for her?"

My mother shrugged. "Not particularly, but I think she should marry a priest of Ba'al. Then when she takes your place, she can make him a High Priest without needing to train him. At least your Akhab was a quick study." She paused and began to scrutinize me in her particular manner. "You look exhausted."

"Thank you, Ama. It is how every woman loves to be described."

"I only mean that I can see what a toll these past years have taken on you, and I sympathize. I do not mean it any other way, Yezeba'al. How are things now that Yoram is king? Is he a good king?"

I could not help but to roll my eyes. "My son is fickle and changeable; at times, relying on me completely, at other times seemingly against me in all things."

"No wonder you are exhausted."

With a quiet sigh, I pursed my lips. Then I said, "It is frustrating, the way he changes his opinion so frequently."

"Wasn't that a trait of his father?"

"No, not like this, Ama. Akhab often tried to placate everyone, sometimes to his detriment, because he wanted everyone to have their needs met. With Yoram, I think he is trying so hard to prove himself to the other men, seeking their adoration and respect…and

567

then suddenly realizes how much he still needs me. I am honestly beginning to doubt the stability of his character."

She raised her brows and then took a sip of her wine. "Is he truly that bad?"

"You know Yoram has always been the most difficult of my children."

"Yes – he was the one who was born backwards and upside down, was he not?"

Again, I nodded. "He almost killed me coming into this world."

"Even so, I find it hard to believe he is so difficult now. He always seemed such a gentle boy – so generous, caring, and polite."

"That was true when he was a boy, but it is only one side of him." I shook my head. "Now, I think sometimes I do not even know him. He cannot even make up his mind about which gods to worship, and his devotion changes depending on which god his current lover worships. I do not think he knows his own mind in anything."

"Esar said he has heard that Yoram has you doing everything for him."

"It is not altogether untrue. He often leaves the management of the kingdom to me and the ministers while he entertains himself with his wives and concubines, only to come back to take over everything when he has lost interest in them or has begun to quarrel with his recent favorite." I paused and again shook my head, this time with a sigh.

"I thought Zyah's stubbornness was frustrating, and sometimes his arrogance," I continued, "but in all other ways he was a good enough king and might have become truly a great king had he lived long enough to prove himself by his deeds... Yoram is proving to be far more difficult to work with than I had expected. The first year went well, but now the more time he spends with his women, the less time he has for the kingdom and the more he relies on me; and the more time he spends with his men, the less he trusts in me to advise him – until he takes interest in another favorite among his women, and then who does he leave the kingdom's governance to...?"

My mother tipped her head knowingly then got up for another drink, pausing to check mine. Although still holding the cup while I talked, I had not drunk any of it. While she went to fill her cup for a second time, I continued, "And even his favorite is constantly

568

changing to the point that he causes jealousy and bitterness among them."

"Jealousy and bitterness between the king's women are not unusual, Yezeba'al," she said while still at the table.

"It is more extreme than anything I am used to seeing, Ama. He practically pits them against one another and enjoys the way they fight over him."

Returning to her chair, she said, "He sounds like a typical young man if you ask me." She pulled her legs up onto the cushions and leaned casually on the arm of the chair with her elbow as she sipped her drink.

I shook my head. "Zyah was the exact opposite – I could not get him interested in anyone but his concubine."

"Yes, I remember you telling me. How is the girl now, anyway? And her children? Have you heard from her since she returned to Aram?"

"She has written to me only once..."

"Sounds like someone I know," she teased.

Ignoring her remark, I continued, "...assuring me they arrived safely and were getting settled with her family. She thanked me for the gifts I sent with them. That was all I heard, but I am not surprised. I pray for her and the children every day, and hope that I might see them again, although I doubt it will ever come to pass."

At last, I paused to sip my drink. Just then, my sleeve slipped down on my left arm, revealing the scars; her eagle eyes narrowed on them. She grabbed my wrist to get a better look, careless of the wine that spilled on my hand. "Yezeba'al! What is this? What have you done to yourself?"

I yanked my arm away and set down my cup, using the hem of my veil to wipe the spilled wine from my hand. "It is nothing. It was an accident."

"That does not look like an accident. You have been well taught how to cut without leaving scars when you need blood for a ritual. How could you have grown so careless?"

"It was when Akhab died," I explained. Then I murmured, "I was trying to...resurrect him. Of course, it did not work. I grew desperate, and then...this."

She looked at me with pity in her gaze.

"Don't pity me, Ama. You know I hate it when people pity me."

"I knew you were ill after you lost him, but did not think... Is that what it was?"

I said nothing; only averted my gaze, not wanting to admit how low I had fallen then.

She put her feet on the floor and set her cup on a table then reached across to take my hand. "But are you all right now? Do I need to be concerned?"

Pulling my hand away, I said, "No, Ama. I am fine now. Mostly." I sighed. "I miss him, of course, but I know that my life did not end when his ended, and that I must go on for the sake of the children and the kingdom. It's lonely sometimes, though, without him."

"Have you not taken a lover?"

Now, I sighed heavily. "I have, but none of them are satisfying. Not really, anyway. They all take and do not give enough in return. Some of them try, but most seem only interested in pleasing themselves, with no consideration at all for whether I have enjoyed them as much as they enjoyed me. I shall never find Akhab's equal. He never left me unsatisfied."

"Most men are like that, Yezeba'al." She smirked. "Why do you think I prefer women?"

"But I am not like you in that way, Ama."

"You were when you were a young maiden."

I gave her a look. "Only because I could not have what I truly desired – they were all I was allowed. For good reason, of course, but that does not change my natural inclinations. I have had some priestesses since then, but it is more...functional than anything. It is not the same and I cannot find it wholly satisfying – not the way it is when I am with a man. One that knows how to please a woman, anyway." I rolled my eyes.

She snorted. "That is a rare thing, indeed. But what sort of men have you been consorting with? Surely, you can find one who pleases you?"

I sighed heavily and thought about the disappointing string of lovers. "The first was one of Akhab's brothers. Asa. You met him when you came to us: the Minister of Ceremonies. An artist. He wrote many songs and poems about me, especially in the early years when I first married Akhab."

570

"Oh, him. Yes, I remember him. He bears a striking resemblance to Akhab, so I can see why you would be drawn to him. But...there were others?"

"Yes. There have been many," I answered, as a warmth spread across my nose and cheeks. "But none of them can satisfy me – most do not even try. After a while, I came to realize that they were not even truly interested in *me*. I was merely a notch on their belts. Their desire for me was more about being able to say that they have bedded Akhab's queen, and a goddess incarnate – nonsense like that has come back to me, from those at court who listen."

"This should not surprise you, Yezeba'al."

I held myself, and tears began to slip down my cheeks. "I feel so ashamed – so disgusted, for allowing myself to be used in such a way. But I have been so lonely, Ama."

"I understand, but you have been consorting with the unworthy. You must not pollute yourself with lesser men."

"They were princes, noblemen – not kings, of course, but..."

"I do not speak of rank and bearing," she cut in. "I speak of the spirit. Have you forgotten about all that, in your loneliness? Have you forgotten the gift of the Ba'alah, whose essence lives within you? *Sexual union is not about physical pleasure*; it is about healing and restoring the balance of spiritual energies within the body. Pleasure is only a byproduct, and that is where you have been going wrong. I think perhaps it came so naturally to you with your husband because he was your true and equal counterpart – you Ba'al. These other men you have consorted with, no matter how highborn, are not your equals in spirit. They could not give back to you in equal measure because they do not have what *you* need to be restored.

"When you lie with them," she continued, "you give them the gift of Ashtarti's healing love, but you need to be restored afterward."

"Who but my husband could restore me?"

"Another priest of Ba'al," she said simply, as if it were obvious.

"You mean like the one you and Abbu had executed for daring to lay his hands on me, at my urging?"

"That was different. You were a maiden then. It was imperative that we protect your integrity. You know that, Yezeba'al."

"You did not have to kill him, though. You could simply have banished him or stripped him of his rank. After him, I could not even think of lying with another priest of Ba'al. I have barely even allowed

571

myself the pleasure of friendship with them, staying mostly in the company of the priests and priestesses of Asherah – Ashtarti."

"Asherah, Ashtarti, Ishtar – it does not matter what name you call her, Yezeba'al. I know what you meant. In Egypt, she is Aushet; the people of Opir call her Adi Shakti. It is all the same, you know that."

She paused and lifted her cup to her lips. Then she continued, "You must move beyond that incident and find a priest of Ba'al to satisfy your needs. He will never be as good for you as your High Priest and husband was – unless you decide he is worthy to become your new High Priest – but any true priest of Ba'al can hold his energy long enough to have a healing union with you, and you are in desperate need of that healing. You have been giving too much of yourself without receiving anything of substance in return, and you are out of balance. That is why you feel so wretched. Only a union with Ba'al himself, or one of his worthy representatives, can restore you."

"I have friends who are priests of Ba'al, but I could not imagine copulating with them, not even for ritual purposes. They are as brothers to me. I have no desire for them."

"Those you have at Shomron, perhaps, but there are many priests of Ba'al here and at Tzidon, and elsewhere. Certainly, there is one who can fill your needs." She reached across to place a hand on my knee. "Do not give up hope – you will find him. In the meantime, do not taint yourself with unworthy lovers. If you cannot consort with one who is able to connect directly with Ba'al, you would be better off celibate, or in pleasing yourself."

I sighed heavily and rolled my eyes, annoyed with those options.

After taking another sip of her drink, she admonished, "You are not a common priestess, Yezeba'al. Only one of Ba'al's priests should ever enter the sacred body of a high priestess. Yet you have been allowing unworthy men to enter you – to use you – as if you were a common priestess. Even common priestesses must seek union with Ba'al to restore themselves after they have given the blessing of Ashtarti to lesser men."

"But I thought they were able to restore themselves through prayer and meditation?"

She shook her head. "That is only the first part – what they must do to cleanse their bodies and prepare for their divine union with Ba'al. Remember, only Ba'al can heal his consort, as only she can heal him. That is what you have been missing."

I furrowed my brow. "Why did Daneyah not teach me these things?"

"It was never intended for you to be a common priestess, and therefore you did not need to know, for you were only ever meant to serve your husband as a high priestess."

"You are a high priestess, yet you know these things."

She confirmed with a nod. "She would have told you, had it become necessary – as it has now. With your husband gone, everything has changed. Now, you need a priest who can take on the role of Ba'al for you, both on the altar and in your bed. No more unworthy lovers, Yezeba'al, no matter how much you are drawn to them. Your body cannot discern what is good for the spirit, and neither can lust fulfill the divine within. Let your spirit choose your lovers – only then will you be satisfied."

She got up and patted my knee again before she walked toward the drink table to refill her cup for a third time. I became lost in thought. She left me with much to consider. Soon we were so caught up in the final preparations for my brother's coronation, however, that I did not have time to think about anything else.

25

Matters Spiritual and Corporeal

The people of Tzidon mourned the death of my father, who had been a good king, but they rejoiced in the coronation of his successor. My brother Esar looked every bit the part of a king as he knelt in the Temple of Ba'al Melkorat for his anointing. The sacred ceremony was conducted by a senior priest of Ba'al and my mother, in her role as High Priestess of Tzidon. The only people outside our family who were allowed to attend were the clergy and nobility; all of us knelt with our hands pressed together as we bore witness. The anointing ceremony began with the sacrificial offering of a pure black bull that was led into the temple draped in a purple cape and dressed in floral wreaths. Once it reached the altar, it was anointed and prayed over before its throat was slit by the presiding priest of Ba'al, an aging man with long white hair down his back. The other attending priests stood chanting or moved about performing other lesser tasks.

Once its spirit was severed from the flesh, some of the attending priests helped the head priest place the bull upon the altar in the usual manner. It was set aflame so it would arrive in the underworld and summon the Ba'alim to our presence, in the hope they would bless Esar's reign. The smoke from the offering was white with only a bit of grey, indicating their acceptance. Once it was received, the anointing could take place. My mother smiled proudly as she pressed the holy oil to his hands, breast, and forehead, after which the priest of Ba'al did the same. I stifled tears as I observed the sacred moment, both out of pride for my brother and sorrow for the loss of my father. This ceremony reminded me also of the anointings of my sons and the losses I had sustained for those to take place.

After the anointing, we rode in a procession that took us through the streets of the two cities, the celebration split between them evenly. The slow-moving procession departed from the temple at Zour around midday and concluded after a mercifully short sea voyage from the northern port there to the southern port at Tzidon. My children and I were fourth in line behind the new king, who was driven in his chariot with our mother beside him, followed by his Melkah who sat upon an ivory-inlaid chair on a litter behind their eldest son, my brother's successor, who was a grown man and drove his own chariot.

My children rode with me in a chariot that I drove myself, thinking of Akhab and grateful for the time he took to teach me this skill. Ba'alesar was twelve and could also drive, so I let him take the reins whenever my arms tired, but I was eager to show myself capable and to represent my goddess as the patroness of chariots. Nine-year-old Azba and eight-year-old Abshalom stood on either side of us, splendid in their rich attire. They enjoyed waving to and blessing the crowds, who rejoiced at our passing with more fervor than they showed to their new king, especially when they saw me driving the chariot myself. It was as my mother had said: I had forgotten how much my father's people adored me, their goddess incarnate.

Some of the people wept and called out to me for my blessing as we passed, which I offered with gratitude, struggling not to also weep. I could not help but compare it to my last procession through Yerushalayim. Even the most recent coronation processions through Shomron were not so glorious, tainted as they were by the sorrows of my husband and son's too early deaths. My father, on the other hand, had died an old man after being ill for quite some time; his people had loved him, but there was nothing unnatural about his death to overshadow the glory of his son's ascent.

After we stopped in one of the courtyards at Tzidon, where the chariots and the queen's litter could be collected, my brother looked at me from across the way with an open-mouthed grin that suggested his excitement and relief that it had gone so well. I smiled and gave him a nod, to hide that I was in fact quite exhausted. Then I gathered my children, and we went inside to freshen up before the feast.

Kora and our other attendants had gone ahead to meet us at the palace in Tzidon. While she fixed my hair, my two youngest children rambled on about the procession to their nurses and guardians, who smiled politely as they straightened and readjusted the children's hair and regalia.

Azba was especially enchanted by the way the people appealed to me. She told Kora, "They called out to Ama, 'Ba'alah! Ba'alah! Bless us!' and they were in tears when she smiled upon them and raised her hand in blessing! Even our own people have not been this joyful to have her blessing."

"It is all right, Azba," I said, glancing at her with a fond smile. "Our people have grown used to seeing me regularly. The people here have not seen me in many years; that is why they rejoice more."

"They also believe in you," said Kora. "The people of Yisrael, even those who worship the Ba'alim, do not fully understand what it means for you to be Ashtarti incarnate. I do not think they can appreciate you the way the people here do."

"Perhaps not," I said with a shrug, "but I have grown used to it. Of course, it does feel good to be properly adored. I forgot how much the people here loved to see me."

Kora's voice took on a wistful yet informative tone as she said to my children, "Your Ama used to be carried through the streets of Zour, Tzidon, and Gebal once a year, for the celebration of the Feast of Ashtarti every spring. From the time she was a small child – even smaller than you, Abshalom – she was dressed in the richest garments and jewels, her face painted beautifully, and escorted in a procession much like the one you saw today, so the people could behold their goddess and receive her blessing. My own Ama was her nurse, and she was also a priestess of Ashtarti, and she accompanied your Ama on these processions. She told me all about the way the people clamored just to get a glimpse of the small girl whose mere presence blessed them. It was even said that their illnesses could be cured, just by a single glance from her in their direction."

"I think you have elaborated on the story a bit over the years, Kora," I teased. "I doubt I healed anyone just by looking at them."

"I think you are just being modest, Yezeba'al," came her retort. Then she said to my children, "Do not listen to your Ama – just this once. What you witnessed today was the way it always was when the people of Tzidon saw her. Though she is beloved of them, the people of Yisrael do not realize how blessed they are to have her as their queen – and how blessed you are to have her as your mother."

"I am the one who is blessed, to be your Ama," I insisted, smiling at my two youngest children. At twelve, Ba'alesar was too old to be present while I was changing, so he was in his own quarters doing the same.

Azba came up to stand beside me, smiling at our reflections in the mirror as Kora twisted and pinned the last lock of hair to the back of my head. I watched her gaze rest on her own reflection then, and realized how much she resembled me. I had not noticed before, but of all my children she had inherited my looks the most. Seeing our reflections side by side, it was almost as if I was looking at a younger version of myself. Our eyes met in the mirror, and we shared a smile. It was good to have this time with my children once again, even if much of it was taken up by all the pomp and ceremony.

All three of my children were permitted to attend the feast along with their cousins, my brother Esar's many children, but they were sent to bed when it grew late and the revelry took on a mature atmosphere. It was just as well, because there was one guest whose presence came as an unwelcome surprise, and it left me feeling bitter rather than merry.

"What is *he* doing here?" I demanded in a low voice, sitting on a cushion next to my brother at the head table, where he had returned for refreshment.

He followed my gaze to where Hadadesar, the King of Aram, was sitting with a group of other men, all of them playing a game with carved figures they pushed around a board with a small rake. He had not been at the ceremony in Zour, and neither had he been part of the procession, so I was shocked when I saw him enter the feast and heard him announced.

"He is family," Esar replied nonchalantly, picking flakes of roasted lamb from a legbone.

"As is the King of Assyria, yet I do not see him here among your guests."

Esar wiped his fingers on a linen cloth and then crossed his arms over his chest, giving me a look. "He is my ally."

"He is *my* enemy. You could have at least warned me ahead of time."

"Would you have come, if I had?"

"No."

He held up his hands. "That is why I did not tell you."

577

I turned my head and raised my eyes toward the ceiling with a heavy sigh.

"Come, *akhatu*. I want us to heal this rift between you and our cousin. We are better off united than we are as enemies – especially in the face of common and more powerful enemies." His expression became grim then and he lowered his voice. "Assyria grows stronger with each passing year."

"Assyria is not my enemy."

"Assyria is everybody's enemy. I believe Shalmaneser poses an even greater threat than his father ever did. If it comes to war, we will need all of us to fight together."

"If it comes to war, I will counsel my son to keep Yisrael out of it."

"You cannot keep Yisrael out of it, if Shalmaneser shows up in your kingdom with a great army bent on conquest."

"He will have to take Aram and Ammon before he can take Yisrael. They are a buffer between us. And if it comes to that, Yisrael will have time to prepare and gather our own true allies. Aram has never been trustworthy – not since Hadi took the throne. I will never consider him an ally."

"You cannot keep your son from being a man."

"Who put the Moabites in their place less than two years ago? My son has already established himself with a great victory in battle."

"Ah yes: the Wolf of Moab." He almost smirked at the nickname some had taken to calling Yoram.

Ignoring his amusement, I insisted, "I am not trying to keep him from being a man – I am trying to keep him *alive*. It is my duty, just as it is my duty to bring peace."

"How can you bring peace if you insist on being enemies with Hadi?"

"He is the one who insists on making of himself my enemy, by antagonizing my family and my kingdom."

Esar chuckled. "You mean that little prank he played with his servant, the one they called Naaman?"

"That was not a harmless prank, Esar. The man was a leper. He could have spread his disease to all of us at court, and throughout our kingdom. He even tried to bring gifts, but we turned them away, for they were surely tainted with leprosy."

"Do you truly believe Hadi meant to bring contagion into Yisrael by sending him?"

"Yes, I do believe that was his intention."

"They say the man was healed," said Esar. "By one of your prophets."

"The prophets of Yahowah are not my prophets."

"He resides and works throughout your kingdom. Forgive me, Yezeba'al. I thought that made him one of your subjects, and one of Yisrael's prophets." He paused to take a drink, and then said, "No matter which god he prophecies for, he healed a leper. That is something to be remarked upon."

"I do not know whether or not the man was healed, nor do I care – that is not the point. The point is that Hadi meant to cause trouble in my kingdom, as he has always done. Whether his intention is to harm or simply to have a bit of fun is irrelevant. His little games have always had serious consequences and have cost people their lives. If not for him, my husband would still be alive. I will never forgive him for taking Akhab from me."

"Was it his arrow that pierced your husband's flesh? Forgive me, *akhatu*; I will not blame the man for what was essentially an accident, for the King of Yisrael was unknown in the battle. Or am I mistaken, having heard that he was in disguise when he went in his chariot?"

I paused and looked away, as a sudden ache had seized my chest and settled in my throat. Swallowing it and exhaling slowly, I turned back to my brother and looked him in the eye. "Akhab was Hadi's target from the moment he became my husband. He has never forgiven Akhab for being the one who was chosen by our father to take me as a wife. And according to the King of Yehudah, and the generals who were witness to the battle, Hadi had charged his men to find Akhab and do all in their power to end his life. It does not matter whose arrow pierced his flesh; in the end, it is Hadi's intent that matters."

With that, I got up and walked away. I needed to go out into the garden for fresh air, and to get away from all the noise of the people who were clustered inside the feast hall. That is when Hadi came to me, attempting to make amends in his usual self-serving manner.

I was standing by a pool, watching fireflies lighting up the surface of the water and the air around me. It was beautiful and I felt as though Akhab was there beside me, that we were watching it together. The moment was ruined, however, when I heard my cousin's voice from behind me, "Shalom, Yeza."

While I whirled around to face him, he continued, "I had hoped for the opportunity to speak with you."

"Go away, Hadi. I have no desire to exchange words with you."

I turned my back on him, but he still came to stand beside me. "I am sorry about Akhab. When I heard how hard his death hit you, how you were near to death yourself, I felt terrible about the whole affair."

Now I turned on him, piercing him with a sharp gaze. If only I had my dagger on me then, I would have thrust it into his heart right there, no matter the consequences. "From the moment my betrothal to Akhab was announced, you hated him. You hated him, and you sought to bring about his end the moment it was in your power to do so."

"It was not my fault he made war against me at Ramot."

"It was absolutely your fault! You started the whole affair — constantly stringing him out with false promises, after *you* made war on us. But when you knew you did not have what it took for you to defeat him in his own land, you devised a way for him to make war against you, and at last you got what you desired." I spit at his feet. "I curse you, Hadadesar. May your treachery come back to haunt you in your own time."

When I moved to walk away, he grabbed my arm above the elbow, and said, "I am not finished with you, Yeza. Akhab may be in the underworld, but I still do not have what I desire."

"You are not worthy of what you desire," I replied, yanking my arm away.

"I am *Bar-Hadad*," he said in Aramaic, standing proudly over me with his fists upon his waist. "Son of Hadad — your Ba'al."

"Whom you do not even worship," I reminded him.

"You should have been *my* wife," he growled.

"My father knew that you were not worthy — no matter what name you were given by your father when he tried so hard to convince my father to marry me to you." I paused and affected a tone of mock sympathy. "Poor Hadadesar; you have never gotten over being

580

rejected." I drew out the final word by each syllable, the greater to sting.

At last, I left him confounded. He did not come back into the feast hall for quite a while; no doubt he was licking his wounds and hiding his shame in the dark veil of night. When he did return, he went back to his friends, the other princes and kings who had been invited to celebrate my brother's ascension. He pretended to be in good spirits, but I could feel his burning gaze upon me throughout the night, and occasionally caught him before he had the chance to turn away.

I refused to acknowledge him, instead turning my attention back to my mother and the other women with whom I gathered, smiling, and laughing with them so he could see how little I cared about his wounded pride. As soon as my brother retired from the feast, I made my own departure to the solitude and safety of my private residence, surrounded by the eunuchs to keep unwanted visitors away.

Hadadesar did not remain at Tzidon for more than a couple of days, staying only until the feasting ended and after sending frequent requests to see me, all of which were denied. I was relieved when he returned to Damaseq, while we moved onto Gebal to continue the celebrations there. Now, I could enjoy my stay without his unwelcome presence inhibiting my movement around the palace grounds. When I grew tired of the endless days of feasting, I excused myself and went to the palace library.

The library in Gebal was the most impressive collection of written works I had ever seen, larger even than the ones at the palaces in Tzidon and Zour. Hundreds of clay tablets lined every wall on shelves. Desks for study set up behind screens amidst endless rows of cedar shelves full of scrolls stacked upon one another and organized into diagonal slots filled with related texts. Priests and priestesses of the Ba'alim came here regularly for study, and some were even appointed to keep the writings from becoming disorganized. Scrolls and tablets of larger works had their own tables where they were kept and could be studied without being moved to another location.

Once a place of refuge for me, I had spent many hours there immersed in study when I was a girl. I was only seven the first time I was allowed to visit the library at Gebal, but I walked along the shelves, awe-struck and overwhelmed by the wealth of knowledge I knew must be stored there. At the time, I had only just begun to learn how to read and write Akkadian, so I was most keenly drawn to the clay tablets that were covered in the language whose characters I recognized but still could not decipher. There was one tablet left upon a table, and I lifted the corner to get a closer look, but the harder I tried to read what it said the more my head began to ache.

Finally, I gave up. When I set it down, the weight caused it to drop and the sound of hardened clay thumping against wood resounded through the chamber.

"Yezeba'al!" Daneyah chided, as she returned her attention to me. "Be careful with the tablets! They are unfired clay and may break easily."

"Why do they not fire them so they will last longer?"

She was stunned by my question, as if momentarily wondering the same. Then she pursed her lips and took me by the hand to lead me away, instructing me to stay away from the tablets until I had learned more respect for them. I was eager to learn how to read those tablets, though, and to discover the wisdom they possessed. I took my Akkadian lessons more seriously after that day, but when I was finally able to read the tablets, I found that the same stories and knowledge they possessed were transcribed on the scrolls I had already read, and so I lost interest in them. Scrolls were far easier to store and to read than clay tablets, anyway.

Glancing at the tablets along the walls, as I entered the library one morning all these years later, I clicked my tongue on the back of my teeth as I thought of these things. Once so fascinated by them, I did not know why we even bothered to keep them now, when the clay could be reused for newer communications. It seemed a waste of space, when there were scrolls on the shelves that contained everything they had and more: the scribes who had copied them onto papyrus made commentaries in the margins to compliment the original texts, expanding on and interpreting them.

None of those stories were of interest to me now, however. With the coronation duties out of the way, I had time to research some of the things which my mother and I had previously discussed

582

about the sexual nature of Ashtarti and her relationship with her divine counterpart. I thought I had been taught everything there was to know about my gods and the nature of their essences, having forgotten about the scrolls that had once been forbidden but were now open to me. There was still so much for me to learn. My disappointment at finding my education so incomplete could be remedied now by what was locked away here in chests stored under the tables in the palace library.

I did not have time to get completely caught up in my research, however, for I would be returning to Yisrael within a fortnight. Once I found the scrolls needed, I began making copies of them to take back to Yisrael for further study. I went to the library every morning, at the time of day when there were seldom others around, so I could have solitude while I worked. This solitude was occasionally interrupted, but I paid little attention to those who entered and they, likewise, knew better than to disturb me. They knew who I was and quietly paid their respects, but otherwise carried on with their own work.

Then came the day when a priest I had never seen at the palace appeared, and although he dressed the same as the others, for some reason he stood out from them. He did not see me at first, for I was sequestered in the back of the chamber and partially obscured behind a screen. When I heard him enter, I paused from transcribing to observe him as he searched through scrolls on the shelves, humming and occasionally murmuring to himself. He was young, perhaps mid-to-late twenties, with a well-trimmed goatee and thick dark hair that fell in curls to his shoulders.

By his loin cloth, which was long and white with wide strips of blue at the front and back, I knew he was a priest of Ba'al. Like all his kind, he did not wear anything on his upper body except for bracelets and armbands, and a gold amulet in the shape of a bull's head hung over his chest. He was handsome, but I did not want him to see me. I admired him from my hidden place, absentmindedly playing with my opal scarab pendant and bringing my stylus to my lips while I scanned his perfectly bronzed skin and athletic form.

He searched casually, as if trying to find something with which to pass the time. I might have gone on watching him, without him ever realizing he was not alone, but then I dropped my stylus. The noise alerted him to my presence as it bounced and rolled across the tile floor. Immediately, he stopped murmuring and straightened. Then he turned to look at the stylus that had rolled into the middle of the floor. His gaze followed the path it had made, and then he leaned to the side to look beyond the screen where he spotted me. I was frozen and wide-eyed.

"Forgive me," he said, meeting my gaze from across the chamber. Then he walked over to where the stylus lay and stooped to pick it up. "I did not realize anyone else was here, or I would have been quieter. I hope I did not disturb your study." He brought it to me, held it out, and watched me curiously. "Your stylus, *Rebitya*."

He used the common title for a priestess, and I quickly surmised that he did not recognize me in my casual attire. Meeting his gaze with a smile, I slipped the scarab pendant beneath the collar of my dress and took the stylus, thanking him. I was not used to people holding my gaze in such a bold manner; it pleased me to hold his interest without being recognized.

"Forgive me," he murmured, "I have not seen you at the temple before. Do you...work at the palace?"

My smile broadened and I shook my head. "I am visiting from Yisrael."

"Ah, you must serve the Ba'alah Yezeba'al. Of course, it makes sense that she would have brought some of her own priestesses in her entourage. What..." He paused as if to reconsider. "Do you mind speaking to me? I do not wish to impose on your leisure time. I am called Daryoush, by the way."

Again, I shook my head. "I do not mind, Daryoush."

Relieved, he sat in one of the empty chairs beside me and looked at me with interest. "What is she like, the Ba'alah?"

Still surprised that he did not realize I was the subject of his inquiry, I raised my brows. "That...is an unusual question. Why do you ask about the Gebirah of Yisrael?"

He chuckled. "Gebirah Azra has summoned me because she wants to introduce me to her. I will be meeting with them soon, in fact."

"Is that so?"

"Yes," he answered with an amused tone. "Is that so hard to believe?"

"No, I suppose not. Only, I find it interesting. Why does Gebirah Azra want you to meet the Gebirah of Yisrael?"

He cleared his throat. I noticed a flush come to his cheeks and the bridge of his nose. "She...wants me to...heal her. You know, ritually."

I nodded in understanding, and my gaze passed over his form, admiring him freely. I certainly found him to my liking, but I was forty-one and thought, surely, I would be too old to be of interest to him. What if he did not find me to his liking? Why should he do this when he had never laid eyes upon me before this moment?

"Do you...want to lie with the Gebirah of Yisrael?"

"It is my duty," he answered, "as a priest of Ba'al."

"Of course, and I am certain you will do your duty without question. Even so, that does not discount your own...interests. What are your thoughts on the matter?"

He smiled faintly and his gaze took on a faraway look. Then he leaned his elbow on the table and sighed heavily. "To be honest, I am not certain of it. I have heard she is a great beauty, even at her age and after having many children, but...I know nothing about her."

"She is a queen – is that not enough?"

"I have no interest in her title. I am more interested in *who* she is, not what she is. It is said she is the incarnation of Ashtarti, which I suppose would explain her beauty – if it is even true. I suspect it is an exaggeration."

He looked at me, as if to see what I might say on the matter. It was strange to be talked about in such a way, and I was not sure what to say. I could hardly reveal myself now, though, for I did not wish to embarrass him. Besides, I wanted to know more about his thoughts on the matter without him feeling the need to lie to placate me.

"Did you not see her at the coronation?"

"I did but she was far away. I couldn't really see *her*; all I could see were her gleaming jewels and opulent regalia. She certainly looked like a queen, perhaps even a goddess, but...how could I get any sense of who she is just by looking at her? In order to really see someone, we have to look into their eyes, you know – see their soul."

He paused and our eyes met, and for a moment he was lost in my gaze. "You have beautiful eyes..." Then he seemed to return to his senses, and began rambling nervously, "Forgive me. Please, do not say anything to the Ba'alah. I do not mean to be irreverent – I hold her in the highest esteem, from what I know of her. And of course, I will do whatever is asked of me. It is my duty as a priest of Ba'al to restore the priestesses of Ashtarti when they have depleted themselves through their work. Although I have never been asked to perform the ritual for a high priestess before, let alone one who is said to actually *be* the goddess incarnate. I suppose it cannot be much different, and I should be honored to have been chosen for this undertaking."

"Then what is your hesitation?"

He sighed. "My Gebirah expects me to do more than perform a healing ritual. She wants me to return with the Ba'alah to Yisrael if she is pleased with me."

"But you do not want to leave your homeland. I can understand."

"It is not that," he answered. "I do not mind going to Yisrael, I suppose. I have nothing to hold me here, except familiarity." He paused. "The part that frightens me is that, if I do this, I must swear myself to the Ba'alah alone. I will not be her husband, but I may only have her for the rest of her life or mine."

"That is a lot to ask, especially when you do not know her." I paused, choosing my words carefully as I went on. "I suppose she would also be troubled by this, as she does not know you any more than you know her, and she would not wish to keep you tied to her in something like marriage without your consent."

"You are remarkably understanding." He met my gaze when I looked up, and for a moment he was lost again, but then he pressed his lips together and looked away. "I'm sorry. Perhaps I should not be telling you all this, especially as you are in her service." He looked up at me again. "You know her well, I assume."

I smiled and momentarily looked away. "I know the Gebirah of Yisrael quite intimately..." Then I saw the way his face brightened, and quickly added, "Not *that* intimately. I mean..." I giggled. *Actually...yes, that intimately.* This was all too amusing.

He watched me with a crooked smile. "You have a beautiful laugh."

I looked at him curiously, wondering if I should reveal myself now or continue to deceive him. Then he asked, "Would you...tell me about her? Enough for me to know what to expect when I meet her?"

I considered his question. "I will tell you only this: she will never force a man to lie with her, not even for ritual purposes. If you

586

do not desire her, you must tell her truthfully. She will not hold it against you."

"Will she not have me executed for offending her, or something?"

I almost laughed but managed to suppress it. "She will appreciate your honesty. You must trust in her mercy, for she is not unreasonable – she strives very much to be as benevolent as the Ba'alah she represents."

He looked up and his smile broadened. "I do not know about her, but I feel I can trust you. Thank you. Forgive me – I do not know your name."

I smiled playfully and told him, "Ask the Gebirah of Yisrael when you meet her."

He earnestly met my gaze. "I know that if I swear myself in service to her, I can never have anything more than friendship with another woman, but...may I ask for her permission to speak with you again?"

For the first time since Akhab, I felt a stirring in my heart. I had forgotten how it felt to be moved in such a way – not lust, but something deeper. A sense of possibility and excitement that was entirely removed from mere carnal desire. "You do not need to ask – you have my permission."

A relieved expression came over his face, and he said, "I will do anything the Ba'alah asks of me, if it means that I may speak with you again."

I looked out the window and suddenly realized the time. I was supposed to be getting ready to meet my mother – and apparently this priest. "Forgive me; I must...go tend to the Gebirah." It was not a lie, for I would be tending to my mother.

He watched me get up, and I could see the sudden melancholy in his gaze. I gently placed a hand upon his shoulder, hesitating only for a moment before letting my palm rest there. His breath caught in his chest as he looked at my hand, and then up at me.

"Do not be afraid to meet her – I am certain she will find you to her liking."

He took my hand. "May I confess that I find you to my liking?"

I smiled. "I find you to my liking, too."

"Will the Ba'alah become jealous?"

I giggled. Then I closed my eyes and gently shook my head. "We shall meet again soon, but now I must go."

He pressed my fingers to his lips and when I slowly pulled away, I felt an ache in my chest. I could hardly breathe as I hurried off. It felt so unreal. My mother had always been a keen matchmaker, but how could she have known we would take to one another like this? I still wanted to be angry with her, but I had not felt this light in years.

When I arrived at my chamber, my mother was there waiting. She had been pacing but stopped the moment I appeared. "Where have you been? Have you forgotten the audience I have arranged for you?"

"I have not forgotten, Ama," I said, hurrying behind the dressing screen. Kora immediately came and began to help me undress.

"You should have been here sooner. We will be late."

"We are queens – we cannot be late." I peered out from behind the screen at her and smiled. "Did you not tell me such a thing once?"

"Yes, I believe I did. But there are *some* things for which even queens must not be late. This is too important an audience to keep him waiting."

"What sort of audience is this, anyway? You never told me who I am meeting with, and for what purpose?"

She came to stand nearby, and her eyes scanned my naked form, just before Kora wrapped me in a plain underrobe. "You are so thin, Yezeba'al. Are you eating enough?"

"I eat plenty," I answered shortly, while Kora draped me in my richly embroidered outer robe.

My mother hummed. "You take after your father then. He was always lean."

"You did not answer my question."

"We are meeting a friend of mine."

"What sort of friend?" I wanted to see how much she would admit to me.

"A priest. He is like a son to me, and I believe you will enjoy his company."

"A priest?" I asked, holding out my arms while Kora wrapped and tied the sash around my waist.

My mother nodded.

588

"A priest of Ba'al?"

"Yes," she at last admitted. "He is willing to heal you, if you find him to your liking."

"I should curse you for arranging all this behind my back."

"Wait until you meet him, Yezeba'al. Then you can decide whether to curse or bless me."

I walked up to her and took her by the arms. "I already have, Ama. And I bless you." I brought my lips to her cheek, and then went around her to my dressing table to put on my jewelry and to touch up the kohl around my eyes.

"Wait," she said, twirling around and coming to me. "You have already met?"

"I was in the library," I explained in a sing-song voice. "He did not know who I was, but he spoke to me and... Ama, I have not felt this way since Akhab."

She regarded me with a knowing smile. "I suppose you did not reveal your identity while you were there?"

I turned to face her now that I was ready and could not stop smiling. "He wants to speak with me again. He thinks I am a priestess in service to the Gebirah of Yisrael, but he finds me to his liking. *Me*. Not the Ba'alah. Not the Gebirah. Just me."

"Why would he not?"

"I would have thought myself too old for him. Surely, he must be younger than some of Akhab's sons. I could be his mother."

"He is in his twenty-ninth year, I believe," she said. "He is quite old enough. Besides, you have retained much of your charm and youthful spirit. It is no wonder he was enchanted by you – as I knew he would be. You must have had a great deal of enjoyment in fooling him as you did. Now, come. We must go."

He was already waiting in my mother's private audience chamber when we were announced, having been brought there ahead of time so as not to keep us waiting. He went down on his knees and bowed in reverence while we entered together. It was only after we were seated, and my mother bade him to rise, that he looked up at me. He started at first, stared at me in disbelief, and then his lips parted the moment recognition hit. His eyes scanned me as if searching for some sort of trickery. I met his gaze and smiled apologetically, as my mother began.

589

"Well, Daryoush," she said in a playful tone, "I was going to introduce you to my daughter – but it seems the two of you have already met."

His eyes sparkled as he met my gaze, and I stifled a laugh. Then he answered, "Yes, Gebirah Azra. Although, I had no idea who I was speaking to."

We turned to each other now, and I said, "I hope you can forgive my little game at your expense, Daryoush. If it is any consolation, I meant everything I said."

"Ba'alah," he said, kneeling with a hand over his heart and bowing his head. When he looked up at me again, he smiled as if still coming to terms with it. "I could never hold anything against you, least of all a harmless prank. It was my fault anyway, for being presumptuous, so it is I who should be begging your forgiveness, my Ba'alah."

"There is no need. I quite enjoyed myself with your presumption. I hope you will continue to be open with me, as if no rank separates us, especially when we are alone together."

We carried on for quite a while with our playful banter before finally discussing the particulars of the arrangement.

Because I was a high priestess, Daryoush had to first be purified and reconsecrated so that he could enter into me without blemish. In preparation for our sacred rituals, we spent a day in fasting and prayer, starting at sundown. Then at sundown on the following day, we were taken to the temple for his purification rite and, if all went well, our coupling. I was dressed in a white hooded prayer robe and taken to kneel upon the dais on one side of the altar, surrounded by a group of priestesses who acted as my attendants, much like the maidens who attend to a bride at her wedding. My mother, as the reigning High Priestess at Tzidon, performed the rite while the rest of the assembly, made up only of high-ranking priests and priestesses, raised incense, beat drums, and chanted.

First, she anointed me and circled me with incense. Then she went to the other side of the altar where Daryoush knelt. She had her own ritual dagger, nearly identical to mine, which she used to draw a small amount of blood from his breast. His blood was mixed into a small bowl with oil of frankincense and set aflame upon the altar as an offering to Ashtarti. If the offering was accepted, the mixture would ignite and consume the blood, indicating his worthiness for the ritual to proceed.

The mixture ignited with a sudden burst, after which my mother stepped back. I held my breath, the drumming and chanting stopped; everyone waited in silence until it was consumed. Tears burned my eyes while I watched, thankful that it appeared the offering was accepted. We would only know for sure once the flames went out, at which point my mother approached the altar and peered into the offering bowl. Having found the blood consumed, she used a cloth to lift the heated bowl and exposed the interior to the rest of us, as she proclaimed: "He is worthy! Ba'alah be praised!"

All at once, the assembly erupted into praise. I released my breath and looked across the altar at Daryoush, who was also looking at me. We shared a tender gaze and soft smile, perhaps both of us consumed by the gravity of what was about to happen: excited yet nervous, like a newly married couple on their wedding night. I hoped he was not having second thoughts, but he appeared calm, and it gave me courage.

My mother anointed him with holy oils and said prayers over him, circling him with incense. Then she bade him to rise and led him to me; the others parted to let them pass. When he stood over me, my mother took my hand and placed it in his. Then he raised me to stand and looked into my eyes. There was an intensity in his gaze that drew me to him.

While we stood together before the assembled clergy, Daryoush swore himself to my service: "Ba'alah, from this moment I am yours. To you alone I give my oath: my flesh is yours, my blood is yours, my spirit is yours, and my soul belongs to you alone. I promise to protect and serve you for as long as we live. So may it be done according to your will."

I accepted his vow and then I was made to drink an herbal concoction. It was the same elixir I drank before the sex rite was performed on the high holy days each year, which heightened the intensity with which we were drawn to each other and opened us to further ecstasy. When he led me toward the altar I followed without hesitation, desire swelling in my loins as it visibly swelled in his.

He gently lowered my hood and began stripping off my robes, leaving me in nothing but the jewelry I wore. Those who were in

591

attendance performed their supportive duties, drumming, chanting, and worshiping in the dim chamber as we came together on the altar: a union of the divine in the flesh. The moment we reached satisfaction – I came first, followed only seconds later by him – the congregation fell silent. The only sound in the chamber was the echo of our voices raised in ecstasy. Then he draped himself over me, his head resting on my breast, as we caught our breaths and settled. I had forgotten how invigorating it was to have this experience. An effigy could never compare to a real man.

Afterward, we dressed and knelt before the altar together, leading the congregation in a prayer of thanksgiving. Then I invited him to dine with me in my quarters. Apart from discussing our future, we laughed together about the way we had met, only a day before. He admitted that he would have found it impossible to resist me and to keep his vow if I were not the Ba'alah herself.

"Even at the risk of death?"

He chuckled, not realizing the seriousness with which I asked the question. "Yes, my Ba'alah. Even at the risk of my very soul, I would have had you, if you would let me."

"I would never ask such a thing of you," I said, looking away.

"You would not have to – I give myself freely to you."

A tear slipped down my cheek. He must have noticed, because suddenly, he got up from the cushion and came around the table to kneel beside me and take me in his arms. "Forgive me – I did not mean to upset you."

I shook my head and wiped my tears, mindful of the kohl around my eyes and trying not to smear it more than it likely already was. "It is not you. Only it reminds me of something from my youth."

Then I told him about the first priest of Ba'al with whom I had been infatuated, and how he died because of it. Daryoush was remarkably patient and for the first time since losing Akhab, I truly felt comforted by my lover. He showed genuine interest and care, and he listened without judgment.

"You are not to blame for the choice he made, and the consequences that were enacted by others. He knew the risk: likely better than you. You cannot blame yourself, Yezeba'al."

He touched my cheek and smiled at me. We could not help but for our hands to stray and our lips to come together, and soon I took him to my bed.

592

After making love, he lay beside me and stroked my bare flesh, gazing at me in awe. "I've heard tales of your beauty all my life, but I never believed them."

"So, you said."

"Yes, I suppose I did. I would not have said so, if I had known who you were then."

"I know. That's why I did not reveal who I was. I wanted you to be honest with me. I want you to always be honest with me, Daryoush."

"Can I be honest?"

I nodded.

"I never believed those tales, but now I see they pale in comparison to the real beauty lying here beside me."

"You've already had me," I teased. "You do not need to woo me."

"Should a man not always continue to woo his woman even after she is his? Not that you are mine, for I have no right to you, except for what you choose to give."

I smiled sadly as I thought of Akhab. "My husband used to say such things to me, and he lived by them all his days…with only a few exceptions, for which I have forgiven him." I gazed at him. "You remind me a little of him. Not in looks so much, but in character. The way you look at me, the way you move, the way you speak…and the way you make love. I never thought I could find that again with any man."

He pulled himself over me, still looking into my eyes, and brought his fingers gently to that place between my thighs. I trembled at his touch, and whispered, "Take me to paradise." He nodded and kissed his way down my breasts and belly, moving lower to deliver his worship. Then when he was sure that I was ready for him, he came into me once again, and we made love through much of the night.

In Tzidon, I began to live openly with Daryoush; we made no secret of our devotion to one another, and there was no need to, for everyone there understood what we were to each other. We would not have quite the same experience in Yisrael, unfortunately. By the time

I returned to my kingdom two weeks later, word had gotten to my son about us, and he made it clear that he disapproved of the affair. When my entourage entered the palace at Shomron he did not come to welcome me home but instead sent the Lord Steward to meet me. When I went to hold court the next day, I presented Daryoush to the king and introduced him as my spiritual advisor at court – normally a position taken by a priest or priestess of Ashtarti, the first of which had been Daneyah.

Raman the priest had been Daneyah's successor and served me well; I intended to keep him on. When I spoke to him on the matter of appointing Daryoush as a second advisor alongside him, he liked the idea, especially as there was not enough representation of Ba'al at our court now that Akhab was gone. The other priests who attended took only a minor role, advising if they were called upon but not in an official capacity, having no true position of leadership at court. Daryoush was mature and experienced enough to take on that role, and amenable to the idea. I was pleased to have both a servant of Ashtarti and a servant of Ba'al at my side in court each day, to strike a balance and to provide support whenever I felt overwhelmed and outnumbered by the ever-growing Yahwists in my son's court.

Yoram, for his part, did not mind me having my own advisors and support, but my choice of a man whom I had taken openly as my lover displeased him. He remained cool toward me and barely concealed his hostility toward Daryoush, glaring at him and shutting him down any time he spoke to anyone but me. Believing he would eventually get over it, I said nothing to the king and carried on as if I did not notice his behavior. After all, there were more important things for us to consider than the king's petty jealousy.

With the end of summer fast approaching, we had the Feast of Ba'al to plan. For the first time since Akhab died I would be able to perform the true awakening ritual at the temple again: I had decided to make Daryoush High Priest, for he was worthy. Not everyone at court understood what this meant, but my son did and when I made the announcement, he did not receive it favorably. He was not in a position of spiritual authority, however; as I reminded him, he was merely a worldly king and, therefore, had no say in my decision. It was the one place where I held all the power, and soon Daryoush would hold his own share of that power.

The awakening ritual went well, and the people rejoiced to have a new High Priest at my side. The Yahwists, meanwhile, having heard specifics about what went on at the Temple of Ba'al on high holy days, were disgusted and outraged. The zealots stirred up the people against us. After the feast, we received reports of the desecration of our altars that were set upon the high places throughout the kingdom. Many of the Yahwists, even those not previously prone to zealotry, demanded the destruction of our monuments and threatened rebellion if they did not get their way. By the end of that summer, in fact, Yoram had to put down a rebellion in the southern provinces near the border with Yehudah, where there was the highest concentration of Yahwists.

When he returned to Shomron about a week before we were due to leave for Yezreel, I congratulated him on his victory. He responded with a bitter remark about my activities being the cause of it. But then he was surprised when I broke down and wept.

"Ama? I'm sorry. I did not mean to upset you..."

I shook my head, trying to collect myself. "No, it is not that..."

"What is it then?"

"I received word from Yerushalayim, just this morning. Your aunt and one of your nieces have passed away."

Then I told him about the rampant illness that had swept through the city following the first of the winter rains. Aya and one of my seven-year-old granddaughters, my namesake, were among those lost to the pestilence. My daughter Atalaya had also been gravely ill but had managed to recover; Akhaz and Yahosheba had thankfully avoided infection but were grieving the losses of their grandmother and sister. Yahosheba was especially distraught at the death of her twin. Her mother, having lost her own twin, was able to provide comfort and solace in a way that no one else could, but how could one ever truly be consoled from such a loss? I was devastated; but more than anything, regretted that I could not be there to console my daughter in her grief.

Yoram was struck by the news and asked if I would go to Yerushalayim to console Atalaya and the others. I shook my head. "Not after the last time I went, and now with the Yahwist upheaval...I will not take such a risk going to the heartland of Yahwist sentiment."

"That is probably for the best," he said, the bitterness returning to his voice. "Of course, you have brought it on yourself."

He walked away before I had the chance to respond. Then he shut himself away for the rest of the week, declaring it a period of mourning. He came out once or twice to meet privately with his council without my knowledge, however; I heard about these meetings only after the fact but did not know what they were discussing. I assumed it had something to do with what had happened in Yerushalayim, but I would soon find out that was not the case.

As we approached the city of Yezreel with our entourage a week later, I sat up in my litter to marvel at the strangeness of the cityscape. Something about it had changed. Then suddenly I realized what it was: the obelisk was missing.

Every year since my husband had constructed it there to honor our gods and our love for one another, the great obelisk cast its shadow across the city and the surrounding landscape as it rose toward the heavens like a finger of the earth reaching up to touch a finger of the gods. But now it was gone, and the city appeared flat without its crowning glory. I was horrified and alarmed, especially because I had not expected it to be missing.

By the time I arrived at the palace, the king had already gone inside, so I could not ask him about it right away. Shmuel was there, however, so I went to him and demanded, "Where is the Obelisk of the Ba'alim? What has happened to it?"

The young Lord Steward's eyes grew wide, and the bridge of his nose turned red, and then it spread across his cheeks and to his ears. He turned his face toward the floor, and murmured, "The king had it taken down and destroyed, Gebirah."

"What?" I could not at first comprehend what he was telling me. "Taken down?"

He nodded once. "Yes, Gebirah."

"It must be put back," I demanded.

"Gebirah, there is nothing left of it – the king ordered its parts dismantled, the stones defaced to be reused elsewhere."

Why would my son do this? When the shock began to fade, I said, "Where is the king?"

596

"In his quarters, Gebirah. He said he does not want to be disturbed, for he is exhausted from the journey."

"I do not care if he does not want to be disturbed – *I* am disturbed. Go and fetch him at once! Tell him his *mother* demands to speak with him."

Shmuel looked horrified and uncertain – obey the king's orders or mine? At last, perhaps when he glimpsed the fury in my gaze and decided mine was the more immediate danger, he went himself to see the king. I was in my quarters, my heart aching as I stood out on the terrace and looked toward where the obelisk had once been, when the answer came. It was not Shmuel but one of the eunuchs who arrived to tell me the king had refused my summons and would summon me when he was rested. That is how the message came to me, but I had little doubt what he had told them to say was far less respectful.

Recognizing that my son would not be moved, I summoned Daryoush instead. When he came to me, I told him about what my son had done – this was his first time at Yezreel, so he had never seen the obelisk and would not have known anything was missing. He listened as I paced and cursed and, when I had completely exhausted my fury, he sat with me on the edge of the bed and held me as I wept: ever patient, ever loving.

After a time, I sat back and looked at him. "I am sorry you must see me like this."

"Yezeba'al, my love, it is all right. It is what I am here for."

"No, but you should not have to be in the middle of this, hearing me lament about my dead husband when I should be pouring my love onto you, for you are here now."

"I *am* here now," he said, slipping his arms around my waist, "and I love you, even when you are angry, even when you are sad, even when the walls of the kingdom are falling around you. And do not think that I could ever be jealous of your husband. I know that you loved him before you knew me, and that you love him still. Love does not end. And I know that your love for him does not, in any way, diminish your love for me."

"Then you are not angry or jealous?"

He chuckled. "Why should I be?"

Inhaling deeply, I fell into his arms again and rested my head upon his shoulder. "I praise the Ba'alim every day for bringing me to you."

He moved the hair from my shoulder and kissed the top of my head. Then he said, "I still cannot believe that I am the man who gets to have you. I do not feel worthy."

Sitting up, I said, "You are the first worthy man I have met since my husband died, Daryoush. That is why I have cast them all away and not summoned them back to me since I found you. Do not think so little of yourself, my love. You deserve all things – certainly all of me."

He reached out to take my face in his hands and drew me into a kiss. I closed my eyes and savored the softness and sweetness of his lips, and then a tremor came over me. When I opened my eyes, he was watching me with hunger in his gaze. He was not Akhab; but the same love-light shone in his eyes, and I knew the source of it came from my divine counterpart. Each time we made love, it was the same bliss.

Yoram summoned me the next afternoon. Perhaps he hoped my anger would have abated by then; it had not. I went to him in his private audience chamber, where he sat on high with a lordly air and a barely concealed smirk: proud to believe he had put me in my place. Instead of paying homage as he expected, however, I marched up the stairs of the dais and slapped him across the face.

"How dare you," I growled. "That monument was a gift from your father. It was consecrated to our gods."

"It offends the people," he replied, turning his face from me.

I scoffed. "What people? A few loud-mouthed Yahwist zealots? Who cares if they are offended?"

"I care, for they are *my* people."

"So are the Ba'alists, and there are considerably more of us than there are of them. What will you do next, tear down our temples and what remains of our altars upon the high places just to please the few?"

"You know I would never do that, Ama."

"They will expect it of you now that you have caved into their demands! Would they have done the same for us if the roles were reversed?" I paused for him to consider. When he did not answer, I continued, "They are not like us – they will not be satisfied to let us worship in our way. They will not stop until they have destroyed us and everything we hold dear. We do not go about demanding their monuments be taken down."

"The Yahwists do not have monuments."

"Their altars, then. What difference does it make? We do not interfere with their worship, neither should they interfere with ours. They have no right to make these demands – and you would be well within your right to ignore them."

"I gave them a concession, in good faith."

"You desecrated holy ground!"

"Like you desecrate my father's memory?"

I was stunned. "That's what this is about?"

"Yes, Ama." He nodded. "I could handle your secret dalliances – I did not like it, but I accepted it, because it was done in secret. But to publicly take a lover, to declare him the High Priest of Ba'al – an office previously only held by my father in Yisrael..."

"I understand your upsetment at what you must see as your father being replaced, Yoram, but you must understand that a high priestess needs a high priest. Ashtarti needs her Ba'al. There has not been any balance in this kingdom since your father died. That is why the rains have been so sparse. With Daryoush, I am restoring that balance."

"You are strutting him around at your side like a loyal hound!" he roared. Then he pushed over a table next to his throne on which a tray of victuals had been set. I jumped as his golden cup and the matching tray clattered onto the stone floor. Ceramic shattered, wine spilled, and pieces of fruit rolled and scattered. The slaves present quietly approached to clean it up, while Yoram continued his tirade. "Consorting with him on the altar at the temple! Putting your twisted love affair on display for all to see! That I cannot abide in my kingdom! Your perversion will bring ruin upon us all!"

"Those are sacred rituals!" I protested. "Not some baseless perversion!"

"That is not what the Yahwists think of your behavior."

599

"Why are you so keen to obtain their favor? What do they know of our rituals? What do they know about anything?"

"Nothing – but that is not the point! The point is that *they* think it is wrong, and they will tear apart the kingdom in their outrage if it continues."

"They thought it was wrong when I was performing these rituals with your father, too. I do not care what they think – neither should you. I am serving my gods, whether they like it or not."

"You are not a temple prostitute!"

Stepping toward him, I said coolly, "Priests and priestesses are *not* prostitutes. I thought you understood that."

"They exchange sexual favors for money. How is it different?"

"It is a spiritual exchange, not a carnal one! You should know this from your own experience: the men who go to these priests and priestesses seek healing and enlightenment through a union with our goddess. If it was about sex, they would go to the tents and houses where they can receive such services for a shekel or two."

He sighed heavily and rubbed his beard. Then he said, "If it is so sacred, what they do, then why do they only provide it to the men who pay? Why do they not give freely to whomever needs that healing?"

"For the same reason a mason must charge for his services, or a healer for his. All money given to the temple is an offering to pay for sacrifices and to support its function and its ministry. Most people will not give an offering out of the goodness of their hearts, Yoram. They want something in return."

He scowled and waved his hands dismissively. Nevertheless, I persisted, "The priests and priestesses who live and work there need to eat. They need clothing and a place to live. And the temple itself must be maintained – the stones washed, the idols adorned, the roof repaired, and the lamps kept burning. All the things that go into keeping it functioning *for the people* and for the glory of the Ba'alim. No one is forced to pay for it, but those who use it choose to pay for it in their own way, and that is not for you but for them to decide if it is worth it."

I turned to walk away, but then he said, "They are calling you a wicked woman, Ama. What am I to say to that?"

Stopping, I turned to face him and spoke calmly. "Say nothing. They do not deserve a response, for it only feeds them in their hate."

600

"Do you not care?" he seemed unable to believe.

"I have learned not to care," I answered with a bitter smile. "They have always called me wicked; from the moment I arrived in this kingdom, the Yahwists have hated me."

"And why is that?"

"Because I refuse to bend to their will and abandon my gods."

"Yet you have chosen not to hate them – not to act against them unless they threaten the kingdom. Why?"

"They do not understand our ways. They curse what they do not understand. I cannot hate them for that. In fact, I pity them for being shackled by their faith to their jealous god."

He fell silent. When he looked up again, he said, "And what if I do not understand? How can I defend you, if I do not understand your ways; for they are not my own."

For a moment, I was startled. "Are you a Yahwist, then?"

His chest rose and fell, and he stroked his beard as he considered. Then at last he sat back in his throne, and said, "No, but his ways make more sense to me than your own."

At last, I was speechless. I wondered where I had gone wrong with his education and upbringing. But as I looked at him – observed his hardened and disinterested gaze – I realized it was not my failing. Understanding only comes to those whose hearts and minds are open. His was closed tight. There was no sense in wasting my breath trying to persuade someone whose mind was already made up.

Suddenly, his voice rose from the silence. "I will not interfere in your worship, Ama. But I will not condone it, either. The next time Yahowah's followers come to complain about your activities, you will have to deal with them yourself. I have more important things to do – as you have said, I should only concern myself with corporeal matters and leave spiritual matters to you and your counsel." He waved carelessly. "You may go."

I bowed my head in acquiescence, and then I went away, eager to return to my quarters and to seek solace at the altar of my goddess. My son had hurt me deeply by destroying the obelisk, and even more by admitting now that he was not a believer in my faith. My disappointment could be consoled, however, with the bitter satisfaction that at last he had made a wise decision as king by promising to leave spiritual matters to me.

601

26

No Love Lost

Yoram kept his promise to step back from concerning himself with spiritual matters; he did not interfere with or condemn my religious practices again after that day. He also refused to admit anyone to court who came with a complaint about the same; instead, those complaints were diverted to my counsel. Daryoush and Raman handled most of the complaints themselves, only escalating them to me when my greater authority was needed. Neither would he pass laws affecting religious practices, other than to reaffirm those his father and myself had already put into place. The only time he intervened was when it affected his management of the kingdom directly, such as the occasional rebellion or riot that needed to be put down. Soon, however, it would become necessary for Yahwists and Ba'alists to put aside our differences and unite against a common enemy.

Throughout the winter and spring, the King of Aram sent raiding parties into Yisrael to cause trouble along our eastern borders. The princes of the provinces dealt with this nuisance the best they could with their own armies; nevertheless, it became necessary for Yoram to send reinforcements to better secure our borders against further attacks. It was clear that Hadadesar was trying to provoke us into war with his kingdom. Thankfully, on the advice of his council, Yoram did not take the bait: his men were put under strict orders not to cross the borders under any circumstances, not even to pursue fleeing enemy soldiers.

The king also sent for the prophet Elisha, seeking not so much his prophesying but the intelligence brought to him by his numerous connections. Aharon was the one who encouraged us to seek Elisha's help. Coming out of his retirement when he heard from his son and wife what we were dealing with, he explained to us that, like Eliyahu before him, Elisha was in contact with a network of people who were able to gather information better than our own associates ever could.

It was how Eliyah had always managed to find his way to us, and how Obadyah reached him when he was in hiding.

Wild men, lepers, beggars, orphans, widows, paupers, and the occasional prostitute: these were the sorts of people our kind did not associate with and, as such, they were inconspicuous enough to go unnoticed. Prostitutes were especially useful in this endeavor, for they could enter enemy camps to entertain the lonely men who were desperate for female companionship. The King of Aram's officers talked freely around them because it was believed they were too witless to understand anything or too insignificant to warrant attention. With a little help from alcohol, it was easy to get these powerful men to open their lips and share details of their plans as they complained about the orders that they received from their king in Damaseq.

These were the ideal gatherers of knowledge it seemed, and the zealots had long made use of their skills while claiming all their prophets' knowledge came from their god. Elisha continued to insist that it was Yahowah who supplied his knowledge; we allowed him to think we were convinced, even though we knew otherwise. Now that we were aware, we decided to make use of the prophet's network — both to gather intelligence and to spread misinformation to our enemies and their agents. It was effective and soon the attacks stopped. Even I could not help but to thank Elisha for his service to us; he begrudgingly accepted our thanks, including even the gifts that were offered to him as a token of our gratitude.

We hoped that would be the last we would have to deal with the King of Aram and his mischief. Of course, as I suspected, that would not be the case. It was now the fifth year of Yoram's reign. The court returned to Shomron at the end of spring and, as always, commenced its return with the Feast of Ashtarti. The three-day feast had only just ended when Hadadesar himself returned to plague our kingdom once again.

It happened while we were holding court. Be'ulah's chair to the left of Yoram's throne was empty. Still exhausted from our latest revelries, she had taken leave. It was afternoon, and we were in our last audience of the day: a group of merchants had come to request lower taxes on imported goods. Yoram listened intently to their concerns, but I was eager to be done for the day, especially because Daryoush and I were still expected at the temple to bless the newly

603

made idols before they could be sold to devotees. I had just begun to nod off when suddenly the obnoxious call of shofars and horns began to resonate from the ramparts surrounding the city and the palace complex, alerting us to the presence of an approaching threat.

It was too early in the year for a sandstorm, so we knew it must be either a rebellion or an invasion. Soon afterward, messengers from the governor of Shomron came to inform us of a large army that was now approaching the city. "Men and horses and chariots as far as the eye can see!" they claimed.

"Any idea who they are?" asked Yoram.

I whispered to my son, "Seventy gold pieces it's the King of Aram."

"Agreed," he muttered.

Meanwhile, the lead messenger answered, "It is not certain, Melekh, but by their standards I would say it is the King of Aram, along with the kings of Qedar, Ammon, and Arwad."

Yoram glanced at me, and I smiled triumphantly. Whenever I won a bet, he had to donate my wins to the temple to pay for a sacrifice.

Turning back to them, he asked, "Have any messengers come to the gates yet?"

"No, Melekh. Lord Amon has ordered Captain Mattiyahu to close the gates and not permit anyone to enter or leave the city. They maintain a defensive stance, but he is awaiting your orders, Melekh."

Yoram considered. Then he said, "Go. Tell Lord Amon to command his captain to maintain the current stance and not permit anyone to enter the city, not even if they claim to be a messenger. For now, I will send General Yehu to accompany you, to make an assessment and deliver a report. Then I will come and assess the matter for myself."

He indicated for Yehu to follow the messengers. They all bowed to the king and departed. Then Yoram rose and addressed the guild merchants, "My lords, we shall revisit your matter again at a later time and day." Then he raised his voice to address the rest of the assembled court: "My lords, court is dismissed; return to your families and prepare your households. We are under siege. If you are needed, I will send for you. Men of the high council, you will return at first light."

While the assembled courtiers and ministers filed out, I rose and went to Raman, asking him to go to the temple and inform them that in light of these developments, Daryoush and I would not be coming to the temple to bless the idols that day. Then I went to my lover. He slid his arms around my waist, kissed me, and asked if I was all right. I nodded, and then we spoke together softly, until Yoram called to me, and I went to him.

"The King of Aram – he is your cousin, Hadadesar, with whom we stayed in Damaseq when Abbu was still alive?"

"Yes," I confirmed with a nod. "One and the same."

Yoram fell silent for a moment. Then he lifted his head. "He laid siege to us before, and Abbu twice defeated him. How did Abbu do it the first time he laid siege to us? I was too young then – I do not remember the details."

I smiled bitterly. "It was only a siege the first time he came to our kingdom – the second time, he never made it this far. The siege ended because I went to the King of Aram, at his command."

"You gave yourself to him?"

"No, you fool," I said with a scowl. "You think I would have made a harlot of myself? And that your Abbu would have allowed it?"

"I do not know! I thought that's what you meant..."

I hissed.

Then he asked, "Did he know you left the city?"

"Of course, he knew. He gave me permission, and I went, and I was able to meet with the King of Aram as a diplomat."

"And you got him to leave?"

"No," I answered. Then I sighed. "But I was able to slip away to Yezreel, assemble the army, and get messages to all the princes of the provinces, to bring their armies to Shomron. With all our combined forces, along with those already stationed here, we were able to defeat them. Your Abbu had the King of Aram fleeing like the coward he has always been."

He smirked. Then he asked, "But how did you slip away without being seen?"

"I didn't," came my reply. "As I said, I went to Hadadesar – first in a failed attempt to convince him to leave. The second time, I went with Zubira and we convinced him to let us leave under pretense of a...female emergency."

"And he believed you?"

605

"Yes, we made it incredibly convincing. I will spare you the details unless you insist on hearing them."

He grimaced. "No, I will trust you on that." After a pause, he said, "Well, you may go now – but be prepared for a summons, if anything should change."

I bowed my head and waited for him to leave, and then I returned to Daryoush. We walked together back to my chamber; along the way, he asked me about Hadadesar. "I did not realize you were cousins."

"Yes, our mothers are sisters," I explained.

"No love lost between kin?"

I chuckled. "It is a bit more complicated than that, I'm afraid. Hadadesar is in love with me – or fancies himself in love, anyway. I believe the only reason he is obsessed with me is because he has never had me, but he has always wanted to have me and has never forgiven me for almost letting him. That was before Akhab and I, of course... We were practically children, but old enough to feel desire and to act on it, had I not stopped him before he could take me."

"He sounds like a dangerous man. I am glad the king will not let you go to him."

I playfully punched his bicep, and then he grabbed me by the hands, turned with me so that my back was against the wall, and pressed himself against me. I smiled and met his gaze as if to challenge him; he kissed me firmly on the mouth, and I melted into it. Then I gently bit his bottom lip. He growled, and then he tickled my waist and at last I conceded victory to him. Sliding my arms around his shoulders, I met his gaze, and urged breathlessly, "Take me, Daryoush. I need to feel you inside me."

With a slow nod, he took my face in his hand, brought his lips to mine, and we shared one breath. Then he led me the rest of the way to my inner sanctum, where I sent my maids and the eunuchs away. We undressed each other slowly and I took him to my bed.

Early the next morning, the ministers and generals returned to court, along with the governor of Shomron who had been summoned. After discussing the situation with Lord Amon, Yoram commanded him to permit messengers to enter the city, and then

606

consulted with his ministers while we waited for messengers from the invading forces to arrive. When they came, the messengers confirmed what had already been assessed: Hadadesar and the three accompanying kings had come to lay siege to Shomron. The King of Aram demanded the city be given unto him and for Yoram to send his mother and the best of his wives, his gold and all his riches; or they would not leave, and neither would they allow anyone to enter the city to bring us aid or sustenance.

"Let me go to him," I whispered to my son, thinking this was my chance to finally kill Hadi.

"What? Ama, have you gone mad?"

"Let me go to him, and I'll make him leave."

"Out of the question," he said firmly. "You admitted yourself, that did not work the first time. I will not let you out of this city."

"He only wants to talk with me."

"He does not want to speak with you – I know what he wants from you. Aharon told me about the King of Aram's obsession with you, and I will not let you be put in harm's way."

I tried again to speak, to suggest we could pay him to leave, but was interrupted when the king raised his voice in anger: "Silence, woman! This is not a spiritual matter – you are not to speak on matters outside your expertise."

Daryoush was standing beside my throne and placed his hand on my shoulder, gently squeezing, for he knew I was deeply offended and about to lose my temper. He had seen my son and I fall into bitter arguments at court many times. It was seldom to my benefit. His gesture reminded me of this, and so I breathed deeply and placed a hand upon his own and glanced back at him in thanks. He gave a discreet nod, and then I turned my gaze forward as my son responded to the messengers.

"You may tell your master, the King of Aram, that I will not give into his demands. He may think me only a boy, but if he provokes me, he will learn why I am called the Wolf of Yisrael and Devourer of Moab."

I resisted the urge to roll my eyes, while he waved the messengers away.

Once they were gone and the doors closed to any unwelcome ears, Yoram addressed the men: "My lords, what say you to this? Should we go out and make war upon these kings?"

607

The Minister of War, General Dawid, was a tidy man with white-streaked black hair and a well-trimmed beard. I had briefly taken him for a lover after Akhab died, but like most of my former love affairs it did not last long. We parted on good terms, however, and as a man of war I had a great deal of respect for him. Upon my son's inquiry, Dawid stepped forward, and said, "Melekh, we do not have enough men stationed here at Shomron to do battle against the King of Aram's forces."

"We would be better off staying the course," another of the ministers agreed.

"Natan," Yoram called to his half-brother, the Minister of Commerce.

Natan stepped forward, "Melekh?"

"What is the current state of supplies here in the city? Do we have enough to withstand a siege?"

I sighed heavily and could not resist rolling my eyes.

"That depends on how long the siege lasts, Melekh," answered Natan. "I will need to make inquiries to be sure but based on my current knowledge we have enough to withstand a few months, if we are sparing in our use of it."

To my surprise, Yoram seemed cheered by this answer. He relaxed on his throne, and said, "Ah, good! Then we should be fine. Surely, they cannot lay siege to us that long."

"You cannot be sure of that," I spoke up, at last losing my patience. "The enemy is outside the city walls. *They* can receive supplies, while we cannot. They may also take from those who come here not knowing we are under siege, and raid nearby cities and villages. Under these circumstances, they can lay siege to us a great deal longer than we can survive without aid."

Yoram sighed heavily – was it his disappointment at facing the reality of our situation, or his annoyance at me for pointing it out? His tone was acidic when he asked, "And what would you have me do? The Minister of War himself, who was appointed at your recommendation, said we do not have the force to do battle."

"We do not," I agreed. "So, we will have to do something within our means to make the Arameans leave." *If Hadi's dead, his army will return to Aram*, I knew.

"I am not giving into his demands," said Yoram, turning his face away.

608

"I am not telling you to give in, Melekh," I insisted. "What I am suggesting is that we use diplomacy, which is our one advantage."

"And how should we do that?"

My plan was simple – I would offer myself as tribute and then kill him instead. Men like Hadi were easy to fool, for they thought with the wrong head. He would be so consumed with thoughts of love-making that he would fail to see the dagger until it was plunged into his heart. I smiled at the thought, but only said, "I will go to him as a diplomat, and offer tribute for him to leave."

"No. You will not leave the safety of the palace walls, let alone the city."

"The king is right, Ba'alah," said Dawid. "Forgive me, but it is too dangerous for you to take such a risk. If we send anyone, it should not be you."

"I have done it before, and with a degree of success. Need I remind you all that it was due to my efforts that the King of Aram was defeated the first time he invaded our kingdom?"

"Ba'alah," said Dawid, "with all due respect, that was a risk that should never have been taken."

"It worked."

"Times were different then," he said simply.

"How were they any different? My cousin, the King of Aram is the same man he was ten years ago – a spoiled prince with the temperament of a young boy just out of the nursery."

Some of the men snickered, but Dawid was not amused. "Ba'alah, I fear you underestimate him. He is aware that you have deceived him before and will not trust you. If you go to him now, what is to stop him from taking you hostage and demanding the city for your safe return? Or worse?"

I almost laughed. "You overestimate his capabilities. Hadadesar is a fool. He is all talk, and he is easy to manipulate. I have known him since we were children together in the nursery – I know what to say to get him to do whatever I want, and he will do it because he is in love with me. Neither does it require anything indecent on my part – only the promise of it, which will never be realized."

"Clearly, my mother enjoys toying with Ben-Hadad," said Yoram. "Nevertheless, I believe you are right, General Dawid. It is not wise to continue dangling carrots before a starving horse."

609

I scoffed but said nothing.

Meanwhile, Yoram continued, "I will not grant the Gebirah permission to leave the city and put herself in jeopardy on this foolish mission. No one is to leave the city under any circumstances unless they have been commanded by me."

"I am the one thing you have that the King of Aram wants."

"And now that you are a widow, Ama, he thinks he can have you," Yoram retorted. "The only thing that stopped him from taking you before was that you were married to my father."

I was about to speak, but he cut me off.

"You may know your cousin better than I do, but I know the minds of *men* better than you. I know what he is thinking, and you would be unwise to put yourself in harm's way by going to him. I will not allow it, and that is final."

I tried one last time to speak, but then he raised his voice, commanding, "You will obey! Another word on this matter, and I will have you confined to your quarters!"

Again, Daryoush gently squeezed my shoulder, but this time I shrugged his hand off.

"I understand, Melekh."

Then the men continued the discussion without my input, and nothing was accomplished.

The siege dragged on for weeks and soon turned into months, stretching over the length of the dry summer and into the rainy months of autumn. Each day, when the king went out to patrol the walls with his men, I went onto my terrace to look out beyond the city. From there, I watched the enemy chariots on their patrols harassing travelers and preventing them from approaching the city. We received reports that they surrounded caravans, commandeered their supplies, and stole their women, killing the men who tried to stop them. The bodies were stripped and left for carrion; it never took long for the vultures and wild dogs to appear, to fight over the dead until there was nothing left.

Even from afar, seeing this chilled me to the core. I turned away and withdrew to my private altar, where I donned my prayer robe, lit incense, and knelt to say prayers for the dead. As High

610

Priestess, I led the people in prayer each day and performed blood rituals at the temple every evening with my High Priest at my side. All the priests and priestesses of the Ba'alim were encouraged to increase their service to our gods and to the people.

Sacrifices at the temples were made each day, asking the Ba'alim to save the people of Yisrael. The roasted meat was distributed to the people to be consumed and to strengthen them in the coming days of famine that were inevitable. Eventually, there were no suitable animals left for us to sacrifice, and so the sacrifices stopped, and the people were left to fend for themselves. As supplies within the city dwindled, driving up the price of everything, the people began to grow desperate.

Inside the palace, we had all that we needed from our gardens and granaries and livestock, but it was necessary to maintain a strict rationing of resources that had a profound effect on everyone used to indulging themselves. I rarely indulged, so not much changed for me; I continued to eat only what I needed, a practice of all priests and priestesses that encouraged holiness. However, I was irritated by everyone else's irritability. I had little patience for their sullen moods and frequent complaints, especially when the common people of the city had even less and were truly suffering.

The worst of it came when one of the nobles approached us with the complaint that his slaves were dying of hunger. "What are we to do? Serve ourselves?"

Yoram looked at me helplessly. I had a barely concealed sneer when I looked at the nobleman, and said, "What a tragedy that would be for your wives and daughters. Perhaps if you and your family cut back on your own consumption, there would be enough for you to feed your slaves to keep them alive and healthy enough to serve you."

He was clearly affronted when he answered, "You want us to starve alongside the slaves, Gebirah?"

"You will not starve from eating less when you are accustomed to eating more than is necessary. Even here at the palace, we are rationing our food stores to ensure that everyone who serves us has enough to eat. Not one of our slaves or servants has died as a result of famine."

"I have a large family, Gebirah."

And a large waist, I thought. Then I said, "As does the king. What of it?"

611

"I cannot afford to feed the slaves from my own coffers!"

"Pity. Then I suppose you will have to learn how to live without them."

"You expect me and my sons to till the fields and care for the animals? For my wives and daughters to sully their hands working in the kitchen, scrubbing the floors, and washing the linens?"

"If you refuse to feed your slaves and let them die, then you will have no other choice."

He threw up his hands, and said, "I cannot believe this! My family has served the House of Omri for three generations, yet you refuse to help us!"

"And I cannot believe the extent of your callousness, caring more about being served than the lives of the people in your service, and their families who mourn them. If you would rather starve your slaves than eat a little less, you have brought it on yourself, and we have no pity for you."

I waved my hand to dismiss him, and the eunuchs began to escort him out. He snapped at them, "I can see myself out!" Then he straightened his robes and stalked out, while the servant he had brought got up and hurried after him.

When I looked at my son, he was giving me a look, so I asked, "What?"

"You could have at least tried to help him..."

"Help him do what? To starve his slaves? I will not condone his greed. Neither should you."

"I only mean that you did not have to be so hard on him, Ama."

"Do not lecture me. That man is an uncivilized brute, unworthy of the people who serve him."

"He was angry."

"Let him be angry. He only has himself to blame. I gave him advice; he refused to take it. What more can we do for him?"

He sighed and sat back on his throne, and then nodded in understanding. Then we went on with the business of the day: reports on casualties within the city from disease or famine, casualties from the latest Aramean assault, and damages from their attempt to break down one of the city gates with a battering ram. Builders within the city were already hard at work on repairs and were confident that it would hold during the next assault. This would likely not be for a few days, they reported, or however long it took for them to rebuild the ram after our forces managed to destroy it with boulders and flaming torches dropped from the walls above.

Between assaults, messengers went back and forth between our court, the governor's office, and the city watch. Hadadesar continued to send his messengers; his demands grew more outrageous as did his blustering. The High Council continued to advise the king not to give in to his demands, and not to allow me to engage in any diplomatic missions. On this, Daryoush and Raman agreed, remaining in opposition to me and insisting that it would not end well if I went to Hadadesar.

When I continued to argue my case, the king finally sent me away and forbade me from attending court or leaving my quarters until further notice. Angry that Daryoush took Yoram's side, I then refused to see him. I would neither summon nor permit him to come to me unless he came with Raman in the capacity of my counsel. Admittedly, it was difficult not to have the comfort of his touch to help ease the loneliness of my imprisonment. Many times, I almost called him to me, but I remained strong in my resolve. Besides, I had others who could provide solace of a different kind.

Unlike the last time I was confined to my quarters, following the Nabot incident, this time I was allowed to have my friends and children come to me. Azba and Abshalom came to me frequently, providing much needed comfort. Ba'alesar was often at his elder brother's side, though, being now thirteen and considered a man. He was frequently at court, permitted to observe but not to take part in the decision-making. Occasionally, as Akhab and I had done with Zyah and Yoram when they became old enough to attend court, I called upon him to offer his thoughts, giving him the opportunity to think carefully about important matters and challenging him to reconsider his position whenever it was flawed. Because of his calm demeanor, considerate nature, and strong intellect, I often thought he would have made a better king than Yoram, although I never said this aloud.

In truth, though, Ba'alesar would truly have hated being king. Power was not something he craved; even if he would have been better suited intellectually, the pressures of managing the kingdom would have weighed more heavily upon him than they did upon his father or his elder brothers. He was a cheerful youth and a capable warrior, but his interests lay more in music and poetry than politics and warfare.

When he did come to me, he often brought his lyre and reclined on a bench near the window. Listening to his music, especially his voice as it deepened, reminded me of peaceful evenings when Akhab was alive. My husband had often made music while I occupied myself in my usual manner at leisure: answering correspondence, reading, writing, or mixing ingredients to make the balms, cosmetics, and sacred oils I used daily. Now, while I did these things, it was Ba'alesar who made music while the children played.

Occasionally, he paused and looked up to watch his younger brother and sister as they raced around the chamber in mock battle, weaving between me and Kora and the handmaids as we all went about our various tasks. I was mixing ingredients for my tinctures and cosmetics, and once or twice had to raise my voice to remind the children not to bump into the table where I was working. When Abshalom pretended to slay Azba with his wooden sword, Ba'alesar asked playfully, "Will you slay every maiden in Yisrael, Abshalom?"

"No, *akhu*," said he, too young to understand his brother's rather inappropriate pun, "for she is not a maiden!"

"I am so!" she protested.

Meanwhile, Ba'alesar laughed. "What is she then?"

"She is the King of Aram, and I have defeated him."

"They shall call you the Hero of Yisrael."

Chuckling as I passed by carrying a small chest of elixirs that I had just finished mixing, I remarked, "Better than the 'Wolf of Yisrael', as the king has taken to calling himself."

Ba'alesar glanced at me with amusement. Then he said, "I thought his men gave him that name. Did they not, Ama?"

"No, hardly," I answered, looking back at him as I locked the cabinet where all my elixirs were stored. Then I came to sit with him, saying, "That is what he says, of course, but Dawid told me Yoram declared it himself by the fire one night at their camp: 'They shall call me the Wolf of Yisrael after this', so he said." I laughed bitterly. "If they call him that, it is only by his will and not their own. That is why it is so ridiculous. Your Abbu never went about giving himself such foolish names, I'll tell you that. He did not need such a name to strike fear into his enemies' hearts; his real name spoke for itself."

614

Abshalom came to stand beside me, and I put my arms around him, drawing him into an embrace. He leaned into me with his arm around my shoulders, and said, "I want to be a great warrior like Abbu one day."

"No doubt you will be if you keep up your practice," I agreed. He bent to kiss my forehead, and then his sister called to him, and he returned to battle.

Ba'alesar chuckled and looked down at the instrument in his hands. "I suppose Abbu would be disappointed in me for choosing the lyre over the sword."

"Not at all. Your Abbu loved making music – do you not remember?"

"Vaguely, I suppose," he answered, setting the lyre aside.

"He appreciated the arts of the mind and body in equal measure, and he would be as proud of you as he would be of your brothers. Of all his brothers, he was closest to those with whom he could share his love of music and song."

"Like *Abakhu* Asa?"

I answered with a nod. Then I said, "You would make a suitable replacement for your uncle one day."

He straightened his posture. "Truly?"

"Your brother the king agrees with me."

Suddenly, Yoram's voice rose from across the chamber, as he entered without warning. "With what do I agree?"

"Yoram!" cried Abshalom and Azba, dropping their wooden swords and running to their brother. He braced for the impact as they came crashing into him for an embrace. Then he placed both his hands, one each, atop their heads and shook them playfully. They giggled and reached up to grab his wrists, as if to stop him.

"Were you at war together?"

"Yes," answered Abshalom.

"And who was winning?"

"I was," Azba declared.

"No, you weren't! I defeated you the first time, and I would have defeated you again. She's the King of Aram, and I will defeat the whole army of Aram for you, *akhu*."

Yoram chuckled. "I believe you would if you could, Abshalom." Then he said, "Now, it is a beautiful day – you should take your swords and go make battle in the garden with our other siblings. I must talk with Ama about some important matters."

They did as they were told. When they were gone, his playful demeanor sank in an instant. He sighed, hung his head, and his shoulders slumped forward as he came to sit with me and Ba'alesar.

"What has happened?" I asked with a degree of concern.

"First," he replied, "what was it you were saying I agreed with, when I came into the chamber?" He laced his fingers together in his lap and waited, watching me as if he might catch me in a trap. If I had anything to hide, it might have unnerved me.

"That Ba'alesar would make a suitable Minister of Ceremonies one day."

"Oh, yes of course." He relaxed now and smiled at his brother. "It is true, and if our uncle should retire from his position or...leave it vacant for any reason...I would be glad to appoint you." Then he added, "When you have a few more years of experience at court."

Cutting in, I said, "Now, what is it you needed to speak with me about?"

He sighed heavily and leaned forward, resting with his elbows on his knees and his hands balled up on his cheeks as he stared at the floor. "Our people are starving, Ama."

"Yes," I answered calmly. "I did tell you this would happen."

He sat up and glared at me for only a moment, before resting his back against the chair and looking out the window. Then he spoke without turning to me, while I got up and walked across the chamber toward the drink table. "Natan tells me that the price of food and fuel at the market is beyond reason. The people are desperate enough to eat a donkey's head, and they'll pay eighty shekels for it! Eighty shekels – for a donkey's head!"

"Yes, I heard you the first time," I said, pouring myself a drink. Taking a sip, I grimaced; the wine had turned sour. Nevertheless, I swallowed and returned to my seat, drink in hand: nothing could go to waste in these conditions.

"Our men continue to hold the city, but each time I send messengers out they are captured and killed or returned to us with warnings and more demands. Not one of them has managed to slip away, to call for help. What more can we do? We have prayed to the Ba'alim, made sacrifices to them at the temples until there was nothing left to sacrifice, and they have done nothing for us. I have

616

consulted every prophet of Yahowah within the city, followed their advice, and none have given me a solution or a suitable answer – least of all that wretch, Elisha, son of Shapat."

"I could have told you that."

He looked at me with a burning gaze. "Do you know what that man said to me today when I summoned him to court?"

"No, since I was not there," I answered, and my tone was noticeably bitter. I had not been welcome at court for several weeks by then. "What did he say?"

"That this whole thing is my fault for permitting the worship of Ba'al in my kingdom."

"He would say that," I murmured, turning away.

Yoram continued, "That it will not end until every worshipper of Ba'al and Asherah has left this kingdom. That I should send you and every man and woman at my court and in the city who bows down to them to the King of Aram, that he may remove you from this kingdom once and for all. That Yahowah will only intervene when all of you have gone from the city."

At this, I let out a sharp laugh. "The zealots have made this threat every time our kingdom has been in peril, and every time we have gotten through without taking such extreme measures. As you can see, I am still here, and the number of our worshippers has continued to rise while the worshippers of Yahowah dwindle. Yahowah has nothing to do with this – he has lost his power here."

"Ama, what are we to do? Obviously, I am not going to do what Elisha has told me to do, as it is ludicrous."

"You could follow his one piece of advice: send me to the King of Aram."

"You know I will not do that."

"Send me to his camp, and I will make him leave."

"How will you do that?"

I looked away. "That is my business."

"Will you make yourself a harlot? Or better yet, pledge to become his wife and serve him for the rest of his days? You know I would not allow it."

Slamming my cup on the table beside my chair, I snapped, "Is everything we women do about sex, Yoram?"

"No, but you certainly seem to make it so. The goddess of love is a fine prize, so they say. *Love.* I am disgusted by what the men say about you."

"You should know better than to listen to talk. I am devoted to Daryoush now, and serve only Ba'al, as is my duty and my highest honor. Besides, I am too old to become a king's wife."

"Not if it is the King of Aram. He would love to add you to his women, so I've been told. As would a few other kings I know. Yehoshapat himself could not stop speaking to me of your beauty when we were riding together to Moab. 'Talk to your mother, boy,' he kept telling me. 'Convince her to return to Yerushalayim and work with me for the betterment of our two kingdoms.' Do not think I did not understand what he meant by this."

I only chuckled. "I do not know what is more amusing – that he thinks I could be persuaded to change my mind on that matter, or that he thinks you could command me to do so."

"I could command it," Yoram insisted, "but I would not, and I told him as much: I said that I knew what he was implying and that, although I am many things, I am not the sort of man who would make a harlot of his mother."

My brows raised in surprise. "You said that to the King of Yehudah?"

"Yes."

"You have more gall than I gave you credit for, Yoram. Forgive me for having doubted you – of course, you would defend your own honor, while you keep silent about mine."

"I cannot defend a woman who dishonors herself."

My lips parted in disbelief as I watched him rise. When he was gone, Ba'alesar spoke for the first time. "You let him talk to you that way, Ama? Why? Is it because he is king?"

A faint smile came to my lips then, and I turned to my son. "It was a good retort. I do not agree with it, but it was good. Besides, I have learned not to argue with stone."

He met my gaze, and I could see that he was thinking. Then he asked, "If you could go to the King of Aram, if my brother would let you, what would you do to make him leave?"

"I would kill him."

618

He laughed aloud, but stopped suddenly when he saw that I was not joking. "Wait, you are serious? Ama...? How could you murder a king surrounded by his army?"

Now, I smiled darkly. "Make him believe that I intend to make love to him, and then before he has the chance to take me, I will slit his throat. I will give him as a sacrifice to Ba'al: I will use my ritual dagger to slay him."

"You have been thinking this through for quite some time."

I gave a nod.

"Do you even know how to slit a man's throat?"

I shrugged. "I have performed the sacrifice of many animals. How different can it be? One need only apply...a little more pressure. With a sharp enough blade, I can perform the task with relative ease."

"How will you escape his camp?"

"I will go on a night when the sky is dark, and the moon is black. I will stay long enough for them to think that we are making love while I perform my ritual, and then I will slip away before anyone has the chance to find him."

"Yoram will never let you do this."

"I know. That is why I have not told him of my plan."

He looked at me thoughtfully, rubbing his bare chin where eventually a beard would grow. Then he asked, "Have you sought the advice of your counsel? Are the signs favorable?"

I turned my face away. "Raman and Daryoush will not support me in this. They have both said it would be to my detriment. I could be killed; I am aware of that...of the risks."

"Then I am glad my brother will not let you go. If even the Ba'alim do not support this endeavor, it should not be undertaken."

"You and all these men would keep one woman alive and let the city starve? I do not believe that is what our gods would ask of us. I would sooner give my life than to allow it."

I got up and walked toward the door to my inner sanctum, where I stopped and turned back to say, "I must commune with Ashtarti. Take your brother's advice: go out and enjoy this fine day."

He watched me as I closed the door between us, and then I donned my prayer robe before entering the sacred space where my altar awaited me.

619

27

Night Eternal

Winter soon turned to spring. *We should be moving to Megiddu by now*, I thought bitterly, as I watched the almond trees bloom, yet still the siege dragged on. Unable to convince my son and the council to let me meet with the King of Aram as a diplomat, I began to plot how I could slip away and take matters into my own hands. Kora and the captain of my eunuchs were the only people who knew the details, as it required both to help me see it through. In the early planning phase, I had also told Daryoush, who had by now returned to my favor, but he still refused to support me. When he threatened to go to the king before I could put my plan into action, I pulled back and said he was right and convinced him that I knew it was folly. Then I seduced him to set his mind at ease and never spoke to him about the matter again. Nevertheless, I continued to work with my conspirators. When all was ready, I waited and prayed for a sign that I should act.

At last, the sign came.

It was just before twilight when Yoram came to me in my chamber a few days after my final preparations had been made. I was in my study, working on my chronicle, when he appeared after being announced. Without looking up, I said, "I am surprised to see you here so late."

I paused to dip my stylus in the bowl of ink. The firelight deepened the shadows that danced across his dark features.

"Ama, you will harm your vision, working in such dim light."

"I have been working like this for years, my son. If it was going to damage my vision, it would have done so by now." I paused and observed a tear in the collar of his tunic. It hung open across his chest, revealing the sackcloth he wore underneath. He was so like his father in that way, always punishing himself. Seeing this, I blotted the tip of my stylus on a cloth and set it on the desk alongside the papyrus I had been working on. "What happened?"

He staggered into the chamber and pulled up a chair alongside mine, a confused look on his face. "When I was out on my patrol this afternoon, a woman came to me and said that she had…eaten her son with another woman, who had convinced her that if she agreed to do this, they would eat her son the next day."

I grimaced, at first disbelieving what I had heard. Then as the horror set in, I brought my hand to my face. "Hunger has driven the people to madness."

"Indeed. She told me this in complaint, for the other woman had hidden her son when it came time to…eat him the next day. The woman came to me, not in despair for her son, but in outrage that the other woman had not kept her end of the bargain! So…" he indicated the tear in his tunic, "this happened. I could not believe what I was hearing, and I swore to make Elisha pay for what his god has allowed to happen to the people of this city."

"What did you do?"

"I sent Shmuel ahead to ensure I could make my way to the prophet's house without being accosted, intending to cut off his head, but when I arrived, he was not afraid. He was in the presence of some of the elders of the city, who had gone to him for advice and solace. I said to him, in the presence of these men, that as his god had permitted this to happen, why should I trust in him any longer? Do you know what he said to me, Ama?"

When he paused, I said, "No, as I was not there…"

"He said that he had a message from Yahowah."

I rolled my eyes. "They always do."

"He said that Yahowah promised to deliver us – that by the time night falls tomorrow, there will be enough food to feed the whole city again, and that the prices will fall, even in the marketplace here in Shomron."

"Tomorrow?" I raised my brows in surprise. "Truly?"

"That is what he said, but I do not know how that could be. Shmuel was incredulous. He said that was impossible, right in front of Elisha. So, the prophet said that he would see it with his own eyes but that he would not himself get to eat of that food."

"What did you say?"

"I did not say anything, for it seems impossible. Do you believe it is possible, Ama?"

621

"You are asking the wrong person, Yoram," I said, getting up and blowing out the lamps. Yoram got up and followed me out into my bedchamber, where Daryoush was resting on the bed with a bowl of pomegranate seeds to keep him company. Nearby, Kora worked quietly, mending a tear in one of my gowns. I had forgotten she was still there, for I had not yet dismissed her. She paused from her work and nodded to pay her respects.

Meanwhile, Yoram said to me, "I know you do not believe in the power of Yahowah, but do you believe that this siege will soon end? What do the Ba'alim say? You speak to them, do you not? And you hear them when they speak to you?"

I sighed heavily now, draping myself across the bed beside my lover. He offered me the bowl of seeds, and I declined. Then he set it aside and rolled over to pull me into his arms. Yoram looked away, barely managing to conceal his irritation, as I kissed my lover on the mouth. Then I turned back to my son.

"Yes, they speak to me. And yes, I hear them sometimes, but it is not as some say: I do not hear their voices in my ear, the way that I hear yours or anyone else's. When they answer me, it comes…" I drew in a breath and considered how I might describe it so that he could understand, "…as a whisper deep in my mind. An impression. Not words, exactly, but thoughts in their most abstract form that I must decipher in order to understand. Then from this, I know what they want me to do or say."

"How can you be certain that it is the Ba'alim, and not your own thoughts, telling you what you want to hear?"

"Because they do not tell me what I want to hear, and I do not actively devise what is communicated. It comes to me spontaneously and, many times, they tell me the opposite of what I want them to say – what I hope they will say."

"And on this – the siege – what do they say?"

I sat up and noticed Daryoush also watching me earnestly. I did not want to reveal to either of them what I was thinking, so I remained vague. "They say that the siege will end when we take action against the King of Aram."

Yoram's eyes lit up for the first time in months showing excitement and hope. "Do they say that I must lead the men against him outside the city? Shall we go to battle, despite our numbers being significantly less?"

622

I breathed in and shook my head. "No, I do not believe that is what they meant." Then I placed a hand to my forehead. "My mind is too clouded to receive the full message. I do not think you should act unless I am certain that is what they ask of you."

"Tomorrow then? If what Elisha says is true, that the siege will be over by this time tomorrow, then I must rally the men and take the fight to his camp."

"Perhaps, Yoram. But for now, you must sleep on it. Let me come to court in the morning, and I shall tell you then what they say."

He nodded slowly. "Very well. You may return to court and to your usual duties. Your confinement is at an end."

I rose and went to place a hand on his cheek, and then I kissed his other cheek. "You have my gratitude, Melekh."

His face reddened a bit and then he turned away. "Yes, well, I shall leave you for the night. Shalom, Ama."

"Shalom, shalom."

He turned, and said, "Shalom, Kora."

"Shalom, shalom, Melekh," she answered with a sweet smile.

Then he turned and walked away, deliberately ignoring Daryoush. I turned to my lover and met his gaze with my brows raised. He waved dismissively, and then he positioned himself to lay his head in my lap. I stared ahead as I ran my fingers through his hair, letting them tangle in his curls, but my mind was elsewhere.

"Where are you, my Ba'alah?" he asked, turning onto his back and staring up at me.

Smiling, I took his face in my hands and pressed my lips to his. Then I urged him to lift his head from my lap. I got up and went to look out across the terrace at the final glow on the horizon as the sun disappeared behind the hills. Daryoush came to stand beside me.

"What a beautiful sunset," he said, wrapping his arm around my back and resting his hand upon my hip.

"There is no moon," I observed, pulling away and going to the ledge, where I stared into the deepening shadows of twilight.

He came to stand beside me, and said, "Yes, it is going to be a dark night."

I said nothing as I gazed across the garden at the cypress trees, black fingers raking across the golden sky that soon became awash with crimson.

"Yezeba'al, come back to bed. Let me make love to you until dawn."

"Not tonight, my love. I am tired." I placed a hand upon his jaw and then gently tugged at his beard. "I am going to bed – to sleep."

"What? But it is still early."

"You forget I am in my forty-second year."

"That has never stopped you from enjoying the night before," he insisted.

Meeting his gaze apologetically, I insisted, "I am tired, my love."

At last, he conceded. "Then I shall come to rouse you in the morning."

He followed when I pulled away and went back inside, where I began to undress. He watched for a moment as Kora came to help me, and then sighed. "I will go, but will you promise to permit me to your presence when morning comes?"

If I am still alive, I thought, hoping that I could pull off my plan without the necessity for self-destruction. If I managed to kill Hadi but his men discovered me before I could escape, I had determined to end my life rather than allow myself to be captured, tortured, raped, and murdered. My actions against Hadi would be considered an act of war; my lofty title could do nothing to protect me if that were the case, yet I was prepared to do whatever was necessary.

Not wishing for him to read my thoughts, I smiled, and said, "Of course. I am already looking forward to you rousing me."

He came to take my naked body in his arms, his hands gliding across my flesh. I trembled and ignored the ache between my thighs. He looked down at my breasts and smiled. "Are you sure I cannot rouse you yet tonight?"

I pulled away and reached for my robe, which Kora held up for me. Covering myself, I said, "No. Now, be gone, for I long only to sleep."

He sighed heavily. "Very well. Shalom, Ba'alah."

"Shalom, Daryoush."

"You will not wish me shalom, shalom?"

I draped myself across the bed, clutched one of the cushions and gazed at him mischievously. "Not unless you promise to behave."

"I promise – I shall behave *only* until I come to you again in the morning."

"Very well, then. Shalom, shalom, Daryoush, my love." I kissed the tips of my fingers at him and watched him leave, hoping I would be there to greet him in the morning. After closing the door, Kora turned to me, and we shared a knowing look.

"Tonight?" she asked.

I gave a single nod and got up.

She inhaled deeply, her chest rising and falling with the action. Her voice shook. "Are you certain of this?"

"The signs are favorable. It is time. Even the prophet of Yahowah has promised we shall be delivered by this time tomorrow."

"I only wish there was another way..."

"I cannot allow my people to starve, and to eat each other out of desperation. This has gone on for too long. There is no other way." I paused to peel off my robe again. "Help me to dress. Then inform Captain Eliezar that it is time. You remember the phrase?"

"The moon sleeps in night eternal."

"Good," I said with a nod. Then I sighed, "This is going to be a long night."

"I shall not get any sleep until you return."

"Please go home tonight and try to get some sleep. I do not want you up all night with worry. You can return to me in the morning. Besides, if I am found gone before I return and you are still here, you would receive some of the blame. If you are at home because I dismissed you, you cannot be blamed."

She nodded. "You are right, Yezeba'al. I will do as you ask of me."

I thanked her, and then she went to fetch the clothing she had acquired from one of the slaves in her house and hid amongst the linens in my bathing chamber. Meanwhile, I pulled out the box where I stored my ritual dagger. I took it out and carefully touched the blade to ensure it had not lost its edge since the last time I sharpened it. Then I smiled and prepared to strap its sheath to my thigh, where it would remain hidden beneath my robes until needed.

The robes Kora acquired were short-sleeved and plain, of a coarse brown cloth that only reached just above my ankles, which was typical for the robes of female slaves. My hair was combed and left loose, but Kora helped me wrap a kerchief around it, fastened at

625

the base of my neck the way she often wore her own. We giggled like girls playing a prank, for a moment forgetting the gravity of the situation. Then I slipped on my riding boots and tucked my scarab seal beneath the collar of my robes until it came time for me to reveal my identity to the King of Aram's men.

After being dressed, Kora admitted the eunuch captain into my chamber. He entered, wearing his own disguise to hide his armor. When he saw me dressed as a slave, he stopped short, clearly startled. "Ba'alah, I do not believe you will need to worry about being recognized. You do not look at all like the Gebirah of Yisrael – or even a nobleman's wife, for that matter."

"Impressive, is it not?" Kora asked with a smile. "The only thing that gives her away, apart from those boots, is that her complexion is too perfect to be that of a common woman, and she still smells of myrrh and cassia."

"No one will look too closely, I suppose," I said, holding out my arms. "They will not see past these wretched clothes. Why do they itch? Do people truly wear such things every day?"

Both laughed, and then Kora said, "Yezeba'al, you are spoiled. There, I said it."

I stuck out my tongue at her, and then we laughed. She came to embrace me and held my face in her hands to look upon me. I forced a smile and said, "I shall return to you, dear sister, if all goes well. And if it does not, we shall be together again in Ertsetu."

"I pray to the Ba'alim that it does not come to that – that they will spare your life and accept the King of Aram alone as a sacrifice."

"Tonight, I send his soul to Ba'al. Let it be done to me and worse by the will of the gods, if I do not make it so by the end of this night." I turned to Eliezar, who waited for my command. "You are certain the way is clear?"

"I have prepared the way for us, as we discussed, Ba'alah. No one suspects a thing."

I gave a single nod, and then I took a deep breath. "All right. Then let us be off."

We had planned our route weeks earlier. As the captain of my eunuchs, Eliezar knew every passage within the palace grounds and the surrounding city. All the eunuchs, just like the city guards, knew

626

how to move through Shomron unseen, using a series of chambers and passageways inside the walls that connected the palace grounds to the barracks and watchtowers, and to the rest of the city beyond. The passages that connected the city to the palace grounds were heavily guarded, so we had to take a different route that led us not into the city but through the slaves' quarter. These passages were cramped and dark and the ceilings were low. Thankfully, Eliezar went ahead carrying a torch, so that any cobwebs we encountered would be burnt along the way.

When we emerged after putting out his torch, we were in the kitchen gardens. It was deserted after sundown. From there, he led us to the place where the channel that fed water to the orchard and gardens flowed out through a tunnel in the thick defensive wall. That was where we would make our exit, as we had planned; he had loosened the grates in advance. I removed my boots to keep them from getting wet and he strapped them to his back as we crawled on our hands and knees in the shallow water. I could feel the water rushing forward, flowing against me and pulling at my clothing.

When we reached the other side of the wall, where there was a second grate, the water was cold, as was the night air. With my robe soaked through, I shivered after emerging on the other side of the wall. The channel led us out upon the rocks overlooking the stream into which the water poured in a gently flowing cascade. Having gone first, Eliezar stood on the edge of the channel to help me up and prevent me from falling. Taking my hands, he whispered, "Watch your step, Ba'alah."

I scraped my knee getting up and sucked air through my teeth, but otherwise kept silent. Blood soaked through my robes, but the night was so dark that I would not see it until much later.

"Are you all right, Ba'alah?" he whispered, still holding my arms while I stood alongside the waterfall, looking around in amazement. We were outside the city. In the distance, I could see enemy patrols on the road with torches, but we were obscured in darkness and far from their view.

Gently removing his hands from my arms, I gave a nod.

He returned my boots and whispered, "We shall have to climb down, as you recall."

I nodded as I held them up. "That is why you had me wear these."

While I knelt to put them on, he eyed my boots as if to determine whether they would be good enough for the climb, and offered, "I can carry you on my back if need be."

Although it was high up, I was unafraid. I said, "I shall be all right. I can manage."

With a nod, he started toward the edge, saying, "I shall go first – that way, I may catch you if you slip. Watch your footing along the way, Ba'alah. It may not look like much, but do not underestimate it."

We began the climb down the steep, rocky slope. Eliezar climbed down with ease and made it to the bottom in under ten minutes. I took a bit longer. It was harder than I thought it would be. By the time I reached the bottom of the craggy slope, I was out of breath. My arms and shoulders ached from the exertion, and my forehead was damp with sweat. Nevertheless, I was fueled by determination and bolstered by a great sense of accomplishment.

"Ba'alah, you have done well," said my eunuch, grinning at me in the dark as I steadied myself and caught my breath.

Smiling broadly, I whispered, "How many queens can boast they have done such things at my age?"

"Not many queens can boast they have done such things," came his reply. Then with a bow, he said, "You astonish me, Ba'alah."

I had to stifle a laugh, as I replied, "I astonish myself. I admit, when you first told me of this plan, I thought it would not be possible for me to do any of this."

"Yet you agreed to it anyway."

"I had to try. I must do whatever I can to protect the people of Shomron. And I believe the Ba'alim are with us. It is only through them that I have been able to do this."

"Ba'alah, you are not finished yet," he reminded me.

"Yes, you are right. We must keep going then. Which way is it to the camp?"

"This way," he said, and we began to round the slope upon which the palace compound rose to meet the endless night sky. As we walked, a chill breeze blew, and I began to shiver in my damp clothes. I probably looked as miserable as I felt, and I began to wonder if we would even make it to the camp without being murdered by Hadi's men, who would likely not believe I was truly the Gebirah of Yisrael.

I hoped my seal would be enough to convince them, but they were probably not even literate.

I looked up to the sky, searching for the star of Ashtarti, only to find it was obscured behind a cloud. It seemed a bad omen, but I pushed forward, determined to have my revenge and not wanting to appear cowardly before Eliezar. Following close at his heels, I realized that although he had served me all these years, I had never really seen him until now. I knew only what my previous captain had told me when he recommended Eliezar as a replacement upon his retirement.

"You are larger than the other eunuchs I have seen," I observed. "You almost appear to be a man."

"I was a man once," he admitted. "Served as a member of the city watch at Megiddu. Lived in a village outside the city." He fell silent for a moment. "I had a wife and daughter."

This took me by surprise. "Why did you leave them to become a eunuch?"

"They were killed by a mob of zealots while I was on duty."

"I am sorry."

"It is not your fault, Ba'alah. You saved me, in fact. I lost everything. Had no hope. Wanted to die. Then you came to Yisrael. And I wanted nothing more than to serve and protect you, so I became a eunuch. I worked hard to distinguish myself until I was promoted to the captain's second. Then he retired and now here I am with you. Now, I know I am blessed by the Ba'alim, for they have allowed me to serve you – Asherah incarnate."

I remained silent for a time, thinking. Eliezar was not only loyal and dutiful – he was fearless and seemed capable of anything. I had a newfound respect for him. Just when we began to round a bend in the path approaching the road, I was about to speak, but we heard boots scrape against gravel. Eliezar stopped suddenly and thrust out his arm to stop me from moving forward. Then a voice came from the darkness, "Who is it that goes there?"

Suddenly, two armored men emerged from within the brush. One of them lit a torch and then they looked between us, their hands poised on the hilts of their swords, as if prepared to draw. Thinking we would not understand any other language, the one who spoke addressed us in Hebrew. "You are not of the king's men. What are you doing traveling outside Shomron by night? Have you come to deliver supplies to the city? Or are you messengers being sent out? Answer for yourselves."

Moving Eliezar's arm aside, I stepped forward, and addressed them in Aramaic. "I am Ba'alah Yezeba'al, Gebirah of Yisrael." I began to add, "I want to be taken to the King of Aram," but before I could finish the men began laughing.

Switching to Aramaic, one of them said, "If you are the Gebirah of Yisrael, I must be the Pharoah of Egypt!"

The one with the torch added, "And I am the King of Assyria!"

They continued laughing together, while I and my eunuch exchanged glances. Then the one who called himself Pharoah came forward and tried to put his hands on me, saying, "Why don't we get better acquainted, hmm?"

I swatted him away as Eliezar came forward to shove him back, saying, "Keep your hands off the Ba'alah, you filth!"

The men drew their swords, and false Pharoah said, "Who are you to lay your hands on me?"

"I am the Ba'alah's Captain of the Guard."

Before anything could happen, I stepped between them, and said, "Boys, please. There is no need for that. It is clearly a misunderstanding. Put down your swords and let us talk as friends, shall we?"

"Who are you really? You do not talk like a slave and you wear kohl around your eyes."

"I told you who I am. Notice, I wear no collar. Instead, I wear this, to show you who I am." I pulled out my scarab seal.

They looked closely. When one of them reached out to touch it, I slapped his hand away. Then the one with the torch said, "A winged lion and a lotus. Those are symbols of royalty."

Then false Pharoah asked, "How do we know you did not steal it when you concocted this tale?"

"Why would I pretend to be the Gebirah of Yisrael and ask you to take me to the King of Aram?"

False king put in, "Maybe you're a whore, looking to make a bigger profit."

I smirked, but Eliezar was clearly affronted. "You call the Ba'alah a whore?"

630

"Eliezar, it is all right," I assured him. "They do not know any better – and they would not be the first to call me such, however misguided."

Then false king said to his companion, "I don't suppose a slave wears riding boots of fine leather…"

They looked at my boots, and I lifted the hem of my robes enough to show them fully, while false Pharoah said, "I have never seen a woman wear riding boots."

"They are too small to be the boots of a man," said false king.

"Perhaps they are the boots of a youth."

I rolled my eyes, and said, "They are my boots."

Meanwhile, the one with the torch continued to argue with his companion. "They are too decorated to belong to a common child, though."

"They were commissioned for me," I insisted, "as a gift from my husband, Melekh Akhab, made by the finest leather craftsman in Yisrael."

"Maybe what she says is true, and she really is the Gebirah?"

"We cannot just take a woman claiming to be the Gebirah of Yisrael to the king. If she turns out to be false, he will kill us both."

"Take me to him. He will know me."

They considered, and then false Pharoah said, "If we do take you, we must take you as prisoners."

"Very well," I said. "I give you permission, as long as you swear not to harm us, and take us straight to Hadadesar."

"No, Ba'alah," Eliezar said, speaking Akkadian so they would not understand. "If you let them tie us, I cannot protect you should they try something."

"They will not," I said with more certainty than I felt. Then, once they gave us their word, I allowed them to tie my wrists and put a rope around my neck as a leash. It was degrading, but they apologized as they did so and were gentle in their manner. They did the same to Eliezar, who allowed it only because I commanded it. I could see by his expression that he still did not trust them, but they kept their word.

At the camp, I held my head high, ignoring the jeers and lusty stares of drunken soldiers as we passed. First, we were taken to see the king's steward, Hazael, a weasely little man whom I had never liked. He recognized me and led us the rest of the way to the King of

Aram's tent. When we arrived, the guards outside looked at us dubiously when they were told who we claimed to be. Nevertheless, they permitted Hazael to go inside and speak to the king. Soon afterward, Hadi himself stepped out to look at me with a hardened stare. When he saw my face, recognition softened his gaze.

"Yeza, it really is you! What are you doing dressed as a slave?"

"Hadi," I greeted him. "It was the only way for me to get out of the palace without calling attention to myself. My son the king would not let me come to see you."

Switching from Akkadian to Aramaic, he said to the men who brought us. "Come; bring her inside."

There were others in his tent: two of his bodyguards, Hazael, and three other kings. The kings were Basa of Ammon, Gindibu of Qedar, and Matinuba'al of Arwad, all of whom had fought alongside my husband in the bid against Assyria. I was not surprised by the presence of Basa, who had always had his sight set on the wealth of our kingdom. I was pleased that the King of Hamat was not present, having kept his alliance with us intact. The three kings sat drinking and looked at us with interest when we entered. Then Hadi said, "It really is my cousin, the Gebirah of Yisrael. Look, she has dressed as a slave to come to me without her son's permission! Can you believe I am so important to her?"

I resisted the urge to roll my eyes, while he commanded the men, "Remove this bondage from her. She is a queen, and my guest, not a prisoner."

Gindibu, the eldest of the kings, had gotten up to bring Hadi his cup. They whispered together as the men removed my bindings. Then Hadi went to set his cup on the large table that was in the center of the tent, covered in scrolls and lamps and writing supplies.

My hands freed, I rubbed my wrists and then removed the mantle from my hair to let it loose. Meanwhile, the King of Qedar bowed his head to me and smiled through his grey beard. "Gebirah Yezeba'al, it is good to see you again."

"I would say the same to you, Melekh, if you were not laying siege to my son's kingdom."

"Eh, well...it is nothing personal, Gebirah. A necessary alliance."

"You might have chosen to ally yourself with Yisrael instead of attacking us."

"You do not take the threat of Assyria seriously, Gebirah."

"So," said Hadi, cutting in. "What brings you to my camp in the middle of the night?"

"You have demanded my son the king send me to you. Well, now I am here."

"Yes, but he did not send you."

Forcing a smile, I walked up to him, placed my hands upon his chest, and gazed into his eyes. "Would it surprise you if I came to lie with you, at last?"

His breath came in sharp and, as I pressed my body against his, I felt the eagerness in his loins. I smiled and carefully reached down to stroke the bulge in his tunic. Then I whispered, "Send the other men away."

He smiled and looked down at me, and I was certain I had him convinced until he seized my wrists, turned away, and went to the table. He lifted his drink and, still with his back to me, commanded, "Hazael: search her."

A stab of horror shot through my core as the guards came to take hold of me. The one who held me by the arms apologized, while the steward put his hands all over me. Hadi leaned his back against the table and, after taking a drink, watched with a thin smile. I held my breath when Hazael slid his hands up my thighs and came upon the dagger. He pulled up my robes then, to reveal it.

Hadi set down his drink again and clapped slowly, as the steward unstrapped the dagger from my thigh. Then Hadi said, "Really, Yeza? Did you think I would not have you searched? I knew you came here for vengeance and not love-making."

The guards released me, certain now that I had no other weapons. I straightened my robes, and said, "I brought it for protection – nothing more, Hadi."

Stepping close to me and caressing my cheek with his fingertips, he said, "Swear it, on the holy seed of your Ba'al."

Unable to take such an oath, I looked away and said nothing.

He smirked and walked back to the table. "I have not forgotten the promise you made to me before the fountain in the garden at Tzidon. I could kill you."

"You would not dare to kill the mother of a king."

"That boy is hardly a king. Everyone knows it is you who truly runs the kingdom." He looked to Hazael, and commanded, "Hold onto

633

the dagger. And take the eunuch outside. Chain him to a tree until I am finished with her."

"No!" Eliezar protested, as the guards took hold of him.

"Come along, you," Hazael said to my eunuch, and they forced him out while I stood silent. I was still coming to terms with the reality that I had failed my mission, and now I was at my cousin's mercy. He had outwitted me, at last. All I could do was pray for the Ba'alim to protect me and preserve my life.

Once the soldiers had removed Eliezar, Hadi looked to his bodyguards. "Stand watch outside and let no one enter. And tell the other men to stay on high alert – the Gebirah of Yisrael is not to be trusted, and her presence may be intended as a distraction. If anyone approaches our camp – be they young or old, armed or not – they are to be killed on sight."

"It will be done, Melekh," answered his guard captain. Then he signaled to the others, and they went out. Now, it was only me and Hadi with the three other kings, who watched the scene play out with great interest. Basa seemed especially eager to watch what was going to transpire; he was sitting on the edge of his seat, drink in hand, black eyes reflecting the flames of the lamps.

Hadi loomed over me, circling like a vulture. "You have more grey hair than the last time I saw you. Are the pressures of running the kingdom for your infant son too much to bear, Yeza?"

"Yoram is hardly an infant – he has sons of his own and more on the way. He has been quite fruitful."

"Good for him. You must be proud. But it must be hard for you to see your children taking the place of your youth."

"I am quite comfortable, actually. I do not mind growing old in body, for I am ever youthful in spirit yet with the confidence and wisdom of age."

"Was it wisdom that brought you here?" His eyes sparkled with mischief.

Again, I said nothing.

"How is your priest of Ba'al these days? I heard you made him High Priest."

I smiled. "I find him most satisfying."

"And that is why you have come to me?"

"You know why I have come to you."

He stopped circling and stood over me. "And yet you failed."

"Have I?"

Suddenly, he grabbed the hair at the back of my head, and said, "You think you are the cat, Yeza, but if you have come here to toy with me, I will show you who has the bigger claws." He released me, and said, "Now, I want you to get down on your knees and beg for mercy." He placed a hand on my cheek and attempted to caress my lips with his thumb, saying, "Use that mouth for what it's good for and, if I'm satisfied, I will let you live."

I pulled away from his touch. He laughed and went to the table for a drink, while I asked, "Are we not getting to be too old for this, Hadi?"

"You are right, Yeza," he agreed. "This has gone on long enough. So, now that you have lost: shall I take you by force, or will you give yourself to me?"

I spat at his feet. The other kings laughed, and Basa said, "She told you, *akhu*."

Hadi glared at me in contempt.

Then, changing tactics, I claimed, "I have come to tell you there is an army coming to destroy you, Hadi. I had hoped to take your life myself, of course, and leave your men to the mercy of our allies..."

"She is lying," said Basa.

"No. What I am saying is quite true: if you do not leave, the armies of Yisrael and our allies will destroy you all."

"What allies?" asked Basa. "All this time we have laid siege to your kingdom, and none have come to rescue you."

"The Pharoah of Egypt and my brother the King of Tzidon, the King of Yehudah, the kings of Ashkelon and Elam... Even your old friend the King of Hamat, whose daughter is my son's Melkah – they are all coming."

Hadi grunted in disbelief, but I could see the uncertainty in his eyes.

"They will arrive in under two days' time," I continued, "and they will crush you."

"Impossible," he finally said with a wave. "I have men posted at every gate. You could not have gotten word out, let alone received word from your...allies."

"But do you have them posted by the channels leading out of the city, through the grates in the walls?" I smiled triumphantly.

635

He looked stunned. Then he said, "You are lying."

"How do you think I got to you without being seen leaving through the city gates? We have been sending and receiving messages in this way for weeks, and now your time is up."

"I do not believe it."

I shrugged. "All right then. Stay and you will soon find that I have outwitted you again. I always win, Hadi."

He stood looking toward the ground with a sneer. Then suddenly, his gaze shot up and he came forward to grab me by the throat, just below the jaw. He pulled me around and shoved me back against the table. Sparks shot up my spine and my knees buckled, but his hold kept me from falling. He growled as he looked at me. Then he grinned and I knew what he was thinking. He began kissing me forcefully, bringing his hands down to touch my breasts and tearing at my robe.

I bit down hard on his bottom lip. When he yelped and pulled away, I grinned, the taste of iron on my tongue. Then he snickered and came at me again, dragging me toward the bed. I fought him, while the other kings watched with a mixture of excitement and horror.

After wrestling me down on the bed, pinning me by the wrists, Hadi forced his knee between my legs and brought it up between my thighs to keep me from closing them. Then he looked up at the other men, shouting, "Help me hold her down! Hold her down and I will let you have her when I am finished!"

The other kings looked at each other uncertainly. Even Basa's grin had faded.

"Help me," I pleaded, hoping to appeal to their gentle natures when they hesitated. They looked at me, but they would not meet my gaze. "Please, help me!"

At last, the King of Qedar protested, "She is a queen!"

"And I am a king! Damn it, woman!" He paused to slap me, as I continued trying to wrestle away.

"Let me go!"

He slapped me again and I fell silent but continued to struggle against him.

"I want no part in this," said Gindibu, and he left the tent while the other two came to subdue me. One of them removed my boots while the other held down my wrists long enough for Hadi to tear off my robes until only my beaded necklace with the opal scarab remained. But even that could not ward him off. Then he removed his own clothes, perched over me, and forcibly opened my legs.

"No!" I wailed hopelessly. Then the air was knocked out of me, and I was being ripped apart, body and soul.

The other two kings released their hold on me and backed away, watching in horror until even they could not bear to see the assault of a queen. Then they fled like Gindibu. The whole camp must have known what was happening to me; yet no one came to my rescue.

Defeated, I fell still and silent, closing my eyes against the burning tears and waiting for it to be over. I no longer had the strength to fight once he was inside me. All my power, all my courage – everything I had been given, everything I had worked so hard for was taken from me in that moment. No longer a queen, a goddess made flesh; I was merely a woman, an aging widow, at the mercy of a man stronger than I could ever be. I had never felt so weak, so powerless in all my life.

When it was over, he held my face and kissed my cheek, his body heavy upon mine. "Thank you for that. It was all I ever wanted, Yeza. We could have avoided so much, if you had just given it to me the first time I asked." Then he pulled himself off me and lifted his tunic, using it to wipe the sweat from his body and began getting dressed, while I lay still on his bed, breathless and trembling. I was still too shocked to move or even to weep.

Fastening his belt, he watched me with a smug expression. I averted my gaze, but I could see him from the corner of my eye. Then he came to me and caressed my cheek. "Do not worry, Yeza. Your Ba'alim have not abandoned you. My Ba'al is stronger tonight because I gave him the better sacrifice: my favorite son."

Horrifed, I gasped and looked at him in disbelief. His expression was one of mild regret. He sniffed once or twice. Then he turned his gaze to meet mine and smiled darkly. "The price was paid, the blessing received. I am glad it was worth it – although, his mother may not think so." He chuckled, and said, "Not that it matters. She's only a concubine."

Fresh tears blurred my vision and I turned away, unable to look upon the face of evil. Then, at last, I managed to speak. "The gods will judge your actions, Hadi."

637

"Perhaps. I do not care, Yeza. Ba'al Rimmon likes tender young flesh. He has judged me and found me worthy: I have gotten what I came for, and that is all that matters to me."

"Then will you leave?" I asked through a fresh wave of tears.

He plopped down into his chair, lifting his leg to rest over the arm of it. "No, I think I might stay. I rather like the idea of enlarging my kingdom. Unfortunate about your sons, though. I shall have to kill every one of them. Oh, but do not worry – they will be burnt as offerings when I convert the altars of your temple to my Ba'al. Their blood will consecrate the altar to him, and I will feast upon their flesh before I take your little daughter as a wife. How old is she now? Ten? Good enough."

I spat at him. "You will not touch her!"

"How will you stop me? With your little dagger? You'll never get it back."

"I will never stop trying to kill you, Hadi."

He got up with a growl and came to kneel on the edge of the bed then grabbed me by the hair on the back of my head. I cried out and whimpered. He sneered. "Still need to be put in your place, woman?"

He yanked my hair and threw me aside then began to remove his tunic. I tried to get up, but he slapped me hard across the face. I fell back on the bed. Then he held me down and forced his knee between my legs again, while I continued to struggle against him. This time, however, I was still too sore and weak to fight him for long; he easily overpowered me, and I soon gave in.

When it was over, I turned onto my stomach with my face hanging off the side of the bed. My ears were ringing, my head ached, and I was nauseated. I closed my eyes to stop the feeling that I was caught up in a whirling sandstorm.

Hadi returned to stand over me after having dressed. "Clean yourself up and get dressed. Then you may return to your palace. You're free – until I take the city."

He walked away, leaving me alone in the tent.

I curled up on the bed, held my stomach, and wept. Once I was able to get up, my hands shook as I reached for my robes and slipped them over my broken body. Warm tears stung, flowing like channels down my cheeks; they gathered in the crevice of my lips before making their final descent. I paused to wipe them with the back of my hand and looked for my boots. Finding them on the ground, I put them on, and then I carefully draped my mantle over my disheveled hair, using the edge to soak up more tears and wipe the kohl from my cheeks.

Except for the ache in every muscle, the pain in every joint, and the stinging between my bloodied thighs, nothing felt real to me as I made my way out of the tent. Two guardsmen stood on either side of the entrance. They straightened when I emerged. I jumped.

Hadi was standing by a campfire nearby, silent and brooding. The flames danced in his black eyes while he lifted a cup to his lips and sated his thirst. The other men nearby did not speak to him, but their eyes all fell on me – briefly – before they looked away. Only one of them dared to approach me. It was the King of Qedar.

"Are you all right, Gebirah? Do you need help returning to the city?"

Despite my shame, I lifted my head, inhaled deeply, and fixed him with an accusing gaze. "Where were you when I needed assistance? Do not come to me with your false gallantry, Gindibu. Now, I can manage without."

Eliezar was unchained from the tree the moment I emerged from the tent, but Hadi's bodyguards remained on high alert and watched him closely. They had confiscated his weapons and did not return them. My eunuch spat toward Hadi, who smirked but otherwise ignored the gesture. Then he came to offer his arm, but I held up my hand. He bowed his head and followed closely as I made my way through the camp, ignoring the stares that followed me along the way.

28

Aftermath

Kora came to rouse me at the same time as always the next morning. I had gotten in a short time before sunrise and, though exhausted, was still awake. Her relief at seeing me alive was overshadowed by the shock of seeing how broken I was. Soon after she appeared, Daryoush tried to come to me as promised, but I did not want him to see me in this condition, so Kora went to send him away. When she returned, I told her what had happened, and she held me as I wept. Then by the time the handmaidens arrived, I pulled myself together and nothing more was said on the matter.

Normally jovial and doting, the handmaids were stricken when they saw me and remained silent as they helped me bathe and dress for court. My bruised cheekbone was obscured with a mixture of face cream and powdered gold carefully applied after everything else was in place. It was not perfect, but it helped. The stares I received from Yoram, Be'ulah, Daryoush, Raman, and the few others who were near enough to notice suggested it did not hide the bruising as well as I had hoped. Nevertheless, I was determined to carry on as if nothing had happened, my dignity intact even if my soul lay in pieces.

Everything went on as usual, until a messenger came from the King of Aram. It was the same boy who had come before, only now he came bearing something wrapped in fine cloth, which he handed to Aharon. Even before it was unwrapped, I knew what it was.

"What is this?" Yoram demanded.

"A gift, Melekh. For the Gebirah Yezeba'al. The King of Aram says: 'She left her dagger in my tent when she came to me last night.'"

The boy paused, while gasps and whispers rose up and spread as a wave throughout the assemblage. Shmuel held the cloth open, my ritual dagger lying in his hands, and looked at us with uncertainty. The eunuchs came to retrieve it, examining it for any signs of poison or other falsehood, before allowing it to be presented to me. I waved it away, turning my face to hide my shame. Then it was taken off to be given to one of my priestesses; it would need to be cleansed and reconsecrated before it could be used ritually again, and I did not even want to look at it.

"He also says that..." Again, the boy paused, this time glancing at me with a troubled expression, before he continued, "he says that he enjoyed her company, and thanks her for blessing him. That is what my lord says."

The boy lowered his face to hide the redness in his cheeks, and I thought that even he must have known what it meant. The whole camp must have heard what had been done to me, and his message delivered with my dagger ensured our court had an idea of what went on in the King of Aram's tent as well. Hadi was stripping me of what little dignity I had left.

Yoram's gaze burned through me when I dared a glance at him. Then he turned to the boy, and said, "Tell your lord that he will soon receive *my* blessing – the blessing of the Wolf of Yisrael, which shall come to him swiftly."

I leaned over, and whispered, "Tell him your allies are coming."

"What?"

"Your allies," I hissed between clenched teeth.

"Oh." Then Yoram lifted his head, cleared his throat, and raised his voice. "Tell him also that my allies are coming. And together, we shall repay him for his gift."

The messenger bowed and then departed with that message. We expected to hear back from the King of Aram, but the messenger did not return and so we carried on with the business of the day. Mostly, we listened to the petty complaints of the nobles in the city, and a recounting of more complaints of the common people, brought to us by the governor who had received them from his administrators; all of which we could do nothing about while the siege persisted.

There was some good news, at least, which came not long after the court was dismissed that afternoon. A messenger from the city watch came before us, and said, "Ba'al be praised, Melekh: three of the kings and their armies have pulled out, leaving the Arameans alone."

"What?" asked General Dawid, standing with the other ministers below the dais.

Yoram looked at the messenger wide-eyed, rubbing his beard. "You are certain of this?" The messenger nodded. Then the king said, "You are sure it is not a ruse?"

"Indeed, Melekh!" the messenger answered jubilantly. "They were seen leaving with their standards. Only the standards of the King of Aram remain in the camp with his army."

"Dawid," Yoram called.

"Yes, Melekh?"

"Do we have the men to defeat the Arameans on our own?"

General Dawid looked uncertain but ultimately shook his head. "No, Melekh, I do not believe so. I will have to get an estimate of the size of his army without those of the other kings, but I still do not believe we have the forces needed to defeat the Arameans without outside help. The men we have stationed in the city are small, and they have grown weak with famine."

Now Yoram's countenance fell, and he slumped on his throne. "Go. Take account of how many are left with the King of Aram and report back to me when you are more certain. That will be all for the day."

He nodded to Aharon, who then announced that the court was dismissed. Exhausted and in pain, I rose from my throne and eagerly took my leave, but Yoram accosted me in the corridor. "You deliberately disobeyed me. When I told you not to go to Hadadesar's camp, not to leave the palace. What did you do — make a harlot of yourself?"

I slapped him for that. "I did *not* permit what was done to me. How dare you even suggest that I went there willingly for that."

"But you did go willingly."

"Not for that!" Then I covered my mouth and turned away, trembling as I struggled not to weep. I had barely been holding myself together as it was; now, what little strength I had left was crumbling.

"If that is not why you went to him...why did you go, Ama?"

"He found a dagger on me, Yoram," I said, turning back to face him. "Why do you think I was there? I wanted to slay him for being the cause of so much misery and death. I wanted to drive that blade into his heart, slit his throat, and watch him bleed to death. To see the lifeforce drain from his eyes when the spirit was severed from his

642

flesh. I wanted him to pay for taking your Abbu from us..." A sob escaped from my throat, and I had to turn away again.

After a long pause, my son came up behind me and placed his hands on my arms. I jumped at first, but then I realized it was only him and that I was safe, and I allowed him to embrace me.

"I am sorry, Ama," he whispered. "Forgive me for being unable to protect you when you needed it most."

I shook my head and placed a hand over his. "This was not your fault, Yoram. If I had listened to you, it would never have happened."

"No, you cannot blame yourself. How could you know he would do this, when he has had many opportunities before and not taken them?"

"I should never have trusted him. I knew he could not be trusted but...still, I did not believe he would..." Unable to say it, I stopped and covered my mouth again.

Yoram sighed heavily and looked past me down the corridor. Then he said, "I will make him pay for what he has done to you."

"There is nothing you can do."

"I will take all of the men who are stationed here and make battle."

"They will be slaughtered, as will you, and then the rest of us will be left to Hadadesar's whims. Is that what you want?"

"Then I will go alone, and send ahead, and challenge him myself."

I scoffed. It was almost a laugh.

"He will face me, man to man."

"And he will crush you like the insignificant ant that he thinks you are."

"I am the Wolf of Yisrael!" he roared, hitting his chest.

"Oh, stop it with that stupid nickname!" I said finally. "You cannot go after him. Just let it be, Yoram."

"How am I to prove myself as king and a capable warrior if I do not defend you, Ama? If I do not seek retribution for what has been done to you?"

"I do not need you to seek retribution! I need you to stay alive and rule your kingdom – that is what I need you to do. Do not make me go through the pain of losing another son, I cannot bear it."

"You will not lose me, Ama."

643

"You do not know that, and it is a chance that you should not take. A chance you cannot take."

"Why can't I?"

"He is a king."

"And so am I."

"You cannot simply walk into his camp and kill him."

"Is that not what you tried to do?"

"Obviously, I failed!"

Inhaling deeply, he brought his hands together in front of his face. "If I challenge him to fight me..."

"You will die by his hand."

"Why are you certain I cannot defeat him? Am I not a capable warrior?"

"Of course, but so is he, and he has more experience than you. He is likely expecting you to retaliate, and certain he can win. I made the mistake of underestimating him. I do not advise you do the same."

Finally, he threw up his hands. "Why do you not want me to avenge you? After what he did, you should be begging me to murder him."

"I want him dead, Yoram – yes, I want to murder him myself for what he did. But there are more important things."

"Than your honor?"

"Yes!" I insisted vehemently. "The wellbeing of your kingdom, for one. That should be your priority – it *must* be your priority. I will take care of myself."

"And the King of Aram?"

"We are at a disadvantage. Let it rest." Then I continued to my quarters, and he did not follow me.

Daryoush tried to come to me again, but again I had Kora turn him away. He would not force his way into my chamber, but this time he stood outside and called, "Ba'alah! Please! Do not turn me away!"

Kora paused from closing the door and looked to me for direction; I could see that she was torn. Sitting at my dressing table after washing my face, trying to ignore the throbbing ache within my cheek, I gave her none. She waited with the door ajar, while he continued his lamentations.

"I can only imagine what has happened to you – it is obvious, what you went through. But I am not here to chide you. I am only here to comfort you because I love you. Yezeba'al, I love you more

644

than life itself, and it pains me to think of what that beast has done to you. Please. Do not shut me out."

Needles stabbed my eyes, and I closed them against the pain. Then I exhaled and hung my head and waved for Kora to let him enter. I rose as he entered, and he rushed to embrace me, but my body still ached, and I cried out from the force of his passion.

He pulled away immediately. "My love, did I hurt you? I'm sorry." Then he gently took my hand, examining the bruise on my cheek. I averted my gaze so as not to weep. He was angry; I felt the rage beneath his sorrow and saw it by the way his jaw tensed. His body trembled as he held back from saying what he was thinking because he knew it would only upset me. In that way, he was like Akhab—he often knew what I needed without me telling him and responded naturally. He knew at that moment I did not need an avenging champion; I needed tenderness. I did not need his passion; I needed his companionship.

Once supper was brought to us, I thanked Kora and dismissed her for the night. It took me a while to speak openly, but my lover sat with me to eat and eventually I told him about everything that had transpired. He listened patiently and held me when I began to weep. Afterward, he lay in my bed simply holding and caressing me and, at last, I was able to sleep.

Some hours later, in the middle of the night, we were roused from our slumber when a eunuch came to deliver the king's summons. I was still dressed in the underrobes from my court regalia, over which I slipped a simple robe, and threw on a mantle as I walked out the door. I did not even bother to dress my hair or cover my face with cosmetics. As my advisor on the High Council, Daryoush accompanied me. Raman met us as we approached the king's private audience chamber. I went to him, and asked, "What is it, Raman? What has happened?"

He looked at me in shock when he turned around and his gaze fell on my cheek. For the first time he saw just how badly I had been beaten by the King of Aram, but he knew better than to say anything. Instead, he pushed down his anger and shook his head. "I do not know, Ba'alah. Only that the king has summoned the High Council."

Then he paused to let me enter ahead of him, as the doors were opened to us.

Yoram was standing by the window when we entered, with Shmuel, Lord Amon, General Dawid, General Yehu, and a few officers from the city watch. There was an air of excitement and uncertainty among them but when we entered, they fell silent. I stopped and looked at them all, trying to ignore the intensity of their stares, and then Yoram came to me.

"Ama, something has happened."

"Obviously. What is it? Why are you all here looking astonished?"

Yoram, unable to speak, waved over one of the gatekeepers to explain it to me. He was one of the younger officers. He approached reverently and bowed his head, saying, "Ba'alah, it is an honor to serve you." When I nodded, he continued, "A group of lepers came to us this night and told us they had gone to the King of Aram's camp and...found it empty."

"What do you mean, 'empty'?"

"Ba'alah, no one was there! The horses and donkeys were still tied up and the tents were standing, but there was not a single man about."

Yoram, who had his hand over his mouth, lowered it now, and asked, "Ama, what do you think? Is it a trick? Do you think Ben-Hadad has paid these lepers to fool us into believing they have left?" He started to pace now. "When in fact they are waiting in the field for us to leave the city so they may capture us and take the city from under us?"

"It does seem hard to believe that they would leave with their camp still intact, and so suddenly..." I was too stunned to complete my thoughts. When one of the men offered me a chair, I sat and stared at the floor in wonderment. Then I looked up at the rest of the men. "Perhaps they believed the lie...what I said to them last night when I was there."

"Ba'alah," asked Dawid, "what did you say?"

"That our allies were coming to destroy them."

"Who?" asked Yehu, with his usual lack of deference. "Who did you tell them was coming? None of our allies have sent aid."

I struggled to assemble my thoughts and put them into words. I spoke slowly, as I recounted, "The Pharoah of Egypt and the kings of Tzidon and Hamat, and others... I said that we had gotten messages that they would arrive in a day or two, all of them together."

"Yes, but why would you say that when it is not true?" Yehu demanded. "And why would they believe it?"

"I was desperate to say something, anything to make them believe I still had power over them... They had seized my dagger, having searched me, for he knew that I had come to kill him. The King of Aram, I mean."

Yehu balked at this, but Yoram rebuked him. "General Yehu, that is my mother. You will show her proper courtesy."

"Forgive me, Melekh," he answered with his hands out. Then he sighed, turned to me, and bowed stiffly. "Gebirah, I beg pardon."

I waved dismissively, for I was used to his behavior. I knew his apology was not genuine because he had never liked me. He made little secret of his distaste for my religious practices, although he never openly denounced me.

Now, though, everyone was looking at me after what I had revealed. Finally, Dawid said, "Ba'alah, it is a good thing you said this. Perhaps the other kings believed this and that is why they abandoned the King of Aram. And now, left alone without the other kings' armies to back them, he and his army have indeed fled."

"*If* they fled," Yoram countered. "We still do not know if it is true. What good is the word of lepers?"

"But Melekh," Yehu spoke up, "did not the prophet of Yahowah tell you that we would be delivered on this day?"

"The prophet says a lot of things that do not come true, Yehu," my son reminded him. "I know you believe in him, but I think he was only trying to buy time and save his skin."

"But if it is true that the Arameans are gone and their camp is empty, perhaps there is food and drink. We should not sit back and stay here to starve if we are free to leave. Let us send some men on horses out of the city – they will soon die anyway, as will the rest of us. We might as well send a few scouts to see what has happened, and if it is true that we are delivered by the grace of Yahowah."

I scoffed at this. "If we are delivered, it is not by your god, Yehu."

"It was one of his prophets who spoke to the king of deliverance!"

647

"Yet it was by my actions, led by the will of my gods, that our deliverance was carried out. By *my* word such fear was planted in their minds, that they should flee."

"You think that your idols are more powerful than my real and living god..."

"That is enough, you two!" Yoram roared. "I will not have you bickering over who has delivered us – if, indeed, we are delivered. Neither do I care which god, if any, is responsible. All we know is what was told to us by the word of some lepers who are not even allowed to enter the city. In desperation, they may have gone to the King of Aram and sold themselves to his bidding for a bit of food, that he might deceive us by them. Until it is confirmed that Aram has fled, *no one* has delivered us."

He paused and swept his gaze across all who were gathered. No one spoke, until the king said, "General Yehu, I do agree with your suggestion that we send scouts to discover whether there be any truth to what the lepers have said. I leave you to choose the men who will embark on this mission. That is all. In the meantime, the rest of us will wait here."

Yehu bowed to the king and left to obey his command, taking the gatekeepers with him. Once he was gone, while the other men talked, I got up and went to my son who was leaning against the table and looking at the map laid out there. Keeping my voice low, I said, "That boy needs to learn his place."

Yoram sighed. "That *boy* is a man, and one of my best generals. Not to mention, he has been one of my closest friends since childhood."

"He cannot be trusted. You do well to keep him close, to keep an eye on him, but do not let him walk all over you."

"I rebuked him, did I not?"

"Yes, and you should continue to rebuke him, but I would suggest you give him less power. Keep him on a leash. There are others who can command your chariots."

"Yehu is loyal, Ama. He may serve a different god than you, but I would trust him with my life. And I know him better than you."

"Sometimes love can make us blind to the truth, Yoram."

He sighed heavily and continued looking at the map without a response, but I could feel the heat of his anger. I decided it best to let it drop and went instead to speak with my advisors. They had been talking together with some of the other men, but when they saw me approaching, they turned to me with a bow of their heads.

"Raman, Daryoush, what do you think of all this?"

"Ba'alah," said Raman, "I think what you did was brilliant — although I advised you against it and wish you had not put yourself at such risk."

"It did not have the outcome I had intended, I suppose," came my reply, "but it was worth the sacrifice if it got them to leave. At least, I am alive to see it play out. May we be delivered."

"Amen," they both replied, as did some of the other men who had been standing nearby listening.

One of the younger officers approached, knelt before me, and asked, "Ba'alah, will you pray over us?"

I nodded, and then the men who were devoted to the Ba'alim gathered around to kneel before us. Two of the men who were uncertain also came, and by the time all who were interested in my prayers gathered, there were seven in number. My son remained at the other end of the chamber, standing by the window, and looking out into the night. Raman and Daryoush also knelt before me, making it nine who gathered before me. I blessed them as I called on Ba'al to hear us and grant us his peace. After our prayers, I led them in song, and that is how we passed the time until Yehu returned. By then, it was near sunrise.

When he entered, the general knelt before the king. Yoram went to him, bade him to stand, and asked, "What did you find, my friend?"

Still kneeling, Yehu answered, "Melekh, it is as the lepers spoke: not a man living was at the camp. It was left behind, as if they had all vanished into thin air. Two of the scouts went in pursuit of the Arameans, having found signs that they had fled in their chariots and by foot, and that they were in a hurry when they left. Only a few of the horses and donkeys were left behind, those that were not fit to flee. They left all their tents and much of their belongings, and food — enough to feed an entire army!"

"Enough to feed the city," Yoram replied. Then he smiled, as if he still could hardly believe it. "This is unbelievable. We are truly delivered."

Overcome, I dropped to my knees and threw up my hands. "Praise Ba'al!"

649

Most of the men repeated my praise. Then Yoram came to me, and said, "I'll settle for praising you, Ama." I took his hands, and he helped me to rise. Then he brought my hands to his lips, and said, "I cursed you for disobeying me, but you were right to do so. You risked your life for us all, and your quick thinking may yet have been enough to fool them into thinking they had to flee. Although, I still cannot believe it."

"It was the Ba'alim who guided me, Yoram. I could never have done it on my own. Nor could I have done it without the aid of Captain Eliezar, who I feel deserves a reward for his loyalty and bravery."

"He was with you the whole time?" There was anger in the roughness of his voice.

With a nod, I said, "He did all he could to protect me. He could not have prevented what happened." Then, aware of all the eyes on me, I looked away to hide my shame.

Yoram inhaled deeply and then turned to the officers who were there. He chose one from among them to go out and guard the gate with a few other men. He also sent messengers to tell the people of the city that the siege was ended and to help themselves to what the Arameans left behind.

The people were so hungry and overjoyed that they stampeded out of the city, and we later heard that the officer Yoram had chosen to lead the guards at the gate was trampled in the frenzy, later dying of his injuries. Rumors began to spread about a man who was close to the king having doubted the prophet's message about our deliverance, and that it was he who had been trampled as a divine judgement. That, of course, was untrue for it was Shmuel who had expressed doubt. The man who was trampled was hardly known to the king, but Yoram sent condolences to his family with a stipend to ease their pain, and even provided him with a funeral worthy of one greater than he had been in life.

And so, we were delivered. Yahwists claimed that the soldiers of the King of Aram fled because Yahowah caused them to hear the sounds of a great army approaching and believed that our allies had come to deliver us. I assumed it was a result of the other kings abandoning him, and Hadi deciding not to take the risk of staying if

650

what I had said about our allies turned out to be true. Either way, no matter what the cause, we were spared, and we went to the temple to give thanks. But there was still much that needed to be done to fortify the kingdom against further assault and to protect my children.

Remembering Hadi's threat about my daughter, I decided to send Azba'alah to my mother in Tzidon, where the King of Aram could never touch her. At first, when I proposed this solution to Yoram in the king's study, he was opposed. Without my knowledge, he had already begun negotiations for her to enter a diplomatic marriage. I was furious that he would conduct these negotiations behind my back, to which he responded, "I am king. It is my duty to find a suitable husband for my unmarried sisters."

"And I am her mother! I should at least have some say in her future!"

"Yes, you are her mother—and that makes her more valuable than my half-sisters."

"We need her to remain in Yisrael, to replace me as the spiritual leader of our people."

"Yet you want to send her to *your* mother in Tzidon?"

"Only to complete her training and to keep her safe from the King of Aram's clutches! It is not permanent!"

"Ama, I know how close you are with Azba—that is why it is necessary for me to make these considerations in your stead. You have said that I allow my emotions to cloud my judgment when it comes to Yehu—"

"That is different."

"It is not different. In fact, as her mother I believe you are even less capable of making the right decision concerning her future."

"That is not true, and you know it! I know how to make the hard decisions concerning the wellbeing of my children. *I am sending her away*—as her mother, *that* is the last thing I want to do, but it is the right thing in this instance."

"Then perhaps she can be wed to one of our cousins in Tzidon, to strengthen our alliance with my uncle."

"No. I want her here to be High Priestess of Yisrael when I am gone. There is no one else suitable for that position—none of your wives, none of the other priestesses. The High Priestess of Ashtarti must be of her bloodline."

651

"Choose one from among my daughters to replace you then. Raise her as your own."

"Do you know nothing? A high priestess cannot be descended from the male line, Yoram. I am certain you were taught all of this, but I see you paid no attention whatsoever to your lessons concerning our religion."

He rolled his eyes to the side. "Forgive me for not taking an interest in things that were of no consequence to me."

I closed my eyes to maintain my composure. Then I said, "As High Priestess and her mother, Azba's future is *my* decision to make—not yours. That is the way these things are done. My marriage, Atalaya's marriage—these were arranged with my mother's and my consent. It cannot be any other way. My father and your father understood this and would never have made such arrangements on their own."

Yoram sighed heavily, while I continued, "You can use your other sisters for diplomacy, and your own daughters when they come of age. Azba is mine; you will not take her from me. She will go to my mother to be trained as my replacement, and she will return to us when her training is complete and the King of Aram is dead. My mother has already agreed to take her."

His expression turned to fury, and his voice cracked like a whip. "You arranged this without consulting *me*?"

Although I had jumped from the sudden anger in his voice, I raised my chin in defiance, and answered calmly, "Yes. She is the daughter of a high priestess—that takes precedence over being the daughter and sister of a king."

I could see that Yoram did not like this, but at last he consented. "Fine. Do as you will. I will let you have this one concession but understand that I will not tolerate your meddling and disobedience anymore after this. I am your king, and I expect you to defer to me in all other matters that affect the wellbeing of my house and my kingdom."

While his command grated on me, I held out my arms in defeat. "As long as you defer to me on all religious matters, Melekh, we are in agreement." I bowed my head, and then I turned to leave without waiting for his dismissal.

Apart from sending a score of priestesses responsible for Azba's education, administrative needs, and entertainment, I sent four daughters of some of Akhab's concubines to continue serving her as handmaidens. I charged Daryoush and Ba'alesar to escort her and her retinue to Yapo, where they would be met by ships my mother sent to carry them to Tzidon. Daryoush would accompany them, stay for a month tending to religious matters at the Temple of Ba'al in Zour, and then return to me; Ba'alesar would remain with his sister to help protect and look after her until I deemed it safe for them to return to Yisrael together.

Although it was technically closer to Aram, they were safer at Zour because the Arameans lacked the means to attack an island fortress surrounded by a powerful navy. They were men of the field, not men of the sea. Nevertheless, the decision to send Azba to Zour was carried out with little fanfare and my mother agreed to keep my daughter's arrival as quiet as possible, to avoid drawing unwanted attention to her presence there. Even her departure was quiet. It was only Yoram and Abshalom who joined me in the courtyard, where the traveling party assembled the morning of their departure.

This was a difficult parting. My visits to my childhood home were rare even before I became Gebirah; it could be many years before I saw my son and daughter again, and by then they would be grown. It was especially hard with Azba, for she was the one to whom I had grown closest of all my children, the one who was to follow closest in my footsteps, and she was still only a girl of ten years. I held her face and smiled upon her with tears in my eyes, saying, "You have done well, my daughter. When it is safe for you to return to Yisrael—when the King of Aram is dead and no longer a threat to our family—you will be a consecrated priestess of Ashtarti. We shall rejoice at your return."

"Yes, Ama," she answered with as much courage as she could muster. Although her voice shook and there were tears in her own eyes, she did not weep. She knew what was expected of a princess of Yisrael and future high priestess—like me, she would have to be the strength of her people one day, even though she would never be queen.

Seeing her in that moment, as I held her out to look at her one last time, my eyes stung. I understood the pain she was in and the strength it took to hold back. I stroked her cheek, and said, "I see in you the woman you will become. I am proud of that woman, Azba'alah. Never forget who you are and where you are from. You are a daughter of Akhab ben Omri. There is strength in that name." I pressed my fingers to her heart, "And in our blood. Call on that strength whenever you are in need."

She lifted her chin and drew up. Then at last I broke down and pulled her into my embrace. She buried her face in my robes and squeezed my waist. When we came apart, some of her kohl was smudged. I used the edge of my mantle to wipe it away and dry her eyes before I kissed her, and then I pressed her toward her elder brother. Ba'alesar placed a hand on her shoulder and gave me a single nod, then took her to her litter. That was when Abshalom ran to embrace her, and he was crying. My heart ached to see it, and I wondered if it was selfish of me to keep Abshalom with me when he and Azba were so close.

My family is being torn apart, I thought with some bitterness as I watched my children in that moment. Once Azba and Ba'alesar departed, I would have only Yoram and Abshalom left of my children with me in Yisrael. My only comfort was in knowing the others would return.

Once Ba'alesar had helped Azba into her litter, Yoram went to say farewell and give her his blessing. Meanwhile, Ba'alesar returned to embrace me one final time.

"Take care of your sister," I whispered.

He squeezed me tighter. "I will, Ama. You have my word—no harm shall come to her as long as I am there."

"I shall miss your music, my son. The palace will be much quieter without you here."

"It will give your hired musicians more to do then," he quipped. I laughed, and then I kissed him.

After saying farewell to my son, I went next to Daryoush. He gently pulled me into his arms and lifted my chin to draw me into a tender kiss. Then his thumb lightly slid across the ugly yellow mark upon my cheek where the bruise had been darkest. "I look forward to the day this sign of abuse is gone from your lovely face...but I know the scars upon your heart will take longer to heal. I give you my word, that I shall remain true while I am away. I belong to you, my Ba'alah, in body and soul."

We had not made love in weeks, for I was still sore and anxious, sensitive to touch. This was not normal for either of us, but he was remarkably patient; he never pushed or pressured me in any way. Whenever I apologized and suggested he find solace with the priestesses at the Temple of Ashtarti, he was quick to remind me that he loved only me and that I should not worry—that it was not the only reason he cared for me, and he was willing to go without for as long as it took me to heal. That made it easier for me to gradually come back to him, and now as we stood together before his departure, I smiled in gratitude. "I hope that when you return, I shall be ready again for...intimacy. I am beginning to miss it—to miss *you*. I think that is a good sign."

He ran his thumb over my lips and kissed me again. Then he breathed in, and said, "I shall miss your scent."

"It is only my anointing oil."

"The scent of a holy woman," he said, bringing my hand to his lips. "The scent of a goddess made flesh. The oil does not smell as sweet on the flesh of other holy women."

"Do you ever miss those days, of serving the priestesses of Ashtarti?"

He shook his head. "You are the only priestess I desire, Yezeba'al. The others are handmaids compared to you."

I let him kiss me again, and for the first time since Hadi took everything away from me, I felt a stirring of passion in my loins. It seemed a cruel twist of fate, that he would be gone when I was at last coming back to life. It would be a long month.

He rubbed his nose against the side of my neck once again, and then pulled away, saying, "I will return in time for the Feast of Ba'al."

"I look forward to your homecoming, my Ba'al."

"As do I," he said, bringing my hand to his lips. Then he looked at me with longing and held my hand a moment longer before stepping away to join the traveling party. He climbed upon his horse, assessed the state of the assemblage, and raised a hand to signal they were ready to leave. Then he looked back to wave one last time, while a single horn was blown to announce their departure. Ba'alesar rode in his chariot alongside Daryoush at the head of the entourage, while Azba's litter followed a few paces behind; the curtains were drawn so that she would not be seen as they made their way through the city. Once my lover and my children were out of view, I turned away to see Yoram fixing me with a hardened stare.

"What?" I snapped, wiping my tears away with the edge of my mantle.

"You should have been more discreet," he rebuked. While I scoffed and rolled my eyes, he persisted, "For an unmarried widow to show such open affection toward a man as though he was her husband—it will cause talk."

"Let them talk," I said bitterly. "I am not a young maiden in search of a husband, Yoram. I am an old woman. A high priestess. And he is my High Priest. It is a higher union than that between husband and wife."

"Abbu—"

"Was my High Priest and my husband. There is no comparison, I know. But Daryoush is all I have now. I do not expect you to honor him in your father's place, but you honor me as your mother." I raised my voice to continue, "And so, you will not rebuke me, for I do not answer to you."

"I am your king!"

Having started to walk away, I stopped and sized him up with my gaze, a bitter smile upon my lips. "Yes; my king, but *not* my god. It is only Ba'al I answer to—you should know that by now, Yoram."

With that, I headed to the temple to order a sacrifice for the safety of my children on their journey.

A short time after my children left for Zour, another Yahwist rebellion arose in the southern provinces, along the border with Moab. The news came while I was at temple overseeing preparations for the upcoming feast, so I was not present when the king met with his ministers. Yoram sent General Yehu to put down the rebellion. When I learned of this, I went to the king in the hope that there was still time to correct his error, only to find it was too late.

We were in the king's chamber. Yoram was seated in the window with one of his dogs, illuminated by a pattern of light and shadow caused by the cedar screen. It was the same window from which Zyah had thrown himself; I struggled not to think about it while his less capable successor sat there, stroking his dog's head, and fixing me with a cynical gaze. "He has already gone, Ama."

"Then send after him." I was furious, but kept my tone measured.

"I will not send after him. I have chosen Yehu for this task, and he will carry out my orders, as he always does."

As inconsistent as he could be, once Yoram's mind was made up, there was no changing it. Aware that I had lost, bitterness crept into my tone again. "You should have sent Dawid. He is loyal to us."

"Yehu is loyal to us."

"Yehu is sympathetic to their cause. He is one of them."

"He is *not* one of them. He is ours. And his success at putting down these rebellions with minimal bloodshed is commendable. Are you not the one who normally advocates for diplomacy over bloodshed?"

"Yes, but there is a difference between diplomacy and duplicity. When he goes to them and they listen to him, he is undermining us. I do not trust him to have our best interests at heart, and neither should you."

"You do not trust him because he serves a different god than you."

"I do not trust him because he continues toying with my son's heart! His loyalties are fickle—and you are too love-struck to see that he is using you to further the Yahwist cause."

His jaw tensed and there was darkness in his gaze. His voice low yet firm, he commanded, "Get out." When I did not move, he raised his voice in anger, "I said get out! You will obey me, woman, for I am your king!"

"A king who needs constantly to remind his subjects that he is a king is no king at all." Then I turned my back to him, ignoring the sound of things crashing in the chamber behind me. I was never moved by his tantrums as a child; I would certainly not be moved by them now.

After performing a ritual purification, I went to Akhab's tomb to pray and commune with him for the first time in months. I brought the customary offering and, after lighting the lamps, placed it upon the dust-covered altar amidst old forgotten offerings as I knelt upon the rug. It was another disappointment to see the altar in such a sad state without me to tend to it. Zyah had been so faithful, but Yoram could not be bothered with ritual, not even to honor his father. I felt

657

a stab of guilt for having neglected my husband's tomb, erroneously thinking that the king would continue to care for it in my stead.

I cleaned up the altar before I lit incense and spoke the usual prayers and incantations. Then I apologized to my husband for neglecting him, after which I sat in silence for a long time before I was finally able to put all my thoughts into words. I wanted desperately to feel something, but I was so hollow, so empty.

Finally, my voice cut through the deathly silence; small and fragile, like pieces of glass from a shattered vase. "I miss you."

Fresh tears pierced my eyes—at last, I felt something. I looked down at my hands in my lap, and forced myself to continue, "I keep myself busy; I pretend to be fine." I paused. My lips began to quiver. "But I'm not fine. I cannot do this without you, Akhab. Everything is falling apart, no matter how hard I try to hold it all together. And now..."

I had gone there intending to tell him about Yoram and Yehu and the rebellion. It seemed safer ground to tread. Instead, I broke down and told him about what happened with Hadi—it was the first time I had been to the tomb since that awful night. I confessed my feelings of shame and how powerless I felt, how hopeless I was beneath the façade I put on to get through each day.

"I am supposed to be the strength of our people, but how can I be strong without you beside me? *You* were my strength. My protector. What happened with Hadi...that would never have happened if you were still with us, Akhab. He would never have dared, but our son..." I shook my head. "He is not you. He is not capable of protecting me. He is not capable of protecting his kingdom. He makes enemies of his allies, denies our gods, and lets the Yahwists push their way and trample us underfoot. He will not listen to reason and is incapable of discerning who to trust and who to cast away."

I inhaled sharply as another wave of sorrow crashed over me, threatening to drown me. "He is not a good king. I fear we are all doomed. And I wonder if, in the end, it is all my doing. Have I failed us? Have I failed him? Have I failed our kingdom? Our children?"

When I could no longer fight the urge, I sank to the floor, buried my face in my hands and wept. Then I collapsed onto my side and, after exhausting my tears, lay still and unmoving in the loud silence of my husband's tomb. I do not know how much time passed, for I fell asleep with exhaustion. I was awakened when Eliezar came looking for me, his voice echoing down the stairs and the narrow corridor. "Ba'alah? Ba'alah, forgive me—I know you do not like to be disturbed when you are here, but much time has passed..."

I pulled myself up to sit in time to see him enter, carrying a torch. The chamber was dark otherwise, the lamps having long gone out. His keen eyes swept the chamber before falling upon me. He said nothing, but I knew what he was thinking.

"I am all right, Eliezar," I said, rubbing the tiredness from my face and massaging the ache from my neck and shoulder. "I must have fallen asleep." I shook my head. "Sleep evades me when I crave it, but it always finds me when I least expect it."

He continued to watch me with a dutiful expression. "May I help you to rise, Ba'alah?"

With a single nod, I held out my hand. He took it and pulled me up with little effort, while still holding the torch in his other hand. Such strength he had in his arms! It surprised me. I swayed a little once I was on my feet. Eliezar reached for me, but again I assured him I was all right. Then I looked at him with a smile, and said, "Say what you are thinking."

Now, he let his lips turn up. "A moment ago, you talked of sleep evading you until it finds you unaware. I was thinking that comes with age."

A chuckle rose in the back of my throat. "Come now, Eliezar— you are not yet old enough to know what comes with age."

"I am getting there, Ba'alah. I am thirty-seven."

Wrinkling my brow, I said, "Surely, you are not that old!"

He gave a nod. "But I am, Ba'alah."

I hummed. "Well, you are still a young man compared to my forty-three," I quipped.

Now, he laughed aloud. "Six years is not so much, Ba'alah."

I grinned. "That is true. Especially at our age," I winked, then raised my chin and looked toward the passage that led out of the tomb. Taking the lead with his torch, we emerged into a dark night. This left me momentarily disoriented because it had still been light outside when I had gone down into the tomb. I quickly shook it off as we returned to the palace.

When I entered my quarters, one of the handmaidens came to me right away, dropping to her knees. "Ba'alah, a messenger arrived from Yerushalyim, with a letter from Lady Atalaya." She held out the flattened papyrus scroll bearing my daughter's seal, the clay pressed into the cord with which it was tied. I took it and carried it to my inner sanctum, where Kora was instructing one of the younger handmaids in the care of my garments that were being put away. They stopped when I entered, but I waved for them to carry on and went into the study to read my daughter's letter. Kora followed me.

"Ba'alah?"

Looking back to see her standing hesitantly in the doorway, I beckoned for her to enter then continued lighting the wicks in the oil lamps. "It is a letter from Atalaya. I'm hoping it is good news."

"I received a letter from Ruta, as well," said Kora, coming all the way into the chamber. "My daughter reports that Melekh Yehoshapat is in poor health."

"Yes, he has been for some time now," I replied, as I sat at my desk and broke open the seal. "Has his condition worsened?"

She nodded. "It would seem so, yes. Ruta informs me Atalaya suspects he will not live another year—no doubt her letter will say much the same. I suspect that is what the messenger has come to report."

"Is he with the king?"

"He was, earlier," she replied. "Now, everyone has retired for the night."

"Yes, of course," I said, gesturing at my forgetfulness. Then I looked down to scan my daughter's letter. I raised a brow. "They are making preparations in anticipation for the inevitable. Yehoram has already taken on much of his father's duties…" Then, as an aside, I added, "which will soon be officially his anyway." I paused to read some more, then summarized, "The king is in good spirits, overall. He seems not to be troubled by the approach of his passing… He is eager to be done with." I chuckled and set the letter aside, taking the time to light another lamp. Then I lifted the letter again and squinted to see it better. I smiled. "Akhaz is in good health, taking well to the bow, and already driving a full-sized chariot! I cannot believe it!"

"He has always been taller than other boys his age," Kora observed with a smile.

"Yes, I suppose you are right. It is hard to believe ten years have passed since I became a grandmother for the first time." I sighed wistfully and kept reading. "Yahosheba is also in good health—praise

Ba'al. She remains as doting and dutiful toward her mother, as always—such a good, sweet child, our little Sheba."

My smile faded as I thought of her twin, my namesake. It had been two years since the spring fever had taken her and Aya and scores of other people in Yerushalayim. I laid the letter on the desk with a sigh and sat back, staring at the darkness outside the window. I did not share my current thoughts, instead pushing them away as I rose and stretched my back. "Well, I shall continue reading in the morning."

Pausing by Kora, I placed a hand on her arm just below her shoulder and looked upon her with a sad smile. "Thank you, Kora."

"For what?"

"For everything you do for me. Now, it is late, and you should be with your husband and sons while it is still just the three of you together."

She smiled and breathed deeply. "Yes, it is hard to believe Shmuel is taking a wife."

"You will be a grandmother soon enough," I menaced with a playful look in my eyes. Then we returned to my chamber.

"It's about time, though, considering my age," Kora said as we walked.

"You are only a few months older than me!"

"I know, but looking between us, one would think I am much older!" She pulled off her headscarf to unfurl a mess of grey curls. I raised my brows and my lips parted in surprise, while she smirked. "You see, Yezeba'al, why I say nothing when you complain of your strands of silver!"

"I shall never complain again," I said, feeling chastened as she began to rewrap her hair. "Here, let me help."

"You do not have to do this," she said, although she allowed me to take over.

"I know. I want to," I answered with a smile. "You do so much for me; it is truly the least I can do."

"You do more than you give yourself credit for, Yezeba'al," she said, turning back to me when I had finished. "You have given me and my family a good life, for which we are grateful. You have the greater duties to which you must attend—what we do for *you* is the least *we* can do to make your life easier."

661

"Well, if you should ever wish to retire," I said, trying to mask the sadness I felt at such a prospect, "never hesitate to speak to me on the matter and I will ensure the king provides you with a marvelous stipend as a reward for your lifetime of service."

"I swore an oath to serve you to the end of my days. I am not dead yet. Unless I am unable to serve, I will maintain that oath."

We embraced tightly before she departed, leaving only the handmaidens who were assigned to serve me that night. Wanting to be alone, I sent them to their sleeping quarters—a small chamber attached to my own, close enough to still be of service if I needed anything in the middle of the night, although I seldom did.

I went out onto the terrace overlooking the quiet gardens. Only the sound of running water and the occasional hoot of an owl disrupted the stillness of the night. Even the peafowl, often so loud during the day, were silent in their slumber as I leaned with my elbows on the terrace and looked up at the blanket of stars spread across the indigo sky. It was glorious to behold, and I was ashamed that I had not spent much time on my terrace at night since Akhab...

"We used to spend so much time out here at night, looking at the stars together," I murmured, thinking that perhaps he could hear me. I closed my eyes against the sting of tears, and yet I smiled faintly thinking of those happy days. I wondered if I took them for granted, foolishly thinking they would never end and Akhab would always be at my side. I thought of Daryoush—sweet, doting, dutiful Daryoush. How I loved him. I was so grateful to him. Yet, I could never love him the way I loved my Akhab, and I felt guilty for that. Was I depriving him of what he deserved, by keeping him devoted to me? I was loyal to him in body, yet my soul still ached for my husband.

I looked down at the garden and wondered briefly what it would be like to fall. Then I closed my eyes again, breathed deeply, and released those evil thoughts and feelings when I exhaled. I longed for deliverance—to be reunited with Akhab, my Ba'al—yet I knew my place was here, for as long as the Ba'alim willed it to be so. Yoram needed me, as much as he liked to pretend otherwise; and Abshalom was still too young to be without his mother, even if my other children were far away and could live without me. Against my desire, I pulled away from the edge of the terrace and returned to my chamber. Perhaps in my dreams, my husband would come to me again and give me peace.

Daryoush returned two days before the opening of the Feast of Ba'al. As I had hoped, I was able to provide him with the passionate homecoming he deserved and both of us needed. Afterward, we lay together in satisfied harmony, and he told me everything about the journey and how well my children were settling into their new temporary home by the time he left Zour. Azba and her grandmother were getting on well, and Ba'alesar enjoyed getting to spend time with his cousins and the uncle whose name he shared. Both children were looking forward to seeing how the Feast of Ba'al was celebrated and observed in the kingdom where our Ba'alim were most valued and worshipped, as neither of them were old enough to remember the glory days of our celebrations at Shomron when Akhab was still alive. Our Ba'alim feasts were still remarkable, to be sure, but they were a shadow of their former selves without a king who truly supported and believed in them. At least, I had my new High Priest with whom I could share the rituals, and we still had brilliant Asa to oversee the festivities.

Once all that had concluded, the court moved to Yezreel but I went instead to Megiddu. By the fifth year of Yoram's reign, he was spending less time at Megiddu and I was spending less time at Yezreel; he could not bear to see how the people of Megiddu favored me to him, and I could not bear to look at the naked skyline at Yezreel, to see the glaring absence of Akhab's monument. Besides, I had always preferred our palaces at Megiddu, which were more modern and spacious and comfortable than the old fortress at Yezreel.

There were, in fact, two palaces at Megiddu: the old palace, which had been used by all the kings of Yisrael since at least the time of Shelomoh, and the new palace built by Akhab's father and improved upon Akhab's ascension when he decided to make it the center of our family life. Upon his ascension, Zyah gifted the new palace to me and allowed me to set up my own court at Megiddu, because he knew how dear it was to me and Akhab. He would make the old palace the center for his own family; Yoram had chosen to do the same.

663

Few Yahwist zealots came to Megiddu in those days. Under me and Akhab, it had become a thoroughly Ba'alist center of religion, art, and culture that continued into my sons' reigns. As such, Daryoush and I could live together openly there with the support of our neighbors and friends. Apart from continuing our religious duties at the Ba'alist temples and holding court, we kept up a rather busy social life at Megiddu, hosting frequent entertainments for the city's elite just as Akhab and I had done. The only difference was that Daryoush was not interested in sport, so when those entertainments became tournaments, he sat with me to watch the other men compete in the chariot races and war games that Akhab always took part in.

I enjoyed having my lover in the royal pavilion, where I sat on a throne and he in a chair beside me. We were never alone, of course. There were always six courtiers seated on cushions, my four eunuchs standing guard, and a small yet varied group of attendants to keep cups full, fans waving, and cushions from going flat. Whenever we grew bored of the games, food, and company, my lover and I slipped away for a quick passionate interlude somewhere nearby, close yet far enough away from the others to avoid being observed. Then we returned feeling refreshed to watch the conclusion of the tournaments.

It was a shock when we returned from one of those interludes to find the king seated on the throne I normally occupied. Yoram usually preferred to stay at Yezreel among his soldiers and courtesans; he came to Megiddu only for the winter tournaments and to see his wives, and even that was rare. When he did come, he always competed with the other men, as his father had done before him. He never sat in the pavilion with us.

The governor of Megiddu and his concubine were among the six favored with permission to join us in the pavilion that day. They gave us a warning look when we emerged through the curtained doorway still clasping hands, our fingers laced together. We had been giggling like a pair of young lovers, until we noticed Yoram just before he turned his head to examine us with a look of disdain. We immediately released each other's hand, and Daryoush dropped to his knees to bow before the king. I remained standing and smiled.

"Yoram, what a pleasant surprise. I did not expect to see you here. Have you come to compete?"

"No, Ama," he said, glancing at Daryoush but not giving him permission to rise. Then he turned his gaze to me, and said, "I was surprised to find you missing when I arrived. I will not ask where you have been, nor what you have been up to—I will say only that I do receive reports of your activities, and I am not pleased by your behavior here."

He must have been referring to the extra awakening rituals I had been performing with my High Priest at the Temple of Ba'al. Although not severe, there had been an on-going drought for years, ever since Akhab died. Now that I had a new High Priest at my side, with the support of the other clergy Daryoush and I decided to step up our efforts to awaken Ba'al and bring the drought to an end. It seemed to be working—there was more rain than usual that year— but without Akhab, the awakening rituals were not as effective. Daryoush could not hold the essence of Ba'al as well as Akhab had, so it required more frequent couplings at the temple. Not that we minded the extra work.

I turned my gaze to the side. "Of course, you have been spying on me. I should have expected it." Then I looked at him, and said, "Will it surprise you if I do not care what you think of my activities? You see for yourself, the effects of our cause—the drought is coming to an end, Yoram. Beyond that, what I do here with my lover is none of your concern—we are doing nothing outside the laws of Yisrael."

Before he could respond, I added, "But surely, you have not come here to rebuke me."

"No, I have not. I have come to inform you that General Yehu has returned from successfully putting down the rebellion and has brought with him a messenger bearing news from Yerushalayim: Yehoshapat is dead."

After taking it all in, I replied, "I am surprised you came here yourself when you could have sent a messenger."

"The last messenger I sent, Ama, you kept waiting for nearly a week before you saw him."

I shrugged. "I was informed it was not urgent."

"Have you nothing to say for the King of Yehudah?"

Looking away, I said, "Not in particular."

Yoram frowned. "He was Abbu's friend. I thought he was your friend, as well."

665

"I will send my condolences to the new king. Will you be attending the funeral?"

"No, I am sending a contingent to represent us. Yehoram and Atalaya will be coronated together this coming spring, and of course Akhaz will be named Yehoram's successor."

"I want to be there for them."

"Yes, we will go together for the coronation, Ama."

I glanced at Daryoush, still on his knees. Annoyed that my son was not giving him permission, I bade him myself to rise. He looked uncertain, but my son did not object, and so he rose to stand beside me. Then I slipped my hand into his, and said, "As my spiritual advisor, I want Daryoush to accompany me, Melekh."

Yoram glared my lover, so I was surprised when he said, "Fine, but you will be discreet. You know how the Yehudans feel about such things, and I will not tolerate you bringing about more talk by flaunting yourselves before them. If you so much as bat an eye at him in public while we are there, Ama, I will banish him from the kingdom of Yisrael."

Forcing a smile, I bowed my head and held out my hands in acquiescence. "As you wish, Melekh."

He raised a finger, indicating for me to sit in the chair next to the throne.

Trying to hide my resentment at being made to take the lesser seat, I bowed my head in gratitude and sat down. Then I cleared my throat, and asked, "Will you be staying for the tournament?"

"No, I must return to my court at Yezreel."

"You neglect your court here."

"You mean *your* court?"

Ignoring his scathing tone, I continued, "If you stay away too long, they will grow to resent you."

"They have you, Ama: their goddess incarnate. They do not want or need me here."

"They need their king. If they do not want you, it is because you do nothing to curry favor with them."

"I should not have to—"

"In fact, you do the opposite. You give more to the zealots than you do for our people. They have taken note of it, and they do resent you for it. Instead of trying to earn back their favor, you alienate them further by neglecting them as you hide away at Yezreel playing with your soldiers, instead of managing your kingdom."

"I do manage my kingdom!"

"*All* of your kingdom—not just your armies and the people you like."

"You favor the Ba'alists!"

"I am their High Priestess. My duty has always been first to them. But you are their king. The people of Megiddu need their king as much as everyone else."

"You seem to be managing the needs of the people of Megiddu just fine without me!" He swept out his hand to indicate the governor and the other nobles in the pavilion, all of them now watching us more than they were watching the tournament.

"This is an important city," I said smoothly, keeping my voice low so that they would not overhear. "You cannot dismiss the nobility so easily. And your wives..."

"I do my duty. I have many sons to prove that. Let it be enough."

"Yoram."

"No, Ama. I do not want to talk about this. I command you to be silent."

I smirked and glanced at my guests, who silently offered their respect and support. They resented him also for the way he treated me, their adored patroness, but I would not tell him that or it would only further enflame his envy. Neither would I remain silent.

"You should have brought your ministers to hold court here, at least while the tournaments are being held. Then you might stay and enjoy yourself for a change."

"I do not have time for revelry," he said, finally rising from the throne.

You might be a better king if you did take time for revelry every now and then. It was not only the people of Megiddu who were growing to resent the king's lack of interest in their lives. He was aware that his popularity among the people of Yisrael was at an all-time low, while mine was soaring, at least among the Ba'alist majority. Instead of voicing my thoughts, however, I got up and bowed again to let him pass. I let out a sigh of relief when he was gone, and then I sank into my throne. Daryoush sat in his chair and took my hand, squeezing it before he brought it to his lips. I offered a grateful smile.

"You are my peace, Daryoush. Have I ever told you that?"

"All the time, my Ba'alah."

"I apologize for my son's behavior toward you. He is most unfair and ungrateful. And he wonders why he is losing the favor of his people." Then I remembered his previous admonition toward me. "How dare he tell me I am not allowed to show my favor to you while we are in Yerushalayim, just to appease a few ignorant zealots!"

"We will never have his support, but I do not think he is being unfair. We can control ourselves while we are in Yehudah. I will not allow myself to be sent away from you by breaking the king's commandment—he is not asking much."

"It is not about *what* he is asking—it is about the way he commands me. I do not appreciate his tone and his self-righteousness."

"He is the king."

"His father was king. Akhab never treated me or any of his women that way. I do not know where our son gets it from."

"Perhaps he comes by it naturally," Daryoush said dryly.

I turned my gaze to the side and smiled wickedly. "If he ever dares to exile you, I will follow wherever you go, my love."

"You cannot, and you know that. You are the Gebirah of Yisrael."

"I am High Priestess of the Ba'alim first."

"And Yisrael needs her High Priestess."

With a reluctant nod, I admitted, "You are right, Daryoush. That is why you are my spiritual advisor, and I need you at my side."

"And that is why, for the duration of our stay in Yehudah, we can behave ourselves in public. I will still come to your bed for worship if you summon me while we are there."

"I will summon you every night, and you will make love to me until dawn—and I do not care if every zealot in Yerushalayim hears the sounds of our lovemaking."

"Yezeba'al," he said sternly, not without affection. "Do not be intentionally contradictory. We do not want to cause trouble—neither with your son, nor with the people of Yehudah. We already have enough to worry about with the zealots here."

"I am tired of these strictures against us. What right do they have to tell us what we can and cannot do together? I am the High Priestess—you are my High Priest."

He tipped his head to the side. "Of course, and our people understand this. But you know there are some who do not—even the king struggles to understand the sanctity of our union. In Yehudah, I am certain we will encounter a great deal more of them who see it differently than us. The Yahwist cult has always been strongest there."

"Were it not forbidden by the law because I am Gebirah, I would take you as my husband and be done with it—then not even the zealots could say we are doing anything wrong."

"They would still find a reason to be against us."

I studied him while he turned his head to watch the men in the field. Then I asked, "Daryoush?"

"Hmm?" He turned back to me. "Yes, my love?"

I began fidgeting with the edge of my mantle. "Are you...happy here with me? Living like this? And don't say yes simply to please me."

"I was not going to."

I looked up, my lips parting in surprise.

He was smiling. "I was going to say *yes* because it is true."

Relief washed over me, and I relaxed as he took my hand. "I love our life together, Yezeba'al: serving our gods and loving each other the way they intended for us. I do not need the law to tell me it is acceptable to love you, when the Ba'alim have deemed it acceptable. I do not see anything wrong with our union, and neither should you. Do not let worldly principles and Yahwist sentiments cloud your judgment. I am devoted to you, my Ba'alah—not because I must be, but because I want to be."

With a smile, I pulled him to me as I leaned over to kiss him on the lips. Then with our elbows resting on the arms of the throne, he held my face, and we pressed our foreheads together. In our own little world, where even the people surrounding us could not intrude, the last of my worries finally collapsed.

669

29

Outside Influences

Atalaya was glorious in her coronation regalia. She stood beside her husband by a pillar in the Temple of Shelomoh, while the High Priest of Yahowah anointed them with the same holy oils with which I had been coronated so many years before. My eyes blurred as I beheld my daughter, the High Priestess of the Ba'alim in Yehudah, now also its Melkah. Her new title suited her. If only we could convince her husband to erect a true temple to our gods, so that she could perform the most sacred of our rites. Unfortunately, the people of Yehudah clung more fiercely to their god than even the people of Yisrael, and Yehoram was more cowardly than my Yoram was inconsistent. He preferred our gods but believed in the supremacy of Yahowah in his kingdom. It was for that reason, above all others, that his marriage to my daughter had grown cold: Atalaya was unforgiving of such weakness.

Publicly, there was no sign of trouble in the marriage of Yehudah's new monarchs. There was talk, however, of the new king's apparent frailty: he did not look well in his coronation regalia. Yehoram had never been strong the way that his father and uncle had been, but neither had he appeared physically weak until now. It was shocking when we arrived at Yerushalayim a few days before, to see that the new king of Yehudah was a shadow of his former self: his once bronze skin had paled, and his intelligent eyes had lost their spark.

Standing in a place of honor among the other heads of state and their representatives, I heard whispers about how ill the new king looked in comparison to his wife, who clearly outshone him in health as well as character. She was much-admired, but he was only to be pitied. One king I overheard had objected to that sentiment, saying, "Melkah Atalaya is the one you should pity, having to be married to him. She deserves a strong man to be her husband—a warrior, fit to share her bed."

"Hush, you idiot," his companion whispered. They were standing not far behind me, somewhat to the left; although I faced forward, with only a slight shift of my gaze I could see them from my peripheral vision. He pointed. "That is her mother, the Gebirah of Yisrael. She might not like to hear what you are suggesting about her daughter, hmm?"

The men fell silent then, and I feigned ignorance as the ceremony continued. I nearly smiled at their obliviousness: Atalaya had never shown an interest in warriors of any kind, preferring the more cultured and intellectual man when she was even interested in a man at all. When their marriage had begun, they seemed well-suited for one another. Now, knowing how far they had drifted apart, and seeing how sickly the king appeared, I cast my gaze around at all her husband's brothers and nephews, and at his other sons. Akhaz was the eldest of Yehoram's sons, but he had no other by Atalaya.

We were in the garden after the celebrations had concluded when I broached the subject with her. It was not the same garden where Hosha had drunkenly attempted to seize me. This was the women's garden and, although we were sitting apart from the rest of the king's women, we were surrounded by them and all the king's children. The garden was abuzz with voices and laughter, but it was stifling because there was very little breeze in the enclosed space. I much preferred our gardens at Megiddu and Shomron which were more open and newer in design. Atalaya had also complained about it a great deal in the early years of her marriage, but now she seemed used to it.

Seated on a cushion, she was dressed in a simple robe that left so little of her flesh bare, I wondered how she could stand the heat even with her attendants fanning her. I had never cared for the strict southern conventions and dressed as I often did in whatever fashion appealed to me that day. As it was unseasonably warm, I was dressed in a Sidonian gown of thin purple linen that exposed my right breast and hugged my form: not much was left to the imagination. At first, when I had appeared in the garden wearing that gown, the other women were scandalized but by now their interest had thankfully faded so that my daughter and I could talk, while my youngest son played with his niece and nephew nearby.

Watching the two boys, who were the same age, I said in a hushed tone, "The king is not looking well these days."

671

I heard Atalaya take in a sharp breath. When I turned my gaze to look upon her, she had lowered her face and was fidgeting with the edge of her mantle. "The death of his father has been...difficult for him. He is often tired, isolating himself in his private quarters, and not eating well. But it is only his grief. His physicians believe that he will recover his health by the end of the year."

"That is not all that is wrong with him," I said, glancing around to be sure we were not overheard. "You know it as well as I do."

She exhaled and looked away. "His physicians say—"

"What they are paid to say. One need only look upon him to see his health is in decline. If he dies—"

"Akhaz will inherit the throne."

"*Akhaz is only a boy of ten years.* And while I am certain you could hold your own against Yehoram's other wives, it is too much of a risk not to have other sons in the line of succession." I paused to sip from my cup, watching the children at play. They were still so innocuous, unaware of all that was at stake. "Will Yehoram's brothers accept your son as their king?"

"Of course. We have their full support."

I smiled knowingly. "You have already reached out to discuss the future with them. That is wise. But are you sure you can trust them not to put their own interests ahead of what is good for the kingdom?"

"They know *my son* is what is good for this kingdom, and they trust me to guide him – with their involvement."

I hesitated to say what I was thinking next, but it needed to be said. "And...if he should die without heirs? What then? You have no son to replace him."

She looked down at her lap, and her cheeks reddened. "I am in the process of seeking a suitable wife for him. As soon as he is old enough to wed and mature enough to produce heirs, he will take a wife."

"You should have more children."

"I do not want more children, Ama."

"You need to secure the dynasty."

"It is secure."

672

"You have *one* son—if something happens to him before he can produce heirs, your husband's other sons will inherit the throne. Or one of their uncles will take it by force, unwilling to submit to a child-king. Is that what you want?"

"I have the utmost faith Akhaz will grow to manhood and produce heirs."

"That is my hope, as well, but that is not a guarantee. Yehoram has many brothers and sons and cousins and uncles—all with their eyes on the throne of Yehudah." With that, I held out my hand, sweeping it to indicate all the sons and brothers of the king still young enough to be in the women's garden: they were only a small fraction of the competition Akhaz would face, were he left to rule before reaching manhood.

Atalaya scoffed. "It will not happen, Ama."

"You do not know that with any certainty. I once thought the same as you, but I made sure to provide my husband with plenty of sons to ensure the survival of *our* line."

"You worry too much. What happened to Zyah..." She paused and looked down, but not before I had glimpsed the pain on her face. "That will not happen here."

"That is not a chance you should take. Many things may cause the death of a king. Our line needs to be preserved. It is our duty to put the needs of our kingdoms and family above personal happiness."

"That is easy for you to say—you and Abbu were well-matched."

"You and Yehoram—"

"Performed our duty. Now, we prefer to live separate personal lives."

"And you may continue to do so, but you should at least come together long enough to give him another son or two."

"Your mother only had two children—you and my uncle. Our bloodline in Tzidon is secure. It will be the same here."

I shook my head. "You are taking too great a risk. As the chief wife of the king, you must preserve the kingdom for your children."

"And I have done so."

When I was about to speak again, she cut me off. "I will not hear any more of this, Ama. Do not meddle in my affairs." Then she got up and walked away, followed by the ladies who were appointed to her service that day.

I sighed heavily and looked to my young granddaughter, who had paused from her play and was watching with concern. Smiling to put her at ease, I beckoned to her. She came to me with a sweet smile and placed her hands upon my thigh as I gently brushed some loose hair away from her cheek. "*Amami*, is Ama all right?"

"She is well, Yahosheba. Do not worry a thing about it."

"Are you all right?"

"I am well, my child. But tell me, have you begun yet to train for the priestesshood?"

She nodded bashfully.

"That is good."

"Ama says that I am to become a priestess like her and you."

"Yes. You will become the High Priestess of Yehudah one day, when your mother can no longer perform that duty. Her sister, Azba'alah, will replace me in Yisrael one day. Together, you will ensure the goddess Ashtarti continues to be honored and worshipped here as she has always been."

She nodded but lowered her gaze. "Ama says the people of Yehudah call her Asherah."

"That is true, but in Tzidon, she is called Ashtarti. I prefer to call her by that name."

"Ama says that Asherah is married to Ba'al, but Abbu says she must marry Yahowah instead so the people of Yehudah will continue to honor her."

I furrowed my brow. "Your Abbu says this?"

She nodded. "It is what *Ababu* Hosha said." Then she looked down and her cheeks became flushed. "Ama says we are descended from Asherah and Ba'al, and that you are the goddess incarnate and that *Ababu* tried to marry you when *Abumi* Akhab died, because he wanted to make Asherah wed Yahowah so the people would stop fighting."

"Is that so?"

Her dark eyes found my gaze. "Is it not true, what Ama said?"

"It is true, but I did not know that was what your *Ababu* meant to do when he...spoke to me last. And it is not right to force the goddess to take another husband when she has one already: her true husband and mate is Ba'al. She can wed no other."

"But...*Ababu* said that her husband is dead, and she needs a new husband to guide her."

674

"*Ba'al is not dead!*" Yahosheba jumped at the fierceness of my tone. Realizing myself, I softened it, as I went on, "Ba'al yet lives, but he was cursed by his rival and is trapped in Ertsetu – Sheol – for part of the year."

"When the rains do not come?"

I nodded, relieved that she understood this—so she had not been completely misled by her father and grandfather's insanity. "He returns to his bride each year and brings the rains with him whenever they are successfully reunited in the flesh."

"Does *Abumi* bring the rains when he comes back to Yisrael?"

I brought my hand to my lips, attempting to stifle a laugh even as my eyes stung with tears. "*Abumi* Akhab cannot return to Yisrael, for his body has died—but his soul lives in Ba'al, and Ba'al comes to me through my High Priest, although he cannot stay as he once did. But I know in my heart that he will return in another form, in another lifetime, as will I—as we already have—and we will be united once again. And one day, I know the curse on his soul will be vanquished, and Ba'al will never have to be taken from Ashtarti again, and they will live together for eternity in perfect harmony and bliss."

"Will *Ababu* also return?"

"I do not know. He was only a man—he was not a god incarnate."

"Only the gods can take new forms?"

My lips parted and I regretted that I had no definite answer for her. Did other souls take on new forms, as well? It was not something I had ever thought to wonder until now. I knew only what I felt and experienced—that I had lived before and would live again, and that the same was true for my husband. At last, I admitted, "Perhaps, but I do not know all the answers, Yahosheba. No one in the form of a man can know all the answers. We are limited in this place, in these bodies. They are frail in their understanding."

"Even for a goddess incarnate?"

I nodded. "Even for a goddess incarnate. Now, that is enough questions for the day. You have a keen mind, Yahosheba. That is a good thing, but *Amami* is tired and needs her rest. Go and play with your brother and uncle, hmm?"

675

She threw her arms around my neck, and we kissed before she ran off. Then I pulled myself from the cushion and went to my guest quarters to find my lover, eager for the comfort of his embrace.

Daryoush and I had behaved perfectly while at Yerushalayim, such that no one there would ever have known we were lovers if not for the fact they had heard about the nature of our relationship beforehand. Yoram continued to treat him with barely concealed disdain, but he was received with all the respect his station commanded and treated well throughout our stay in Yehudah. Nevertheless, it was a relief when we could return to our usual openness at Megiddu, while Yoram went to Shomron with the rest of the court to resume the governance of our kingdom.

Our concerns for the kingdom of Yehudah could not yet be put aside, however. We were only a few days returned to our routine when we heard that Edom had rebelled against Yehudah's new king. It all happened so fast that Yehoram did not even have the chance to rally his troops and send for allies. Edom was now an independent kingdom, its former governor proclaimed king. There was talk that Yehoram would attempt to recover Edom, but it seemed unlikely in his condition.

Atalaya reported that his health continued to decline; apart from his previous symptoms, he complained of chest pain and was often seized by coughing fits that left those around him anxious for the future. Without a strong king, Yehudah was more at risk than it had ever been throughout Yehoshapat's reign. I worried for my daughter and sent to her, but she sent back that apart from the king's health, all was well within Yerushalayim. She was working with the king's ministers and training Akhaz for his future role, and measures were being taken to secure the borders while ensuring the loyalty of the other provinces. As usual, Atalaya was unconcerned, and I hoped she was not overestimating the abilities of her husband's ministers and generals to keep the kingdom from collapsing altogether during this tumultuous period.

It was not only Yehudah that struggled in the period following the death of Yehoshapat. Soon the loss of Edom seemed of little concern compared to the growing instability throughout the region.

Over the next three years, Yisrael and Tzidon remained stable during this time, but many of the other kingdoms around us were not. To the south and east of us, the nomadic Qedar tribes, who had long been united under Gindibu, were increasingly at war as factions arose among them, pushing for an alliance with Assyria. Gindibu had to appeal to the kings of Aram and Ammon to help him keep the tribes united under his rule, and soon the *de facto* king of Edom began to offer his aid to the same. Fearing an alliance between our enemies and the Qedarites, Yisrael and Yehudah began to tighten our own alliances with Egypt, Kush, and the kingdoms along the western sea. As such, we were beginning to feel increasingly cornered, though hoping the eastern kingdoms would remain too preoccupied over the ever-growing Assyrian threat to bother with our kingdoms in the west.

Then, after these three years of mounting tension, came shocking news from Damaseq: my cousin Hadi had been murdered by his steward, Hazael, who had set himself up as Aram's new king. My joy at the death of Hadadesar was overshadowed by reports that the prophet Elisha was at Damaseq when the murder took place, amidst rumors that Hazael had declared himself a follower of the zealous Yahwist sect. Elisha had seemed less threatening to us than Eliyahu, but now we began to wonder if he posed an even greater threat than his predecessor. Fearing the zealots might again begin to work against us in our kingdom, I made one of my increasingly rare appearances at court. With the support of his ministers, I urged my son to send out an edict that would tighten the laws against seditious preaching and to have executed any prophets known or believed to speak against us.

Shaken by the murder of another king by his own servant—however deserved in this case—my son agreed, and the second great Yahwist purge began. Ever the master entertainer, Asa had envisioned turning these executions into a public spectacle the likes of which had never been seen in Yisrael. He suggested that, apart from providing entertainment to the masses, it would also inflict fear into the hearts of any who could be swayed to the zealous cause. Most of the ministers were in favor of it, and to my surprise, Yoram was delighted by the idea. Once the purge began, he attended many of the executions himself and, according to the reports brought to me, quite enjoyed himself—the bloodier the better. While I approved of these measures, I withdrew once again to my palace at Megiddu with my lover and our priestly court, eager to partake in our more spiritual forms of entertainment.

Meanwhile, I decided it was time to bring Ba'alesar and Azba'alah home to Yisrael now that my cousin was no longer a threat. I sent a message to my mother and daughter at Tzidon, informing them that I would soon be arriving to escort my children home, and requesting ships be sent to meet me at Yapo in a fortnight. When the time came, I traveled with Daryoush, accompanied by Kora and my usual entourage. Upon boarding at Yapo, I was greeted by the captain and Kourosh, a young priest of Ba'al in my mother's service who turned out to be Daryoush's younger brother.

Daryoush was pleased to be reunited with the youngest of his brothers, a man of twenty-three years, and to introduce me to him for the first time. I found Kourosh to be a respectable and capable young man if a bit shy. Apart from having been appointed by my mother to escort us to Zour, Kourosh had been charged with delivering a letter from my daughter, written on a scroll of papyrus in her own hand and bearing her seal. The shy young priest could barely get himself to meet my gaze when I accepted the letter and thanked him for it. As I took it to my cabin, where I would read it after I had the chance to settle in, Daryoush teased me, "My love, I think my little brother is enamored of you."

"Too bad for him, I am smitten with you," I teased him back, tugging at his beard. I dropped the letter on a table, just before he grabbed me around the waist and, growling, drew me toward the bed. The ship would not be leaving until morning, so we had time before the seasickness consumed me.

After making love with Daryoush, I slipped on a thin robe and broke the seal on the papyrus, while he poured us drinks. I smiled, accepted the cup he offered, took a sip, then placed it on the nightstand before I began reading the letter aloud:

"To the most esteemed and holy Ba'alah Ashtarti, Yezeba'al Gebirah Yisrael, from her most devoted daughter Azba'alah, priestess of Ashtarti: I thank you for your dear letter, Ama, and look forward to our reuniting after these years apart. You will be pleased by the progress I have made under the tutelage of my dearest *Amami* Azra, and the fondness I have developed for her as my mentor and esteemed guardian. As you know, I have for two years now been practicing my sacred profession in preparation for my eventual role as a high priestess of the Most High. In my time here, I have also developed a deep love for Tzidon and her most loyal people, most especially for a certain priest of Ba'al whom you will soon meet."

I paused and looked over the top of the papyrus at my lover, who smiled back, while I continued reading aloud: "With the support of my grandmother, the most noble High Priestess of the Ba'alim in Tzidon, and my uncle the King of Tzidon, I have decided to marry this man and to make him my high priest when the time comes for me to replace my dear *Amami* as the High Priestess..."

I stopped, for a moment unbelieving of what I read. I looked up to reread in silence from the beginning of the sentence, and then continued to read aloud from where I had left off: "...of Tzidon. Forgive me, dearest Ama, but I will not return with you to Yisrael. It is my greatest desire to remain in Tzidon, where I will serve the people of the Ba'alim without prejudice and threat of expulsion or bodily harm."

Finally, unable to read any further, I crumpled the papyrus in my fists. "Ugh! Can you believe it, Daryoush? She wants to stay in Tzidon!"

"I...cannot blame her," he said, getting up and coming to me.

"What?" I turned an accusing gaze on him and shrugged his hands off me.

"Yisrael is a difficult place for our people, my love. Especially as the zealots continue to sway the people against our gods. You have often complained of it yourself."

"No! You cannot support her in this! She is abandoning our people there!"

"It does not matter what I think, love. The Gebirah and Melekh support her."

"My mother... Of course. My mother put her up to this! It is in my daughter's hand, but the decision entirely belongs to my mother! She has no one to replace her in Tzidon—she has never cared for the alliance with Yisrael! Never wanted me to be made High Priestess there! She accepted it, but only because I was eager for it. I am certain this was her plan all along. She conspired to take Azba from me and reshape her in her own image! She cannot do this to us! I'll not allow it! How dare she meddle in our kingdom's affairs!"

"Yezeba'al, please," Daryoush attempted to calm me. Nevertheless, I continued railing against Azba's decision and my mother's scheming for much of the night, until I had exhausted my rage. By the end of it, my fury had turned to lamentations for our people in Yisrael and I wept bitterly. By the time we set sail in the morning, I was fast asleep. Daryoush stayed beside me for much of the voyage, holding back my hair whenever I was sick, and leaving me only when Kora was there to tend to me. It was a relief when we were moored at the southern docks at Zour for the night, giving me time to recover from the voyage before meeting my family—and going to war—the following morning.

My normally docile, obedient younger daughter surprised me with the force of her passion and determination. Once the greetings were out of the way and we had been escorted to my mother's quarters in the palace, I wasted little time turning all my fury upon my mother, only for her to hold out her hands. "Do not look at me, Yezeba'al. This was entirely Azba's decision."

I scoffed. "Azba is only a girl of fourteen years—too young to know her own mind and make such decisions."

"You were a girl of fourteen when you made the decision to marry Akhab, and by all accounts it was a happy decision."

"The decision was made *for* me, and I consented. That is not the same thing."

She shrugged. "What of it? Azba wants this and so do I."

"It is not about what Azba wants."

"No, of course not—it is about what *you* want. As it always is."

"It is about the kingdom of Yisrael! About our people there—the people who need our presence most, and you would have her abandon them in your selfishness!"

Standing by helplessly, Azba finally raised her voice above ours: "Enough!"

I had not once heard my youngest daughter's voice raised in such a way, and I suspect neither had my mother, for we both were silenced and turned to look at Azba in surprise.

"Will the two of you kindly stop bickering and let me speak? This is about *my* future, is it not? My life, my profession, my

680

happiness—and yes, our people need guidance. But, Ama, I am not the one to give it to them. Not in Yisrael. I cannot go back there. I will not."

"Your happiness is important to me, daughter, but we have a duty to put the wellbeing of our people above personal happiness. What *is* it about your generation that does not seem to understand?"

My mother could not help herself, cutting in dryly, "I would have said yours was the same."

I turned a sharp gaze upon her. "You are not helping!"

"I do not intend to," she shrugged. "Forgive me, Yezeba'al. I am on your daughter's side in this matter. You will find you are outmatched."

Azba turned a look of gratitude upon my mother, which only angered me further. I tensed my jaw and had to take a deep breath to maintain my composure in the face of such bold opposition. "She is *my* daughter! I make the decisions for her! That has always been the way of it! You have no right." I held up my palm to indicate my unwillingness to hear anymore from her and turned to my daughter. "Azba'alah, you are coming back to Yisrael with me and your brother. There is no point in arguing against it and seeking allies, because it is not your decision to be made. You will replace me as the High Priestess of Yisrael. You will be the beacon for our people there when I am gone."

"No!" she insisted vehemently, clenching her fists and stamping her foot on the floor. "I am not leaving Tzidon. I am not leaving the people here without a high priestess—for they are the *true* people who never waver in their devotion. And I am not leaving my husband nor taking him to face opposition in Yisrael as you have faced!"

The argument on my tongue was silenced at once. "Your...husband?"

"Yes, my husband," she insisted, her chin raised defiantly even as her eyes filled with tears. "We were married before the Ba'alim a few days before you arrived. I am already with child by him. And I refuse to let my child be born and raised in a kingdom that will never truly accept us and our ways."

My mouth fell open in a wordless question as I turned to my mother. It was clear by her expression that she had known all along. "You...allowed her to carry on with a man to whom she was not married? I recall a time not so long ago when a man was executed for even considering carrying on with me in such a way!"

"Yezeba'al, this is different. She was not betrothed to a king."

"Who is he? Who is this man who has violated my daughter? *Where* is he? I command for him to be presented to me at once!"

I noticed my daughter's gaze fall upon someone across the room. I turned to see Kourosh's bloodless face, his body trembling, where he stood beside his brother. Daryoush was looking at him, too. Narrowing my gaze, I demanded of my lover, "Did *you* know of this?"

Daryoush turned to me, a look of surprise on his face. He shook his head. "Yezeba'al..."

"Do not use my name, Daryoush—you will answer me as your goddess and your queen, for that is all I am to you in this moment."

"Ba'alah," he began, taking a step forward.

My daughter rushed before me then and fell to her knees, "Ama, please! He did not know any more than you! I swear to it— Kourosh was under my command, not to speak a word of our marriage or relationship to anyone, not even to his brother. Do not blame anyone but *me*—not *Amami*, not even Kourosh, who is the love of my being. As Abbu was to you, so he is to me! *They* did not do anything that I did not require of them."

"My mother—"

"*Amami* did not know he was coming to me—not at first. I told her only when your letter came, and when I knew I was with child."

"He violated you!"

"No!" she insisted, shaking her head. "He came to me because I asked him to. *I* was the one who brought him to my bed. He acted only upon my encouragement. He would never have dared otherwise."

I clenched my fists at my side and pressed my eyes shut, trembling as my self-righteous wrath was countered by my understanding of her words; words which echoed my own from so long ago. How could I blame her for doing what I had once tried to do? How could I blame him for falling for her, loving her, as my first priest of Ba'al had done the same for me? Would I be like my own parents and demand his life be taken for doing what came naturally to lovers? Would I jealously punish them for getting away with it? Would I take away my daughter's happiness when such things are so fleeting in this world?

682

Breathing out the last of my rage, I opened my eyes and looked upon my daughter and her husband. "I will accept this marriage, but only under one condition: you will both return to Yisrael with me, and you will serve there when I am gone, as it was always intended."

Azba went to her husband, taking his hand and leading him toward me, even as the young man continued trembling. Daryoush stepped forward with them, perhaps fearing I may yet lash out at his younger brother; or perhaps he was attempting to sooth his brother's fear. When they approached, Kourosh dropped to his knees and prostrated himself worshipfully. Weeping, he begged, "Ba'alah, I meant no disrespect. Thank you for your mercy."

"We will not return with you," Azba said, firmly meeting my gaze. Her husband rose to his knees and looked up at her with eyes wide, as she continued, "I have made my decision."

Rather than be incited to further anger, I almost laughed. "You are not at liberty to make that decision, Azba. It is mine to make—and the king's. And you have already broken the law by taking a husband without first seeking his approval."

Taking a step closer, she said, "If you force me to return to Yisrael, I will leave the moment you are gone to be with Ba'al. I will not serve there. I will return to Tzidon with my husband and our children, and you will not have your way." I was about to speak, but she held up her hand, and continued, "But…if you will permit me to stay in Tzidon with my husband, and for us to raise our children here together…I will come to Yisrael to take over for you when you are gone, provided I have daughters to leave here in my stead. I give you my word, Ama. Let that be enough."

What could I do? I did not doubt the truth in her words. She had bested me, and I realized then that I had always underestimated her. Atalaya, her elder sister, I had always seen as the strong one; the clever one. I had seen Azba'alah's outward beauty and the gentleness of her character, but I had overlooked her cunning. She had never had reason to outwit me until now. My gaze fell on her abdomen—there was the slightest protrusion, which I had not noticed before, for she had kept her mantle about her. I cupped my hands over my mouth. Then I looked up to meet my daughter's gaze— my youngest daughter, now soon to be a mother. Could I blame her for wanting to do what she thought was best for the child in her womb?

"You may stay in Tzidon, to raise your children here, so long as you permit me to visit you from time to time."

Suddenly, I felt a warm hand on my shoulder. It was Daryoush. I did not even realize he was standing beside me. Now, when I looked at him, Azba offered me a slight nod and a reassuring smile. I took his hand, and then I turned back to my daughter who was urging her husband to his feet. When he was standing at her side, she held his hand, lacing their fingers together, and turned to me. "Ama, Kourosh and I would be pleased if you would come to our home as often as you like and stay as our most honored guest." She placed a hand over her heart and bowed her head graciously.

And so, it was decided that my son Ba'alesar would return to Yisrael with me to serve in his brother's court, but Azba'alah and Kourosh would remain in the kingdom of Tzidon to raise their family and serve the Ba'alim there until such a time when she would come to Yisrael to replace me as High Priestess. Meanwhile, I would visit as often as I could.

My mother was amenable to this plan, which Azba'alah herself had devised, and even I could not deny the genius of it. Provided she and Kourosh had at least two daughters come of age, both the kingdoms of Tzidon and Yisrael would have high priestesses to safeguard the people's devotion to the Ba'alim, just as the kingdom of Yehudah would have the same from Atalaya and any granddaughters she might have through Yahosheba. Ironically, once I got used to the idea, I could not be more pleased with it. By the time I returned to Yisrael, I had faith and hope for the future of our three kingdoms. If only I had not underestimated our rivals and their ability to lead the people of Yisrael astray.

30
Legacy

When the news came from Tzidon that Azba'alah had safely delivered a daughter, who was given the name Shammuramat, I rejoiced. With her birth, I now had twenty-two grandchildren of my blood yet living, of whom fourteen were legitimate. If my sons had any other illegitimate children, I was not aware of them. My mother had informed me that Ba'alesar, now approaching his eighteenth year, had kept the company of several women while in Tzidon, so it was likely he had left behind at least one illegitimate child. With such a bountiful progeny, I gave thanks to my god in the Temple of Ba'al at Megiddu, never forgetting what he had done for me when I thought I might never have a single child of my body.

From my own private coffers, I paid for the sacrifice of three bulls, ten calves, twenty-five lambs, forty goats, and ten-score quails and doves that would be used to feed my guests at a banquet I hosted in the honor of my newest granddaughter. Every time a legitimate grandchild was born, I hosted a feast in their honor and invited all those who had earned my favor by their loyalty and service to us and to the Ba'alim. As always, I put my brother-in-law and former lover in charge of planning the affair. Now that he had come of age, Ba'alesar joined his uncle Asa in the planning. I was pleased to see he was as naturally gifted as Asa and would make a fitting replacement when the time came.

Daryoush and I presided over the banquet at the head table, which was set up outside in the courtyard. There was more room for all the guests, and we could see the moon and stars overhead on this perfect, clear night. We were watching an exciting show with acrobats and fire dancers, which followed a musical performance led by Ba'alesar and the court musicians, when Captain Eliezar approached with an anxious expression. His position as the captain of my eunuchs exempted him from prostrating himself before me,

685

especially where matters of security were concerned. He knelt beside the cushion where I sat, bowed his head, and spoke quietly so as not to be overheard by my guests. "Ba'alah, forgive the intrusion."

Setting down my cup and keeping my gaze on the performance, I clapped and smiled so as not to cause alarm from those of my guests who noticed him speaking to me. "What is it, Eliezar?"

"I have arrested three eunuchs who were, just now, caught attempting to permit the entry of a group of zealots into the palace."

Although I raised my brows in surprise, I kept my expression calm and glanced at Daryoush, who was not as practiced at keeping the concern from showing on his face. I took his hand and squeezed to remind him of the necessity not to cause alarm. Meanwhile, I spoke to Eliezar, "And what of the zealots?"

"Most of them were captured, Ba'alah, but several fled before they could be apprehended. The city watch has been alerted and is searching for them. Should they be hiding within the city, they will be brought to justice."

"Not many would knowingly shelter zealots in Megiddu. What was their intent?"

"I do not know for certain, Ba'alah, as they have yet to be interrogated but...they were found with weapons and apart from interrupting the festivities, I believe their main intent was to assassinate you."

Daryoush cursed aloud, and I could feel the heat of anger emanating from his body. Again, I squeezed his hand reassuringly, while Eliezar continued, "Ba'alah, I suspect this is not an isolated incident. With your permission, I would like to launch an investigation to determine if there are any others among our ranks who were involved, including those who may have Yahwist sympathies, and to execute those who give me cause for suspicion."

I smiled and raised my hand at the acrobats and fire dancers as they concluded their performance, while nodding to Eliezar's request. "Arrest them, question them, but do not have them executed until I have had the chance to survey all the evidence against them."

"Ba'alah, with all due respect, I think if there is even the suspicion of Yahwist sympathies among my own ranks of eunuchs, it should not be tolerated. They should be executed or imprisoned at the very least."

686

"I do not hold Yahwist sympathies against any of my subjects, Eliezar. Neither do I care which of the gods they choose to worship." He was about to speak, but I held up my hand and raised my voice. "If you hear them speak against me or the king, have them executed for sedition—but if they can worship their god and remain loyal to us, so let it be. I will not incite further resentment from the Yahwists by making martyrs of them without just cause."

I waved to dismiss him. Although I could tell he was not pleased with my decision, he bowed once more before rising and hurrying away. Noticing some of the guests watching me with unease, I reached out to take a handful of roasted pine nuts from a ceramic bowl. The act would not only make it look as though I was not worried but would also provide a means of working away the built-up tension. Then I gazed fondly at Daryoush, but he did not return my smile.

"Are you sure it is safe to dismiss Captain Eliezar's concerns?"

"I have not dismissed his concerns, Daryoush. I have advocated for caution, so as not to overreact. There is no need to add to the growing tension between our factions. After the last purge, Yahwist sympathies are on the rise. The only way to temper this is to show that we are not against *all* Yahwists—only the zealots, who seek to cause trouble in our kingdom."

"But Yahwists among the eunuchs..." He shook his head. "They are responsible for protecting you, the other women, and your children and grandchildren who are here with you. I do not think it is overreacting to put a stop to any threat to your wellbeing and the safety of your family."

"I agree. That is why I am permitting him to investigate, and to execute anyone who is found to be guilty of zealotry. But I will not have them executed simply for having sympathy for the Yahwists, neither will I have them punished for worshiping as they choose. I do not believe they are incapable of worshipping Yahowah *and* being loyal to us. Yahowah and his worshippers have always lived and worked alongside us, for many generations. It is only those who are unwilling to accept us and actively work against us who are cause for concern, and I have faith they shall be rooted out and judged accordingly."

687

He was about to speak, but I rose from my cushion. My sandals were brought to me. I slipped my feet into them and beckoned to Daryoush. "Walk with me."

After a pause, he got up and slid his feet into his own sandals. Then I took his arm and we walked into the inner palace, followed closely by four of my eunuchs as always. Those appointed to guard me personally were of the highest caliber and well-trusted by myself and Eliezar, so I was not afraid that they were involved in the previous incident. Before leaving us, Eliezar had given them clear instructions, and they were on high alert so that I did not have to be. We went to my private apartments and there I drew my lover into my arms, kissing him firmly on the mouth. He tried to resist, at first, but I soon wore down his stubbornness. After some heavy kissing, I smiled and met his gaze.

He said to me, "Were you an assassin, you could disarm me in an instant with those eyes and that smile. I would be dead before dawn."

"I intend for you to be," I whispered teasingly. He understood the euphemism and a smile snaked across his lips, while I continued, "The only thing you should be worried about tonight is making love to your goddess." I carefully dropped to my knees and moved aside his loincloth. Grinning up at him as I took hold of his aching member, I said, "Let me ease your suffering, my love, and then you will ease mine."

He shuddered as I began. Soon all else was forgotten.

Eliezar continued his investigation and uncovered a substantial infiltration of zealots within the ranks of his eunuchs at the palace, but it seemed to be concentrated within the lower ranks. With my full support, those eunuchs were executed and replaced, but any Yahwist eunuchs who were deemed to show no signs of ill-will toward me or my family were allowed to continue in their positions under intense scrutiny. I permitted them to worship openly, and they repaid me with increased dedication, which I rewarded with gifts and favors, raising them above many of their brethren. Eliezar still did not trust them, but I insisted it was the best way to smooth over any potential weakness their devotion to Yahowah might create. It seemed to me that if they were treated well, it would increase their dedication to me and my family, regardless of which god they worshipped.

Security issues aside, I was able to focus on my family again, which continued to grow. Over the next three years, Azba'alah gave birth to two more daughters, born within a year of each other. I visited when I could and delighted in my granddaughters, but when she revealed she was again expecting, I admonished my youngest daughter not to destroy her body by too many pregnancies too close together, particularly at such a young age. She reminded me of how many children I had given to her father, and that it had not destroyed my body. I reminded her that I was older by the time I had carried the first of my children to term and that there had been more time between each birth in most cases.

When she continued to dismiss my concerns, saying only that she enjoyed being pregnant, I summoned her husband to my quarters. There, in the presence of his elder brother, I admonished Kourosh to take care with my daughter, giving him advice on how to prevent pregnancy to give her body time to heal between each child. The poor man still regarded me with terrified awe. Daryoush reclined on cushions and laughed as he observed his brother's reddened face and inability to look me in the eye while I described the various ways he might engage in sexual intercourse with my daughter without impregnating her. "She seems to be so blessed with fertility," I concluded with a wink.

"Yes, Ba'alah," he stammered, bowing his head. "I receive your counsel with gratitude and shall put it into practice with Azba's wellbeing at the forefront of my mind, as it always is."

"Good. I am glad you understand. You may go now. Oh, but one more thing, Kourosh."

"Yes, Ba'alah?"

"Do not let my daughter push you around, especially on these matters. She is strong-willed and lusty, as I always was..."

Daryoush snorted, and corrected, "Are."

"But you are her husband," I continued, ignoring him, "and you must also guide her. She does not always know what is best. You must work *alongside* her, not *for* her. If you are to be her high priest one day, you must be her equal. You are not her servant, Kourosh— remember that."

"Yes, Ba'alah," he answered meekly. Then I waved him away and he scurried off, while I raised my eyes toward the heavens.

Daryoush rose from the cushions and came to draw me into his embrace. "You enjoy him being afraid of you."

"Well, perhaps a little. I do find it amusing, I must confess, but I do wish he would have more courage. He will not be able to perform his duty as high priest if he does not overcome his shyness."

"He is not always this shy."

"Only with me?"

"You are the goddess incarnate, and he is married to your daughter—he probably fears you may smite him should he displease you in any way."

I chuckled. "Even if I could smite him, I would not dare, for it would hurt you and Azba, and all their children."

"Did you ever think you would have so many grandchildren?"

"There was a time I feared I might never have any children of my body, but Ba'al heard my prayers and blessed me far greater than I could ever have imagined. Of all the things for which I could be proud, I am most proud of my children and grandchildren. Though my heart shall one day cease to beat and these walls around us may fall, by the grace of the Ba'alim, I will live on through them. They will be my legacy."

Pulling my body against him and pressing his hips to mine, he said, "You are the sexiest grandmother I have ever known."

"Have you known many grandmothers?"

"Well, not in that way. You know what I meant, Yezeba'al." He lifted my chin with his forefinger and drew me into a kiss. I shuddered and then looked into his eyes with a hopeful gaze. He smiled and led me to the cushions where he had been reclining before, and there, paid homage to his goddess.

Approaching my fiftieth year in the eleventh year of Yoram's reign, I would soon be able to add great-grandchildren to my ever-growing progeny. Now that she had reached the age her mother was when she married into the house of Yehoshapat, my granddaughter Yahosheba was to be married. Yahoiadah, the newly appointed High Priest of Yahowah at the Temple of Shelomoh in Yerushalayim, was the man chosen by her parents. Her elder brother, Akhazyah, was also to take a wife that year: a young woman, Zibiah, who was the daughter of the prince of the province of Be'er Sheba in southern Yehudah.

While I attended the wedding of my grandson in Yerushalayim, I did not come for the wedding of my granddaughter three months earlier, because I was not pleased that Atalaya would permit her to be married to a priest of Yahowah. It felt like a betrayal to marry a priestess and descendant of Ashtarti to a representative of the brother and rival of Ba'al, especially when there were kings who served our gods that would make for a more suitable husband. Atalaya argued that it would heal the rift that had grown between our factions. I did not agree, and so I remained in Yisrael when the time came for Yahosheba to wed Yahoiadah, although I sent a substantial gift and wished them a fruitful and happy marriage.

Yahoiadah turned out to be a gentle and doting husband to my granddaughter. I softened to him after I consulted several Ba'alim priests and priestesses to hear their prophecies concerning my granddaughter's new husband. They all spoke favorably of the match. This prepared me so that, when I met him while in Yerushalayim for Akhazyah's wedding, I could be fair in my assessment of him. He was polite and honored me as the Gebirah of Yisrael and grandmother to his new wife, but I sensed he was not as open to our ways as was his predecessor.

Testing the water, I told him of the Ba'alim prophecy concerning him. "When you married my granddaughter, I consulted my priests and priestesses on whether it would be a favorable match. It is said that you will safeguard my lineage in Yehudah."

"Forgive me, Gebirah, but I do not put my faith in false gods. What your prophets say is true, but it is hardly a prophecy. It would be a surprise if I did not protect your lineage, for it is also mine, considering your granddaughter is my new wife."

Although I felt the sting, as no doubt he intended, I offered a nod and a smile in reply. Then I excused myself and went to my daughter, while Yahoiadah went to his wife. After his disparaging remark about my gods, I was surprised by the care and devotion he showed to Yahosheba. She seemed likewise smitten with him, and I did not doubt she would soon be with child. I only hoped he would not attempt to convince her to abandon our gods and the priestesshood

691

in favor of his own, and I wondered if the Ba'alim prophecy was correct after all. Yahoaidah would protect his children, but would he teach them to hate the gods of their ancestors? Would he raise them to work against the cause I held so dear to my heart? Prevent my granddaughters from becoming priestesses of Ashtarti, as was their birthright?

Taking my daughter aside, I said, "You did not tell me Yahoiadah was a Yahwist zealot."

"He is not a zealot, Ama."

"He called the Ba'alim false gods. Is that not the language of a zealot?"

Atalaya sighed heavily. "What did you say to him, Ama?"

"What did *I* say to *him*? I complimented him—told him of the prophecy I was given in favor of him—and in return, he insulted me."

"You should not have spoken to him of prophecy."

"Why? Does he not depend upon the prophecy of his god?"

"Of course, but you still should not have said it. Why could you not have merely said it was a pleasure to make his acquaintance, and be done with it? You already insulted him by refusing to attend his wedding."

"I am the High Priestess and Gebirah of Yisrael. My duties keep me very busy, as you well know."

Atalaya smirked. "Ama, we both know you could have made it to Yerushalayim for the wedding if you had wanted to come. Instead of saying you could not get away, you should have at least claimed illness as the cause of your absence. You know, it hurt Sheba that you were not there. You should have come for her, regardless of who she married."

"You should not have allowed Yehoram to marry his daughter to a zealot."

"Who happens to be the High Priest of Yahowah," she added.

"Why not a priest of Ba'al? Even the lowest of them would make for a more suitable husband than even the highest of Yahowah's priests."

"In Yisrael, perhaps, or in Tzidon but not in Yehudah. He is a more fitting husband for her than some foreign king, and I wanted to keep her near to me. I could not bear the thought of her living at some far away court where I might never see her again."

692

I lowered my gaze. "It was never my desire to send you away from me. Nor your sister, who has chosen to stay away. It broke my heart for you to leave us."

"I am happy here, Ama. Do not think I am ungrateful for the sacrifices you have made for us and for our father's kingdom. But Yahosheba is my only daughter now. Forgive me if I am unwilling to lose her, too."

She faltered, and I reached out to touch her arm. Then she threw her arms around my waist and rested her head upon my shoulder, for a moment not caring that we were queens. It was undignified, but it felt good to hold my first daughter again, and I permitted it. I had wanted to continue to argue my case, but realized as I held her that it was unfair to continue battering her with my upsetment—especially when the wedding had already taken place. It could not easily be undone, no matter how many reasons I had to dislike it. Besides, this was a happy occasion. It should not be marred by my misgivings about the future. *All will be as it is meant to be*, I told myself, and then I put those thoughts from my mind.

The weddings of Atalaya's children came so close together for good reason: Yehoram's condition was worsening, and it was thought that he would be dead within the year. He coughed up blood and his body was wasting away, such that he could barely stand for his son's wedding. He had to be held up when his time came to bless their union, and he could barely get the words out before he was seized by a violent coughing fit. The ceremony was concluded soon afterward, and then the king was whisked away to his bed, while Atalaya presided over the festivities. She informed me, when I expressed my concerns about contagion, that the king was kept mostly in isolation to avoid spreading the illness to his family. He was king only in name by now. Akhaz had been working alongside his mother to manage the kingdom, in preparation for his ascension.

Much to everyone's surprise, Yehoram managed to live another year or so, long enough to learn of the birth of a son to Akhaz and Zibiah. It seemed he held on long enough to know that his kingdom was secured by the birth of an heir to his successor. The son was named Yehoash, but everyone in the family called him Yoash. He was a healthy boy with strong lungs. When I traveled to Yerushalayim for the celebration of his birth, I stood with the other women outside the main chamber for his circumcision and was

693

surprised by the robustness of his cries that we could hear echoing throughout the temple when the procedure began. Zibiah, his mother, nearly fainted at the sound of her son's wailing, but I and Atalaya held onto her, while her own mother held her hand and reassured her that her son would be well.

Yahosheba was heavy with child by this time. Once we had calmed her sister-in-law, I went to check on my granddaughter, for I noticed her looking faint. She smiled weakly when she saw me approaching, and I took her aside to find a chair. I helped her ease into it, after which she held my hand, and said, "Thank you, *Amami*. I thought I would be stronger."

"You are strong, Sheba. It has been a long day, and in your condition, I did not expect you to make it this long without sitting."

She rubbed her enormous belly. "I do hope this child comes soon. I do not know how much longer I can bear the weight of him on my hips."

"Do you believe it will be a son?"

She nodded. "The prophets have looked to the stars and observed the signs. They say it will be a son. They knew also that my nephew would be a son."

At her urging, I brought my hand to her belly, to feel where the child moved. I smiled as I stroked what seemed to be a knee jutting out from the side, and asked, "If it is a son, what will you name him?"

"I would like to name him Akhab, but Yahoiadah wants to give him a different name. Dawid or Yahoshua are his favorites. We are undecided."

"It is customary for the mother to name her children."

She smiled knowingly. "Did my grandfather not choose the names for my mother and her brothers and sisters?"

"Well, we named them together—as you are doing with your husband. I suppose it is best for both parents to be pleased with the names of their children," I conceded. Then the child shifted in his mother's womb, and I pulled my hand away. "What will you name your child if she turns out to be a girl instead?"

"Elisheba," she answered without hesitation. "We have both agreed on it, for it was his mother's name and it resembles my own. It will give honor to us both."

694

"I think that is a lovely name. I look forward to meeting Elisheba."

When I received word from Yerushalayim a month later that Yahosheba had given birth to a daughter and named her Elisheba, I was not surprised that the prophet had been wrong. I wrote in my letter that it would give her and Yahoiadah time to decide on a name for their son. I sent a gift with my letter, with the promise to come to see her and my great-granddaughter as soon as I was able to make the journey. That would come sooner than expected, for it was not long afterward that the news of Yehoram's death came to us while I was with the court at Shomron for the Feast of Ba'al.

Yoram was unable to make the journey, but I traveled to Yerushalayim to represent our kingdom at the funeral of my nephew and son-in-law. I stayed long enough to attend my grandson's coronation, happy to have this time with my daughter, my grandchildren, and my newborn great-grandchildren. Atalaya was as doting a grandmother as she had been a mother. When Yahosheba brought her daughter to the nursery at the palace to see us, Atalaya sat on a rug with Yoash while he attempted to lift himself onto his knees. While she helped and encouraged her grandson, I cradled sleepy Elisheba in my arms as her mother proudly looked on. In that moment, I was happier than I had ever been, except perhaps when I was a new mother and had Akhab at my side.

Do you see this, Akhab? I asked in my thoughts. *What we have created together?* Gently stroking Elisheba's cheek and watching Yoash briefly succeed at holding himself up, I thought back to that precious moment after our twins were born, when my husband sat beside me on the bed, and we cradled them in our arms. Tears welled in my eyes. *This is our greatest legacy, my love.* I closed my eyes and breathed deeply.

"*Amami*, are you all right?" asked Yahosheba.

Opening my eyes in slits, I smiled over at my granddaughter. "I am well, Sheba. Only thinking how beautiful it all is, and wishing your grandfather was here to see it."

"I wish I knew him. Ama speaks so highly of him, and of his love for you."

"He is with Ba'al now, and I know he is at peace. It is not easy, wanting to be in two places at once."

"You mean, you long to be with him while you are here?"

695

I closed my eyes again and nodded. "If only there was a way for us all to be together, in both this world and the next—to move between the two worlds with ease, and to stay in either of them for as long as we like."

"Is that not the way of it, though? For Ba'al and his Asherah? For her to be here, and him to be there for part of the time before they are reunited again in eternity?"

"Yes," I answered, turning to look at her with a hint of pride. "You do remember the story. I hope you will teach it to her and to her brothers and sisters."

"I promise to teach them, *Amami*. It is a beautiful story. Do not think that because my husband is devoted to Yahowah, I would forget my own heritage. He will raise them to worship his god, but I will raise them to honor our own, as well."

"Honor them," I repeated. *But not to worship them*. My heart ached, for I understood the meaning perhaps better than even she who had spoken those words. I hoped I was wrong, but for a moment I could sense the direction of the winds were no longer in our favor. Ba'al was being erased in Yehudah, and his consort was being recast as Yahowah's wife. But Yahowah had always been a jealous god. How long would it last before even she was erased?

After I returned to Yisrael, I settled into my usual routine, spending most of my time at Megiddu and traveling to Shomron or Yezreel only when my duties to the kingdom required my presence. Yoram's wives and concubines continued to bear him children, often several each year, and I was present at the births of each of his legitimate children as I had always been. Only his favorite women and children travelled with him to wherever he held court; the majority continued to stay behind at Megiddu where I would visit them often, showering my grandchildren with gifts and affection and ensuring they were being educated properly. By the time I was in my fifty-second year, which was the thirteenth year of Yoram's reign, I had thirty-seven legitimate grandchildren of my blood and eight more on the way.

Azba'alah was expecting her fifth child that year and hoping for a son. I had every intention of going to Tzidon to be with her for the birth, but then Yoram invited the King of Yehudah to meet with us at Megiddu during one of his rare appearances there. I postponed my trip so that I could see my grandson. He would be staying as a guest at my palace because it had more room to house his entourage. Those who were unable to be housed there were set up in the king's palace across the city.

Akhazyah was a charming young man who adored his grandmother and his uncles in Yisrael. I was pleased to have him as my guest. As we sat together on my private terrace overlooking the gardens, which he much admired, I said, "You may walk through them any time, Akhaz. If you are here for a while, I can have my gardeners provide you with advice on how to improve the gardens at your palaces. I know there is not much to be done for the gardens at Yerushalayim, being you have such limited space, but the gardens at your other palaces may benefit from the advancements that have been applied to our gardens here. For how long will you stay?"

"I am uncertain, *Amami*. I suppose it depends on how long it takes for the Gilad campaign to be concluded."

"The Gilad campaign?"

"Yes, you know, the campaign to take back Ramot from the Arameans. Did...my uncle not tell you of this?"

"No, he did not. Is that why you are here?" I exhaled. "I see. That is why the king invited you to Yisrael."

He looked away shamefacedly, perhaps realizing that his uncle had meant for it to be a secret. By nightfall, I was at the king's palace, upbraiding him in his study while his ministers and scribes waited outside. No doubt they were listening through the door. Yoram claimed it was not truly meant to be a secret. "It was only temporary, Ama, while the plans were being made. I was going to send a message to you once our armies departed from Yezreel next week."

"You arranged all this without consulting me?"

"I did not need to consult you—war is not a spiritual matter."

"This is different! Your Abbu died trying to take back Ramot!"

"That is why I did not want to tell you."

"Because you knew I would tell you it is folly."

"No, because I knew you would allow your emotions to cloud your judgment."

697

Feeling bitten, I fell silent and took a deep breath to calm down. "Have you consulted with the prophets? Even if you will not take my advice, will you at least seek their counsel?"

"I do not care for the counsel of priests or prophets. I care only about the counsel of my ministers and generals—they know war, and they believe we can take back Ramot and restore it to Gilad, as it was always meant to be."

"This is folly. You cannot go to war at Ramot! You will be killed!"

"Ama, I am not my father," he said calmly, gazing out the window as the violet hands of twilight took hold across the evening sky. "I will not die in battle at Ramot. I intend to finish what he began. I am not an old man, as my father was when he went into battle for these lands. I am in my twenty-eighth year, and this new king Hazael is not the warrior Ben-Hadad was—I am confident he will be defeated and those lands in Gilad which are rightfully ours will, at last, be returned to us."

Nothing I could say would dissuade him from his cause. As Gebirah, it was my duty to manage the kingdom for my son in his absence, and so I had to postpone my trip to Tzidon yet again. I did not know how long I would be detained, but I knew my daughter was due to give birth any week now. So, I sent Ba'alesar and Abshalom together with letters and gifts for their sister, grandmother, uncle, nieces, and cousins. They took Kora's youngest son, Ezra, who was their servant and closest companion since childhood, and the three men left Megiddu together with their entourage at the same time Yoram left to meet his nephew and their armies at Yezreel.

Alone at Megiddu with what remained of my son's court, now most of them men with whom I had seldom worked and had no part in electing to their lofty positions, I felt more isolated than I had in a great many years. I had Daryoush and Raman to stand beside me as I held court, traveling across the city each morning when the court was in session at the old palace, but I felt once again the isolation I had as an inexperienced young queen left in charge of my husband's court so many years ago. Once again, I faced a group of hostile men who looked upon me as a foreign woman with gods they rejected and views they refused to accept. My experience, which was greater than theirs, meant nothing to many of these men who behaved as though it was an insult to be left with a woman to lead them. I realized then that I had been away from the king's court for far too long. I should never have left my son to manage the kingdom on his own.

Shmuel was there at least, in his role as Lord Steward, and I was grateful to have his aid in dealing with the ministers. He knew them and their ways better than I and was able to smooth over their distrust of me. He was a follower of Yahowah like many of them and had worked alongside them these past years. He was also not a Yahwist zealot, for he had been raised to respect all the gods and even to call on the others when their aid was needed. Best of all, he knew how to placate even the zealots without hurting or alienating the rest of us. He loved his mother and my sons and even me, so I was not afraid to put my trust in him, for he knew our hearts and respected our ways, despite our differences. It was my trust in him and those like him, however, that encouraged me to overlook such differences in others.

It was while listening to a bitter dispute between two neighboring estate holders over the ownership of an ewe that a messenger arrived from the king. The moment I saw the youth enter, recognizing him, I rose from the throne and held up my hand to silence the bickering nobles. Shmuel stepped down to dismiss the landowners, telling them to return the next day, and then brought the messenger forward. The boy knelt before the dais and bowed low, as I sat once again on the throne and affected a calm demeanor.

"Rise. You have an urgent message from the king?"

The boy did as commanded. "Gebirah, the king was injured in battle at Ramot. He assures you that he is alive and that his physicians say he shall recover, but commands the court be moved to Yezreel, where he has been taken to be healed of his injuries. He wishes also to have his esteemed mother at his side, for the wounds are great and he bears much pain."

Although I felt much relief in that report, especially knowing how much of a fuss Yoram often made over the smallest of injuries, I did not hesitate to obey the king's command. I dismissed the court, ordering those who were fit to travel with us to prepare for the journey. I gave them until dawn of the next day. I then sent a reply with the messenger to my son, assuring him we would arrive by dusk the following day and offering words of comfort. Then I went to the women's quarters to see my son's Melkah, who was laid up with child. Be'ulah rarely attended court, even when the king was at Megiddu, and I knew she would be unable to travel in her condition. She had never taken well to pregnancy and lacked my stamina. Nevertheless, I wanted to inform her first, of all Yoram's women, that the court would be moving to Yezreel and that I was required to go with it.

Propped up with cushions upon a low bed, she smiled weakly when my arrival was announced. Everyone else in the room stopped immediately to pay homage, but Be'ulah held out her hand to me as a child might reach for its mother. I reached to take her hand and brought it down onto the bed as I sat beside her. Before telling her anything of what happened to Yoram, I looked at her swollen belly and smiled.

"You look well, Be'ulah."

"Ama, it is good to see you. But should you not be holding court? One of the eunuchs said there was a messenger from the king?" She looked worried, no doubt thinking what I had at first feared when I saw the youth.

"He is alive," I assured her. She relaxed then and brought a hand to her belly. The baby was moving all about, making her belly shift to-and-fro. I reached out to place a soothing hand upon the restless infant still in his mother's womb, and said, "He was injured in battle, but is recovering at Yezreel. The court must go to him there, by his command."

"But, Ama, I am to be delivered any day now. Does that mean you will not be here to attend the delivery?"

"I will try to return for the birth if there is time for a messenger to reach me. Send word as soon as the pains begin."

She nodded in understanding, but a bitterness stole across her face. "Yoram would take you from me now when I need you most. Are his injuries severe?"

"Not likely. The messenger reports that the king is in a great deal of pain, but you know how he is. Once I see that he is well enough, I shall appoint one of his concubines to keep him company and he shall likely forget that he ever requested me. Then I shall return to you, I promise."

"I fear this child will be the death of me," she lamented.

"You said that the last time," I observed with affection. "The last three, in fact."

"I wish he would stop coming to me." She seemed not to have meant to say what she was thinking aloud, for suddenly I heard a sharp intake of breath and she looked at me as though I was a venomous snake waiting for an excuse to lunge at her. "Forgive me, Gebirah. I meant no disrespect."

Rather than be angry, I chuckled wryly. "There is no need to apologize, Be'ulah. It is not uncommon for wives to feel this way, especially with husbands who are so fickle and uncaring. Yoram is my son, it is true, and my king—Ba'al preserve us from his folly—but I know what he is like, and I cannot say that I blame you. However, you must take care not to say such things, lest it be heard by the wrong ears."

She nodded in understanding.

"Now, rest. I shall send word when I am on my way back to Megiddu if I do not hear from you first. I have no intention of staying with the king if he does not truly have need of me." I leaned forward and glanced around, lowering my voice. "I, too, prefer to remain at a distance from his fussiness and changeability."

"I cannot believe the way he lashes out at you, at times," she confided in a low voice. "Your patience with him is remarkable. I hope our sons do not behave in this way toward me one day—I do not believe I could be as patient with them as you are with him."

"I do not believe you will need to be. Your sons are far stronger in spirit."

I did not stay long with her, for I went immediately to find Zubira. She was one of the last of Akhab's widows to remain with us, most of the others having gone to live with their children's families at their estates spread throughout the kingdom. Her sons, of which there were two, served as generals in the army, but her daughter had become a priestess and served at the Temple of Ashtarti in Megiddu for a few years before returning to the palace as a midwife. I would leave Zubira and her daughter in charge of looking after Be'ulah and the other women who were in a similar condition.

Zubira had aged beautifully, but she had long abandoned wigs in favor of her natural hair, enjoying the wisdom that her greying curls bestowed upon her. She wore them in tight braids, the silver strands woven throughout. Her face was mostly unwrinkled, though.

701

She was still only forty-five, after all. Having been braiding the hair of one of Yoram's wives, she smiled broadly when she saw me appear, and handed the task off to one of the other wives while she came to embrace me. We kissed cheeks, and then she said, "Yezeba'al, I am glad you have come. I want you to see this new style I have developed—I'd like to try it on your hair next."

"There is not much time, I'm afraid. I can see it, but it may be some time before you get to try it on my hair."

"Can you not wear it to court tomorrow?"

"I will be journeying to Yezreel tomorrow. Yoram is there, recovering from injuries sustained in battle, and has commanded me to bring the court to him."

"You need me to remain here with the other women?"

I nodded. "There is none I trust as well to oversee the women's needs and keep order among them. Besides, I assume you would like to stay with your daughter while she tends to Be'ulah and the other pregnant women?"

"Yes, I would like to be with her," she answered with a nod. "Thank you, Yezeba'al."

"I do not know how long it will be, but I have promised to return as soon as I can, so that I may be present for the birth of Be'ulah's child at least. Send word as soon as you suspect her time is near."

"I suspect it already *is* near. My daughter says it could be any day now. Speaking of which, have you heard yet from Tzidon about Azba?"

"Nothing yet. Her brothers are with her, but she is still waiting for the pains to begin. I think it will be another week or two before anything changes. I wish I could be with her, but if I can at least be here for Be'ulah, that will make up for it. I think, sometimes, she needs me more than my own daughters."

"She did not know a mother's love as your daughters have," Zubira observed. "And she was so young when she came here, as I was, but she has never been good at making and keeping friends. Now that she is without her sister, she is very lonely."

Shalima had died in childbirth some years ago, leaving a single daughter and two sons. Of all his women, Yoram may truly have cared for Shalima, and he had taken her death hard. It had brought him closer to Be'ulah, at least, but now they were at odds again. That was not surprising, considering he had been growing closer with General Yehu once more, as Yehu had become more openly affectionate with him in the last several months. It made Yoram happy, but it left me uneasy, for I still did not trust Yehu.

As expected, Yoram was not nearly as badly injured as I had been led to believe. It would be a week or two before he could walk again, but he was more concerned about having lost the onyx from his signet ring than he was about his injuries. "I am certain that I would not have been injured had the onyx not come loose from my ring during the battle. You know, they say it has strong protective properties."

"I know," I answered patiently, smoothing out the blanket on his bed. "I am the one who gave it to you."

"Oh, that was you? I thought Abbu had it commissioned for me."

"No, Abbu was the one who presented it to you. I was the one who commissioned it. Do you not remember us sitting together while you designed it? I thought it was your leg that was injured in battle, not your head."

He seemed not to notice the jest. Instead, he continued fussing. "What if it is never found? I think I shall die without it. What if it falls into the hands of my enemies?"

"Then I shall commission a new one."

"But it won't be the same, Ama. That one was infused with my essence – like yours." He indicated the opal scarab hanging from its beaded necklace, and continued, "It is connected to me, much as a horse is connected to its rider."

"You will survive without it if need be. And the new one will become infused with your essence all the same."

"I have asked Yehu and the other generals to be on the lookout for it. They have charged the troops to search for it, as well."

"Instead of battling the enemy?"

"Well, no. They will continue to battle, but they know to look for it and, if it turns up, to give it to the right man to ensure it is returned to me."

"The right man. Do you mean your nephew, the King of Yehudah?"

"No, Akhaz is on his way back to Yezreel. His men have sustained severe losses, so Yehu suggested he pull out."

"Yehu? Why Yehu?"

"Because he is the one I appointed."

"You have left Yehu in charge of your troops?"

"Yes, and I have the utmost confidence in him. If he does well and we take it back from Aram, I may promote him to Governor of Gilad."

"Are you sure that is a good idea?"

"Why not? He is a superb leader."

"That is just what he needs to build a following that he can use to turn against you."

"Why can you not set aside your differences long enough to see that Yehu is for us."

"I am not the one who is unable to set aside 'differences', as you call them. I have plenty of followers of Yahowah in my service, and I trust them with my life."

"Then why is Yehu any different?"

"You know why. He is a zealot. He has made his feelings about me and our gods quite clear on numerous occasions."

"But that does not mean he cannot serve me and our kingdom faithfully."

"Greater men have been executed for less."

"He has never spoken against you—only your activities at the temple, and I cannot help but to agree with him on that point."

"I am not arguing with you about this again, Yoram." With that, I rose from the edge of the bed where I had been seated.

"I do not agree with what you do, Ama, yet I do not stop you. I let him have his beliefs, and I let you have yours. Why can you not be satisfied? I am sick to death of both of you!"

"You think I enjoy trying to hold everything together while you do all you can to let it fall apart? I just want to be left in peace!"

Turning my back toward him to hide the tear that had broken free and now slipped down my cheek, I walked toward the window and looked out. It was a beautiful day, and there were children playing in the streets below. I found myself wishing my children could all be young and innocent again—that we could return to those halcyon days when Akhab was still alive and all our troubles, though many in number, seemed somehow less ominous. Now, I felt crushed by the weight of it. Forcing back tears, I hardened my heart and turned back to Yoram. "I am leaving tomorrow."

"What? Why? I still need you here."

"You do not need me here, Yoram. You have Shmuel and soon you will have your nephew, the King of Yehudah."

"*I* need you, Ama."

"Your Melkah needs me. I received word from Megiddu. Zubira's daughter is certain Be'ulah will be delivered of her child by the end of the week, and it is my duty to be with her."

"It is your duty to be with me!"

"Do not be so selfish, Yoram. You are not dying, and you have plenty of others here to support you in the management of the kingdom: men who will not listen to reason when it comes from the mouth of a woman, for they are as stubborn and misguided as you."

He barely managed not to make a pout. "Will you return to me here after she is delivered?"

"No. I will stay at Megiddu."

He sighed heavily. "Of course. Back to your own court of harlots and sorcerers."

I scoffed and raised my eyes toward the ceiling. "I suppose that is what Yehu calls us? And you permit him to speak this way about my friends? About me, your own mother?"

"I do not permit him to speak this way."

"You do not punish him, nor reprimand him."

"I tolerate his differing views."

"You tolerate his disrespect. That only emboldens him, and it will embolden others in time, if it has not already."

I walked toward the door as if to leave, but he called out, "Ama, wait! Please, I do not wish for us to part in this way. I...understand what you are saying. In fact, it is in part because of his lack of deference toward you that I wish to make him Governor of Gilad."

"You wish to reward him!" I said, raising my hand and laughing bitterly.

"No, I mean to send him away where he will not be able to cause so much trouble and warring between us. I love him and want him near to me, but you have always counseled me to put the good of

705

the kingdom above my personal happiness. I am, at last, prepared to do that. I want you to be at court more often. Things have not been going well without your constant presence."

I wondered how long it would take for him to change his mind and decide he did not need me anymore, but I did not say what I was thinking. Instead, I went to take his hands and brought his fingers to my lips. Then I pressed his hand to my cheek, and gazed at him with all the affection I could still muster for the son who, for the past thirteen years, had treated me so wretchedly. Then I said, "I love you, Yoram. But I will never return to court unless you are rid of all the zealots whom you have raised into its ranks."

Scowling, he pulled his hand away. "Fine. Go back to your glittering palace and your court of sycophants and your harlotry! Then you can tell *me* who is not putting our kingdom first."

You are impossible to work with! I wanted to shout. Instead, I backed away and bowed to him, as my king. But as I took my leave, I paused in the doorway and turned back. "Such a king your brother would have made, if only he was still here with us."

Then I left and, as the door was closed, I heard him yell out before something crashed upon the other side of the door as if thrown against it. I felt very little for my son in that moment; only the sadness of what could have been, and the torment of wondering where I went wrong with him.

31

Deliverance

Peace. That is how I would describe the quiet moments after lovemaking, when two lovers lay side by side, gazing into eyes filled with affection, talking in whispers, caressing, and breathing in each other's scent. Nothing else in the world exists in these moments: all their troubles are far away; all their past loves cease to rend their hearts. There is only the two of them, lost in a world of their own creation, a world of light and love and peace like no other. It is a world full of hope and possibility and wonder. I never thought I could feel that peace with any man except my husband. Yet here I am with Daryoush, my head upon the cushion beside his and the afternoon sun coming through the window to warm my flesh, and I feel all these things. I breathe deeply, and the peace fills my lungs.

"What are you thinking?" he asks, gazing upon me and running his fingertips across my tingling flesh.

I tremble at his touch. "I am thinking of writing a poem."

"A poem?"

"About love." I turn my gaze to meet his, and smile.

"Do you love me, Yezeba'al?"

"You sound like a young woman," I tease, "infatuated yet insecure about her lover's affections. It is unbecoming of you."

"The question still stands."

I pause, wondering if I should leave his question unanswered. I do not care for the sort of games which pin me down and try to force me to answer in a certain way: even when the answer I would freely give of my own accord is the one they seek. The peace is gone, and now I feel trapped, which causes me to become irritable and restless. I sit up to pour a drink from the ceramic pitcher on the bedside table. Before bringing the cup to my lips, I sigh heavily, as if the act may dispel the frustration I now feel with my youthful lover.

He sits up and pulls himself over to me, while I continue to sip my drink. "Yezeba'al? Have I done something wrong?"

"You should not ask such things of me, Daryoush."

"It was only a question, and one that should not be so difficult to answer."

I set the cup down hard upon the table. "It is *not* difficult to answer—only I should not have to. After all these years together, you should know the answer. I say it all the time and show it in countless ways. If I am lacking in affection, tell me; but do not play games with me, Daryoush. I am too old for such things."

Silence falls between us. I sense his wavering as guilt and shame overtake his confusion. Then he sighs. "Forgive me, Ba'alah. You show more love and affection every day than I deserve; it is that unworthiness I feel in myself that causes me to be weak in faith."

He reaches for my hand, which rests palm-down upon the bed. I pull away, but only so that I may turn toward him and lie down beside him once again. His gaze momentarily falls upon my breast. I pretend not to notice as I reach out to stroke his cheek, letting my fingers trace the edge of his well-trimmed beard.

"You are young and foolish sometimes," I say to him. Then I permit a faint smile to touch upon my lips. "But yes, I do love you. More than I ought—not because you are unworthy, but because you distract me from more important things."

"Nothing is more important than love. Not even the temple. Not even the kingdom."

His black eyes are flecked with golden-brown when the light touches them. I love it when he looks at me with such intensity and smiles, while his hand reaches out to rest upon my naked hip. Although the bedlinen is still draped over his lower extremities, I notice a particular movement from beneath the sheet which, taken with the way he gently tugs at my hip suggests he is eager to make love again. I could be persuaded, but I will not give into him so easily. He must work for it, especially after he has shown such weakness of faith.

"You are supposed to be my advisor!"

He reaches out to stroke my cheek and runs his fingers through my hair. "Then let me advise you in the ways of love, my Ba'alah." He draws me into a kiss.

For a moment, I forget that I am supposed to be angry with him, and I let him kiss me. Then I pull back my head, and say, "I have still not forgiven you for your weakness of faith."

"Then I shall have to earn my absolution."

He moves closer and brushes his lips across my breast. I turn onto my back and raise my arms and close my eyes to enjoy the sensation as he cups my breast and begins to gently bite and suck. He is a masterful penitent. I tremble and gasp as desire pulses through me, rippling out from wherever his lips and his fingers touch my bare flesh. His eager body presses against mine when he comes up to bring our lips together. He knows he has been forgiven for his trespass because I give into him fully. We are very near to making love again when the door opens suddenly.

"Ba'alah," Kora calls out in a strained voice. "Forgive the intrusion. It is a matter of urgency."

Before I am even sitting up, I hear heavy boot falls and Kora begins to protest. I gasp and reach for the bedlinens to cover my nakedness. Thankfully it is only Eliezar, his expression grim even as he averts his gaze. "Ba'alah, forgive me, but it cannot wait. A group of chariots have arrived from Yezreel. One of them bears the King of Yehudah, but he is pierced with arrows. He may be dying even as we speak."

"Akhaz!" I say in alarm, as I rise from the bed. "My precious grandson." Kora brings my robe and helps me into it, while Daryoush jumps up to put on his loincloth. I do not wait for him. As soon as Kora is finished helping me into my sandals, I take off to follow Eliezar down to the courtyard where the charioteers await. They carry the banners of Yehudah, but there are none bearing the banners of Yisrael.

"What has happened? Where is the king?"

"Ba'alah." I am relieved when General Kaleb, one of Zubira's sons, steps forward with a bow. There is a scratch on his cheek, perhaps from an arrow having grazed him, but he is otherwise unharmed. His mother will be equally relieved, but there is no sign of his brother. "Melekh Akhazyah is in the gatehouse," he explains, pointing. "He has been gravely injured."

"And my son?" I look at them. No one answers. "The King of Yisrael! Where is he?"

The men shift uncomfortably. They still seem to be in shock, or perhaps they are afraid to confess what has happened, especially in the face of a mother's fury. None of them speak, until at last one of

709

the King of Yehudah's generals explains, "Gebirah, forgive us. Melekh Yoram is dead, at the hands of his general."

The news hits me like waves that crash upon the rocks at the fortress of Zour. My memory of that storm the night before I left Tzidon to become the wife of the King of Yisrael flashes before me, as I try to make sense of what the men are telling me.

"There has been a coup, Ba'alah," Kaleb explains, his voice intense with alarm. "It happened outside the city, at Yezreel."

"The kings of Yehudah and Yisrael went out to meet a large group of men who were approaching. Messengers were sent to find who they were and if they came in peace, but those messengers did not return."

"It was a trick. The man leading them was General Yehu."

"He spoke against you, Gebirah, saying there would be no peace while you are permitted to practice your religious duties at the temple."

"He shot the King of Yisrael in the back as he tried to flee! And then he commanded his men to attack the rest of us! They listened to him, as if *he* was their king!"

"Melekh Akhazyah also tried to flee, as did the other men. Most of them did not make it, Ba'alah. My brothers... Forgive us..."

"Melekh Akhazyah was shot through with arrows but has made it this far. They took him into the gatehouse to tend to his injuries, Gebirah."

They continue to recount the tale of what happened, but I no longer understand their words over the din of my own inner turmoil. *Betrayed.* I feel caught up in a whirling torrent. *We are undone.* I begin to fall, but familiar hands catch me.

"Yezeba'al!" It is Daryoush. He is holding me to his body. I did not hear him arrive, but of course he must have caught up with me and Eliezar and the rest of my bodyguards.

"My son is dead," I feel my lips murmur, as I am led to sit upon a nearby ledge, along a pool filled with blooming lilies and other water plants. I hear the buzz of insects. My mouth is dry, but my face is wet. My voice sounds hollow, unfamiliar. "Yoram is dead." I look up at the crowd of men surrounding me, their familiar faces painted with concern. "My grandson? Akhazyah?"

"He is in the gatehouse, Gebirah."

710

They look at me as if I have gone mad. I remember now that they have already told me, although I still cannot believe it. I never trusted Yehu and, in a sense, always knew it would come to this, but not in this way, not so soon. I wipe the tears from my cheeks. I must regain my composure. Now is not the time to crumble. *My grandson. I must see him.*

I rise. "Take me to the King of Yehudah."

The men lead me to the gatehouse. The gate that leads out into the main thoroughfare of the city is closed and barred, but the small doorway to the right, which leads to an antechamber that is used for storage, is open. They direct me through that doorway, but Kaleb goes ahead to tell the men who are with their king, "Stand down. Make way for the Gebirah of Yisrael." They do not need to be reminded that I am grandmother to their king.

I am assaulted with the smell of iron when I enter, but it is too dark for me to see until my eyes adjust to the change. There is enough light coming through the open doorway and the windows that look in from the courtyard, although the number of men trying to peer inside blocks some of the light. The soldiers and eunuchs who are near begin to wave them off, telling them to disperse, while I go to my grandson. Akhazyah is lying on his back on a bed of straw, breathing heavily and barely moving.

His armor has been removed and there are several dark patches across his flesh, concentrated in all the places where his cuirass would have come apart to allow freedom of movement. I realize the dark patches are blood from where the arrows pierced him. The arrows have been broken, their bloodied shafts laid aside. The arrowheads that did not pierce too deeply have been removed, but some of the heads are still embedded within his flesh. I know enough to understand that if they remove these arrowheads, he will bleed out and die more quickly. They have left them in place to keep him alive long enough for me to see him.

"Akhaz?" My voice rises from within me, sounding like that of a child. My eyes feel as pierced as his flesh appears.

He groans and his eyes flutter open. "Ama?" His voice is faint and his lips tremble. He studies me for a moment before recognition registers in his gaze. Then he whispers, *"Amami."*

I kneel beside my grandson. He reaches for my hand, but his grip is weak. *He is not long for this world.* For a moment I am

711

overcome with grief. While my tears begin to fall, I whisper breathlessly, "You should not have been here. You should be in Yerushalayim, raising your son and making more sons. You should not have been brought into my son's folly."

"*Amami*," he attempts to speak. I can sense that he wants to tell me about Yoram. I can feel his anguish, the helplessness he must have felt when his uncle fell before his eyes, and the fear of death that arose within him as he fled for his life. As he fled here, to find me and warn me of what is coming—for if Yoram is dead, I have little doubt Yehu intends to kill me next.

"Shh," I encourage him through tear-streamed lips. I bring his hand up to my heart and press his knuckles there as I hunch over, trying not to fall apart. *Now is not the time*, I remind myself. *There is still too much to be done before it all ends*. I look at my grandson and cover his lips with my fingers. "Do not speak. There is no need."

"Yehu..."

"Yes, my son. I know. He is coming for me. He is coming for all of us."

Akhazyah closes his eyes and seems to nod as he begins to relax. His breath grows shallow with each rise and fall of his chest. I wonder if this is what it was like for Akhab when he bled to death from his wounds. The stinging returns to my eyes but I force back the tears with every bit of my strength. Suddenly, Akhazyah inhales sharply—it is almost a strangled sound, and I am alarmed, but the other men nearby seem to understand what is happening. They have seen the deaths of many men who have fallen in battle. As he exhales, he falls still and I stare at him, waiting for him to stir but knowing he will never breathe or move again in this form.

I feel a hand upon my shoulder and startle. I turn to see Daryoush gazing at me in sorrow. Again, I had not realized he was there, but he must have been next to me the whole time. Still somewhat in a daze, I say, "The King of Yehudah is dead. The King of Yisrael is dead."

"Yehu commands the entire army of Yisrael," said Kaleb. He is standing in the doorway. His voice is acid when he speaks of Yehu's betrayal. "Those who refused to join him were slaughtered without mercy."

"He is calling himself king," said the general from Yehudah, "claiming a prophet anointed him to lead the people of Yisrael."

"Ba'alah," says Eliezar, stepping forward. "We must get you out of the city."

"No," I shake my head. "There is no time."

I rise. Daryoush rises with me. He is still holding my hand and looks at me imploringly, while Eliezar continues, "If we slip away through the tunnels beneath the city…"

Ignoring my eunuch captain, I reach out to touch my lover's cheek and smile with a teary-eyed gaze. I do not say what I am thinking just yet, but I am preparing to send him away before the enemy arrives.

"How long is it from Yezreel to here?" I ask.

Kaleb answers, "An hour and a half, Ba'alah, if one rides fast on a horse. It takes a bit longer by chariot—possibly two hours."

"Did they pursue you when you fled?"

"After they riddled my king with arrows, they fell back toward Yezreel." This time it was the Yehudan general who answered. "As far as my men could tell, they were not pursuing us. But by Yehu's words against you, I have no doubt he will come for you next, Gebirah. When they realize you are not at Yezreel, they will come here."

I nod in understanding.

"Ba'alah," says Eliezar. "There is still time to get you safely out of the city, if we leave now."

"No. If I flee, they will pursue me. They will pursue me, and then all will be lost."

"Will you try to hold them off?"

I shake my head. "This city cannot handle a siege. There are not enough men here to keep out the entire army of Yisrael."

"Yezeba'al, what are you going to do?" asks Daryoush. He knows me better than any man, except for my husband. He can see my mind working.

"I am going to meet with the traitor. I must dress for the occasion."

The men exchange glances. No doubt they think I have gone mad if they had not thought so before. It is not time yet to reveal what I am thinking, but I turn to Akhazyah's general. "You must return to Yerushalayim with the body of the king. Prepare him for the journey, but do not tarry, lest the traitor arrive while you are still here. May the gods be with you."

713

The men of Yehudah kneel as I depart, followed by Daryoush, Eliezar, and the four eunuchs appointed to guard me that day. I beckon for Kaleb to follow. As he walks alongside me toward the palace entrance, I say, "Go to the king's palace to alert Melkah Be'ulah and the other women about what has happened. Rally all the king's women and children who are there, including your mother and sister. Bring them here to my palace, as it is further from the main gate and closer to the spring. Send word to my quarters when you have arrived."

"Yes, Ba'alah," he responds with his hand over his heart. Then he whirls back toward the courtyard as the rest of us continue walking through the palace corridors in haste. Daryoush moves up to walk alongside me. "So, you will try to escape through the tunnels to the spring?"

I do not answer his question, for it is not what he will want to hear. Instead, I say, "Go and find Raman. Bring him to my quarters and make haste."

He obeys and turns the other way, while I continue to my quarters. Kora and the other handmaids are at work, arranging my wardrobe, putting away the sumptuous robes and dresses that have been returned from the wash. They stop when I enter, and I beckon to Kora. She comes to me, and I quietly inform her, "There has been a coup at Yezreel."

Alarm rises in her throat. "Our sons?"

"The king is dead. I do not know the fate of Shmuel, but as he was so often at Yoram's side..."

She nods solemnly. I place a comforting hand upon her arm, for we have both lost a son today. Then I turn to address the handmaids. "You are all dismissed from my service. Return to your families. Tell them they should flee from the city and take all their valuables, for the army of Yisrael is being led by a traitor this day. If the city is attacked, you and your families will be targeted for your wealth and your loyalty to me."

The handmaids gasp and murmur fearfully. They are the daughters of Megiddu's nobility. Some are even daughters of the House of Omri; one is Asa's granddaughter, betrothed to Ba'alesar. After addressing them all, I single her out by wagging my finger at her. She comes immediately to me, and I ask, "Your *Ababu* Asa is still here in the city?"

714

She nods. "Yes, Ba'alah."

Asa had taken a leave of absence from court the moment I retreated from Yezreel. He was eager for a break from all the backstabbing intrigue of the factions my son encouraged with his inconstance, preferring my court at Megiddu to that of the king. I am relieved that he is still here. If he had stayed at Yezreel with the rest of the court, or returned there without my knowing, he would likely already be dead.

"Good. His leave of absence may yet preserve him. I do not need to tell him, but I will tell you so that you understand the severity of what is coming. When a king is murdered by one who seeks to usurp his power, all the men of his House are in danger of being slaughtered to prevent them from laying claim to the succession. For the women of his House, it is often far worse." I lay a gentle hand upon her cheek. "I do not want that to be your fate."

She nods. "I understand, Ba'alah."

"I want you to tell your family to come here to my palace. Do you understand? Do not flee through the city gate with the rest of the nobility. I have other plans for you. Now, go. And make haste."

After all the handmaids have hurried away, Kora returns to me, and I say, "You must go, too. Take your husband and flee from the city."

"Aharon is too frail for travel, Ba'alah."

"Kora, you must go *now*. If you stay here, you will surely die."

"I am willing to stand beside you and take that chance."

Damn her... "Kora, I appreciate your devotion, but I do not expect to survive this. I must protect the people that I love."

"General Yehu...?"

"Is no doubt on his way to kill us all."

She nods in understanding. She has always known of and shared in my distrust for Yehu. She knows he is a zealot. I do not need to tell her what he and his men will do to her, my closest friend and confidant. Nevertheless, she says, "Yezeba'al, I will not leave you."

"Kora."

She cuts me off, her voice like a knife. "I am sworn to you for life! I will not leave your side. If you die, I shall die with you. I pray my husband will be spared due to his age."

Tears cut my eyes once again. "You cannot."

715

She smiles. "You will need a handmaid to serve you in Ertsetu. Who better to serve you than me? Besides, my mother will be there, and I long for her embrace. And Shmuel…"

With that, I throw my arms around her shoulders and pull her into a tight embrace, kissing her cheek. Then I say, "Come with me." We go into my study, and I gently command, "Shut the door." She does so, while I sit at my desk, pull out one clean sheet of papyrus and begin cutting it in two. Then I lay the pieces flat, and Kora comes to pour ink from the small container in which it is sealed, while I reach for my stylus. Before she is done pouring the ink into the basin, I dip my stylus and begin to write, first to Atalaya:

By the time you receive this message, I will most likely be dead. The enemy has infiltrated our ranks. Your brother the king and your son have been slain. The traitor is on his way to slay me even as I write this to you now. My daughter: the safety of our people, the future of these realms, and the preservation of our divine bloodline rests in your hands. You must do whatever it takes to preserve the life of your son's heir, and to guard his throne from those of his brothers who would seek to take it for their own. May the gods continue to bless and preserve you, my daughter. Remember all I taught you. The time has come for you to take your rightful place. Draw on your strength.

After writing this, I hand it off to Kora who begins to blow on the ink, while I write a second letter to Azba'alah, almost word-for-word except for the parts about her son and the throne, which are only relevant to the Gebirah of Yehudah. Meanwhile, Kora begins to roll the first papyrus then folds it in the usual manner and wraps it with a woven cord. As I am making the last stroke on the second letter, Daryoush arrives with Raman. I lay down the stylus and rise from my chair as they enter. Kora takes the second letter and does the same as with the first, while Raman kneels before me. "Ba'alah, I am at your service."

"Raman, my friend," I say, taking his hands and bidding him to rise. But then I go to the door and, opening it, look out to see

Eliezar speaking with the other eunuchs who are all waiting anxiously. I beckon to him, as well.

"Ba'alah?" asks my captain of the eunuchs, stepping forward.

Keeping my voice low, I say, "Direct the others to stand watch at the entrance to my quarters. I do not wish for them to hear what is being said within this chamber. I need you to stand watch outside the door to my bedchamber, so that they will not attempt to return to listen."

He nods and carries out my orders. I wait until they have all gone. Now, it is only me, Kora, Daryoush, and Raman left within the innermost chambers of my quarters. Daryoush asks, "My love, what are you going to do?"

"I have written letters to my daughters," I explain as I return to my desk, unclasping the scarab seal from around my neck. "I need you and Raman to deliver them." I press my seal upon the clay that Kora has placed over the cords, leaving behind the imprint of my name and the symbols of my royal and divine status. Then I return the seal to my neck as Kora indicates which letter is which. I hand the one that is meant for Atalaya to Raman, instructing him, "Take this letter to my daughter in Yerushalayim. Take one of the swiftest horses from the stables, and do not tarry, for if news reaches Yerushalayim before this letter reaches the Gebirah of Yehudah, the king's son will be in danger from those who would take the throne for themselves."

He nods, but I am not satisfied that he understands the seriousness of his charge.

"Raman, *no one else* in Yerushalayim must hear about what has happened until *after* this letter reaches Atalaya. Do not reveal who you are or what is your mission, and do not return to Yisrael unless you get word that it is safe."

"Yes, my Ba'alah. I will tell no one, and I will not stop along the way but to rest my horse and take sustenance. I give you my word: the Gebirah of Yehudah shall hear of this before anyone else in Yerushalayim."

Smiling at him with tearful gaze, I say, "Thank you, my friend."

Raman is a deeply feeling man and devoted to me, so when it comes time for him to carry out his duty, he is unwavering. I have always known that I can count on him. I am not surprised that he

717

accepts his charge without a fight, saying, "It has been an honor to serve you, Ba'alah. I hope we will meet again soon."

"We shall all meet again in Ertsetu," I answer with a smile.

He nods and tucks the letter away, rises, then hurries off while my lover looks at me incredulously. He knows what is coming, and says, "I will not leave without you. Yezeba'al, you cannot stay here and let them kill you. Tell me you will escape with the rest of the king's women. That is what you are planning? For all of you to escape through the tunnels before Yehu arrives?"

Still smiling, I go to my lover. I take his face in my hands, draw him into a kiss, and then I say, "I love you, Daryoush. I have enjoyed our time together—they have been some of the happiest days of my life. But I am eager to be reunited with my Ba'al in Ertsetu; there, to spend eternity in his embrace until such a time that I must return once again to a life in the flesh."

His eyes are now filling with tears. He looks at me as though he is beginning at last to understand but still does not want to leave me. I am grateful for his devotion and loyalty.

"You are free now to love again. I release you from your oath."

"I could never love another as I have loved you."

"But if the chance should arise again, as it did for me, I hope that you will take it and know that you have my blessing."

"I will never find your equal."

"I pray that you will find better," I whisper before I press my lips to his. Then I say gently, "You must go. Ba'alesar and Abshalom will be arriving on the ships at Yapo before the day is out. By morning, they will be on their way here—on their way to certain death, unaware of what has happened. I cannot let them die with the rest of us."

"You are not dead yet."

"My love, but I am. My fate is sealed. But for you and for them there is still a chance. Their fate, and the fate of my bloodline, rests in your hands now. I need you to do this for me if you have ever loved me."

"I have always loved you, from the moment I first laid eyes upon you."

"Then you will do as I ask. And if you will not—if you cannot—then as my servant you will do as I command. You will go to Yapo and meet my sons, and you will tell them all that has happened here, and you will have them turn the ships back to Tzidon and you will go with them to deliver this message to my daughter." I hand him the papyrus. "Tell my brother the king to send more ships to collect Melkah Be'ulah and the others, who I will send to Yapo to wait for safe passage. None of you should ever return to this cursed place."

He accepts the letter and looks down at it in his hands before tucking it away. Then he looks up at me, and a single tear slips down his cheek. "What will you do now?"

"I will dress for battle."

"You have armor?"

I chuckle. "No, my love. But my armaments have served me well over the years, and they will serve me one last time. Kora, prepare my finest gown and jewels."

She nods and slips away, while I turn back to my lover. I kiss him once more, and then I pull my hand from his face and step back. "Go now; do not let me die in vain."

Daryoush gazes upon me, and then he bows. "Ba'alah, I have been blessed by your favor. I will not let your faith in me be mislaid. May your death be swift and may Ba'al wrap you in his embrace. I will pray for your soul's peace every day until we meet again."

I press my hand to my heart in thanks. He turns and then he is gone, and I am alone in my study for what I am certain will be the last time. Looking around at all the scrolls and tablets on the shelves, I wonder if the zealots will preserve them or put them to the flame. There is nothing here that would be of interest to them, and much of it preserves the truth of Yahowah's origin and place among the gods. It would not serve their strange belief in their one and only jealous god.

I turn my gaze toward the little wooden chest where I keep my chronicle. I will give it to Zubira and ask her to take it to Tzidon, in the hope that it will survive with the rest of my and Akhab's legacy. I have kept it up to date as much as possible, but there is not time to add this latest happening. *It will be for another to tell what has happened here this day. My time is spent.*

I go out through the open door to my chamber, where Kora has laid out my richest clothes and jewels as though I am to dress for court or a banquet. There is not much time by now, I am certain, but I have just enough to dress and arrange my hair and paint my face so that if I die – and I am certain that I will – it will be with my

719

dignity intact. I am the daughter of a king, the sister of a king, the grandmother of a king; I was the mother of two kings, and the wife of a king. I am the Gebirah of Yisrael and, more importantly, the High Priestess and Divine Consort of Ba'al. If my enemies are prepared to take my life, they must know without question whose life they are taking.

By the time I am dressed and have finished lining my eyes and painting my face, I look every bit the part of a queen. I wear a sumptuous gown of purple cloth, cut in Sidonian fashion; a purple mantle is pinned beneath my gilded headdress, and golden sandals adorn my feet. My fingers and toes glitter with bejeweled rings, all of which I am certain will be stolen after I am dead. I reach up to touch the opal scarab seal which hangs over my heart and say a silent prayer for the Ba'alim to ensure my death comes swiftly.

While I finish lining my eyes with kohl, there is a quiet knock on my door. I nod for Kora to open it. I am relieved to see it is Zubira and not a messenger coming to tell me that the traitor's army is approaching the city. She is dressed not as the widow of a king, but as a lowly traveller – the perfect disguise. I can tell by the redness in her eyes that she has been weeping, no doubt after learning that her youngest son is dead alongside his half-brother, the king. I go to embrace and comfort her, but she says, "I am not the only mother who is grieving this day." Then she stops and scrutinizes my dress. Her lips part and she looks back up to meet my gaze. "By what Kaleb told us, I thought you meant for us all to escape through the spring?"

"I mean for you and what is left of the House of Omri to escape through the spring. Apart from your son, I will send the most trusted eunuchs to guard you, and you will wait in the tunnels beneath the city until it is safe for you to make your way out through the spring."

"Then you will not be coming with us?"

"I cannot."

"Why, Yezeba'al? It makes no sense for you to stay."

"It makes sense, because it will give the rest of you a chance to escape while I am distracting Yehu."

"Can you not distract him some other way?"

720

"Zubira," I say, taking her by the arms. "This is the only way to ensure the rest of you survive. He is after me. I am the target of his hate. I am the one who needs to die so that he will be satisfied, but the whole of our husband's house does not have to die with me."

She looks down. Then she nods in understanding. When she looks back up, there are tears in her eyes. "You have been a good friend and sister to me. And a mother when I still needed one. I cannot imagine life without you here."

"You will not be here—you will be in Tzidon, my brother's kingdom. I have already sent ahead, to inform my brother of what has happened and beg for him to send ships to collect you at Yapo. Daryoush will deliver the message, and they will come back for you. That is my hope, at least. If the ships do not come within a day or two, you are to travel south. Go as far away from here as you can manage with so many children and infants traveling with you. It will not be easy, but there is no other way. If you stay here, Yehu will kill all the men and boys. He will force the women and girls to marry him or give them to his men to be ravaged."

She raises her chin. "I will lead them all to safety. You have my word. And if you should somehow survive…I pray we will soon be reunited."

I smile faintly, knowing it is not to be. I pull her into an embrace, squeeze her tightly, and whisper, "I will always be with you." Then I kiss her cheek and pull away before I start to cry and ruin my kohl. "Is Asa's family here with the rest of you?"

She nods. "Everyone is waiting in the courtyard."

"Good. Remember my instructions. When word comes of Yehu's approach, all of you are to go down into the tunnels and escape through the spring, and head for Yapo to await the ships from Tzidon."

"Will Yehu not figure out where we have gone and try to stop us?"

"Yehu is fueled by hate. He will come first to my palace to find and kill me. I have sent word that he is not to be prevented from entering the city. I do not want there to be a battle, and I am hoping that the lack of resistance will convince him that we are unaware of his treachery."

"You have always been good at scheming, my friend. It would be frightening if you were not on our side."

721

I smile but turn my face toward the floor. When I raise my head again, I am composed. "Go, Zubira. Deliver my instructions and guide our family to safety."

"I will, Ba'alah," she answers, straightening to her full height. We stand together in this way, facing each other as two queens of equal standing. I have always known that were it not for Akhab's devotion to me she would have been his queen, for she was one of his favorite wives and herself the daughter of a great and powerful king.

Once she departs, I start to pace by the terrace, wondering how long we will have to wait. Surely, Yehu will not tarry too long at Yezreel before coming here. At last, I tire of pacing and try to relax. First, I closet myself away to pray at my private altar and anoint myself for death. I prepare a bowl of qaneh-bosem, breathing in its fumes, and at last the anxiety begins to fade and my sense of peace returns.

Then I go out to casually drape across the cushions on my bed and begin snacking on grapes. Kora sits with me, her hands ever filled with some task involving needle and thread and a piece of clothing. We talk and laugh quietly, as though nothing is amiss. It is only the two of us in my chamber, along with the four eunuchs who I have called back now that there is nothing more to hide. They stand at attention, trained to be alert while appearing unaffected, but I notice the way they shift nervously from time to time, beads of sweat upon their foreheads and their brows.

The palace is eerily quiet. Except for the hum of our voices, the occasional call of the peafowl in the garden, or the howl of dogs roaming the streets outside the palace walls, there is no sound. Having nothing more to say for a time, the silence is drawn out. I think about Daryoush and Raman, wondering how far they have gotten, and if they were noticed making their way out of the city. Likely not, if they were able to slip into the crowd of people fleeing, most of them my friends: nobles and their families, and those of my priests and priestesses I discharged for their safety, urging them by messengers not to stay or they will die. No wonder it is so quiet. Not just the palace is empty—half the city must have fled by now.

I glance at my eunuchs, wondering what they are thinking. If they have noticed that Daryoush is missing, they have not indicated curiosity or concern. It is not unusual for my lover to be absent. His duties at the temple often keep him busy. Even now, the priests and priestesses who have opted to remain with us at Megiddu are burning a sacrifice upon the altar of Ba'al. I can smell the odor of roasting flesh and sacred oil and, when I look out the window, a river of smoke flows across the deep blue sky. Soon it will be evening. Will I live to see the sun set one last time?

Suddenly the silence is broken by the call of a shofar in the distance. It is answered by a horn from somewhere in the city, and soon others join the call. Closing my eyes, again I touch the seal and breathe deeply, sending a silent prayer up to the Ba'alim, that they will strengthen me in this, my final hour. May my death be swift, my slayer just, the stroke of his sword precise. *My husband, I will be with you again soon. And from Ertsetu may we never be parted.*

Forcing myself to remain calm, I put another grape in my mouth, careful not to let it touch my painted lips. I bite down. The sweet liquid pours onto my tongue and slips down my throat when I swallow. Then the door opens, and Eliezar enters quietly. He bows his head. I clear my throat.

"Speak," I command, rising from the cushions.

"Ba'alah, there is an army approaching the city. They carry the banners of Yisrael."

"It is Yehu," I reply. "It took him long enough. He must have searched the entire fortress before he realized I was not there. Does he truly believe we do not know what has happened? That he approaches not as our friend but as a traitor who has killed his king— like Zimri."

Everyone knows about Zimri, the commander of chariots who murdered King Elah and shut himself up in the palace at Tirzah, where he ruled as a usurper for seven days. He is hated to this day, his name a euphemism for a traitor. It was Akhab's father, Omri, who laid siege to the city and avenged the rightful king before the people chose him to start a new dynasty. Now, it seems that dynasty is ended after only two generations. Is it my weak-willed son who is to blame, or me for not having guided him better?

"Have they begun their descent?" He knows what I mean. I do not speak of the plan to evacuate the members of my family who are here in the city; not in front of the other eunuchs, whose loyalty may fade once I am dead, lest they inform Yehu of their whereabouts in the hope that it will curry his favor.

723

Eliezar gives a firm nod to confirm that they are on their way down the long stairway to reach the tunnels that lead to the spring. "There is still a chance, Ba'alah. I can send word to close the gates."

"My previous instructions remain in effect. There is to be no resistance. I would like to avoid bloodshed—apart from my own." I grin. Eliezar looks away. I sense his disquiet. "You do not have to stay here to die with me."

I had asked him to go with the others, but he refused to part from me. It was the first time in all our years together that he ever disobeyed my command. Now, he is committed to die with me. "Ba'alah, I am sworn to you for life."

"I hope that if you are still alive when I am dead, you will give yourself over to the traitor's cause." I cast my gaze around the chamber to the other four eunuchs who are present. They exchange uncertain glances, when I say, "All of you. When I am dead, you are free from your oath of service to me. Let me die swiftly, and do not seek to avenge me."

"We will defend you with our lives, Ba'alah." Eliezar gives the others a sharp look. They avoid his gaze, but I do not blame them for fearing death and considering mine the more appealing instruction.

"There is no point in giving your lives for a woman who is already dead," I answer pointedly, as I walk toward the terrace to look out.

The garden is peaceful, illuminated by an orange glow from the sun as it travels closer to the horizon. Even the deepening shadows are not ominous. Nothing about this day would suggest what is about to happen. Were it not for my grandson and the last of his men arriving here to warn us when they did, we would have no chance to shelter from the approaching storm. Now, I am certain the last of my children—two sons and two daughters—and those of my grandchildren who are now waiting in the tunnels beneath the city will survive. My bloodline, the sacred bloodline of the gods themselves, will not die with me.

I turn back to Eliezar. He still looks defiant, but I reinforce my command. "When they come for me, even when they raise their swords to strike me down, I command you to stand down. Do not die trying to save me."

He comes to kneel before me and takes my hand, breaking protocol. "My life holds no purpose without you, Ba'alah. I have no wife, no children, no family. I leave no one behind."

Still holding his hands in mine, I say, "You are a warrior, Eliezar. Surely, there is still need in this world for your kind—if not here, then somewhere else. Be assured: you have not failed me. It is my time. But it does not have to be yours."

For the first time in all the years that he has served me, I see the captain of my eunuchs weep. He presses my hands to his lips and to his cheeks, and I pull him to me as a mother would a weeping child. For a moment, he permits himself to lean against me and cry. It takes all my strength not to cry with him, to see him weep openly in this way, but I am always mindful of my kohl.

After a short time, Eliezar seems to remember his duty and recovers his strength. He pulls away, wipes his face, sniffs, and rises to his feet. "Ba'alah, I am at your command."

"I command you to live, my friend."

He nods in understanding. "I will do as you ask of me."

"Good. Now, go out and resume your position. Inform me when the traitor's army has crossed the threshold into the city."

He leaves with a nod. Then I go to Kora, who is standing by the wardrobe after putting away the gown she has been mending. Her back is to me, her hands still on the doors of the wardrobe she has just finished closing. I notice that she is trembling. "Kora."

She turns to me. She has been crying, but now she wipes her eyes and returns to the stoicism she had affected earlier. "How may I serve you, Ba'alah?"

"You do not have to stay," I whisper. "There is still a chance for you to escape—to join the others waiting in the tunnels."

"I will not leave you, my Gebirah."

"Soldiers are cruel to those they have defeated—especially toward women."

She is almost laughing. "I am too old to be of interest to the soldiers, Yezeba'al."

"You do not know that with any certainty. I cannot bear to be the cause—"

"When we were girls, growing up together in your father's kingdom, I swore to serve you to the end of your days."

"The end has come. I release you from my service."

"The day is not yet done. I will serve you 'til your heart beats no longer. I will not let you face your death alone, for you have been good to me as you were good to my mother before me. We will all be together in Ertsetu very soon."

"Are you afraid?"

She shakes her head. "It is not death that I fear—only the manner in which it is delivered. But I am with you."

I throw my arms around her neck and pull her into an embrace. Then, stepping back, I move my hands up to her face and kiss her cheeks, once on each side. "Thank you for your service to me all these years, Kora. I love you as if you were my own flesh and blood."

A moment later, Eliezar returns. "The army has entered the city, Ba'alah. It is indeed Yehu that is leading them."

"Then it is time." I nod to Kora and the others. They follow me as I make my way through the palace, to the audience chamber. "Eliezar, stand watch at the base of the stairs, but remember my command: do not try to stop them when they come for me."

He nods, and I turn to climb the stairs that lead up to the gallery overlooking the street below. Kora and my four bodyguards follow close behind as I make my way to the window. Normally whenever I come here to address the people of the city, there are crowds of worshippers gathered to see me and to shout their praises, eager to receive my blessing. Now, the streets of Megiddu are empty. Any of the people of the city who have stayed behind are shut away inside their homes, their doors likely barred, and their shutters tethered. There is nothing—only the dogs left behind to go hungry, already roaming the streets in search of scraps and fighting over whatever they manage to find.

Savage beasts, I think with disdain. Then I hold onto the edge of one of the windows and lean out, looking for any sign of Yehu and his men moving through the city. Clouds of dust rise from between the buildings. They are not far. I step back, but I do not move away from the window. I want him to see me as he approaches, and to feel the weight of my judgment bearing down on him, even if he feels no remorse for his treachery.

When at last he appears and I see him riding in my son's golden chariot at the head of the army of Yisrael, anger fills me with an intense heat from within. He sees me there above in the window

726

even before I call out, "Shalom, Yehu! Or should I call you Zimri? Do you dare now approach your queen in the chariot of my son, your king whom you have slain?"

"Shalom, my Lady!" He offers a mock bow with his hand over his heart as the chariot comes to a stop. It is being driven by the same man who once drove the chariot for my son. Yehu glances at the man, and then smirks up at me. "Looks like it is my chariot now."

"Yoram trusted you! Loved you! And you have shown yourself to be unworthy by your treachery. I told my son not to trust you."

"He should have listened to his mother."

"Did you ever truly love him, or did you always plan to betray him in the end?"

At last, the smirk fades from his lips, and he lowers his face. "It is unnatural for a man to love another man in that way. I did what I had to do."

Although I have always suspected it, this pains me more than anything to hear. I close my eyes against the sting of tears and will them away. Then I breathe deeply and look down at the traitor again. "Have you no honor as a man? No faith?"

"I have put my faith in Yahowah, the God of Yisrael, and he anointed me by the hand of his prophet. I, not your son, am the true anointed King of Yisrael. As proof, Yahowah has bestowed victory upon me this day. What has your Ba'al done for you, *Yezebel?*"

I bristle. The Yahwist inclination to bastardize my name has always bothered me, but today it is as if he twists the knife in the wound already inflicted by the deaths of my son and grandson. It takes every ounce of strength in me not to roar. Instead, I bare my teeth and growl, "My name is Yezeba'al. And even as you betray me this day, Yehu, I am your queen. And when you put me to the sword in the name of your god and his prophets, I am your queen. I am Yezeba'al, Gebirah of Yisrael, High Priestess and Consort of Ba'al; and you are a scheming traitor."

He grins. "Only for as long as it takes for my army to fight its way into your palace, killing all who are foolish enough to resist its advance. My army is the larger one, now that Yoram and his men have been put to sword. Yoram is dead – as you will soon be too, *Yezebel.*"

I raise my eyes and frown. I will not tell him that I have already given him his victory. I must continue to stall for as long as possible while my grandchildren and their guardians escape through the tunnels. I need to keep the traitor focused on me and my palace. His patience appears to be waning, however.

"You may as well give up now. Surrender and we can avoid the onslaught."

I scoff. "And die a coward? No, Yehu; I will not go tail-tucked to the grave, whimpering like a dog to my death. Send your men to act out your treacherous deeds. Let us see how long it takes for them to reach my inner sanctum. I will be waiting."

I turn and step away, but he calls me back, again by that false name. I pause and return to the window, waiting for him to speak. Why do I get the feeling he is trying to keep me at the window? I scan the rooftops and the streets for signs of archers ready to strike but see none. I place my hand on the windowsill and cast an imperious gaze down on him. "You have my attention. Say what you're going to say."

He glances around uncertainly, shifting in his chariot. "I will send them: the whole army. At my command, they will tear down the palace walls if they must – of that you can be sure. But first, let us see what your eunuchs think of their sentence, shall we?"

Now I cannot hide my confusion. I look at the four eunuchs who are there with me. Two of them are looking out the other windows, scanning for immediate danger, while the other two remain in their place by the door to the stairwell. Then I look back to Yehu, affecting an air of confidence. "They may be eunuchs, but you know as well as I, they are as much men as any of your soldiers."

"We shall see," he answers with a snakelike grin. He then makes a gesture to his cupbearer and pauses for a drink, after which he calls out, "Eunuchs! Is your devotion to the Whore of Ba'al such that you will die for her?"

Another glance at my eunuchs perhaps betrays my unease. Their dutiful expressions give nothing away. I turn back to Yehu and chuckle. "It is their duty to defend their queen."

"As it was mine to defend Yoram; yet here we stand." He grins, pleased to have twisted the knife yet again.

Unwilling to show him any weakness, I raise my head in defiance. "Not everyone is a Zimri."

"Perhaps not; but every man has his price."

"Careful, Yehu; your own men may turn on you, by that logic."

He tightens his grip on the reins. "Eunuchs! Once again, I ask, will you die for this woman? I offer forgiveness if you heed my call: betray the Whore of Ba'al, and I will spare you; defend her, and you will perish alongside her this day. You have my word – the choice is yours."

"The word of a man who betrayed his king. Why should they be any different? How are they to know you will not embrace them with one hand and plunge a knife into their backs with the other as you did to my son?"

"Because I have no quarrel with them. It is you I am after, *Yezebel* – only you who stands between me and the throne of Yisrael this day."

"And all who would defend me. I am not going to make this easy for you, Yehu."

His gaze shifts to my right, and he smirks. "You don't need to because I've already paved the way."

In that moment, I become aware of a presence looming behind me to my right. I step away and begin to turn, to confront my would-be assailant, but am seized by another who has come up from behind me. It is one of my eunuchs. He takes hold of my arms, as the other moves to help him. A third approaches with a bloodied dagger in hand. Kora is lying on the ground nearby; her throat has been slit. Blood pools beneath her head and neck. I do not see any sign of the fourth eunuch and think he must have fled when Kora was assaulted.

Crying out from the shock, and horrified that my most trusted eunuchs would turn on me, I pull back thinking the one who killed her is about to stab me to death while the other two hold me by the arms. For the first time, I feel the sharp thrust of fear rise from within me. Tightening his grip on the dagger, he looks at me with murderous intent but when I meet his gaze, he falters.

"What are you waiting for?" Yehu shouts from outside. "The Whore of Ba'al must die!"

The dagger is lowered. "Gebirah, forgive me."

"What are you doing, you fool?" cries the eunuch to my left.

"Eliyas, this is for Yahowah!" hisses the one to my right.

Taking advantage of his hesitation while the other two are still holding me by the arms, I kick the one with the dagger away from me. The force causes me to lean backward out the window. I cry out as my headdress comes loose and crashes into the street. There is laughter from the men below.

One of the eunuchs lets go of me and stumbles away. The other nearly loses his balance but maintains his grip even as he steadies himself. But when I grab at the straps on his armor, he lets go of my arm and clutches the window frame. I twist away, only to find myself suddenly looking out at the men and their chariots below. The sight of it makes me feel lightheaded and I hold the windowsill to steady myself.

Do not be afraid. Let it happen.

Then I hear Yehu's voice, exhausted and impatient. "Just throw her down! For the glory of Yahowah!"

I am still looking down at him, still processing what he said, when they take hold of my arms once again from behind. I gasp as I am pulled forward and the ground beneath my feet disappears. I cry out and then I am thrust out upside down and falling. I hold my breath and close my eyes. Then there is an explosive blow to the right side of my skull, seconds before the rest of my body collides with the pavement.

Ears ringing... Pain, everywhere all at once...

Everything fades, and then...

Akhab.

Epilogue

itting on the stone docks at Yapo, whispered prayers upon her lips and eyes glistening, Zubira pulled her shawl tighter around her shoulders. Twilight was falling as she looked out across the harbor, watching the lanterns on incoming ships alight. She had heard it proclaimed only a short time ago, while eating at the inn, that Gebirah Yezeba'al was dead. It was said that the queen was thrown from a window – some claimed it was at Yezreel, and that her body had been eaten by dogs there just as the zealot Eliyah had prophesied. Zubira knew it had not happened at Yezreel, for she had left Yezeba'al at her palace at Megiddu, after the queen's grandson had arrived nearly dead from the arrows that the traitor's men had pierced him with as he fled.

It was strange, she mused, how quickly rumors spread. She hoped the bit about the dogs was not true. If the queen's body was missing, perhaps Yehu's men had desecrated it and concocted the story about the dogs so as not to bring the wrath of her powerful relatives down on Yisrael. Or perhaps one of the faithful took her body away to be given last rites. That was Zubira's hope, but either way she sensed it did not matter so much to Yezeba'al, as long as she was reunited with her husband in Ertsetu.

"Ama." It was Kaleb, now Zubira's only surviving son. She smiled sadly when she turned to see him coming. He sat down beside her, and they looked out across the harbor in silence for a while before, at last, he spoke softly. "It is growing dark. I do not think the ships will come tonight."

"Her soul is at peace," Zubira said, turning to look at him. Her face was wet with tears, but she was smiling. "I know it. I feel it. She is reunited with Akhab."

Kaleb sighed and looked down at his hands. "Ama, what if the ships never come?"

"They will come for us, Kaleb. I know they will come."

Raman stood silently as Atalaya wept bitterly over the papyrus scroll he had delivered. He had known the Gebirah of Yehudah since she was only a girl, still living with her parents in Yisrael, but he had never seen her weep. Not once. She was deeply emotional; that he had always known. He still remembered seeing her laughing with her brothers and their parents in Melkah Yezeba'al's private quarters at Megiddu, entertaining them with her wild antics; the expressiveness in her face and her voice whenever she sang hymns or recited poetry, and the passion with which she performed sacred ritual dances under the scrutinizing gaze of her mother and the other priestesses of Ashtarti. She was her mother's daughter in every way, only she had always seemed the more extravagant of the two and, therefore, less prone to weep.

After reading the letter, she had at first seemed to be in a state of disbelief. She began badgering him with questions, as though she was hoping he would tell her something—anything—to contradict what her mother had written. When, at last, she began to comprehend what had happened in the kingdom of Yisrael, Atalaya tore her clothes and shrieked and cursed and wept unto the heavens. The papyrus had fallen from her hands as her torrent began and now it lay undisturbed beneath the desk at her feet, even as she upended every small thing within her reach, leaving her study to appear as though a great storm had passed through it. Then she sank into her chair and fell weeping across the surface of her desk, careless of the spilled ink staining the sleeves of her sumptuous robe.

Raman stood there, steeling himself against the ache in his heart that was only made worse after seeing the pain of this great woman who had lost her mother, son, and brother all at once. He stood there, unable to soothe her pain because it was not his place, yet unable to leave because he had not been dismissed. And so, he closed his eyes and he prayed silently for the souls of the dead and all who mourned them. He prayed, as he had so many times since the moment his Ba'alah had placed that wretched scroll in his hand and asked him to be the bearer of the worst news the Gebirah of Yehudah had ever received in her entire life. And it broke him to see her break.

When she had exhausted her tears, she sat back in her chair and stared vacantly toward the window, breathing deeply. Then suddenly she turned to him, her composure regained, and said, "You have always been a loyal friend and servant to my mother, Raman.

732

Thank you for obeying her last command. You may go. You are welcome to stay here for however long you need to recover, but I do not encourage you to stay for long in this kingdom, for I cannot guarantee your safety in these unenlightened times."

"Ba'alah," he answered with a bow. Then he left her, eager for some food and rest.

Daryoush stood at the bow of the frontmost ship as the royal fleet sailed into the harbor. It was a beautiful morning. As the ships were eased into their landing, he scanned the people on the docks, praying that everyone made it to Yapo, as planned. No one there looked royal, but then he assumed they would not because they could not risk drawing attention to themselves. Surely, they would have travelled in disguise. How was he to find them? What if Yehu's men found them first? If he arrived and no one was waiting, was he to wait in the harbor for a day or two, or turn back to Tzidon at the risk of leaving survivors behind?

Then he spotted an old, bearded man seated on some crates and smoking from a pipe. The man in question was not dressed in his usual finery and his beard was not as trim and well-kept as it had always been, but Daryoush was sure it was Asa. When the man rose and waved at the ships, which sailed under the banner of the King of Tzidon, Daryoush felt hope that the royal refugees had made it safely out of Megiddu. He prayed that, by some miracle, Yezeba'al was with them.

When at last he was able to disembark, Daryoush nearly ran to Asa. "Please, tell me she has come with you."

Asa's eyes said what his mouth did not seem able to communicate. Daryoush sighed heavily and lowered his face to hide the fact that his eyes were filled with tears. He felt sick. Then suddenly, Asa's hand was on his shoulder. "She was brave up to the end, I heard it said. And everyone made it out, as she intended. We are all here." He paused. "She is with my brother now, in Ertsetu. Let that bring you some peace. It is all she ever wanted."

"How did she die?"

Asa looked away. "They threw her from the window. Her own damned eunuchs. No one can be trusted, these days – least of all,

Yahwists. Anyway, come. It was difficult to find lodging for everyone, with so many fleeing from Yisrael all at once, but we managed. We arrived before most of the other refugees, so none of us had to sleep on the streets."

He waved his hand to indicate all the people crowded into every alley and lining the outside of buildings. Daryoush asked, "Who are they? Why are there so many?"

"Ba'alists. No one wants to stay in Yisrael under the usurper's strict Yahwist regime. In the cities and villages east of here, his followers have been murdering every Ba'alist they can find, tearing them from their homes and beating them in the streets, desecrating the temples. It is a bloodbath, so I have heard it said. The 'judgment of Yahowah', the zealots are calling it. They are rejoicing in the streets. The whole kingdom is falling apart."

"Then let it burn," said Daryoush. His throat was tight and his mouth dry. His temples throbbed. "Let Yahowah have his kingdom. There is nothing left for our kind here."

"It's a shame, though. My brother and his wife held it all together for so many years, built it up and brought it to life. They made the kingdom magnificent. Now, everything they made is being obliterated."

"Not everything."

Asa looked at him, confused.

"Their children, grandchildren, and great-grandchildren survive. As long as they live, the greatest of what they made together will go on. That was the most important thing to her. That is why I am here – to collect the last of them. Now, it is all that matters."

Yahosheba was surprised when the messenger arrived from the palace in the middle of the night. Her mother had requested her presence immediately, and she was to tell no one of her summons, except for her husband. After sending a message to Yahoiadah, who was likely already asleep in his own quarters, Yahosheba went with the messenger from the palace to meet with her mother. She was surprised to be taken to the king's study. She was not aware that her brother had returned from Yisrael.

The messenger left her when one of the palace eunuchs opened the door to the study to admit her. When she went inside, the door was closed behind her and she saw that it was only her mother who was there. "Ama? Where is Akhaz? Has he returned from Yisrael?"

"No, my daughter. He is not here. It is only me—and the king." With that, Atalaya beckoned to someone who was hiding behind the desk. It was a nurse cradling the infant prince, Yoash, who was just over a year old and asleep in his nurse's arms. The loving aunt looked at the boy in surprise. "Yehoash! Ama, what is all this about? You said the king was here—"

"The king is here, Sheba. *This* is the king."

"What about Akhaz? Did he fall in battle?" She brought her hand to her lips, as the realization hit. "Is my brother dead?"

"They are all dead," Atalaya lamented. "My son, my mother, my brother Yoram…"

"What? How can this be?"

Without a word, Atalaya handed the hastily scrawled papyrus letter to her daughter. Yahosheba read what was written and fell back against a column as if bowled over by a great wave upon the sea. Tears welled in her eyes, and her voice became like that of a little girl. "*Amami?*"

"As far as her messenger is aware, she did not survive. I have not yet received any official news from Yisrael one way or the other—but no one must know yet that the king is dead. Do you understand me, Sheba? Tell no one, until I have done what I need to do."

"Ama, I don't understand."

"Take Yoash to Yahoiadah."

"My husband?"

"Ask him to take your nephew into hiding at the temple, telling no one who he is until such time that we may safely reveal him, when he may take his place as King of Yehudah."

"Ama, what are you going to do?"

"I must secure the realm against the other men of your father's house, who will see themselves better suited to rule than an infant king. When I am through, there will be no other contenders to the throne but he, and I will rule in his place until he is old enough to be accepted as king."

"What?"

"Now, go."

"Ama, wait. You cannot have them all killed! Every man in Abbu's house?"

"If I do not, his house will fall into chaos as the other factions break into a war over the throne, and Yoash will be smothered in his cradle while he sleeps. He is the rightful king, but he is too young to defend himself and I cannot count on any but you and Yahoiadah to protect his identity and preserve his life. In the meantime, I will do whatever it takes to preserve his throne."

"Ama, are you sure of this?"

"Of course, I am sure. It is the only way. Now, go. And tell no one about what has been spoken here. He is a nobody. An orphan. He will be raised to serve your husband at the temple, where he will learn how to read and write and pray. When I believe it is safe for him to return to the palace as king, Yahoiadah will reveal him, and I will continue to guide him until such time that he is able to rule on his own."

Following her mother's instruction, Yahosheba took her nephew and his nurse from the palace in the dark of night. The hidden king was, indeed, raised at the temple to serve the High Priest who was secretly his uncle. Yehoash was doted on by Yahosheba, and by the nurse who became his adopted mother, and he lived a good life away from the palace.

In the meantime, Atalaya ordered slain every man, woman, and child of the royal house of Yehudah and their supporters, replacing those of influence with members of her own Ba'alist court. She declared her lover, Mattan, the High Priest of Ba'al and began performing all the sacred rites at the Temple of Ba'al that she had never been able to perform during the reigns of her husband and son. Surrounding herself only with those who shared her views and supported her taste for vengeance, she implemented a strict anti-Yahwist regime that made the Yahwist purges of her parents' reign seem trivial by comparison.

Atalaya ruled for six years until she decided it was time for her now seven-year-old grandson's whereabouts to be revealed, to take his place to rule Yehudah at her side. Being the High Priest of Yahowah, however, Yahoiadah did not wish to give the young king to

736

his grandmother so she could teach him her ways. Instead, having raised Yehoash to follow Yahowah and to loathe the Ba'alists, and having made a secret covenant with many powerful men in the kingdom who were sympathetic to the Yahwist cult, Yahoiadah betrayed Atalaya.

When the time came for Yehoash to be given unto his grandmother, instead Yahoiadah had him brought to stand before the pillar at the temple where kings were anointed. Surrounded by the soldiers of the households of all the men with whom he had made a secret covenant, Yahoaidah anointed the boy and declared him the true king. Then he encouraged the young king to make a covenant with Yahowah, that he and all his people would be Yahowah's people and not tolerate the worship of Ba'al or any of the other gods in his kingdom. When Atalaya appeared at the appointed time, she was shocked to find her grandson making this covenant, and she cried out against Yahoiadah's treachery.

Yahoiadah commanded the soldiers who surrounded the king to take Atalaya out of the temple and to put her and all her followers to the sword. Then all the followers of Yahowah that had been in hiding came out into the streets. They gathered in mobs and went into the city to the Temple of Ba'al to kill Mattan and all the other priests of Ba'al, destroy their idols, and desecrate their altars.

Seven-year-old Yehoash, the new King of Yehudah, was the son of Akhazyah of Yehudah and the grandson of Yehoram and Atalaya. He was the great-grandson of Yehoshapat of Yehudah and his queen Atalaya, daughter of Omri, King of Yisrael. He was also the great-grandson of Akhab, King of Yisrael, and his queen, Yezeba'al, High Priestess and Consort of Ba'al. He ruled Yehudah for many years. Although he supported the Temple of Yahowah and worshipped in his ways, he did not permit the destruction of the temples of Ba'al and the other gods that were set upon the high places throughout his kingdom.

The descendants of Yehoash ruled Yehudah until it was conquered by the Assyrians about two-hundred years later. But even as they fled into hiding or were taken and dispersed with their people into the lands of Assyria, the descendants of Yehoash continued to flourish for many more generations. **According to the genealogy found in the Gospel of Matthew, one of these descendants was Jesus of Nazareth.**

Appendix

Glossary

In Alphabetical Order

Abbu – Father.

Ababu – paternal grandfather (literally 'father's father').

Abakhati – paternal aunt (literally, 'father's sister').

Abakhu – paternal uncle (literally, 'father's brother').

Abarakkum – steward, administrator (of a palace, temple, or private household).

Abumi – maternal grandfather (literally, 'mother's father').

Akhab –Ahab King of Israel, and husband to Jezebel.

Akhatamu -maternal aunt (literally, 'sister of my mother').

Akhamu – maternal uncle (literally, 'brother of my mother').

Akhatu – Sister.

Akhazyah – Ahaziah, a son of Ahab and Jezebel; also, the name of one of their grandsons. Both son and grandson became kings.

Akhimelekh – a title, meaning 'Brother to the king'.

Akhu – Brother.

Ama – Mother. (The scholarly consensus for the Akkadian word for mother is "ummu," but I have chosen to go with the Sumerian original on which the Akkadian and many other languages are based.)

Amabi – paternal grandmother (literally, 'mother of my father').

Amami – maternal grandmother (literally, 'mother of my mother').

Apiq – Aphek, an ancient city in the Plain of Sharon.

Ashtarti — Astarte, the Canaanite (Phoenician) goddess of healing, sexuality, and fertility; patroness of hunting, chariots, and war. Associated with storms, the sea, the moon, and the dawn and dusk star (the planet Venus). Also known as Ishtar, Auset (Isis), Aphrodite, and Shakti in various cultures and mythologies. **Asherah**, known by her followers as the Queen of Heaven, was her Hebrew equivalent, but they were originally two different goddesses whose identities became merged by Jezebel and Ahab's time (much like the gods El and Yahweh).

Atalaya — Athaliah, daughter of Ahab and Jezebel; also, one of Ahab's sisters.

Ba'al — Canaanite title for a god, meaning 'Lord' or 'Prince'; used only in the context of divinity. Thus, when human rulers took this title, they were inferring on themselves divine status. (When not used as a title, it can also mean 'husband'.) (See *Melkorat*.)

Ba'alah — Feminine form of Ba'al; a title given to Canaanite goddesses. (See *Ashtarti*.)

Ba'alim — Plural form of Ba'al / Ba'alah.

Ba'al Zebul — Ba'al Zebub (Beelzebub), the god of healing and sickness, and the patron deity of Ekron.

Be'er Sheba — Beersheba; Be'er Sheva in modern Hebrew.

Damaseq — Damascus, then the capital city of the kingdom of Aram (modern-day Syria).

Dawid — David.

Debarim — Deuteronomy, one of the five books of the Torah.

El — The supreme god of the Canaanite pantheon, father to Ba'al and Yahowah. During Jezebel and Ahab's lifetime, the identities of El and Yahowah had begun to be conflated by the push for monotheism by some of Yahowah's followers.

Elisha — Elisha the prophet, Eliyah's successor.

742

Eliyah / Eliyahu – Elijah 'the Tishbite', leader of the prophets of Yahowah in Israel during Ahab's reign.

Ertsetu – The underworld, the resting place of the dead. *Sheol*, in Hebrew.

Ethba'al – Father to Jezebel and King of Sidon. He was originally a priest and powerful warlord who became king of Tyre after he killed the usurper, Pheles. After becoming king of Tyre, Ethba'al conquered Sidon and Byblos and declared himself Melech Tzidonim 'King of the Sidonians'.

Gebal – The original Phoenician name for Byblos.

Gebirah – Queen Mother (Hebrew), mother of the reigning king; of higher rank than *Melkah*.

Gilad – Gilead, the lands east of the Jordan River.

Hamat – Hamath, capital of the Hittite kingdom by the same name, now part of modern-day Syria.

Hawah – Eve, the first woman and the mother of humankind, according to Hebrew mythology and the Biblical book of Genesis.

Kerem-el – Mount Carmel, a range of mountains that are the location of an ancient vineyard and many sacred valleys and grottos.

Kir Kharaset – Kir Hareseth, a city in the Kingdom of Moab; razed during the reign of King Joram as retribution for the kingdom's rebellion against Israel. (2 Kings 3:25)

Melekh – King, or "my King".

Melkah – Queen, or "my Queen." The king's chief wife: of higher rank than the king's other wives, but lower rank than his mother (see *Gebirah*).

Melkorat – A Canaanite fertility god and consort to the goddess Astarte; from the Phoenician *MLQRT*, known to scholars as Melqart (also sometimes spelled 'Melkart'). Lord of the Underworld, he is associated with storms and the sea, the sun, the life-death cycle, fertility, and the cycle of the seasons. The name Melkorat is an epithet, meaning 'King of the City.'

His true name is Hadad. In the Ugaritic texts, he is called Ba'al Hadad, or simply Ba'al. He is one of the sons of El.

Metushelak – Methuselah, from the book of Genesis, purported to be the oldest man to have ever lived.

Miqwah – a ritual bath made from a spring or groundwater well. In the ancient Levant, these 'living water baths' could often be found along major roadways for use by travelers throughout the region. (In modern Hebrew, 'mikveh'.)

Moshe – Moses, the prophet who led the Israelites out of Egypt.

Mot / Motu – a god of death, "he who eats the souls of the dead." He is in an eternal rivalry with Ba'al, who seeks to preserve the souls of the dead from Motu's greed.

Nabot – Naboth "the Jezreelite," who owned a vineyard in Jezreel.

Obadyah / Obadyahu – Obadiah, Ahab's steward who hid many prophets of Yahowah in caves during the anti-Yahwist purges.

Opir – The land of Ophir in the Bible, believed by some scholars to be India.

Pesakh – Passover, the feast celebrated every spring to commemorate the release of the Hebrew people from bondage in Egypt in the time of Moses.

Qaneh-bosem – Cannabis; used ritually, medicinally, and recreationally throughout the ancient Levant.

Qayin and Hebel – Cain and Abel, the sons of Adam and Eve in the creation story from the book of Genesis.

Ramot – Ramoth, a wealthy trade city in the land of Gilad (Gilead).

Rebitya – "My Lady," reconstructed from Phoenician *RBTY*. Used only for priestesses: indicating a woman of learning and a spiritual teacher, much like the Hebrew 'rabbi' and its modern female counterpart, 'rebbetzin'.

Serapim – Seraphim, the highest order of angels (messengers of the gods).

Shabbat – Sabbath, a day of rest.

Shelomoh – King Solomon, an ancestor to both royal lines of Israel and Judah, including Ahab and Jehosaphat.

Sheol – The underworld, the resting place of the dead. *Ertsetu*, in Akkadian.

Shomron – Samaria, the capital city of the northern kingdom of Israel; also, an alternative name for the kingdom itself which would have been used more frequently then. *For simplicity, I have chosen to use the name Yisrael when referring to the kingdom and Shomron when referring to the city.*

Tzidon – Sidon, a city in modern-day Lebanon that was once also a Canaanite kingdom.

Yahowah – Yahweh/Jehovah (YHWH), the god of Israel; originally a storm god and one of the sons of El. Around the 9th century BCE, a zealous faction of his followers began to deny the existence of other gods and goddesses altogether, and the identities of Yahowah and El were conflated.

Yahoiadah – Jehoiada, the High Priest.

Yahoram – Jehoram, successor to King Jehoshaphat of Judah.

Yahoshapat – King Jehoshaphat, a ruler of the southern kingdom of Judah, and a close ally to Israel during the reigns of Ahab and his successors.

Yahosheba – Jehosheba, wife of Jehoiada and aunt to Joash.

Yam HaMelah – The Dead Sea. In Hebrew, literally, "Sea of Salt."

Yapo – Jaffa, the ancient port city that is now part of Tel Aviv in modern-day Israel.

Yarden – Jordan, the main river that flows through Israel.

Yehudah – Judah, the southern kingdom, the capital of which is Jerusalem.

Yerushalayim – Jerusalem, capital of the southern kingdom of Judah.

Yezeba'al – Jezebel, daughter to King Ethba'al and wife to King Ahab.

Yezreel – Jezreel, the city and fortress located in the Jezreel Valley of northern Israel. Tel Yizre'el in modern-day Israel.

Yisrael – Israel, the northern kingdom; also known in the 9th century BCE as the kingdom of Shomron (Samaria).

Yoash – Joash/Jehoash, son and successor of Ahaziah of Judah.

Yoram – Joram, a son of Ahab and Jezebel.

Zhou – China, as the kingdom was called during the Zhou dynasty.

Zour – Tyre, one of the great Canaanite (Phoenician) city-states and a center for trade, along with Sidon.

Acknowledgements

First and foremost, I would like to thank you, dear reader. Of the scores of novels you could have picked up and read, you chose mine for this round and I am incredibly grateful. I am especially grateful if you made it all the way to the end of this very long story – I know it was not a light read by any means, but neither was it intended to be. If you made it to the end, I commend you for your perseverance.

Next, I would like to thank my reviewers, teachers, and mentors – anyone who has contributed to my writing career or this book in any way. Most especially, I would like to thank the brilliant and talented author Kimberly L. Craft. Kim is my mentor, editor, partner in crime, and dearest friend in all the world. (She also made the amazing trailer for *The Book of Jezebel*; one-handed, because she had a broken arm at the time, and so it was truly a labor of love and a sign of her dedication.) Her honest and professional feedback, her willingness to discuss all things Jezebel, 9th century BCE Israel, linguistic and Biblical history, and so on were invaluable. Honestly, none of this would have been possible without her love and support, both before and during this project.

Above all, I would like to thank all my friends and family for putting up with me becoming a ghost throughout the research, writing, and editing phases. I especially want to thank my children for making me laugh and giving me much-needed breaks from working to remember what is truly important in life. Every day, they inspire me, and give my life its greatest purpose.

Finally, I want to thank my cats for being warm and soft, for cuddling at my feet or on the pillow beside me while I work from the comfort of my bed, and for making me laugh at their antics. Their purr-fect presence makes every day extra special.

Thank you all for your unceasing patience while I'm half-way in another time and place. I love and appreciate each and every one of you more than words can possibly express!

About the Author

R.M. Watters is the author of *The Book of Jezebel*. Her works include literary historical fiction, fantasy, and poetry.

When not spending time with family or writing, she can often be found biking, hiking in nature, studying linguistics, researching historical places & people, solving cryptograms, or playing video games and relaxing with a glass of red wine or a gin & tonic. She earned a BA in English Literature from University of Central Florida and an MFA in Creative Writing at Southern New Hampshire University.

She lives in sunny Central Florida with her family.

Learn more at *www.rmwatters.com*.

Made in United States
Troutdale, OR
03/29/2024

18823967R00463